THE MAKING OF A GOOD MAN

A GOOD MAN

Frank W. Travis

 **New Generation Publishing**

Dedication

This novel is dedicated to the memory of the late Terence Flanagan. For fifty-eight years, from when we first met at Junior Technical School at Easter 1949 until Terence's death at Easter 2007, we shared hobbies: hiking, camping, cycling, then boat-building, sailing and fishing, in all of which he was an ideal companion. When fishing out-at-sea he was dauntless: no matter the cold, the rain, the frost, the snow, or how severe the wind or the roughness of the sea, we went out together undeterred and returned with magnificent catches. He is sorely missed.

Terence Flanagan, on right, and the author, with one of the many catches of 20+ pound cod that they used to take regularly from the Firth of Clyde over the winter months, in years gone by.

The author

The author was born in Manchester in 1935. After graduating in Mechanical Engineering from the University of Manchester Institute of Science and Technology, he completed a graduate apprenticeship at the aircraft manufacturers A.V. Roe & Co. of Oldham, and then worked as a research engineer within the company's Engineering Research Division. Following this he returned to UMIST as a member of staff, also pursuing research into the use of explosives in the forming of metals, gaining an MScTech and then a PhD. Next he took up a Senior Lectureship in Production Engineering at the University of Strathclyde, Glasgow.

Soon after moving to Glasgow he developed an obsession for sea fishing on the west coast, on one winter's day catching a 46 pound cod out in the Firth of Clyde, the Scottish record then, as now, being 46 pounds and half-an-ounce (46.03 pounds!) On another occasion he won the British and International Skate Championships, fishing in Loch Broom out of Ullapool in a force 10 gale, catching a common skate weighing 136 pounds. However, as is the usual practice in academic life, he then, reluctantly, moved on elsewhere for promotion, but resolved to return to Scotland in his retirement.

He then held professorial appointments at universities in England, Singapore and Hong Kong. He was awarded the higher doctorate of DSc for having established through his research publications an international reputation in the industrial aspects of the high-speed forming of metals.

In 1975 he founded Journal of Materials Processing Technology and continued as the Editor of the journal until 2003. He has been awarded two gold medals, one for "Lifetime achievements in materials processing research and education" and the second gold medal, with an embedded Zirconium jewel, along with appointment as Distinguished Visiting Research Professor of the University of Silesia, Poland, for his support of Polish materials processing researchers. He was also awarded the Professor Fryderyk Staub "Golden Owl Award" by the World Academy of Materials and Manufacturing Engineering.

Whilst working in Singapore he found a second obsession, Chinese language and culture, taking classes on two evenings each week for four years and then, at the age of 57, arranging a year's unpaid leave from his post to take a one-year full-time post-graduate diploma in Chinese at Durham University. He has visited some twenty different cities in China, presenting papers at research conferences and lecturing to gatherings of university academic staff and research students.

4

In retirement, he and his wife live in the tiny village of Arrochar at the head of Loch Long on the west coast of Scotland. His present hobbies include: working in his Chinese garden and maintaining the Chinese pavilion that he built there using traditional roof tiles that he brought back with him from Hong Kong; visiting Strathclyde University - which appointed him Visiting Professor upon his return to Scotland in retirement - to lecture to Chinese research students, research fellows and visiting academic staff; and playing on his beach with his two border collies, Callum and Jamie.

Foreword

A large number of people have supplied the author with information concerning Chinese history and culture or have supported his visits to Southeast Asia and China. It is not possible to acknowledge the help of all of them, but those in particular who must be named are: his one-time colleagues Professors W.B. Lee, C.Y. Tang and K.C. Chan of Hong Kong Polytechnic University and Assoc. Professor Tan Ming Jen of Nanyang Technological University, Singapore; Professor Z.R. Wang of Harbin Institute of Technology; Professor D.Y. Yu of Chongqing University; Professor Y.M. Huang of National Taiwan University of Science and Technology; Professor Hong Hocheng of National Tsing Hua University, Taiwan; Professor Y.T. Im of Korea Advanced Institute of Science and Technology; Professor Yi Qin and Emeritus Professor R. Balendra of Strathclyde University, Glasgow; and Professor M.S.J. Hashmi of Dublin City University.

He apologises in advance to native Chinese speakers and readers for the mutilation that he has probably wreaked, inadvertently, on their language within the pages of this novel. The Chinese have a saying that learning is a life-long process but, in respect of Chinese language and culture, the author was a very late starter and was, and still is, a very slow learner: the proficiency in Mandarin that he bestowed on the main character of the book, Alex, is much greater by far than his own. However, he doesn't think that he needs to apologise to non-native Chinese speakers and readers for any such mutilation, as they will know from their own experience how difficult it is to learn this complex, fascinating, and beautiful language.

Pronunciation

Ai Li: '*Ai*' as if "eye"; and '*Li*' to rhyme with "lee"

Beijing: '*Bei*' as if "bay" and 'jing' to rhyme with "sing"

Ceanncropic : '*Ceann*' pronounced as "can" and '*cropic*' to rhyme with "topic"

Chonghai: '*Chong*' to rhyme with "song"; and '*hai*' to rhyme with "sky", with slight aspiration of air with the "h"

Chun Feng: '*Chun*' to rhyme with "moon"; and '*Feng*' to rhyme with "sung"

Feng Shui: '*Feng*' to rhyme with "sung"; and '*Shui*' as if spelt "shway", ro rhyme with "bay" ('*Shui*' is commonly pronounced incorrectly in the West as "shoe-ee")

Fu Rong: '*Fu*' to rhyme with "two"; and '*Rong*' to rhyme with "song"

Hong bau: '*Hong*' to rhyme with "song" with slight aspiration with the "h"; and '*bau*' to rhyme with "cow"

Irn Bru: pronounced as "iron brew"

MacKay: "Kay" to rhyme with "sky"

Kok Lun: '*Kok*' to rhyme with "sock"; and '*Lun*' to rhyme with "moon"

Loh Yung Tsui: '*Loh*' as if "low"; '*Yung*' as if "young"; and '*Tsui*' as if spelt "swee"

Mei Hua: '*Mei*' as if "May"; and '*Hua*' as if spelt "hwa", with slight aspiration with the "h", and with the "a" as in "apple"

Polis: 'pol' to rhyme with "pole"; 'is' as in "hiss"

Qiangwei: '*Qiang*' as "chee-ang", with '*ang*' to rhyme with "sang"; and '*wei*' to rhyme with "say"

Qilin: '*Qi*' as if "chee"; and '*lin*' to rhyme with "tin"

Qin: pronounced as "chin"

Siew Tung: '*Siew*' as "see-oo" with 'oo' to rhyme with "two"; and '*Tung*' to rhyme with "sung"

Wang Yu Tian: '*Wang*' to rhyme with "sang"; '*Yu*' pronounced as "you"; '*Tian*' as "tee-enn"

Xiao Maque: '*Xiao*' as "see-ow" with 'ow' to rhyme with "cow"; and '*Maque*' as "ma-q-eh", with the 'ma' as in "match", the 'q' as in queue and the 'eh' as in "echo"

Xinghong: '*Xing*' pronounced as "sing"; and '*hong*' to rhyme with "song"

Ya Zheng: '*Ya*' with the 'a' as in "apple"; and '*Zheng*' as if spelt 'jung' to rhyme with "sung"

Ying Hong: '*Ying*' to rhyme with "sing"; and '*Hong*' to rhyme with "song" with slight aspiration with the "h"

7

Yu Wing: '*Yu*' pronounced as "you"; '*Wing*' as if in English

Zhang Chor Eong: '*Zhang*' to rhyme with "sang", with the '*Zh*' pronounced as if "j" as in "jack"; '*Chor*' to rhyme with "law"; and '*Eong*' as "ee-ong", with the 'ong' to rhyme with "song"

Note

With words ending in "g", such as '*Hong*', the "g" is stopped short in the nose, to give it a nasal sound, as is the case with some words in French, rather than for it to have a final slight 'grunt' of air as when the word is pronounced in English, which, when greatly exaggerated, sounds like "Hong-ge"

Prologue

The year is 1942; the place is the "Pleasure Beach" in the seaside town of Blackpool sitting at the edge of Morecambe Bay on the Fylde Coast of north-west England.

**

Madge and her friend Mary had come down from Glasgow by train on that morning and were to return on the last train of the evening. The day out hadn't been easy to organise, as since she and her husband, Jamie, had got married they had lived with his mother, Cathy, in her Govan tenement house,[P:1] and with Jamie now away at the War, Cathy watched over her like a hawk to ensure that she didn't get up to any mischief. Cathy's husband had gone down to England to find work ten years ago and hadn't returned or been heard from since, Jamie, her only child, then becoming the main interest in her life.

The tenement house was a small place, with just a living room, two bedrooms, a tiny kitchen and a toilet, but no bathroom. If anyone wanted a bath, they had to go to the local public bathhouse, or use the galvanised metal bath in the kitchen, so baths were taken relatively infrequently, the more private parts of the body usually being washed quickly using a bowl in the kitchen sink when no-one else was about.

After Jamie had returned to his unit from embarkation leave two weeks earlier, Madge had pretended to be depressed at missing him, and had done her best to try to win Cathy over, but to no avail. Cathy had continued to regard her as woman of dubious morality who had ensnared her son in marriage, but this was only partly true: Jamie had asked her to marry him because he feared that whilst he was away at the War some man working in a reserved occupation, such as at the Bishopton Ordnance Factory, would pay her compliments and listen attentively to what she had to say, and then persuade her into bed with

---

[P:1] "Up Oor Close: memories of domestic life in Glasgow tenements, 1910-1945" by Jean Farley, published by White Cockade Publishing, ISBN 0-9513124-5-6, provides the first-hand accounts of twenty-seven contributors living in a Gasgow "tenement house" – in other parts of Britain this would be called a "flat" – covering such aspects as: The Tenement House; Beds and Baths; Doing the housework; Cooking the Food; Entertaining and Celebrations; Up Oor Close; Roon Oor Back; Doing the Shopping; Weddings and Funerals; Childcare and Babycare; Illness, Remedies and Death; Then and Now.

him.

They had had a small wedding, with just Mary, Cathy, Madge's sister Mollie and her husband, and half a dozen friends as guests, with the wedding tea being provided by Cathy in the living room of the tenement house. Madge's father had gone off with a younger woman many years ago, leaving her mother to bring up Madge and Mollie as best she could on her own. When her mother died over four years ago, Madge and Mollie had continued to stay in the apartment at Port Glasgow, but then Mollie had brought her man into the front bedroom with her.

For a while the three of them had lived in relative harmony, but then the man had started to become a nuisance. Whenever Mollie was out, he would find an excuse to squeeze past Madge in the tiny kitchen, rubbing against her with a mild apology. He then started to touch her: nothing much, just on her shoulder as she was sitting in the living room, but one time he had slid his arm around her waist and given her a kiss on the cheek as he left for work, and on another occasion he had patted her backside as he left. Madge had found the situation stressful, as she knew that he was trying to get over the difficult stage of her acceptance of physical contact between them, after which there would be no holding him back. Not that she feared men, but as an attractive young woman could always find a man for herself, even in wartime, there was no point in stealing Mollie's man and incurring her sister's wrath.

After the ceremony and the wedding tea, they had all walked down to the "Buckie Inn", where Jamie had proceeded to drink himself into a state of extreme drunkenness, which was not unusual for a newly-married man in that area. Indeed, everyone present, men and women, were soon very drunk, and had started to make the usual vulgar banter. The evening continued in the same, but steadily coarsening, style and a good time was had by all.

His mates in the Yard had conditioned Jamie's views of marital responsibility: 'Keep her ill-shod and well xxxxed and you'll have nae problems!', although the originator of this advice must surely have given it as some kind of masochistic bad taste. Similarly, his guidance on romance and foreplay had been no better: 'Nae bother, just get it stuck in!'

At closing time, Jamie and Madge, along with Cathy, had left their friends outside the pub, with much hand-shaking, and then, as the distance from their friends increased, with the raising of hands and arms in salutation, and the shouting of further ribald remarks. It had been a good evening, with not even one word of anger having been passed between any of the family members and guests, which was not always the case for a wedding in some parts of Glasgow, as the coming together of two families could bring old enemies into contact, and then into conflict. However, after a good set-to the night before, the erstwhile combatants would often greet each other warmly in the pub on the next evening and say to each other 'Och, that was a grand nicht last nicht, so it was!'

They had then made their way back to the tenement house. After Jamie and Madge had said goodnight to Cathy, and had gone on to the back bedroom, Jamie had stripped off down to his socks, which he left on as usual, and then staggered about the room in a drunken state, before clambering into bed, pulling Madge into bed alongside him. She had then had to succumb to his feverish grasping, and to his beer-smelling slobbery kisses. He had smelt sweaty from the over-stimulation of the beer and the excitement of being in the noisy company of his friends. Madge hadn't realised that Jamie was capable of drinking himself into such an inebriated condition: although he would stop off at the pub for "a few drinks" with a crowd of his workmates after leaving the Yard on pay day and always got 'well oiled', he was never disgustingly or incapably drunk.

Jamie hadn't shown this lack of sexual finesse before, or more accurately, in the short time that he and Madge had known each other, he hadn't really had the opportunity to do so. As soon as Madge had decided that he would do for her, she had kept a firm control on his behaviour, lest he should cool off if she allowed him to 'sample the goods', which she knew well is the usual way of men, bastards so they are! However, to keep him interested, a couple of times after he had given her a goodnight kiss in some secluded spot, she had let him lift up her skirt and have a quick fumble, but she had never let him go further than that.

Despite Jamie's attempts to persuade her, Cathy would never go out and leave him and Madge alone in her tenement house, so Madge didn't have any problems on that score: Put simply, she wasn't so keen on Jamie, nor was she very interested in sex, although she knew that once they were married she would have to comply with his demands. Such is a woman's lot!

Jamie didn't have a great interest in personal hygiene. It was only when he was called up into the army that he started to wear underpants and a vest. Prior to that he had worn the same old trousers every day for work, week after week, so that they gradually became stiffer and smellier. His teeth, like those of many people in the poorer parts of Glasgow, were rotted and mis-shapen, so that his breath was often offensive. Madge didn't question these things, as they were quite common amongst the poorer families in the city. Life was hard and there wasn't widespread attention to dental hygiene. Indeed, it had once been the practice for some parents to go to great lengths to find the money to pay for a daughter to have all of her teeth removed as a wedding present, not only those that were decaying and discoloured, but also those that were still sound, so that she could go to her wedding with a beautiful smile showing her white even teeth, the envy of all of her friends, and also so that she would be spared any dental expenses in the future.

Whilst Madge was not enamoured of Jamie, a man is still a man, and so she was prepared to marry him, but she thought that he might, at least on this special night, have thought of her, and made an effort to introduce an element of romance. He had spent the rest of the night snoring and farting and belching off his bellyful of ale. Madge had looked at him with disgust: 'Drunken sod!' Why had she married him? It certainly hadn't been for love and it hadn't been for financial gain, as Jamie's job didn't pay well and the amount he brought home was even less on account of his calling into the pub with his workmates on pay-day. There was usually a crowd of women waiting at the Yard gates on pay-day to try to get most of their husbands' wages from them before they went to the pub, as by the time that they had staggered home late that night they could often have spent a substantial amount on drink and cigs, and sometimes on gambling: money that would have been better spent on food and clothing for the kids.

Jamie wasn't handsome, and he was rather short, but she wasn't bothered about his lack of height, as many men in the Clyde Valley were on the short side, due in part to having been brought up within a polluted environment and having lived a poor life-style, with jam-on-bread or toast "pieces" [1] (see the Appendix) as major items of diet, and with sugar-rich "tablet" - which in other parts of Britain might be called "fudge" - when they were lucky, along with the occasional fish supper or scotch pie, but rarely fruit or vegetables. For a treat the mothers in the town might buy them a shortcake "piece", and on a special occasion a "Millionaires' shortcake piece", which was a normal shortcake piece covered with a thick layer of soft caramel followed by a thin layer of chocolate. With luck, this would be accompanied by a bottle of "Irn Bru", a clear orange-tinted fizzy drink, which was declared to be "made in Scotland from girders!"

As the male children reached working age, they encountered harsh working conditions, where within the factories and shipyards the already-polluted air was further polluted by welding fumes and fumes from the blast furnaces, casting shops and heat-treatment baths. Just as badly, those employed in the mines suffered damp and often wet conditions, with stale air and coal dust, and spent little time in the daylight and fresh air. Not that life was easy for young women: those who weren't soon saddled with a bunch of kids found themselves employed as cleaners, or working long hours as sweat-shop machinists, or employed in some other low-pay low-esteem job, with little regard for their welfare or their comfort.

Everyone in the area worked long hours, and smoked heavily to help to overcome the tedium of the repetitive work that they were called upon to carry out. Those who didn't smoke were pressed to do so by their smoker friends, where a refusal to accept a cigarette could cause offence, so it was easier just to accept and join in with the crowd: no point in letting your mates think that you were a bit odd or stand-offish. Heavy drinking was standard with the men: a man who couldn't drink himself into a totally-inebriated condition was regarded by the other men, and by quite a few of the women, as a 'pansy', and was open to scorn and ridicule. Better to be a 'proper man' and get your drink down you just like the other men do!

However, the living conditions weren't as bad as they used to be. Madge's hometown of Port Glasgow used to be called "the town of little people", as many living there were bow-legged from rickets, due to the lack of money with which to buy decent wholesome food. It was little wonder that many in the Clyde region felt bitter about the indifference of the British Government to their general poverty. The only really big people in Scotland came from the Highlands and Islands, which provided the huge policemen, the 'polis', who kept law and order in Glasgow and in the other big Scottish cities.

Jamie had pale sandy hair with the usually-accompanying fair skin, which was marked by the ravages of untreated acne. The main reason for her marrying him had been the remark of Mary when she herself had got married: 'Never mind Madge Hen, I'm sure that someone will want you one day, your no' a bad-looking lass, although you're getting on a bit!' Madge had burned at Mary's remarks, but she was aware that at twenty-five years of age most women were married and dragging a couple of kids around with them, with another one on the way. She would show Mary! Within three weeks she had picked up Jamie at a dance and was going steady with him, with the wedding arranged within a further month.

Indeed, Madge was a good-looking woman, a very good-looking woman. She was 5ft 2inches tall, with an eye-catching figure, a small well-shaped mouth, white even teeth, high cheek bones, and grey/blue eyes set in a slim pleasant face. She had long straight fair hair that she parted in the middle and let fall down to her shoulders, rather like the film star Veronica Lake. Her legs were long and slim, and her skin was clear and fresh, without the blemishes from which many of the women in that area suffered. She looked so sweet and gentle that many - those who didn't know her very well - even considered her to be a nice friendly person, but her appearance was deceptive, as she was as hard as nails inside, and more than a match for any man who earned her displeasure.

However, when she wanted to secure some favour or concession from a man, of whatever age, whether an office junior, a shop-floor workman, or a foreman or manager, she could turn on such charm as to have him almost drooling with pleasure. Needless to say, any other woman who was in the vicinity could see through her antics, and many a head was shaken in disapproval: 'dirty little slut!'

Madge had been glad when Jamie had been called up and she no longer had to endure sleeping in the same bed as him. Working as a storeman in the Yard, Jamie had thought that he wouldn't be conscripted for military service, "called-up", as shipbuilding was a reserved occupation, essential to the War effort. However, it seemed that the Yard could cope with one less storeman, whilst the Army needed more men for a forthcoming offensive. Both his foreman and the manager at the Yard knew that he was a slacker, so they didn't make a case to retain him: perhaps the Army would be able to knock him into shape for service in the trenches. He had had the chance in the past to become a riveter, which would have meant better pay and more security against the call-up, but it also would have meant his having to do more demanding work, so he had turned the job down. Anyway, off to the army he had had to go.

When she was thirteen, Madge had lost her virginity to an older boy. He had told her that he loved her and asked her to "prove" her love for him, to which, after a few times of refusal, and his threats to walk out on her, she had reluctantly agreed. He had led her into the toilet at the end of the court at the back of his mother's house, where he had immediately pulled down her knickers, sat her on the front of the toilet seat, lifted her knees and then entered her, ejaculating within a minute, without making any declarations of love or even kissing her or showing any other signs of affection. Indeed, his only objective had been to add another 'notch to his belt' by making her yet one more of his conquests.

Madge had been completely unmoved by the experience and found it messy, disgusting and pointless. After a repeat performance, again without the display of any affection, his interest had cooled and he had sought the attention of another girl. This would have been bad enough, but he had bragged to all of his mates about having 'had' her, which had led to a number of them thinking that she was an 'easy lay' and propositioning her at every opportunity. Madge had smarted at this treatment, and resolved that no other bastard man would ever take advantage of her again. As the years passed she didn't weaken in her resolve, and stood no nonsense from any man. She was hardened and insensitive, and with a cutting tongue when this was called for.

After Madge had left school, at fourteen years of age, she had got a job as an office junior in a cable-winding company in Greenock. This was fine to start with, and she enjoyed the teasing and mild sexual innuendos of the two young male clerks in the office, but then one of the junior managers had started to take an interest in her. On one occasion when no-one else was in the office, he had asked her to bring some stationery to him from the stockroom, knowing that this particular item of stationery was located on a high shelf at the rear of the room, out of sight of anyone entering the office.

He had followed her into the stockroom just as she was attempting to reach the material by standing on a small stool. Coming up behind her he had placed his hands around her waist to hold her steady. When she had taken hold of the required item and started to step down from the stool, he had let his hands slide up from her waist to her breasts, whilst retaining his firm grasp of her. When on a second occasion he had again requested a further supply of this item, she had let the procedure repeat itself until the item was in her hands, and then she had given a backwards kick to his testicles, upon which he had grunted, let go of her and stepped back. Madge had smiled sweetly at him and then marched pertly out of the stockroom, whilst he glared after her, muttering 'The vicious young swine!' He didn't bother her again.

When she had got to about seventeen she had started to go the local dances with some of her friends, where she would often let some unsuspecting man pick her up. She and the man would get a pass-out card, or a have an ink-stamp applied to the back of their hands, to allow them to re-enter the dance hall later in the evening, and then they would go to one of the pubs that invariably stood on a nearby corner. After the man had bought her a few drinks, and they had flirted and joked together, with some suggestive remarks having been whispered into her ear, she would agree to go round to the back of the pub with the now-aroused man, for a kiss and a cuddle. To encourage him further, she would let the man fondle her breasts, and even run his hand down the front of her dress and into her crutch. Sometimes she would also let him guide her hand down to the swelling in his trousers, but she never went any further than that.

At this point she would call a halt and say that she was going back into the dance hall. The enraged man would call her a "time-waster" and other less-polite names, all of which were indeed appropriate, but she would just laugh. When the word got around about her behaviour, she and her friends would move on to another dance hall. What she got out of this behaviour her friends didn't know, but the explanation was quite simple. Madge didn't care which man it was whom she tormented: in her eyes, they were all bastards, useless randy bastards, and they deserved what they got! "Let them piss off and play with themselves!"

After the declaration of War, with many men being drafted into the forces, there was a need for women to take over some of their duties in industry. Madge had got a job as a machinist at the Bishopton Ordnance Factory, where she was trained initially to use a turret lathe to machine ordnance components. She soon completed the training, and took her place on the production line, her long hair tucked safely inside a turban to keep it away from the rotating work-pieces.

While most of the woman took to wearing trousers, or "slacks" as they called them, Madge carried on wearing a skirt, so that the men in the factory could catch sight of her legs as she bent over the lathe, or reached down into the bin for another work-piece to machine. She was very proud of her legs. With the virtual non-availability of silk stockings during the war, she used to dye the visible part of her legs a gentle golden brown, and then use her eyebrow pencil to draw lines down the back of her legs to simulate seams, so that when not inspected too closely the impression given was that her legs were indeed encased in real silk stockings. She quite enjoyed being at the Ordnance Factory, as it gave her the opportunity to torment a lot of men.

After clocking-on one morning, on her way to the machine shop, she had passed by the Maintenance Electricians' Bay, where one of the men, holding a length of electrical wire in his hand, had called out to her 'Hey Hen, I need someone to pull my wire for me, will you do the job?' Without pausing in her stride she had called back 'Get one of your mates to do it for you. I've heard that you spend all of your tea-breaks pulling each other's wires!' The men roared at this! Madge soon became the favourite of the men in the factory. She was indeed "a real prick-teaser", no mistake!

After a while she grew bored with the monotony of machining the same work-pieces day in and day out, and worked her charms on one of the older foremen to get him to find her a more interesting job. As luck would have it a position became vacant for someone to drive the overhead crane in the Assembly Bay. She was duly instructed in the use

16

of the crane and, after a test, was awarded a Certificate of Competence. When she climbed up the steel ladder to the control cabin at the top of the crane, the men in the vicinity would cluster at the foot of the ladder to look up her skirt, and the same when she climbed down. One day, feeling full of devilment, whilst up in her cabin she removed her knickers surreptitiously. Climbing down the ladder at the end of the afternoon shift she gave the cluster of men a view that they had never seen before and would never forget, the details of which, greatly embellished upon, spread throughout the pubs and clubs that evening like wildfire.

The next morning all of the men in the Assembly Bay were waiting at the foot of the ladder for her arrival, but when Madge appeared she was also wearing slacks, and she wore them every day thereafter. The event passed into legend. The men declared that Madge was "the biggest prick-teaser in the factory by far", with a large measure of admiration in their voices.

Madge had pretended to be depressed by Jamie's return to the Army from leave and had told Cathy that she needed a break from her life of nothing but working all day in munitions at the Ordnance Factory followed by sitting around in the tenement. She told Cathy about Mary's suggestion to join her on a day trip to Blackpool. Cathy had been against this, telling her that now she was a married woman she should sit at home with her in the evenings and at weekends until such time that Jamie could return. Madge had laughed, saying that no possible harm could come to her whilst she was with Mary.

Early that Saturday morning she and Mary had met at Glasgow Central Station, where in the Ladies' toilets they had changed from the dull old clothes that they had arrived in into the much more sexy clothes that Mary had brought with her in her bag. Mary had been given two pairs of virtually-unobtainable silk stockings by a friend with contacts in the black market, and had given one pair to Madge. Mary had many such friends, but Madge knew better than to inquire.

As she drew on the stockings, taking care to check that their seams were straight, Madge contemplated her legs, her best feature. She attached the tops of the stockings to her suspender belt. Her knickers, of white cotton, had shorter legs than was usual, and were close fitting, hugging her bottom tightly, and were highly provocative. She was pleased with what she saw, and knew that she looked attractive and would have no trouble in drawing a man when they got to Blackpool, as neither would Mary. She drew off her wedding ring and slipped it into her purse. Mary noticed this, and did the same herself. All set, they had then boarded the train for the journey south in a state of great excitement and anticipation.

Coming out of Blackpool Central Station on arrival, they had turned left and made for the sea front, only a few hundred yards away. First there was the main road to cross, then the track upon which the electric trams ran, and then the promenade. The trams were sleek and streamlined, not like the noisy, swaying, clanking monsters that ran on the Glasgow streets. They ran smoothly and almost noiselessly, like whispering ghostly machines from another planet! The atmosphere was magical, with the sun shining down and the seagulls whirling overhead emitting their loud raucous cries. The two women were thrilled!

The promenade was wide and sweeping, with bracing sea air coming in from the Irish Sea. Here there were no fogs such as those that stopped the traffic in Glasgow, and left the old and the unwell gasping and coughing, and the undertakers rubbing their hands in gleeful anticipation. The Blackpool beach was clean and sandy and ran without interruption for miles, both north and south. When the tide went out, those on the promenade claimed that they could "hardly see the sea, it was so far away", but in reality it did not withdraw as far as the tide did at Southport, just a few miles to the south. A favourite game for the adventurous was to go out to the extreme low-water mark at low tide, and then enjoy the thrill of having to race back as the incoming tide increased its speed.

This was great fun, but without danger, as it would take the tide more than six hours to flow up the gentle and smooth gradient of the beach to achieve the six or eight feet to the high-water mark, and should a mist be seen to be descending it would take the cautious beach-walker only a five-minute scamper to be back on the promenade, while for romantic couples strolling together on the beach at dusk, the street-lamps on the promenade were like glowing beacons, lighting their way back. However, only a few miles further north into Morecambe Bay, the situation is different, with great danger facing the incautious or unwary [2].

Running out to sea from the Blackpool promenade are three piers, South Pier, Central Pier and North Pier, spaced well apart along the length of the promenade. All three offer a range of attractions, the main of which are variety shows that feature the top entertainers of the day. The longest and most popular pier is North Pier, opened in 1863, which runs out a great way from the promenade, even beyond the low-water mark, enabling the visitors, at all states of the tide, and under all weather conditions, to stride out to the pier's end, glorifying in this magnificent British invention that gives them command over the sea. The floor of the pier is made of timber decking, with spacing between the planks that, although small, gives the visitors a feeling of danger and adventure.

For a small charge they could proceed beyond the decked part of the pier to a lower-lying jetty that was floored with cast-iron grills, of even wider spacing, so that only hardy fishermen, or the more spirited visitors, would venture onto it, particularly in rough weather, when waves would crash up through the grills and soak all present. Madge had heard that at one time boats used to sail from this jetty, some even carrying passengers to and from the Isle of Man.

The fishermen, clad in oilskins and sou'westers, and shod in sturdy boots or 'wellies', "wellingtons", with one or two pairs of thick woollen socks underneath, would brave all weathers; rain, sleet and snow, cold winds, come what may. Most had packs of sandwiches and vacuum flasks, and made theirselves comfortable on little folding camping stools. When the fishing was slow, as it often was, they would go for a little walk to see how the other fishermen were doing, or to exchange information on recent catches.

Most of the fishermen flung out their three-hooked paternoster terminal tackle using stiff split-cane beach rods, although a few used hand-lines, and had to swing their tackle around their head before releasing it. This had to be done carefully, as if the line should be gripped too close to its end there was the danger that one of the hooks, swinging on its trace, could hook the angler's hand as the line was released: regard also had to be taken for other anglers in the immediate vicinity.

Although the locally-dug lugworms were alright for catching the flatfish that inhabited the sandy waters of the bay, they were no match for the writhing centipede-like ragworms that were used elsewhere around the coast. Madge had once sailed 'doon the watter' from Jamaica Street Bridge in Glasgow to Gourock - where the River Clyde opens-out to become the Firth of Clyde - on a kids' outing organised by a local church, and had seen fishermen digging for 'rag' and 'lug' in Cardwell Bay. They were plentiful and in one hour, using a fork, a fisherman could expect to catch about sixty of them, which were more than enough for a day's fishing. However, those in the know caught really big ragworms at the "Shitey Pipe" in Greenock, where untreated sewage flows into the river. At low water, digging down around the end of the exposed sewage pipe into the foul beach, the latter festooned with shreds of toilet paper and newspaper that had been used for the same purpose, fierce ragworms of up to about fifteen inches in length were plentiful.

Exhibitionists amongst the fishermen would bring the ragworms close to their jumpers, whereupon the worms would extend their formidable pincers and grip the jumpers tightly, determined not to let go. The fishermen would then parade around the promenade so adorned, to the horror of passers-by. However, on Blackpool North Pier, the inactive lugworms, with their black swollen tail-ends, which soon leaked fluid to become little more than shrunken skins, had to suffice.

A feature of the North Pier was the "Indian Pavilion", an un-roofed glass-enclosed sun-lounge where, sitting in deck chairs, the visitors could listen to performances from a small stage set at its western, seaward, end. Others just read their newspapers, warm in the sun, but protected from the breezes that blew in from the sea. It was elegant! The seats in the sun lounge were highly prized, and once occupied were likely to remain so until it was time for tea: it paid to be early. Just how many romances have blossomed amongst the unattached middle-aged and old-aged folk sitting in the lounge will never be known, but there must have been a great many!

In good weather the Blackpool beach was solid with day-trippers and holidaymakers. Deckchairs could be hired at the top of the steps leading down to beach from the promenade, but on bright sunny days these were all soon gone. On the beach men sat with knotted handkerchiefs on their heads, drinking tea from cups brought over with filled teapots from stalls on the other side of the promenade, against a deposit for their safe return. At some time during the day the families would go for a paddle in the sea, the men with their trouser legs rolled up and the women with the hems of their skirts tucked inside their knickers: no-one stood on their dignity!

The children were usually persuaded by their parents to remove their shirts and vests to catch the sun but were told after a couple of hours to put them back on again. Some of the women would roll up the bottom of their blouse and turn down the collar, but modesty did not allow them to reveal more of their bodies. However, the men were different altogether. Not normally seeing much of the sun, nor even of daylight in some occupations, due to spending most of their time indoors in a factory, with the standard three nights a week plus Saturday-morning overtime, and having little appreciation of the harmful effects of prolonged exposure to sunlight, many of them would strip to the waist and prostrate themselves from morning until teatime, determined to catch all the rays of the sun that they could.

At the end of the day, they would troop up the beach as red as boiled lobsters, to spend a painful evening applying Calamine lotion to sunburnt faces and necks. Those who had taken off their shirts and vests would suffer even greater discomfort, that could not be eased by Calamine: they would spend a painful night in bed, unable to sleep and unable to take the pressure of the blankets on their blistering bodies. However, when the men got back to work on the following Monday morning, they were the envy of their mates, as having had good weather was the main talking point of a holiday, and what better way of demonstrating this than by a massive shedding of dead skin?

An attraction for the kids on the beach was the donkey rides, where for a modest charge the owner or his assistant would walk several of the donkeys, with kids on their backs, a few hundred yards along the beach and then back again. Pop and ice-cream vendors toured the beach. Usually there was a Punch & Judy show somewhere nearby. There was no problem in entertaining the kids.

Blackpool was the favourite holiday place for most of the people of the north-west of England, and for many Glaswegians too. It did not have the elegance of Southport or Bispham, nor even of Morecambe, but the working class loved it. On the Wakes' Week of the nearby Lancashire cotton towns, most of the population would transfer en-masse to Blackpool, passing each other on the promenade and making frequent exclamations such as 'Hello Alice, Hello Arthur, fancy seeing you here!', to which the inevitable rejoinder would be 'Eee, it's a small world, isn't it!'

Madge and Mary had crossed over to the promenade, and turned right, heading north, as Mary wanted to go up Blackpool Tower, and she would pout if she didn't get her own way. Blackpool tower, a tapering steel structure built in 1894 and rising to 518 feet, was copied from the Eiffel Tower in Paris and was originally intended to be called "The Blackpool Eiffel Tower". It is an elegant Victorian landmark. Children travelling by train from the industrial towns of the north-west of England to Blackpool would stand at the windows of their carriages, even though they were might be twenty or thirty miles away, risking getting soot or grit in their eyes from the steam locomotive up in front, for the chance to be the first to spot the tower in the distance.

The tower typifies Blackpool: confident, bold, brash and cheerful, and it gives the town a character all of its own. It is said that it was designed in such a way that in the event of structural failure, it would not fall along the promenade, nor backwards across the busy streets lying behind it, but across the promenade and into the sea! To whom this statement is intended to give reassurance is not known!

The ride up the tower in the small cabin had been breathtaking. As the ground had fallen away, Mary had started her usual squealing and yelling. She wasn't a very bright girl, but she was usually jolly and good company, so Madge had let her carry on. They had admired the extensive views from the viewing gallery at the top of the tower. On most days it is possible to look 18 miles north-north-west over to the town of Barrow-in-Furness, with the Isle of Walney lying just off it, on the west side of Morecambe Bay; and on very clear days to look some 55-60 miles north-west to the Isle of Man or look east to the Pennine Range. Those going up the tower were highly impressed: 'Better than the view from the Eiffel Tower any day!', although most of those who exclaimed this had never been outside of Lancashire, unless it had been on a day trip on a chara' to the Yorkshire Dales or North Wales, or on a boat trip to the Isle of Man.

After the two girls had decided to return to the ground, Mary had pretended to be helpless and frightened of crossing the small gap between the floor of the cabin and the floor of the viewing platform, whereupon a young man standing close by had held her hand and was rewarded with a beaming smile. However, he didn't respond, and as they reached the ground and the cabin door opened she had turned away, disappointed.

Next they had visited the large indoor zoo within the tower building, where many of the animals were pacing up and down in their cages in a dispirited manner. Mary had said that the place 'smelt of pee', as indeed it did, so they had left and had a snack at a nearby café.

Across the road at the back of the tower building was a large open-fronted shop where an amiable middle-aged man was demonstrating the making of Blackpool Rock. At the end of his performance, he had said in a straight voice 'The special feature of this shop is that we also make rock for one of the cities of our great ally-in-arms, Russia.' and had held up a stick of rock that at its end clearly displayed a name in what looked like Cyrillic characters.

The audience had smiled politely at this old 'chestnut', except for Mary, simple soul that she is, who had exclaimed 'Fancy that!' which brought grins to the faces of the others present. When she had quickly realised her mistake, she had felt mortified, and promptly marched Madge out of the shop, exclaiming 'The stupid old English fart!' When the need arose, Mary could curse with the best of them! Madge's giggles at this outburst had soon brought Mary round, and, smiling at each other, they had decided that it was time for a drink and an ice-cream sundae at one of the seafront cafés.

They had then gone on to the Winter Gardens, where-middle aged and middle-class visitors were enjoying an elegant tea dance. This wasn't of interest to Madge and Mary, so they had walked back towards the station and found themselves once again at the sea front, this time turning south along the promenade, soon coming to the "Golden Mile".

This was a major attraction of the town, but it didn't have the majesty of the Tower, or the sophistication of the Winter Gardens: it was a miscellany of amusement arcades and sideshows. In the 1890s, Blackpool Beach had been overflowing with stalls and entertainment of all kinds, so that in 1897 the Corporation had announced that in future, only donkeys, camels and boatmen could operate there, along with ventriloquists, Punch & Judy shows, magicians and stalls selling Blackpool Rock, sweets, soft drinks, ice cream and oysters. As a result of this decision, all of the other stallholders had moved to the forecourts and gardens of the Victorian villas directly opposite across the promenade.

In some cases what had been the gardens of the villas had been totally or partially lightly roofed-over, and slot machines set on each side, with a central passage-way leading to bigger games and competitive games within the house proper at the rear. The competitive games included such as horse racing, where each of some nine or ten seated players would roll their small wooden ball down a ramp, an inclined board at the end of the ramp causing the ball to fly up into the air, and then fall into one of several curved troughs, the difficulty of landing in the increasingly-smaller troughs being reflected in a greater forwards-displacement being given to the player's model horse, running in a race against the horses of the other players on a big board mounted on the far wall. It was exciting and good fun.

Intermingled with these amusement arcades were other attractions, such as: the Tattooed Man; the Fat Lady; the Strong Man; the Gypsy Fortune Teller; the booths of the photographers who worked the pavements outside; the kids' talent shows; and the Spiritualist. The latter was of especial interest to Mary, who was a mug for anything 'from the other side'.

They had paid the entrance fee and gone in, just as the performance was about to start. After a flowery and glowing introduction from his assistant, the "Master of the Unknown" came onto the small stage and stood in front of a lectern. He remained silent as he gazed solemnly at the audience to quell any nervous hilarity that they might be feeling. There was always the chance that a few in the audience had had a drink, and he wasn't going to allow his performance to generate into a comedy show. He had seen the film "The Thirty-Nine Steps" starring Robert Donat, in which "Mr. Memory" had had to endure the ribald comments of the drinkers sitting at the bar of the music hall in which he was performing, and that wasn't going to happen to him. No fear!

The audience was soon sitting quietly and attentively. He then

23

lowered his head into his hands and was silent for a whole minute, during which time the audience had begun to get agitated, then he had said 'I feel a strong presence from the other side. Someone is trying to contact one of you. Has one of you been ill?' There was a rapid show of hands from the grey-faced amongst the audience. Good, he could play this lot! 'I see a name, is it Joan or Jean?' This time there were lesser hands raised, but he noticed that two of those who had raised their hands appeared to be sitting alone, judging from their lack of communication with their neighbours.

He couldn't have gone wrong in the choice of names, as Joan and Jean were amongst the most common names of ladies of their age group, with Bill, John and Arthur being their male counterparts. He had then said 'You have lost a loved one. He is trying to say something to me from the other side. No, the contact is fading.', first giving hope of contact with the loved one, then dashing the hope, but all along intending finally to restore contact and give the audience what they wanted to hear.

In this way he was employing the psychological sandwich that is used by hospital staff after breaking the news to the family of someone who had just died: 'He was very weak and we didn't think that he would pull through', at which the faces of the relatives would show their grief, 'but then he rallied and fought back and we really thought that he had a chance', upon which their faces would brighten, as they all knew that old Jack wouldn't have given up easily, 'but finally the strain was too much for him, and we lost him.' This technique eased the grief of the bereaved relatives, who liked to think that old Jack had gone down fighting, losing out in the end against overwhelming odds. He had always been a grand scrapper had old Jack!

The audience had begun to squirm in their seats in frustration. 'But no, I am making contact again!' He looked in turn at the two women who had raised their hands a few moments earlier: 'Joan, you have been asked to keep your chin up, and I am told that Bill, is it Bill?' A confirmatory 'Yes' from one of the two women had the audience frozen in their seats. 'Bill on the other side is doing all that he can for you. You are not to forget him, as he won't forget you, He sends you his love. Ah, the contact is fading.' He had then placed his head in his hands again, weak from the mental effort that he had just made. Arthur had turned to Alice and said 'By gum Alice, this makes you think! How could he know all that?'

At this point his assistant had passed slips of paper round the audience, and asked them to write down their problems for the "Master of the Unknown" to contemplate, then to fold their slips so that they could not be read by anyone else. The "Master of the Unknown" was to learn of the problem by means of his spiritual attributes, the slips being just to confirm the correctness of the problems after he had responded to them. He placed the folded slips onto the lectern in front of him. He then started to respond to what he stated to the audience was the problem in the first of the as-yet unfolded slips, but actually what he said was pure nonsense and had nothing to do with the audience's problems. When he had finished his response he asked the audience for confirmation of the accuracy of the response. However, what the audience didn't know was that when he responded to this 'first', fake, problem, this particular problem would be claimed by a stooge at the back of the room, who hadn't forwarded a folded slip of paper with the details of a problem on it.

Having successfully responded to the problem, to the grateful and loudly-outspoken thanks of the stooge, he had unfolded the first slip and made a pretence of reading what the audience believed to be the stooge's question, after which he placed the 'finished' slip down on the lectern with a dramatic theatrical gesture. Thus he had read the first genuine problem before even commencing to use his 'supernatural skills' to determine what the problem was, and then to answer it! So it went on, his knowledge of the problems of the audience appearing to be uncanny. Alice had said to Arthur 'That man has a divine gift. We have seen a miracle performed here today!'

Next Madge and Mary went into a kids' talent contest, won by a show of hands by a skinny little boy of about eight, with a mop of curly hair, wearing a skimpy bathing suit, playing the "Warsaw Concerto" on an upright piano, just out-doing the impersonation by a cute little girl of about ten of Shirley Temple singing "On the good ship lollipop". The little girl, who had been well applauded, had erupted into tears as the decision was announced. Still, if she wanted to make her way in the entertainment world, she would have to learn to accept disappointment graciously and with a smile.

Leaving this show, they had gone back to the roadside, where they had been 'snapped' by a spiv-type photographer sporting a trilby hat and a pencil-line moustache. The girls were pleased and flattered to have been 'chosen'. He had handed the girls a card, telling them that the photograph would be available at his kiosk in two hours' time. Before he moved on, he had asked them to pose for a second shot, 'in case the first shot doesn't come out', and this time he had actually clicked the shutter.

They had then stopped at a seafood bar, where Mary had cockles in vinegar on a little dish, whilst Madge had shrimps. Both of these delicacies are caught locally, the cockles by raking the sand after the tide has gone out, where they lie just beneath the surface awaiting the tide's return, whilst the shrimps are caught in about one-to-two feet of water in close-mesh beam nets pulled by massive shire-horses.

The locals also catch these sea-foods themselves, and on most days a few people can be seen raking the sand at the water's edge with a garden rake or hand-fork. Sometimes they would place a flat board, called a "Jumbo board", on the sand and then vibrate it with their feet or by means of two attached upright handles, the history behind this being that at one time some cockle-pickers had brought a young boy along with them, and had sat him on the sand in a galvanised tub to keep him out of mischief. His unsuccessful attempts to climb out had vibrated the tub to such an extent that the cockles below had thought that the tide had returned, as great numbers of them were lying on the surface when the tub was moved away.

Other locals, wearing chest-waders, or if they were hardy enough, wearing just shorts and deck-shoes or sandals, would push smaller versions of the small-mesh beam net close inshore, in perhaps six-to-twelve inches of water. However, the use of open-toed sandals was not to be recommended, as this brought with it the danger of being stung by a stone fish or a weaver fish, lying just submerged in the sand, but with its dorsal fin raised, where a sting from the fin can cause excruciating agony, and possibly the need for a visit to the hospital. In many cases the pain is so severe that the injured person is unable to communicate to others the source of the problem. Many professional shrimp-catchers have a blackened thumb or finger from having been stung by a stone fish or a weaver fish that had found its way, along with the catch, onto the sorting table.

Both the shrimps and the cockles had tasted gritty from the sand grains that inevitably could not be washed from them, even after boiling, but they were delicious. On offer at the seafood bar were also winkles, mussels, and even more expensive varieties of seafood such as crabs, crayfish and oysters. Seeing the latter, Mary, never missing the opportunity for a little vulgarity, had reminded Madge of the old joke about the alleged aphrodisiac properties of oysters, which a woman had claimed were exaggerated, seeing as her husband had consumed half-a-dozen of them the night before and only three of them had worked!

Further along the way they came to a "Health Machine", where the sick were invited to have their electrical resistance measured, under the astounding premise that one's resistance to illness can be measured by one's resistance to electrical current! A middle-aged woman, dressed in a white overall to give her 'medical credibility', assisted a grey-faced old lady onto the stand of the machine and helped her to grasp firmly, one hand on each, the two upright metal bars that made the electrical contact with the machine.

'You haven't been well have you dear?' she had asked, as the indicator of the machine displayed a low reading. 'No, I haven't' replied the 'patient', but she appeared to have gained some satisfaction from her illness having been recognised, not having had the courage to visit the local doctor, choosing to ignore the many symptoms of illness that she had displayed over recent months. Despite the 'ill-health' deduction from the result of the ridiculous 'test' on the Health Machine, it was unlikely that she would visit the doctor until her illness had progressed so far that very little could be done to save her. 'I don't want to waste the doctor's time.' she would say. Sadly, such was the way of many of the working class, particularly those who couldn't afford the cost of a consultation, and there were many in this position.

The next place that they had visited was a slot-machine arcade, where they had passed to the back of the arcade, in which there was a shooting gallery. It was not the traditional shooting gallery where airguns are used to shoot at painted paper targets, but a projection-type system where images of Hitler and his fellow leaders of the Nazi party, Ribbentrop, Goebbels, Himmler, Goering and the rest, were projected onto a screen. Aiming the rifles caused a marker to move over the image, and when the trigger was pulled a mechanical piercer punctured the strip of film that was projecting the image, providing a mark on the image to show just where one's shot had 'landed'. At the end of the game, the punctured strip was delivered down a chute, so that it could be taken away as evidence of the owner's prowess as a marksman.

Mary had squealed for a chance at the machine, but had put up an abysmal performance. As she had prattled on in her usual way, a hand had reached over from behind her to take the rifle, and a deep American voice had said 'Excuse me Ma'am, but let me show you how we US of A soldiers deal with these Nazis!' Mary had stood back as the US soldier put his coin into the machine and then, in a short time, selectively demolished Hitler and the rest of the bunch. Mary had trilled with delight, proclaiming 'Well, seeing as we now have you Yanks on our side, we have nothing to fear from this war!'

Madge had then moved further into the interior of the building, leaving Mary to complete her conquest of the soldier. After a couple of minutes Mary had come over and told her that the Yank wanted her to spend the day with him, and asked if she minded. Madge had assured her that she had no objection, as this had been agreed before they had set out, just saying that she would meet her at the station half an hour before the return train to Glasgow was due to depart.

Mary and her new friend had then left the arcade, and after a few seconds Madge started to follow them out. It was then that she saw him, an American soldier, standing in the gloom at the far side of the room, staring intently at her. As she had walked out of the arcade she was disappointed that he made no attempt to speak to her, but was pleased when she noticed that he was following her.

She had continued to walk south along the Golden Mile, until she came to Madame Tussaud's waxworks and next to it the Huntsman Hotel. She had entered the hotel and gone into the Best Room, where she had asked for an "Oh Be Joyful", which was the name adopted by the locals for the sweet stout manufactured by the OBJ company. He had followed her into the Best Room, where he had asked for a whisky, receiving the inevitable refusal from the barman: 'Don't you know? There's a war on!' Such drinks, and many other things as well, were available on the black market, particularly in Blackpool, but a Yank turning up at a public house had no chance! He had settled for a half-pint of bitter and went to sit at the back of the room. After finishing her drink, Madge had gone to the Ladies' room and then straight out of the hotel. The soldier, however, had been quick to follow.

At the end of the block was the "Fairy-Land Grotto" where, in a beautifully-created underground cavern set into the front of the building as if on a stage, there were eight or so little 'gnomes', sitting in a row at a workbench as workers on a production line, all of them busily engaged in different tasks in the extraction of pearls from oysters. As each oyster shell was cracked open, the pearl, represented by a bright little light bulb, was removed and then passed along the line via other gnomes to its eventual storage place: a very impressive and industrious little factory! This magical scene was supported by the grinding of the mechanisms that controlled the actions of the gnomes, and by a hurdy-gurdy-type tune that was exactly appropriate for the setting.

Those entering the Grotto passed by the cavern to a small landing stage, where they boarded tiny boats floating in a narrow channel. Driven by an unseen underwater mechanism, the boats took them on a journey past wondrous fairy-tale scenes that delighted children and brought a smile to the face of even the most serious of adults. It was innocent and delightful! Madge had paused to look at the gnomes at their work, and smiled. The Golden Mile was cheap and cheerful and a bit seamy, but it had a charm and vitality all of its own.

She had then carried on south, reaching the seafront boarding houses with their neatly flagged, gravelled or tiled gardens, although a number of them also had minute areas of closely-cropped grass. The houses gave the impression of tidiness, order and prosperity, not like some of the terraced houses that she had seen through the train window whilst coming down from Glasgow that morning, which clearly needed attention to their structure and paint-work, and where the gardens were overgrown and neglected.

There was nothing scruffy or neglected about these sea-front boarding houses: their paintwork was clean and fresh, and the views through the windows were of bright, well-furnished rooms. There would be a dinner gong in the hall to summon the guests to the dining room, although a call up the stairs would have sufficed. However, that would not have been sufficiently genteel and certainly not what the guests expected.

One place, the "Craig-y-Don", had caught her eye. It had a novel glass 'drinking' bird standing on a small table in front of the dining-room window, the bird, balanced on a pivot, constantly bending down, taking a drink from a glass of water sitting in front of it, and then rising up again. Of how it worked Madge had had no idea [#3], but it enthralled her, as it did most of the passers-by.

She would have loved to have been able to stay there, and get up in the morning to a cooked breakfast, and then stroll down to the pavement coffee stall at the corner, where she could watch the world go by, and let it see her in return. Indeed, she would have loved to have been able to stay in any one of these grand boarding houses, and enjoy a brief period of middle-class living, but this was beyond the means of Mary and herself

Carrying on south along the promenade, passing the South Pier, the Lifeboat station and approaching the outdoor swimming-pool, Madge finally reached her intended destination, the one attraction that no holiday-maker or day-tripper to Blackpool would ever miss: the Pleasure Beach! This is a huge complex of various amusements, along with places at which to eat and drink. There are side-shows, shies, games of chance, thrilling rides; indeed everything that anyone could wish for. Madge ignored all of the other attractions, and made her way to the Fun House, which stood on slightly higher ground towards the back of the complex.

The Fun House was a big rectangular building of about 40ft height, devoid of windows and ornamentation, and resembling a suburban cinema or a warehouse. However, the plainness of the front of the House was relieved by a long opening at about 20ft from the ground, which provided a balcony on which a couple of dozen people, mostly youngsters, were cooling-off from their frantic activities inside the House and shouting and waving excitedly to those passing by. A hubbub of shrieks, laughter, and loud excited conversations came from within the House.

Madge made her way towards the entrance, at the side of which stood a big glass-fronted and glass-sided case. Sitting within the case was a human-size fat old clown with a little clown sitting on his knee. The fat old clown wobbled and shook as he roared with laughter, but the little clown just rocked to-and-fro without a sound. The old clown's laughter, however, was not full-bodied and sincere, but mechanical and tinny, like that on the record that was played often on the wireless, "The Laughing Policeman". The tinny sound was not surprising, as the fat old clown had sat on his throne-like seat, wearing his ornate crown, and laughing, for a great many years, during which time the record producing his laughter had become old and scratched. However, protected by the glass case, and with the case itself sitting partially in the shade of the House, the painted wooden faces of the two clowns, and the traditional gaudy harlequin tunics that they wore, were bright and well preserved.

Stopping in front of the case, Madge bent down, as if to view the little clown better, but what she really wanted to do was to look into the glass front of the case to see if she could see the image of the soldier reflected in it. He was there, as she knew that he would be, standing about twenty feet away. Madge had decided earlier that the Fun House would give the solder the best chance to make his move: with luck, she would soon find out! She squared her shoulders and walked quickly over to the entrance...

Part 1: Scotland

Chapter One

Madge paid the admission charge and passed through the turnstile into the Fun House, her mind pre-occupied with the image of the soldier that she had seen in the glass of the clowns' case. He was young, tall and lean, and whilst not exactly handsome, had a look of quality about him that can only be acquired by an active and healthy outdoor life-style. Madge couldn't but compare his appearance with that of her husband Jamie, but then he hadn't been born and raised in a slum area of Glasgow, with poor housing and poor food and in a polluted environment.

Once inside the House, the visitors found themselves on a stage, and had to run the gauntlet of various ordeals before they could proceed onto the floor of the House: they had to walk between piled-high columns of barrels, which wobbled precariously as if about to fall down on top of them; they had to walk along a path of contra-rotating disks, which threatened to throw them off their feet; they had to walk over a bridge of rollers, where every step forward ran the risk of their rolling back to the starting point; and they had to walk over a floor that sank beneath them.

However, after they had overcome these challenges, there was one final ordeal for the ladies. As they walked forwards on the stage towards the short flight of steps that would take them down to the floor, in the mistaken belief that the different ordeals were over, a blast of air under the control of some hidden operator would come up from between the floorboards and blow their skirts up into the air. Madge knew of this particular ordeal, and as her skirt arose around her, showing her new silk stockings, her suspender belt and her skimpy knickers, she squealed and twirled, making an apparent attempt, but carefully failing, to hold down her skirt. The eyes of the group of middle-aged men watching from within the Hall glistened with lust: this is what they had come to see! Madge turned and caught sight of the soldier in the act of running his tongue over his parted lips: she glowed!

Madge then stepped down onto the floor: not pausing at the barrel roll, where people rolled and tumbled together in clusters within a barrel of some 9ft diameter and 20ft length revolving around its horizontally-set axis, as they tried to reach the far end; nor did she pause when she reached a runway where two huge concave sheets, each fastened to a launching platform at one end and to a common central island at the other end, trapped the cautious, the secret being to be bold and rush with full energy from one of the launching platforms to the central island, and then, without pausing, to rush to the far end over the second concave sheet. Those who were trapped at the bottom of one the sheets had to be helped to reach one or other of the launching platforms safety by grasping the hands held down to them from the short guard-wall running above each side of the sheets. Many a 'trapped' young lady who had to be hauled to safety by a young man ended up making a new friend!

She carried on past the centrifuge, an almost horizontally-mounted disk of about 25ft diameter with a low padded wall around its rim, where those brave enough to give this fearsome ordeal a try, sitting with their backs against the wall, were trapped in place by the high centrifugal force developed as the wheel rotated at increasing speed, the slight inclination of the wheel to the horizontal imparting a periodically increasing and then decreasing gravitational affect, which left them reeling when they alighted. Finally, she came to the slides at the far right-hand side of the Hall.

There were four slides, of shining metal, the two inner slides running from about the half-height of the Hall, with the two outer slides running from the full height. Madge climbed the right-hand-side steps leading to one of the full-height slides, with the soldier following behind her. After Madge reached the top of the steps and sat down at the edge of the platform, she started to 'do a Mary', in crying out 'Oh, I can't!' knowing that this technique had always worked for Mary. Immediately the soldier slid down behind her, putting his legs around each side of her and his arms around her waist. 'Have no fear Ma'am' he said, as he pushed the two of them off the platform before the attendant could stop him, as "tandem sliding" was expressly forbidden.

As they gained speed down the slide Madge screamed with excitement, thrilled that the soldier had made his move. Coming to a stop at the end of the slide, she stood up and lost her balance and swayed, so that he reached out and drew her against him to steady her: she was delighted to feel his erection pressing against her back as he held her firmly, enjoying the moment! 'Hold on there Honey!' he said, the sound of his slow deep voice sending a tingle of excitement through her.

She turned and looked up into his face and saw that he was smiling, a kind gentle smile that showed his perfect white teeth. His short-cropped dark curly hair, and his dark brown eyes and olive skin, gave an indication of his likely South-American origins. He was absolutely lovely! She told him her name, and learned that his name was Joel. He looked so handsome in his uniform! It was made of a lightweight good-quality material, not like the coarse fabric of the ill-fitting battledress that Jamie wore. Although the day was warm, he carried his greatcoat with him, neatly folded over one arm. When he spoke to her, it was in a respectful humble tone, always addressing her as "Ma'am", which made her feel special.

She thought how Joel's gentle manner of speech contrasted with Jamie's guttural Glasgow accent. Not that in Govan anyone spoke any differently, nor was this important. What really annoyed her was that Jamie could not complete a sentence without swearing. Not long ago one of the kids in the close had interfered with his bike, so that he couldn't use it to get to work. Jamie had come into the tenement in an enraged state, and explained the reason in a remarkable display of the use of one basic swear-word in a range of grammatical forms: as an adjective, a noun, an adverb, a verb, and then again as an adjective; set between the words 'Some - - has - - my - bike!'

Whilst Madge had winced at his use of bad language, Cathy had responded with righteous anger at what the kid had done, employing her own imaginative use of swear words: like mother, like son! However, such minor acts of vandalism were a common enough occurrence in the area where they lived, or as the Scots say, where they "stayed".

Joel suggested that they walk around the Pleasure Beach together, seeing that they were both on their own, to which Madge agreed readily. As they walked he made polite conversation, but seemed rather nervous. To put him at his ease, she started to tell him a little about herself, but glossing over her background and presenting a much nicer picture of herself. She realised that Joel was only about eighteen or nineteen years old and knocked off five years from her own age, telling him that she was twenty. She also modulated her voice, to sound more like a modest and inexperienced young girl, unfamiliar with the ways of the world. Joel was clearly taken with her and smiled and laughed at her every word.

Soon they came to the "Grand National", a roller-coaster named after the famous horse-race run each year at Aintree. Two carriages sitting on railed tracks were lined up level with each other at the foot of a steep incline, awaiting being boarded by passengers. Joel insisted that they give it a try and, despite her initial protests, Madge allowed him to usher her through the turnstile and into one on the carriages. After a minute or so, the two carriages rolled forwards together a few feet under gravity, and then the chain mechanism running between the tracks engaged with the carriages and started to drag them up to the top of the incline.

The whole structure of the ride was made just of timber beams and the carriage started to vibrate and sway. Madge clasped Joel's hand in mounting concern. As they approached the top of the incline, they had a grand panoramic view of Blackpool sea-front. Madge started to squeal with mounting fear. Reaching the top they passed under a board declaring "They're off", and the carriage started to gain speed, swinging to the left and approaching the first of the 'hazards', "Beecher's Brook", named after one of the jumps in the Grand National. The track fell away, and Madge and Joel became weightless, held in their seats only by the safety barrier that they had folded down onto their laps before setting off.

Both Madge and Joel groaned in fear, which was intensified as the carriage started to climb up the other side of the dip, when they then suffered an excess, as opposed to a deficit, of gravity. However, there was no relenting: the carriage swung from side-to-side and dropped down into one valley after another, then immediately climbing the other side. Finally, the carriage rolled from a great height towards a wall set square across the track, where spectators watched their progress towards them, with fascination, through big glass windows. Madge feared that they would crash into the wall and screamed out loud, but at the last moment the track dropped away and they passed through a tunnel beneath the wall, her fear of crashing being replaced by her fear of being beheaded by the roof of the tunnel.

As they pulled in at the end of the 'race', Madge noticed that the other carriage, which had originally been on their left, was now on their right, and she couldn't see how it could possibly have passed from one side to the other. She asked Joel how this could be so, but he couldn't give an explanation. Both Madge and Joel were thrilled and excited by the experience and, after alighting, stood with their arms around each without embarrassment. As they moved apart, Joel took Madge's hand in his in a perfectly natural manner. Madge squeezed his hand and gave him a beaming smile, which made his heart lurch. God, she was lovely! By this time Madge was captivated by Joel, and she understood the reason for the oft-quoted resentful view of the British servicemen of their American allies posted to Britain, usually expressed as their being 'over paid, over sexed and over here!'

Madge and Joel tired of walking around and made their way to the lounge in the "Casino" at the entrance to the Pleasure Beach. Madge chose a quiet corner whilst Joel went to the bar to order drinks. By now, conversation between them flowed naturally and easily. Madge learnt of Joel's early life and of his family, and what his plans were for after the war and, in return, he asked her about herself. She told him of her life in Govan and her hopes for the future, but she didn't mention Jamie. She described her war work at the Ordnance Factory, and how she was qualified to drive an overhead crane. He was impressed and listened attentively to all that she had to say.

After a while they stopped talking. He moved his seat closer to hers and reached out for her hand. Joel was not like any other man she had known: he was so gentle. He was little more than a youth, a long way from home and having to face doing a man's job. She felt an ache in her heart that she had never felt before. Short as their acquaintance had been, she realised that she was experiencing a new sensation: for the first time in her life she was falling in love. They decided that they wanted something to eat, so they left the bar and bought fish and chips, wrapped in the traditional newspaper, from a nearly stall and sat on an empty bench to eat them.

Later, Joel slid his arm around Madge's shoulder, drawing her head again his chest. For a long time they didn't speak, the closeness of their contact being all that they needed. Eventually, Madge became concerned with the passage of time and the need before too long to meet Mary at the station. She had also started to feel a desperate need for Joel to show in a more physical manner his obvious attraction to her. She knew that he was young and inexperienced and that she would have to help him to show his feelings. The strong desire that she herself felt for Joel was new to her, and also a little frightening. Never before had she felt this way about a man.

They decided to make their way back to the centre of the town. As they crossed over to the promenade Joel took her hand again. Approaching a quiet spot, he turned and kissed her. In mounting excitement he put his hands around her body and drew her close. Madge didn't want the moment to end, but it was lost when a small boy approached them, followed by his parents. The little boy walked up to Joel and with a cheeky grin on his face asked 'Got any gum chum?' knowing that this American soldier would probably produce a strip of chewing gum for him, as would most American soldiers over in Britain when so asked. However, Joel shook his head and smiled, before the mother caught up with the boy and led him away, remonstrating with him for being so presumptuous.

They started to walk towards Central Pier, which was near to Central Station where she was to meet Mary, but to avoid bumping into her on the promenade she suggested that they walk on the sands. Underneath Central Pier the sand was soft and clean, having been washed by the recent high tide, but with a few dimps lying here and there that had fallen through the spaces in the decking of the pier. Joel stopped and spread his greatcoat on the sand. Madge needed no persuasion, and lay down and then drew Joel down beside her.

They lay together for a few moments, and then they reached for each other, kissing gently at first, but then with increasing passion. After a few moments Madge realised that Joel was uneasy about making his next move, probably fearing rejection. She reached down for his hand and drew it up and laid it across her breasts. Joel's response was immediate: he undid the buttons of her blouse, slid a hand into her brassiere and then gently cupped her breasts in turn. Madge gasped, and drew Joel's hand out, alarming him that he had gone to far, but no: Madge eased her brassiere over her breasts and pulled Joel's head down to her. His mouth found one of her nipples and he sucked it into his mouth, which caused her to moan. Joel then started to fondle her lower body.

Soon Madge was strongly aroused and moaned at such volume that Joel felt that the people walking on the decking above them would hear her. He tried to slip down her knickers and was pleased when Madge raised herself from the ground to make this easier, but he was thwarted by her suspender belt. Madge realised this and sat up and unfastened it, then carefully rolled down her silk stockings and placed them to one side: they were too valuable to be treated carelessly! She then raised her hips again, and helped him to remove the impeding garment.

Joel's hands were gentle and manipulating and soon she was experiencing a depth of feeling that she had not known before: she ached for him to 'take' her. She helped him to remove his lower clothing. Within four or five seconds the two of them were stripped from the waist down. Joel moved over her, slowly and carefully, and then she drew him close, helping him to enter her, which he did with consideration, whilst at the same time expressing his love, in contrast with the brutish manner that she had always experienced with Jamie.

She felt the warmth of Joel inside her. As he started to move, Madge's arousal intensified to fever pitch and she began to wail. Soon they were both crying out with emotion. Joel, with great effort, delayed his climax until Madge's cries became incoherent as she approached her own climax, which she experienced as a sudden spreading through the whole of her vagina of the immensely pleasurable sensation that she had experienced during Joel's foreplay, but this time of such intensity as to be almost painful. They climaxed in unison, Madge giving one last desperate moaning wail.

Although Madge was the object of desire of many men, and could have had her pick of them whenever she so wished, this was the first time, married woman that she was, that she had experienced a climax. Neither the man who had deflowered her when she was young, nor her husband Jamie, had attempted any form of foreplay, nor had they had any consideration for her own needs, but had simply used her body for their own selfish satisfaction. Brutish ignorant inconsiderate swine! Her love for this young sensitive American soldier swelled within her.

Afterwards, as they lay together, Joel whispered soft words of endearment into her ear, unlike Jamie, who usually rolled over as soon as the act was completed and was asleep within minutes. Madge lay quietly, feeling fulfilled and loved, and marvelling at the sensation that she had just experienced. She hadn't known that lovemaking could be such an exciting and emotion-churning experience. She felt a desperate need to see Joel again, no matter what it took, or what lies she would have to tell, to bring about their reunion. She realised that the time for her to get to the station was becoming short, and gently eased Joel away from her. Their passion spent, they dressed, almost in embarrassment, and then they returned to the promenade.

Joel had to go south to his barracks close by Squires Gate Aerodrome and agreed that he should get a tram, which would take him almost the whole way back, whilst Madge still had enough time to walk back to the station. As they clung together, they expressed their love for each other, kissed one last time and then agreed that they would meet in the Huntsman at noon four weeks hence, although how she would arrange this Madge didn't know.

On the train back to Glasgow Madge was silent, despite Mary's attempts to get her to talk about her day, her mind filled with thoughts of Joel. However, Mary chatted on happily about her own new friend. Madge was careful to sit still in her seat for the whole journey, lest the heat of the carriage should cause the residual scent of her and Joel's lovemaking to come to Mary's attention: better that Mary, even though a close friend, should know nothing that she could pass on to others at a later date. They reached Glasgow in time to catch the last bus to Govan, and as soon as Madge reached home she slipped into the kitchen and washed herself and her underwear at the kitchen sink.

The next morning Madge gave thought to the next visit to Blackpool to see Joel, and decided that on the coming Monday she would raise the subject with Mary, perhaps suggesting that they should pretend that they had the intention to spend the day in the city, visiting the 'Barras' Market along the Gallowgate, and perhaps the Museum and Art Gallery in Kelvinside, whilst instead catching the train south to Blackpool, although Cathy would be unlikely to accept that the two girls would be interested in anything so cultural as the Museum and Art Gallery. She would have to wait and see.

However, these things were not to be. Three weeks later she received a telegram advising her " ... regret to inform you that your husband Pte. James Alexander MacAlister was killed in action ... ' She also realised that her period was overdue. At that same moment Joel was embarking for action in the European War Zone.

Chapter Two

As the weeks passed, Madge resigned herself to being pregnant, but she didn't tell anyone of her condition. She knew that of all people, she mustn't let Mary know, as Mary couldn't keep a secret to herself for as long as it took her to walk the length of the street. Fortunately, her one-night stand with Joel had followed soon after the departure of Jamie, so that there was no reason for anyone to think that the baby wasn't his, although Madge herself knew that it wasn't, as Jamie hadn't approached her for sex for the whole of his leave.

It didn't take Cathy long to realise the cause of Madge's attacks of sickness in the mornings, and she questioned her, but the confirmation wasn't well received: 'What are you going to do with a wee 'un about the place, needing its arse wiped every five minutes, and what are you going to do about your work?' It was clear that Cathy had no intention of helping out.

Since the news of Jamie's death, Cathy had become increasingly sour and hostile towards Madge, feeling that with her son gone there was now no need for her to put up with Madge any longer, and now this! A snotty-nosed little shit-bag running around the place, getting underfoot! No doubt Madge would in due course expect her to mind the little shite, so that she could go back to work or go out with her friends. Not a chance!

This situation continued. Eventually Madge told Mary about her pregnancy, but Mary wasn't interested. Indeed, she became quite cool towards Madge, as her husband had been criticising her for her failure to conceive, and only the night before, as a result of his workmates teasing him about not yet being a father and implying that he wasn't up to the job, had called her a 'sterile bitch!'

Madge had to give up her job at the Ordnance Factory, not feeling well enough, and not being sufficiently motivated, to get herself out of bed and on her way in time to catch the bus that was laid on for outlying workers. Still, she had her war widow's pension, and she got by. A couple of times during the day she would walk down the stairs and along the "close", the passage-way from the street that gives access to the stairs to the upper floors, and runs to the rear of the tenement block into the "court", the area of common ground at the back of the tenement block. A group of the wives from the other tenements in the block usually gathered there to gossip, such meetings being the extent of Madge's social life. Not that the conversation was very interesting, being mostly a tirade against the landlord from one and then another, with much nodding and many an 'Och aye!' from the listeners.

As her term approached, she wondered what she was going to do. Cathy wouldn't be of any help. Her communication with Madge had withered away as Madge's pregnancy had advanced, the most that she had to say now being just grunted monosyllables. Her sister wasn't interested, having her own problems, with her own man having taken up with another woman. Madge had started to retain fluid and her ankles had swelled up, so the doctor recommended bed-rest. Her life had reached a low ebb. From time-to-time she thought of Joel, and of how much different her life might have been if she had been able to see him again.

She wrote to the authorities at the camp where Joel had told her that he was based, enclosing a letter addressed to him, asking that it be forwarded, but all that she could provide to identify him with was his first name, approximate age and physical description, along with a few vague remembrances of their conversation relating to his home background. When her letter arrived at the camp the officer in charge of the mail office tore up the enclosed letter and then replied to Madge to the effect, indeed truthfully, that there was no man of that description on the camp. There was nothing else that she could do, as the US Army, just as the British Army, was notoriously unwilling to put a pregnant woman or a young mother into contact with her erstwhile lover, instead posting the man off elsewhere if he were still on the camp and then denying knowledge of any man on the camp fitting the description.

Eventually her time came. She had prepared as best she could and the local midwife was on call when the need arose. Within two hours the midwife had delivered a baby boy, which she put alongside Madge in the bed. Cathy, who had been sitting in the kitchen during this time, came up for a reluctant look at the new arrival, and was shocked to see that it had a full head of curly black hair and olive skin, totally unlike the hair and skin of her son Jamie. She remembered her first glimpse of Jamie after he had been born and recalled his pale skin and his ginger hair. Madge also had pale skin and fair hair, so how could their union have produced a baby with this appearance? She turned to look at Madge and said 'What on earth is this then? This little shite was never put up there by my Jamie's cock!'

The midwife had experienced this situation before, although much more often since the war had started. She said to Cathy 'Now listen here Hen, kids are born with black hair, but it soon comes off. Just you away and make a cup of tea for all of us.' Cathy did so, but her last gaze at Madge was full of suspicion and malevolence. Later Mary came to the tenement, and also commented on the baby's colouring. She had had her suspicions about Madge's pregnancy for a long time. Although scatter-brained and shallow, she had a fair grasp of human nature and not only that, she remembered Madge's reluctance to talk about her day out in Blackpool after they had separated, and her generally preoccupied manner on their return journey home on the train. She might be a little bit dim, but she could put two and two together. A cruel smile crossed her face as she said to herself 'The deceptive little cow! Well she won't get away with this nice little performance much longer!'

A few days later the court was buzzing with the news of Madge's baby, which she had registered in the name Alexander William MacAllister, and how it didn't in the least resemble her husband Jamie. Knowing of her earlier friendship with Madge, the women asked Mary what she thought. 'Well' said Mary, affecting a non-committal voice, 'I'm not making any accusations, but not long before Jamie was killed me and Madge spent the day at Blackpool. In the evening we got separated, but I know that Madge met a Yank and was planning to see him again.'

The women were thirsting for more, and tried to entice Mary on, one of them asking for the rest: 'What do you mean, do you think he xxxxed her?' Mary couldn't resist telling what she knew: 'Well, coming back on the train she didn't speak a word to me and seemed lost in her thoughts.' She paused, thinking that she had already said too much, but then she couldn't resist delivering her punch line: 'And I got a whiff of that particular smell coming off her, if you know what I mean, like when you've been with a man.' The women knew what she meant! They assumed indignant expressions of outrage and disgust, one of them expressing what they all felt: 'The dirty little bastard, going with one of they xxxxing Yanks!' Thereafter Madge's new baby, whom she called Alex, was known locally as "the little Yank".

Madge knew that she could not stay much longer in Cathy's tenement, so she made inquiries of the local women as to any rooms that might be available, but without luck. Eventually, when they were on their own, one of the more realistic and compassionate women in the court suggested that she try the local branch of the 'Sally Army'. The next day Madge took Alex along to the Salvation Army Hostel, where the superintendent interviewed her. The woman was a kindly considerate soul, who had joined the Salvation Army after her fiancé had been killed in the Great War, and had since then devoted her life to the service of others. She listened patiently to Madge's story, although she had heard it all before over the last couple of years. Why do young women get themselves into this situation?

Since her Henry had died on the Somme in the Great War, she had

41

not entertained the thought of any other man, although for several years, whilst she was still young, many had shown interest in her. For her, taking another man would be being disloyal to Henry's memory. She could live without emotional involvement, but thoughts of Henry were rarely out of her mind, particularly during sleepless periods during the night.

Sometimes, lying in bed, her sadness at the loss of Henry would cause her to feel such sexual despair that she would lift up the hem of her night-dress and seek relief, calling out Henry's name as she reached her climax, not that she and Henry had ever been so intimate: just holding hands, walking arm-in-arm and the occasional kiss were all that they allowed themselves, pending Henry's return from the Front, when their love would be able to bloom, unrestrained.

After Henry's death, her sense of 'unfair denial' at the termination of the natural progression of their love to the full physical relationship that she had so patiently awaited had caused her initially to continue this natural progression in her thoughts, but eventually that hadn't been enough, and she had sought comfort by tactile means: this comfort was all she needed of life, other than her work. On particularly stressful days, she would look forward to temporary reunion with her long-dead Henry that night, and this was enough to keep her going.

The superintendent decided that Madge, along with Alex, could have a room in the hostel, but took pains to point out that this would only be on a short-term basis, until Madge could get herself sorted out with accommodation of her own, and find a child-minder who could look after Alex to enable her to return to her job at the Ordnance Factory.

The following week Madge and Alex moved into the hostel, although all that this involved was bringing along a couple of carrier bags of Alex's baby clothes and a cardboard suitcase of her own things. Cathy had watched her as she had prepared to leave. Standing on the doorstep she shouted a final insult after Madge as she left: 'Piss off with your wee Yank then, you whore!'

Of the watching women, not one had said a kind word or a word of farewell to Madge as she had walked away from the tenement block. They remained together in a cluster long after Madge had gone, to discuss what an immoral woman she was, although, had it been known, a few of them had strayed themselves whilst their men were away at the war, but then, they hadn't made the mistake of becoming pregnant!

Although the hostel was clean and tidy, it was bare and cold and smelt of disinfectant. The other mothers were uncommunicative, preferring just to take their meals in the dining room and then retire to their tiny bed-sit rooms, not bothering to sit in the common room. Madge realised that they all felt a sense of shame at the predicament in which they now found themselves, as she herself did.

One time she tried to make friends with a young Glasgow girl with a coloured baby that she suspected was the result of a transient relationship with an American serviceman, feeling a bond between them because of her own situation. She paused by the dining table where the girl had her baby on a seat next to her. 'My, he's a lovely wee fella!' she said, reaching for the baby's hand. The girl quickly drew the child away, in an instinctive act that reflected the distrust of other people that had pervaded her mind since her US soldier had abandoned her.

The young girl had been reluctant to tell him of her condition, even though he had professed undying love for her, and had told her many times of how he would take her back to the States after the war, and about the house with a kitchen filled with labour-saving gadgetry that he would buy for them, and how he would show her how to cook chicken the way that he liked it.

To a young girl who had only ever eaten chicken once before as a Christmas treat, and for whom the facilities in the family kitchen comprised a cold tap and a gas cooker, this was sheer fantasy! She had longed for the day when she could accompany her young man back home to meet his folk, and it had been in this frame of mind that she had yielded to his advances.

When she had eventually told him about the baby, she had expected him to be delighted, as by the time that they went back to the States they would be a ready-made family, even though she would suffer some criticism in the meantime from her own family and neighbours. Still, she could stand that, as she loved him desperately, and once they were in the US the episode would soon be forgotten. However, he had seemed stunned, and had sat in silence. She knew that the news would come as a shock to him, and was prepared for this, but expected that after a little while he would brighten up and start to relish the thought of early fatherhood.

After some minutes he had stood up and said that he had to get back to camp, but would see her soon. This had been ten months ago, and there had been no communication from him since. Her inquiries of the camp had come to nothing. He had gone and that was that. Her parents had been disgusted and angry when they learned of her condition and didn't show any concern or sympathy. Their only interest was how best this appalling incident could be hushed-up so that they could retain their standing within the community.

The young girl's father was a lay preacher at the local 'Wee Free' Church and was overcome with shame at the thought of what his parishioners would think of him. Although her mother would have liked to have shown some support, her awe of her God-fearing husband had been too great, so she had made discreet inquiries of the authorities that might be able to help her daughter: 'For one of the unfortunates at the church, you understand.' she had said, in a pious voice. When a place in the Salvation Army Hostel had been offered, the mother had taken her daughter along to the Matron's office and then departed, not to return again.

As the days passed, Madge grew increasingly more lonely and despondent. Alex was a quiet baby, but she had little time for him, mostly wanting just to sit down and rest. The Matron would often chide her. 'Come on then young woman, sitting on your backside won't get your baby changed and his nappies washed!' Madge didn't know what to do. She didn't feel any affection for the child, and she resented the firm authoritarian manner of the hostel staff. She felt that in their eyes, she was no more than a young trollop, with loose knickers-elastic and round heels. How had she got into this position?

Her depression grew. Mary came to visit her one day, but was appalled by the morbid and silent Madge. After half an hour Mary found an excuse to get up to leave, but at the door she paused, with something yet to say. After a moment, she asked Madge 'You remember the Yank you met at Blackpool, is he Alex's father?' Incredulously, even though Mary was the instigator of the torment that Madge had had to endure, she clearly wanted to hear Madge remove any doubt regarding Alex's conception, to ease her feeling that perhaps she could have been mistaken.

Madge's muttered response, 'Yes', led her on to ask 'But how can you be sure?' Madge raised her eyes to look Mary full in the face: 'I had a period a few days after Jamie went back to the army, and there was no-one after that but Joel.' Mary had her answer, and also confirmation of the name of the Yank: she left the hostel satisfied with the outcome of her visit and didn't ever come again.

Madge's sister also came to visit, but also just the once. Eventually Madge was no longer able to rouse herself and lay in bed most of the day, oblivious of her surroundings and of Alex. Under proper circumstances Madge would have been fussed over by parents and friends, but there wasn't even one person to give her any affection. The staff of the hostel, good as they were, were greatly overworked and had only limited time to give to any of their inmates.

Day by day, Madge's mental condition deteriorated. She would sit on the edge of her bed deep in her own thoughts, not hearing the remarks or questions that the staff addressed to her, and having to be shaken by the shoulder before she would give a response. She didn't bother to go to the dining room at mealtimes and ate little of the food that an understanding member of the staff brought along to her room on a tray. Her face became thin and her cheeks sunken. She no longer had any interest in her appearance. Much as the staff could see her deteriorating condition, they were at a loss as to what to do, except to hope that with the passage of time she would begin to make some kind of recovery.

One day Madge got up, dressed, and then walked out of the hostel, leaving Alex in his bedside crib. For four hours she roamed the streets, past all the Victorian-built four-storey tenement blocks, with their strong red sandstone facing, past the pubs, the betting shops, the corner grocers' and greengrocers' shops, and the fish-and-chip shops, until eventually she came to the banks of the River Clyde. Sitting down on a bollard at the edge of a quay, she let her thoughts roam. A young man on the deck of a passing boat paused in his work to give her a wave and shout a cheeky but pleasant remark at her, but she neither saw nor heard him.

Soon her brain started to pound and her ears to roar. Her vision became blurred. Constantly her thoughts turned to Joel. She relived their meeting and their single beautiful act of lovemaking. She cursed the fate that had thwarted their arrangement to meet again: he would have thought that her declaration of love for him had been insincere and that he had been no more than just a day's entertainment to her. She saw again his warm smile, his strong white teeth, his lovely brown eyes. It was as though he were standing there before her!

Her emotions ran wild, her eyes flooded with tears. She moaned with anguish and despair. Calling his name, she stood up, and opening her arms to receive him, she stepped forwards into his embrace ...

The crew of a passing Police launch recovered Madge's body from the river off Greenock three days later. For the second time she had taken a trip "doon the watter", but this time it had been in death. The Coroner pronounced the obvious verdict: 'Suicide whilst the balance of her mind was disturbed.', then expressing his regret that no-one had been able to do more to save her.

There was some delay in arranging the funeral, as although Madge had not been religious, she had been born into the Catholic faith, and as she was assumed to have committed suicide, the local priest initially was not disposed to sanction her burial in the graveyard of the church: however, he eventually relented and agreed to conduct the funeral service. At the graveside were just Madge's sister, the Matron, one staff member who had taken particular care of Madge, the young girl who had rejected Madge's gesture of friendship and now felt remorse, and Mary. Although Mary had pleaded with Cathy to come with her to the funeral, Cathy had refused: 'Let the little whore rot in Hell!'

The priest droned on in an uninspired manner, having already conducted two funeral services that day, with two more to follow. He mouthed all the usual platitudes, and quoted God's name countless times, saying that Madge was now 'Safe in the bosom of the Lord.' and that 'She has gone to a better place.', the truth of which latter statement was beyond doubt, as recently life had been intolerable for Madge. There was not to be a funeral breakfast, nor was a headstone to be erected in due course. Madge was gone, and that was all that there was to it. The assembled mourners departed in their different directions, never to meet again in Madge's name.

Alexander William MacAllister was on his own in the world. Poor sod. Poor wee sod!

Chapter Three

The week after his mother died, Alex was moved into the local orphanage. Not that he was aware of the move, but he missed the sound of her voice and the warmth of her breasts as he suckled. For most of each day he lay silently in his cot, and when it was time for him to be fed he was reluctant to take the bottle. The nurse in charge of the baby ward called him a 'difficult baby' in a sharp tone that made him cry, which brought the further comment 'What a little mard-arse you are!'

From time-to-time prospective adoptive parents would come and look around the ward, but they never stayed long at Alex's cot: his obvious mixed parentage was something that they couldn't accept. Most of them were embarrassed about adoption, and were reluctant for their family and their friends to learn that they were contemplating this possibility. The few people in whom they confided would make sympathetic noises, but eventually would say 'Do you really want to take on someone else's baby?'

Had they have confided in their families this would have been even worse, as even the humblest of families was opposed to going outside of the bloodline. As for adopting Alex, with his obvious non-white ancestry, this would have been doubly daunting. Not being able to make their wife pregnant was regarded as a lack of masculinity on the part of the man, so many who would have made good and loving parents lacked the courage to make the necessary commitment.

The man would have heard the sniggering remarks of his workmates to others who had mentioned their interest in adoption. 'Can't you get it up then?' Likewise, the man's wife would not have been spared by the women in the court: 'Why don't you do what the farmer did when he couldn't get his hen broody? Try another cock!' There was much unsolicited advice: 'Have a few good drinks before you have a 'do' to help you both to relax.', or that the couple should 'Have sex with the wife's feet propped up on a pillow so that the 'cum' flows in instead of out.', upon which one of the woman piped up with 'So your husband will come instead of went.', paraphrasing the verse about the man from Kent in the well-known rugby song, to the great amusement of the other women. They also had to suffer the conceit and implied superiority of those who had several children: 'I'm so fertile my Angus only has to look at me and I'm pregnant!' Fecund, but insensitive creatures! Adopting a child was not a step to be taken lightly.

Weeks passed, whilst Alex remained in the orphanage, unloved and unwanted. His late mother's friend, Mary, who had not conceived after a couple of years of trying, had been to see the doctor, who had referred her to a specialist. After making an internal examination, the decision of the learned man was that there was no obvious reason why Mary should not conceive, and he suggested that her husband, Alf, should himself visit the doctor for examination.

When Mary had put this to Alf, he had exploded with rage: 'I can xxxx as well as the next man!' he had roared, and thereafter refused to discuss the matter. Mary grew despondent with longing for a child. There was no-one with whom she could discuss her problem. One day, feeling more than usually depressed about not having had a child of her own, she made her way to the orphanage and asked to see young Alex.

The superintendent, never one for missing the opportunity of placing one of her charges, brought Alex into an empty side room and laid him on a cot, then removing his nappy to show Mary that he was not lacking in any respect. Mary's heart lurched at the sight of this strong fine baby. The superintendent could see that Mary was enchanted, and said kindly 'Why don't you bring your man in to see him?'

That evening Mary waited until Alf had had his meal and time to put his working day behind him before she told him of her visit to the orphanage. 'He's the most beautiful wee man, with all the parts he is meant to have, but bigger than I would ever have imagined. You would love him!' Alf just grunted, guessing what was coming: 'Shall we go and see him this Saturday afternoon?' After raising the topic again several times during the following few days, and going out of her way to be nice to him, and telling him how great it would be for him to be able to take his son fishing in the river, and to see his team, Partick Thistle, play at Firhill Stadium, he agreed, but with great reluctance.

Saturday afternoon came and the two of them walked to the nursery, Mary carrying a cuddly-toy to give to wee Alex. The matron received them warmly, confident that she would soon have placed one more charge, and repeated what she had done when Mary had visited earlier, in removing Alex's nappy and exposing him in all his manliness. Mary cooed, but Alf was non-committal. Eventually, he commented 'He's a wee bittie on the dark side.' and suggested that they leave and think it over, which Mary knew was his way of saying "no". The superintendent knew this also, and sadly escorted them off the premises, taking the opportunity of whispering to the obviously distressed Mary 'I'm so sorry my dear.'

Over the next few weeks Mary remained silent and despondent, so that even her insensitive husband knew that she was deeply troubled. When he could stand no more of her silence, he agreed that he would go and see the doctor about their failure to conceive. The doctor referred him to a specialist at the local hospital, who spoke to him for some time. A nurse gave him Alf a small beaker with a cloth cover and then led him to a side room to provide "a sample", having the audacity to say to him as she left the room 'If you need a hand, just give me a call.'

He closed his eyes, and thought in turn of the many young women in the neighbourhood who in the past he had copulated with in his imagination, until eventually he achieved an erection. With his eyes still closed he started to masturbate. The side room that he was in, on the ground floor, was separated from the main road by a privet hedge, iron railings, and then the pavement. Being an old Victorian building, the windows were very tall sash windows, with the bottom part fitted with frosted glass, but the top part fitted with normal clear glass.

The hospital was some distance away from the traffic lights. Normally, the traffic would have flowed past the hospital without impediment, but the closing of the outside lane for road-works had caused the traffic to back up from the traffic lights for some considerable distance. He opened his eyes to see the upper deck of a double-decker bus that had drawn up level with the side room. The people on the upper deck looked down at him with curiosity, being able to see only his head and shoulders, wondering what he was doing. He closed his eyes again, and got on with the job, eventually achieving success.

The findings of the investigation were that he had a low sperm count and that the possibility of his fathering a child was not high. Mary was dismayed by the news, and again raised the question of adopting wee Alex, but Alf was adamant: 'No, no, xxxxing no!' he had raged, and then had gone off to the pub, coming home late in the evening, drunk and aggressive.

Mary thereafter never raised the subject again, but the seeds of hatred of her husband were planted in her heart, and grew slowly but surely, day by day and month by month. After two further years she left him and went off down south to serve as a Land-Army girl. Within three months she was pregnant by one of the hands at the farm to which she was assigned. Mary felt no shame in her condition: indeed, her joy knew no bounds. Her new man was kind to her, and she was going to have the baby that she had longed for so desperately, and for so long. Life was good!

Time passed by, whilst Alex grew up in the orphanage without the close contact with parents that ordinary children take for granted. Usually he would sit deep in his own thoughts, speaking only when spoken to, not making any initial approaches. The other children were mostly like that, as they were all in the same position. There was no rivalry between them and they grew up regarding each other as an extended family, but regrettably regarding the matron and her staff as outsiders, even though these good people tried to build up a relationship with the children in the little time that they had to spare from their duties.

The living conditions of the children were good: the orphanage was warm, there was clean dry clothing to wear, albeit coarse and cheap, and there was good wholesome food to eat. The only things lacking were brothers and sisters, the love of a mother, the reassurance of a father, and the fussing of a granny or an auntie, to make them feel special: they knew that they were different from other children.

When Alex grew older, he would walk with the other children in a crocodile, holding hands in pairs without embarrassment, into the town, or sometimes on an infrequent visit to the park or to the swimming baths. As they passed groups of children playing in the streets, the children would call after them, cruelly 'Orphanage bastards! Got no ma! Got no pa!' Yes, they knew that they were different, but there was nothing that they could do about it.

Once a year there was a treat for the children, when they were taken by coach about twenty miles west of the city to the village of Bridge of Weir, there to visit "Quarrier's Homes."[3:1] The Homes was an orphanage that had been established in 1881 by a Glasgow benefactor, William Quarrier, who was himself an orphan and knew at first-hand the loneliness and isolation that orphans can feel. He had set up the orphanage as several individual 'homes', each housing a small group of children as a family, with a housekeeper acting as the mother, these homes together constituting a village.

As the coach passed beyond the outskirts of the city, those children making the visit for the first time were astonished to see semi-detached and detached houses with their own gardens, filled with flowers, shrubs and blossoming trees. Further into the journey they passed fields of growing crops and even some fields containing herds of sheep or cows! They called out to each other to look at the wondrous sights that came into view around each bend in the road.

The Homes were located a couple of miles out of Bridge of Weir on the Kilmacolm road in an idyllic setting, with rolling hills and tall strong trees. Waiting for them in the car park were groups of children accompanied by their 'mother', each group waiting to 'adopt' three of

---

[3:1] The "Quarriers" has since grown dramatically, and is now a major charitable organisation, with its headquarters in Edinburgh, It currently has 85 projects underway, in Scotland and England, and also internationally: see www.quarries.org.uk.

four children for the day. These children were first taken back to their 'own homes' for a lunch-time meal, after which they played games in the grounds. The visitors soon bonded with their families-for-the-day and the grounds rang with their excited cries and laughter.

The culmination of the day was a tea party in their own homes, when they enjoyed sandwiches, cakes, jelly and ice cream, and lemonade. It had been a lovely day out for them. The memory of that marvellous day remained with Alex for a long time. If only there could be more homes like "Quarrier's Homes!"

Alex reached five years of age, when it was time for him to attend school. He was taken along to the school by the matron, who was received respectfully by the headmaster, Mr. McKitterick, whilst Alex himself was told to stand in the background. After a little social chit-chat with the matron, Mr. McKitterick called Alex over: 'Come here boy!' he ordered, in a loud authoritative voice. Alex approached the headmaster, obediently, but fearfully. 'Now young feller-me-lad,' the headmaster boomed, assuming a jocular man-to-man voice, to which Alex was totally unaccustomed, 'What's your name then?' Alex had not been encouraged to speak in the orphanage, just doing as he was told without question and avoiding contact whenever he could. He hesitated. The headmaster spoke again, but this time aggressively. 'Come on then, speak up! We don't want any dummies in this school!'

Alex mumbled his name. Mr. McKitterick turned to the matron, saying that he would soon have the boy "pulled into shape." After the matron had left, the head said to Alex 'Listen here boy, when I speak to you, you answer loud and clear, and say Sir.' Alex remained silent, in bewilderment as to what to say or do. The head bent down so that his face was close to Alex's. 'Answer boy!' he raged, 'or you will feel my strap on your bare arse before many minutes have passed!' Alex was petrified. A wet patch appeared at the front of his rough serge pants, and then a stream of urine ran down his legs and formed a pool on the floor. The headmaster was beside himself with fury. He grasped Alex by his ear and marched him down the corridor to the infants' class, where he was told to stand in front of the class, his lack of bladder control being obvious to all of the other children in the room.

The class teacher was a middle-aged woman named Mrs. McIver. She was not a good teacher and had difficulty in keeping her charges under control. One of her strategies in trying to enforce discipline in the class was to pick on a sensitive child and then subject this child to humiliation until he or she cried, this having a frightening effect on the other children, each fearing that they would be next to suffer this fate. Alex was to be her new weapon in the enforcement of class discipline!

She told him to sit at a vacant seat on one of the two-child desks on the front row, so that she could have him close to hand the next time that class discipline needed to be enforced.

Alex sat quietly, dejected and humiliated. For the next few days he suffered the ridicule of his classmates, but gradually this ceased, and he eventually became accepted by the rest of the class, except for one boy, Angus MacKay, who sat behind him. This boy, a head taller and almost a year older than Alex, and the acknowledged 'cock-of-the-class', tormented him relentlessly by whatever means possible.

One morning as Alex was copying down into his exercise book some sentences that the teacher was writing on the blackboard, he felt a violent pain in his backside. Inside each of the children's lift-up-top desks was an assortment of pens, pencils, erasers and other miscellaneous items. Angus MacKay had pulled the metal nib from one of his pens, jammed it into the small gap between the sole and the upper of the front of one of his boots, and then swung his foot forwards to jab the nib into Alex's backside. Alex knew from his time in the orphanage that a complaint would lead to severe repercussions, not just from the boy in question, but from the class as a whole, so he remained silent. The jab was repeated twice more before break-time came.

Once in the playground he challenged his tormentor, who just laughed and played up to the group of classmates that had gathered to watch: 'This little bastard is from the orphanage. His mother was a prostitute.' Neither Alex nor the boy knew what a bastard and a prostitute were, but they both knew that they were bad offensive words. Alex leapt at the boy, swinging his clenched fists, with great luck landing a blow on the boy's nose. Blood poured, and the boy roared with pain, his eyes filling with tears. The eyes of the assembled pupils widened in shock! Realising his advantage, Alex again struck the boy on the nose, this time taking careful aim and having the satisfaction of landing such a solid blow that his arm became numb. The boy was demoralised, and lay on the ground bleeding and moaning. Having got over their initial fright, the children shouted with excitement.

Mrs. McIver, who was on playground duty, came running from out of the school to see what all the noise was about. She could see that Alex was involved, he and his tormentor being at the centre of the surrounding children, and asked him what had happened, to which he replied 'He fell over Mrs. McIver.' Mrs. McIver then turned to the surrounding crowd of children: 'Is that the truth?' Without exception they all said that that was what had happened. Mrs. McIver then asked

Angus MacKay 'Why are you greetin' boy?[3:21] Did you fall over?', to which he too replied 'Yes, Mrs. McIver.' The children all knew that to give any other answer would lead to trouble for all of them: best to say nothing.

Alex had learnt three important lessons at school that day. Don't accept any form of bullying or your life will be made Hell; aim for the nose, which will cause your opponent's eyes to fill with tears, his blood to flow and his courage to wane; and, finally, when you have your opponent at your mercy, deliver such a blow as to make him think twice before initiating a future confrontation.

The infants had a new 'cock-of-the-class'! Alex was delighted in the outcome of his fight with his tormentor, and his new fame. The rest of the children vied to be his friend. Alex thought that if his education were to continue in this way then perhaps school would not be so bad! Alex became sought out by the rest of the boys, and encouraged to go along with them to the boys' toilets at each break-time, where the current fashion was to see who could pee the highest up the dividing wall between the boys' and the girls' toilets. Most of the boys could reach about one-and-a-half times their own height, but, unfortunately, the few boys who had been circumcised couldn't take part in this event, for technical reasons! This height was accomplished by the standard practice of pinching the end of the foreskin between the thumb and first finger, passing urine to inflate the foreskin into almost a sphere, and then using the other hand to squeeze the inflated foreskin quickly so that a high-speed stream of urine is discharged.

At the top of the dividing wall was a metal ventilation grill. Alex directed his stream at the top of the wall, and was rewarded by some of the stream passing high up it: indeed, some even reaching the grill. Unfortunately, some of the stream passed through the grill and was followed by a horrified shriek from an unsuspecting girl sitting on the other side of the wall. After a stern warning by the headmaster at assembly on the following morning, the practice was officially banned, although this didn't stop the odd few boys from trying it once again if there was no sign of authority around, or of any girls entering the girls' toilets.

At playtime the girls would play hopscotch. There was a paved area close by the girls' toilets that they marked out with pieces of chalk

---

[3:2] In the Glasgow area, "greetin' not only means to welcome someone or to make a welcoming remark or send a welcoming message to them, but also to cry: this latter usage is consistent with that in the works of Burns.

collected surreptitiously from the small tray running along the bottom of the blackboard, when leaving the classroom. When the teacher in charge of playtime had nothing better to do, she would complain about the chalk marks, but this was really unnecessary, as come the next fall of rain, which occurred almost daily in the Clyde Valley, the chalk marks would be washed away quickly.

Other times they would play with skipping ropes, chanting a traditional question-and-response in time with the skipping. A favourite chant was Solomon Grundy"[3:3]:

> Solomon Grundy,
> Born on a Monday,
> Christened on Tuesday,
> Married on Wednesday,
> Took ill on Thursday,
> Grew worse of Friday,
> Died on Saturday,
> Buried on Sunday,
> That was the end of
> Solomon Grundy.

When the playtime supervisor was not about, and one of the students had a ball, the boys and girls would play a simple game together. One child would be appointed "It". He or she would turn their back to the rest of the group, who would decide amongst themselves who was to have the ball. They would then put both of their hands behind their back and call out 'Ready!', upon which "It" would turn around to face them and then ask them in a sing-song voice 'Who's got the ball, who's got the ball?' whereupon the group would produce first one hand from behind their back, display the open palm, with the response 'See, I haven't got it!', then replacing one hand by the other and repeating the response: 'See, I haven't got it!' After this they asked their own question of "It": 'Alla-balla-boosha, who's got the ball?'

"It" would then have to decide, from their giggling and tittering, which of them was holding the ball and would demand to see the hands of the chosen one. Sometimes when "It" made the correct choice, the chosen one would want to show only one hand at a time, which "It" wouldn't accept, and there was then much squealing and protesting.

[3:3] This is an 1842 children's nursery rhyme by James Orchard Halliwell-Phillipps, in which the seven ages of man are presented as though occurring in a single week.

There were many other games that the children played.[3:4]

One day, one of the boys sang to them a rude little song that he had learnt from one of the older boys, which went down well:

'There is a happy land, far, far, away,
where the monkeys scratch their bum,
three times a day.
Oh, you should see them run,
with their fingers up their bum,
when the farmer gets his gun,
three times a day.'

The boys were elated with this song[3:5] and sang it every time that they met in the playground, provided that the teacher on duty was not within earshot.

As time passed, Alex's confidence in himself grew. Not that he was an outwardly assertive boy: indeed, he had little to say and wasn't of an openly bullying nature. His silence and the gaze from his soft dark brown eyes caused discomfort. He would fix his eyes on a child he was talking to and listen attentively, but without reaction, such that often the other child would falter, become embarrassed and run out of words. Not only was he the cock-of-the-class, he was now its acknowledged leader.

As the weeks went by the boys added other songs, but with the passage of time these songs became of a 'rugby-club' nature, such as such as "The ball of Kirriemuir", and 'The good ship Venus", but it is doubtful if all of the boys understood the meaning of the words that they were singing. They sang these songs every playtime, with the girls hanging about close by, ready to be shocked, but determined not to miss a word.

As might be expected, on one occasion one of the songs was overheard by the playground supervisor, who reported the matter to the headmaster. The outcome was that the headmaster declared that in future, organised games would be arranged for the playtime breaks, the girls playing Rounders and the boys playing French Cricket.

[3:4] Such other games that the children played, and songs, rhymes and saying that they enjoyed, are described comprehensively in: "The Singing Street" by James T.R. Ritchie, published by Mercat Press, ISBN 1 841830 15 5; and in "Doh, Ray Me, When Ah Wis Wee", by Ewan McVicar, published by Birlinn, ISBN 13 978 1 84158 558 1.
[3:5] Surprisingly, the first line of this poem is identical with the first two lines of the serious poem "There is a happy land" by Andrew John Young (1885-1971), a Scottish poet and a member of the "Wee Free", i.e. the Scottish Free Church. His "Collected Poems" appeared in 1936 and his "Complete Poems" were revised in 1974.

Nevertheless, the songs continued to be sung at clandestine meetings in the boys' toilets, mainly as a show of solidarity and a protest against the authority that forbade them this simple pleasure.

Mrs. McIver no longer tried to use Alex as a stick with which to beat the other children into obedience. On the last occasion on which she had tried, Alex had fixed her with his stare, answering her questions, after a pause, slowly and with the suggestion of a smile about his lips. Mrs. McIver could see that the other children were aware of the battle of wits between herself and Alex, and became flustered, her voice increasing in pitch as she tried to assert herself, without success. Thereafter, she left Alex in peace.

Pleased with his success in facing-down Mrs. Mc Iver, Alex re-instituted the singing of playground songs. The children carried on singing each playtime until one day the playground supervisor noted the cluster of children, and came along to investigate, in time to hear one of the verses of "We're off to see the Wild West Show" being spoken by one of the boys in the style as would be used by a fairground barker. The playground supervisor, a recent member of the teaching staff, was aware of Alex's confrontation with Mrs. McIver from staff-room gossip, and decided to take no action other than to send the boys and girls to their own areas of the playground.

In his sixth year at school, Alex became increasingly more aware of girls as sex objects, not as just a strange kind of child to be teased on account of wearing plaits or gymslips and being somewhat different 'lower down'. In the orphanage the girls had been segregated from the boys, and even in school there was segregation, with the girls entering and emerging by one door and the boys by another, and with separate, although adjacent, toilets. Whilst the playground was mixed, the teacher on playground duty took care to ensure that there was no excessive fraternisation, quickly sending the boys and girls back to their area areas of the playground.

When Alex reached about twelve years of age, he found that disturbing changes to his body were occurring. He started to get an involuntary erection at any time and in any place, that he was completely unable to control. He was a well-developed lad for his age, with a relatively large penis and with a big bushy growth of pubic hair, whilst none of his classmates, as yet, were so generously endowed.

Once a week he and nine of his classmates would go along to the communal bathroom in the orphanage, where they would take a bath in one of the ten small square tiled baths set into the floor around the walls of the room, under the watchful eye of the nurse, a big well-built woman of about thirty years of age, with large, shapely breasts. Alex was fascinated by the nurse's breasts, as also were most of his classmates, and the mere thought of them would cause him an immediate erection.[3:6] He began to fear bath-day, and as bath-time approached he did all that he could to keep his mind occupied with thoughts other than of the nurse's breasts. This was always unsuccessful, and he was always obliged to leave the changing room with his hands trying their best to cover up his manhood, and then immerse himself in the bath-water as quickly as he could.

On one, final, occasion, he was so eager to get into the bath that he slipped, and had to fling out his arms to steady himself. The nurse's eyes widened in wonder, and then she tried to suppress a smile, but without success. Thereafter, Alex was allowed to take a bath in a private cubicle

Alex had discussed sex with the boys in the orphanage, and knew that sperm played an important part in the procreation process, as did condoms, known to the boys as 'French letters' or 'wally-bags'. The lads knew this from having found wally-bags on odd occasions in the boys' toilets or in the corners of the playground, which had been used on the previous evening by young couples who would help each over the school wall after the school had closed. It was agreed by all that the man wore a wally-bag so that he could discharge his sperm into it, after which, by some vague as-yet unexplained process, the woman's egg also found its way into the bag. After a period of 'fermentation' the baby was conceived, rather in the way that a haggis is produced within a skin - the stomach of a sheep - after a suitable period of boiling.

However, Alex was not the only boy in the class who had made this discovery of sex, although not with a girl. They had all learnt to masturbate, and in their playtime teased each other with statements that masturbation made hair grow on the palms of the hands, upon which all of the boys looked down involuntarily at their palms, or made the eyes weak so that one had to wear glasses, which brought howls of laughter down upon the poor boys in their midst who were wearing spectacles. 'Who're your best friends?' they would say to each other, 'Mrs Hand and her five daughters?'

The few non-masturbators amongst the boys had a problem of their own: "wet dreams", or nocturnal emissions. After a night of lurid fantasies, they would awaken to find a wet or drying whitish patch on the front of their pyjama bottoms, and they would then have to sneak the soiled garment into the laundry basket, trying not to be noticed

---

[3:6] The stage of being embarrassed by one's involuntary erection is something that all young boys pass through.

when so doing by their roommates and the staff. Even at their age, sex was not without its difficulties!

Alex entered his final year. The teacher was Mr. Gilbraith, who was a tall angular man, with intense beady eyes. He carried a short stick with him, with which he would strike his desk to draw the attention of the class, or to emphasise some particular point in his lecture. He was a much-feared man, who didn't tolerate indiscipline. He was known for being a Scottish nationalist, and could be seen speaking at street-corner meetings around Govan on Saturday afternoons.

He would patrol the isles between the desks, slapping his stick held in his right hand across the palm of his left hand. No-one spoke out of turn with Mr. Gilbraith! It was said that even the head was in awe of him and never questioned his actions, even when he had slapped a cheeky pupil across the face and an angry dockland father had turned up at the school to seek retribution.

Mr. Gilbraith was charged with the teaching of history within the school, and would do so with enthusiasm, recounting the rise of the Roman Empire and the Greek Empire, and the development of civilisations world-wide, and discussing the spread of the influence of different ancient cultures on the present-day Scottish race. However, from time-to-time he would return to dwell in particular upon the relationship between Scotland and England. One day he was warming to his favourite theme of the cruelty of the English to the Scottish clansmen in the 1700s, and came to the battle of Culloden.

Alex, who had been watching through half-glazed eyes, with his mind far distant, came to attention at the description of how, when a group of Scottish clansmen has been overwhelmed and had taken refuge in a barn, the English soldiers had set fire to the barn and burned the Scots to death [4]. Without thinking, he shouted out 'The bastards!' The rest of the class sat in horrified silence! No-one had ever before used bad language in the presence of Mr. Gilbraith and they feared the worst. Mr. Gilbraith's eye lit up! He walked over to Alex's desk, whilst the class watched fearfully. He bent so low so that his face was level with Alex's, and only inches away. 'The bastards! Yes, the English bastards!' he growled.

As the class left at the end of the afternoon session, Mr. Gilbraith asked Alex to hang on for a moment. Once they were alone he said to him 'I can see that you are a true patriot. I am pleased with your devotion to your country. There are some books that I have that you may enjoy reading. I'll give them to you tomorrow and you can tell me what you think of them when you come in after the weekend.'

Alex collected the books from Mr. Gilbraith on the Friday

afternoon, stuffing them under his jacket before he left the school. He took the books into the orphanage, keeping out of sight of the matron and her staff, then putting them under his spare clothes in the locker at the side of his bed, pending the morning, when the older boys would be allowed to go out into the town for a little while to prepare them for their forthcoming advancement into living away from the hostel, whilst the younger children would be kicking a ball or otherwise entertaining theirselves in the orphanage yard: he did so surreptitiously, as he suspected that some of the orphanage staff might not consider the books to be appropriate reading material for a young boy. Come the morning, the dormitory would soon be deserted and he could read undisturbed.

In the morning, when all the other boys had left, he sat on his bunk and started to read. One book in particular took Alex's interest. It was concerned with the history of the Scottish nation, and included a discussion of Scotland's national language, Gaelic, emphasising the independence of the Scots as a proud and freedom-loving race. Indeed, to guard against attack from the Scots, the Romans had built a wall, Hadrian's Wall, running east—west for some seventy miles from one coast to the other, with a walkway on top of the wall so that the legionaries could move quickly from one place to another in the event of attack. Along the course of the wall were guard houses, and at regular intervals there were gateways to enable forages to be made by the legionaries against the Scots. Military stations, with such amenities as running water and under-floor heating, were built along the length of the Wall.

For more than a century the Romans had tried to conquer the Scots, at one stage even building a lesser wall, the Antonine Wall, about a hundred miles further north, but they weren't able to hold it against the Scots and had had to retreat to Hadrian's Wall. The book described how one of the mightiest military forces in human history, the Roman Empire, had conquered and then ruled a major part of the earth's surface, but after conquering most of Britain its legions had met their match in the fierce Scots living in the North. Alex's national pride swelled as he carried on reading.

The book went on to say that even after the decline of the Roman Empire and the abandonment of the Wall, the troubles of the Scots were not over, as the English ruling classes later tried to force them into union. Alex read of William Wallace, of Bonnie Prince Charlie, of Scotland's alliance with France against their common enemy, England, and of the many battles that the Scottish clans had fought to retain their freedom.

As Alex read, he started to quietly mouth obscenities against the

English, but before long he was speaking them out loud. He read of how the English had built a military road, now called the "Rest and Be Thankful Pass" at the head of Loch Long, to enable their troops to advance more quickly north in the event of an uprising by the Scottish "rebels". Finally, Alex read of what Mr. Gilbraith had told the students in his class, of the Battle of Culloden, where a band of Scots had taken refuge in a barn from the English soldiers, who had been told to give them no quarter. When the Scots would not come out to their deaths, the English soldiers had burned them alive. Alex moaned with anger!

He read that subsequent to the battle, the English had banned the Scots from the wearing of the kilt, so that one clan could no longer recognise those of another clan and thus whether they be friend or foe, as the clans on many occasions fought each another over cattle and other matters. He read also that the English had banned the Scots from the bearing of arms, so that one clan could not defend itself from another. Further, he read that the English had banned the use of the Scots' own language, Gaelic. Alex's face was flushed with rage and he ranted 'English bastards! Xxxxing English butchers!'

Although he carried on reading, of the clearing of the highlands, and of the later acts of injustice heaped upon the Scots by the English, this did not promote any increased reaction from Alex, as by this time he was filled with xenophobic hatred of that evil race from the south, although he had not yet met a single member of that race. He longed to confront them and make them pay for their past atrocities against the Scots: 'The xxxxing English bastards!'

Within a couple of hours Alex had been transformed from the average Scot who loves his country and enjoys a mild jibe at the English into a ranting and raging xenophile: such is the power of brainwashing. No longer for him the patriotic schoolboy humour of the Glasgow Empire theatre: 'What's the best thing that ever came out of England? The train to Glasgow!' and no longer for him the joke about the mean absentee Sassenach[3:7] landowner, who after a good day's grouse shooting on his highland estate had poured his gillie a tiny whisky from his hip flask, asking 'Would you like something with it?' with the reply from the gillie 'Aye, I would'na mind a wee bittee more whisky!'

At the end of the school day on the following Monday, Alex stayed behind to give Mr. Gilbraith his opinion of the books. Mr. Gilbraith's

---

[3:7] Alex, in common with many Scots, used the name "Sassenach", derogatorily, to describe the English, but most Scots are Sassenachs, as this is the Gaelic word for those who cannot speak the Gaellic language.

eyes widened and his eyebrows rose in delight as Alex expressed his fury at what the English had done to the Scots over many hundreds of years, and were still doing at the present time. 'Alexander,' he said, never before having addressed a pupil by his personal name, 'there is a small group of like-minded people who meet of a Saturday morning in the back room of the Rosicrucian Hall. Would you like to attend?'

Alex accepted the invitation. At the meeting Mr. Gilbraith gave an address to the assembly, on the theme of how Scotland is not given the international recognition that it deserves. He spoke of how, in arrogance, the English speak of "England" when they are referring to Britain, such that in the recent War, despite the death in action of many brave Scots, even the Germans spoke of "fighting the English". As he warmed to his theme his voice began to quiver with emotion and righteous conviction. Alex was thrilled to think that he had been befriended by such an eloquent, knowledgeable and patriotic man.

Mr. Gilbraith spoke of the enslavement of Scotland by the English, and of the martyrs who had fought for the regaining of Scottish independence, men such as William Wallace, 1270 to 1305, who in 1297 rallied the clans in an attempt to oppose and prevent the conquest of Scotland by English invaders; Robert Bruce "Good King Robert", 1274 to 1329, who won a great victory over the much-larger and greater-equipped English forces at Bannockburn in 1314, forcing the English to recognise Scotland as an independent kingdom; and Charles Edward Stuart "Bonnie Prince Charlie", 1720 to 1788, who raised an army to attack England,but from lack of support was forced to retreat to Scotland, where he suffered defeat at the bloody battle of Culloden Moor in 1746, leading to the English forbidding the Scots from the wearing of the kilt, the bearing of arms, and the speaking of their native tongue, Gaelic.

Alex listened with rapt eyes and with a patriotic stirring in his breast, whilst many of the audience shouted "Aye!" and "English bastards!" as Mr. Gilbraith's words moved them to anger. He spoke of the depopulation of the Highlands, which had led many Scots, in desperation, starving and in poverty, to leave their native land, which caused the audience to howl and stamp their feet with anguish and frustration. Mr. Gilbraith was a magnificent, impassioned and stirring orator!

Moving forwards in time, he went on to speak of the countless achievements of the Scots, and the products of their skilled work, such as in the building of ships, of locomotives, of boilers, of bridges and of much, much else, all helping to raise the standard of living in Britain and countries worldwide. He spoke of the invention of the steam engine by the Glasgow University technician, James Watt, 1736 to 1819, which had been capitalised upon by the English; of the pioneer of anaesthetics, James Young Simpson, 1811 to 1870; of the inventor of the telephone, Alexander Graham Bell, 1847 to 1922; of the discoverer of Penicillin, Alexander Fleming, 1881 to 1950; and of the inventor of television, John Logie Baird, 1888 to 1946.

He drew attention to the continuing scientific achievements not only of native Scots, numbering only some five million, but also including their direct descendents in other countries, the latter, it must be accepted, numbering considerably more, who together have been the recipients of eleven percent of all of the Nobel Prizes that have ever been awarded. Alex and the rest of the audience applauded this magnificent performance!

He then turned from science to culture, lauding Scotland's most famous poet, Robert Burns, 1756 to 1796, reciting from Burns's work in an emotional and impassioned voice that brought tears to the eyes of the gathering. He spoke of the architect, designer and artist, Charles Rennie Macintosh, 1868 to 1928, who was born as one of eleven children in the Townhead area of Glasgow, and went on to become recognised as one of the most talented men to have emerged from the city, his work combining Scottish traditions with the style of Art Nouveau and the simplicity of Japanese forms.

Finally, he spoke with regret of the many fine graduates of Scottish universities who are seduced annually into going down to work in England by better salaries and working conditions; in particular physicians graduating from such as Edinburgh University, who are sorely needed in Scotland's major cities to fight the diseases caused by poor housing, poor diet, unhealthy working and living conditions, and the general neglect of the Scots by the English government. This caused the exhilaration of the audience to subside.

Not wanting to end the gathering on a gloomy note, he then held up a road atlas of Britain, opening it at Page One. 'What is wrong with this atlas?' he asked. When no-one was able to answer, be continued: 'When we read a book or a newspaper, we start at the top. Even the Chinese, who read from right to left, start at the top. Why then does this atlas not start at Scotland, at the top of Britain, and then run down to England? The answer is simple: English arrogance!' The audience chuckled at this, partly to relieve the tense atmosphere that had built up during his presentation, but the point was noted: arrogant English bastards!

To end his presentation, Mr. Gilbraith introduced Alex to the gathering, asking him how the Scots might throw off the English yoke and enable Scotland to become a free, independent nation. Alex thought for a moment, and then in a firm clear voice replied 'We need to fight for our independence Sir, there is no other way.' Mr. Gilbraith and the audience applauded vigorously and beamed smiles upon Alex. As they all left at the conclusion of the meeting, whilst several people complimented Mr. Gilbraith on his address and said what a grand pupil he had in Alex, others patted Alex on the shoulder. One man spoke for the rest: 'With a few more loyal lads like you, Scotland's future will be in good hands!'

When Alex got to school on the following Monday morning, Mr. Gilbraith was there waiting at the gate for him, his face beaming with smiles. 'Good morning, Alexander! May I say how impressed my friends were with you on Saturday: "A fine young man" they all said to me.' He walked alongside Alex across the playground to the Boys' entrance to the school, then saying to him 'We will be holding an open-air meeting this coming Saturday afternoon. Would you like to attend?' Alex was flattered that such an erudite man as Mr. Gilbraith should ask him to attend this forthcoming meeting as his companion, and quickly accepted his invitation. 'I'll meet you here on Saturday afternoon then, at three o'clock,' said Mr. Gilbraith in parting, 'but wrap up warm as it gets chilly after a while standing in the open.' With a last smile at Alex, he strode off into the school.

Come the Saturday, Alex arrived at the school to find Mr. Gilbraith waiting for him there, carrying a small stool and a satchel. A little while later a saloon car arrived and they got in. Alex recognised the driver and the two other passengers from the meeting the week earlier, and responded to their friendly greetings. After a short journey Alex realised that they were in George Square, the main square in Glasgow, with the Glasgow City Chambers sitting squarely and impressively along its eastern side. After ten minutes, apart from Alex and Mr. Gilbraith, the group had built up to twelve, all men, and all carrying placards bearing such messages as "Scotland for the Scots!", "Remember 1746!" and "Home rule for Scotland!" Alex was thrilled to be involved!

Mr. Gilbraith then mounted his stool, whilst the rest of the men formed a circle around him, all facing outwards and all holding up their placards. Although there were only a few people passing through the square, he began his address: 'Friends! Fellow Scots! I speak to you today on a matter of grave concern to all of us who love our beautiful country. Too long have we struggled under the yoke of English imperialism. It is time that we took up the banner of William Wallace and of Bonnie Prince Charlie and demanded our freedom and our independence.'

His group nodded vigorously to each other and proclaimed 'Aye!' and 'Indeed!' with fervour. Slowly, a small crowd developed to listen to Mr. Gilbraith, who was inspired by their presence and began to speak with increasing eloquence and passion. A group of young lads, fresh from the pub after having been to the match, stopped to listen, their eyes lighting up with the prospect of some ribbing of the speaker. They started to listen earnestly to Mr. Gilbraith's words and, fuelled by alcohol, their nationalism was soon aroused and they too began to shout expressions of support.

The increased noise and the size of the crowd drew the attention of two passing policemen, big burly men, one a sergeant and the other a constable, who pushed their way through to the front of the crown and told Mr. Gilbraith to get down from his stool. 'You have no authority to hold a public meeting here.' said the sergeant, 'Be on your way or I'll arrest you.' This treatment incensed the crowd. One of the crowd shouted 'I fought the Nazis for the right of free speech. Leave him be!' The young football supporters joined in with abusive remarks about the police, whilst the crowd became restless and angry. The constable now forced his way through the crowd and ran to a nearly police box to telephone to the station for reinforcements, advising 'The crowd's turning ugly!'

With the roared support of the crowd, Mr. Gilbraith refused to step down from his stool, despite the repeated warnings of the sergeant. After a few minutes the sergeant lost his patience and, to calls of police brutality, pulled Mr. Gilbraith off the stool, who then stumbled to the ground. Whilst grovelling on the ground he came across his satchel, filled with leaflets that he had intended for himself and his group to hand out after his address. He picked up the satchel and swung it at the sergeant, catching him a blow on the side of the head that caused him, in turn, to stumble.

At that moment four further policemen arrived and tried to arrest Mr. Gilbraith and the members of his group. The crowd was incensed and immediately joined in, pushing and jostling the police until all of the police officers were forced to withdraw. Alex, now standing out of risk at the edge of the crowd, watched these goings-on with trepidation.

His in-built fear of authority and his institutionalised upbringing left him feeling overwhelmed by the confrontation taking place in front of him. It was more than he could cope with. As more policemen arrived he moved away from the crowd guiltily, feeling that he was abandoning Mr. Gilbraith and his group, but his defection wasn't noticed, as by this time Mr. Gilbraith and five others were being dragged into a police van.

He made his way back to Govan on his own, in desolation.

It had been an unexpectedly disturbing day for him. Although his admiration for Mr. Gilbraith, and his support for Mr. Gilbraith's crusade, were unshaken, Alex decided to stay clear of gatherings of this sort for the time being. Perhaps at some time in the future, when he had grown a bit bigger and put on more weight and muscle, so that he would be better able to defend himself and play a more active role, he might again take part in such public activities.

However, Mr. Gilbraith's teachings had done their mischief, and Alex's xenophobic hatred of the English was now firmly and deeply rooted in his mind: 'English bastards! Xxxxing English bastards!'

Chapter Four

Alex had a last confrontation a few weeks before he was due to leave school. One of the boys who was also in the orphanage, and felt that he should therefore support Alex, came to him during the playtime break to tell him that Callum Robertson, a boy who in the past had made unkind comments about the orphanage inmates, had been telling the other kids that his mother had told him that Alex was "known in the neighbourhood as the Yank on account of his mother having been xxxxed by a Yankie soldier".

At the mid-morning break, Alex strode over to the boy with firm even steps. The boy paled as he saw him coming, guessing the reason. Alex stopped and stood squarely before him, then saying in a low menacing voice 'What is my name?' Callum stuttered his name, to which Alex responded with 'And what is the name that your Ma called me?' The boy was reluctant to speak, so Alex took a further step towards him, repeating his question. This time Callum said 'She said that the women in the court called you "the Yank", but she didn't make it up, she had heard it from all the other women.' Alex replied 'Your Ma is a lying cow! Repeat my words out loud.' The boy hesitated, so Alex took a final step that placed his face only inches away from Callum's face: 'Repeat my words!

Callum was torn between loyalty to his mother and fear of Alex, eventually muttering the required words, but in a quiet voice. Alex said 'Louder!' Callum repeated the words louder, but Alex was still not satisfied. By this time a crowd had gathered around them. 'Shout them out so that everyone can hear!' With tears of shame running down his face, Callum did as he was ordered: "My mother is a lying cow!" The name "the Yank" was never uttered again, as everyone feared receiving the same treatment at the hands of Alex as had Callum. Alex had learnt something new. He could inflict pain and suffering on someone else by other means than physical violence: by humiliation. Nevertheless, he intended at some time to visit old Mrs. Robertson to find out what more she knew about this Yank, and also to teach her a lesson that she wouldn't forget in a hurry.

The time came for Alex to leave school to take up a job, and also to leave the orphanage. Mr. Gilbraith used his influence to get Alex a job as a junior storeman in Govan at a Ships' Outfitters and the superintendent of the hostel found him lodgings, also in Govan, with an old widowed lady. Things were looking good. Although the widow didn't like him to be late coming in of an evening, he had much more freedom to do as he wanted to do than he had ever had before. Many of the lads that Alex had grown up with in the orphanage also had lodgings in the area and they all used to meet in the evenings.

One day one of the lads put the idea to Alex, who was the acknowledged leader of the group, that they should go to Ibrox's football ground on Saturday afternoon, where an increasing number of fans were parking their cars in the nearby side streets. For a 'tanner', "sixpence", they would offer to look after a car and save it from damage by "the hooligans who live in this area". The idea was greeted warmly by the group, which was usually at a loose end on Saturday afternoons anyway.

The next Saturday the group arrived at Ibrox's ground early and split up into pairs, a smaller boy pairing with a bigger boy, the smaller boy being the spokesman whilst the bigger boy was evidence of the muscle that they would bring to bear on anyone out to cause damage to their clients' cars. To their delight, more than a half of those approached paid over a tanner. One driver told one pair to "Piss off!" returning after the match to find two of his tyres deflated. The pair came back again for the next match, and were unfortunate to be seen by the same irate driver, who advised them 'Leave my car alone you little bastards!' this time returning to find one of his tyres slashed. Although they saw him at subsequent matches, he never again abused them, and paid over his tanner without a word. Great!

In Govan there were the usual street gangs that were present in most areas in the Clyde valley. It was easy to see which gang was in residence in any particular area by the symbols and slogans painted on the gable-ends of buildings, on bus shelters and on the doors of garages, such as "Ya bas rules!" Some of the gangs were of long standing, with sons joining the gangs that their fathers had belonged to in their own youth. Often inter-gang violence broke out, with the members of the gangs fighting each other with knives, steel combs with sharpened teeth, and bicycle chains that they carried around their necks out of sight. Whilst this was indeed violent, and left many a youth with scars and bruises, it did not match the violence of earlier generations. The "Bridgeton Axemen" in their time had carried small axes hidden within their clothing, and had no hesitation in using them; whilst the battles in the east-end of the city between rival gangs of many hundreds in the 20s and 30s, using clubs, bottles and 'cut-throat' razors, led by "razor kings", left many severely injured or disfigured. [#5]

Because of his reputation, Alex was often asked to join one or another of these gangs, but he didn't do so. He would return violence for violence with relish when the need arose, but he preferred personal violence, when he could enjoy the punishment that he was inflicting upon others, not gang warfare where he would be fairly anonymous. He was also more interested in using his own small gang to make money.

Of late the gang had been losing interest in just making tanners at the Ibrox ground, feeling that this was kid's stuff and he needed to find a way to let them earn greater amounts of money. They couldn't afford drink, and had tried alternatives, such as milk through which they had bubbled town gas until it curdled and turned lime green, but this had tasted revolting and left them feeling ill. Eventually he hit on the idea of offering protection for the owners of cars in the relatively more prosperous areas beyond Govan over towards Paisley Road West. He had been over that way once with the gang on a cold winter's day and they had gone into the close of one tenement block to get out of the biting wind. Within minutes a group of residents, no doubt some kind of citizens' mutual-protection group, who had been in contact with each other over the telephone, had emerged from their apartments and ordered them, in an unpleasant hostile manner, to be off on their way.

They didn't want the likes of Alex and his gang near their property. They lived in tenements with 'wally closes', meaning that the closes and the staircases were tiled to half-height with good-quality hard-glazed coloured tiles, and often there were stained-glass windows on the landings. Alex hated these "jumped-up bastards", who considered themselves to be superior to him: they didn't want 'keelies', rough uncultured common people, hanging about their tenement block! They spoke in a 'posh' manner as though they had 'yorries', "marbles" in their mouths, and they threw in Scots dialect[4:1] each time that they met, to indicate that although they now lived in a relatively well-to-do district, they were still good down-to-earth decent Scots folk at heart. 'What a 'dreich' day it is today Heather!' they would say if the weather should be inclement, with the reply 'It is indeed Mary. It's enough to turn one into a sour dook!', meaning a miserable person.

After the hurling of some abuse, the gang had left, but smarting at their treatment. Alex considered these residents fair game for what he had in mind! He had the gang members equip themselves with spring-loaded centre-punches, the legitimate engineering use of which is to make a small indentation in a metal sheet or block at a required position in order to locate the point of a drill, and thus prevent it from sliding and scoring the surface of the sheet or block that was being drilled.

These tools are small, about the size of a fountain pen, and when pressed hard against a firm surface first load an internal spring, whilst

---

[4:1] See, for example, "Scots Dictionary" published by Harper Collins, ISBN 0-00-710134-1.

further pressure causes a hardened steel indenter to be released, which is driven by the spring to strike the surface at high speed, sufficient to make a small but adequate indentation. However, when the tool is deployed against a brittle surface, such as the window or windscreen of a car, the impact causes the glass to shatter.

The following Friday evening the gang went into action. Walking along the chosen street at about 30 feet apart, so as not to attract attention, each member of the gang spent the two or three seconds necessary to operate the tool against the windscreen - this being the most expensive item to replace - or the rear window of a parked car, then carried on along the street as if nothing had happened. The next day the younger and smaller, and thus apparently more innocent, members of the gang approached the owners of the damaged cars and in polite voices offered for themselves and their friends to maintain a watch on the cars on Friday and Saturday evenings for five bob a week. Most owners paid up: those who didn't had a repeat visit two weeks later, when the replacement window was subjected to the same treatment.

Before long, every car owner in the street was paying protection money. Over the months, knowledge of the scheme that Alex was operating passed by word of mouth among the youth of the area, and soon he had enough gang members to be able to include three further streets in his operations. Things were going well, and his local reputation was soaring. Not only that, he was starting to become the centre of attention of the female gang-followers in the area.

Alex had not had any involvement with girls since he had left school. Most of the girls he had known then had matured at a greater rate than the boys, as is usual, and were now interested in older and more physically-developed boys, whilst Alex and his gang had not yet experienced their growth spurt. Further, the older boys were involved in more serious gang activities, which added to their attraction. However, Alex's sexual urges were increasing day-by-day, and were directed now to full-blown sexual activity, rather than to a quick fumble.

One girl, Liz, had attached herself to the gang and, because he was the leader, had shown particular interest in him. One evening after the gang had decided to call it a night, she asked Alex to walk her home, some distance away on the other side of the district. Normally he would have refused, but the itch in his trousers made him interested. After they had walked for some time, Liz started to push matters. Was he afraid of girls? Did he have a regular girlfriend? Did he think she was pretty? After a while she caught hold of his hand and they walked together hand-in-hand, in silence. Nearing where she lived, she asked him if he wanted to kiss her goodnight. When he said yes, she led him down a side road and behind a run of garages where in the gathering gloom they were safe from view.

Alex pulled her towards him and gave her a long kiss, to which she responded by putting her arms around his waist and drawing him hard against her. Following another kiss, Alex inched up her skirt and put his hand into her knickers, running his open hand down her smooth belly until he reached her pubic hair.

At this point a car came around the corner, the driver intending to park it in one of the garages. Alex withdrew his hand and Liz hurriedly re-arranged her clothing: it was likely that the occupants of the car were some of her neighbours, and if her father should learn of her goings-on with Alex there would be Hell to pay!

Liz seemed very pleased with their goings-on behind the garages and asked him if she could see him again the following evening, to which he agreed, He realised that the time was getting late and so left her and ran to catch the last bus home.

Seven o'clock found Alex and Liz behind the garages again, Liz displaying such readiness to do whatever he wanted that he was determined to get the two of them into a situation where he could strip off her clothes and have proper full-blown sex with her without fear of disturbance. The opportunity came sooner than he had expected. His landlady told him that a week hence she was going to see her sister, who had been ill, and asked him if he look after himself until she returned on the following day. Great!

He bought a packet of condoms from the local barber's shop in readiness. When the day arrived, he took a bath, put on clean underwear and a clean shirt, and then sat waiting impatiently for Liz to arrive. Reflecting her eagerness, she arrived early. With needing to be asked, she followed Alex up to his bedroom, where as soon as the door was closed he pulled her to him and proceeded to take off her clothes, item by item, until she stood completely naked in front of him.

He then took off his own clothes, aided by Liz, whereupon Liz, without further ado, lay back on the bed. He followed her down and drew his body up over hers. As he entered her, she groaned with delight, which increased in intensity as he began to pound her with strong hard strokes. Alex felt his climax approaching and knew that he should stop to put one of his condoms, but he couldn't bring himself to do so. He said to himself that he would withdraw at the last moment, but when the last moment came he instinctively and convulsively drove hard home into her, delivering his sperm as far into her as he could.

His ardour cooling rapidly, he cursed himself for being such an idiot, and swore to himself that he wouldn't see her again, but Liz knew better. However, a couple of days later, Greg, a boy from the orphanage who had become Alex's right-hand man, said to him that one of the gang, "Shug"[4:2], had borrowed the keys to his father's car-repair premises and had "knocked-off" Liz on the back seat of one of the cars. Alex was wild! If that trollop Liz was making herself available to all of the gang, he wasn't going to put himself at risk of being claimed as the father of any kid she might drop! That was the end of his relationship with Liz, but he was still concerned until the passage of time put him in the clear of any risk of having made her pregnant.

Within a few months Alex and his gang were starting to reach the time when youths grow into men, both physically and emotionally. Their heights were increasing and their bodies were filling out. They also were assuming the 'tough man' attitude that typifies many Glasgow hard men: walking along the street with their fists clenched with the knuckles facing forwards and their hands at their sides with the elbows bent outwards. The message that they gave to the public at large was 'Get out of my way if you know what's good for you!' When a group of them walked along the pavement, it was now enough to make most people cross over to the other side of the street.

The women gossiping in the doorways of the different apartment blocks that they passed would say to each other 'They young lads is becoming a hard bunch of bastards, so they are!' upon which the others would all nod in agreement, the older ones having seen the transformation from young tearaways into hardened criminals many times before.

Although Alex and his gang were not particularly big men physically, nor did they have exceptionally good muscular development, they had the mental qualities that have long characterised the men of the Glasgow region: they were intransigent, unyielding and fearless. Just as with their fathers and grandfathers, and generations before them, from the days of Roman conquest and on through the centuries of English imperialism, they would not back down from confrontation, nor yield or grovel to any man.

During the two World Wars, these qualities had stood Britain in great stead, and many a German regiment that had been ordered to hold

---

[4:2] Anyone with the name "Hugh" in Scotland, and particularly in Glasgow, is usually given the nickname "Shug" or "Shuggie", just as throughout Britain anyone christened "William" is usually, informally, called "Bill". Other popular Scottish nicknames are "Tam" (instead of the English "Tom") for "Thomas"; and "Rab" (instead of the English "Bob") for "Robert".

its lines had quailed at the sound of the pipes and the sight of Scots advancing relentlessly and fearlessly towards them, bayonets at the ready. In peacetime, however, when the Scots wanted better working, housing or environmental conditions, and stood up against the management or the establishment to secure them, these same qualities earned them the name of "trouble-makers", "rabble-rousers" or "commie-bastards". Such is life!

The gang members were thrilled with their new power and the possibilities that it offered them. Their hormones were fired up and they began to crave excitement. Most times when they met they discussed the ways to overcome an opponent, their preferred means, but not yet put into practice, being the head butt and the kick in the testicles, the "balls". On meeting they would simulate the head butt, known colloquially as "the Glasgow kiss", in grabbing the lapels of the other's jacket, or the collar of his shirt or jumper, pulling it down and drawing him forwards, and at the same time propelling themselves upwards, until they had the height to drop the flat of their forehead squarely onto the bridge of the other's nose, but under these practice conditions stopping short of actually delivering the blow. Other times they would pretend to deliver a kick to the other's balls, again just drawing short of actually making contact. They were like young lion cubs, practising combat continually, pending the day when they would put what they had learnt into practice.

Whilst they still worked the car-protection scheme two nights a week, it had become boring to them, and they wanted to see some action. In anticipation, the gang had equipped themselves with "Stanley" knives, having razor-sharp one-inch-long retractable blades: not of great use for stabbing, but perfect for inflicting horrendous swiping cuts to the face. One evening Alex and a couple of his gang, equipped with their Stanley knives, took the bus into Glasgow city centre and mooched about the main streets, looking for trouble. Walking along Argyle Street from Gallowgate, they passed under the railway arch known locally as "The Heilermen's Umbrella" on account of the large number of Highlanders working in Glasgow who used to congregate there as a meeting place out of the rain.

As they turned right towards Central Station, Alex heard what be though must surely be an English accent. A large man was asking the way to Queens Street Station, just a few minutes walk away. Alex went up to the man and asked him if he was English, learning that he was. This was enough for him. His hatred of the English, cultivated by Mr. Gilbraith, still festered strongly within him. He asked the man 'Do you know where the hospital is?' When the man said that he didn't, Alex drew his Stanley knife from out of his pocket, slashed it across the man's face and said 'Well you'd better find out hadn't you!'

News of Alex's assault on the Englishman got around the rest of the gang, who were highly impressed. However, what Alex really wanted was not just to assault an Englishman and then run away, but to see an Englishman helpless on his knees before him. Having now drawn blood, he was keen to draw more. The next week several of them went into Glasgow city centre again. In one of the pubs they visited, they heard an improbable story that earlier in the evening an Englishman had complained of being short-changed by a barmaid, and had then smashed a glass and thrust it into her face. Alex and his gang were incensed! Whether the story was true or not made no difference to Alex: he thirsted for vengeance!

In the next pub that they went into, of all things, there was a party of English rugby players, up for a competition. Alex and his gang sat a couple of tables away, so that they could listen in on the conversation. One of the Englishman, whom Alex took to be the captain from the run of the conversation, was a big well-built young chap, but overweight, no doubt from eating all the good rich food that Mummy cooked constantly for him. He spoke with an affected southern drawl that set Alex's teeth on edge. The conversation was all hearty, manly, rugby-club stuff that was designed to show what grand fellows they all were.

Alex's blood ran hot, and he ached for the chance to smash the smugness from the man's face. His chance came when the man went to the Gents'. After about a minute, he followed behind him, and entered just as the man was washing his hands. Alex said colloquially 'Where d'y cum frae?' which drew a blank expression from the man. Alex tried again, this time changing his words and speaking more slowly: 'Where do you come from?' The Englishman understood and replied in a cultivated accent 'From Wednesbury actually,' but added, unwisely, 'not that that is any of your business.' This was all that Alex needed. He replied in a low guttural voice 'Don't use that tone with me you English bastard!' Had the man not drunk quite so much, or been so confident in his height- and weight-advantage over Alex, he might have realised the danger that he was in, but instead he moved up to Alex and prodding him in the chest with his forefinger said 'Now come here, you can't use ...'

Further words were lost as Alex grabbed hold of the lapels of the man's jacket and went through the routine that he had practised so many times before. As his forehead crashed down on the bridge of the man's nose, he had the satisfaction of feeling the crushing of cartilage. The man fell back against the wall in obvious distress, but Alex, remembering his lessons from the orphanage, set himself squarely before the man and took a well-aimed kick at the man's testicles, delivering a sound blow. The man gasped with pain, but this initial pain was nothing compared to what he would feel several seconds later, as the testicles are by far the most sensitive part of a man's body: in due course the pain would be excruciating.

The man collapsed onto his knees, whereupon Alex brought one of his own knees up under the man's chin, feeling the breaking of the jawbone and the cracking of teeth. The man then slid down onto the floor, puked out the contents of his stomach along with some broken teeth, and then remained motionless. With his hands shaking with nervous excitement and exhilaration, Alex walked from out of the toilet, beckoned his gang to join him, and then walked over to the man's team-mates, saying to them in a polite mock-concerned voice 'Your friend's in the toilet. I don't think he's feeling very well.', after which he and the gang left.

Following Alex's treatment of the Englishman, his gang lionised him. However, this gave him a problem in that they expected him to provide further entertainment for them. From time to time one of the gang would suggest that they go "queer bashing", but Alex was not in favour of this, as all the queers that he had ever met had been of a soft, gentle disposition and wouldn't fight back if taunted: what he wanted to do was to challenge harder men, who would give him the opportunity to put his violent streak into action.

Of late, the gang had taken to each consuming a bottle every evening of 'lannie', which was the local name for "Lanriq Cream", the cheap wine that had taken the place of whisky amongst the working class as an economical 'carry out' for maintaining one's state of drunkenness after closing time. In the course of time 'lannie' drinkers would usually move on to "Buckfast Tonic Wine", fortified to 15%, known locally as "wreck the hoose (house) juice!" or "commotion lotion!" What the Abbot and his Benedictine monks at Buckfast Abbey, Devon, thought about the great demand for their product from the poorer areas of Glasgow is not known, but they must have been pleased at this recognition of the merit of their product, as the Glaswegian knows a good drink when he tastes one!

One evening, after they had each consumed their bottle of 'lannie' and were feeling the effect, the gang went to a dance-hall in Gorbals, a part of Glasgow noted for violence, much more so than their home locality, Govan. Alex and two of the gang went to the gents', which in dance-halls of that type was a place where one needed to be on one's guard: many of the men in the dance-halls were sexually aroused, and

74

frustrated in not yet having achieved success in picking up a woman. They were like stags in rut, desperate to mate and enjoy the relief of discharging their sperm.

The aggression in the gents' was pervasive. A sideways glance, or an accidental contact whilst passing by, could lead to a violent flair up, which could escalate in seconds to the exchange of blows or to the use of weapons. Keep your eyes straight ahead, watch your step, and don't make any remarks, was the best advice under the circumstances for most people. However, Alex and his two gang members were thirsting for action, and sauntered in with contempt on their faces. Let any of these local pricks make a move and they would soon be sorry!

Whilst they were in the gents', one of the gang, Fergie, had tried to get off with a local girl, but had been warned off by a group of local boys for "trespassing on our patch". Just as Alex and his two gang members were leaving the gents', or as it is known colloquially, the "piss-stone", there was the sound of trouble in the hall. Alex and his two lads rushed out to find that Fergie, along with three others of the gang, were being attacked by four locals. Apart from their Stanley knives, before setting out that evening, Alex and his mates had armed themselves with bicycle chains, which they were wearing under the lapels of their jackets. Alex and his two lads drew out their chains, and ran to the group of fighting men. Coming upon the locals unexpectedly, Alex was able to strike one of them across the side of his head, the chain then wrapping itself around the man's face, to leave a scar that he would carry for the rest of his life. His two mates had similar success, so that within a few seconds only one local man was still in the conflict: the man whose girl had been chatted up, and who had started the trouble.

Fergie then produced his Stanley knife, at the sight of which the local man's eyes widened in fear. Backed by Alex and the rest of the gang, Fergie moved in, slashing his knife down across the bridge of the man's nose, to produce a shower of blood. The local man cried out in pain and shock, and tried to stem the flow of blood with his handkerchief. Alex and the gang left the hall hurriedly. There was sense in this: do what you have to do and then go! Better to leave whilst their opponents were still in confusion than to give them the chance to consolidate and seek retribution.

Alex and the gang were elated with their success, and felt that they were invincible. The next evening they went into the Argyle Inn, where they ordered seven pints of heavy. When the landlord had served the beer, Alex just said 'Put it on the slate.' They drank the beer in arrogance, and then left to go on to the next pub. However, as soon as they had left, the landlord went into the back room and spoke for a few minutes on the phone: he had decided that he should explore the possibility of gaining protection. The "free beer" period was soon to come to an end!

At the end of the evening, after having had free beer in four different pubs, some of the gang went off home, whilst Alex and three others decided that they wanted a fish supper. They went along to the "Hong Kong Fish and Chip Shop", where the proprietor, 'old Mr. *Chan*', was serving his last customer. Mr. *Chan* was not really very old, but his hard life in the past had left its mark on him. He had spent his earlier years living in Kowloon, Hong Kong, close to Boundary Street, which marks the boundary between Hong Kong and the New Territories.

As the eldest son of seven children, he had had the responsibility of taking care of his aged parents, and had spent all of his working days employed in the family hardware business. His life was filled with orders and deliveries, and with attending to the demands of the shop. Time passed by, and before long he found himself to be forty-five years old, but still unmarried.

The young daughter of the proprietor of a nearby shop caught his eye, but he doubted his prospects, as the young girl was little more than twenty years of age. Eventually his aged parents died, and free of his parental responsibilities, he had ventured to express his interests in the girl, *Chun Feng*, to her parents. Whilst her parents were aware of the age difference, they knew that *Chan* was industrious, with the proper respect of a Chinese man for family responsibilities.

Eventually, *Chun Feng* was persuaded to meet with *Chan*, under the chaperonage of an elderly aunt. *Chan* was at a loss as to what to say when faced with *Chun Feng*, and spent most of the time in discussing trivial matters, such as the recent monsoon, and the havoc caused by the floods. However, he eventually realised what a mess he was making of his opportunity, and said simply to *Chun Feng* 'You are a beautiful young woman whilst I am a middle-aged man, but if you will consent to be my wife, I will devote my life to ensuring your happiness and prosperity.'

Chun Feng, who had not had any previous suitors, was flattered by his proposal and, recalling her parents' earlier assurance of his earnestness and industriousness, agreed to become his wife. Their engagement was duly celebrated, with *Chan* agreeing to provide ten tables, each of ten settings, for the wedding breakfast, which satisfied the bride's parents. The wedding took place with great ceremony and with all the usual traditions, *Chan* having to give the bride's family a nominal payment for her, and giving each of the guests a '*hong bau*', a "red packet", containing money, in appreciation of their having graced the ceremony with their presence.

The married couple continued with the *Chan* family business, but soon *Chan* became subjected to the attention of the local *tong*, "gang", which wanted weekly 'protection' money, although against what risk was not made clear. After having had paid this protection money for a few months, *Chan* found that the payments were bleeding him dry, and was concerned as to what to do, particularly as *Chun Feng* was now pregnant.

Time passed, and *Chan* was getting desperate. After *Chun Feng* had given birth, *Chan* asked her father for advice. Following a few minutes of contemplation, his father-in-law told him to get away from the situation by emigrating to Britain, where he, *Chun Feng* and their baby daughter, *Mei Hua*, could start a new life. Although *Chun Feng* was reluctant to leave her aging parents, her siblings - three brothers and two sisters - assured her that they would take care of them, so she told *Chan* that she and the baby would accompany him to Britain.

Chan looked at Alex and his gang with his usual deadpan expression. He had been a good-looking man in his youth, strongly built as are many Cantonese folk, with a broad and deep chest, but now his hair was thinning, and he was running to fat. His upper eyelids, without a crease in them, as with all Chinese, were puffed from his long hours of working over hot fat. He had experienced much discrimination in his time in Britain, but had learned not to show his feelings, carrying on his life day-by-day with fortitude and with the support of his Buddhist convictions: "Treat others as you would hope to be treated by them. If someone commits an offence against you, they have lost their moral integrity, whilst if you do not retaliate, your moral integrity remains intact."

Chan waited for Alex to order. Alex said 'Four fish suppers' but then added, with uncalled-for offensiveness, 'Chop Chop!' which drew titters from his companions. Mr. *Chan* looked at him with disgust, but said nothing: these barbarians weren't worth words. After having received the fish suppers, Alex said, for the fifth time that evening 'Put it on the slate.' Old man *Chan* repeated the price, upon which Alex said 'You have a great big plate glass window there Mr. *Chan*. Don't waste your time worrying about the price of four fish suppers when you should be worrying about your window.' Mr *Chan* shouted at them 'Get out of my shop and don't ever come back!'

The gang left laughing. *Chan* had come to Britain to find a better life for his wife and *Mei Hua*. Adjusting to a new life in the West had been difficult, but he and his wife had succeeded, and had been blessed by the birth of a son, *Xiao Jun*, which had satisfied Mr. *Chan's* obligation to his ancestors, in carrying on the family line. However, his wife had died five years ago, and since then he had lived only for his children. He paid for protection, but if he should call on his protectors for a transgression that amounted to only four fish suppers, he would lose out, as once protection is called upon, a realistic charge would be imposed for the time that his protectors would be involved. The money he paid over in notes every week was no more than a fee for remaining 'in membership'.

Chan turned to see *Mei Hua*, a slightly-built girl of twelve years of age, in the doorway to the back room, where she had been standing since she had heard his voice raised in anger. Her eyes were wide in fear and in concern for her father. He spoke to reassure her, but the fear remained in her eyes. *Mei Hua* was a gentle placid girl by nature, but at that moment she felt only intense hatred. Who were these men who could be so cruel to the person she loved most in the whole world? Tears flowed down her cheeks.

Chan put his arms around *Mei Hua* and sought to comfort her. He spoke to her softly in Cantonese, telling her that all would be well, and that one day they would sell the shop and find a nice little apartment in the Chinese part of the city, where they could live in peace. *Mei Hua* ceased her crying and tried to smile at him, saying that she was now alright, and had got over the shock, but her heart was filled with loathing for the evil *gui lo*, "white devils", and, young as she was, she cursed them silently in the few swear words that she knew.

Alex suddenly remembered his neglected 'appointment' with Callum Robertson's mother. He left his three gang members at the end of the street, and made his way to the court at the back of Mrs. Robertson's apartment. He had intended to settle the score with her for a long time, and tonight, replete with four pints of heavy and a fish supper, he was in the frame of mind to do so.

The walls in the court were old, with crumbling mortar, so with little effort Alex kicked a brick loose. He put it beneath his jacket and walked round to the front of the apartment block and stopped in front of Mrs. Robertson's ground-floor kitchen window. He was not visible standing in the gloom of the evening, but Mrs. Robertson could be seen clearly through the window: although only middle-aged, she was fat, with a big, full bust that rested on the table as she and Callum sat reading the evening newspaper.

After a quick look around, Alex flung the brick at the window, not waiting for the sound of breaking glass as he set off round the corner out of sight. He carried on around the block and reappeared at the front a couple of minutes later, where Mrs. Robertson, her son Callum, and a couple of neighbours were standing decrying this wanton act of hooliganism. Alex stopped short, and exclaimed in a theatrical mock-English voice 'Oh dear, Mrs. Robertson, you appear to have had a spot of bother!' Mrs. Robertson wasn't fooled by this and shouted to her son 'He's the bastard what done it! Sort him out Callum!' Alex simply smiled at Callum, and when the latter made no move towards him said 'Well I must be going. We Yanks don't like to hang about all evening making social chit-chat. I'll be around again soon Mrs. Robertson.'

The two neighbours were aghast, but didn't say a word. True to his word, two weeks later, when the window had been repaired, he made another visit and put another brick through it. The next day Callum stopped him in the street and asked him to call round and see his mother, who wanted to apologise to him for any remark she might have made about him inadvertently.

When Alex arrived at the Robertson's tenement, he was let in by Mrs. Robertson, who led him along the lobby to the kitchen, where Callum was standing looking embarrassed and uncomfortable. Mrs. Robertson asked him to sit down, and then went into a long story of the hardships of being a widow, soon blubbering as she spoke, with her bust heaving with emotion. Callum remained standing, cringing with shame, but saying nothing. Alex let her run on, enjoying the spectacle of the two of them, servile and pathetic, trying to wriggle their way out of his disfavour.

On the subject of his mother's relationship with an American, he learnt only what Mary had told the women in the court at the time of his birth. However, he wasn't bothered about this: he wasn't really interested in his parentage, the sole purpose of his visit to the Robertsons being just to see them crawl. He enjoyed this feeling of power, albeit it that he was exercising it over just two simple folk. However, one day the whole of Govan would show him fear and respect, or else!

Alex was thriving on his life of cruelty. He was the direct result of his poor upbringing, his harsh environment and his mind-poisoning education. The Glaswegians are intelligent, ambitious, creative people. By and large, those who turn to crime are those who have not been given the opportunity to succeed in other fields. There is the saying that "The Devil finds mischief for idle hands to do", but it would be equally true to say that "The Devil finds even greater mischief for idle minds to do".

Had Alex been given the support of a loving family; had he been given the encouragement to do well at school; had he been guided into an apprenticeship or trade; he would not have taken up a life of crime or developed into such a mean, evil person. There is no way that he, or any other young Glasgow lad with a similar level of intelligence, would passively accept his lot and be content just to drift through life. It was inevitable that Alex would turn to crime as a means of self-expression, and to win the esteem of the community within which he lived, to the loss of society in general. He had never been treated as an individual, or asked for his opinions. He had never been fussed over by someone close to him. He had never experienced the warmth and support of a family. He had never felt or given love. He had no respect for any man or woman. He had no conscience, no sense of fair play, no sense of justice, no sense of decency, no sense of shame. He had no guilt or remorse or fear of retribution for any of his actions. He enjoyed violence for itself, not needing any motive, implied insult, or any other reason or excuse for perpetrating violence upon others.

In particular, he had a deep-rooted hatred of the English, and was dedicated to inflicting as much harm upon them as possible, but this didn't stop him from harming any other person, Scot or foreigner, who crossed his path. He had no redeeming features whatsoever. Irrespective of the reasons for his failings, there was just one conclusion that could be drawn: Alex was an utterly wicked man.

Chapter Five

Alex's job at the ship's chandlers had started to bore him. He stood at a counter all day, attending to the customers' needs: checking the availability of the item in the stock inventory; finding the shelf and bin from which to retrieve the item; checking with the customer that it is indeed the item needed; and then finding the price and checking it into the cash register. Sometimes the customer had an account with the chandlers, so that all that was needed was for him to ask the customer to sign a receipt form, and then to pass this form to the clerk in the back office for processing. It was boring.

However, sometimes someone came in who was self-employed. Alex would ask if it was a cash purchase, and if no-one was about, he would say 'Do you want a receipt?', when if the answer was no, he would ask for a lesser amount: the customer knew what the game was, and kept his mouth shut. Such transaction didn't go through the company's books, the cash just disappearing into Alex's back-pocket.

Over the course of time, there became an increasing disparity between the stock that the company had on its inventory and the stock that was actually present on its shelves. After one inventory check, conducted in secrecy during the annual Glasgow-Fair holidays, a substantial discrepancy was uncovered. The company then hired a man with some experience of the industry, and appropriately dressed, to call in during a quiet period and make a cash purchase. Alex fell for the trap and was fired, but he was fortunate in that the matter went no further. Had the company been able to find any evidence relating Alex to the previous stock shortages, he would have ended up in court.

In a similar way, Alex's gang members became bored with the jobs that, with their lack of education, were all that were available to them. One by one they packed in their jobs and relied on the 'buroo', usually reduced to just 'broo', this being the local name for the bureau that dispensed unemployment benefit. From time-to-time the staff at the 'broo' would call them in for interview, to see what progress they had made with job applications. If the staff at the 'broo' weren't satisfied with their progress, they would threaten to withdraw benefit until the person in question had indeed attended an interview.

This was a nuisance to the gang members, but if they displayed a general lack of enthusiasm and intelligence at the interview and didn't respond sensibly to any questions that they were asked, most times they wouldn't be offered a job. Even if they were offered a job, after a few days they could stop turning up for work and when they were questioned at the 'broo' they could claim that the work was too demanding, or making them ill, or that the other workers were ganging up and picking on them. Any reason would suffice.

Soon Alex and the gang were finding that the 'dole' money from the 'broo' wasn't enough to cover their main social activity, drinking, which had now extended to drinking themselves into a state of inebriation on several evenings a week. Recalling their evening of 'free beer' some time earlier, they decided to try this again. Alex and his gang made another visit to the Argyle Inn, where Alex repeated his previous order: 'Seven pints of heavy.' and gave the same response to the request for payment: 'Put it on the slate.' The landlord went into the back room and made a quick phone call.

Within a quarter of an hour a car pulled up outside and four rough-looking men got out. From the car-boot, they each withdrew a shortened pickaxe handle and slid it inside their jacket. As the first of the men entered the pub he looked the landlord in the eye, who gave a quick glance over to Alex and his gang. The man glanced at the gang himself and then at the landlord, who gave a confirmatory nod. The man said 'Right lads!' to his companions, whereupon they each drew out their pickaxe handles, strode over to the gang, and proceeded to deliver blows to the heads of all of them.

Within seconds Alex and his gang were lying on the floor, either unconscious or groaning in agony. In pairs the men dragged the gang members outside, and then into the side lane next to the pub: if the incident should be reported to the police, the landlord would be able to say that he knew nothing about it. However, it was unlikely that it would be reported, as most passers-by knew when to keep their mouth shut.

The men shook one of the gang into some state of awareness and asked him which one of them was the leader. With a pointed finger he indicated the unconscious Alex, and then fell back onto the ground. Two of the men dragged Alex over to the car and bundled him into the back seat. When he came to, he found himself propped up in a chair in a sparsely furnished room. Opposite to him was a man sitting behind a desk, whom he recognised as Joe Bannion, who controlled the organised crime in the district.

Joe stared at Alex without speaking. No-one was allowed to cross Joe, and Alex realised that the pub must have been under Joe's protection. He head ached and he felt sick, not just because of his physical assault, but because he feared for his life. Joe continued to stare at Alex, who realised that the first words must come from him. 'I didn't know you minded that pub Joe.' he said, and then added words that he had never spoken before: 'I'm sorry.'

Joe Bannion was a typical Glaswegian: short, but strongly built. What was different about Joe was that since rising to the top he had taken to always wearing a dark suit, a crisp white shirt, a smart tie and black shoes. He kept his hair short and regularly trimmed, he shaved daily and he kept his fingernails clean. Joe maintained an immaculate appearance, to let the world know that he controlled his gang by the power of his iron will and not by his physique. Not that he had ever jibbed at physical means as, in his earlier days, he would rush in with fists flailing and with feet kicking, but if trouble should ever arise nowadays he would only have to send his gang out around the local pubs and they could be back within the hour, along with a dozen hard men ready for action. However, trouble rarely arose, as Joe believed in keeping vigilant and putting down any potential problem before it became serious. Joe used to tell his gang with a smile on his face 'A stitch in time saves nine.' but he was referring to a stitch in the face of a trouble-maker.

Joe didn't feel any malice towards Alex, who reminded him of himself when he was Alex's age, before he had risen from amongst the many petty criminals in the vicinity to become the acknowledged top man. He now controlled gambling, protection, prostitution and the resetting of stolen goods. Over the years he had learnt to be hard on transgressors, as any lack of suitable punishment on his part would be seen as weakness, and there were many who would eagerly leap into his seat, given the chance.

After a couple of minutes' silence, he said 'I know of your racket with the cars. I know everything about you.' Alex wondered what was to come next. 'I tolerated you on my patch because you were just small time, but now you are starting to cause me problems.' Another two minutes' silence, then 'I'm taking over your car racket. In future I want half.' Alex brightened at these words and he replied 'Does this mean that I am one of your mob now Joe?' Joe laughed. 'Cheeky young bastard, yes you are!' Alex was quick to seize the opportunity. 'Can I bring in my gang to work under me? They are used to the car racket and don't need much of a cut.' Joe stared in admiration at Alex. Only two minutes ago Alex had clearly feared for his life, but now he was dictating terms. He would have to watch this young upstart!

He decided to give him a good lesson. 'Yes, come back here tomorrow night and I'll give you your orders.' Alex moved to get up and leave, but Joe told him to sit down again. He then said 'You don't think that you can get away without punishment do you? I have my reputation to consider.' Joe signalled to two of his men, who grasped Alex's shoulders, pinning him to the chair. Joe got up from behind his desk, walked over to Alex and gave him several vicious swipes across the cheeks with the back of his hand. He then bunched his fists and burst Alex's upper lip, followed by giving Alex a punch in each eye, which by morning would produce two lovely black eyes. Taking out his wallet he tossed two large notes into Alex's lap. 'Go round to the Argyle in the morning with your lads, order pints for each of you, and then pay the landlord all you owe him. He needs to see what he is getting for his money if I am to keep my reputation.'

Alex's gang were still under shock from the beating that they had received, but when he told them that now they all work for Joe Bannion they soon brightened up. They were in the big time now for sure! The landlord looked suspicious and uneasy when they entered the Argyle and ordered beer, but he took reassurance from the state of Alex's face and the blood-matted hair and bruising of his gang. When he received the money owing to him he was delighted: Joe stood for no trouble for those under his protection!

The word got around that Alex and his gang were now part of the Bannion 'empire'. Although he and his gang paid for their beer when asked, many times their new reputation earned them a free pint from a landlord wanting to stay on the right side of them. Life had never been better and they looked forward to a career of profitable crime. However, Alex had done two things recently that he had never done before in his life: he had felt fear, and he had apologised. Perhaps he was not incorrigible, but only time would tell.

The first thing that Joe did when Alex reported for work was to find just how profitable that Alex's car protection was. After some discussion, he then said 'Right, that seems straightforward enough, and no risk. We'll double your area of coverage. Can your lads cope?' Alex assured him that they could, and was delighted that the doubling of his protection would make up for Joe's fifty-percent cut.

When he told the gang, they were likewise pleased. Now that they were Bannion men their standing in the community was vastly enhanced, and they benefited not only by the recognition and deference of others, but also by the increased attention of not just the young girls who had hung around his gang in the past, but also that of their elder sisters, who hung around the more successful and professional criminal fraternity.

As Joe got to have more confidence in Alex and his gang, he brought them into other areas of his business activities: sending them out in pairs to collect his protection money; and to collect his cut from the pimps who operated the prostitutes in the area. A real test came with one landlord who had decided that he wasn't going to pay any more protection money. The landlord's bar was filled each evening by tough shipyard workers, who had assured him that if there should be any trouble they would pitch in for him.

Joe decided to send Alex and his gang along as a test of their mettle. Alex and six of his lads arrived at the pub in the early evening, armed with Stanley knives, knuckle dusters, lengths of chain around their necks, and short clubs pushed into their belt at the back of their trousers. They went into the bar, where eight of the shipyard workers were drinking. The landlord knew who had sent them, and simply said 'Yes?' to which Alex replied 'That's a good range of whiskies you've got on that shelf. Do you never fear that someone will put a bottle through them?' The landlord responded with 'If they did they'd get their xxxxing heads kicked in.' The shipyard men got to their feet to emphasise the point. Alex picked up a heavy porcelain ashtray that was on the counter and sent it crashing into the shelf of whisky bottles, smashing not only some of the bottles, but also the glass mirror behind them. At the same time his gang withdrew their clubs.

The shipyard men, who had been promised a night's free booze in reward for their assistance, leapt forwards, three of them falling instantly from blows to the skull, whilst a fourth backed off nursing a broken collar bone. The remaining four workers stopped in their tracks in confusion. This wasn't what they had expected! They had been told that Alex and his gang were just a bunch of kids, not hardened villains. One of them headed for the door, saying 'bugger this!', soon followed by the rest of the workers, who helped their injured colleagues off the premises.

Alex said to Greg 'Would you like to choose a whisky?', upon which Greg picked up a bar stool and hurled it at the remaining whisky bottles on the shelf. Alex then invited each member of the gang to do the same, whilst the landlord watched in silence. Alex said to him as they left 'You could do with some protection. I'll send a man around tomorrow to arrange it.'

Alex and his gang had taken to calling in at one of the local pubs at the end of each evening, to chat and to enjoy a few pints together. They would sit at a table close by the bar, discussing the day, but inevitably the conversation would turn to sex. One of the gang had been extolling the virtues of virgins, but another claimed that woman, like car engines, perform better after they have been "well run in". They asked the barman, an older man, what he thought: 'That may be so, but in my experience, an older woman will be more grateful and will do her best to please you, even giving you breakfast if you stay over.' Alex continued with the conversation. 'So you always go for an older woman nowadays?', to which the barman replied 'No, I had to give it up. At my age it got to be like dooking [5:1] with a banana!'

One evening an argument developed as to who could drink a pint fastest, it eventually being decided that this would be determined by the result of a "flying pint" contest. The waiter brought in a tray of pints and placed one before each of them. They were allowed to grasp the handle of the pot, but not to lift the pot from off the table, nor to lower their heads close to the pot. To ensure that there was no cheating, the signal to start was given by a man at a nearby table.

Upon "Go!" they all rushed their pots to their lips and gulped away non-stop. Greg and Alex were the first to empty their pots, but there was an argument between them as to which of their two empty pots had reached the table-top first. After some minutes of bickering, Alex decided to resolve the issue, saying to Greg 'Okay then, let's settle it by having another go.'

Another pint was placed before the two of them, and one of the gang then gave the signal to start. Alex's pint went down at almost the same speed as the first pint, and he slammed the empty pot down on the table top in triumph. However, after Greg had managed to get most of his pint down, he suddenly gagged, puking back into the pot not only what he had just drunk, but also some of the contents of his stomach, including the fish supper - as yet only partly-digested - that he had eaten earlier in the evening. The brim-full pot sitting before him on the table-top was clouded and contained small floating particles. The waiter stopped to look, and then inquired of Greg 'Shall I get you a fresh pot for that Sir?'

Their evening relaxation continued in this manner: endless discussions of sex; boasting of their personal sexual prowess and the size of their members; drinking to excess; telling the foulest jokes that they knew; singing bawdy songs; and participating in whatever contests that one or another of them might suggest - arm wrestling, or farting and belching - the latter two in respect of both loudness and duration. In short, they were like most other young men in their sexual prime, of whatever background: uncouth, disgusting, boorish, completely lacking in culture, refinement and good manners, and indifferent to the effect of their behaviour on others around them. The main hope for the redemption of such young men is advancing age, but not even this is certain, nor is marriage, as the improvement in the behaviour of a new

---

[5:1] The word "dooking" is the Scots equivalent of the English word "plugging" for describing the process of removing the mortar from between the bricks of a wall by the repeated hammering of a chisel.

husband is usually only temporary, as most wives will confirm: old habits die hard!

Joe was pleased with the way Alex carried out his work. He liked his no-nonsense attitude. Joe had started in the same way, working for the top man in the district, gradually gaining his boss's confidence until eventually he was his right-hand man. Joe had learnt most of his lessons from his boss: be hard on transgressors; never show weakness; be seen around the pubs of the district so that nobody ever forgets who the top man is; never have stolen goods on the premises; and never handle doubtful business yourself, leaving this to underlings, so that if anything goes wrong there is nothing that can be pinned on you.

Joe started to take Alex and two or three of his gang out with him once a week, but never on the same night, usually on a tour of the perimeter of his area, so that he could be seen to be in charge, which would deter anyone from trying to move in, as they would then know that if they did, this would lead to gang warfare. Whichever pub they went into, a smiling landlord would provide them with drinks "on the house." On one occasion one of Alex's gang recognised a man he knew and went over for a chat. Joe saw this, and as soon as he, Alex and the others were outside, he rounded on the one who had chatted. 'When you are out with me your job is to look menacing, not to be everybody's friend. Just give a nod in the future and keep your face stiff.'

Joe never took an unnecessary risk or ever let down his guard. His own boss had only made one mistake, which was when he had stored some stolen property in his office overnight. How the police found out was never known, but they came at 3 o'clock in the morning with a search warrant. Joe's boss was given five years in Barlinnie Prison. Joe was left in charge of the gang, and used to visit his boss every week to keep him up to date with activities. Towards the end of his boss's sentence, he visited him one last time. He came straight to the point. 'Whilst you have been in here the businesses have done well. As we agreed, after wages and expenses have been taken out, half of what is left is yours and half is mine.'

His boss just nodded, sensing what was coming. Joe continued. 'However, when you come out I will carry on running the show. I'll pay you ten percent to stay away.' His boss thought for a while, and then asked 'How will that go down with the boys?' Joe smiled at this and replied 'Jamie and Colin are away south on account of a botched job they did on the side. Glen is in clink in Edinburgh for helping a man to keep his wife in line. Rory packed it in because of his asthma, and Pete disappeared six months ago, and is now believed to be at the bottom of the Clyde or under the foundations of a new office block in the city. Most of the gang are new men who answer only to me.' His boss thought for a moment, but realising the truth of the situation, just nodded his agreement. Joe was true to his word, and for several years afterwards made regular ten-percent payments.

From time to time Joe got 'emergency' requests for help. One evening the manager of a ship repair company rang him to say that the foreman of one of his repair crews had just informed him that his crew had taken some bottles aboard. The job they were doing was to complete some engine repairs, and it was imperative that they be finished before morning so that the ship could leave the repair dock on the high tide. A ship in harbour is no good to its owners, with crews lying idle, harbour dues being incurred and business being lost. If repair work isn't finished in time, the repair company stands to lose a heavy bonus and also to lose future business.

Joe told Alex to get together some of the lads and meet him at his office in half an hour. Alex found three of his gang and the four of them set off with Joe in his car. Joe warned them 'No clubs, no knuckle-dusters. They have a job to do and we must keep them in a good enough condition to do it'. As they reached the ship the worried foreman of the repair crew led the group to the engine room, within which they could hear the sound of loud voices and singing. Joe said 'Christ! I hope we aren't too late.' They burst into the engine room, where the surprised repair crew leapt to their feet, but to no avail. The gang was upon them punching and kicking, and in two minutes three of the repair crew were dabbing bleeding noses whilst the remaining four were backed into a corner, offering no further resistance. One bottle of whisky was finished and a second was well down. Joe picked up the bottles and flung them at a bulkhead. 'Back to work!' he ordered, and the men did as they were told.

There wouldn't be any further problems, as the men knew that they were out of line, and risking their jobs. Their foreman of the repair crew simply said to Joe 'Okay Boss. Leave it to me.' As they drove away in the car, Joe was elated. 'The best time I've had in years!' and insisted that they all have a few drinks together before calling it a night.

As Joe started to get to know Alex better, he explained to him some of his views on staying in business. One was never to antagonise the police, as ultimately, with the weight of the law on their side, they would come out the victors. Joe always went out of his way to be friendly with the police, answering their questions civilly, and treating them with respect. He knew that if he ever made a serious transgression he could expect no mercy, but there was no harm in letting them think that he wasn't a bad sort of bloke.

Anyway, Joe was an asset to the police, because in keeping in check any young upstarts in the neighbourhood who wanted to break into the crime scene, he was saving the police a lot of work. They also knew that in the event of some unsavoury act of violence or cruelty, of such nature as the criminal fraternity couldn't condone, he would pass on any information that came his way. Joe and the police maintained a mutual respect.

Alex already knew from his earlier days that one couldn't beat the law, and that there was no point in confrontation with them. He had learnt that no matter how late he was for meeting anyone, he must never run in Govan, or it would be thought that he was running away from a crime. One time, when he was late for meeting some of his gang, he had been stopped by two policemen, who pushed him back against a wall for questioning. When asked why he was running, Alex explained flippantly 'I needed the exercise.' The senior of the two, a big hulking sergeant, prodded Alex in the chest so fiercely that he fell back against the wall and bumped his head. The sergeant then said 'When I ask you a question give me a straight answer, and call me Sir, do you understand?' Alex realised the error of his ways and replied 'Yes Sir. I was late for meeting some friends.'

The policemen were mollified by his response and, after a few cautionary words, sent him on his way. Alex never forgot that lesson. Don't try to be flippant, don't try to be cute, don't try to be sarcastic, don't get angry or insulting, just do what you have to do to get out of the situation before your become more deeply embroiled.

With his increasing confidence in Alex, Joe began to trust him with more responsible jobs. He became one of Joe's collectors, going around the pubs in one area on Friday nights to collect the stakes for the betting on the horses on the Saturday, returning to the pubs on the Saturday evening to hand out the winnings. Joe operated a simple system. Alex and the other collectors waited for the punters in the Gents' of the different bars and entered their stake, choice of horse, and the odds in a receipt book, the top copy being given to the punters and the carbon copy being torn out from the receipt book, then being given on the Saturday morning, along with the stakes, to a clerk in Joe's office, who, after the races had been run, would put a winner's stake and winnings in a brown envelope, simply bearing the receipt number.

Later that evening, Alex and the other collectors, again in the Gents', would hand over the envelopes upon the production of the winning receipts. There was nothing to indicate that gambling was taking place, but to maintain security, one of the bigger locals would wait outside the door of the Gents' in case a stranger to the pub should want to enter. However, he seldom had cause to take any action, as strangers were few and far between in the pubs in the area.

A lot of people in the area gambled, mostly for a little excitement, and the chance to put their knowledge of racing form to good use. However, there were others who had to find some money quickly to meet urgent needs, such as the repayment of crippling loans, another of Joe's business activities, or housewives who had built up a large 'slate', without their husband's knowledge, for drink and cigs at the off-license or for clothes that they had bought through a clothing club, for which they were being pressed for repayment These people invariably bet on outsiders, as winning a small amount would not solve their problem, whilst a successful long-odds bet would get them off the hook.

They would bet all the money that they could draw together: the rent money, the money for food for the coming week, the money put aside for the electricity and the gas. They even pawned all their clothes in the desperate hope that they would be able to redeem the pledge before their husband found out. By these various means they could sometimes amass as much money as Alex earned in a week working for Joe, but after that, if their bet didn't come off, they were destitute.

There were other methods to raise money, but these were either not able to provide cash immediately, or they were illegal or of low return. Traditionally there was the "menodge", where a group of workmates or members of the same club or tenement would put together a sum of money each pay day and then have a draw to determine the week's winner, there being an understanding that once a person's win had come up he or she would continue to make the weekly payment to cover the later wins of others: however, this was sometimes difficult to enforce without resorting to violence.

Another way was to use the 'provi', the "provident society", where a housewife would commit herself to a weekly repayment in return for being provided immediately with vouchers that it was intended that she would exchange for clothing at an appointed shop, but actually she would sell to one of the other housewives. The problem here was to find someone who had the cash to buy the vouchers from her, and at the price that she was asking, albeit that this price was only a fraction of the face-value of the vouchers.

A means for the desperate to acquire money quickly was to break open the lock on their coin-operated electricity meter or gas meter and steal the cash, but they invariably would be reported to the police by the man who came to empty the meter. They would claim that the breaking of the lock and the theft of the cash had taken place whilst they were out. They knew that they would have to make up the missing money, but it gave them immediate cash in their hands for their gambling stake. Should there be an empty tenement in the vicinity, others might wrench out the meter, in the case of a gas meter rupturing the pipes in the process and leaving the house to become an unexploded bomb: this was a constant fear of neighbours whenever a tenant moved out.

Because of the problems of these different methods of getting their hands onto cash, long-odds bets were the favoured practice of those in poverty. Alex would accept the bet, which, as is to be expected from the long-odds given, was placed on a horse that wasn't likely to win, so that the bet was rarely a winning bet. He started to think what a waste it was to pass over these bets to Joe's clerk. One day a man came in with a sizeable stake that he wanted to place on an outsider. Joe accepted the bet. Early on the Saturday morning he tried a few paper-shops some distance away from Joe's office until he found one that sold the same kind of duplicate-entry receipt book as used by Joe and his collectors.

He tore out both the top sheets and the carbon copies for the bets for earlier weeks, and then copied the long-odds bet for that day into the correspondingly-numbered page of the new book, replacing the large bet on the outsider by a small bet on the favourite. Once he had destroyed the 'replacement' top copy, his preparations were finished. As expected, the outsider didn't win, so Alex had successfully 'earned' himself the large stake less the small stake that he had placed on the favourite. A small bonus was that if the favourite won, Alex pocketed these winnings also, as the man who had placed the bet had not put his money on that particular horse! Alex thought that his system was fool-proof: he had made some cash for himself, and no-one was any the wiser, as the pages from the receipt book that he passed over to Joe's clerk bore the correct number, and the punter had simply backed the wrong horse.

Alex carried on in this way for a few months, always taking care not to overdo it and thereby attract suspicion. However, one day a worried looking punter came to Alex to place a large stake on a double: if his first long-odds horse won, the winnings and the stake were to be placed on a second long-odds horse. If both horses won, the winnings would be immense, but the odds against this happening were enormous. Alex took the bet, and later that evening re-wrote the entry for the bet in the corresponding page of his own duplicate book.

The next day, as a matter of course, Alex listened to the news of the races on the wireless, and was shocked to learn that the first horse in the double had won. Horrified, he listened to the account of the second race, feeling less stressed when the second horse got off to a bad start.

The commentator joked about the horse, but changed his attitude when it started to make up ground. At the half-way mark it was lying fourth, but towards the finishing line it began to increase its stride and drew level with the leaders. The horses crossed the line in a tight group, and there was a wait of a few minutes until the winner was declared, during which time Alex sat with laboured breathing, and with his stomach in a knot. As the outsider was declared the winner, Alex realised that his life was in ruins! There was no way that he could get together the winnings due to the punter, nor any chance that Joe would not order the most terrible retribution to be carried out on him: Joe would have him killed!

Alex moaned and groaned in self-pity. He had to get out of town before Joe caught him. He packed his few clothes into his small cardboard suitcase and made his way to the local railway station, but which way to go from there? He couldn't go into any other district of Glasgow, as Joe would certainly find out and come and get him. If he went on from Glasgow to Edinburgh, he would be in new territory and might not be accepted by the gangs there, as they would likely find out how he had deceived Joe, and no gang boss would want to employ a man who is unreliable. He decided to take the train to Gourock, at the end of the 'blue' line running west from Glasgow along the south bank of the Clyde.

Joe received a telephone call from the landlord of the pub where the double had been placed, saying that there was much excitement about the amount the punter had won, and that everyone was eager for the pay-out so that the punter could buy the drinks. The landlord was concerned that Alex was ten minutes late by his usual time of arrival. Fifteen minutes later he rang Joe again to say that the atmosphere in the bar was becoming unpleasant, and asked if he could get over as soon as possible. Joe knew instinctively that there was something wrong, and his fears were confirmed when he couldn't make contact with Alex, not gain any indication from the members of Alex's gang as to where Alex might be. He took a large wad of banknotes from his desk, stuffed them into the inside pocket of his jacket, and left for the pub.

Forcing a smile, Joe entered the bar, asking 'Now who's the lucky winner then?' The punter pushed his winning receipt into Joe's hand. Joe made a big flourish in drawing out his wad. He started to count out notes onto the bar top, smiling as he did so, even though in his heart he was seething: 'Wait till I get my hands on that young yyyy Alex!' Counting out the final note, he said in a loud voice, maintaining a big smile on his face, 'Okay lads, there's a pint for all of you on me.' The men in the bar were delighted: a free pint from Joe, and then further free pints from the winning punter!

The landlord drew Joe to one side and asked him quietly what had happened to Alex. Joe let his fixed smile drop from his face and replied stonily 'Nothing to what's going to happen to him when I get hold of him.' The landlord knew what this meant and said no more. Later that night Joe called in all of his men, including those from Alex's own gang. 'Put the word around the district. I want Alex and there is a reward for the man who finds him.' However, Joe was too late, as Alex had already fled the district. After a couple of days, when it was clear that Alex was not to be found, Joe repeated his order, adding that there was no time limit on the reward. He had his pride and his considerable reputation to consider if he were to remain unchallenged at the top. No-one ever got the better of Joe Bannion, no matter how long it took him to bring them to task!

Chapter Six

Alex travelled west on the train from the city centre, the rail-track soon following the south bank of the River Clyde. For a few miles he passed the shipyards of the upper Clyde, with their huge cranes rising high above the construction bays and the dry docks. Then the scenery became rural as the city was left behind. At one point on the opposite bank of the river was an enormous rock, Dumbarton Rock, atop of which sat a great castle, Dumbarton Castle, that has stood guard on the river for many centuries. During World War II guns were mounted on the rock to prevent enemy bombers from using the river as a path to Glasgow, moonlight reflected from the river providing all the illumination that they needed.

As Alex travelled on, he passed many little places that he hadn't heard of, then reaching the shipyards of the lower Clyde, and the towns of Port Glasgow, Greenock and finally Gourock. As the train approached Gourock station, it ran alongside a big bay on its right, Cardwell Bay, within which were moored a great many boats of a wide range of sizes: small dinghies, sailing boats, motor-sailers, commercial fishing boats, ferries, general-cargo boats, and boats for fishing parties. However, all the views from the train window, including this final nautical scene, were lost on Alex, whose mind throughout the journey had been filled with thoughts of the retribution that Joe Bannion would effect upon him if, or as Alex feared, when, he got his hands on him.

The railway station was adjacent to Gourock boat quay, enabling Gourock to serve as a hub, so that foot passengers could travel to and from different parts of the Firth by boat, or commute to Glasgow by rail. As he left the station, he saw large ferries operating from the end of the quay, and on the west side of the end of the quay, on the opposite side of the quay to the bay, he saw a couple of smaller boats that were busy offloading anglers and their catches.

He made his way from the station towards the town, after a few hundred yards reaching the main road. He stopped at a big pub at the corner on his left, the Bay Hotel, not knowing which way to turn. To the right, heading west, the shops on the roadside started to thin out and he deduced that this way would lead out of town, so he turned left, which would eventually lead him east towards Greenock, although at this point the road was running south to accommodate the sweep of Cardwell Bay.

After a few minutes he came to the Gamble Steps, leading to the Gamble Bridge, a footbridge running from the road, over the railway line and down to the quayside on the other side. Across the road from the steps was the Gamble Bar: as it looked to be a quiet place, Alex went in. There were only three customers inside: two men in earnest conversation at the far end of the bar, and a woman sitting at a table near to the door.

Although many Glasgow pubs had started to draw attention to their provision of a more suitable and better-furnished room where ladies and their male companions could drink undisturbed, Alex was surprised to see a woman sitting in a pub bar on her own. Until recently, the Glasgow pubs would not allow this, which suited many men, who could then curse and swear to their heart's content, free from the recriminations of women who, in reality, could match them in their swearing anytime that the occasion demanded, and it also suited their wives. It was one thing for a man to go out and drink in a bar and come back late in the evening drunk and incapable, but another thing for him to go to a bar where there were women, and not come back until the next morning.

However, the authorities had decided that it was acceptable for accompanied 'respectable' woman to drink in a bar, the measure of respectability being that they were wearing a hat. Thereafter women were to be seen in the bars drinking alongside a male companion, wearing his working cap on their head. That the man was bare-headed was of no consequence, as men were not subject to this requirement. Alex felt, with good grounds, that in any event, women have no place in bars, which are places where hard drinkers congregate, women being catalysts for trouble. The presence of a woman in a bar brings out the animal in a man, provoking him into a 'macho' display of male virility and aggression, leading inevitably to violence. Leave the bars to the men! When Alex wanted to drink he would drink, and when he wanted to fight he would fight: he didn't need the presence of a woman to give him cause or excuse.

The woman was a good few years older than Alex, probably in her early forties, but was still reasonably good-looking, albeit that nowadays it might take her half-an-hour to apply the make-up to try to achieve the look that ten years ago she would have achieved with just a smear of lipstick. Although she was full busted, her breasts sagged, and she was thick around her waist and hips, but she could probably still bring a sparkle to many a man's eyes, particularly if he were emboldened by drink. Her hair was bleached blond, piled into a statuesque mound on top of her head. Whilst she probably looked a sight in the morning, and it took her an hour to set her hair, she drew many admiring glances at closing time from the men in the Gamble Bar and down at the Sailors' Club.

Alex sat deep in thought, not knowing what to do next. He had to find accommodation and, whilst he had enough money to keep him going for a few weeks, he had to find a job. Now that he was out of Govan, the panic he had felt earlier was beginning to subside. The woman's voice brought him round from his reverie. 'You're new to this town then?' she asked. Alex looked up, startled, which didn't pass unnoticed by the woman. He stumbled an affirmative reply. 'Thought so,' said the woman, 'seeing as how you have a suitcase with you, and anyone new in this town stands out a mile.'

Alex was concerned at the thought of his obvious newness in the town. The woman bent forwards and said in a low conspiratorial voice 'If you're on the run, don't worry. You're safe with me.' She liked men in trouble with the law! She continued: 'You look more interesting than the boring respectable shopkeepers in this town, with their meanly-mouthed "Thank you, come again, we do appreciate your business." and their pathetic false smiles. I always say under my breath as I leave their prissy little shops "Kiss my arse!": the pathetic little pricks, counting out their mint imperials, with not a stiff dick amongst them!' Alex winced at her vulgarity.

The woman pushed the conversation. 'You'll need somewhere to stay.' she said, which was becoming uppermost in Alex's mind, 'Get me a G and T,' she said, adding 'a double, and when you come back I'll make you a proposition.' When Alex returned, double G and T in his hand, he sat down alongside the woman at her table. She told him that her name was Flo, and that her last man had ditched her four weeks ago for a younger woman. 'You can stay the night for a trial run, and if it suits you, we can come to a more permanent arrangement.'

Alex was on the point of asking if the trial run referred to herself or to the accommodation, but stopped himself at the last minute in view of the brief period of their acquaintance. They had a few more drinks, and as closing time approached Flo suggested that they make their way back to her place. Passing the off-license she asked Alex to pop in for a bottle of gin and a bottle of tonic so that they could continue drinking when they got back. Flo was already drunk and as they passed a shop doorway, she dragged Alex into it and put her arms around his neck. She was wearing richly-scented perfume, which aroused Alex's sexual urges. He kissed her, and at the same time put his hands around her bottom and drew her hard against his now erect penis. Flo drew away and then reached down and grasped it through his trousers 'Who's a hungry boy then?' she asked. 'We'd better get back quick. No point in wasting a stiffie like this.'

Once back at her apartment, Flo led him up to her bedroom, which was done out in a chintzy style, with heavy rose-patterned wallpaper, and a thick pile carpet. Numerous small toy animals adorned the top of her dressing table. Heavy drapes hung at the window. The whole effect was of vulgar opulence, but Alex was in no mind to notice. He dragged off his clothes in haste, whilst she did the same. As soon as they were naked, Flo lay back on the bed and pulled Alex down onto her.

They kissed for a few seconds, whilst Alex fondled her breasts. Flo took his head in both of her hands and forced it down to her breasts, telling him to bite her hard. He did so, whilst she urged him to bite her harder and harder, which he did until his teeth broke her skin and her blood flowed. Finally she told him to penetrate her. After he had done so, he felt his penis suddenly held in a firm grip. Flo had developed the control of her internal muscles, after much practice - indeed, after very much practice! - to such extent as to be able to apply a grip almost as strong as a handshake: the reputed speciality of French whores. Alex was astounded! After the culmination of the sex act Alex lay awake for some time, wondering what he had got himself into, and whether he would be able to keep pace with the sexual athlete who now lay snoring alongside him. In the morning Alex awakened to see Flo inspecting her bites in the mirror, with obvious pleasure. 'Look what you've done to me, you sex-mad young sod.' she said approvingly. Flo clearly enjoyed masochism in her sex life!

Alex wondered what Flo did to earn her living. 'I'm on the broo,' she said, 'have been for years.' Alex knew all about the 'broo' from his own experience, or so he thought, but he was to learn that there were still one or two ploys that were new to him. He pursued his point. 'But why haven't they got you working, or cut off your benefit?' to which she replied 'Well, every now and then they pricks at the 'broo' tell me to go for a job interview, otherwise they will cut off my cash, but when I get there I say to the yyyy on the other side of the desk "Sometimes I can't bring myself round in the morning. Does it matter if I am a bit late in coming into work?" or I tell them that the buses aren't regular or are sometimes full early in the morning.' Flo continued: 'If that doesn't put them off I ask if I can see the rest room, and tell them that sometimes I come over a bit faint and need to lie down for a while. I never get offered a job.'

Alex recalled his own use of such subterfuge in the past in the avoidance of work, but he was clearly not in the same class as Flo. She was pleased at the affect that her description of her performance of the 'broo' was having on Alex, and went on to say 'When they really insist that I go for an interview, I tell them that I haven't got anything to wear, and then they give me the cash to go and buy something suitable.

Once, after I didn't attend an interview, even though they had paid for a new outfit, I told them that when the money was in my hands, I couldn't stop myself from going out and buying some of the things I had been needing, such as underwear, sanitary towels and the like, and the silly buggers gave me a second helping of cash!'

Whenever Flo went down to the 'broo', she always tried to wangle herself a male interviewer, as she could then go into the intimate details of her menstrual system, and quickly reach agreement as to the immediate cash hand-out needed to deal with her sanitary needs in that respect, before she could be sent for any interviews. Flo was beyond embarrassment! She was delighted with Alex's naïve reaction. Even though he was a hardened Glasgow lad, there was a lot he didn't know about working the benefit system. Should he stay on with her, there was a lot she could teach him, and with her money from the 'broo' and whatever Alex might be able to earn from the boats or elsewhere, they wouldn't be short of a bob or two.

After giving him breakfast the next morning, she sent Alex off to see what work there might be on the boats. That morning there was a lot of activity at the quayside. Five of six parties of about a dozen anglers each were waiting for their boats, with their tackle and bait boxes in their hands, ready to get underway. Boats of all sizes came and went: car ferries went off to the more remote islands; others went just a short trip across the Firth to Dunoon; and there were smaller passenger boats going to local places such as Kilcreggan and Helensburgh. Other boats were carrying goods to and from the ships lying at anchor under repair. A nuclear submarine passed by slowly, looking big, sinister and menacing. There was a constant bustle of activity.

Coming west from Glasgow on the train the day before, Alex had been too pre-occupied to see that the River Clyde had been gradually widening over the last mile or two, to become the Firth of Clyde. What Alex now saw was a magnificent scene: the Firth at this point is about a mile wide, making a great sweeping turn south, with a backcloth of high craggy mountains, separated by sea lochs - long inlets, which in Scandinavia would be called "fjords". Alex had never experienced anything like this before, nor imagined that such a place existed: the scene was awe inspiring! He made his way along the quayside to where several boats were tied up awaiting the arrival of their skippers, before they set off with their parties of anglers.

Just at that moment a big man dressed in rough seafaring clothing walked up to where the "Westering Home" was tied up and started to lower a rucksack tied to a rope down to her deck. Alex asked him what the prospect of work was. Alex had left Govan in his evening working suit, and was over-dressed by the standards of the quayside. Following Joe's example, he had always dressed smartly for work, as Joe had often said to him that this helps in business dealings, at whatever level, but the suit was way out of place on the quayside. The big man looked him up and down, clearly thinking him unsuitable, before he said 'Try the cabin just by the café up on the main road.'

Alex found the cabin, knocked, and then entered. Inside another man dressed in rough seafaring clothing was on the phone, clearly in an argument with the person on the other end. 'Well tell the drunken sod he needn't come to me for a job again when he's sobered up.' Turning to Alex, still angry from his telephone conversation, he asked him curtly what he wanted. Alex told him that he was looking for work, and that he was prepared to put his hand to anything. The man asked Alex if he had any experience of boats, upon which Alex told him of his time working at the ships' outfitters. This clearly did not impress the man, who was looking at Alex's clothing critically. Alex knew that he must say something to excuse his appearance, so he told the man that he had come directly from a night out the previous evening.

The man looked at Alex for a few seconds before saying 'Look. There's a clothing store along the road. If you go up there, buy some suitable clothes and get back here in half an hour, I'll send you out on one of the boats for a day's trial.' Alex rushed off, duly returning in a pair of sea-boots, a pair of jeans, a thick rough sweater and a bob cap. The man, Ernie, was pleased and said to Alex 'That's more like it. What's your name then?' Alex decided that whilst he could still use his first name, it would be wiser to give a false surname, quickly deciding upon the name Alex Campbell.

Ernie led the way to the "Westering Home" where the skipper had just climbed up the steel ladder built into the wall of the quayside that was the means of access to the boat below, and was waiting for his fishing party to arrive. Ernie introduced Alex to the skipper, Big John, and then said to him 'That yyyy Mick is pissed again, his wife's just been on the phone. I'm through with him. Take Alex out with you and let me know how he shapes. If he's any good we'll keep him on.'

At the end of Alex's trial day-out, John made a favourable report to Ernie, who promptly offered Alex a job: so began Alex's life as an inshore seaman. The following day he reported for work early, and spent ten minutes standing on the quay looking at the magnificent scenery.

Over to the right the river leads up to Glasgow, which, whilst not being Scotland's capital city, certainly is the centre of commerce and industry. Alex was enchanted by the view, albeit that he didn't know the names of any of the places. Looking upriver, on the left is the Gareloch, with the large town of Helensburgh, named after the wife of the town's founder, set close to its mouth on the eastern side. In the early days, the rich businessmen living in the town used to travel to business in Glasgow by boat, but nowadays use the train, with its terminus at Queen Street Station close to the centre of the city. Across the loch from Helensburgh is the hamlet of Clynder and nearer to the mouth of the loch is Rosneath.

Directly across the Firth from Gourock is Kilcreggan, and then looking left is the hamlet of Cove, at the mouth of Loch Long. This loch is well named, being about twenty miles long and not much more than about half-a-mile wide at any point. On the left partway along Loch Long is the hamlet of Ardentinny, remembered by the famous Sir Harry Lauder song "O'er the hill to Ardentinny, there to see my sweet lass Jeannie." Beyond Ardentinny another loch, Loch Goil, branches off to the left, with the derelict[6:1] Carrick Castle on its southern shore shortly past its entrance, the tiny hamlet of Lochgoilhead being at the top of the loch. Further round to the left, on the northern coast of the Firth is Holy Loch, with Strone at the north side of its mouth and Hunter's Quay at the south side.

Beyond this point the far side of the Firth was hidden from view from where Alex was standing, so he was not able to see the lovely port and seaside town of Dunoon, with its statue of Robbie Burn's love, Mary, erected on the 100th anniversary of the poet's death, looking out over the Firth. Away to the south, the Firth widens out: Ahead lies the Atlantic Ocean, but bearing west leads to the Isle of Bute, and then on to the Isle of Arran. Continuing west and rounding the Mull of Kintyre leads to numerous romantic islands, some made famous by the fine single-malt whiskies - in particular the Isle of Islay - that they produce from the local water that percolates through peat hags before reaching the distillery, and which are extolled by connoisseurs world-wide.

Alex's reverie was interrupted by a 'friendly' greeting from his skipper, Big John: 'Right then, get your arse moving!' Big John was well named, being tall, broad-shouldered and thick set, but there was no fat on him, due to his having worked the boats for many years. His head and his chin were covered with short grey stubble and a mass of curly

---

[6:1] This lovely 15th Century Tower House, with an intriguing passage-way running around through the middle of its outer walls, has now been re-roofed and restored to occupancy.

grey hair protruded from the neck of his check shirt. His hands were huge and his forearms were like ham shanks, and would not have shamed even Popeye. He was an impressive figure of a man.

Although Ernie had several boats in his fleet, on that day John was again skippering the "Westering Home". Whilst well past its prime, it is a lovely beamy old boat of about 60 feet length. The wheelhouse is forward, with steps at the stern leading down to a small saloon with an adjacent toilet. Mounted around the walls of the saloon are framed prints of ships of yester-year. At one time it must have carried folk in comfort and elegance to and from the harbours and small jetties dotted around the Firth and the lochs. Alex felt a tinge of regret that he had not been around when the Firth was alive with such small comfortable passenger boats.

They were to take a cargo to the Shipbreakers' Yard on the Gareloch, close by the submarine base. On Saturdays and Sundays, and sometimes on one mid-week day, Ernie's boats took out fishing parties, on the other days delivering and uplifting either passengers or all kinds of cargo from the ships in the Firth under repair, or from the harbours and few remaining jetties around the Firth and the lochs. Many jetties had fallen into disrepair after the railways and motorised road-transport assumed prominence in the area, but there was still enough work to keep Ernie's small fleet of boats occupied.

From time-to-time, one of Ernie's boats went to the closer of the offshore islands, although this was not often, as they were limited by license as to how far they could travel beyond the Firth. Also, the bigger "puffers" were more suited to deliveries to the more remote islands, with their ability to run aground at high water on sandy or pebbly beaches in the absence of a harbour or a jetty, floating off on the next high tide [#6].

As they passed by the Esplanade at Greenock on the way to the Gareloch, Alex noticed a large Cross of Lorraine set high up on the hillside and asked John about it, learning that it is a monument to the Free French seamen who sailed out of the Clyde during World War II. John was a very knowledgeable chap and Alex enjoyed working with him, always learning something new. Although the members of Joe's gang had a good knowledge of the local criminal fraternity and of the sporting scene, they were not in the class of Big John in terms of general knowledge. Alex began to appreciate that there was much more to life than a knowledge of racing form and who was due for release from Barlinnie Gaol. Alex settled into working with John and looked forward each morning to what the day would bring.

One day John and Alex made a delivery to the Torpedo Test Station at Arrochar, at the head of Loch Long. On the way they passed several derelict jetties, John bemoaning the decline of sea transport. He told Alex how at one time, not so long ago, holiday-makers could travel by train from Glasgow to Gourock and then embark on a ferry that would take them to Arrochar, where they would disembark and then travel by coach the two miles to Tarbet on the shores of Loch Lomond. There they would join the "Maid of the Loch" that would first cruise the loch and then drop them off at Balloch at its southern end, following which they would catch the train back to Glasgow.

Alternatively, the Maid of the Loch would drop them off at Inversnaid close by "Rob Roy's Cave", where a coach would take them to Stronachlachar at the northern end of Loch Catrine, when they would then enjoy a cruise on the "Sir Walter Scott", following which they would be taken by another coach through the magnificent scenery of "Duke's Pass" in the Trossachs, on their way back to Glasgow. Other excursions involved more extended trips through Loch Fyne, noted for its herring smokeries, where they would visit the lovely little village of Inverary. What magnificent trips these must have been! Alex was beginning to appreciate his Scottish heritage, and how he was an heir to this exceptionally beautiful country.

Further up Loch Long Alex was astounded to see a train high up the mountain on the east side of the loch. There didn't seem to be enough ground for the track to hold on to, with the mountain being so steep. John told him that this was the West Highland Line, a single-track line running north from Glasgow Queen Street Lower Station to Oban or Mallaig. A trip on this train affords a view of some of the most magnificent scenery in the whole of Scotland, particularly in winter, when the leaves have fallen from the trees, enabling the passengers to have a long clear view over the surrounding countryside, and the snow-covered mountain tops: very often, deer can be seen in their natural habitat.

As they approached Arrochar, Alex asked what the meaning was of the big round sign with "1½" painted on it that was mounted on the eastern shore close to the water's edge. John explained that this meant that the spot was one-and-half nautical miles [7] from the head of the loch, and was a marker for the skippers of the recovery boats of the Torpedo Station, when test firings are being carried out on the loch. He also told him that the house sitting above the shore where the sign is displayed had been built around 1890 when the railway line was being built. During excavations for the laying of the track a huge boulder had become dislodged, and had rolled down the mountain-side to demolish the home of a widow and her eight children living at the water's edge.

Fortunately, the family had been out shopping at the time. To compensate the widow for her loss, the railway company replaced her modest house with a much larger and impressive house, "Rossmay House", which is still standing to this day.

There had been other, more serious, disasters in the building of this railway line, and in the building of other lines throughout the country, resulting in the deaths of a number of the workforce, most of whom were buried in unmarked graves. It had been the same in the building of the canal system in Britain, where if a manual worker should die or be killed, he would just be buried in an unmarked grave alongside the canal, with no further thought given. Many of the manual workers were simple illiterate men, a great number having come over from Ireland for the work, so that in a lot of cases nothing was known about them or about any family that they might have, so it was not possible to advise their next-of-kin of their death. There was just the misery of a family waiting for the return of a loved one from over the water, with the eventual sad realisation that he was never going to come back.

Around that part of the loch there were several pontoons moored out in the middle of the loch, but at different distances from its end, that are involved in the test firings. When torpedoes are to be fired, one of the recovery boats would come and chase the anglers from off the water, returning some half-hour later to recover the fired torpedoes. Should anglers be resentful of this intrusion upon their sport and take their time in lifting the anchor and starting the boat engine, the menacing sight of an approaching - and submerging! - submarine was all that was required to hurry them on their way. The torpedoes were controlled by electrical wires, and anglers regularly hooked masses of plastic-covered copper wire, like bell-push wire, having to bring it to the surface before they could free their terminal tackle [#8].

John told him of the various tales that he had heard over the years from the men working on the recovery launches. On one occasion a torpedo had run wild and had shot up onto the road skirting the loch, skittering about amongst the traffic and causing great consternation. There would not be many drivers who could report having been almost torpedoed on a day-run into the countryside! It was said that the impressive sea wall around the boundary of the garden of the prominent "Ardmay Hotel" had been built at the expense of the Admiralty to protect the guests from errant torpedoes.

On their left they passed a mountain with the name "The Brack", some two thousand six hundred feet in height, with its northern slopes running down to Glen Croe, with the River Croe running into Loch Long. On the northern side of Glen Croe the ground rises steeply up the side of Ben Arthur, with its two fine peaks, the more northerly of the peaks being known as "The Cobbler", on account of its resemblance, when viewed from the east shore of the loch, of a cobbler bending over his last, this peak being about two thousand nine hundred feet in height.

To the north of Ben Arthur, the ground falls away initially, but then rise to the even greater height of Beinn Narnain at three thousand and thirty eight feet. John went on to point out that at around the turn of the century, a well-known Scottish climber, Munro, had set out to climb, and then list and describe, all of the Scottish mountains with peaks of at least three thousand feet, setting a precedent for climbers from all over the world to follow, in 'bagging' as many of the 280 Scottish "Munros" as they could.

Because there are many mountains in Scotland that fall just short of three thousand feet in height, a later climber, Corbett, listed and described all of the 200 Scottish mountains with heights of between two thousand five hundred feet and two thousand nine hundred and ninety nine feet. John pointed out that, in their enthusiasm to bag Corbetts or Munros, some climbers would first climb Ben Arthur and then carry on to climb the nearby Beinn Narnain, which he claimed was cheating. Corbett himself had stated that when mountain peaks lie in close proximity to each other, the climber should first descent at least five hundred feet from one peak before starting to climb the next peak, but John gave his own views on the subject:

'The proper procedure in my opinion is first to descent from the peak of Ben Arthur to the loch and dip the toe of your foot into the loch, and only then set out afresh to climb Beinn Narnain, otherwise some of these bloody climbers will soon want to be dropped by parachute a feet hundred feet from the summit of a mountain, and then climb the last bit to claim yet another Corbett or Munro.'

John was a stickler for doing things properly. He was a mine of information, from his many years of sailing the Firth. He told how in 1232 a fleet of sixty Viking longboats led by Magnus of Man had sailed across the North Sea, round the treacherous north coast of Scotland, travelled down the west coast until they reached the Firth of Clyde, and then up to the top of Loch Long to what is now the village of Arrochar. There they had fought and defeated the natives, after which they had dragged their longboats over the two miles of ground until they reached the shores of Loch Lomond, where they had rowed their galleys along the loch, seizing hundreds of cattle. After they had returned to Arrochar[6:2] and had prepared to depart, a fierce storm had sprung up

---

[6:2] Another account says that the Vikings departed from Loch Lomond by sailing their

and destroyed ten of their boats.

Regardless of their aggression, what magnificent, brave and hardly seamen these Vikings must have been! Not all of them returned to their homeland. John told Alex that there is a Viking grave in the churchyard at Tarbet, to which Alex decided to pay a visit as soon as he was able.

Arrochar did not return to being a place of peace after the departure of the Vikings with a large number of the natives' cattle. Many cattle were seized by the inhabitants of Arrochar themselves from the cattle drovers who came down over what is now known as the "Rest and be Thankful" road with their herds, en-route for Glasgow and the big towns to the south. From the thirteenth to the nineteenth century Arrochar had been ruled by the Macfarlane clan, who would lie in wait for the drovers, and then spring out of hiding places with their swords in their hands, shouting their battle cry "Loch Sloy!" following which they would make off with some of the drovers' cattle. Not that Arrochar was always a place to fear. Indeed, the sister of the poet Wordsworth in visiting the village much later had been impressed by the rain, the mountains and the local people, and had also noted how most of these local people, very strangely, carried with them green umbrellas. However, Rabbie Burns had not been so impressed, describing Arrochar as:

" ... land of savage hills,
swept by savage rains,
peopled by savage sheep,
tended by savage people,"

With regard to the Arrochar hills being savage: when looking up at "The Cobbler" during the winter months, the storms of snow swirling around the peak indeed give a clear demonstration of savageness, no-one caught out on the mountain under such conditions having a great chance of survival, so indeed Burns was correct on this point. Similarly, the almost constant rains during the winter - and also for most of the summer! - support his view as to the savage rains. However, when the

---

boats down the river Leven, which latter carries the outflow from the loch down to the river Clyde. It could have been much easier for the Vikings to have used this route, should they have been aware of it, but in times of low rainfall – albeit rare in Scotland! – there would be the possibility that their boats could become grounded in the relatively-shallow Leven whilst they were travelling down the river to Dumbarton, where the Leven joins the Clyde, making the hauling of their boats over to relatively shorter distance from Loch Lomond to the immediately-deep water of Loch Long a more attractive alternative.

sun shines on a clear winter's day, with the sky a clear bright blue, and with The Cobbler clad in a fresh coating of snow, sitting amongst the rest of the Arrochar Alps, with a gentle south-west wind bringing white-tipped waves rolling up the loch, there is no finer sight in the whole of Scotland. Few of the Arrochar people, apart from some of the restless young, would ever want to leave this stunningly beautiful place.

Whilst the sheep are not savage, they are a nuisance to most of the villagers, in that Scottish law allows sheep to run free, the responsibility for keeping them out of the property of the villagers resting with the residents of the property themselves, not with the shepherd, so that during the winter months, when the sheep come down from the mountains, they are often to be seen in the gardens of the houses, chewing grass and flowering plants alike, their tiny hooves relative to their big fat bodies digging into carefully-tended lawns to leave them pock-marked and ugly.

Apart from bringing themselves down from the mountains, the sheep also bring with them a detestable blood-sucking parasite, the Tick[6:3]. Before it has drawn blood, this little creature is not much different in size than a grain of rice, but after it has leapt onto a sheep or some other animal and drawn blood, it is of the size of a pea: then sated, it falls off its victim, to digest its heavy meal, before finding another victim. It has a pointed proboscis about 4mm or 5mm long, surrounded by a ring of little feet. It shouldn't be removed by gripping its body, as this will cause more venom to be injected into the victim, the recommended way being to chill it with a drop of solvent, then to use a knife-blade drawn sideways along the skin to make contact with just the proboscis. Anyone with fingernails long enough to slide under the distended body can lift it out fairly easily, but on account of the extent of penetration of the proboscis, the skin is drawn up some fair way at the same time, and there is a quite loud "plop-type" noise when the parasite comes free. It should be killed immediately, as it is still capable of moving away on its legs and, in due course, of finding another victim.

Anyone with a dog should check it carefully for ticks after a walk in the countryside. As dogs like to run around sniffing at various objects, with their noses close the ground, ticks can often be found on their faces, sometimes even on their eyelids. What is more, ticks can jump

---

[6:3] A small authoritative, entertaining and useful book, written with the visitor to Scotland in mind, covering midges and also other flying blood-suckers such as the Mosquito, Stable Fly, Black Fly and the Cleg or Horse Fly, is "Midges in Scotland" by George Hendry, Aberdeen University Press, ISBN 0-08-036595-7.

from a dog onto its owner: most country people will have found a tick on themselves at some time. Horrid loathsome creatures!

Sheep are charming creatures when newly born, making plaintive little helpless cries that cause women of all ages to smile and coo, but if in adulthood they are carrying a ragged fleece that should have been sheared from them but wasn't, they can look decidedly unattractive. Even worse, should Burns have encountered a ram holding its ground on a mountain path, with its short strong horns and its hostile glassy eyes, he could perhaps be excused for having described then as savage.

Whilst they are regarded generally as magnificent creatures, adult stags present a nuisance, not only on the roads, where they have caused deaths in collision with motorists in the dark, but also to the local residents, where they leap over fences to forage in their gardens, and to the Forestry Commissions, where they eat the young trees set out on the mountains.

Whether or not Burns was accurate in describing the Arrochar people of his day as fierce, this is not the case with the present generation. Calm and self-reliant from living in the relative isolation of the village, with its paucity of shops and services, and limited public transport to the nearest large town, Helensburgh, and having to endure the almost ceaseless downpour of rain during the short days and long dark evenings of winter, and then the long midge-ridden days of summer, the Arrochar people are good, sound and friendly, and not the least bit savage.

As they cleared the quay one morning, Alex asked him how far it was to Kilcreggan directly north across the Firth. Without hesitation John replied 'Eight minutes.' Surprised at the exactness of his response, Alex looked up sharply. John explained: 'When its foggy, eight minutes full throttle, then stop the engine and throw out a line, 'cos' you're there!' Alex did not pursue the point, but suspected that there was more than an element of truth in John's reply.

With each passing day, Alex's admiration of John increased. He deferred to no man, was beholden to no man and feared no man, yet at the same time he was well regarded by all of the skippers on the Clyde and treated by them with respect. There was no stress in his life: basically, he was contented and relaxed, enjoying his work and doing it well. Alex contrasted John's life with Joe's life in Glasgow. Certainly Joe was treated with respect, mainly based on fear, but there was no time for relaxation, with the need for constant awareness of potential threats to his position as a leader in the criminal fraternity. One day Joe, and likely Alex in time, had he not already ruined his relationship with Joe, would have made a careless mistake that he would regret, and which would lead to his downfall.

By this time Alex was beginning to think that perhaps John had the right approach in not worrying about what the next day might bring, but just getting on with his job. He learnt all that he could about seamanship from him. Sometimes, under John's guidance, he started the engine and took the boat from its mooring, and even brought it in at their destination. He learn of the slow response of a boat, compared with the positive steering of a car, the boat responding not just to the wheel, but also to its own inertia, to the wind, and to the tide.

He learnt than in order to get past an obstacle in an emergency, it was sometimes necessary to think of the two 'ends' of the boat as separate parts. Steering the bows away from the obstacle will not necessarily ensure that the stern will also clear the obstacle, as the main action of such steering is to cause the boat to swing just its bows away from the obstacle, the inertia of the boat continuing to propel the bulk of it forwards in a straight line, so that the stern will still be in danger of collision. Once the bows are clear, it is necessary to put the rudder over in the opposite direction, so that the boat will now rotate such as to move its stern away from the obstacle.

Before long, when approaching a mooring or a jetty, Alex could judge when to reduce his speed, and then when to put the engine into reverse, and finally how much burst of the throttle to apply to ensure that the boat comes alongside gently. John showed Alex how to fasten the anchor chain to a small shackle at the foot of the anchor and then, leaving a few links of slack, to fasten the chain to the top of the anchor using a "weak link" made of cord or thin rope, so that in the event of the anchor hooking fast into the sea bed, the weak link will part when enough force has been applied to the anchor line, allowing the anchor to invert and break free.

Alex also learnt from John of the danger of the "sailors' wind". It is very pleasant travelling nicely away from the shore in a small boat, whether under sail or under power, with a gentle offshore breeze on one's back, enjoying the speed and the apparent calm, and there is the temptation to travel just that little bit further. However, when the time comes to turn around and go home, that 'gentle breeze' is now found to be an unpleasant opposing wind, making progress slow and throwing waves over the bows. The shelter of a protective shore or the harbour is never more welcome!

He also learnt silly old fishing humour from John, such as when a good fish was brought aboard, instead of saying 'That's a good one!' John would say 'That's a gudgeon!' which invariably left unknowing anglers bewildered, as a "gudgeon" is a small freshwater fish that under no conditions would ever be caught in the sea. Other times when a fish was brought aboard John would say 'Which way was it pointing?', upon reply then saying 'Okay then, let's go in that direction after the rest of them!' John had a great way of teasing any young angler who got his terminal tackle caught on the sea bed, telling him that he had hooked the plug at the bottom of the sea and cautioning him not to pull too hard lest he pull it out, as if he did 'All the sea will drain out and we won't be able to get the boat back to harbour!' Such simple humour brightened the day for all of those on board.

Fortunately Alex was a quick learner. He borrowed charts and books from Ernie and soon knew of the, albeit few, navigational hazards in the Firth. Being in mountainous countryside, it requires only a small departure from the shore for a boat to be in very deep water, but there are a few areas that needed to be treated with caution. When sailing up the river, it is necessary to remain within the dredged channel, otherwise a boat can easily be grounded on a sandbank. Over the centuries, many cargo ships had returned to the Clyde filled with ballast rather than with a cargo, which they needed to discharge before they could pick up an outgoing cargo. A convenient discharge point was the west side of the mouth of the Gareloch. The continuing discharge of ballast at this point had eventually caused the depth of the water to reduce to such level as to constitute a hazard to shipping.

In the early days, cargo boats had had to discharge their cargo on the shore of the Firth, hence the growth of the town of Port Glasgow some fifteen miles short of Glasgow, but with the dredging of a channel, cargo boats could then proceed right up the river into the city itself.

With John's guidance, Alex studied the rules of navigation at sea, and learnt that power gives way to sail. Whilst he complied with this rule himself, along with all the rest of Ernie's skippers, he couldn't see how this rule could apply to the big ships that use the Clyde, as with their large draught they have to stay within the shipping channels, and with their great mass they require to travel a considerable distance before they can be brought to rest. However, it would be a very stupid person who set his sailing boat in the path of a tanker or a container ship and expect it to try to give way. It was always wiser to give way if in doubt, although a useful practice when approaching an oncoming ship is to check the bearing of the ship: if after a few minutes the angle between the two vessels has increased then it could be safe to pass in front of the ship's bows, whilst if the angle has decreased then the action to take would be to pass by its stern: if the angle has not changed, then turn away, as you are on a collision course!

Alex learnt the different meanings of the many types of buoys, both navigational and those indicating hazards, moored around the Firth. He also learnt the meaning of the various lights, both those carried on board the ships and those mounted on the buoys. Although it wasn't really necessary on the Firth, where navigation was almost entirely by visual sightings, he learnt to use a compass, giving the somewhat embarrassed explanation to John 'Just in case a heavy mist comes down suddenly', which caused John to shake his head in mock despair.

He soon learnt that when proceeding along a channel upriver, the channel-marker buoys on the left-hand side, "the port side", are coloured red; and the buoys on the right-hand side, "the starboard side", are coloured green.

Although not really necessary, as Ernie's boats never ventured far from land and rarely used a compass, Alex learnt the memory-aid to correct the True bearing for the Variation due to the Magnetic influence of the earth and for any Deviation due to the steel of the ship, to obtain the required Compass bearing:

"**T**imid **V**irgins **M**ake **D**ull **C**ompanions."

He also learnt the memory aid to determine in which direction to add the correction for deviation:

"**D**eviation west, **C**ompass best."

so that he wouldn't make a mistake when correcting the true bearing to allow for deviation. Whilst this correction might seem to be simple, when faced with it many people have as little idea as to whether to subtract the variation from, or add it to, the true bearing to obtain the compass bearing, as others have as to which way to turn the clock to change Greenwich Mean Time into British Summer Time in the spring, and then back again in the autumn.

After having learnt something about navigation, Alex decided that he wanted to learn Morse code and also the international system of signalling with flags. He went along to the Greenock Marine College and bought from the book-room two sets of cards, one for Morse code and the other for signal flags. For the Morse cards, on one side was the letter of the alphabet, and on the other side was the appropriate set of dots and dashes, whilst for the flag cards, on one side was the letter of the alphabet together with the special meaning of the letter, and on the other side was the appropriate flag. He studied these cards at every spare moment.

Before long he could recognise and recall the meaning of the flags without delay, although he had some difficulty with Morse code. He grouped the letters to correspond with the progressive change of their constituent dots and dashes and developed simple mnemonics to help him to remember them by. Within a few days he had acquired a reasonable proficiency and, using his knuckles for dots and the palm of his hand for dashes, could tap out simple messages on the chart-table in the wheel-house. He learnt how to start a Morse code message with the call-up signal, aa, repeated a couple of times, and very soon could sound the appropriate dots and dashes for the kind of messages that ships would sent to each other when on the high seas, such as "What ship? Where bound?", finally sending the 'end-of-message' signal, "ar".

Big John scoffed at this, saying that Alex was just wasting his time, as indeed he probably was. However, coming back to Gourock late one evening, they passed Dunoon just as a ferry was leaving the terminal. A car on the quayside was flashing its light on and off, which caused John to ask what the "silly sod" was doing. Alex was delighted to tell him that the driver had just sent the message "Safe journey" to someone on board the ferry. Thereafter, John passed no further criticism of Alex's new interests.

With his knowledge of signal flags, Alex was often able to tell John the message expressed by the flags on passing naval ships, although in many cases these were just single or small groups of letters having a special meaning known only to those on board and those on other ships or ashore for whom the message was intended. John already knew the meaning of several flags, such as "Pilot on board" and "Diver down", but as time passed by he quietly learnt more from Alex.

Alex also learnt the meaning of the blasts on the ship's whistle, more commonly known as the foghorn, of the larger vessels coming up the channels in the Firth, where the intention of the ship to turn to starboard, to turn to port, or to go astern, is indicated by one, two or three one-second blasts, respectively: five one-second blasts means that you are coming too close! In respect of remembering 'port' from 'starboard', the latter being on the left when looking from the stern of a boat to the bows, when first starting to take the helm from John, under instruction, Alex had relied on his having memorised the simple short sentence "There is **port left** in the bottle", but very soon he had no further need of it, responding to John's instructions without delay.

On large vessels, the ship's compass is usually mounted on gimbals within a binnacle, which latter provides it with illumination and protection from the environment. On opposite sides of the binnacle are spherical or rounded supports for the navigator's hands, to steady him or her whilst checking the compass reading. Presumably as a precaution

111

to avoid confusion between "port" and "starboard" under conditions of stress or when a rapid response is required; or when the navigator is relatively inexperienced; the left-hand side support is painted red and the right-hand support is painted green: good, sensible, simple precautions!

Another area of Alex's study was the weather, and he soon became able to predict how the wind would be likely to change during the course of the day: whether it would back or veer, whether it would increase or decrease; and whether there would be rain or mist. The Firth of Clyde is a relatively safe area, surrounded by great mountains that offer a lot of protection from the wind, but it is open to the prevailing south-west wind and there is always the need to know what the wind force and direction is likely to be during the day, before deciding whether to round Cloch Point, or just stay within the inner Firth and the lochs.

Occasionally, with a strong prevailing south-west wind and an incoming tide, a small tidal bore can develop out in the open Firth, but this is very infrequent and such small bores are only a danger to small dinghies of about 12-15 feet length. Fishermen out in such small craft would need to up-anchor and head for the nearest shore, or Dunoon harbour if close enough, upon sighting a bore coming up the Firth from the south.

On one occasion when he and John were leaving the quay to deliver some goods to Dunoon he told John 'Okay then, I'll cast us adrift', which caused John's face to break out in a grin. Alex asked the reason for this, to be told, good naturedly, that the correct terminology was "Cast off", as to "Cast adrift" is to throw the boat, its cargo and its passengers and crew to the mercy of the wind and the tide when there was no alternative, whilst the boat that the two of them were on was quite capable of being motored to its destination.

Alex also learnt the peculiarities of the marine diesel engine, a magnificently reliable and efficient means of propulsion that requires no electrical ancillaries for starting and running. Its maintenance is minimal and inexpensive, and it can give decades of service.

John was delighted with his progress and with his enthusiasm, and started to have the odd drink with Alex after work to talk over the events of the day, and what was planned for the following day. They had become very close friends, enjoying each other's company and their mutual love of the sea. One evening as they left the boat, John asked Alex if he wanted to call in for a drink at the Bay. As they entered the lounge Alex was astounded to see 'James Cagney' standing at the bar, short, in a suit, and wearing a trilby, chatting to 'Betty

Grable'. As he looked around he saw 'George Raft' standing further along the bar, characteristically spinning and catching a coin with his fingers.

John laughed at Alex's evident discomposure, and told him that the pub was a regular meeting place for people who liked to model the film stars. They weren't perverts or misfits: their posing was just harmless fun, and was enjoyed by all who frequented the Bay. After they had had a few drinks, Alex asked John where he had been born, to which, maintaining a straight face, John replied 'The town where the population never changes.' Alex was intrigued by this mysterious answer and asked John to explain. John smiled. 'Port Glasgow, where whenever a young woman gives birth in the town, a young man leaves the town in great haste.' Whilst accepting that Port Glasgow was John's birthplace, Alex didn't believe his 'explanation' for one minute!

Some time and several pints later, as another group of 'film stars' entered the lounge, John said to Alex 'Next week, why don't you dig out that smart suit you were wearing the first time I met you, slick down your hair, and come in tap-dancing and singing "I'm in Heaven, dancing cheek-to-cheek with you", as Fred Astaire? You'd be a hit!', to which Alex replied 'Aye, and why don't you put on a white sailor hat and a stripy vest, stick a pipe in your mouth and a stuffed parrot on your shoulder, and come in dancing a sea-shanty, as Popeye? You'd be a sensation!'

They stayed in the Bay until closing time and had a great evening. However, Flo was beside herself with rage when Alex got home. 'What time do you call this, you useless drunken sod? Out boozing all hours with your new shirt-lifting sailor friends when you should have been down in the pub with me!'

After four weeks Ernie asked John how Alex was getting on, being pleased to learn that John considered him to be sufficiently skilled and knowledgeable to be allowed to take out a boat on his own, provided that John himself would be afloat in the vicinity on one of the other boats, just to keep an eye on him. Ernie was delighted with the news, as was Alex when Ernie past the news on to him.

Chapter Seven

Alex's first time out as skipper came the following Saturday, when he had a fishing party from Yorkshire to take out. The party arrived on the quayside, and made their way to the string of boats that were tied up along the west side of the quay. Other boats, some of which were 60 feet or more in length, such as the "Gourockian" and the "Granny Kempock" [#9], were waiting their turn to come alongside the quay. The anglers passed by boats that were clearly too big for their small party, until they found the one that they were looking for, the "Westering Home". Whilst a bit scruffy, the anglers were pleased to find that it had a saloon and a toilet for the use of the passengers, and was ideal for fishing parties.

Other smaller boats, of about 28 feet in length, were tied up there also, such as the "The Bounty" and the "Golden Dawn", which were fine for a fishing party, although they had only a cabin for the skipper and perhaps a couple of others, but no substantial covered accommodation: however, serious anglers have no use for covered accommodation anyway, as they will be out on the deck fishing, come whatever weather.

The 'fishing captain' called down to Alex, standing on the foredeck of the "Westering Home", to check that everything was alright, and then told his lads to board. As they moved off from the quay, one of the fishermen asked Alex why the "Granny Kempock" was so named. Alex had raised this question himself some time earlier in the "Puffer", the pub where the inshore fishermen congregate, and was able to tell him that it was named after an ancient monument up on the hillside immediately above Gourock, the "Granny Kempock Stone" [#10], having a resemblance to an old lady. At one time it had stood prominently on the hillside, visible in all directions, but it is now partly obscured by tenement houses and other properties.

After Alex had told the angler that the rock was no more than about five minutes walk from where the boats is tied up, the angler said that he would call in and see it after they had disembarked at the end of the trip. In return, Alex asked the fisherman why the party had a 'fishing captain', and was told that this was to try to avoid arguments as to where to fish and when to move on if the fishing was slack, otherwise the day would be spent in argument and they would all go home frustrated. As it was, there were soon dissenting comments when the 'captain' chose to move to a spot that was less favoured by others of the team. Things came to a head later in the morning one of the team asked 'Why the Hell are we going to that dead hole?' He was told by the captain, in no uncertain terms: 'Because I'm the bloody fishing captain and what I say goes!' After this, the day passed without further dissent.

The idea of a fishing party sitting down in the pub to appoint a fishing captain for the forthcoming trip seemed admirable to Alex. On too many trips he had heard the quarrelling and quibbling of all of the fishing party on the boat as to the best fishing marks, leading to all of them going home at the end of the trip disgruntled and unhappy. He had heard that during the War, Winston Churchill had never explained the reasons for his decisions, simply issuing orders, as to have offered an explanation would have enabled and encouraged others to realise that he had thought processes that were no superior to their own, and would have opened the flood-gates to endless procrastination and the voicing of numerous individual opinions: a dreadful situation!

When time allows, as in the pub the evening before setting off on the fishing trip, group discussion is fine, but when an immediate onboard decision is required, then only one man can decide. Alex agreed entirely with the comment of the Yorkshire fishing captain: 'Because I'm the bloody fishing captain and what I say goes!'

Later in the day a party of divers anchored close by, both groups wanting to exploit a wreck lying on the bottom at that point, the divers for artefacts and the fishermen for conger eels. As the divers took to the water, the Yorkshire Fishing Captain shouted out 'Sithee, tha'll scare off the fish. Now piss off or I'll belt thee on tha head wi' a lead weight!' One of the divers, a young well-made Scot, broke away from the group, raised his goggles and then swam over slowly to the part of Alex's boat where the Fishing Captain was standing. He looked the Fishing Captain hard in the eyes, then put both of his hands onto the "gun'les", gunwales, and drew his body up out of the water: He was a fearsome menacing sight! With cold glinting eyes he said, in a deep guttural snarling voice, 'Don't you threaten me you English turd!' whereupon the fishing captain roared with laughter at having got the Scot to lose his temper. The diver turned away in disgust and swam back to his companions: no good wasting time on idiots.

Alex thought that all of the fishing party was balmy, Fishing Captain included. They would make remarks to each other that would have driven any self-respecting Scot to violence, but within seconds they would be exchanging 'cigs' and talking about cricket. Alex's first real introduction to the English, in the form of these Yorkshiremen, had him in confusion, but had he but known, there are many people living in other parts of England who have a similar opinion of Yorkshiremen! [11]

One party of Yorkshiremen that that he met who were fishing from Gourock beach had a mate with them who had lost both of his legs, but who cast out perfectly well from a small rectangular padded board that was set at the water's edge. As the tide started to come in, he asked his mates to move him further up the beach. His mates took no action, but one of the said to him 'Do what King Canute did. Tell it to piss off out!' The man cursed and swore at them, using a range of crude but imaginative expressions, most of which were unknown to Alex, but seemed to have an association with the mining industry. Eventually, with much pretended grumbling, they dragged his board a few feet further up the beach, the whole procedure, swearing and cursing included, being repeated fifteen minutes later, and so on, until the tide turned.

Alex found their strong accent and the colloquialisms that they used, together with the practice of omitting the initial letter "h" from the words that they used, difficult to follow, just as they found difficulty with his own accent. Alex was amazed once again that such behaviour and such expressions could pass between what was obviously a group of good friends. Yorkshire men are indeed very strange, and add substance to the saying "There's now't so queer as folk!"

There were anglers from other areas than Yorkshire that Alex took out. One fishing party from a pub down in Carlisle came up regularly in an old coach with a beer barrel set on a stillage (a timber support) at the back end. After a good day's fishing, the lads would sit supping in the coach to keep them going until they arrived back at their local, when they would then carry on drinking and discussing the day's fishing until closing time, and probably beyond. From time-to-time parties came from further afield: Liverpool, Manchester, Birmingham and Leeds, but rarely from further south, as the anglers from the Midlands find it easier to go down to the south coast for their fishing. Alex got on well with the anglers: they were all honest good-natured men, save for one nasty person who, in a rage and full of self-pity after having lost a good fish, tipped the contents of his tackle box over the side, in full view of a couple of youngsters who were fishing nearby with the minimum of equipment, and would have been delighted to have been given just a small part of the contents of the tackle box. No doubt the angler would have come round by the next trip, and re-equipped himself with new tackle, but Alex squashed this possibility by saying to him 'I hope I don't see you on this boat again', to nods and glances of approval from the other fishermen.

Alex had always believed that the only justification in catching and killing fish was that at the end of the trip they were to be taken home and eaten, and that immediately after capture they should be killed as painlessly as possible and their bodies then put aside. He also made a point with the anglers that immature fish should be returned to the water with the minimum delay, the only exception being if they were badly hooked, where the removal of the hook would inevitably result in the death of the fish, even though returned to the water. This led to the odd rogue angler claiming that an immature fish in his basket had been badly hooked, when the clean mark of the hook in its lip was clear for all to see, joking in an aside to his mates that it had been "badly lip hooked". The laws relating to the minimum size of fish able to be retained by the angler are virtually unenforceable with small fishing parties, but Alex maintained a firm position on this matter.

On one trip a father and his young son aged about eight came aboard. The father eventually caught a small, but acceptable, fish and put it into his bag without first killing it. Feeling bored some time later, the son took the fish from the bag and held it towards his face, making popping noises and opening and shutting his mouth in the pretence of being a fish himself, to the delight of his father, who gazed at him adoringly, and beamed a smile at the other anglers, expecting them to express praise for his son's impersonation, but none of them spoke or raised a smile, viewing both the angler and his son with displeasure and disgust. Alex said to the boy, in a cold clear voice that carried to the rest of the party 'Put it back into the bag sonny. Let it rest in peace, it's not a plaything.', speaking more for the benefit of the father than for that of the son. The father was angry and scolded Alex for having chastised his precious young child: 'It's my fish. I caught it and he can do what he wants with it.' 'Not on my boat' said Alex.

There were other anglers who earned Alex's displeasure. On one trip a loud-mouthed self-opinionated man set himself up in the stern of the boat amongst a group of other anglers. There wasn't really enough room for him to fish there, but he had thrust his way in and the group obligingly made room for him. After he had baited up, he got ready to cast out, whereupon the rest of the anglers in the confined space followed the normal procedure of bending their heads down out of the way. The man cast out, and then settled down to fish, oblivious of the other anglers, who were awaiting some indication that it was now safe for them to lift their heads. When, after a minute or so, one of them did lift his head, the man noticed him and was overcome with amusement: 'What! Are you lot still bending down there?' A stupid inconsiderate man who didn't belong in the company of decent anglers!

Alex held his tongue. Inconsiderate pathetic man! He was reminded of one occasion when a neighbour had called round to Flo's apartment late one cold winter's evening in a state of distress, telling them that his young daughter, a child of about three years of age, had wandered off

117

and couldn't be found. Alex had immediately put on his outdoor clothes and set off looking around the district, calling back to Flo's apartment about every hour or so to see if the child had been found. After four hours, cold and tired, he had gone around to the man's apartment to see what progress had been made in the search, learning when the man opened his front door with a glass of beer in his hand that the child had been found two hours before and was safely tucked up in bed.

The man clearly thought that Alex was an idiot and expressed his annoyance at having been disturbed so late in the evening by Alex's knocking on his door, when the child was now safe at home and in bed, and he had settled down to enjoy a drink! There was no appreciation by the man that, once the panic was over, he should have paid the same attention to calling off the search as he had in calling on the help of his neighbours in the first instance, nor would the inconsiderate creature have befitted by Alex's explaining this to him. Alex realised that there are many people in the world who don't have any understanding of civic responsibility or fairness to those around them. It is no good remonstrating with them: they are irresponsible, of low morality, of low-grade, and deserving of contempt. At the same time, this caused Alex to consider, to his great discomfort, his own behaviour in the past.

One time a group of four anglers brought a bottle of whisky on board with them, and had obviously been drinking heavily before they arrived at the boat. It was a rough day, and as the boat left the quay and headed out to sea, the group went and stood in the bows, shirt fronts open wide to the wind, revelling in the bucking of the boat, laughing as spray was thrown over them, and passing the bottle from hand to hand. They felt that they were indeed a magnificent manly group, not like the other soft anglers, who just stood there like dummies, waiting for the boat to reach the fishing mark, with not a drink between them! However, after half an hour, one of them fell silent and went and sat in the saloon, soon to be followed by the others. For the rest of the trip, the members of that group emerged only temporarily, to 'call for Hughie' over the side on their hands and knees.

As one of them came on deck and bent down over the gun'les to puke, an older fisherman sitting nearby stripped a length of yellowish fat from the edge of his beef sandwich and stuck the end of it up one of his nostrils. Tapping the puking man on the shoulder so that he turned his head round, he inquired with a straight face and in a concerned voice 'Are you alright son?', the sight of the long string of 'snot' hanging from the inquirer's nose causing the abject angler to return to his puking with renewed vigour.

Another angler offered the man advice: 'Best get it up son, better out than in, but if you find a round furry ring in your mouth then swallow hard, 'cos' that's your arsehole!', which brought delighted laughter from the rest of them anglers. Drink and rough weather don't go together, and there is no sympathy given to the drunken angler, nor should there be. He is a nuisance on land and even more so within the close confines of a fishing boat!

Many anglers carry little cans to urinate into when the need arises, but most are sensible and just urinate discretely over the side without any concern, provided that there aren't any ladies or young females present amongst the fishing party. Female anglers retreat to the saloon, usually making their purpose of their visit known to the rest of the party so that they can rest assured that they won't be disturbed. Many of the men take the opportunity of the temporary departure of any females to relieve themselves at the same time: everything runs smoothly. The only noticeable effect of the presence of women that Alex noticed was that the men have to restrain their language, which as all anglers know well, is very difficult should one lose a good fish.

All-male parties were no problem, although on one occasion, after a somewhat modest young newcomer to fishing had held himself in restraint for a couple of hours, he eventually stood close up to the gun'les, fumbling with his waterproofs and clearly feeling uncomfortable. When at last he found what he wanted and was ready to urinate, he attempted to cover his embarrassment by saying to those around him 'I hope that this doesn't disturb the ecological balance.', to which one of the older anglers, with the wisdom that comes with age, replied 'Upset the ecological balance! You and me and everyone else here are part of the ecological balance, so get pissing!'

Although Alex was learning quickly, there were still some things that he had yet to learn. Rounding Ashton Point on one slightly misty day, on his way into the Firth, he was disturbed when the foghorn of the Cloch lighthouse started to sound. He looked down the Firth, but the mist was only mild, so he continued, with the foghorn continuing to sound. The fishing party started to become alarmed at the sound of the foghorn, eventually the Fishing Captain approaching Alex to ask if it was safe to continue out towards the open sea. After thinking for a few seconds, Alex decided that it was better to be safe than sorry, so he turned the boat about. As he did so, the foghorn ceased sounding, which caused him some uncertainty: was it now safe to stay out on the Firth? However, they continued back around Ashton Point to fish off Greenock Esplanade, to the general relief of the fishing party, which then had a good day's fishing, returning to the jetty later in the afternoon with a good catch.

After tying up, bidding farewell to the fishing party, sluicing down the deck of the boat, and generally tidying up in readiness for the following day, Alex walked along the quay to speak to John, who was tidying up his own boat, also in preparation for the next day's work. He mentioned the sounding of the foghorn, expressing his surprise that it should have sounded, as there had been no evidence of fog out on the Firth, nor had there been any warning of fog on the weather forecast. John stopped what he was doing and with a broad grin on his face asked him 'Would that be at about half past ten then?' Alex was surprised, and asked how John should have known should this, as on that day John had taken his own boat to the Gareloch, well out of earshot of the Cloch foghorn. John replied 'Because the lighthouse always tests its foghorn for half an hour at half past ten every Friday morning!' Alex was embarrassed at his mistake, but better safe than sorry!

After he had taken out half a dozen parties of English anglers, Alex began to wonder whether Mr.Gilbraith had summed up the English properly. These anglers harboured no aggression towards the Scots, and came up to the Clyde regularly, all year round, year after year. For the first time he questioned Mr. Gilbraith's teaching. That the English in the past had committed atrocities against the Scots was without doubt, but could the ancestors of these simple friendly men have taken part in such activities? If so, under what conditions of brain-washing and duress? Alex was beginning to think for himself, rather than to accept the paranoid and xenophobic ranting of others, as he had done in the past.

As time went by, Alex began to learn about the various fish and their haunts, and the ways to clean and skin or fillet them and he also became familiar with the variety of birds on the Firth of Clyde: back in Glasgow the only birds that he had ever seen were sparrows, pigeons and starlings.

As well as learning where to fish, Alex also learnt where not to fish, sometimes the hard way. On one trip he set down the anchor in a spot that was new to him, but without taking the precaution of checking his chart. When the time came to move, there was heavy resistance to the lifting of the anchor, which had become engaged with something or other on the sea-bed. Somehow the anchor rope had become tangled around the shaft of the anchor, with the result that the weak link failed to provide its usual protection by snapping: the anchor was stuck fast on the sea-bed!

Alex asked the members of the fishing party on board for help in lifting up the anchor, and was pleased when half a dozen of the lads, a group of miners from Doncaster, willingly came to the bows, whilst the rest, a group of office workers from Cheshire, kept their eyes averted and pretended that they were sorting out their tackle boxes, or otherwise importantly engaged. The group at the bows took up the slack and then commenced a long slow haul, dragging in the rope a foot at a time, and every now and then giving the rope a couple of turns around the Samson post whilst they took a rest.

After an hour they brought the anchor to the surface, to see that it had become engaged in the heavily-armoured telephone cable running between Dunoon and the Ashton shore. He reached down and ran a strong rope under the cable and then tied it around the Samson post. After his helpers had eased off the load on the anchor rope, Alex worked the anchor free and brought it inboard, and then used his knife to cut the rope holding the telephone cable, letting it return to the sea bed. He should have known better than to have put the anchor down at this spot, as the runs of the submerged telephone cables are marked clearly on the charts for this region.

Alex had made a discovery: there are those, mostly such as miners, steel workers and other manual workers, who will identify with someone needing physical help and gladly give a helping hand, whilst there are others, usually white-collar workers, who will draw back. Alex now saw this as the difference between the working class and the lower middle class! He heaped thanks on his 'working class' helpers, whilst at the same time staring with disgust at the rest of the fishing party, the 'lower middle class' group, some of whom, but not all, had the grace to look uncomfortable. This was the first time that Alex had experienced, at first-hand, class differences in the way that people behave. All of the people he had met until he came to Gourock had been of a manual background, as also were Ernie and his skippers. However, although all of these people were manual workers, with callused hands and weather-beaten faces, and would be categorised, often derogatorily, as working class, they possessing many and varied skills and in some instances a lifetime of experience, a feature often overlooked by others in more socially-prestigious occupations. Alex was learning to judge people by their actions, not by their accents or their fine words, or their inherited wealth, or their social standing in the community.

The party he took out one day was a group of solicitors from a law firm in Kelvinside, a prosperous and very desirable area to the west of Glasgow city centre. They arrived in a convoy of top-quality cars, and were dressed in bright bobble-caps, and smart Arran sweaters. Each of them carried an expensive tackle box that also served as a seat. They were a beautifully turned out angling party! As they got to the fishing mark and the anglers proceed to make up their tackle, Alex was astonished at the contents of their tackle boxes: hooks and weights of all sizes, connectors, swivels, traces, lures, cartons of bait, and all kinds of equipment such as spare reels, rolls of spare line of different strength, disgorgers and other miscellaneous items of hardware.

They spoke in cultivated Kelvinside and Byers Road accents, and addressed each other without contracting their personal name to a diminutive, in contrast with all of the lads that Alex had known hitherto, such as Greg, Joe, John and Ernie. Their sentences were enunciated 'beautifully', with "I" pronounced by widening and pulling back the lips to emerge as a strangulated "Aaaye", and with the words rising and falling in melodious cadences. They were so nice to each other that Alex was amazed. When one of them asked the man fishing next to him if he would give him a hook, he did so most graciously: 'Hamish, my good fellow, could you oblige me with a 2/0 hook? There's a good chap.', to which Hamish replied 'By all means my dear Cameron, do please help yourself.'

Some of them spoke normally to Alex, treating him as an equal, despite his harsh and guttural inner-city accent, and giving him the respect that he was due as their skipper for the day, but others had a condescending manner, speaking to him in slow clear sentences so that he would be able to understand them, and treating him as hired help, which he supposed was all that he was to them. Alex resented the presence of the latter on his boat and was glad to see them leave at the end of the day, beaming farewells to each other and carrying their catches with them like courageous hunters returning home from a wild day out on the open sea. They would have exciting tales to tell at this evening's dinner party!

Alex didn't feel inferior, but they irritated him. He was also envious of the education that they had been given, and the protective and discriminating environment in which they had been brought up, that had given them self-confidence, group loyalty, professional employment and a social circle that provided them with all the company that they might need and a suitable women for a wife. He had met, and now knew, the middle-class! 'Lucky bastards!' he would say to himself, but without rancour.

Alex grew to love his life on the boats. He began to recognise the ships that passed up and down the Firth regularly. A fleet of three ships carried raw sewage from Glasgow out to deep water offshore, where they would open the bottom of their huge holds and let their foul cargoes drop down into the depths, when it would undoubtedly be well received by the marine life down there. [13] When they weren't in operation, they could be seen tied up at the Custom's House Quay in Greenock.

On one fishing trip, one of these ships, the "Garrochhead", came down the Firth close by where Alex's party was fishing. Someone on a nearby fishing boat called out to the skipper of the Garrochhead as it drew level 'Ahoy there skipper. What's you cargo?' to which the skipper bellowed back 'Shit!' The next time that this particular fishing party came out on Alex's boat, to fish in the same spot, the eyes of the fishermen were all alert, looking for the first sign of one of the sewage ships.

Eventually one of them, the "Dalmarnock", was seen coming down the Firth. As the ship drew level, the captain of the fishing party, claiming this right as the senior member of the party aboard, bellowed out the standard question in a voice that could be heard a mile away, to receive the standard reply "Shit!" The members of the fishing party were delighted, and laughed and grinned for the next five minutes, with numerous recounts of the verbal exchange between the two ships doubtless being given in the pub when they got back home late that evening. Whenever they came back for another fishing trip, no matter how good the catch, they were always disappointed if they didn't see one of the sewage ships and were able to shout the traditional question. It was considered great fun by all, although the skippers of the sewage ships might be called upon to give this response a dozen or more times a day.

A great range of ships used the Clyde: container ships bound for the container terminal at Greenock; oil tankers bound for the oil terminal at Finnart on Loch Long; ammunition ships bound for the jetty for the MOD explosives depot, known to the locals as "The Base"; built on and below the mountain to the east of Loch Long just north of Finnart; pleasure cruisers operating out of Greenock; car ferries operating between Gourock and Dunoon; smaller passenger ferries carrying goods and passengers to local destinations; puffers travelling to the offshore islands; big powerful tugs operating out of Greenock harbour; numerous small work boats; and fleets of sailing boats from the Clyde Yacht Club on the promenade at Gourock, and from Cove, Inverkip and other places around the Firth.

Alex in particular liked to watch the sailing boats on the days when they had competitions, marvelling at the instant filling of the spinnaker sails as their crews released them to take a following wind after turning at one of the course markers. Not all of the boats had a spinnaker sail, however: when picking up a following wind, some of them sailed 'goose-rigged', setting the fore-sail and the main-sail on opposite beams and allowing them to swing out, fill, and make the most of the wind. Although 'goose-rigged' is the usual term, Alex felt that 'swan-rigged' would be a better term, as the sight of an adult swan advancing under a following wind with its wings part-extended, so that it resembles a great square-rigged sailing ship, is a magnificent sight to behold.

Amongst the pleasure cruisers was the "Second Snark", doubtless named from the book "The hunting of the Snark" by Lewis Carroll, which was built by Denny's of Dumbarton in 1938, a time when the principal means of transportation along the Clyde coast was by passenger ship. Since that time the Snark, which has room for eighty passengers, has operated continuously on the River Clyde and the Firth of Clyde, latterly carrying mainly day-trippers between Glasgow, Greenock, Helensburgh, Kilcreggan, Dunoon, Largs, Milport, Rothesay, Tignabruaich, and Lochranza.

An especial favourite was the "Waverley", the last ocean-going paddle ship in the world. This magnificent ship would carry several hundred holidaymakers from Glasgow, calling in at ports on the Firth down to Largs and Rothesay, and going on to other more-distant places, allowing the passengers to go ashore for a few hours, then returning to pick them up and carry them back to their point of embarkation in the evening. It would motor along majestically, its great shrouded paddle wheels cutting cleanly through the water.

A single accordion player, or a small band, would be playing Scottish airs and songs of the day in the bar, accompanied by the singing, and sometimes dancing, of most of the passengers: the Scots know how to let their hair down when the mood takes them! Other passengers would stand on the decks and wave to those in passing boats or on the shore. During the course of their trip, most of the passengers would enjoy a snack in the tea-room or a hot meal in the restaurant, whilst others would just sit warm and snug in the conformable seats in the lounge, some of them enjoying a drink from the bar, whilst looking through the large glass windows at the changing scenery. A great pleasure for those travelling on the Waverley is to go below deck to see the enormous flywheels, driven by crankshafts and connecting rods of equally impressive size. Small glass windows set into the side of the hull enable them to look at the paddles as they revolve.

Sometimes the Waverley visits ports down in the south of England, but always returns to her home base in the Clyde, and long may she do so. Although herself a truly magnificent ship, the present Waverley is not the first of that name, the original Waverley having being sunk whilst serving the country in the evacuation of Dunkirk during World War II. The present Waverley was built shortly after the war in response to popular demand, the only difference between it and the original being the use of oil instead of coal as fuel.

As his knowledge increased, Alex began to advise those new to fishing, and soon acquired a reputation for being helpful. He was always willing to move to a new mark when the fishing was slow, not like many skippers who, once they have lowered the anchor, just want to sit in the wheelhouse reading and smoking, until it is time to call it a day. Before long, the organisers of fishing parties were ringing up and telling Ernie that they wanted Alex as their skipper for the day, which pleased Ernie immensely, as it ensured bookings in the future. After a good day's fishing, they would thank Alex as they left the boat, and add 'See you next time!'

Alex was delighted with this, and it felt good. Ernie was pleased with him for another reason also: Alex had proven to be trustworthy and could be relied upon to take out a boat at short notice. In this way, Ernie could accept rush jobs without hesitation, in the confidence that Alex would agree to do the job. Life was good for Alex: he had a good boss, a good job, and good mates in the other skippers. For the first time in his life, Alex had friends. He set off for work each morning as happy and contented as could be: his life had never been better. There was only one part of his life that was not going well, and that was his relationship with Flo.

Chapter Eight

Flo had been pleased when Alex had got his job on the boats. This meant that she could now go with him into the lounge of the "Clyde Puffer", where all the inshore seamen drank. She and Alex would call in for an hour most evenings, and would spend the whole evening there on "Free and Easy" concert nights. She used to go there with her previous man, but when the relationship ended she had stopped going, as all of the seamen's women were cool towards her, knowing her reputation and seeing her as a threat. Indeed, at one time or another she had had her moments with a good number of the men who drank there.

At first the two of them had been greeted warmly, and she had been teased and fussed-over by the other men, which she had enjoyed immensely, but as time passed, with Alex's increasing popularity with the rest of the skippers, she began to feel neglected, as after the initial friendly greeting, the talk was all about boats and catches, the events of the day, and what the weather would be like tomorrow. She began to get irritated with the conversation, and would sit there with a set face, which led to her being paid even less attention. To make matters worse, Alex's willingness to do extra jobs for Ernie caused them to miss a couple of "Free and Easy" evenings.

She began to nag Alex: nothing much at first, but with the passage of time the nagging grew offensive, and her voice would be raised in anger and her words punctuated with bad language. Alex tried to make up for the neglect she claimed to be suffering by giving her extra money to buy clothes and other things that she might fancy, but after a while even this did no good. Their arguments became a nightly occurrence.

Often Flo had been drinking when Alex came in, and after she had vented all her anger, and shed many tears, she would become maudlin and want him to make love to her. Alex wouldn't have minded this, but Flo's love-making was becoming lewd, and she would demand actions of him that he found embarrassing. Moreover, the clothing that Flo had bought of late was all erotic: crutch-less knickers, bras with holes in them for the nipples to peep through, gaudy suspender belts.

He was becoming seriously concerned as to where their relationship was heading, and as to what sexual novelties she still had in store for him, but he couldn't bring himself to discuss the matter with anyone. Alex's sexual interest in Flo was beginning to wane, with her crudity and her increasing nagging. Sometimes he couldn't be bothered to respond when she reached out under the bed-sheets and fondled him. This would drive her wild with anger and she would call him a "bloody fairy".

One evening he rejected her advances by saying that he had a stiff back after the heavy work of the day, to which Flo responded with 'Well let's hope it spreads, you droopy-dicked pansy.' She held out one of her hands in front of her, palm down, with all of her fingers held out straight, except for her middle finger, which she held drooped down limply, wiggling it to and fro weakly, ridiculing Alex's recent sexual performance. Rather childlike and pathetically, Alex lost his temper and responded by pulling the sides of his mouth wide apart with the forefingers of his hands, then saying "Clyde Tunnel!", which made her wild with anger. He knew that the end of their relationship was in sight, but he was just about past caring. She had become too demanding and too vulgar: he no longer felt sexually attracted to her and if she didn't change her ways soon he would start to look for lodgings elsewhere.

One Saturday when neither Alex nor John had a fishing party to take out, John asked him if he wanted to come along with a friend of his who had the use of a big van, to go netting down in the south of the country. Alex jumped at the chance, much to Flo's annoyance. 'Aren't you out enough during the week without going out again at weekend, when we should be in the bloody pub?' They met at the quayside at five o'clock in the afternoon. John's mate, Neil, was a strong-looking chap, dressed in suitable rough clothing, and Alex took an instant liking to him. In the back of his van was a pile of netting lying under a boat cover, and sitting on a trailer behind the van was a lovely16ft fibreglass simulated-clinker dory.

They reached their objective, the hamlet of Drummore, in the Mull of Galloway, with its harbour opening into Luce Bay, at the southern tip of Scotland. At nine o'clock, after parking the van by the side of the harbour, they went for a drink in the local. As soon as the pub had closed, and the village had become deserted, they disconnected the trailer and wheeled it down to the water's edge. John and Neil had arranged the trip to coincide with high tide being at eleven o'clock, so high tide was fast approaching. They carried the net down to the boat, spread the boat cover over the stern so that the net would not snag as it was paid overboard, and then 'flaked' the net onto it, i.e. spread it out evenly without tangles.

When the tide had reached its full height, the water covered an area within the harbour of about equal to that of a football field, whilst the harbour mouth was little over forty yards wide. Under the faint glimmer of the moon, John and Neil rowed the dinghy over to the far side of the harbour and tied the end of the net to a timber post close to the water's edge, then rowing the boat back to where Alex was standing, the net paying out smoothly over the stern of the dinghy, needing but the occasional flick to remove any small tangles, so that it fell down into the water as a clean smooth barrier, suspended by the floats that had been strung into it at about eighteen-inch intervals, with a thin lead-line at its base pulling it down taut.

The net was a gill net with a square mesh of about one-inch sides. However, it was not the intention to catch the fish by their pushing their heads through the net until their gills passed beyond the mesh and they could then neither advance nor withdraw, but simply for the net to act as a barrier to retain the fish whilst the outgoing tide drained the harbour dry. Soon the tide turned and the fish in the harbour started to move towards the harbour mouth on their way back out into the sea. Alex and John walked down to the net to see, in the phosphorescence caused by their movement through the water, numerous fish rushing at the net to try to break out. 'Flounders,' said John, 'mullet don't rush at a net like that.'

The net had not been long enough to reach all the way across the harbour mouth, ending some five yards short of the shore. Alex walked into the water to the end of the net and stood guard. Soon, in the light of the moon, he spotted a shoal of some forty grey mullet cautiously feeling their way along the net, in contrast to the mindless way in which the flounders had tried to escape. Grey mullet are noted as a highly intelligent fish, difficult to catch by normal fishing methods using a baited hook, unless both the hook and the bait are of such small size, and the line so thin, as to give the mullet no cause for suspicion. The shoal drew steadily closer, until it was only four or five feet from the end of the net. Alex gave a small shuffle of his feet, upon which the shoal turned and then began making its way along the net in the opposite direction. Alex knew that by the time that the shoal had reached the far end of the net, found it to be above the surface of the water, and then returned, his end of the net would also be above the surface of the water.

A short time later they saw a dark shape approaching the net, with another dark shape, some ten feet behind it, but weaving from side to side. Neil shouted 'Damn! We've trapped a bloody basking shark in the harbour!' Undoubtedly, in the eyes of the three of them, the leading dark shape was the dorsal fin of an almost submerged basking shark[8:1] and [12], whilst the second dark shape, moving with a regular motion from side-to-side, was its tail fin. With held breath they waited for the

---

[8:1] This creature is well described by Gavin Maxwell in his book "Harpoon at a venture", published by New English Library, number 450-01236-0.

inevitable catastrophe when the shark reached the net, but to their amazement the leading dark shape passed beyond the net without the slightest disturbance. The second dark shape, still weaving from side-to-side, also reached the net and passed beyond it. John realised what they had been looking at and started to chuckle, in some measure due to relief. 'It's a bloody pair of ducks.' he said, 'When the first duck makes a small change of direction, the second duck soon changes its direction too, but makes a bigger change, and then corrects its course, hence the swaying tail. If that had been a basking shark, the net would have been ripped apart or else on its way out of the harbour.'

The three men then returned to the van, where they sat and chatted until they dozed off. They awoke at five o'clock in the morning to what sounded like the quiet clapping of a small group of people. They left the van and walked down to the harbour, to be confronted with the sight of many hundreds of fish, either stranded on that part of the harbour that had already drained, or thrashing about in the twenty of so yards within the confines of the net that still contained water. They were somewhat disturbed by the noise, in case an early riser should hear it and come to investigate. Although none of the locals appeared to be interested in netting the harbour themselves, they would nevertheless feel that any fish in it were their property, and John and Neil wanted to keep their activities unnoticed so that they could come back on a future occasion.

Somewhat unwisely, they took the boat and trailer down to the water's edge and used buckets to clear the fish from the dried-out part of the harbour first, and then, as the rest of the harbour dried out completely, they cleared the rest of the fish, including those tangled within the net. This had taken then about an hour, but luckily the only passer-by had been a farmer on his tractor pulling milk churns along on a trailer, and he had still been sleepy enough not to have noticed them. At this point Alex realised that they would have trouble pulling the trailer, the boat and the catch up the rock-strew beach, but Neil told him not to worry.

As they encountered the first rock and Alex went to move it, wondering if it was too deeply embedded in the beach for him to be able to do so without a shovel, Neil told him not to worry, but just to find a suitable rock to jam behind the opposite wheel to stop it rolling backwards: perplexed, Alex did so. John then called the other two to the towing hitch of the trailer, to which he had attached a short length of rope. Upon the instruction to pull the rope transversely, towards the side where the wheel was chocked, the obstructed wheel rose up and over the rock, ready to move forwards again.

Alex was impressed by the ease of the operation, which Neil told him he called "walking the boat", and explained that their rope was attached about 8ft forward of the trailer's wheels, whilst the track of the trailer wheels was only about 4ft, so that they had a mechanical advantage of 2-to-1 when rotating the trailer about the chocked wheel. "Walking" meant that the trailer had a slow oscillatory progression up the beach, but it was worth it. Not for the first time, Alex was impressed by Neil and John's practical knowledge, and, not for the first time, felt uncomfortable about his own limited knowledge of other than crime and violence: however, he knew that under John's guidance, his knowledge of the sea and of inshore fishing was increasing day-by-day.

They drove off north in a state of great glee, estimating the catch as about two hundred flounders of an average weight of one-and-a-half pounds, and about fifty grey mullet at an average weight of three pounds, some six hundred pounds in all. Reaching the town of Girvan, they stopped at a café and had a full breakfast. The next problem was to decide what to do with the catch. As they drove through the town, Alex noticed that a man was preparing for the opening of his supper bar. John asked Neil to stop the van, and then went to the door of the supper bar and attracted the man's attention.

When the man opened the door, John told him, the proprietor, of their catch and asked if he was interested in buying any of it, then leading him to the back of the van. As soon as the man saw the catch, and realised its freshness, he made John an offer for a hundred of the flounders, which John accepted, but he said that he couldn't use the mullet, as his customers weren't familiar with this fish. However, he told John to hang on for a minute and went back inside the supper bar. Returning a couple of minutes later, he told John that he had just phoned a friend who ran a fish shop, who might be able to use the mullet, as his customers were used to seeing less-common fish on his slabs, and would probably be prepared to take a chance. Five minutes later a small van arrived and parked outside the shop. The fish-shop proprietor looked at the mullet and then made a quite low offer for thirty of them, which under the circumstances Alex felt that they should accept. They reimbursed Neil a generous sum for his expenses and then split the remainder of the cash three ways.

As it was still early, and they didn't want to get back to Gourock before the "Puffer" opened, when they reached Turnberry Neil turned off onto the coast road. Travelling along this road they came close by Culzean Castle. Alex had been told that the room in the castle that General Eisenhower had occupied during the second World War had been retained unchanged, and was open to viewing by visitors to the castle. He would have liked to visit the castle, sitting overlooking the sea, but time didn't allow: however, he made a mental note to do so when a suitable opportunity arose.

They followed the A719 and came to "Croy Brae", well-known as the "Electric Brae", located between Croy Railway Viaduct at an altitude of 286ft and Craigencroy Glen at an altitude of 303ft. When travelling from Craigencroy Glen towards Croy Railway Viaduct, the road slopes downhill slightly, but on account of the roadside hedges and the lie of the surrounding ground, the impression is given that the road is actually rising, and that the car and its occupants are being drawn uphill by some mysterious "electrical or magnetic force". John pointed out that they were travelling in the 'wrong' direction for this force to work, so after reaching Craigencroy Glen they turned round and set off in the opposite direction. Sure enough, the impression was very strong that the van was moving uphill under some mysterious force and when they stopped with the van in neutral gear and the handbrake off, the van moved off slowly forwards!

Just two or three miles further they came to a small loop that led to the tiny harbour of Dunure, a beautiful little place offering a safe haven from the rocky coastline in that area to three or four little fishing boats. Further along they came to Alloway, where Robert Burns had lived, his cottage, beautifully maintained, being open to viewing by the many Burns enthusiasts visiting the area from all parts of Britain and also from many other parts of the world.

After passing through the large town of Ayr, with its prosperous suburbs, its clean and attractive town centre, and its great big bustling harbour, they carried on along the coast road, passing through Irvine, Stevenston, Saltcoats, Ardrossan, Seamill, and Largs, before reaching Gourock, where they went straight to the "Puffer". After setting aside the fish that each of them might be able to use personally, or give to friends, they had about seventy flounders and twenty grey mullet left. Once inside the pub, they invited all present to come outside and select such fish as they wanted. Within minutes all of the fish were gone. Not only had it been a great trip, but all three of them had made money from it. John's mate said to Alex that they must do it again, to which he agreed, but judging from Flo's behaviour before he had set off, he felt that it might be better to give any future trip a miss, for a while anyway.

When he got back to the apartment, Alex found Flo in an enraged state. She excelled herself with her vulgar comments: 'What the devil do you think you are doing coming back at this time? It was bad enough having to go out on my own last night and sit like a wet fanny with no-one to talk to, but I thought that you would have come back

131

early enough today to take me along for a sodding dinner-time drink. Now for God's sake let's get down to the "Puffer" before they call time, but I don't want to hear a bloody word about how you and your 'sailor-boy' friends enjoyed yourselves!'

Although he turned down the invitation to go along on the next netting trip, Alex eventually agreed to go with John and his mate on a long-lining trip out on the Firth. The day before the trip Alex had a fishing party to take out, and had used the opportunity to catch about a hundred mackerel himself for use the next day as long-line bait. Alex and John met Neil at Gourock Quay, where they got into his big van and then drove the few miles to a slip several hundred yards to the south of Ashton Point. It was a lovely calm day and they rowed over to the Gantock Rocks lying just off Dunoon. The lighthouse there had been erected after a boat carrying grain had been wrecked on the rocks, and served as an excellent reference point for anglers fishing in the area. Arriving up-tide of the selected spot, Neil held over the side an anchor weight, with two lines attached, at the end of one of which a small buoy was attached, whilst the other line led to the tray of hooks.

Alex rowed vigorously down-tide for a few dozen yards whilst Neil started to pay out the two lines, the buoy restraining the anchor line to flow behind them so that it wouldn't tangle with the bait line. Once the anchor had reached the bottom, the three of them set to in cutting the mackerel into eight or ten pieces each, depending upon their size. Old steel nuts had been attached to the long-line every few yards to make sure that it would sink to the sea bed, whilst every fathom a two-foot length of line, a "snood", was fastened to the long-line, with a 4/0 fishing hook attached to its other end. Alex and John baited the bare hooks quickly as they drew them from out of the basket in which they were stored, whist Neil controlled the steady flow of the long-line over the transom of the boat under the drag of the tide. It was a smooth precision operation.

Fishing from a small boat, should a hook snag on part of the transom, or hook a finger, it is no problem for one of the others to arrest the flow of the long-line over the transom until the problem is sorted out, but when fishing from a big boat, it is not possible to restrain the flow and a hooked man could be drawn over the side. Under these conditions, commercial long-line fishermen would pre-bait the long lines and curl them around the insides of large wicker baskets, using a long metal glove, a "tin hand", to flick the baited hooks over the stern of the vessel. It also paid to keep a knife on hand, so that in the event of an accidental hooking, the line or the trace could be cut.

When the end of the long-line was reached, another anchor line was paid out and after a float line had been attached to the anchor, the latter was then thrown over the side, and that was that for a couple of hours, when the line would be brought to the surface from the up-tide end, and then the caught fish would be removed and the hooks re-baited progressively, as the tide drew them along the length of the long-line. Alex questioned why a second float had been used, Neil explaining that in the event of the first anchor becoming snagged, the long-line could be retrieved by pulling up the second anchor. Further, if they should want to continue fishing after the change of the tide, or in the case of a wind developing that would over-ride the pull of the tide on the boat, driving the boat up-tide, the progressive lifting and re-baiting of the long-line could be continued from the second-float end.

This was the exciting time, as John and Neil, and to some extent Alex, knew from the pull on the line what had been caught long before a section of the line reached the surface. Conger eels would wriggle and writhe and spin around and around, leaving a thin greasy film on the line and the snood, and often a severely twisted and severed snood would come up, without the hook, where a conger eel had bitten its way through the nylon snood to effect its escape. Skate would give a strong steady pull, and were a delight to see as they came up from the depth, being such excellent fish to eat.

Big cod would give a succession of strong pulls, as they swung their heads in different directions to try to shake free of the hooks. The most likely time to lose a big cod is when its reaches the surface, when it is no longer restrained in its movements by the surrounding water, so that whenever a cod was hooked, one of the three would hold a long gaff in readiness, and reach down into the water to hook it as soon as possible: God help the man who doesn't gaff a good fish properly!

On one occasion, one of the anglers on Alex's boat had hooked a great cod, and after about ten minutes had drawn it to the surface, then calling on his mate to gaff it for him. In his nervousness at the sight of such a big fish, the mate had lunged at the cod with the gaff, but only succeeded in hooking the split ring that held the lure attached to the line, and as he drew back the gaff, he pulled the hook free from the cod's mouth. Making just one swirl, the cod was immediately on its way back to the bottom, leaving the angler cursing and swearing at his mate for half-and-hour. Still, this is fishing, and one must be prepared to accept it! However, even the most experienced angler can feel frustration when the carelessness or indifference of a fellow angler causes him to lose a good fish.

The least desired fish caught were the lesser-spotted dogfish, which on some days can take almost every hook on the long-line, thus denying

133

the hook the chance to catch a fish of better edible quality. On this day, fortunately, the dogfish were not so abundant, so they didn't groan when only about twenty were caught, just taking them off the hook and returning them to the water.

Neil's long-line held only two hundred hooks, which is quite few compared with the several-thousand-hook lines put down by commercial fishermen, but after two re-baitings, the three of them were feeling quite tired and decided to call it a day. It had been a good catch: some two hundred pounds of cod of up to eighteen pounds individual weight and fifty pounds of skate of up to eight pounds individual weight, along with three big conger eels: however, conger eels are not considered particularly good for eating, containing a mass of small bones and the taste of the flesh finding favour with only a few people.

After they had returned to shore, they stripped the hooks of bait, engaging the hooks in the long-line by twisting the line so that its three strands opened up to allow the hook to be inserted, and then they flaked the long-line loosely inside a tub, so that it wouldn't become tangled. Finally they coiled the anchor lines and put the dinghy into the back of the van.

The three of them had had a great day. John and Neil wanted Alex to join them in the "Puffer", but Alex declined in view of Flo's outburst on the lateness of his return from their previous fishing trip. He simply took a couple of the cod, asking them to keep for themselves what they could get for them from the customers in the "Puffer." After Alex had departed, John told Neil of Alex's problems with Flo. It wasn't that Alex had ever discussed his problems with him, but simply that John had been around for a long enough time to be able to tell when a relationship was beginning to fall apart.

As it happened, Flo was in a good mood when he got back, and was pleased that he had returned early. After a quick meal, whilst he changed she put on some of her finery and asked him to take her into Greenock, to one of the bigger hotels, where there was to be a "concert night", with professional entertainers, albeit in the later stages of their careers. They had a good evening, with not even one cross word exchanged between them. At his invitation, Flo even got up to sing with one of the male entertainers, and clearly enjoyed his suggestive teasing. Alex realised that one never knew what to expect with Flo: when she was in a bad mood, she was an absolute cow, but when she felt cheery, she was good, lively company.

After a few weeks a free Sunday came along and John asked if he wanted to join him and Neil on a pike-fishing trip to Loch Lomond. He broached the subject with Flo, telling her that he would be back in time for them to go to the pub in the evening, and also giving her a handful of notes and suggesting that she take the train into Glasgow and pay a visit to the 'Barras' Market. Suitably bribed, and after an initial display of pique, Flo reluctantly agreed.

However, realising that Alex had been generous, after they had got into bed that evening, she leant over, gave him a kiss and then said to him 'Thanks for the money Pet, I'll have a nice day out. Whilst I'm there, are there any messages I can see to for you?', the local meaning of this being 'is there any shopping that I can do for you?' Alex was pleased with Flo's attitude: perhaps there was still hope for their relationship.

The three of them met at nine o'clock on the Sunday morning and drove down to the Erskine Ferry, which took them the short trip over to the north bank of the Clyde. They set off north towards Crianlarich, but turned right at the roundabout for Balloch and Stirling. The passed through the tiny village of Gartocharn, and when they reached Drymen, they turned left and drove along the side of Loch Lomond until they reached the village, or perhaps it should be called hamlet, of Balmaha, where they parked the van and carried the dinghy and their equipment to the water's edge.

After twenty minutes of rowing, they arrived at Cromer Bay, about a half-mile north-west of where the river Endrick flows into the loch. The water of the bay is usually only about four feet deep, but varies with the rainfall in the surrounding hills. John picked up a large rock from the shore and tied a short length of rope around it, to use as an anchor when afloat. The day before Alex had got half a bucket of sprats from a seaman from one of the trawlers in Greenock, sprats being white fish of about four inches length that were the usual bait for pike.

For terminal tackle, he had called into a tackle shop and bought a few sets of "snap" tackle, which latter comprise a short steel trace on which are mounted three sets of treble hooks. Two of the treble hooks are the normal curved hooks, but the third hook is straight and points out at a right-angle from the shank, the idea being to push the straight hook into the body of the bait to hold it, whilst the remaining two hooks are to catch the prey. To stop the bait from being flung from off the straight hook when casting out, an elastic band is used to hold the trace firmly against the 'waist', the narrow part of the body of the bait, just forward of the tail. As with all fish, the pike swallows the bait head first, so the three sets of hooks are arranged with their points pointing towards the tail of the bait fish, so that when the drag of the line attempts to pull the bait from the pike's mouth, the hooks quickly engage. A small floating "bung" is used to keep the bait clear of the bottom of the loch, where it could become entangled in the weeds growing there.

Soon all three had cast out and were sitting smoking, waiting for the first 'take'. After about ten minutes, John's bung first bobbed as a pike mouthed the bait and turned it around so that it could swallow it head first, then the bung disappeared below the surface of the water as the pike made off, a common reaction of many creatures when they find food, intended to stop competitors in the immediate vicinity from stealing it from them. The other two drew in their lines and then Alex pulled up the anchor, to give John complete freedom in playing his fish. Not having fishing rods and reels, the three of them were just using the thin orange cord mounted on a wooden frame that is used commonly in mackerel fishing, but this was of no detriment: pike, although fearsome predators, indeed being called by some the "freshwater shark", and able to race after and seize a trolled lure resembling a live fish, are drawn by the smell of a dead bait-fish, and pay no regard to the clearly-visible presence of the line or the trace.

After five minutes, with John playing the fish carefully, giving it line when it ran, and then drawing the line back when it came towards the boat, the pike was able to be drawn alongside, where Alex scooped it up out of the water with a landing net. Altogether the three of them landed seven pike, the biggest of them weighing about fifteen pounds. The record for pike is in excess of forty pounds, with many of above thirty pounds being caught, but most commonly those caught are of about eight to twelve pounds.

Alex looked at the pike, marbled in green and yellow, with their sleek shape and long wolf-like jaws, lined with rows of backwards-pointing teeth: a fish caught within such teeth has little chance of escape! He kept his hands and feet well away from their mouths whilst holding them firmly to allow Neil to remove the snap tackle using a pair of long-nosed pliers. The pike is generally regarded as a serious predator of salmon stock, and anglers are urged not to return them to the water, on some waters the anglers only being granted permission to fish for them on the condition that they follow this directive. However, a poached steak of pike is considered great eating by many and any pike offered will be gladly accepted. Indeed, John told him that in years past, pike were the preferred fish for the nobility, along with carp, with salmon being much too common for them to eat. When a master took on an apprentice or a servant, he would usually state that he would not feed his charges cheap and readily-available salmon more than once a day.

They set off back to Balmaha, with John on the mid-thwart doing the rowing, Neil in the bows, and Alex at the stern. The scenery was magnificent. A pair of swans swam by them, their reflections rippling in the clear water set against a background of bull-rushes and tall aquatic grasses. Alex looked to the north-east, where the skyline was filled by Conic Hill, tinted a faint purple from heather that covered its slopes. Looking to the east he saw the edge of Cromer Bay, that they had just left, and to its right the river Endrick, the biggest tributary, at its southern end at least, of Loch Lomond. Looking along the southern shore of the loch he saw Ross Priory, with its great walled garden and glasshouses filled with exotic plants, and beyond this the mouth of the River Leven, which carries the outflow of the loch down through Balloch to Dumbarton, where it joins the river Clyde on its way to the Firth. Looking north, he saw the great expanse of the loch, reaching for some twenty miles almost to Crianlarich.

The road running on the west shore of the loch branches at Crianlarich, allowing the traveller to turn right and head east for Stirling and Edinburgh, or to turn left and head for Fort William and Oban. About 30 miles along the Fort William road the traveller reaches the magnificent scenery of the Pass of Glencoe [14], believed by many to afford the finest views in the whole of the lower Highlands, in particular that of the range of mountains Buachaille Etive Mor, known popularly as "The Buckle", which attracts many climbers and photographers in all seasons of the year.

In the distance, on the eastern side of the loch he could see the magnificent mountain Ben Lomond, with its two broad shoulders that are covered in snow for most of the winter, with the snow on its northern and eastern faces sometimes remaining un-melted until as late as June or July, when the summer visitors arrive.

There are many islands scattered within the loch: Inchlonaig, Inchcannachan, Buinch, Inchtavannach, Inchcruin, Inchfad, Inchmoan, Inchcailloch, Creeinch, Torrinch, Inchmurrin; where the part of the name 'inch' is the Gaelic word for island. Some of these islands are inhabited, having their mail delivered to them by boat, whilst others are uninhabited but serve as perfect picnic spots for families or parties of friends. The whole setting was one of outstanding beauty and utter tranquillity.

Alex reflected on the use of the Gaelic language in place names. The name of the tiny village on the loch to where the Vikings had pulled their longboats, Tarbet, has the meaning of a strip of land between two masses of water, in this case the strip of land being the two miles between Tarbet and Arrochar and the two masses of water being Loch Long and Loch Lomond. There are several Tarbets in Scotland, although the spelling varies, some of them being spelt Tarbert.

Having just thought of the two masses of water, Loch Long and Loch Lomond, Alex recalled with a smile a conversation that he had had with a visiting English fisherman. During the trip out on Alex's boat, the man and his fellow fishermen had spoken of "Lock Long", "Holy Lock" and "Garelock", in each case pronouncing "loch" as "lock". Alex had put this down to the difficulty that many non-Scots have in pronouncing the word "loch" gutturally, with an almost throat-clearing expulsion of air, but eventually the man had said to Alex 'Tell me, why do you call all these places locks, when they are open to the sea and not land-locked?' Alex had painstakingly described to the angler the difference between a fresh-water loch, such as Loch Lomond, which in England would be called a lake, and a sea loch, such as Holy Loch, which might be described as a long inlet from the sea, and which in Scandinavia would be called a "fjord", although a sea loch could also be no more than just a large bay. The angler had remained confused, turning back to his fishing with a grunt, clearly not having understood, or not believed, a word.

Alex thought about all of the other Gaelic words still in use as place names: 'ben' or 'beinn' for mountain; 'strath' for valley; 'inver' for bridge; and so on, all carrying on from the past, although the spoken language is now used to any great extent only in the Highlands and Islands. Alex thought that perhaps one day there would be a revival in the Gaelic language, if ever Scotland regains its independence from England: however, that day might yet be many years away. Apart from Gaelic, Scotland has many regional dialects or dialects that were spoken in the past, and are now being cherished, the most famous of which is the dialect used by Rabbie Burns, with words such as: 'gang', go; 'wean', child; 'aught', anything; 'mickle', much; 'greet', weep; 'tapsalteerie', topsy-tervy; and a great many others.

Thinking of these Scots words, Alex recalled some of the lines from one of Burn's poems, "To a mouse: on turning her up in her nest with the plough, November 1785", that is known throughout the English-speaking world:[8:2]

> "But mousie, thou art no they-vane,
> In proving foresight may be vain:
> The best laid schemes o' mice an' men,

[8:2] See "The complete illustrated poems, songs & ballads of Robert Burns", published by Lomond Books, ISBN 1-85152-018-X; or, for example, "Robert Burns: selected poems", edited by Carol McGuirk, published by Penguin Classics, ISBN 0-14-042382-6.

Gang aft agley,
An' lea'e us nought but grief an' pain,
For promis'd joy!"

How well Burns understood mankind, with its petty deviousness, its aspirations of grandeur and its scheming! By the association of mice and men, Burns succinctly exposed and debunked mankind as reaching above itself and attempting to assume an unwarranted elevated standing in the order of things. However, Alex considered that the most magnificent of Burn's words, which expose mankind for its weaknesses and insincerity, are:

"Oh, what a tangled web we weave, when first we set out to deceive"

Then too, there was Alex's own 'modern' Scots' dialect, with its own words, such as a "granny", meaning the spinning cowl on the top of some chimney pots, and with its own expressions, some very simple such as "Och, yer af yer heed" meaning that "you don't know what you're talking about", or others that are more complex such as the words to a departing friend: "Lang may yer lum reek", literally "long may your chimney smoke", meaning "I wish you a long life." These words are the everyday usage of the dialect immortalised by Burns.

Thinking about the many different ways in which what is ostensibly the same language is spoken, Alex recalled the words of that great master of the English language, Winston Churchill, who had once said that Britain and America were both united and divided by the same language. Nevertheless, the power of his words was such as to encourage the Americans to give the Allies substantial support in World War II, before they were drawn into the war themselves by the attack on Pearl Harbour.

Alex though that perhaps it would not be for the good of mankind if everyone spoke the same language, as this would then increase the opportunity for mutual lying and deception.

The most friendly and acceptable way to greet someone speaking a language that one cannot understand is with a big sincere smile, supported by the universal 'thumbs-up' sign, made either one-handed, or as favoured in the Far East, two-handed!

Looking again at the surrounding scenery, Alex found it hard to believe that only about twenty miles away was the city of Glasgow, where the best part of a million people work hard to earn their living, but a great many of whom do not often find the time, or have the means, to make their way out of the city to enjoy the outstanding natural beauty of Loch Lomond. He had watched a television programme a few evening previously, where a group of young children had been taken out to the countryside from one of the inner-city slums. Upon their return, when asked what they thought of the countryside, one young girl had spoken for the group, saying with complete sincerity and with disappointment that their day out had been so dull, and so lacking in the basic amenities and pleasures available in the city, that 'There's nothing there: no shops, no picture houses, no supper bars, no nothing, only bare fields and great big mountains.'

Alex smiled at the memory. Indeed there was nothing surrounding them on the loch but bare fields and mountains, but what beautiful fields and mountains! He himself had been no different in his childhood, and he hoped that one day all Scots children would realise what a beautiful country they live in. But for his deception of Joe Bannion coming to light, and his having to flee Glasgow in great haste, he too would have known no better: at the time he had thought that his departure was a dreadful misfortune, but now he was not sure. John too must have been moved by the scenery. As he sat at the oars, the muscles of his bare arms rippling with the strokes, he started to sing, in a strong baritone voice:[8:3]

> "By yon bonnie banks and by yon bonnie braes,
> Where the sun shins bright on Loch Lomond,
> Where me and my true love were ever wont to gae,
> On the bonnie bonnie banks o' Loch Lomond."

Neil joined in with him in singing the chorus:

> "O, ye'll tak' the high road, an' I'll tak' the low road
> An' I'll be in Scotland afore ye;
> But me and my true love will never meet again
> On the bonnie bonnie banks o' Loch Lomond."

John then sang the second verse, whilst Neil and Alex rested their oars to listen to the words more carefully:

> "Where in purple hue, the Hieland hills we viewed;
> And the moon comin' out in the gloamin'
> Twas there that we parted in yon shady glen,

[8:3] See, for example, "Scottish songs" edited by Chris Findlater, published by Lomond Books, ISBN 0-947782-33-2.

On the steep, steep side o' Ben Lomond."

Neil again joined John in the chorus, after which John sang the final verse:

"The wee birdies sing, and the wild flowers spring,
While in sunshine the waters are sleeping;
But the broken heart kens nae second spring again,
Though the waefu' may cease frae their greetin'."

This time Alex joined John and Neil in the chorus, their three voices ringing out over the still waters of the loch, but with no-one to listen to them. When the song was finished, Alex reflected on the love between the man and woman of the song .and the sadness of their separation, never to meet again. [#15]

Alex looked at John, some thirty years his senior, and realised what it must be like to have a father: someone to chat to, someone to discuss the affairs of the day with, and someone to look up to, as he looked up to John. He realised his good luck in having had such a fine man as John offer him his friendship. Life had been good to him of late, and he was grateful.

As he had feared would be the case, Flo was in a nasty mood when he got back. 'Where've you been until this time? There was sod-all worth buying at the Barras and my damn feet are killing me.' He showed Flo the pike and told her that he would poach it following John's advice, but she wasn't impressed. 'Bollocks to cooking them pike, let's piss off to the Puffer before I die of thirst.' Nevertheless, when he cooked some of the pike after they had returned from the pub, and served it with a bag of chips that they had picked up from the supper-bar in passing, she had had the grace to mutter, but only when pressed 'I've eaten worse.', which, coming from Flo, was praise indeed!

Alex was a novice at home cooking, never before having done as much as boil an egg: there was always the café for a bacon sandwich, the supper-bar for a fish supper, and the pub for a pickled egg and a Scotch pie. However, having enjoyed eating the pike, Alex decided to see what else he could cook and asked John what made good eating from the catches that they took on the boats. John thought for a couple of minutes, and then told him of his preference: my favourite meal is fish pie, or as it is known in the Western Isles, "fish champion". It's very easy to make.', giving him instructions as to how to make it.

One his next trip out Alex brought back a nice-sized cod and made a fish pie to John's instructions. On this occasion Flo spoke her praise without having to be encouraged! Emboldened by his success, Alex asked John what else was good to cook. John again thought for a while, and then said 'An old dish from the Western Isles, where nothing is wasted: "Ceanncropic", after which he went on to describe the making of this dish [16]. Alex duly tried using John's recipe, but the result wasn't up to his, or Flo's expectation. However, the fault wasn't John's, but Alex's: he had added too much oatmeal and too little pepper and salt, so that the meal was of rather a bland and unappetising taste, with a texture closer to that of biscuit rather than that of a savoury pudding.

Not daunted, Alex tried his hand at smoking herring to make kippers and haddock to make "Arbroath Smokies". In this he was more successful. He acquired a large can that had contained cooking oil, then he cut off one end and punched several small holes into the other end to act as air-intakes for the fire. Towards the top of the can he made matching holes in two opposite faces to accommodate lengths of 3/8inch-diameter wooden doweling for holding the fish to be smoked, the gutted fish being tied together at their tails in pairs. First he salted the fish by leaving them in a strong brine solution for three hours, then he lit a fire at the bottom of the can using oak chips. When the fire was burning well, he placed the pairs of gutted fish, both herring and haddock, on the rods, and then placed a lid on the can so that the fire was reduced to smouldering and thus to producing smoke rather than flame. With this confined arrangement the method was closer to hot smoking rather than cold smoking, so that the fish were partially cooked upon removal. To play safe, he gave them a further few minutes under the grill, before serving them to a suspicious Flo.

The smoked fish tasted alright, albeit that they tasted more strongly of smoke than their commercial counterparts. However, in the past, the people of the Northern Isles would have relished the taste, as in order to be able to conserve fish over the winter months, they would have put the salted fish into the chimneys of their peat-burning fires for a considerable time, so that the smokiness of the fish would have been much greater than is found palatable by the present generation. Flo ate her kipper without comment, but declined a second one.

With an abundance of herring in the Firth over the Summer months, Alex tried salting a couple of dozen. He placed the herring fillets in a bucket, separated by a thin layer of salt. Within a day the salt had extracted so much liquid from the fillets as to dissolve itself, the fillets then lying in a concentrated brine solution. After four days, Alex took one of them out, to find it almost as stiff as a piece of shoe leather. Despite three boilings, it was still too salty to be eaten. He discussed this with John, who told him that he should have drained off the brine after only a few hours, and then left the fish to dry, pointing out that with a barrel of fish salted and dried in this way, along with a few sacks of spuds and plenty of dry peat for the fire, an Islander of the past would have had no fear of his family going hungry over the cold winter months. 'Our generation is too spoilt in its tastes.' he told Alex.

After that Alex stopped experimenting with fish preserving, deciding to leave it to the professionals. However, come the arrival of the spawning shoals of cod as winter approached, he took back home a big roe-sac and boiled it for an hour or so, before he and Flo ate the roe on toast, finding it delicious. 'Just like caviar!' said Flo, who hadn't ever eaten caviar in her life. However, Alex was glad that he had been able to please her, as this was a rare event nowadays.

Chapter Nine

John and Ernie were delighted with Alex's progress and both had complete confidence in giving him any job that came along, whether it be to take out a fishing party, to deliver an important cargo to one of the naval bases, or just to take a consignment of goods to one of the harbours or jetties of the Firth, or even to one of the nearest islands such as Bute or Arran. He was careful, reliable, imaginative and knowledgeable. However, one day John watched Alex as he tied up his boat at the quayside and was appalled at the un-nautical knot that he used: too sloppy, too many twists and turns, and too difficult to untie after it had carried load.

He called Alex over. 'It's time you learnt a few proper knots, mate', he said to him. There are many well-known knots[9:1], but John did not teach Alex these, concentrating on just the few more-traditional seamen's knots. John also taught Alex a knot used to tie a fishing line to a hook or the shank of a hook, rather like the Hangman's Knot, but with more turns around the main line and with the end tucked in to help to avoid slipping of the line when wet. In two or three days Alex had learnt these knots and demonstrated them to John, who nodded and then asked 'What about learning the most impressive knot of all, the Turk's Head?' referring to the big decorative knot that is sometimes tied at the end of a rope to give it weight for throwing, or to the end of the clapper of a bell to give a secure hand-hold Alex was delighted with the knot and spent all of his spare time over the next few days in perfecting his skill in tying it, at the end of which he was able to tie a good, tight Turk's Head knot in just two or three minutes

John also taught Alex how to secure a deck cargo in a secure, ship-shape way. On one occasion when Alex had gone to great length to lash a cargo with nice, neat runs of rope, running parallel with each other, John pronounced the lashing as too slack. Alex thought that he would have to unlash the cargo and start again. However, John explained that

---

[9:1] A fairly recent book, dividing the knots into seven main sections: bends; binding knots; hitches; loops; slip knots; splices; stopper knots; and trick & fancy knots; is "Knots: an illustrated practical guide to the essential knot types and their uses" by Andrew Adamides, published by Advanced Marketing (UK) Ltd.: ISBN 978-1-90576-507-2.   Another recent, well-illustrated book, "Tying knots", by Egmont Manfred Friedl, published by Hinkler Books, ISBN 978 1 7418 2528 2, describes 25 of the most useful knots, and also covers: materials; coiling and handling; and whipping and splicing. The book is accompanied by a DVD explaining how 35 different knots are tied.

it is difficult to apply a high tension on the ropes when lashing, but how by running a line between two slack lengths and then drawing them together, the mechanical advantage afforded by the relatively low force needed to pull the initially-straight ropes sideways - rather than lengthways - enables them to be tensioned effortlessly.

John had an aversion to ever cutting a rope, and on other occasion when Alex was tediously threading a long rope around other ropes - to avoid cutting it shorter - whenever he wanted to tie a knot, Alex showed him that he could make a "bight", a small loop in the long rope, and just use the loop to make the knots, securing the knots by using the end of the loop to make two half-hitches. As an extras precaution against the knots working loose, finally he ran the end of a rope through all of the bights that he had made, then drawing them up tight. Alex was quick to grasp the time-saving techniques that he had learnt.

Alex was feeling good. He had good friends, appreciating in particular his friendship with Big John; his seamanship was first-class; and he had a responsible job that gave him great satisfaction. He didn't think that there could be anything that could give him more pleasure in life, but he hadn't anticipated what was to come. Arriving at his boat one morning, Alex was perplexed to see what looked like an old mottled rag lying on the quayside. As he approached, the 'rag' uncurled to reveal itself as a scruffy little dog, which looked at him appealingly, wagging its little tail and moving its tongue in and out over its lips to show that it wanted to be friendly. The little dog looked hungry and destitute. Alex reached into his bag and drew out a Scotch Pie that Flo had given him that morning. He broke the pie into pieces and gave one piece to the dog, which wolfed it down and then looked to Alex for more. Alex laughed, and fed the dog the rest of the pie. The little dog was pleased, and wagged its tail so violently that its body shook. Alex bent and stroked the its head, and as a reward received a lick on his outstretched hand, accompanied by even more vigorous tail wagging.

During the day Alex thought about the dog and wondered whether it would still be there when they returned to the quayside. Sure enough, as they came alongside to tie up, it appeared, looked in concern at the people on board, and then broke into vigorous tail-wagging when it spotted Alex. As soon as the boat had been made secure, Alex climbed up the steps to the quayside, carrying his bag. He had saved some of his lunch, and gave the dog half of a beef sandwich. This was soon gone, but Alex had no more to offer. Patting the dog on the head, he waked towards the main road, leaving it gazing after him with sad eyes.

The next morning could not come soon enough for Alex. He asked Flo to give him extra food, saying that the sea air and the hard work was building up his appetite. Flo agreed, but couldn't resist adding 'Let's hope that it does the same for your sexual appetite.' As he approached the boat, the dog appeared from behind a bollard where it had sheltered for the night, and ran towards him, wagging its tail. This time Alex gave it a Scotch Pie and also a chicken sandwich. The dog quickly ate both and then came and sat by Alex's feet, looking up at him with affection. Alex was delighted with the little creature. He left the dog at the quayside and climbed down the ladder to the boat, feeling guilty at leaving it on its own.

The day dragged on, and it seemed ages before he returned for the evening. The dog recognised the boat as it approached, and gave a welcoming bark. Alex tied up as quickly as he could and then scrambled up the ladder. The little dog came and lifted a paw and placed it on Alex's sea-boot, as it to establish its ownership of him. Alex then gave it the remainder of his lunch. As he was feeding the dog, Alex came to a decision. Picking up the dog, he carried it to Gourock Police Station, just two minutes walk away. Entering the station, he walked over to the sergeant on the desk and told him that he had come to report a lost male dog, to which the sergeant replied 'Lost dog? Who would want a scruffy little tyke like that? More likely it's an abandoned dog.'

Alex was furious, but held his temper. When the sergeant had taken down the details, Alex picked up the dog and made as to leave, whereupon the sergeant told him that the dog should be left for collection by the local dog-catcher. Alex would have none of this, telling the sergeant that if anyone reported a lost dog answering to the description they could come around to his place and claim it. Grumbling, the sergeant agreed to this non-compliance with local-authority procedure, knowing full well that it was extremely unlikely that anyone would ever come to claim 'such a runty little sod'. Certainly his own wife, who had a passion for King George Spaniels, wouldn't give house room to this 'probably flea-ridden and worm-infested little cur', so if this fool of a seamen wanted to play dog-minder, that was okay with him.

On his way home Alex called in at the pet shop and bought some tins of dog food, a packet of dog biscuits, a collar and a lead. The shopkeeper asked him if he wanted an identity disk made for the collar, but Alex thought that under the circumstances this might be tempting fate and decided to wait until it was clear that no-one was going to claim the dog: for the same reason, he hadn't yet given it a name.

Flo was in the kitchen making his meal when he arrived back, with a glass of whisky in her hand. Looking up she saw the dog and asked the stupid question 'What on earth is that you've got there?', to which Alex replied with matching studied stupidity 'It's a wee dog.' Flo exploded with rage at being treated as an idiot. 'I can see it's a sodding wee dog, but what's it doing here in my bloody house? What do I want with a runty little cur like that?' Alex told her the story of how he had come by the dog whilst Flo stood angrily with her arms folded and with her face set in a thunderous expression. Flo was unmoved by what Alex had to say, and had the same view as the sergeant, in that nobody would claim it, and asked him what he would do then. Alex looked her squarely in the eye and replied in a firm voice 'Then I will have got myself a wee dog.' He was not going to budge on this matter!

It was clear to the dog that Flo didn't like him, so for the rest of the evening he hung around Alex's feet, looking up from time-to-time to give him a look that could only be interpreted as expressing loyalty and love. He had found a master! Alex left the dog overnight in the kitchen and was pleased in the morning to see that he hadn't performed.

Putting the dog on his lead he set off walking to some common ground nearby. The dog walked nicely at his heels, not pulling or whining, but content just to be out with his master. When they got back Alex gave the dog its breakfast and then it was time for him to go to work. Alex patted the dog's head and told it to be good for Flo whilst he was out, which caused Flo to snort and say 'As long as the little ball of shite keeps from under my feet.'

This pattern was repeated for the next five days, by which time had Alex begun to feel confident that no-one was going to claim the dog, so that he could now give it a name: "Rover", or "Shep", or "Rex"? None of these names seemed to suit. Eventually he settled for "Clyde", as it was on the banks of the Clyde that he and the dog had met. The more he thought about it the happier he was with the name. He asked Flo what she thought, but received only another derisory snort.

She came in one evening to find Alex brushing the tangles out of Clyde's hair. Under both of his ears was a ball of fur that had turned into felt, so that Alex had to use scissors to remove it. 'You great big girl with your wee babby' she jeered, but Alex ignored her. However, when he started to use the scissors to remove tangled hair from around Clyde's rear-end she said 'What are you doing playing with that little bugger's arse-hole?' to which Alex replied 'I'm removing his dinkle-berries. You know what dinkle-berries are, little lumps of shit that have stuck to his fur. All long-haired dogs have this problem, as indeed do some men with hairy arses. The difference is that whilst men have hands and can remove their own dinkle-berries, little dogs need someone to help them.'

147

Flo was speechless with rage and disgust. 'Well don't come wanting to touch me up with those shite-covered hands in bed tonight', to which Alex replied in a serious voice 'Have no fear of that.' Things had reached a low point in his relationship with Flo. Why couldn't she just learn to love his little dog the way that he did? Must she have all of the attention all of the time?

On the following Monday Alex decided to take Clyde with him out on the boat for the day, to save the moaning from Flo every time he returned in the evening about what a nuisance Clyde had been that day. Clyde trotted along happily beside him, pleased to be out. Alex lifted Clyde up and tucked him under his arm as he descended the ladder to the boat. As soon as he was put down, Clyde scuttled around on a tour of inspection.

When John climbed down the ladder, Clyde barked furiously at this 'intruder'. John laughed, and settled on his haunches, to try and make friends. After a couple of minutes, Clyde came over and licked his hand to cement their friendship. Alex and John tried to decide what kind of dog Clyde was. He looked as though he had some terrier in him, and also some Jack Russell, but then again he had a quite long coat and hair hanging over his face, which suggested a touch of West-Highland Terrier. After a while they gave up, but agreed that he was a fine wee dog.

That day they were to take a small cargo over to a ship at anchor out on the Firth. On the way over, Clyde sat on the fore-deck keeping a watch on all that went on. Whenever a boat came close, he barked a warning for it to keep its distance, which amused not only Alex and John, but also the crew on the other boat. After arriving at the ship at anchor, three of its crew came to transfer the cargo, and were met by fierce growling and barking from Clyde. One of the crew said 'That's a grand wee doggie you've got there', at which Alex's chest swelled with pride.

Thereafter Clyde accompanied Alex on every trip. Before long all of the skippers knew him, as did the shore-workers on the various harbours and jetties dotted around the Firth and the sea lochs, all of them giving him a pat and a scratch of his head every time that they met him. He sailed the Firth and the lochs sitting to attention on the fore-deck, whatever the weather, greeting friends with a wag of his tail and strangers with a warning bark. He was soon the mascot of Ernie's small fleet.

On one rough morning John and Alex had set out to deliver a cargo to Dunoon, with wee Clyde sitting as usual on the fore-deck. As they rounded Cloch Point, and into the prevailing south-west wind, a strong gust of wind caught the boat, throwing Clyde from off the fore-desk and into the scuppers, and almost over the side. Alex rushed forward to rescue him, but he was in mental anguish for the rest of the morning as to what he could have done had Clyde been swept overboard. It would be bad enough recovering a man from such a rough sea, but trying to find a scrap of a dog and then getting it on board would have been nigh on impossible.

After a lot of troubled thought, Alex went to the storage area under the fore-deck, where some time earlier he had seen a child's life preserver stowed away. That evening he took the life preserver back to the house and then spent two hours cutting and stitching until he had fashioned it to suit Clyde. Flo laughed and ridiculed him as being pathetic in giving so much attention to such a "useless wee turd". Her hatred and jealousy of Clyde were reaching monumental proportions.

The next day Alex fitted the modified life preserver onto Clyde, who stood stiffly to attention, appreciating that he was being given special treatment. As they walked to the quay, he held himself proud, clearly feeling that he was superior to the landlubber dogs that they passed on the way. When they saw him, the rest of the seamen tried to hide their smiles, as they were all fond of Clyde, as they were also of his master. Thereafter Clyde would sit on the fore-deck, wearing his life-preserver, in all weathers.

After a few weeks, Alex decided to take Clyde to the pub along with him and Flo. As they went into the lounge, the seamen there greeted Alex and Flo, and then vied with each other for Clyde's attention. However, Clyde would have not of it: after a quick lick of an extended hand, he would return to his place at Alex's heels. The fishermen weren't resentful of Clyde's indifference to them: on the contrary, they admired the wee dog for its devotion to its master. Flo sat with her usual po face, in silence. She already had to put up with Alex's popularity, and his being the centre of attention amongst the other fishermen, which meant that she no longer received the fussing and teasing that she craved for, but now she had to play second fiddle to that useless little ball of shite.

She hated Clyde, although he had done nothing to deserve it. As the weeks passed, her hatred became stronger, and she wished the dog out of her life. When Alex wasn't about she would curse and swear at him in a low grinding menacing voice. Sometimes she went out of her way to kick him, but Clyde usually anticipated her intention and took evasive action. Why didn't it run away, or die, or get run over? Was that too much to ask?

Every day the level of communication between Alex and Clyde

increased. After only a couple of months of their living together, Clyde had an understanding of several dozen words but, more importantly, he fully understood the implication of the tones in which Alex spoke the words. He would sit at Alex's feet, listening to the conversation between Alex and Flo, his eyes darting in turn from one to the other. Whenever his name was mentioned, or if a sentence from Alex started with such as 'Well I think I'll take the dog for … ' he was instantly on his feet, ready to go. At the sound of the television set being switched off, he would jump up, in anticipation of being taken for a walk.

Normally Clyde would sit on the other side of the room and look over to Alex, hoping to catch his eye and be invited over for a pat or a scratch. If Alex failed to notice him, after a while he would crawl slowly across the room, his head laid low between his paws and with his ears folded down, knowing that he was stepping out of line. Alex would see him coming, but pretend that he hadn't, and continue reading his paper. When Clyde reached Alex, he would gently lift one paw and place it on Alex's knee, giving him a plaintive look as if to say 'Put your paper down Dad and talk to me.'

However, when Alex came back from the pub and spoke to him in an affectionate tone, he knew that Alex was in an indulgent mood and would not hesitate in jumping up onto his knee to be made a fuss of and to have his tummy scratched. At the same time Alex was starting to recognise the messages that Clyde was giving to him in return. Apart from the obvious messages given by the wagging of his tail, or by his barking, there were subtle messages that Clyde gave, either intentionally or unintentionally. When seeing Alex for the first thing in the morning, it wasn't sufficient for him just to wag his tail. He would make a gentle growling-type noise, but with rising and falling tones. When Alex responded with the same noises, he was ecstatic: they were speaking to each other in dog language! He would then scamper around the room, with his mouth open and his eyes sparkling, with what could only be described as a rapturous grin on his face.

Other times, when telling Alex that he was hungry, he would push his food bowl along the floor with his nose and make a different kind of growling noise, gentle but of a higher pitch, without aggression, but with a suggestion of pleading. Alex could never resist him, and had to endure Flo's constant remark 'You'll turn that little flea bag into a tub of lard before you're finished, you soft bugger.' Often, when Alex was taking a little longer than usual in getting ready to leave for the day's work, Clyde would make a different kind of bark: not a loud, aggressive bark, nor a sharp higher-pitched irritable yelp, but a single, muted "woof", with an expression on his face that said clearly "Come on dad! It's time we were going!"

The movement of Clyde's ears told Alex a lot about what his dog was thinking. If he was feeling guilty, he would drop his ears down, as they were on the morning after Alex had fed him the remains of a curry on the previous evening and he had passed diarrhoea all over the kitchen floor, to Flo's great disgust. Clyde had cringed and shivered as Flo had poured abuse on him, until Alex had picked him up and reassured him in a soothing voice that everything was alright.

Alex dearly loved his wee dog, diarrhoea or no diarrhoea, and he remonstrated fiercely with Flo, telling her that she was an insensitive bastard. Fortunately, Alex, who usually had to work each Saturday and Sunday with fishing parties, had this day off in lieu, and could stay at home and mind Clyde. Flo had stormed off out of the house after this and didn't return for three hours, not that Alex and Clyde were bothered: they had each other for company and sat together companionably.

When Clyde was feeling cheerful, his ears would stand straight up, and he would sit bright and alert, ready and eager for what the day might bring. Other times, when he was feeling self conscious, as he had been the first time that the other skippers had seen him in his life preserver, his ears would turn outwards, with their tips inclined slightly towards each other. When he was embarrassed at having done something wrong, he would fold his ears back over the top of his head, and sit in the corner with his back to Alex, so that Alex couldn't catch his eye. When Alex saw him doing this, he would call him over, and ask him in a kindly voice 'What's up son?' Clyde soon learnt that when Alex called him "son" he was feeling affectionate towards him, and he would quickly get over his embarrassment and give Alex a lick, after which all was well again. He was a loving wee dog, and there was nothing that Alex wouldn't do for him.

Time passed, and almost before Alex knew it, it was Christmas and then Hogmanay. Alex realised that it had been almost two years since he had arrived in Gourock. His present life was good: he had a good job, good friends, the love of a fine wee dog, and the presence of a warm female body in his bed during the cold winter nights. He couldn't say that the relationship that he had with Flo was loving, but when she was getting her own way, she was, at least, a cheerful, albeit very vulgar, soul.

As February approached, John asked him if he would like to attend a Burns Supper that was being organised by the Bay Hotel. A number of the skippers were planning on attending, as was also John's fishing mate Neil. That evening he broached the subject with Flo. After listening to what he had to say, Flo gave him her views. 'If you think I want to sit amongst a crowd of your boring mates, watching you all get pissed and then maudlin over a dead poet, you can think again. I'll go down to the Puffer and spend some time with the living.'

Come the evening, Alex put on his suit and made his way along to the Bay, where he met John and Neil in the foyer. Both John and Neil were wearing kilts, as was appropriate for the occasion, which made Alex feel uncomfortable, as he considered himself to be as good a Scot as the next man. However, they soon put him at his ease, and after a couple of single malts he relaxed and prepared to enjoy the evening. Before long they were asked to take their places in the dining room.

No sooner than were they were settled in their places, they were called upon to stand again, then giving a slow hand-clap whilst a piper led the top-table guests to their places. The Chairman for the evening welcomed them from his place at the top table, after which he give an informal and humorous address during which he outlined the programme for the evening. Then he called upon an invited clergyman, the Minister of the Kirk of Scotland at Dunlop, Ayrshire, who on this occasion was also to be the principal speaker later in the evening, to give a recitation of the "The Selkirk Grace":

"Some hae meat and canna eat
And some wad eat that want it:
But we hae meat and we can eat,
And sae the Lord be thankit."

Following this, Dinner was served, starting with the traditional Cock-a-leekie soup, and as soon as the soup plates were cleared away, the main course would be served: Haggis with champit, "mashed", tatties and bashed neeps! When the Chairman had been signalled from the kitchen that all was ready, he asked the assembled company to stand once again. Then, a piper led in the chef carrying the haggis, a monster weighing some fifteen pounds, held aloft on a silver tray, followed by a third person carrying two bottles of single-malt whisky. The party marched to the head of the top table, to the music of the pipes, and to a further slow hand-clap from the assembly.

As the party reached the chairman, the chef placed the silver tray down in front of him, and the piper and the chef accepted the chairman's offer to take a glass of whisky with him in toasting the haggis, making the traditional Gaelic toast "Slainte mbath", meaning "good health".

The assembled company now eagerly awaited the Chairman's

traditional recitation of "To a Haggis". He was an excellent, well-known public speaker, in great demand at this time of the year for speaking at Burns' Dinners, ensuring a full house and providing a dramatic and entertaining delivery. The company sat down in their seats again and the room fell silent as the Chairman prepared to address the haggis. He was known to be able to recite faultlessly from memory, with a great deal of vigorous play acting, which in view of the amount of whisky already consumed by the gathering, would suit them perfectly. He started his address by complimenting the haggis:

"Fair fa' your honest, sonsie face
Great Chieftain o' the Puddin-race!
Aboon them a' ye tak your place,
Painch , tripe, or thairm:
Weel are ye wordy o' a grace
As lang's my arm."

Alex was perplexed by some of the old Scots words used by Burns, so John explained their meaning to him: 'sonsie', happy or jolly; 'aboon', above; 'painch', paunch; 'wordy', worthy. The speaker then went on to describe the gastronomic delights of the haggis, before reaching the dramatic moment when he took up his knife and slashed the haggis open:

"An' cut you up wi' ready sleight.
Trenching your gushing entrails bright
Like onie ditch;
And then, O what a glorious sight,
Warm-reekin, rich!"

He continued in glowing terms, placing the haggis beyond comparison with the foods of other nations,[9:2] and illustrating the effect of such a magnificent meal upon the eater:

"But mark the Rustic, haggis-fed,
The trembling earth resounds his tread
Clap in his walie nieve a blade,

[9:2] There has been much fuss made in Scotland of a recent claim that the haggis was created in England, not Scotland. It was stated by a food historian that the English farmers used to give their un-saleable animal offal to the widows of the parish, referred to as "hags" - the word is still used for old women at the present time, but now disparagingly - to make "hag's dish", which name changed with time to "haggis".

He'll mak it whissle;
An' legs, an' arms, an' heads will sned
Like taps o' thrissle."

John again explained the meaning of some of the words to Alex: 'walie nieve', fist; 'sned', cut off; 'taps o' thrissle', 'tops of thistles'. The assembly cheered the Chairman soundly at the end of his Dedication.

Alex had never before felt so thrilled in being a Scot, amongst fellow Scots. He raised his glass to Neil and John and toasted their health. After a break, the proceedings began again, leading to "The Immortal Memory", delivered by the Minister. By now everyone was somewhat under the influence of the drink and the magic of the evening, and looked forward in anticipation and excitement to his words.

The Minister was dressed in his dark clerical suit with dog collar, and with his thinning grey hair looked every bit the sombre and reserved man of the cloth. However, within minutes, his humour, sometimes a little naughty for a man holding such office, had them all enthralled. He would make an ambiguous remark, and then stand with his hands clasped and with a saintly expression on his face and his eyes uplifted, the picture of innocence. Alex thought to himself that if the Minister's addresses from the pulpit were half as good as his Address this evening, his services would be standing room only! He had had them all entertained for some fifteen minutes with accounts of Burns' life, taking the opportunity of having them all laughing, in good-natured humour, with tales of Burns' prolific love life. Finally, he spoke of those Scots who have gone away to live in a distant land, and asked that the gathering remember them at this time. As he spoke, there were some in the audience whose eyes became wet with unshed tears.

He ended his address, as is appropriate for a moral leader, by speaking of the international brotherhood of man, and expressing the view that one day the people of the world may live together in peace. To this end, he recited Burns's poem "A Man's a Man for a' That":

"Then let us pray that come it may,
And come it will for a' that
That Sense and Worth, o'er a' the earth,
May bear the gree, and a' that.
Fo a' that, and a' that,
It's comin' yet for a' that,
That man to Man, the world o' er,

154

Shall brothers be for a' that!"

The gathering was moved by the Minister's address, and felt both emotional and nostalgic. In this same frame of mind, at the end of the evening they joined in enthusiastically with the first verse of "Auld Lang Syne":

"Should auld acquaintance be forgot,
And never be brought to mind?
Should auld acquaintance be forgot,
And auld lang syne!"

followed by the chorus:

"For auld lang syne, my dear,
For auld lang syne,
We'll tak a cup o' kindness yet,
For auld lang syne."

The words of the following verse were not known by some of those present, including Alex, but he was thrilled to hear John singing clearly and confidently, as he continued to do so to the last verse:

"And there's a hand, my trusty fere!
And gie's a hand o' thine!
And we'll tak a right gude willie-waught,
For auld lang syne."

Alex guessed that 'fere' means "friend"; that 'willie-waught' means "draught"; and that 'auld lang syne' means "times past". All of those present then linked hands with their neighbours at the table for a final rendering of the chorus.

It had been a great evening, such as to rouse the pride of any Scot in his or her heritage. As the formalities came to an end, the three of them hung on for a last double single-malt. Alex recalled the words of the Minister in speaking of the international brotherhood of man, and said to John and Neil that he wished it were indeed so, and that warring nations could recognise the enemy as being no more than simple men such as themselves.

John reflected for a moment, and then went on to say that there had been moments in the insanity of war when men had temporarily ceased their hostility, recalling the occasion in the Great War when on one

Christmas Day some British and German troops had left their trenches and played football together, the next day returning to their mutual killing. Both Alex and Neil were surprised when John went on to say that he himself had experienced an act of humanity between warring nations during his time in the Merchant Navy during the Second World War, as he hadn't ever before referred to his war service.

He told them that at the outbreak of war, considering his extensive experience of the sea, he had enlisted in the Merchant Navy. Initially, he had been made a cook, and was not pleased at being given this inappropriate job, but once at sea, his skills were soon recognised and he was transferred to more seaman-like duties.

For three years he had sailed out of the Clyde on convoys, but had been fortunate not to have been subjected to enemy action. However, before one departure, just before Christmas, the crew were told that they were to join an important convoy and on no account were they to discuss this with their friends or relatives, or even amongst themselves, in particular in the pub, as "walls have ears." After the cargo had been loaded, they soon guessed where the convoy was headed for, Russia, and what it contained, as could indeed have any sharp-eyed person ashore with a reasonable seaman's knowledge, by watching the loading of the ship, and looking at its draught when fully laden.

The merchant ships for the convoy were tied up at different points at Port Glasgow, Greenock and Gourock. After having been loaded, they slipped their mooring lines at different times during the night, so as not to attract too much attention, and made their way down to the Firth and out to sea. The next day, the convoy, thirty merchant ships in total, assembled off the Western Isles, where they met their escort, eight destroyers. The convoy made its way north for twenty-four hours, before making their eastings, in the hope that it would then be well north of any enemy submarines.

For the first two days, the weather was dull and overcast, which was good, as this made their detection less likely, but on the third day the weather turned still and calm, the sea like glass. The bow waves and the wash from the propellers of the ships of the convoy and its escort stood out brightly and clearly against the flat sea, which caused great concern. In the late afternoon, there was a sighting of a small plane, which could have been an enemy spotter plane, but this was discounted in view of the distance of the convoy from land.

As darkness fell, a bright full-moon rose, which illuminated the whole scene, in the moonlight the whole of the convoy standing out clearly. All of the ships were on full alert. For three hours the convoy moved on steadily, but then without warning there was an explosion from one of the merchant ships in the van of the convoy. Immediately the destroyers took action, searching across the sea, and dropping depth charges at suspected contacts. One of the merchant ships stopped to pick up survivors from the torpedoed ship, in doing so making itself a sitting target. Within minutes it was itself struck by a torpedo and rolled over and sank. Thereafter, no more of the merchant ships stopped to pick up survivors.

By this time Alex and Neil had put down their drinks and were totally engrossed in John's account, oblivious of their surroundings and of the people sitting at the tables around them. John seemed to be lost in his memories, and his eyes had a distant look as he continued.

After another hour, John's own ship was torpedoed and the order was given to abandon ship, the crew managing to launch a lifeboat before the ship sank. The crew of seventeen men crowded into the lifeboat in disarray, wet and with inadequate clothing. Two men had been injured in the attack, one having had one of his legs broken, whilst the second, a young man from the engine room, just eighteen years old, had been badly injured when the ship had been torpedoed, and sat nursing broken ribs and suspected internal injuries, along with a fractured shoulder-blade. The young man was distressed by his injuries and was calling for his mother, so John sat by his side and attempted to comfort and reassure him.

For the rest of the night, the crew sat quietly. John was disturbed by the deterioration in the condition of the young man at his side, who had slipped into a coma. When the convoy had been attacked, a message had been sent for help, so there was the chance that they would be rescued, and he hoped that help could come soon enough to save the young man's life. As dawn arose, one of the crew spotted the periscope of a U-boat close by. After an hour, the U-boat surfaced, and the survivors in the lifeboat thought that they were to be machine-gunned as they sat there helpless. However, they were hailed from the conning tower of the U-boat, and asked if there was anything that they needed. The skipper of the sunken merchant ship shouted back that they had need of medical supplies, blankets and food.

After a few minutes a small inflatable dinghy pulled alongside the lifeboat, the two German seamen manning the inflatable then passing over the requested medical supplies, blankets and food, and finally passing over two bottles of schnapps, with the words "Merry Christmas". After that the German seamen had returned to their submarine, which then submerged, but remained nearby at periscope depth. Clearly, the U-boat intended to wait and see if a rescue ship would come for the survivors, in which case the rescue ship would be an easy target. For the next twenty-four hours the U-boat sat watching and waiting, whilst the survivors, desperate for rescue, but at the same time not wanting to be instrumental in the sinking of a rescue ship, prayed that no rescue ship would arrive. Eventually, the U-boat surfaced, the captain and his senior officers gave a wave from the conning tower, and then it departed. Three hours later a rescue ship arrived, to take them back to the safety of the Clyde and in time for the life of the young man to be saved.

Neil was disturbed, asking what the survivors in the lifeboat had done when the German submariners had waved farewell to them. John replied 'Most of us waved back. They were good men.' to which Alex interjected 'But they or their mates had sunk your ship, and they were waiting in the hope of sinking your rescue ship.' to which John responded with 'That was their job. They were fighting for their country and they had no choice. You, Neil and I and would have done the same. But what they did for us and our wounded was humanitarian.'

John said that after the end of the war he had written to the Admiralty, giving an account of their sympathetic treatment by the enemy, and giving the number of the U-boat. Some months later he had received a reply from an officer at the Admiralty, advising that two months after the encounter of the convey with the German submarine pack, the submarine in question had been sunk in action, with the loss of all hands. John roused himself from his memories. 'There are no bad common folk, only power-mad or inept politicians. If the different races of the world were to see each other living their daily lives, bringing up their kids, and struggling to make ends meet, and if they could have a drink together and talk matters over, there would be no more xenophobia, no more hatred and no more wars.'

Alex looked at John with unbounded respect and admiration. 'What a great man' he thought, 'and how lucky I am to have him as my friend.' He compared John's simple views with the anarchistic, xenophobic views of Mr. Gilbraith, and didn't know what to think. Something told him that John was right in his outlook on the world, but at the same time Mr. Gilbraith had spoken of historical facts in the long-standing conflict between England and Scotland, facts that even almost two hundred and fifty years later could arouse Scottish anger and Scottish nationalism. He would need to think more about this subject, at another time, to try to get his thoughts clear.

By the time that they had finished their drinks and made their farewell, it was getting quite late. As soon as he got back to the house and opened the door, Alex found Flo waiting for him, her face contorted with rage. 'What time do you call this?' she screeched. Alex tried to tell her what a good evening it had been, and how he, John and Neil had had a good chat afterwards, but she would have none of it. 'Yous fishermen are a bunch of shirt-tail lifters. You think more of they pricks than you do of me!' Alex considered her words seriously before replying 'Yes' he said, 'you are quite right. I think more of those mates of mine than I do of you.' Flo turned red in the face with anger and screamed all the obscenities that she could think of, before making her way up to bed. Alex decided to spend the night on the settee. It looked as though his relationship with Flo was indeed reaching its end.

A few days later Ernie asked Alex if he could take a trip over to Dunoon on the Saturday morning to deliver some goods to a local hardware shop. Alex agreed, but decided that he would leave Clyde at home, as the dog had seemed off-colour for the last couple of days. Flo was annoyed when she learnt of this, as she had intended to go to Greenock Market on that morning.

Alex said goodbye to Clyde and walked over to the door, with Clyde's eyes following him, his face filled with dismay and disappointment at not being allowed to go along too. Feeling guilty, Alex forced himself to leave. He would make it up to Clyde when he got back by taking him a long walk along the promenade and then along the shore. They would soon be the best of pals again.

Flo's anger at Alex, and her hatred of Clyde, increased as the morning passed. She poured herself a double gin, and then a second, which helped her to build up her resentment at having been denied a shopping expedition. Soon she was openly cursing Clyde, who ran under the table in fear. Flo decided to bring the dog into line and teach it who was boss. 'Come here you little bastard!' she howled, but Clyde, petrified, stayed where he was, with a pool of urine spreading on the floor beneath him.

Flo got the yard brush and used it to stab at Clyde in an attempt to force him to move. When this didn't work she got on her hands and knees and reached under the table to try to grab Clyde's collar. Catching hold of his ear, she started to pull him out. Clyde yelped and pulled loose. At Flo's next attempt to grab him, in desperation he nipped her wrist, not to inflict injury, but to give her a warning that he had had enough. Flo screamed, but more in anger than in pain. She toppled the table out of the way and caught hold of Clyde by his collar. 'Got you, you runty little swine!' she howled.

Flo took down Clyde's lead from behind the door and fastened it to his collar. Then she took him out onto the street and set off walking towards the Veterinary Surgery. Clyde tried to hang back, but Flo dragged him along with repeated curses. Along the way she huffed and puffed to maintain her anger. The vet's waiting room was empty, so Flo rattled on the door to the surgery until the vet emerged. This wasn't the regular vet, but a locum who was standing-in for a few days. Flo said to him, in a great state of indignation 'I want this vicious dog put down. It just attacked me and it can't be trusted.'

The locum had had little experience, and wasn't sure what to do. The dog looked placid, yet he knew that some small dogs can be snappy, and Flo was adamant. He asked her if it was her dog, and when she said it was he decided, against his better instincts, that he had no alternative but to agree to her request. He took Clyde into the next room and sat him on the table. He looked such a sad little dog, with big appealing eyes. The locum shaved a small area of Clyde's leg so that he could more easily locate a vein, and then prepared the lethal injection.

In his disturbed state, the locum made a mess of the injection, causing Clyde some pain. Clyde yelped, but was then embarrassed at the fuss he had made and licked the locum's hand and gave him an apologetic look, after which he sagged and died. The locum rushed over to the sink and vomited. He had become a vet to save the lives of sick animals, not to kill a gentle and friendly wee dog like Clyde.

After she got back to her house, Flo poured herself a large gin. She fumed to herself and prepared what she was going to tell Alex when he got back. She would show him the bite mark on her wrist and tell him what a dangerous little bastard he had brought into her house! Looking down at her wrist, she was dismayed to see that the faint mark left by Clyde's little nip had almost disappeared. She rubbed hard on her wrist with her other hand in an attempt to restore the mark, but to no avail.

Her confidence in facing Alex with the fact that she had had his wee dog put down began to fade, even another double gin doing little to restore it. A cold fear started to creep over her. What had she done? The noise of Alex's key in the back-door lock drove her last thoughts of defending her action from her mind. As he came into the room she busied herself with washing a few pots in the sink. Alex looked around and then asked her 'Where's Clyde?'

Flo mumbled a few words to the effect that she had let him out into the back court, upon which Alex walked out of the back door calling out Clyde's name. He returned a few minutes later, concern written all over his face. As he closed the back door he noticed that Clyde's lead was not hanging in its usual place, and realised that something was amiss. He walked over to Flo and turned her round to face him, asking again, but this time in a slow deliberate voice 'Where is Clyde?'

Flo babbled a few words, upon which Alex repeated his question, but this time in a loud angry voice, at the same time shaking her shoulders violently to make sure that she would tell him the truth. Flo screamed her explanation for Clyde's absence at him. 'The little bugger bit me for no reason. We can't keep a biting dog, it wouldn't be fair to the neighbours. I had to take him to the vet's to be put down.'

Alex's eyes glinted as he asked 'Where is this bite?', upon which Flo slowly raised her wrist, where there was not a sign of a bite to be seen. In the past, when she had been losing ground in confrontations with her lovers, as a last resort Flo would throw herself upon their mercy. It had always worked, so she tried it on with Alex. With her face flooding with tears, she begged his forgiveness.

Flo waited for his rage to explode, and looked forward to the string of abuse and the tirade of blows that would fall upon her, after which they would both cry, before making up and going to bed together: she had found before that sex under these circumstances is exceptionally good. Alex made no move, which was not what she had expected. By now her previous lovers would have attacked her, blacking her eyes and bursting her lips.

She became concerned by his cold staring eyes, and tried to provoke him into action. 'Why did you want a runty gutter-tyke like that wee bastard anyway? I'll get you a proper man's dog like a Bull Mastiff or a Doberman.' Still Alex made no movement, continuing to stare at her with a look of intense hatred. Flo knew that she had lost him. Alex turned round and mounted the stairs, returning a few minutes later with his case.

He knew that he would have to leave Gourock, not only to get away from Flo, but also because be couldn't bear to continue with his life there without Clyde. How could he go out on the "Westering Home" without wee Clyde standing on guard on the foredeck? As he opened the back door, he threw his keys down onto the floor, and then he left.

Flo poured herself another large gin and then contemplated her situation. She had been in this position before, but had always been able to move on and find herself another man, and she would do so again now. She remembered the young seaman who always passed a pleasant word to her at the "Clyde Puffer" when Alex wasn't about, although his eyes had more in them than just a friendly interest in her.

She looked at herself in the mirror. Her eyes were swollen with crying, but otherwise she didn't look too bad. She would go into the "Puffer" this evening and sit in solitude at the bar. The young man would be certain to see that something was wrong, after which she would look up at him with her sad tear-filled eyes and tell him that Alex had run off with a younger woman. Tonight could be his lucky night! She went upstairs to decide what she would wear, and also to check that the bed was tidy, just in case. Yes, tonight could be his lucky night!

After leaving the house Alex walked to the vet's. As he entered, the receptionist looked up from her desk to tell him that the morning session was just closing, but he ignored her and walked into the surgery. The locum also started to tell Alex that the morning session was finished, but Alex interrupted him: 'You put my dog down this morning. I've come for the body.' The locum's hasty glance towards the back room told Alex what he wanted to know.

He strode over to the door and entered. In the corner were two plastic bags. Alex looked into the first, to find the body of a poodle, but in the second he found Clyde's body. In life, Clyde's extrovert personality had made him seem a bigger dog, but lying in death he looked tiny and nondescript. Alex flinched, but then picked up the bag and walked to the door. The locum stood in the doorway and tried to remonstrate with Alex. 'Now look here, you can't just barge into my surgery like this and ...' but Alex pushed him aside and walked out into the surgery and then into the street.

Carrying his suitcase in one hand and the plastic bag in the other, Alex walked west out of the town along the Ashton shoreline. After half an hour he reached Ashton Point and then the Clock Lighthouse. Some houses were being built at the foot of the hill rising from the road. Alex spotted the night-watchman's cabin and walked over to it. As he approached the cabin the night-watchman emerged and stood waiting for him, a look of suspicion on his face.

The night-watchman preferred not to have dealings with the public, just wanting to do his rounds and then sit in peace in the cabin with a mug of tea. Alex simply said 'Lend me a spade.', an order rather than a question, to which the night-watchman raised his eyebrows and was about to refuse, but then he saw the pain in Alex's eyes and he suspected what might be in the plastic bag. Without saying a word, he reached into the cabin and produced a spade, silently handing it to Alex and taking Alex's suitcase and putting it into the cabin.

He watched Alex climb the hill, thinking of his own old dog that had died the previous year. The dog had used to come to work with him in the evenings, where they would make the rounds together, and then sit companionably by the coke brazier. He still missed the old dog. From force of habit, for a few weeks after the dog had died he would sometimes call his name when it was time to make the rounds, after which he would grieve for his old friend. He knew how Alex must be feeling. 'Poor sod.' he said quietly, and then shaking his head he repeated it. 'Poor sod.'

Alex climbed higher and higher. Soon the Firth opened out to view, but Alex was in no frame of mind to notice. Eventually he reached a point where the hillside was little more than a mass of rocky outcrops. It was unlikely that there would ever be any building development at such a height. He put down the plastic bag by an outcrop and started to dig. The ground was filled with small rocks and the going was slow, but after an hour he had made a hole three feet deep. He lifted Clyde's body from the plastic bag, and then laid one half of the bag at the centre of the hole, and then placed Clyde's body on it, with the intention of just folding the other half of the bag over Clyde's body to form a cover, before filling in the hole.

Clyde looked so small and forlorn lying at the bottom of the hole. He had been such a sociable little dog and such a grand friend in life that Alex couldn't bear the thought of leaving him lying alone in this lonely spot in death. He picked up a big rock and placed it close to the outcrop. Then he found a smaller stone that he could grip firmly in his hand. Placing the palm of his left hand down on the larger rock, he set the cutting edge of the spade over the first joint of his little finger and then leaned the spade against the outcrop.

Swinging the smaller stone high into the air in his right hand, he brought it down onto one of the shoulders of the spade. There was a brief flash of pain, then numbness. Taking the severed tip of his finger, he placed it between Clyde's front paws. With tears streaming down his face he scratched Clyde's forehead, the way that Clyde used to like, after which he filled in the grave.

Afterwards he tidied the ground to leave no evidence of digging. He didn't mark the spot, as it was unlikely that he would ever return. He was content that over the thousands, millions, and thousands of millions of years that the world might yet exist, Clyde's body and part of his own body would lie together undisturbed. They would go on together into the future.

Alex wrapped his handkerchief around the end of his severed finger, and then retraced his steps down the hill. The night-watchman saw him coming and brought out his suitcase, silently exchanging it for the spade. Alex patted the man's arm and just grunted 'Thanks', his emotions not allowing him to say more. The night-watchman picked up his mug and watched Alex as he made his way along the road back to Gourock. 'Poor sod' he said to himself, 'Poor bloody sod.'

Alex made his way along to the railway station at Gourock Pier, with the intention of catching the train to Glasgow, but first he wanted to see Ernie and John to tell them that he was leaving. When he reached Ernie's office, the door was locked, so he walked along the quayside looking for Alex. He climbed down the ladder attached to the quay and went aboard the "Westering Home", but Alex wasn't there. Walking to the bow of the boat, he saw one of Clyde's turds lying in the scuppers.

The day before he had taken the boat over to a military installation that was patrolled by guard dogs, so fearing for Clyde's safety, he had kept him fastened up in the saloon until after they had departed. The day afloat must have been too long for the wee dog, and he had had to perform before the boat could arrive back at Gourock, much as it would have embarrassed him to do so. Alex was overcome by this last physical evidence that Clyde had ever lived on this earth. He picked up the turd with streaming eyes and gently dropped it over the side. He watched it as it sank down into the water, then he turned and made his way off the boat.

Finally, he walked along to the Puffer and looked in, but neither Ernie nor John were there, nor were any of the other skippers with whom he would have been able to leave a message. With reluctance, he made his way to the railway station, sad that he had not been able to say goodbye to his friends, but also feeling distraught at the loss of Clyde and with his mind numbed with the pain in his severed finger. He would make contact with Ernie at his office once he had settled in somewhere else, but at this time he had no idea as to where he would go when he reached Glasgow.

Since arriving in fear and panic in Gourock close on three years ago, Alex had experienced many new emotions: respect; the satisfaction of honest work; friendship; and the love of another living creature, Clyde. He had suffered grief and shed tears at Clyde's death, and would never forget him. He had arrived in Gourock an evil man, but now he was leaving as a quite good man. Whether he would ever make a truly decent man was still to be seen, but there was hope. Yes, there was hope!

Part 2: England

Chapter Ten

As the train neared Glasgow Central Station, Alex began to wonder where he should head for next. It would be foolish to stay in Glasgow, as Joe would soon learn of his whereabouts from one of his contacts. He decided to take a train to Edinburgh: whilst it would not be wise to stay in Edinburgh, as news of his arrival in that city could filter back to Joe, once there he could decide whether to head north for Aberdeen or Dundee, or head south for Newcastle and the rest of England. He pondered on what heading north would offer. All that he knew about the north was that there was the linoleum industry at Kirkaldy, and the offshore oil industry at Aberdeen, neither of which appealed to him. On the other hand, England was an unknown quantity, but he knew that Joe had no contacts there and would not be likely ever to find him.

Alighting from the train at Glasgow, Alex bought a single ticket to Edinburgh's Waverley Station, and then went to the station bar, where he ordered a half-and-a-half and a pack of sandwiches. His little finger was starting to give him pain, and although the fingertip had been severed cleanly at the first joint, he felt dizzy and faint from shock and stress.

The whisky deadened the pain a little, so he went to the bar for another. The barman looked at Alex's white strained face and wondered whether he should ask him if he was alright, but decided against it: 'Leave the customers alone with their own problems.' had been the advice of the manager when he had been given the job, and he had found this to be good advice.

Alex boarded the train, feeling better for the food in his stomach, but nevertheless still feeling weak and stressed from the constant throbbing of his finger. Where kind of place was he going to? What was he going to do? These thoughts occupied his mind for most of the journey. The accents of the staff on the train brought home to him that he was entering a 'foreign' country, and he remembered the teachings of Mr. Gilbraith, saying to himself 'What on earth am I doing here amongst all these Sassenachs?'

It was mid-evening when the train pulled into Newcastle Station. Alex decide that he needed a drink, but he didn't go into the first few pubs that he came across, but walked a little way until he found a quiet side-street pub, where he felt that he could sit in peace whilst he decided what to do. He asked the bar-lady for a pint of heavy, to which she responded with a laugh. 'You'll not get a pint of heavy in this town Jock. Will you settle for a pint of Exhibition bitter?'

The woman had not meant any offence, and he realised that his order and his accent identified him clearly as coming from north of the border. She was a good-looking woman, probably in her early thirties, with a pleasant, slightly-chubby face, and a full bust, albeit that she was just a little overweight: she would probably have to struggle to control her weight, but she looked nice. Alex tried to smile back at her, but the throbbing in his finger turned the smile into more of a grimace.

The woman's expression changed to concern. 'Are you alright flower?' she asked. Alex told her that he had been to a farewell party that lunch-time, and had got very drunk, waking to find himself on a building site with the tip of his little finger missing. The story sounded implausible, but the woman accepted it and expressed sympathy. She came from behind the bar and ushered him into a corner, telling him that she would come off shift in half-an-hour, and would then take him to the Emergency Department at the hospital to get his finger attended to.

When her shift finished, the woman called Alex over to the bar and told him to meet her outside, after she had cashed-up and put on her top-coat. She said that her name was Aggie, and he told her that he was called Alex. They took a taxi to the hospital and followed the signs for Emergency, where the receptionist asked them to take a seat. Aggie started to tell him about herself. She was married, but her husband had left her and their son Luke a year ago to live with a young woman from where he worked. She had stayed on in their flat and managed to pay her way by serving behind the bar for a couple of hours in the evening to supplement her wages as an assistant at a department store.

Alex asked her what Luke did in the evenings when she was out working and she told him that he stayed with a neighbour. Aggie then asked him what he himself did for a living, and he told her how he had worked on the boats at Gourock and what a grand life it was. 'If it was so grand, then why have you come down here?' she asked in the direct but un-aggressive Geordie style. Alex mumbled a vague unconvincing reply, from which she deduced that a woman had been involved, and decided not to pursue the matter further.

Their conversation was interrupted when his name was called by a nurse, who took down the particulars of the injury. When he said that he had no recollection of how the injury had actually occurred on account of being dead drunk at the time, she looked at him unbelievingly. He was told to return to his seat until the doctor was ready to see him. When his turn came Aggie insisted on going along also, and the two of them followed the nurse to a side room, where she told them to wait outside, whilst she went in to brief the doctor. After a couple of minutes she came out, gave Alex a disapproving stare, and told them to go in.

The doctor had doubts about Alex's story that he had been too drunk to recollect how his injury had occurred, and questioned him until he was satisfied that no-one else had been involved. After spending a few minutes cleaning up the injury, the doctor told Alex that fortunately it was a nice clean separation at the first joint, with no bone fracture being involved.

He gave Alex a local anaesthetic, and then an antibiotic injection, by which time Alex was feeling the worse for wear: he had had a long stressful day. Finally, after a few more minutes, during which Alex sat with his eyes closed, the doctor drew the skin up over the part-joint and carefully stitched the loose folds together. The nurse bound up the finger and told Alex to return in the morning for it to be checked.

As they left the hospital, Alex tried to thank Aggie for what she had done for him and for having volunteered the information to support his story, but she quickly dismissed this 'What's a few white lies if it helps someone out, like?' As they neared the corner of the street, Alex said that he must find somewhere to stay for the night. She replied that he could stay with her if he didn't mind sleeping on the settee. With a laugh she cautioned him 'No funny business mind!' but it was clear to both of them that Alex was in no state for anything of that kind.

Aggie led the way to the bus stop where she told the conductor 'Two to the Wall.' When Alex looked at her questioningly, she explained that her flat was in a recently-built housing development at Byker, called "The Byker Wall". Alex smiled at the anology draw between this "Wall" and the magnicent "Hadrian's Wall", a defensive fortified wall built about nineteen hundred years, running for 73 miles from what is now a suburb of Newcastle, "Wallsend" across the width of the country to the Solway Firth. A good example of Geordie humour!

As soon as they got to her flat, Aggie told Alex to sit down on the settee whilst she made him a cup of tea and a sandwich, but by the time that she had come back from the kitchen he was sound asleep. She lifted his feet and swung them onto the settee, and then covered him with a blanket.

Before she turned out the light, she gave one last look at him. Her family had always chided her for being a soft touch, willing to take in any lame duck that came her way. They had said that she was soft in the head for having tolerated her husband's wandering eye, and that she herself had brought about his running off by giving him too much freedom. She smiled down at Alex, poor injured man, and said in a quiet gentle voice 'Good night flower. I hope you'll feel better in the morning.' In his introduction to England, Alex had fallen lucky in meeting such a kind good-hearted soul as Aggie.

He awoke in the morning stiff and aching, and with his finger throbbing, to find a young boy of about eight or nine years of age, presumably Luke, staring across at him from one of the chairs on the other side of the room. Luke immediately recited what his mum had instructed him to say, in a desperate monotone, worried in case he should forget a single word. 'Brew yourself a pot of tea. You'll find some eggs, bacon and sausage in the fridge. Don't forget to go to the hospital to have your finger seen to. Mum will be in at half-past five.'

Having delivered his message, Luke relaxed, sat back in his chair and smiled: he was very responsible for his age. Alex smiled back at him in return. He had not had any previous experience of kids, and wasn't sure about how to talk to them. 'So you're Luke?' he inquired, for want of something better to say. Luke nodded. 'Why aren't you at school?' Alex asked, in response to which Luke began a long tale about the school's central-heating system having broken down and the kids being told to stop at home for the next two days.

Alex eventually said 'Okay then' to stem the flow of words, 'you can show me where the hospital is later on.' having been too tired and stressed the previous evening to have taken proper note of its whereabouts. Again Luke nodded, but added that he would have to telephone his mum to tell her where he was going to. They had got off to a good start.

After Alex had had breakfast, they set off for the hospital, deciding to walk rather than take the bus, as it was a clear bright day. As they crossed the road, Luke took Alex's hand without embarrassment, which caused Alex some confusion, as he couldn't understand how on their short acquaintance Luke could put such trust in him.

No-one before had ever put any trust in him, or shown any affection for him, discounting the affection that Flo had professed to hold for him, and he was at a loss as how to respond. To overcome his embarrassment, he swung their joined hands backwards and forwards in time with their steps. Luke chatted on, not needing any encouragement, telling Alex all the events of his daily life, of the problems with bullying at school, and of his old uncle Matt, a retired miner who lived nearby. Alex listened to Luke with interest.

After about a half-hour they arrived at the hospital. Leaving Luke in the waiting room, Alex walked to the reception desk, from which he was directed to the doctor's waiting area. He was soon called into the doctor's room, where the doctor examined his finger, finding that all appeared to be healing well, and that Alex needn't return for another week, unless he felt that there was something that needed immediate attention. Picking up Luke on the way out, Alex decided that they should spend the rest of the day together, and asked Luke what he wanted to do. Luke didn't hesitate: 'Let's go to the Exhibition Museum at the Town Moor.'

A short bus ride took them north of the town to the museum, which was housed in an attractive old building, sitting comfortably in its own grounds on the outskirts of the city. It was not as big as might be found in the inner parts of a city, nor did it seem to have the same level of patronage. However, upon entering, Alex was amazed at its contents. He had not visited a museum before, even though he had spent most of his life not very far from Kelvingrove Museum, which is one of the finest museums in the world, not just in terms of the exhibits, but also in respect of the building itself.

In the entrance hall of the museum, hanging high up from wires attached to the ceiling, was a minute flying machine, a "Flying Flea,"[10:1] with a fuselage that seemed to him to be no more than four or five feet in length and three feet in width, with the wings also being similarly short, that had actually flown, but had been found to be aerodynamically unstable, with a disastrous tendency to nose dive. They read that it was not actually an aeroplane, but an autogyro, where, unlike a helicopter, the rotor was not powered, but secured its rotation, and hence the lift imparted to the craft, by the forward motion imparted by the propeller.[#17]

They stared in incredulity as this creation of man's engineering skills. Luke asked Alex a few questions about the craft, which Alex, in embarrassment, was unable to answer. He regretted the limits of his own formal education and general knowledge. Whilst in Govan he had never been stumped for an answer to a problem, although the answer had usually involved some act of brutality; similarly, despite having been able to cope with all the problems of skippering a boat whilst at Gourock, this did not help him at all in answering the questions of this young boy.

[10:1] When the Exhibition Museum was closed some years ago, the Flying Flea that had been on display there was "sent down south". The author has searched the internet to try to locate this particular machine, but without success. The Turbinia however, is now housed in a prominent and fitting setting in a new science museum in the centre of Newcastle-upon-Tyne.

They moved on further into the museum, and in one exhibition hall came across a marvellous exhibit, the "Turbinia", the first-ever turbine-powered ship, that had led to a revolution in marine propulsion, achieving unheard of speeds of approximately 40mph, the required power having to be transmitted through nine separate propellers. She was beautiful! [18] Alex was awed with admiration for the creators of this magnificent machine: those who had had the vision of such a craft; those who had designed the ship; those who had built it; and those intrepid men who had sat in its bowels as it raced into naval history. Luke too was entranced by the Turbinia, as he had been by the Flying Flea. Alex suddenly became aware of the skills and knowledge that other men possess, and he felt humble. He himself was skilled, but only in brutality; and knowledgeable, but only in criminal folklore.

The two of them stood hand-in-hand as they gazed in wonderment at this marvellous example of man's inventiveness. Alex had never before had any interest in science and engineering, just taking for granted all the achievements of mankind made in these fields that had come into his life: the electricity that gave him light, power and heat; the telephone; the camera; the petrol engine, the diesel engine, and countless other wonders. He had been interested only in creating fear and shame in his fellow men, although, to his credit, more recently he had become a skilled inshore skipper.

Alex regretted that he had not paid attention to his studies in his school-days, instead of being concerned only with his standing amongst the other children. He looked down at Luke and felt a protectiveness that he had not experienced ever before. Luke should be encouraged to take a part in such developments in the future, and he resolved to raise with Aggie her plans for Luke's future, albeit this was hardly any part of his business in view of his having only just met her.

Their next call was at South Shields, on the southern bank of the river Tyne as it reaches the sea. Directly opposite on the northern bank is North Shields, with its fish quay. They walked from the bus stop at the centre of the town along Ocean Road, with its almost continuous run of eating places, mostly Indian and Asian, on its southern side. The first restaurant had been opened to satisfy the demands of the many sailors returning from the Orient and also foreign sailors docking in the Tyne. It would take a lover of oriental food many weeks of nightly dining to work from one end of the road to the other.

Reaching the seaward end of the road, they came to the first lifeboat in the world, sitting under a sound roof to protect it from the weather, but open to view from all sides. It was a robust boat and, naturally for its day, was oar-powered. Alex felt a surge of admiration for the men from the North East who had taken this boat out to sea in all kinds of weather to rescue souls in distress. They must have been men of exemplary courage.

Close by was a smart hotel sitting on the promenade, the "Sea Hotel", and directly across from it was a park. On a boating lake inside the park were several model boats, some sail powered, and some powered by small engines, both electrical and petrol. Luke was enthralled, and watched them with wide eyes. Around the perimeter of the lake was a small railway line, on which ran a model steam train pulling three carriages filled with children and adults. The driver of the train, as also the men working on the rolling stock in the station yard, were dressed in the appropriate clothing of boiler-suit and peaked-cap, stained with oil and coated with coal dust, matching their counterparts who used to man the real-life steam locomotives on the national railway system, before steam power was superseded by diesel-power and electrical-power.

Many of the men were miners who had built the model engines and rolling stock themselves during their periods above ground. That men could work deep down in the earth, day-after-day, and yet retain the enthusiasm to carry out the meticulous construction of such examples of precision engineering during their spare time astounded Alex. Although he was new to the north-east, he felt a growing respect for the 'Geordies'. Despite living in an area of national neglect, exemplified by the Jarrow March of the twenties down to London in a peaceful protest about their living conditions, these men maintained their dignity and their integrity, and filled their non-working time with creative and skilled hobbies. They did not feel the need to turn to crime, or to violent protest, but accepted what they had got and lived happy, fulfilled lives. Alex was impressed by them, and again saw the weaknesses and the lack of value of his own earlier lifestyle.

When they got back that evening Luke was bubbling over with what they had seen that day, which brought a smile of pleasure from Aggie. She turned to Alex and gave him a look that clearly said "thank you". Since his father had left, Luke had been missing male company, as Aggie knew well, and this day's outing had meant a lot to him. During tea Luke sat next to Alex and chatted about what they had seen, whilst Aggie sat quietly listening, not checking his rapid outpouring of words, but letting him enjoy recounting his experiences. Any misgivings that she might have had about inviting Alex to stay with them for a few days were forgotten: moreover, if Alex wanted to stay on a more prolonged basis, this would be alright by her, and certainly it would be by Luke.

The next day, Saturday, was Aggie's day off from the department store. After breakfast, the three of them went shopping in the town, amongst other things calling in at the grocer's to buy some peese-pudding, which caused Alex to smile. Aggie explained that if a housewife had boiled a joint of ham, she would save the stock after the ham had been cooked. She would also boil some split peas until they were cooked, drain off the water and add the stock from the ham, and then continue to simmer the mixture until the peas 'fell' and became a thick yellowish mush, "peese-pudding", which can be eaten hot as one of the vegetables with a main meal, or eaten cold on a sandwich with the cooked ham: either way, it is delicious.

She also bought some "stottie cakes", which also caused Alex to smile, then explaining that a "stottie-cake" is rather like what those in Scotland might call a "bread roll", others might call a "bap" and those down in northern England might call a "barm cake", except that it is larger and flatter and more doughy.

When Luke asked his mother to buy him some sweets, Aggie responded with 'Na! You've been eating too much ket recently', from which Alex deduced that "ket" referred to sweets, biscuits and the like. He had a lot to learn yet about the north-east. However, he soon found that the Geordies and the Glaswegians have many words in common that are not used in other parts of Britain, such as "bairn" for child and "clarty" for dirty.

During her conversations with the shopkeepers and with several friends and acquaintances she met in the town, Aggie bewildered Alex with some of the local dialect. 'Away man!' she said to a woman friend, an expression of incredulity that was used for men, women, and even young children. She also used the word "Pet" as a term of fondness, in just the same way. All of the people she met, the same as Aggie herself, seemed incapable of sounding the letter "t", such that 'cartoon' wasn't pronounced in the way to which Alex was accustomed of 'car-toon', but as 'cart-oon' with a glottal stop to the 't' so that it was cut off short in the mouth. It was the same with 'Rita', which was pronounced 'Reet-ah', with the 't' again being cut off short. The letter 'h' was omitted from the front of words as a matter of course. To take the sharpness off questions and statements, 'like' was added at the end, such as 'Where are you going to, like?'

At one stage in the shopping Aggie and Alex found themselves standing in a queue behind a mother and her teenage daughter, the latter apparently unable to decide whether to go off to meet her friends or stay with her mother. In exasperation her mother eventually declared 'If yer ganna gan, gan; if yer nae ganna gan, away wi' us', which Aggie translated as meaning 'If you want to go then go, if you don't then come with me.' A simple decision!

Alex listened in fascination to the conversations going on around him. Everyone sounded happy and well balanced, with their exchanges being free of aggression, cynicism, bitchiness and rudeness, and all made in good humour. Alex soon came to the opinion that the Geordies are grand considerate people, unlike the first impression that he gained of them - that they are hard and aggressive - from their 'uncultured' and difficult-to-follow accents on the train down from Edinburgh.

He felt uncomfortable when he remembered that back in Govan he had been proud of being hard and aggressive and had despised others who weren't. Alex started to realise that prejudices, as in the case of the views of Mr. Gilbraith, or initially unfavourable impressions, as in his own case, are of no value: one must mix with the local people to see their true worth. He felt that he would enjoy life in the north-east, and the company of Aggie and Luke.

Alex asked Aggie as to why the people from Newcastle were called Geordies, learning from her that this had originated in the early 18th century, when the Newcastle people had supported George I and George II in opposition to the population of the rest of Northumberland, who supported the Scottish Jacobite rebellions. He teased her: 'You silly buggers', he said, 'missing the chance to become Scots!' upon which she uttered a rude remark under her breath, which caused Alex and Luke to roar with laughter. Aggie was a grand soul, and marvellous, cheerful, company.

On the following morning, Aggie told him that it was the long-established practice for old Matt, their next-door neighbour, to come for Sunday lunch. When Matt came round Alex was surprised to see that he was wearing a smart, though old, suit, a shirt and a tie. Matt was a slight man, with his hollow chest and his cough indicating the complaint from which he had been forced to retire prematurely from the mines: silicosis. He was in his late seventies, but little else was known about him, any questions being stalled by a polite but uninformative reply. He shook Alex's hand and sat down next to him at the dinner table. They chatted cordially, Matt asking un-inquisitive questions, to which Alex had no trouble in responding.

Matt was clearly one of the family, with Luke calling him uncle, but in reality, Granddad would have been more appropriate. He didn't seem to resent Alex's presence: indeed, his attitude was welcoming, as though he was aware of Luke's need for a father figure rather than for a grandfather figure. He also seemed to realise that Aggie needed to have a man about the place who was young enough to appreciate her

173

feminine qualities.

After dinner, the two men sat together on the settee, with Matt recounting his life down the mines to Alex. As a retired miner, Matt received a monthly coal allowance. Not needing all of it, he had arranged for half of it to be dropped off at Aggie's. This was a great help, and in return she did little things for him: cooking the odd week-day meal, and doing jobs around his flat that he couldn't manage himself, such as washing curtains and any sowing that needed to be done. He was also willing to keep an eye on Luke whenever there was the need. Matt had maintained contact with some of the miners from his colliery, and told Alex that, if he wanted him to, he would arrange for them to go down one of the mines together, so that he could see what the working life was like there. Alex thanked him, not realising quite what this might entail.

Come the Monday morning, Alex asked Aggie where the nearest Labour Exchange was, so that he could go and see what jobs were on offer. Arriving there, he read the notices on the various boards, but none seemed suited to his experience, apart from the need for a security man, a 'bouncer', in the evenings at a local club, for which his time as a Glasgow gang man would have come in handy! One described a job working on the fishing fleet operating out of North Shields, but although Alex had had experience on boats, and had taken out many fishing parties, this had been on an amateur basis, and he knew nothing of commercial fishing methods, or of the equipment that is involved. Still, if there was nothing else more suitable, he would give this job a try.

Eventually, one job caught his eye: an international removal firm required a warehouseman at their local depot. Alex joined the queue of people waiting to be interviewed, and after going through the formalities with the clerk on the other side of the desk, including a telephone call to the company, he set off for interview. The manager was waiting for Alex when he arrived and wasted no time in showing him around and explaining the duties associated with the job. These were mostly menial or clerical, but Alex didn't mind: once he had got the job he might be able to find something better.

Upon his accepting the job, to start on the following morning, the manager shook Alex's hand and led him to the door. His final words were 'This may not be the best job in the world, but for the right kind of man, the prospects are good. Make a success of it and you could move up the ladder.'

Following the job interview, having got his immediate problem of a job sorted out, Alex rang up Ernie in his office at Gourock to explain the reason for his sudden departure. The phone was answered by Ernie's wife who, once she realised who was on the line, adopted a cold hostile attitude. 'Oh, it's you is it?' she said, 'I wondered when you would be looking for your wages.' Alex was confused, and asked her what she was talking about, but then realised that he hadn't drawn his week's wages at the time he had left Gourock. 'You needn't have worried.' she said, 'Flo was in first thing yesterday morning to collect them for you. You're a bit of a shit the way you left Ernie in the lurch. He had to cancel a job yesterday and one again today on account of being a skipper short.'

Alex started to try to explain his sudden departure from Gourock, but she cut him short and put the phone down. When Ernie came in that evening she didn't tell him the exact run of the conversation with Alex. 'That bastard Alex was on the phone this morning asking for his wages, but I told him that Flo had been in for them.' Ernie asked if Alex had given any explanation for his behaviour, but she just told him 'He started some tale about not being able to help it, but I didn't waste any time on him.' For a few minutes Ernie sat silently, then he said 'The bastard! John was upset this morning about not knowing what had come over Alex. He loved him like a young brother you know, and the swine just 'upped-and-offed' without a word.'

A few weeks later, true to his word, Matt told Alex that he had arranged for them to go down East Herrington Colliery, Sunderland, on the following Saturday. Came the day, they caught the bus to Newcastle city centre, and then the bus on to Sunderland. Matt explained the rivalry between the city of Newcastle and the town of Sunderland, most vividly expressed in the support of their respective teams, Newcastle United and Sunderland AFC. On the days of a local derby, either at St. James's Park, or at Roker Park, the atmosphere in the centres of Newcastle and Sunderland is intense.

Despite the very short distance apart, the Newcastle people don't consider the Sunderland people to be Geordies, but refer to them as "Mak'ems". This term arose from time when the Weir was the largest shipbuilding river in the world, which caused the Geordies to make what they thought was a criticism 'You only mak'em, but we use'em!' However, the term stuck, and the Sunderland people now happily refer to themselves by this name. Because of this intense rivalry, very few people move from Sunderland to Newcastle, and vice versa: if a local girl marries a man from 'the other place' and goes to live there with him, she is regarded as having virtually emigrated. However, the apparent hostility in their rivalry is not real: whenever Sunderland AFC or Newcastle United are playing a team from outside of the region, the local team would be given the support of their long-standing rival.

Apart from its reputation at one time for shipbuilding, Sunderland had had another 'first', in being the place of the first reported death from the plague, brought ashore by rats from ships arriving in the harbour, a girl of the family name of Hazard being buried in the grounds of what was then St. Mary's Hospital. Later, this hospital was financed by local miners and shipbuilders giving thrip'ence[10:2] each week from their wages in return for free care and medical treatment, a forerunner of the National Heath Service.

The beaches along the east coast are all storm beaches, with great waves rolling in when the wind is from the east. Along the stretch of shoreline from the mouth of the Tyne to the mouth of the Weir and then along to the mouth of the Tees there are large expanses of clean sand, but speckled with coal from the washings of the mines. Often people with sacks could be seen on the shore collecting this "sea coal". For many poor families this was a source of free fuel whenever money was very short.

A few miles south of Sunderland is the small town of Seaham, with its huge harbour that had been build to meet the demands of the mining industry for the shipment of coal, but the intended development of Seaham for this purpose hadn't taken off. The complex structure of great walls dividing the harbour into inner and outer harbours now just serves a small collection of inshore fishing boats, whilst the town itself, with its bracing winds coming in from the sea, remains a quiet peaceful backwater.

Hartlepool, further south along the coast in Teeside, has a somewhat tarnished reputation, in that during the Napoleonic War the inhabitants had hanged a monkey washed ashore alive from a boat, in the belief that it was a spy! However, they don't take kindly to being reminded of this!

When Alex and Matt reached Sunderland, they caught the Durham bus, after they left the town first passing the hamlet of Offerton Village. Before the first of the bridges over the River Weir had been built, Offerton was the first place where the river could be forded, and was the place where all traffic, human, animal and mercantile, made the north—south and south—north crossing of the river. It is alleged that Mary Queen of Scots had crossed the River Weir here on her way to imprisonment. Early records show that in its prime the village had boasted four pubs and one-hundred-and-fifty houses, including a house

---

10:2 Equivalent to 1.25p in present-day sterling, but constituting a substantial part of a man's wages in the late 17th – early 18th Century.

where Oliver Cromwell had stayed. However, with the building of the down-river bridges, the importance of the village had dwindled, along with its population, such that at the present time there are no more than nine houses, with not even a single pub! Those of the inhabitants of the village wanting a drink now have to walk to either Hastings Hill, or to the lovely unspoilt old pub down by the river at Cox Green, the "Oddfellows Arms".

The next sight that they saw was the Penshaw Monument, a huge classical Grecian-type construction in the style of the Temple of Diana at Ephesus but of twice the proportions, sitting on top of Penshaw Hill, built by public subscription in the memory of John George of Lambton, the first earl of Durham, the foundation stone having been laid in 1844. The building comprises essentially twelve columns with a walkway with side-walls on each of its long sides, with a steep ramp running up to the middle and a matching ramp running down the other side on each of the short sides, unfortunately there being no side-walls alongside or at the foot of the ramps.

At one time visitors to the monument could climb up a staircase inside the next to the most south-westerly corner column, but following the death of a fifteen-year old boy in 1926, the staircase was closed to the public. The boy had run up one of the ramps, and then down the other side, but had stumbled and fallen 70 feet to his death. It is hard to imagine why anyone would have designed a building with protected walkways on two opposite sides, but with unprotected ramps linking them.

The next place they reached was Shiney Row, from where they would have to walk the remaining few miles to the pit. Alex was intrigued by the names of the local villages and hamlets: Newbottle, Philadelphia, Washington. Matt told him that the original hamlet of Washington, now surrounded by housing development, contains Washington Old Hall, the birthplace of some of President Washington's family, and is a popular attraction for American tourists. Even close to where Aggie lives is a place with an American counterpart: the tiny village of New York.

When they arrived at the colliery, they were met by Fred, a younger ex-colleague of Matt, whom Matt greeted enthusiastically with 'How are you marrer?' which Alex learned was the local word for "mate" or "friend". Matt replied 'Canny, and you?' Alex was surprised at the used of "canny" to mean well, and when used to describe a person to mean that he or she is a nice person, as back in Scotland "canny" was intended to mean sly or scheming.

Fred took them to be fitted out with overalls and a helmet with a lamp attached, the battery for the light being mounted around the waist. They then joined a group of miners about to go down the shaft. As the miners entered the cage, Alex was surprised by their unconcerned attitude, but realised that whilst this was new and exciting to him, it was an everyday occurrence for the rest of the men.

The cage dropped down into the darkness for what seemed an extraordinary length of time, until it eventually came to a stop. They then found seats in one of a string of small open carriages running on a metal track and after quite a long journey they reached the end of the line. Alex was surprised by the length of the journey, but Matt explained that some of the workings in the pit were very old, and the constant removal of coal from the seams had moved the coal-face back many miles, but rather than sink a new shaft for immediate access to the coal-face it was cheaper to use underground transport to deliver the miners to their workplace. Indeed, in the colliery operating beneath the sea, many miles out from the coastline between Sunderland and South Shields, there was no alternative, as a new shaft could not be sunk out at sea!

Fred led them for close on twenty minutes down a tunnel that was little more than head height, until they came to an opening on one side of about three feet in height. Fred asked 'Are you ready then?' the meaning of which was lost on Alex, and then without waiting for an answer he dropped to his knees and clambered into the opening. Matt followed and then Alex, who, expecting the tunnel to be short and no more than an opening into another shaft, was surprised that it stretched away into the distance. On one side was first a conveyor belt of not more than a couple of feet in width, and next to that was a small metal track.

Alex followed Fred and Matt as they crawled beneath a succession of hydraulic jacks set at about a yard apart. The space below the jacks was little more two feet in height and he couldn't lift his head high enough for the lamp on his helmet to shine ahead. They moved forwards, passing under jack after jack, until Alex was horrified to hear, and then see, a monstrous circular cutter of about three feet diameter, mounted on a powered carriage, with its axis set horizontally, advancing towards them along the metal track, cutting out coal from the seam, the coal then falling onto the conveyor belt.

After the cutter had passed by, the jacks pushed the conveyor belt and the track forwards into the coal face, ready for the next pass of the cutter. The jacks, in turn, including the one under which Alex was lying, then relaxed and advanced, and as they did so the now-unsupported roof behind them collapsed. Alex was petrified! He had been counting the number of jacks that they had passed through, and was desperate to get out of the tunnel. However, as they reached about the seventy-fifth jack, Fred stopped and said, with relish, suspecting the fear that Alex would be feeling, 'This is halfway through. The lads think that this would be a good place for us to hold our wage negotiations with the Coal Board. Don't you agree?' Alex felt sick with claustrophobia and tried to keep his voice calm, muttering some kind of agreement to Fred's question, but saying to himself 'The malicious old swine, why the Hell doesn't he get us out of here?'

Having enjoyed his terrorising of Alex, Fred started off again, with Alex counting every jack, until eventually they reached one-hundred-and-fifty, when they emerged into a tunnel of head height. Matt could see that Alex had been shaken by his experience, and said to him 'Have no fear lad, you have been through about as frightening a situation as this mine can offer, barring a fall-in of course, and pray God we can do without one of those.' Matt told him that of out all the men employed in the mine, only three men at a time worked on the coal face with the automatic cutting and recovery system. On the way back home, Alex thought over the visit, and resolved that in view of the claustrophobia that he had felt, he would never set foot down a mine again. At the same time his admiration for the men who went down the shaft of this and other collieries in the north-east, and indeed in other parts of England and in Scotland and Wales, was enhanced.

How these modest and unassuming men could submit themselves daily to such fearful conditions and yet emerge after each shift as rational calm human beings, eager to continue with their main hobbies of model making, growing leeks, racing their whippets, singing in a choir and playing their instruments in brass bands, was beyond him. They were incredulous! Sod Mr.Gilbraith and his xenophobic beliefs that had corrupted Alex's mind for so many years!

Alex had been interested to hear the dialect words that the miners had used on their visit to the mine, and asked Matt about them the next day. Matt told him that they were speaking "Pitmatic".[10:3] As an example of Pitmatic, he sang for Alex a well-known Geordie song:

"Come here me little Jackie noo aa've smoked me baccy,

10:3 Pitmatic is a collection of words and phrases, many original, spoken with unusual vowel sounds in the Northumbrian dialect, that arose in the mining industry of the North-East of England in the late 19th century with the industrialisation of the region. Many of these words and phrases remain in local usage in the North-East, adding greatly to the individuality and character of the region.

Hev a bit o' crackie 'till the boo-at cooms in.
Dance ti thi Daddy, Sing ti thi Mammy,
Thoo shall hev a fishy on a little dishy,
Thoo shall hev a bloo-aater when the boo-at cooms in."

Matt then introduced him to some Pitmatic words and phrases: "bait", the snack that a miner takes down the mine to eat whilst working; "singin hinnie", a rich cake loved by mining families, so named for the sound that it makes whilst being baked on a griddle; "brassies", iron pyrites found in the coal seam; "keeker", a man who checks that the coal is being worked properly; "lowe", a pit candle; "neives", the fist; "double neives", the clenched fist; "reek", smoke; and "peck", a measure of quantity of coal, where forty-one gallons equals one peck; eight pecks equal one bole, and twenty-four boles equal one chauldron. Whilst these terms were mostly new to him, he recalled "reek" from the Scottish expression of farewell, "Lang may yer lum reek"; and "neive" from Burns' "To a Haggis", that he had enjoyed listening to in John's company at the Burns supper.

Warming to his theme, Matt told Alex more about life down the pit. 'Did you see any netties, "toilets", whilst you were down the pit?' he asked Alex, who replied that he hadn't. Matt told him that indeed there were no toilet facilities down at the coal face, and that if a man wanted a crap he would just do it onto the paper that his "bait" had been wrapped in, and then throw the paper onto the conveyor for it to find its way to the surface. If there should be a new man further along the path of the conveyor, one of the more mischievous men would call out to him as the paper and its contents approached 'Quick man! Grab my bait!' One expression that Matt used often when Alex had got the wrong meaning of something that he had been told, was 'Na! You've got it arsefanical!', the meaning of which Alex soon worked out for himself.

Alex felt that the English were fine people, at least those from the north-east, as he had not yet encountered enough people from further south as would enable him to form an opinion. He reflected upon his good fortune since arriving in Newcastle: he had been befriended by a young woman and was happy to play the role of father figure to her son; he had made friends with a grand old man; and he had a job that he enjoyed. Alex was changing: he had lost his unfounded hatred for the English; he was now a more rational and clear-thinking man; and be was becoming a better man. There was now a possibility that he would one day become a good man. A distinct possibility!

Chapter Eleven

A couple of weeks later, Laurie, one of the drivers at the removal company, told Alex that he was to make a delivery of heavy engineering goods on the coming Saturday to a company down in Manchester, and that he could come with him if he wanted to. Laurie knew a comfortable boarding house where they could stay for a modest charge, and in the evening they could visit a local pub. Alex immediately accepted. On the Saturday, Alex arrived at the depot in good time, to find Laurie just driving out the already-laden lorry.

They set off for Wetherby, then on to Leeds, after that heading over the Pennine Range, then descending towards Oldham. Coming down Oldham Road towards Manchester, Laurie told Alex something about the district that they were going to visit, West Gorton, that he had learnt from the factory manager on his last visit: "It's an area of heavy industry and slum housing built at the time of the industrial revolution. However, when Beyer Peacock, locomotive builders, built their factory here in 1854, Gorton was just a village of 2000 inhabitants, set in meadowland.[11:1] The range of heavy engineering work carried out in the area is impressive. Apart from Beyer Peacock, there is railway-engine work carried out at Gorton Tank on "tank engines", the compact and unglamorous locomotives - compared with their main-line passenger-carrying counterparts - that serve as work-horses in many industries, such as in mining, timber mills, manufacturing plants and construction, the employment of saddle-tanks or side-tanks mounted on the outside of the boiler of such engines enabling the elimination of a tender."

Laurie was a mine of information and continued with his account. "In the vaults of the local pubs after work, the conversations are all about such activities as the manufacturing and assembly work carried out for the Admiralty in the production of the massive barrels for 16-inch naval guns[19]. The local populace has an exciting day whenever an ingot is to be forged into a naval gun. Two locomotives are used to move a line of bogies carrying a white-hot 250-ton ingot across the busy Ashton Old Road from Armstrong Whitworth's North Street Works to the forge at Whitworth Bessemer Works, whilst Whitworth's

---

11:1 The growth of the industry of West Gorton and its eventual decline is reported in "A history of Gorton and Openshaw" by Ernest France, ISBN 0 9515528 0 5, extensively illustrated and with much relevant detailed data, published by Mr. French after seven years of research following his retirement in 1981. The book is believed to be now out of print.

traffic men hold up the trams and stand by with warning flags, with heat shields having being set up along the route to protect the spectators from the intense thermal radiation from the massive ingot."

Alex, in his ignorance, believed that all of England was quite affluent, but as they reached the district he saw through the lorry window that the housing area surrounding this throbbing industrial activity was one of greyness and bleakness. There was not a blade of grass or a single tree to be seen in the district, the pavements being entirely covered with huge granite slabs edged by equally huge granite kerbstones, and the streets being entirely covered with granite setts, more commonly called "cobble-stones".

Laurie told Alex that these cobble-stones have to be re-laid from time-to-time, following the bursting of a water main or such-like. After they have been set out, the cobble stones are hammered down with a large double-handled tool that resembles a small horizontal battering ram, and then the spaces between them are filled with pitch, this being contained within a tank mounted on a trailer, and heated to a runny consistency by a coal-fired burner set within the lower part of the tank. The smell of the hot pitch is considered to be a cure for bad chests and to give relief to those suffering from whooping cough. The local mothers bring their children close to the tank to breathe in the hot fumes.

During the summer months the pitch softens, whereupon the local children prise it out from the gaps and roll it into balls, in the process usually getting some of it onto their clothes or stuck to their hands: for those few who could afford it, butter is the common, but not very effective, means of removal. Alex drew Laurie's attention to the depressing, poverty-stricken sight of the area, to which Laurie replied "Fortunately, those living here knew of nothing else and so accept the environment without question. Indeed, when these close-packed streets of terraced houses were first built the occupants must have been delighted with them, with a sound roof over their heads, a warm hearth to sit in front of, water on tap, and a lavatory just a few yards away down the back-yard. At least the majority of these houses have both a front door and a back door, not like many others of that period, which had been built back-to-back. But times change, old houses develop faults and become damp and unhygienic. The living conditions of these people certainly should be improved." Alex concurred entirely with these views.

Alex was surprised that the district should be so similar to Govan: heavy industry, poor housing and general poverty: it seems that not only does the Westminster parliament neglect Scotland, but it also neglects the health and welfare of the residents of part of one of the major cities down here in England! Alex started to realise that, with his upbringing, he had much more in common with the ordinary people of this area than he could ever have imagined. His anger rose, not, as in the past, against the English generally, but now against the British government!

The streets were set out generally orthogonally, and at the corners of the streets, and partway along in the case of longer streets, were tall cast-iron posts with a cross-arm on which a light fitting sits in a glass-and-metal housing. Laurie explained that: "The lights, running on town-gas, are turned on each evening and off on the following morning by a "lamp-lighter", a man who comes round with a ladder which he leans against the cross-arm so that he can reach to turn the gas flow up or down, the flame being maintained by a pilot light. Other people act as a "knocker-up" where for a small weekly charge they come round early in the morning and tap on the bedroom window with a long pole until an occupant of the room makes himself or herself visible. The houses have no heating other than that provided by an open fire in the living room."

Laurie got into his stride as he explained: "There is no electricity, meagre lighting being provided by means of gas mantles. Hot water can be obtained by filling a small tank forming part of the one-piece cast-iron fireplace, drawing the water off through a tap as required. Food can be baked in a small oven, also forming part of the cast-iron fireplace, located at the other side of the fire. Soups and stews can be cooked in a cauldron hanging from a hook on one end of a short arm, the other end of the arm rotating on a strong spigot mounted on the fireplace, the cauldron being swung to different positions over the fire to regulate the temperature. Although a few people use the public bathhouse, baths are usually taken on Friday night using a galvanised mild-steel bath, albeit always called a "tin bath", set before the fire: father first, then mother, then each of the kids in order of seniority. This practice is the source of the common jocular expression "Don't throw the baby out with the bathwater", suggesting that the baby might be overlooked in the murky bath-water when finally it is time to empty the bath. After their Friday bath, the children are usually given a dose of syrup-of-figs to "keep the bowels open". When the weather conditions are conducive, the smoke emitted from the chimneys of the factories in the area soon causes a dense fog. This alone is bad enough, but as all of the houses have a coal fire in constant use, the residents take the opportunity of a fog to set fire to the soot that is building up in their chimneys by pushing a few sheets of burning newspaper up them.

Dense black choking smoke billows out, but so what? Everyone else is doing it! Also, why incur the expense of a chimney sweep when they can do the job themselves for nothing? The result is that the fog becomes so dense that, even in the middle of the day, on some days it is impossible to see more than about six feet ahead, with soot and grit soon settling on the pavements to be crunched underfoot by those passing by."

Alex was disturbed at what he heard and asked him if this lead to poor health of the residents [20], with the reply "The effect on the health of the residents is serious in terms of their contracting bronchitis, asthma, emphysema and other respiratory diseases, whilst some say that the fogs lead to the young having an insufficient intake of vitamin D, which leaves them susceptible to developing rickets. However, as the expression goes: ignorance is bliss!"

Laurie knew the district well, having made earlier deliveries to the district, and he soon located the company that he wanted, Crossley's, manufacturers of heavy diesel engines, where the goods were quickly unloaded. After this, they went to the boarding house and had a lie down in their shared room, followed by a wash and brush up and a change of clothing. Next they went to a nearby café where they had fish and chips with mushy peas, along with a delicacy that Alex had not seen before: a 'pudding', which consisted of minced beef in a rich gravy, set within a small suet-lined aluminium bowl and then fitted with a suet lid, the assembly being cooked by placing it for a set time in a pan of boiling water. After this meal, which was accompanied by bread and butter and a mug of tea, they were all set for the evening.

They made their way to one of the local pubs, the '"Birch Arms Hotel". In this area however, there was a pub on almost every street corner. The main street of the district, 'Clowes Street', although only about half a mile long, has so many pubs on it that no-one has ever been known to have completed a pub crawl from one end to the other, despite numerous attempts. Tonight there was to be a competition darts match between the pubs of the area, organised by "Sportstopics", a local sports-leaflet. Laurie knew the landlord, Mike, from his previous deliveries to the area, and introduced Alex to him. Mike was a friendly outgoing chap, about ten years older than Alex. They chatted for a while, as trade was still slack at this time, Mike telling them something about the pub and its history.

He had taken over the pub from his father who had become landlord early on in the war. Despite the food shortages, Winston Churchill had insisted that the pubs should continue to be supplied with their basic commodity, beer, in order that the home front would be able to relax in the evenings, and thus return to work each morning invigorated and able to maintain their daily production of war materials for the armed forces. Winston was known to have had a liking for his own relaxant, a glass or two of whisky, so everyone appreciated his efforts to ensure that their own relaxant, beer, was available to them at all times. Naturally, whisky, which anyway had never been of great demand by the working classes, was unavailable.

Most working class pubs only had a license to sell beer and wines, and not a license to sell spirits, so that the general unavailability of spirits had passed unnoticed. There were a couple of times when the supply of beer ran short, which caused the workers from the nearby factories to stop at the pub on their way home, rather than to return later in the evening and find the pub drunk dry. They would queue up outside the pub waiting for opening time, whilst inside the bar staff would draw seventy or eighty pints and line them up on the bar top, ready for the rush when the doors open.

Mike told them that in his dad's first week as tenant, he had 'barred' twenty individuals. Whilst this sounded incredulous, in reality the twenty people concerned were the members of two warring families who had been barred by the previous landlord, and had returned to the pub on the first night of the new tenancy to claim the customary free pint from the new landlord, during the course of the evening their grievances with their old enemies often resulting in renewed outbreaks of violence. However, such outbreaks of violence were conducted without the use of weapons and with regard for fair play, so that at the end of the evening the combatants could return to their homes having had a good night out, and with a few black eyes amongst them to show to their workmates in the morning. The next night they would have to find a different pub to drink in. Never mind, there were enough other pubs around!

After so much trouble in his first week, Mike's father had acquired a sold rubber truncheon, which he kept close-to-hand under the counter for when it should be needed, and he also changed the hanging of the swing-doors at the entrance to the pub to make them open outwards, so that at the first signs of trouble he could quickly bundle any trouble-makers out of the pub and onto the pavement: if the trouble-makers were very drunk, the doors also served to some extent as a 'non-return valve'.

Alex asked Mike about the protection that the police might have offered, receiving a derisory snort in reply. Mile told them that they were never there when needed, but later on Friday and Saturday evenings they would come into the pubs in pairs, being invited by his dad into the back room, where he served both of them with a free pint and slipped them a packet of twenty cigs each. They would be on their way in five minutes. With the pubs being so close to each other, it was a poor night when they couldn't both sup five or six free pints and pocket enough cigs to keep them going for the next few days.

They got to talking about the poverty in the area, Mike's tone became serious: "A great number of families in this area are poor. Some of the kids take off their footware, usually wellingtons, "wellies", or if they are lucky, leather boots, upon returning home from school, then going out to play barefooted. Most of the boys wear woollen jerseys with high-buttoned necks, and short trousers made of very coarse and stiff material. In wet weather the bottoms of their wet trousers rub and "chap" their legs, which is very painful. Underpants are virtually unknown. The girls fare no better, with gym-slips of coarse material being the standard attire, which again cause chaps on the legs. Amongst the poorest families, usually those with the most kids, whilst the children wear clothing for school that is appropriate to their sex, in cases where there is a preponderance of one sex amongst the children, the youngest of the minority sex will often have to change out of their school clothes when they return home, to play out in the discarded clothing of an elder child of the opposite sex, which in some cases leads to personality problems with the child as it grows older. From time-to-time one of the local churches will hold a Jumble sale on Saturday morning. Mothers will start to queue an hour before the doors open. As soon as the door key is turned in its lock they force their way in and seize an armful of clothing, which they then take into a corner where they can check its suitability without the risk of it being snatched away: rather in the way that a dog acts when it is given a bone in the presence of other dogs. Come Monday morning, the children of the family depart for school in their 'new' clothes: what matter if the jacket had been intended for a child of the opposite sex so that the buttoning is the 'wrong' way round; what matter if the shirt or blouse has a tear in the sleeve; what matter if the shoes are two or three sizes too large, so that pieces of cardboard have to be put inside them to make them fit; their 'new' clothing attracts only favourable comments from their classmates."

Alex was sympathetic when he learnt that some of the mothers quite frequently receive a note from the teacher informing them of the infestation of their children's hair with "nits", and the need for them to keep an eye on the kids in case they should be wriggling on their seats or fiddling with their backsides, an indication that they have worms: this was not an infrequent situation back in the orphanage. Another

186

similarity between Govan and West Gorton! The mothers particularly dread the weekly visit of the rent collector and the dept collector. When these men are expected, usually on the evening of their husband's pay day, the mothers will keep the kids in the kitchen, where they can't be seen, and threaten them with horrendous consequences should they utter a sound when the knock comes on the door.

Often a thwarted rent-collector or debt-collector will return unexpectedly when the family is in the living room, and there are sounds coming from within the house. The eldest child will then open the door, with the security chain in place, and advise him through the small gap that their mother has gone out for the day and won't be back until late. It is a very good day indeed when the rent-collector or debt-collector can collect what is due and also something off the arrears.

Many of the families rely on the pawnbroker. The wife will get some money from her husband on pay day before he goes off to the pub, and then go round to the pawnbroker's shop, with its customary three big brass balls hanging above the door, and redeem an item that she had pawned earlier in the week, usually the husband's best, and only, suit, before the pawnbroker puts it into his window for sale, as is his right with an unredeemed pledge. Come Monday, when their husband has spent the last of his wages in the pub, and the wife needs money for food for the kids, she will return the same item, to pledge it yet again. This might go on for years, with the amount of money lost in redeeming the pledged item exceeding by far the value of the item: a dreadful poverty trap.[11:2] Mike recounted a story that he had been told by his father about a local pawnbroker who was untypical in being soft-hearted. One old lady used to come in regularly on Monday morning carrying a shoe box in which were her husband's shoes, and just as regularly she would redeem the shoes on Friday evening. This went on for years, until one Monday morning, when after her husband's working boots had finally fallen apart, he had had to go off to work in his shoes. She didn't know what to do, but eventually decided to place a house brick in the shoe box, as the pawnbroker no longer looked inside

---

[11:2] The author is dismayed by the insidiously-seductive advertisements appearing on UK television in recent months showing beautiful young actors with smiling faces and gleaming white teeth, offering to equally-attractive, happy young 'pretend' customers instant short-time loans, "pay-day loans", at astounding rates of interest, to spend on something that they could just wait a few days for and then buy with their earnings. Inevitably, in many cases this leads to the person taking out further loads when the time comes to pay off the first loan. This is virtually a return to the "bad old days" of frequent visits to the pawnshop. So much for progress!

the box, but just handed over her cash and the pawn ticket. However, as soon as he picked up the box he knew that it didn't contain the usual shoes, but he didn't look inside until after she had gone. Come Friday, she came in as usual and redeemed her pledge, and this arrangement carried on for years.

There was much philosophical discussion in the tap-rooms of the local pubs as to what the pawnbroker should have done. There were some who said that he should have refused to accept the shoe box in the future without opening it up, thereby drawing attention to the old lady's deception, but there were others who argued that he had made so much money out of the old lady in the past, and would make more money out of her in the future, totalling much more than the value of a pair of old shoes, that it was in his best interests to ignore the deception and just carry on as usual.

Gambling on cards in the pubs was forbidden by law, so landlords were careful to see that their customers didn't break the law, keeping a close check on those playing cards to ensure that money does not change hands However, there was a simpler way to gamble illegally, that didn't involve any serious risk. Frequently a customer would leave the pub to place a bet on a horse. All of the houses faced onto the street, but between the rows of houses there was a narrow "back alley" or "entry", to allow the dustbin men to collect the dustbins from the back yards and the coal men to drop off coal, the houses having a brick coal shed at the bottom of the yard alongside the entry. The coal was put into the coal shed through the "coal hole", a small opening fitted with a door, partway up the wall opening to the entry. Those in the know would walk down the entry, make the required knock on the appropriate back-yard door or coal-hole door, place their bet, the door would be shut and bolted, and they would be back inthe pub again, all within a couple of minutes. Against the law, but who cared!

In this district there are "knick-knack clubs", where one of the local wives will arrange with the manager of a local store for her to organise a club, where she will collect from, say, twenty local housewives, two shillings a week for twenty weeks, thus generating a total of two pounds a week, with which she would collect a two-pound voucher from the manager each week. The voucher would be raffled amongst the members each week, the winner then spending her voucher with the store in question.

This should work well, but sometimes the housewives who haven't been lucky in the raffle will grumble and ask the organiser to raise the possibility with the store manager of providing extra vouchers ahead of time. Afraid that the housewives will lose interest, the manager might agree to an early release of the vouchers, with the danger that either the organiser will sell these vouchers herself for cash, or the housewives who have already won will no longer maintain their payments, leaving the organiser in a vulnerable and probably inescapable situation, in which prosecution could result. This is a scheme fraught with risk, no different from the "menodge" that Alex had seen in Govan, but attractive to the poor and desperate.

Some of the poorer families in West Gorton took over empty shop premises for their homes, painting the inside of the large windows with dark green paint, leaving just the top quarter or so clear. It wasn't such a bad situation, as the opaque paint gave them privacy whilst the clear band gave them light. No-one looked down on such families: everyone was poor and so all had to make-do as best they could.

The conversation got around to the marital problems caused by poverty, Mike saying that if a husband had a boring or menial job, or an unsympathetic foreman, to contend with, he would often ask his wife to give him some of the money from the pledged item so that he could then go out and forget his work troubles over a few pints. If she refused she would hear his anger, and if she didn't then comply she could suffer the consequences of a black eye, damaged ribs, or some other injury, often inflicted in the presence of the kids.

Alex had seen this situation in Govan, where sometimes when a wife came down to chat to the other wives in the court she would have a black eye or a burst lip. However, instead of expressing sympathy, some of them would tease her and ask her what she had been up to in order to anger her husband so. They all liked to think that their husbands were 'real' men who stood no nonsense! Anyway, if a man was so angry as to give her a bashing, it showed that he was still concerned about her, otherwise why would he bother?

It was the same with sex. If a drunken husband wanted to have sex and the wife refused because she was afraid of having another kid, her frustrated husband would not take no for an answer and would often become aggressive, so it was easier to comply: in a way, this was another poverty trap. The husband of a poor family had little else to look forward to other than a few pints and sex, therefore it would be unlikely that he would agree to give up these two pleasures, regardless of the consequences.

Thus the families of the poor increased in size, with more mouths to feed, which increased their poverty. Many a man lost his wife in childbirth, which created an even worse situation. The problem was eased to some extent when the older children started to earn a wage. In many families the wife only ceased to have children when she reached the menopause. The men in the pubs used to say, with some truth, 'The rich get richer and the poor get children.'

Because of the Catholic faith of many of the people, the only forms of contraception available to them were the withdrawal method and the rhythm method. It was the same problem with those of the Protestant faith: there wasn't the money available for contraceptives and, as Alex had found with Liz years ago back in Govan, it takes a strong-willed man, even when sober, to withdraw at the instant when all of his hormones are telling him to push forwards. It is no use telling a husband back from the pub and wanting sex that he will have to wait for a few days before he can be accommodated.

Mike pointed out one or two amongst the customers who had started to come in. One little chap, wearing a boiler suit, was caked in soot and black ash. Mike told Alex and Laurie that he works in a boiler room and has never been seen with a clean face. The man was complaining that he had called into the doctor's on his way to the pub and had been reprimanded for having arrived in such a dirty condition. 'I've been working!' he had protested to the doctor, but Mike told them that he had worked only until noon, after which he had drunk in the pub until afternoon closing time, and then gone home to sleep off his ale until the time came to call in at the doctor's, still unwashed, before proceeding to the pub for his evening drinking session. However, despite being a repulsive little creature, he had still managed to impregnate his wife every year for the last eight years. His drinking mates in the vault, impressed by his sexual achievements, often used to say 'Big man big dick, little man **all** dick.'

Another man who came in was described locally as the chap who had brought up his kids "on the one o'clock", this being the starting time reported in the "Sportstopics" racing sheet of a popular race on which bets were placed. Whatever the results of his bets may have been over the years, he had brought up a family of eight talented children, each with a gift for music. The second youngest son, wearing the short wellies that were all that the family could afford in place of shoes, could bring tears to the eyes with his rendition of Al Johnson's hit song "Mammy!" Mike told them that the eldest son, who was closest to his own age, had once told him with glee that he had teased his mother the previous evening by asking her what was for tea. 'What's for tea, you cheeky bugger?' she had exploded, 'Get off your arse and get it toasted!'

Mike himself had suffered some confusing experiences when his family had first moved into the area from another suburb of Manchester. On one occasion his mother had sent him to the local fish

190

and chip shop to buy his evening meal. Upon placing his order with the proprietor, old Mrs. Pearson, she had inquired about his fish, saying to him 'Do you want titotid? He had stood perplexed, upon which Mrs. Peterson had repeated her question. With his continued lack of response, she eventually decided that she was dealing with an idiot child and rephrased her question, which she repeated slowly and clearly: 'Do you want me to hot your fish for you in the fat?'

Mike told them how some of his friends from time-to-time were sent to Borstal Corrective Institutions for minor criminal acts, in the hope that this would teach the culprits to see the error of their ways, but the delinquent boys regarded their stay as in the nature of a training course for their future criminal activities, learning, if nothing else, not to get caught the next time. Upon their return they were treated as heroes by the local boys and accorded a higher status within the community.

Alex and Mike talked about the different accents in the region, and Alex contrasted the accent of most of the men in the vault, which he personally considered as sing-song, drawly and sloppy, with the accent of one of the older men. As this older chap got up to go for a pee, one of his mates said 'Off to play with it again then Walter?', to which Walter replied 'Sithee, hold tha tongue or I'll put m'toe up thine arse, tha spindle-gutted whore!' Mike told Alex that Walter came from the mill town of Oldham, just a few miles to the north of Manchester, where most of the people talk in this way, although not using the particular expressions that Walter had brought with him from the mills. No one there ever caught a bus: it was pronounced "buzz", and "it was" was always "it were". As well as his specialised swear words, Walter has retained some of his habits from his mill days. He still gets up at half past five in the morning, and on summer mornings can be seen sitting on his front door-step at six o'clock, reading a newspaper, where he remains until seven thirty, when it is then time for him to leave for his job as a ganger-man on the Mersey River Board.

Upon moving into the district Mike's parents had arranged for him to study the piano, and had bought him a proper leather music case, with which he was obliged to walk off proudly to his music lessons, but once out of the sight of his parents Mike used to stuff it beneath his jacket lest one of his mates should catch sight of it: it didn't do to be 'posh' in that area! One unfortunate aspect of learning to play the piano was that whenever the regular pub pianist failed to turn up, Mike's dad expected him to stand in. He hated this. He didn't like the kind of music that he was expected to play, which was the popular music preferred by the customers, who didn't listen to what was being played anyway, this just serving as a background noise. Towards the end of the evening a dense pall of cigarette smoke would fill the "best room" where the piano was, such that it was impossible to see across the only-modest-sized room, and his eyes would prick and flood with tears with the irritation of the smoke.

He was also critical of the inane conversation between the customers during their constant flow to the bar and the toilets:

'Hello there Harry! Long time no see. Aw'reet old lad?'

'Aye, I'm aw'reet right Jack. Fit as a flea. How's y'self?'

'Me? Oh, can't grumble. Got t'grin and bear it. The missus aw'reet?'

'Oh aye, now't wrong wi' her. How's your Alice, she aw'reet?'

'Oh aye, she's aw'reet but for a bit of the 'old' trouble. Still, got to keep y'chin up.'

'Aye. Well, I'd better get t'th stone before I piss m'self. See you soon mate.'

After this conversation, they would laugh and move on with a smile of their faces, pleased with their responses in the encounter. Alex thought that at heart Mike was a good-natured friendly chap, but had been young and a bit of a prig. Being a non-drinker, he wouldn't have found humour or intelligence in the words of well-oiled drinkers, albeit that they were jovial and friendly towards him and each other. Alex regarded Mike's snobbish attitude at that time towards the customers as unfair and unreasonable. If they chose to relax after work and get a bit drunk and talk a bit silly, that was their privilege: after all, it was a pub that they were in, not a debating chamber. He risked putting these comments to Mike, who agreed with him, saying 'Yes, you are right Alex. I sometimes think what a young prick I used to be.'

Mike had joined the scout group at the local church, the main attraction of which was that the troop had a brass band. He had been taught to play first cornet, and revelled in playing with the band such stirring marching tunes as "Sussex by the Sea" at local church events, and in the Whit Week processions through the centre of Manchester. The Whit walks were a great Manchester tradition, both those of the Catholics and those of the Protestants, known respectively by the young of their opposite camp as "the cat-licks" and "the prodi-dogs". Mike's band used to lead the Protestant walks through the city centre and past the Cenotaph. The Catholic and the Protestant Walks were held of different days and the weather on the days of the Walks was used as a measure of God's support for the respective churches, a heavy fall of rain on the day of the walk of the 'opposition' leading to gleeful remarks, such as "God knows his own!"

Apart from the annual Whit-week rivalry between the Catholics and the Protestants, the Scouts also had an ongoing rivalry with the local unit of the Boys' Brigade. Should any member of the Scouts or the Boys' Brigade be out on the streets in uniform when a contingent of the opposition marched by on parade, he would have to endure jeering cat-calls and banter until they had marched on: harmless fun really, but somewhat disturbing to those of a nervous disposition!

One weekend the scout group went to camp in Reddish Vale, the scouts sleeping in two bell tents whilst the three scout leaders in charge slept nearby in a small ridge tent. The boys in Mike's tent had been unable to sleep with the excitement of camping out and had started to tell dirty stories. Soon the conversation turned to sex, upon which one of the older boys took out his now-erect penis and demonstrated, to those of the others who didn't already know, how to masturbate. Soon they were all doing it! The news of this must have got back to the scout-leaders, as one of them gathered the boys together the next day and in a state of embarrassment lectured them at great length on the "dangers of self abuse", and how it would "rot the mind if carried out persistently", and would "damage their future as husbands and fathers". Mike said to Alex and Laurie 'Why couldn't he have just said "Try not to wank too much", then we would have known what he was talking about?' Laurie replied 'Didn't he tell you that you will go blind if you don't stop doing it?', to which Mike responded with the old joke 'Well if he had have done we would have asked if we could do it less and just wear glasses.'

Mike also told them about the weekly weekend fights that occurred along Clowes Street after closing time. One night he had been returning home after going to the pictures with a friend, and had stopped to watch a fight outside the Gorton Brook Hotel. Amongst the combatants he spotted a man who drank in his father's pub, Colin Malone, and was dismayed to see that Colin's wallet had fallen from his pocket. He rushed forward to retrieve it and handed it back to him during a lull in the fighting. Colin was pleased, and thanked him courteously and formally, but then noticing that he was needed in the affray, politely asked to be excused and proceeded to knock hell out of the nearest member of the rival faction. However, there was chivalry in the street fights of those days, with no weapons being used, and no-one ever suffering a serious injury, with peace, albeit of a limited nature, being restored by the following evening.

Mike went on to explain that when his father had first taken over the tenancy, the old men in the vault had told him about the after-closing-time activities that had used to go on "in the old days", when all of the men and most of the women wore clogs, which latter have a thick wooden sole with a leather upper. However, the front of the clog is reinforced by a sharply-rounded metal cap, whilst the sole is fitted around its edges with a 'clog iron', a thick almost closed ring of metal resembling a horse-shoe, held on similarly by nails driven through into the sole. When the men and women set off for work early in the morning, the clog iron would ring out on the stone pavement, and sparks could be seen to fly.

One after-closing-time activity was "puncin", where a group of men, perhaps ten to twenty, would form a ring on the pavement outside the pub. One man would then deliver a kick, driving the metal cap of his clog into the calf muscle of the man in front. If the man wanted to remain in the game, he in turn would then kick the man in front, otherwise he would retire. This game of elimination went on until the winner emerged. In the north of England, the word "puncin" has carried forward to the present day as slang: if a man should be involved in a fight, he might say that he gave his adversary "a good puncin", but in this case usually referring to the use of both fists and feet, and certainly not to the use of feet shod in clogs.

An even fiercer game was "purlin", where one man would stand alongside the next man, and then drive his clog, inclined so that the clog iron rather than the wooden sole made contact down the outside of the other man's leg, from high up his thigh to down to his ankle, inflicting in some cases such abrasion, even through the thick material of the man's trouser-leg, that he would be crippled for days and often scarred for life. In the same way as for "puncin", if the man wanted to stay in the game he delivered a similar blow to the next man, until the 'winner' eventually emerged. These two multi-contestant and non-grievance-based contests, seem to be local variants of the Lancashire "purring".[11:3]

Mike told Alex that in his youth he and his mates had used to go to a nearby pleasure ground, "Belle Vue", which was a large complex containing a boating lake, a zoo, an aquarium, fairground rides, amusements, a speedway track, a large concert hall the "King's Hall", and many other attractions, with pubs at the different entrances:

[11:3] Clog fights were common in northern England in the mid-1800s until the 1910s, and men died as a result of their injuries, despite the contests being declared illegal. In Lancashire "purring", which had recognised rules-of-procedure, two clog fighters, usually drunk and bearing a grievance, would climb into a large open-ended barrel, sit on the rim, and then kick away at each other's legs until one of them raised his legs out of the barrel in submission. The winner was declared after three submissions. Whilst clogs were produced as cheap and sturdy items of footware, they also made fearsome offensive and defensive weapons!

Lakeside Entrance, Main Entrance, and Longsight Entrance. People came from far around to spend a day at Belle Vue.

The concert hall presented many of the top performers of the day, an especial favourite being Joseph Locke, whose singing would have the audience spellbound from the opening line:

"Hear my song, Violetta, ... "

although he also sang songs of a more stirring nature:

"I'll join the legion, that's what I'll do, ... "

The concert hall enabled people to see, in person, popular radio entertainers such as Betty Driver;[11:4] Tessee O'Shea, who sometimes called herself Two-ton Tessie O'Shea on account of her large figure; and Tommy Handley. Unfortunately, Tommy Handley would be without his usual supporting players, whose radio characters were well-known for their catch-phrases, such as: "Don't forget the diver!", and the frequent question from the cleaner, Mrs. Mopp: "Can I do you now sir?", as well as that of Colonel Chinstrap, who never turned down the chance of a drink: "I don't mind if I do." Radio audiences would wait eagerly for these catch-phrases, and upon hearing them would turn to each other and smile. The next day at work they would use them in conversations with their workmates.

On some Saturday evenings Mike and his friends would go along to Belle Vue to watch the wrestling, where his favourite wrestler was "Bert Azaratti". Bert was a comparatively small man, who would initially suffer at the hands of his large cruel opponent, but when, as the underdog, the crowd had taken his side and started to encourage him on, he would proceed to demolish his opponent with deft skilled moves, to rapturous cheering. The referee was usually "Dick the Dormouse", a popular man who would first announce the rules of the contest over the microphone, the crown joining in enthusiastically, en masse, with the last of the rules, copying his slow, stern theatrical delivery: ".... by two falls, one submission or a knockout."

An alternative to the wrestling for Mike and his friends was to watch the home team, the "Belle Vue Aces", racing at the Belle Vue motorcycle stadium, led by their captain, Split Waterman. Split was

---

[11:4] The author remembers being present at a variety event in the Hall in the late 1940s at which the young singer and comedienne, Betty Driver, was performing. Betty died in mid-2011, still going strong as the popular barmaid, "Betty", at the "Rover's Return" in the long-running television programme "Coronation Street". What great staying power!

born in 1907 and was a trials rider for BSA before taking up motorcycle racing in 1928, continuing to race until his retirement in 1954. Another great rider and favourite was Jack Parker. Mike's eyes were misty as he told them that these men, clad in leather, wearing heavy gauntlets and strong boots, with their appropriate club emblem, the Ace of Clubs, displayed on a white singlet on their chests, were the idols of the crowd. When they performed the victory lap at the end of a race, riding with their front wheels off the ground, they were cheered wildly by the spectators: they were heroes!

Mike told how the four-man events were thrilling, with the un-silenced engines, burning peanut oil to emit a delightful odour, pushing the bikes around the cinder-covered circuit at speeds of up to forty or fifty miles per hour. Whilst this speed is comparatively low compared to the speeds achievable on flat open roads, it is high for the short circuit of the race track.

No sooner had a rider come out of a corner, than he had to give his bike full throttle over the short distance before encountering the next corner, and then it was a matter of using his steel-shod boot on the track to stop his bike from skidding away as he fought to control it round the tight bend. The cinders would be sprayed up from under his boot, such that at the end of the race grounds-men would run onto the track with rakes to smooth its surface before the start of the next race.

Sometimes Mike and his pals would take in a bottle or two of "VP Cream", a cheap sweet port wine, to enhance the excitement of the event. Mike said that to this day it only took a two-stroke motor bike using peanut oil as lubricant to pass by him on the road to bring back all of his memories.

Mike told them that of the gang fights between the youths of different parts of the district. Up to about a hundred youths on each side would collect together and then gather stones to throw at each other in running battles that swept to and fro over the main roads and side streets, oblivious of the traffic. Recruiters would scour the area to try to increase the size of their own gang. Should a member of one gang be captured by members of the opposing gang, he would be given a quick beating-up and then sent on his way: nothing too severe, a bloody nose being quite sufficient, and ensuring a hero's welcome for the boy upon his return to his own ranks. Alex joined in, giving his description of the gang fights back in Glasgow, but stopped talking when he felt a sudden embarrassment as he remembered his own violent past: better that he should try to forget it.

When not engaged in such fights, the braver of the local kids would sneak onto the railway engines parked in their siding at the nearly loco yard, stealing coal from the tenders to take home, or fog signals to have fun with. The latter, small thin metal disks of about two inches diameter, with short flat wire clips that enable them to be attached to the top of the rails for an engine to explode as it passes over them, are easy to explode by means of a well-aimed half-brick.

Mike told then of a further way that the railway provided entertainment, albeit it of a dangerous nature. The local kids, dragging their younger siblings with them, would pick their way across the usually-shallow Gorton Brook and then make their way over to the unguarded railway lines that carried the commuting residents of relatively-affluent towns such as Marple, Disley and, further afield, Chapel-en-le Frith and other places south of Manchester. Quite often the incoming trains would be halted for a few minutes awaiting clearance to proceed onwards to the city. Upon catching site of an oncoming train, the kids would take off their foot-ware and that of their siblings and hide it nearby, then line up alongside the particular track that the train was running on: there were several tracks, with the constant possibility that a second train could approach at high speed from either direction on an adjacent track.

The kids would quickly assume an appearance of poverty and hunger, which in many cases was their normal condition, and then hold out their hand and implore the travellers to take pity on them with sad cries of "Penny down! Penny down!" They were always successful: they were never moved on by policemen or railway workers or security staff and the lines remained unguarded, and a source of money for the local kids year-by-year. An appalling accident-fraught situation! 'However,' Mike said, 'thankfully I never heard of the occurrence of a single accident.'

Sitting in the passage-way that led to the pub toilets was a group of elderly women, drinking bottled Guinness. Mike told them of three old women who had used to sit there when his father had first taken over the pub. These old women were dressed from head to foot in heavy black woollen clothing and wore shawls, the last ever to be seen in the neighbourhood. They would sit there all evening without moving, passing their money up to, and having their drinks handed down to them from, the bar. At the end of the evening they would get up to go home, leaving behind a strong smell of stale pee and a pool of fresh pee in the dished wooden seats that hadn't quite been able to be absorbed by their heavy clothing. His father, kind and understanding by nature, had used to curse and swear as he went to get the mop and bucket, heavily dosed with disinfectant to mask the smell of the pee, but he didn't ever say a reproachful word about it to the old ladies, explaining to Mike: 'It isn't the fault of the old dears: we all get old!'

The men in the vault were now making their way to the bar to order another drink, for the darts match was due to start and as soon as the Master of Ceremonies announced the start of the match by calling out "Game on", there would be no more drinks served, both in the vault and elsewhere in the pub, until each game had finished. As the first game, played between one man from each of the two teams, drew towards its conclusion, the bar staff quietly started to draw pints and line them up on the bar, ready for the rush of orders before the start of the next game.

The board used in the games was the Manchester board, a small board without trebles and with doubles no more than a quarter of an inch wide, not like the barn-door-size boards that were used down south. The board itself was a cross-section of the trunk of a softwood tree, and was soaked in a tub of water prior to the competition. The markings and divisions on the board were created by tapping lengths of thin flat strip, shaped as required, into the board, so that there was less chance of an arrow being deflected than there would be with a southern board, with its divisions and markings made up of a complete ring using relatively-thick galvanised wire, the ring just being stapled onto the board as a complete item.

The usual game was 301, starting and ending on a double. The scores were recorded in chalk on blackboards set on each side of the dart board, with an appointed member of one team calling out the score, and an appointed member of the other team then confirming the score by calling out "Check". If there should be any noise or conversation whatsoever in the vault, however muted, the MC would issue an appropriate reprimand. At the conclusion of the individual games, the teams played 501 for a gallon of ale.

The match over, there would usually be an exhibition of dart throwing given by an acknowledged expert from within the locality. On this evening the expert first covered the board with a page of newspaper, and then proceeded to put a dart into each double on the board, in numerical order. Considering the time that it had taken some members of the teams to get a double to start and to finish the game, this was a magnificent display. However, there was more to come. The darts expert called over his mate and stood him against the board. He then placed a sixpence,[11:5] which has a diameter of only about half-an-inch, into the corner of his mate's eye. He then walked back to the "oddie", the name for where the dart thrower stands. There was a call

---

[11:5] The sixpence was very similar to the 5p coin, in respect of both size and general appearance.

for silence, and the whole pub became hushed. Alex felt the skin on him arm stand on end! The thrower took careful aim and then threw the dart true to its mark, the sixpence stopping the dart dead, both the dart and the sixpence then falling to the ground. Before the customers in the pub could recover their composure, the thrower's mate made a quick round with a hat, collecting enough money for the two of them to drink all that they wanted for the rest of the evening.

Following the excitement of the match, and then the drama of the exhibition of dart throwing, the men in the vault relieved their tension by starting to sing. First there was "I've got a lovely bunch of coconuts", followed by "In barefoot days", with everybody joining in, and then someone started to sing another song:

'My brother, Sylvest, he's got a lot of hair upon his chest'
(with the assembly coming in with "Big chest!")
'It'd take all the Army and the Navy
to put the wind up Sylvest!'

After this the songs became increasingly bawdy, indeed vulgar, but with everyone joining in with great enthusiasm. Alex was delighted to be in their company: whatever Mr. Gilbraith had said about the English, those living in the north-west of the country, the same as those in the north-east, are good, friendly people.

As the men got drunker some of the Irish amongst them became a little maudlin, and one of them started to sing, in a fine tenor voice, "I'll take you home again Cathleen":

"I'll take you home again Cathleen, across the ocean wild and wide,
to where your heart has ever been, since first you were my bonny bride,"

Although having no Irish connections, Alex felt moved by the beauty of the song and of the singing. The song described how a man had taken his wife with him across the sea to England, when he was forced to leave Ireland to seek work. His wife had been homesick for Ireland, and he pledged to her that one day he would take her back, telling her that he had seen that:

"the roses all have left your cheek, I've watched them fade away and die;
your voice is sad when-e'er you speak, and tears be-dim your

loving eyes."

The song continued. One Irishman sobbed openly, to be comforted by his friend, who said to him 'Don't be ashamed to show how you miss and love your country Michael'.   When the singer had finished this song, he was persuaded, after an appropriate show of reluctance, to sing another lovely old song "Danny boy". This song tells how a young man, Danny, had to leave his wife, Eily, and go over to England to find work, as many Irishmen did, usually because of the failure of the potato crop due to potato blight, a disease which causes the potato tubers to rot in the ground. With a good potato crop, a barrel of salt herring and a stack of peats from the bog, a man and his family could live comfortably throughout the winter: the Irish economy was based on agriculture, so the failure of the potato crop meant starvation.

For two hundred years or more, thousands of young Irishmen folk, mostly men, have left their wives or sweethearts to go over to England or to America, often not to return. Although there were agencies that could send money back to their families in Ireland for them, as they were mostly illiterate peasant folk they could not write back home themselves. Those who went to England were given dangerous manual jobs such as digging the canals that were to provide the means of moving heavy loads, such as coal, iron ore, steel, bricks and porcelain, across the country, and digging the railway tracks and tunnels that were essential to Britain's industrial development

Many were killed, their bodies just being buried alongside their place of work in unmarked graves. [21]   No-one knew their names, other than "Paddy" or "Shamus", so their loved ones back home in Ireland could not be informed of their death, being left just to realise with the passage of time that their man, and provider, was never going to return home. Regrettably, some men, seduced by the better life-style in Britain, set up home with a local woman, and slowly forgot those waiting for them back in Ireland. It was a sad, dreadful situation.

The listeners in the pub joined in with the first verse, in which Eily tells Danny that she knows that he must leave, but begs that he return before too long:

"when summer's in the meadow,
or when the valley's hushed and white with snow",

and that she will:

"be here, in sunshine or in shadow",

then telling him:

"Oh Danny Boy, oh Danny Boy, I love you so."

After this the listeners fell silent, as the singer carried on with the second verse, in which Eily tells Danny that if he is too long in returning, she may be dead:

'But when ye come, and all the flowers are dying,
If I am dead, as dead I well may be,
Ye'll come and find the place where I am lying,
And kneel and say an Ave there for me."

At this point the room fell hushed, and beer pots were placed gently back onto the tables. The eyes of the listeners became fixed on the singer, as he started to sing the last few lines of the second verse:

"And I shall hear, though soft you tread above me,
and all my grave will warmer, sweeter be,
for you will bend and tell me that you love me,
and I shall sleep in peace until you come to me."

As he listened to these tragic and haunting words, the hair on the back of Alex's arms and neck rose, and he felt tears pressing inside his eyelids. One Irishmen, overcome with homesickness, shouted 'God save Ireland and God bless all Irishmen!' which was greeted by cheers from all of those in the room, English, Irish and Alex alike.

Alex had met many Irishmen before in Glasgow, but in his ignorance he had always thought of them in terms of their stereotypical image as amiable and somewhat comical and illogical characters, but now he was filled with understanding and respect for these people who leave the country and the people that they love so much, to work in a foreign land.

Alex had wondered why there is such a large proportion of Irishmen present in the pub. Mike explained that Liverpool was a major port of disembarkation for Irish immigrants, such that a hundred years ago one third of its population was of Irish stock, and that Manchester, being but thirty miles east of Liverpool, had become the home of a great number of these immigrants,[11:6] to serve as a major component of the

---

11:6 The author's maternal grandfather, James O'Neill, who was born in Ireland some

local workforce, but being of illiterate farming stock, having to do the rough menial jobs that were essential to Britain's industrial development. Whilst a short train journey could take any of them to the port of Liverpool and then a few hours on a ferry could take them to Dublin or Belfast, many of the Irish present, mainly those second-generation Irishmen who were born in Britain and those for whom their ties with their Irish kinfolk were weakened by time or commitments but who still felt intensely loyal to Ireland, never undertook this journey, instead keeping faith with their homeland and their fellow countrymen by the singing of such songs, both in the pubs and in the many Irish clubs that are to be found not only in the different parts of this city, but in all of the other cities throughout Britain. Alex was learning more about people, and becoming a better man in the process. 'Yes,' he said to himself, with feeling, 'God save Ireland and God bless all Irishmen!'

Five minutes before closing time, Mike pulled a big glass from under the counter and started to fill it with best mild. It wasn't the dimpled crown pot that was preferred in the north, nor was it the conical glass with an annular swelling towards the top to prevent the glass from slipping out of the hand of the drinker that was favoured in the south: it was simply an unusual two-pint-capacity conical glass. Mike placed the filled glass on the bar top, whilst all eyes turned towards the pub door. The pub became silent. Within a minute the door burst open and a man dressed in overalls and wearing a peaked railwayman's cap strode up to the bar and downed the contents of the glass in one go, to the cheers of all present, then placing the glass on the bar top for a refill.

Mike explained that the man worked on the railways and didn't get off his shift until ten minutes before closing time. By the time that he had got to the pub it was five minutes to go before closing time, so that in order to be able to join in with the spirit of the evening, he needed to do some catching up by quickly downing the first glass, after which he could relax amongst his friends with his refill.

At the end of the evening Laurie and Alex bade farewell to Mike, who wished them a safe journey home. The evening had been an education for Alex. As they made their way home on the following

---

time around 1880, left Ireland in the early 1900s to seek work in England, joining the British Army at the start of the First World War. From his youth, the author was advised by family members that because Grandfather James had left Ireland for economic reasons, i.e. not being able to find work, his children and grandchildren can claim Irish citizenship at any time. This would have been of some comfort to those leaving their homeland, but it is likely that only a few descendents have ever taken this opportunity.

morning, he kept turning over in his mind what would have happened if the dart had landed in the man's eye. Laurie, who was not so bothered, replied 'Then he would put a patch over the blind eye and next week he would put the sixpence in the corner of his other eye. They will still want to have a drink. Life still has to go on.' Perhaps so. Alex shivered at the thought.

Chapter Twelve

Following their visit down the mine, Alex and Matt had become even greater mates. In addition to coming round for Sunday lunch, Matt would call in mid-week, either to sit down for a chat, or to invite Alex to come out for a walk. One weekend, when Aggie had taken Luke with her to the shops, then intending to take him to visit her family, Alex and Matt took a bus to Tynemouth, and then walked north along the cliff edge overlooking Cullercoats, where kippered herrings had first been produced.

Reaching the promenade, they turned north. On their left was a magnificent sweeping Georgian terrace, built in stone and reflecting the wealth of the merchants and business men who had worked in Newcastle in earlier times, and who had commuted daily to Newcastle from their coastal homes, whilst on their right was the ruined Tynemouth Castle that had defended the River Tyne for many centuries, from Viking raids through to the two World Wars. Set behind it is the ruined Tynemouth Priory.

During the World Wars the approaches to the Tyne had been a fruitful hunting ground for German U-boats, which had lain in wait for the ships of the Merchant Navy delivering essential food and war supplies. The charts of the approaches to the Tyne are dotted with the wrecks of such ships that had fallen victim to enemy submarines when only a few miles from home and safety. How well the U-boats that had congregated offshore from harbours and rivers such as the Tyne, lying in wait for defenceless merchant ships, had earned their name "Wolf packs!"

Alex and Matt decided to visit Tynemouth Castle. After looking around the ruins of what once must have been a beautiful building, but which were still able to conjure in the minds of the visitors an image of how the castle would have looked in its prime, they walked to its eastern extremity of its grounds, overlooking the North Sea. There they climbed a flight of steps to reach the top of a run of old concrete bunkers, which Matt explained was an arsenal. He pointed out to Alex the rusted remains of a mechanical system that had delivered shells from the arsenal to a big gun that had been mounted at that point. As a new shell arrived at the surface, it would fall forwards and trip a switch that stopped the delivery system, the next shell being advanced to the surface only when the previous shell had been removed, in this way reducing the risk of a major catastrophe within the arsenal from the activation of a shell by mishandling or from enemy action. Matt lingered over the mechanism in silence for a while, whilst he relived his memories.

He then told Alex that there had been three magazines in the arsenal for two 6 inch guns. He went on to say that in 1905 there was one 9.22 inch gun able to fire two rounds per minute to 21,000 yards - nearly 12 miles - on battleships and cruisers; two 6 inch guns to fire on destroyers; and two 12-pounder quick-fire guns for quick action against fast-moving torpedo boats within the harbour. A search-light was introduced to work with the 12-pounder guns, powered from a purpose-built engine-house.

Responding to Alex's interest, Matt went on to tell him about the enormous muzzle-loading guns, weighing over 100 tons and capable of firing a 1-ton shell, that had been built towards the end of the 19th century at the Armstrong factory in Newcastle, two of which had been set up in Malta and two in Gibraltar in the early 1900s to defend their harbours against the threat posed by the rebuilding and strengthening of the Italian navy. Alex was surprised at the extent of Matt's knowledge, and realised that he must have had previous experience of military ordnance and, in particular, of the ordnance at this castle, almost certainly from during the Great War.

Matt reflected upon the way thousands of men from the north had gone off to fight in the Great War, often enlisting in "Pals" battalions, such as the "Sheffield City Pals", where the entire staff of an office, workshop, or football team, would enlist together to fight side-by-side with their friends and colleagues, taking reassurance from each other's presence. Later, after a number of "Pals" battalions had suffered severe losses during a particular offensive, leaving some towns with a large proportion of their young men dead, injured or taken prisoner, the Army had abandoned the idea of "Pals" battalions and distributed its intake randomly over the whole of the armed forces, so as in turn to distribute future losses over the whole of the country.

Matt told Alex that, in one day, 57,000 officers and men were either wounded or killed in the Battle of the Somme, summing up his view of war with the sad observation 'What an obscene war, with so many young men dead on both sides, all fighting for their country and their families, and in the name of the same God!' Alex didn't question Matt about his personal war experience: if Matt wanted to talk about it he would do so in his own time. He walked on a short way, leaving Matt to his thoughts.

Also at the eastern end of the castle grounds is a cemetery, with big thick headstones from the eighteenth century and earlier, standing up strongly on the headland against the prevailing wind coming in over the North Sea, unrestrained for six hundred miles. Alex stopped at one headstone, bearing the family name "Shipley". The general period of the graves in this part of the cemetery was around 1800, Alex deducing that all of the names probably having been carved before the 1840s.

Alex was surprised to see that despite very heavy erosion, the name "Ann Shipley" stood out clearly. Using a board tht was standing outside a nearly Gardeners' hut, he compared the thickness of the headstone at the level of the carved name with its thickness down at ground level, which indicated that there had been about half-an-inch of erosion of the front face of the headstone. However, with reference to where the front face of the gravestone had been originally, the stone at the bottom of the carved letter "S" had 'retreated' into the stone by about seven-eighths of an inch more than had the surface of the stone at the edge of the carving.

From the other headstones in the immediate area, he saw that the depth of the original carving had been about a quarter of an inch, albeit that the bottom of the carving had not been flat. Why had there been so much more erosion at the bottom of the carving than elsewhere, as the material at the bottom of the hole might logically be thought to be more protected from the wind?

The name "Ann Skipley" was still clear to read, although it had been trans-located back into the virgin material by such a large amount. How was this possible? Moreover, why should the depth of the trans-located hole be greater than when it was carved originally? He called Matt over and pointed out to him this very puzzling phenomenon. Matt studied the headstone for a few minutes and then gave Alex his explanation.

'This headstone is made of sandstone, which is a very soft stone that is easily eroded. The wind coming in at this spot can sometimes be travelling at fifty miles an hour, or even more in really bad weather. Whilst the wind is coming in over the North Sea it can pick up salt spray from the waves, and it can also pick up sand from the beach. When this particle-laden wind strikes the headstone it acts like a mild sand-blasting machine, such as is used to clean the buildings in the town centre. In this case the blasting, although mild, has acted continually for more than a hundred and fifty years, so the erosion of the soft sandstone isn't surprising. When the wind hits the corner of these carved letters, it can be deflected sideways, so the wear is less there, and similarly when it hits the corner of the gravestone, but when it hits a flat surface where the air can't move to one side as easily, a lot of the particles it is carrying carry on moving forwards and strike the surface of the stone, causing wear. In the case of the air deflected from the side of the characters into the bottom of the carving, the whole of the particles can do no other than strike the bottom of the carving, making it much deeper.'

Alex was impressed with Matt's explanation. Although not having had much in the way of formal education, Matt was the deepest thinking and wisest man that Alex had ever met. He thanked his luck for having given him such a fine man as a friend. However, this is the way of the North East, where there are many men and women who didn't have the opportunity for extended education in their youth, with the boys having to leave school at an early age to work in the shipyards or down the pits, and the girls to go into domestic service or factories. Nevertheless, these people are highly intelligent with immense reasoning power, a great knowledge of practical matters and also a deep understanding of human behaviour.

Apart from these mental attributes, they are also very family minded and are always there to support each other, young or old. They keep their minds active with hobbies and interests and lead a contented life. Unfortunately, their unassuming manner and their unsophisticated dialect leads to their qualities often being unappreciated by those from elsewhere, but what magnificent people they are!

After they had finished their visit to the castle, Matt, always a mine of information, told Alex that Northumberland has the greatest concentration of castles in the whole of Britain, built as staging posts and as strongholds from which to venture north against the Scots. However, it was not all one-sided, as on many occasions these very castles had been subjected to siege and sacking by Scottish armies. Alex was pleased that, because his ancestors had resisted the enforced union with the English for so long and had fought so bravely, such enormous and expensive structures as the castles in Northumberland and elsewhere had had to be built.

Sometimes they walked as far as Whitley Bay, where Alex would hear Glasgow accents similar to his own: Whitley Bay was a popular holiday place for Glaswegians. Their days-out together drew Alex and Matt even closer. They both looked forward to the next trip and to another day in each other's company. With their increasing familiarity they would poke fun at each other and make unflattering remarks about each other's home country.

One day, after they had decided to walk up to the north of Whitley Bay and walk over the causeway to St. Mary's island, Alex said to Matt 'Come on Dad, let's get a move on or the causeway will be under water when we get there!' Matt stopped dead in his tracks, and replied in an angry voice 'Less of the Dad, you young bugger! I can match you any day!', mistakenly thinking that Alex was mocking him for his advanced years. Alex was dismayed, thinking that Matt had objected to being called dad, and replied in an unsure, embarrassed voice 'I'm sorry Matt. I didn't mean to offend you, it's just that I've come to think of you as the dad I never had.'

Matt's expression softened, and he walked up to Alex. Placing his hands on Alex's shoulders he said 'That's alright son.' The two men looked at each other in silence for a few moments and then hugged each other. Eventually Matt said 'Come on then, or else everyone will think we're a pair of brown hatters.' and with the tension eased, they both laughed and then carried on with their walk.

That night, back in his own flat, Matt opened the chest of drawers in his living room and took out a small cardboard box. After a short search he took out a faded photograph showing a smart young First World War soldier, standing alongside a seated young woman of great beauty. He gazed at the photograph for several minutes, his mind lost in memories, and then he said quietly 'You would have loved Alex, Beattie. He's the son we always wanted.'

Matt then put the photograph back into the box and returned it to the chest of drawers. He had left his sweetheart Beattrice to go off to fight in World War I, suffering the atrocious conditions at the front and even spending his twenty-first birthday in the trenches. Against the odds, he had survived the conflict and had returned to marry his loved one. They had set up home in a small terraced house in Pelaw, and he had got a job down the mines.

After only a few months Beattrice told him that she was pregnant and they both waited in eager delight for the birth of their first child. However, there were complications, and the baby was still-born. Beattrice developed septicaemia and died three days later. After the double-funeral of his wife and his child, Matt carried on his life without regard for those around him. His fellow miners knew what he was suffering and in kindness left him to come to terms with his loss in his own way and in his own time. For many months Matt cursed the God that he had earlier believed in, for having brought him unscathed through the war only to lose his child and the only woman he had ever loved. He lay awake at night, his thoughts filled with what might, and should, have been: a loving wife and a fine young child, and a bright future for the three of them together.

Despite numerous opportunities, as there were many young widows or fiancées of those lost in the Great War who would have welcomed his attention, he never wanted another woman, seeking only the companionship of his fellow miners, many of whom had lived through the same conditions at the front as himself and with whom he felt a bond. However, after all these years, he felt that he and Beattie now had a son, Alex, and said a silent prayer of thanks to the God that he had rejected so long ago.

On some weekends when the weather was good, Matt, Alex, Aggie and Luke would go out walking together, either to the shops or to the local park. Alex rejoiced in the smiles that they received from passers-by, who saw them as a nice family group: granddad, father, mother and son. He relished his observed status as father, and would put his arm across Luke's shoulders as they walked along. Aggie would watch the two of them laughing together and teasing each other, feeling happier than she had felt since her husband had left her. The thought of her husband could bring sadness to her and a cloud to her face. She had loved him dearly and had been distraught when he had left her for another woman, despite the regular assurances of her friends and family that she was better off without him, and would one day meet another man, one who was loyal, kind and good.

Aggie felt that she would soon have to make up her mind about Alex, for she knew that he loved Luke as a son, and several times she had caught him glancing at her with a look on his face that meant only one thing: he wanted her as his woman. It wasn't that she didn't have any love for him, but she was still married and lived in hope that her husband still loved her and might one day want to return to her and Luke.

Aggie came in from work one evening to say that she had seen a notice in the paper-shop advertising a "Mystery Coach Tour" on the following Sunday. They all thought that this was a grand idea, so Aggie went along to the shop and booked the last four seats. Come the Sunday they met the coach outside the paper-shop, after which the coach set off in a westerly direction, towards Carlisle.

Partway along, at the town of Hexham, they turned north on a lesser road until they came out on the Military Road, running parallel to, and in some places on top of, the remains of Hadrian's Wall. Along this road were little hamlets such as "Once Brewed" and "Twice Brewed", although how and why they had been given these strange names even Matt didn't know.

They eventually reached the parking place for "Housesteads", a Roman staging post on Hadrian's Wall. Leaving the coach they trekked for about a quarter of a mile up to the Wall. Housesteads covers a large area, with the remains still to be seen of living quarters, latrines, bath-houses and grain-stores, with the living quarters heated by means of the floors being set on short columns, the space between the floor and the ground having warm air passing through it from external fires.

Despite many of the stones from the Wall and its staging posts and watch towers having been removed some hundreds of years ago by farmers for use in constructing their farm buildings, and by civil engineers in building the Military Road, the function and size of the many different buildings can be seen clearly. Luke was intrigued to see the way that the water from a stream had been led into one building for use first in a washroom, then led away to open-channel latrines, finally the body-waste and waste water running out of the building and continuing on its way down the stream. This was an early, albeit primitive, example of the flushing of lavatories, the modern flush-toilet having been introduced during Victorian times, when the pioneering work of a man named "Crapper" gave rise to the expression "I'm going for a crap.", still used commonly, albeit informally, at the present day.

Matt told Alex that the Wall had been build to repel the fierce northern tribes, but couldn't resist adding that in recent years there had been the suggestion to rebuild the Wall to enable the monitoring and control of the Scottish football supporters as they travelled south on away-matches, these supporters being noted for their 'exuberance' before, during and after a match. Alex checked that he was out of ear's reach of Aggie and Luke, and then with a grin on his face whispered to Matt 'Get stuffed!', which caused Matt to chuckle. Alex then countered by saying that at least the Celts had successfully resisted the Romans 'rather than rolling over onto their backs like your side did!' Then, with honours even, they let the matter rest.

Next the coach took them to Corbridge, to see the Roman supply town of Corstopitum. This was of similar construction to Housesteads, with grain-stores, barracks, latrines, washrooms, and the houses of the commanding officer and his subordinate officers. There was a quite modern museum nearby that contained many relics that had been unearthed in the vicinity. Alex stood in front of a large stone tablet on which were carved many Latin characters. An adjacent notice explained that the tablet had been erected by a group of officers in memory of one of their colleagues. He was moved to think that, so long ago, men would go to such lengths to honour and to remember a good friend and comrade.

After taking lunch at a Corbridge pub, the coach set off again, this time heading east towards the coast. Reaching the coast road, the coach headed north until it came to the village of Bamburgh, and shortly beyond it, to the Grace Darling Museum. This was a small but interesting museum, telling how Grace and her father had rowed out in heavy seas to rescue the crew from a ship that had run aground on the rocks of the Farne Islands. She had become a national heroine, and a shining example to woman everywhere as to what womankind is capable of doing when the need arises.

After this is was time to return to Newcastle. As they made their way along, Alex noted several village names ending in "ington" and asked Matt why this was so. Matt told him that there are many hamlets and villages along the east coast with names ending in "ington", such as Cramlinton, Bedlington, and Ashington, and that this resulted from some of the Vikings arriving here from over the North Sea having settled in the area, "ington" meaning "family farm of", so that Ashington originally meant the family farm of a Viking called "Ash". Matt was indeed a mine of information.

Alex was happy with the way that his life was going, apart from feeling an increasing urge to tell Aggie of his feelings for her. On the odd occasion that he taken hold of her hand in an innocent manner, after a minute or two she had found an excuse to withdraw it. He didn't know what that to do next. Contrarily, his working life had gone from strength to strength. The depot manager had been impressed by his dedication to work, and his obvious intelligence, and had soon promoted him to special responsibility for the North-East delivery of household effects from abroad. All was going well.

However, one morning the manager called him into his office and told him of a problem that had arisen. There had been two claims for missing goods, made some time after delivery, where the owners in both cases had signed at the time of delivery that all of the goods had been off-loaded. The manager didn't know what to do, but was concerned in that the same pair of delivery men had been involved in the two cases.

Alex asked if there was anything unusual that the two deliveries had in common, to which the manager replied 'Nothing really, except that, in both cases, there had been some slight confusion, in that the person ticking-off the boxes as they were being carried in had thought that there was one box missing, but the matter was soon cleared up when the missing box was found, safe and sound. He asked Alex to think about the matter over the weekend and then come in to see him again on the following Monday.

Alex turned over the problem time and time again in his mind, eventually deciding that the answer lay in the list of goods to be delivered that the owners had signed for as being off-loaded in full. He considered the ways in which the owners could have been deceived into thinking that all of the goods were present, whereas in reality one carton of the delivery still remained within the delivery van. Late on the Sunday evening the explanation came to him, and he couldn't wait to put the explanation to his boss on the following morning. After having listened to Alex for a half-hour, and discussed the matter for a further half-hour, the manager rang up the local police station and asked to speak to the inspector in charge. Later in the day he went down to the station, and spoke again to the inspector, who was accompanied by two detectives. They agreed a plan to be implemented at the first opportunity.

Some two weeks later, a consignment of overseas goods was scheduled for delivery in the area, the manager assigning to the job the two men of whom he had suspicions. As their delivery van entered the local area, a nondescript old car, with two plain-clothed detectives in it, quietly took up a position some distance behind the van. Arriving at the house, the delivery men gave the owner the list of goods to be delivered, and asked him to stand by the front door and tick off each box as it was taken into the house.

The men had decided earlier that they would steal a box of crystal glassware, such items, whilst being expensive, not being likely to be missed until some time later. During the unloading, whilst carrying in the boxed television set, the delivery man called out the number of the box containing the crystal, whereupon the owner ticked off that number. The unloading went on, until the last box was taken into the house, whereupon the owner pointed out that there was one item not ticked off, the television set.

The delivery men expressed concern, and the wife, looking worried and feeling tired, queried the husband as to whether he could have made a mistake and not entered a tick against the TV as it was being carried in. The children were impatient, as they wanted to sit and watch their favourite programmes. After a further few minutes, the delivery men started to shuffle and look at their watches, pointing out that they were due back at the depot. Suddenly one of them said 'Wait a minute, I'm sure I carried the television set into the living room!'

They all made their way into the living room where, sure enough, the set was found safe and sound within one of the boxes. The faces of the delivery men were wreathed in smiles at the problem having been 'solved', whilst the wife smiled weakly at the husband in relief. The children merely muttered to each other what an idiot their dad was. The husband was still not convinced that the full number of boxes had been unloaded, but when confronted by the now hostile late-to-check-in faces of the delivery men, the pleading face of the tired wife and the exasperated remarks of the children, he yielded and signed for a full and complete delivery.

As the delivery van drove off, the small car parked some distance away moved off also, and followed the van, which did not go back to the depot, but to a side road off the main road, where the box of crystal glass was unloaded and taken through the back door of a shop, after which the delivery van set off on its way back to the depot. One of the detectives in the car got out and walked to the main road, where he noted the name of the shop, then ringing up the police station on his radio telephone to ask for the issue of a search warrant. The two detectives waited to see if the box would be brought out from the shop, whereupon they could legitimately ask to see its contents. However, nothing happened.

After two hours two uniformed officers arrived in a patrol car with the search warrant and the two detectives then knocked on the shop door, whilst the two uniformed officers stood guard at the back door. Apart from finding the box of crystal glassware inside the shop, the detectives also found numerous other stolen items. Ultimately the two delivery men and the owner of the shop were sentence to a period of imprisonment by the Crown Court.

At Alex's request, the manager of the removal depot didn't allow Alex's part in the recovery of the stolen property to be made known generally, but he called him into his office after the trial to shake his hand warmly and to tell him that the Board of Directors had asked him to pass on to Alex personally the news that his advancement within the company was assured. Alex didn't tell anyone about his part in the recovery of the stolen property or in the arrest of the thieves concerned. He didn't want praise, but more so, he didn't want any of the friends or relatives of the convicted men to learn of his identity and exact revenge on Aggie, Matt or Luke.

His strengthening relationship with Matt enabled Alex to talk more openly about his past, and of the violent hatred that he used to feel for the English. Matt said simply that he had been brain-washed, and that those doing the brain-washing had not got their facts right. Alex protested that the atrocities committed by the English on the Scots, such as at the Battle of Culloden, were historical facts, beyond dispute. Matt thought for a moment before giving his reply.

'Yes, the English soldiers did kill the trapped Scots, but only under orders. The soldiers of the day were just ordinary village lads, most of whom hadn't been outside of their own village until they signed up. They had no understanding of the political situation between Scotland and England and had been told that the Scots were rebels, bent on the destruction of the union between the two countries. They were not permitted to think for themselves, nor could they question their officers as to the reasons why they were faced with having to fight and kill the Scots: the only thing that they knew was that if they didn't obey their orders they would be subjected to immediate execution. What else could they do?

The brain-washing of servicemen carried on then has carried up to the present day, including during the Great War and during World War II. Why would both the Allied and the Axis forces in the Great War believe almost to a man that 'Right and God' were on their side without having been brainwashed? The evil-doers were the ruling classes of the period, both Scots and English, with the soldiers being just pawns who carried out their orders.

Why should the present-day ordinary Englishmen and Englishwomen be held responsible for actions committed under the orders of the ruling classes of almost three hundred years ago? Whilst the English ruling classes were subjugating the ordinary Scots, they were also subjugating the ordinary English working class: sending the seven "Tolpuddle Martyrs" to Australia, away from their wives and children, just for wanting to form a trade union to improve the working conditions of farm labourers; and sending in the cavalry at the "Peterlee Massacre" to a peaceful meeting of "Luddites" - so names after Ted Ludd, who 38 years earlier, in frustration, had broken two knitting frames with a hammer - to protest against the poor economic conditions arising from the industrialisation of the textile industry, resulting in the killing of fifteen protesters and the injuring of several hundred other protesters.

The ruling classes made slaves of the ordinary people of many nations throughout the world, including those of both Scotland and England. You Scots should regard the ordinary Englishman as a brother and fellow sufferer, not as an enemy to be vilified. The main cause of racial hatred and xenophobia is fear and ignorance. Would you want young Luke to be hated by your fellow Scots?'

Alex was taken aback by Matt's sustained outpouring and his depth of feeling. He hadn't looked at the situation from this point of view before, but had simply accepted without question all that Mr. Gilbraith and his ilk had poured into his unquestioning ears. Virtually all of the English that he had met since arriving in Newcastle had been good honest folk, who had received him warmly and welcomed him into their company as a friend. Alex turned to Matt and said simply and sincerely 'Yes Matt, you are right.' Alex had finally and truly overcome his instilled deep-rooted hatred of the English!

Matt's spirited words had left him breathless, and he sat quietly, his shrunken chest heaving in trying to draw air into his damaged lungs. Alex watched him with concern, cursing the bosses and the government who had sent brave men, such as Matt, back from both of the world wars to labour deep underground in ill-ventilated dust-ridden mines. There were still social injustices to be overcome but, given time, he believed that the Labour Party, or if that party should not be in office, then some future government, would surely fulfil the promise made to those returning from the Second World War to provide them with "a country fit for heroes to live in." Without realising it, Alex had transferred the anger that he had always felt for the deprivation that he had seen in Glasgow, away from the ordinary English people and onto the nation's political leaders, past and present, of whatever ilk, Scots and English alike.

Over the next few months, Matt and Alex's outings became less frequent: instead, they spent their time together just talking. Alex could see the deterioration in Matt's health, and this depressed him greatly, as he loved this old man dearly. Matt's condition continued to deteriorate, and soon he was confined to bed, with a regular visit from the doctor. Alex went to see him each evening, and they would sit and talk, until Matt's flagging strength and prolonged bouts of coughing told Alex that it was time for him to leave. The day came when it was obvious to Alex that Matt didn't have long for this world, and he could tell by the despair in his eyes that Matt felt this also. He sat and held the old man's hand in his own, and when Matt fell asleep he leaned forward and kissed him on the forehead, whispering 'Goodbye Dad, I love you and I'll never forget you.'

Aggie arranged to stay with Matt the following day. Upon Alex's return from work, her anguished face as she met him at the door told him all that he needed to know. Matt had slipped into unconsciousness and died that afternoon. Alex went into Matt's bedroom, and looked down at the slight figure lying in the bed. Matt had not been a big man in life, but his knowledge and personality had made him a man of great presence. The shell of a man lying there bore no resemblance to Matt in life.

The funeral was arranged for two days hence. At the funeral there were only a few mourners: Alex, Aggie, Luke, two men from the Miners' Institute, four of Matt's mates from the pit, a representative of the British Legion and one former fellow serviceman from the Great War. Time had taken away many of the men who had served with Matt at the Front.

The minister, a fresh-faced young man, spoke of the courage of the "heroes" of Matt's generation, who had given up their jobs and left their wives and families to go to the Front and fight for the good of their fellow men, but Alex was unmoved: what good had it done Matt, and what of the hundreds of thousands of young men who hadn't returned from the conflict, or had returned disabled, or severely mentally or physically handicapped? The sooner the politicians of the world do their jobs properly and negotiate peace, rather than send off young men to become "heroes", the better: the world can do without young men, on both sides of a conflict, being send away from their loved ones to suffer home-sickness, mental and physical hardship, fear, grief at the loss of comrades, injury and death. It's a sick world! He said a silent prayer to Matt, telling him that should there be an afterlife, which both he and Matt had doubted, they would meet and enjoy each other's company once again.

After the funeral, Alex, Aggie and Luke returned to their apartment, where Alex sat in front of the fire, deep in his thoughts of Matt, his recently found, and now lost, Dad. When Luke said goodnight to him, he only uttered a quiet 'Goodnight lad' in reply, hardly being aware of Luke and Aggie's presence in the room. He stared into the fire for two more hours, whilst Aggie sat and watched him, distressed at seeing him in such grief and not knowing what to do for the best. However, as bedtime came, she realised that she alone could ease his suffering. Stopping at the bottom of the staircase, she turned to him and said 'I'm going to bed now love. Don't be long in coming up.'

Alex muttered a reply, poked the fire, replaced the fireguard and made his way upstairs. Reaching the top of the stairs, he saw that the door of Aggie's room was open, and realised the meaning of her words to him only minutes before. He walked across the landing and into her room, closing the door quietly behind him.

The following day Alex went round to Matt's apartment to clear it out. The furniture was old and of little value, so Alex decided that it would be best to give it, along with the few pots and pans, kitchen utensils, and the newer of Matt's clothes, to the Salvation Army, which would arrange for its uplifting and its distribution to the needy. The local council could come and collect the remaining items.

Alex looked in the chest of drawers and found a small cardboard box. Lifting the lid, the first thing that he saw was a small velvet-covered box, and the next thing a single sheet of ruled paper, on which Matt had written his Will, duly witnessed by a member of the Miners' Institute. The Will said simply "I leave everything to Alexander James MacAlister." In the box was a bankbook showing that over his working life Matt had accumulated a sizeable sum of money. Next was a small cloth wallet containing Matt's war medals. Finally there was a faded old envelope, inside which were several documents and a photograph of a uniformed man, who must have been Matt during his service in the Great War, standing alongside a seated young woman. Looking through the documents, Alex first found a marriage certificate for Matthew Paul Connaught and Beattrice Alice Wilson, and then, sadly, a death certificate for Beattrice Alice Connaught.

Alex realised that Matt had been only twenty-three years old and Beattrice only twenty-one years old when they had married, with Beattrice dying in childbirth whilst only just twenty-two years old. Below the envelope containing the documents were two dozen or so letters sent by Matt and Beattrice to each other whilst Matt was at the front. Alex sighed at the simplicity yet sincerity of the love that the letters conveyed. Two young people in an awful situation, dreaming of the life that they would have together when Matt returned from the war.

After reading just a few of the letters, Alex felt that he had no right to pry into their private world, and returned all of the letters to the box: perhaps he would read them at some time in the future, when he had come to terms with the loss of Matt. He felt distressed that poor Matt had lived for close-on sixty years in isolation since Beattrice's death, without the love of a woman, or the warmth of her body in bed alongside him to comfort him during cold winter nights.

Alex picked up the cardboard box, along with the only other of Matt's personal possessions that he wanted to keep, Matt's strong leather belt with a big brass buckle that he had worn to the pit. It was the kind of belt that could serve a miner all of his working days, and then be passed on to his son or grandson to serve them, in turn, all of their own working days. Matt had obviously valued it and looked after it, from the gloss of the leather and the gleam of the brass buckle. Alex would treasure this belt to the end of his own days.

He walked along to the local bank and asked to see the manager. Once seated inside the manager's office, he showed him the Will and the bankbook, then telling him that he wanted the deposit in the bank account to be transferred to a new account in Luke's name. The manager didn't query the simple Will or Alex's request, but simply filled in the details of the new bankbook and handed it over to Alex. When Alex got back to the apartment he handed first the velvet box to Aggie. Inside the box was a beautiful gold chain and locket that had belonged to Beattrice, her wedding-day gift from Matt. She opened the locket. It contained two photographs, one of Matt and one of Beattrice, taken when they were newly-wed. Her eyes filled with tears and she muttered 'I have never owned anything so beautiful. I will treasure it all my life.' Next he gave her the bankbook, saying that he had also found this amongst Matt's possessions. It was fitting that Luke should have Matt's money, as Matt had been as a grandfather to him. Alex himself had received the greatest gift of all from Matt: his love as a father.

217

During the following months Alex experienced happiness and contentment as he had never known them before. Although his life was tinged with sadness of the loss of Matt, he now had a woman and a son of his own. Luke had accepted that Alex and his mum had entered a new phase in their relationship, and he was happy for them. Although Alex would have liked to, he could not bring himself to ask Luke to call him dad, for he was aware that Luke still had thoughts of his father. Nevertheless, the relationship between Alex, Aggie and Luke was a close as anyone could wish for. When they went out together, Luke would walk between them, holding each of them by the hand.

Alex began to think that he would like Aggie to have his child, and raised with her the question of her seeking a divorce. Her response was one of confusion. Much as she loved Alex, she had always harboured the hope that one day her husband would return to her and Luke. She forestalled Alex by saying that she needed time to come to terms with the idea, so Alex let the matter drop for the time being.

Alex realised that he had been living with Aggie and Luke for over a year and was surprised that so much time had passed. Life continued well for them as the months continued to pass by, but one day Alex noticed that Aggie seemed prepossessed, becoming flustered when he asked her a simple question. He thought at first that she might have been experiencing early symptoms of the menopause, or that she might have an illness that she didn't want to disclose to him. He even thought that it could be the unpleasant weather that they had been having for the last few days: that the cold winter winds blowing in from the North Sea were depressing her.

Eventually be became so concerned that he sat her down in the chair and demanded to know that was wrong with her. Aggie simply stood up and went over to the dresser, taking an envelope from one of the drawers, then handing it to Alex without a word. He took out a single sheet of paper from the envelope, finding it to be a letter from her husband Jack, who explained that the young woman he had run off with had left him, and that he wanted to return to Aggie and Luke.

Alex looked into Aggie's eyes, seeing the distress that she was feeling. After all, Jack was her legal husband and the father of her son. She knew that Luke still missed his father, even though at the same time he loved Alex. Jack went on in his note to say that he wanted to call round to the flat on the coming Saturday afternoon.

The atmosphere between Alex and Aggie was strained for the rest of the week, even Luke sensing that something was wrong. On the Saturday morning Aggie took Luke out shopping, whilst Alex attended to a wobbly shelf in the kitchen. Towards noon Aggie returned, having left Luke at a friend's house on the way home. Alex and Aggie spoke formally and politely to each other, with none of the previous warmth that had typified their relationship, both of them feeling embarrassment at the situation that they were in. Alex asked if he should leave the apartment before Jack arrived, but Aggie asked him to stay to meet Jack.

The time passed agonisingly slowly, but at 1 o'clock there was a knock at the door. Aggie opened it and asked Jack to come in. As he entered the room he glanced at Alex guiltily, but then pulled himself together and introduced himself to him. There was a period of silence, whilst all three stood avoiding eye contact, until Alex said 'This is a matter for you two to sort out. I'll go down to the pub and be back in an hour.'

At the pub he downed two pints, but three quarters of an hour after he had left the apartment he got up and walked out of the pub and down the street until he came to a house with a note in the window "Lodger wanted. Inquire within". He sensed that Aggie's decision would go against him, and he didn't want any delay in moving out of the apartment and into other accommodation.

When Alex got back to the apartment, neither Aggie nor Jack would raise their eyes from the floor: the decision was clear. He said to Aggie 'I'll go and pack my case.', returning to the room a few minutes later carrying the same small case that he had brought with him when he had arrived two years ago. Through her tears Aggie tried to explain the reason for her decision to him, but he cut her short gently. 'Jack is your husband and Luke's father. There is no need for an explanation.'

As he made to leave the room Jack called for him to stop, and then walked over to him and offered him his hand. 'I'm sorry Alex.' he said with sincerity. 'You have been good to Aggie and Luke. I hope that the future will be good to you in return.' Alex grasped his outstretched hand, smiled a reply and then left.

The next day Alex told the depot manager of his problem and of his decision to leave the area, after having completed the statutory four weeks' notice. The manager was dismayed, for he had developed a soft spot for Alex and knew that he would miss him. Alex's leaving would also be a loss to the company. He left his office for a few minutes, and then came back with a circular from Head Office advising of a vacant post of Deputy Manager at the company's office in Singapore. 'You deserve this job Alex.' he said, handing him the circular. 'I know that you can handle it. Let me put your case to Head Office.'

Four days later the manager called Alex into his office to advise him that the Board of Directors had approved his appointment, at a generous salary, and further had suggested that rather than complete his period of notice at the Newcastle branch, he should join a ship leaving the Tyne for Singapore on the following Monday, using the six weeks aboard the ship en-route to Singapore to familiarise himself with company policy and with the nature of the company's business in the Far East. Alex accepted the post without delay, and thanked the manager profusely, who would hear none of it, still being grateful for Alex's major part in sorting out the thefts that had caused him so much concern only a few months before. They parted with a handshake, with the manager wishing Alex 'All the best.'

Alex called by Aggie's apartment on the way back to his lodgings that evening. Aggie invited him in uneasily, and both Jack and Luke, whilst greeting him warmly, looked at him apprehensively. Alex told them of his new appointment in Singapore and of his departure three days hence. All three of them congratulated him sincerely, and Luke came forward and clasped his hand without embarrassment, telling him with wet eyes 'I'll miss you Alex, you are my best pal.'

Both Aggie and Jack smiled at this. Alex bent down and kissed Luke on the forehead, telling him 'Now you be a good lad to your mum and dad, or I'll be back on the next boat and come and tan your arse for you.' This broke the tension of the moment and they all laughed, then following Alex to the door, waving to him as he walked away up the street.

Three days later Alex boarded the ship. After the cook/steward had taken him to his small cabin, he lay on his bed and reflected on his life. What on earth was he doing here on this ship? What on earth was in store for him in Singapore? Eventually the ship got underway. Alex put on his top coat and walked to the bows of the ship through the flurries of snow that had been falling for the last few days, then standing at the guard rail looking at all the places with which he had become familiar during his time in Newcastle.

Eventually, the ship drew level with the North Shields Fish Quay, lying on the port side; and then it approached the harbour sea-walls, with "The Groyne" at South Shields lying on the starboard side; and the open sea directly ahead. Standing on the Groyne was a group of three figures: a man, a woman and a child. The figures started to wave vigorously and Alex realised who they were. He waved back in turn, and started to walk back along the starboard-side deck towards the stern, whilst the group started to walk along the long curving sea-wall on the south side of the river. For a short time, whilst they waved and waved, the combined speed of their walking offset to some degree the speed of the ship, but then Alex reached the stern and the group fell behind. As the ship went out onto the North Sea, Alex and the group continued to wave until they could no longer see each other. Alex made his way back to his cabin.

Whilst a better man than when he had left Glasgow, Alex had come to the North East still prejudiced and hard. Leaving the North East now, he was a changed man. He had found in Matt the father that he had never had, and had grieved at Matt's death. He had found a wife and son in Aggie and Luke, and then lost them, but he had not shed tears at the loss, as they were now reunited with Jack, husband and father, and looking forward to a life of happiness and fulfilment together. He had lost his paranoid hatred of the English, and had learnt to take people as he found them. In short, he had finally become a kind man, a thoughtful man, a good man.

Part 3: Singapore

Chapter Thirteen

After he had watched the coastline disappear from sight, Alex walked back to his cabin and again lay down on his bed. What lay ahead? He had not left the shores of Britain before, but now he was to travel thousands of miles, not only to a different continent, but also to a tropical island lying only about one degree north of the equator. He had learnt that the majority of the population of Singapore is Chinese, followed by Malays, Indians and then a sprinkling of Europeans. He had also been told that the country is hot and humid. What an enormous change this would be from his life up to the present time.

He picked up some of the company information that he had been given relating to overseas employment, and thumbed through it until he came to the section on "The Far East". This section had obviously been written by an old-fashioned time-served expatriate, with its warnings:

"Avoid close contact and familiarity with the local population, and always remember that one is a representative of one's country and must therefore behave with decorum and dignity at all times. Despite Singapore being a hot and humid country, one must maintain the company dress code and a suit and tie must be worn at all times whilst on company business, the only exception to this being at informal or sporting events, when a white open-necked shirt and white shorts are permitted. One must not go barefooted, and knee-length white stockings are to be worn with sandals and other casual foot-ware. Whilst it is expected that staff will bring their spouses to company functions, unmarried male staff are not to be accompanied by ladies of the local populace."

The section went on at length in this way, the author's name given at the end, to Alex's dismay, being that of the manager of the Singapore Branch, to whom Alex was to report directly: Major Horace Smedley (retd.). 'Damn!' he thought, 'What have I let myself in for?'

The journey from the Tyne, first down the east coast of England, then through the English Channel and then down past the Bay of Biscay, passed uneventfully. There was only one other passenger, a widower, Mr. Harrison, who had been employed by the company for thirty years and upon his early retirement had been granted as a farewell gift a round trip: Newcastle, Singapore, Hong Kong and back

222

to Newcastle. Mr. Harrison was determined to enjoy his trip and spent most of his time creating a record to give him something to look back upon during the cold winters awaiting him on his return to England. Daily, he would log their progress and enter records of the weather and of passing ships. 'We will soon reach the Straits of Gibraltar, and then the Suez Canal and on into the Red Sea!' exclaimed Mr. Harrison excitedly, enjoying every minute of the voyage.

Mr. Harrison was actually quite a nice man, but Alex found him rather dull and after three days, feeling guilty, he tried to avoid him as much as possible, whilst still being very cordial to him whenever they should chance to meet, such as when taking a stroll around the deck. However, he was still obliged to enter into conversation on the progress of the ship and like matters at meal times in the Officers' Mess, to which both himself and Mr. Harrison has been granted temporary membership. The junior officers were young, outgoing, and full of anticipation as to their success with the young ladies that they would entertain when they made port. The skipper was a good deal older and did not fraternise with either the junior officers or the passengers, taking his meals in his cabin, either alone, or with his immediate subordinate, when they would discuss the ship's business. Alex soon settled down on board, the monotony of the voyage being eased by the playing of cards with the off-duty officers in the mess, and in listening to his radio in his cabin.

Gradually they progressed towards the equator, eventually passing by the south of Ceylon, the weather becoming warmer by the day. Alex took to sitting on the fore-deck, finding it pleasant to sit out in the sun after having had to suffer the start of the depressing English winter before leaving Britain. The view from the fore-deck was boring, with the ship sailing out of sight of land and of other ships for most of the time. Alex said to himself 'Who in their right mind would want to be a sailor?'

The remaining days passed uneventfully, and then it was Christmas, with the Christmas-day lunch to be eaten in style, so the cook/steward informed him. Thus advised, Alex came along for the Christmas lunch dressed in a lightweight suit, a white shirt and a tie, as did Mr. Harrison, whilst those amongst the officers who were not on duty at the time, and able to attend the Christmas lunch, looked splendid in their formal dress. The captain himself joined them on that day and presided at the head of the table. The cook/steward did them proud, serving a meal of roast turkey with all the trimmings, followed by Christmas pudding and white sauce, and then mince pies. In contrast with his usual reserve, the captain did the rounds with whisky and gin, and then with brandy, whilst the cook/steward kept them all replenished with beer.

As the atmosphere became more relaxed, Alex, who was seated next to the captain, asked him if he didn't find the sea-going life a strain, especially for a married man. The captain, who by now was well oiled, replied 'No. After three months at sea, my wife and I have two weeks of re-union, and I mean frequent re-union,' emphasising the word "union" and at the same time winking at Alex to make his message absolutely clear, 'and then I come back to sea for a well-earned rest!' The captain later went on to mention that he was looking forward to their arrival in Singapore, as he had a couple of 'young friends' that he would be meeting again. Alex reflected upon his earlier view. It seemed that there were indeed some compensations for a life at sea!

On Saturday nights, those of the crew who were not involved in ship-board duties would congregate in one of the state-rooms below deck. Whilst taking a last walk around the deck, Alex saw a long-haired 'woman' dressed in a sexy ball gown go down to one of the state rooms, where she was received with loud cheers. He couldn't understand this, as to the best of his knowledge there were no women aboard. The next morning he raised the question with the cook/steward, who explained that the ship was a long time out of port and that the men 'have to entertain themselves as best they can.', no more needing to be said!

When they reached the west coast of Malaya and made their way south, the weather became more hot and humid. They could see flying fish skimming over the surface of the sea. These fish would leap off from the crest of a wave at great speed, and then glide through the air on their large extended pectoral fins for twenty yards or more, before diving into another wave, quickly emerging to repeat the performance again and again.

Mr. Harrison became more excited with each passing day, advising Alex as to the name of various places on the coast. 'Oh look! There's Penang!' he exclaimed, as an island came into view, and then scurried off to make an appropriate entry in his diary.

As they approached Singapore, Alex received a message over the ship's radio that he was to be met upon arrival by a young man, *Wang Yu Tian*[13:1], who was to be his assistant, and who would help him to settle down both into Singapore and into the company. Finally they reached Singapore, approaching the docks on Keppel Road, right at the southern coast of Singapore island, immediately opposite the small

---

[13:1]Throughout the novel, Chinese words are set in italics.

island lying only a few hundred yards off Singapore itself, called Pulau Blakang Mati. This island was noted for its big guns "facing the wrong way" during the Japanese advance down Malaya and the subsequent surrender of Singapore, during World War II. However, this was an unjustified criticism, as these guns had been placed to counter an attack on Singapore from the sea, and even if they had been "facing the right way" the hills of Singapore, albeit low, would have impaired their effective firing on the advancing Japanese, who soon crossed the causeway from Malaya and made their way towards the city centre.

As the ship tied up, and the gangways were moved into place, Mr. Harrison came over to Alex to wish him success in his new life in the orient. 'I envy you.' he said, 'If I were twenty years younger I would do anything to take the opportunity that you have been given.' Alex responded cordially to Mr. Harrison's kind words and wished him in return a happy and enjoyable voyage. As they shook hands in farewell, Alex realised a great truth. For all that Mr. Harrison had seemed to him to be a dull person, he was an enthusiast and was happy in his enthusiasm. He would always have an interest to pursue, whatever that interest might be, and he would never be bored with life and sit gloomily in a chair complaining about the weather, or the television programmes, or the neighbours' kids kicking a ball in the street.

Enthusiasm is one of the most important of human qualities, and an important element in all of the major achievements of mankind. If a person found a topic that fascinated him or her and led to that person wanting to learn more, indeed perhaps to devoting the rest of their life to its study, in other words to develop an obsession, this was to their own good and to the general good of mankind. Many advances in medicine, in the sciences and in the arts have been the result of one person's obsession. Too many people living a routine and uneventful life criticise others with the ability to immerse themselves in a topic and pursue it in great depth to the exclusion of all other interests, without realising the value of such people to society.

Alex wished that he had been more friendly towards Mr. Harrison and listened more to what he had told him as the voyage had progressed. He resolved to write a letter to him once he had become settled in Singapore, sent via the company offices in Newcastle, telling him of his experiences and observations of his new country.

Alex scanned the small crowd standing on the quayside awaiting the ship's arrival. Amongst the crowd he noted a relatively tall, slim, western-suited young Chinese man, who looked his way and then gave a welcoming smile. Alex was pleased at his first view of *Wang Yu Tian*, having feared that he would be encumbered with a dour Westernerhating oriental, who would be a thorn in his side. As soon as he had passed through the Disembarkation Hall, and loaded his two suitcases onto a trolley, he made his way over to *Wang Yu Tian*, who extended his hand to him and expressed the hope that Alex had had a good journey and was happy to be in Singapore.

The comments of Major Horace Smedley (retd.) faded to the back of Alex's mind as *Wang Yu Tian* spoke to him in such a friendly way and he shook the extended hand warmly. When *Wang Yu Tian* addressed him as "Mr. MacAlister", Alex reciprocating by calling him Mr. *Tian*, at which "Mr. *Tian*" smiled broadly and told him that the Chinese family name comes first, *Wang*, meaning "king", being his family name, although *Ong* and *Wong* also have the same meaning.

He asked Alex to call him George, having, as do many other Chinese, a western personal name preceding his Chinese name, as non-Chinese find this easier to remember and cope with in dealings with the company. Alex then reciprocated the gesture. However, George's face clouded over and he said that the company, meaning the major, discouraged over-friendliness between staff, and that it would be better if he were to call him Mr. MacAlister. Alex compromised by saying 'Okay then George, let it be Mr. MacAlister during working hours, but Alex at all other times.', which brought a relieved smile to George's face. They had got off to a good start, and Alex had learned something about Chinese customs, and also about the oriental mind, which is that is does not favour immediate or easy familiarity. His education in Singapore had begun!

They made their way out of the building and George called a taxi, giving their destination as a short string of what was, to Alex, high-pitched rasping unintelligible sounds. Alex asked George what language it was and George told him "Hokkien", explaining that there are many Chinese dialects spoken in Singapore: *putonghua,* the "people's language", often called Mandarin, but in countries that have their own national language, such as Malaya, it is called *hanyu*, "Chinese language"; *guangdonghua* "Cantonese"; Hokkien; Teochew; Hakka; and others, depending on which part of China the speaker or his or her forebears had come from.

To try to avoid communication problems, not only between the different Chinese racial groups, but also between the Chinese, the Indian and the Malayan citizens, English was promoted as the business and commercial language. However, whilst this was convenient for the British administration, it did little for many of the non-English-speaking immigrants to Singapore from China, Hong Kong or elsewhere, who were too busy trying to earn a living to be able to acquire a knowledge of both written and spoken English.

With the promotion of the Mandarin dialect as the national language in China to improve communication between the speakers of the many different dialects, there was pressure on Singapore to follow suit, with Mandarin being taught in the schools, but this was often to the detriment of Chinese family life. The grandparents may have been immigrants from a part of China speaking a dialect other than Mandarin, and too old to learn English, whist their children would do so, but at the same time retain a knowledge of their native dialect.

When the grandchildren came along however, those who were English-educated would be taught English in school to a high degree of fluency, which was important to their chances of advancement under the British administration and within the British-orientated business and commercial environment of Singapore, and they would also learn some Mandarin, but they would have only very limited, if any, knowledge of the native language of their grandparents. Those grandchildren who were Chinese-educated would be taught Mandarin and to a lesser extent English, and also would have little or no knowledge of the native language of their grandparents. In both cases, conversation between the grandchildren and the grandparents was almost impossible or very limited.

Further, a great many of the non-Mandarin speakers who spoke Cantonese, the major dialect of southern China, were disturbed by the promotion of Mandarin to the detriment of their own dialect, as were the speakers of Hokkien and other minority dialects. This provoked great resentment, just as it would do if the people of Scotland were told that they had to stop speaking their "Scots" dialect, or to acquire a southern accent, or perhaps to speak German, as was often said, perhaps not so convincingly, would have been the case should Britain and its allies have lost the last war. Indeed, Alex realised, this was close to the situation in the 1740s when the Highlanders were forbidden by the English to speak their native language, Gaelic. However, in the case of Singapore the intention was not repression, but working towards the commendable situation where future generations of Singaporean Chinese will be able to speak a common Chinese dialect.

The cooling breeze of the ship had helped Alex to cope with the increasing heat and humidity as they had made its way to Singapore, but now ashore he found the heat and humidity torturous. Soon both the front and back of his thin shirt were wet with perspiration. George smiled and told Alex that within a couple of weeks he would acclimatise and that in the meantime he should try to accept the conditions.

George said that before they went to the company-house that had been assigned to Alex he would introduce him to Chinese food. After a short journey they arrived at a tiny eating place that was no more than a kitchen at the back, a small inside room and four or five tables set outside. They sat outside under a large umbrella, with locals sitting at the tables around them. He looked over to them and returned their smiles.

These were Chinese people living in their own country, confident and relaxed, brightly dressed, and with many of the older ones in ethnic clothing. There was not the reluctance of the Chinese to make contact that he had experienced with the few Chinese that he had met in Scotland, and with a guilty feeling he remembered why, bringing old Mr. *Chan* and his daughter to mind. What an ignorant swine he had been to the two of them! One day he would go back to old *Chan*'s shop in Govan and apologise for his behaviour. This eased his guilt and he settled down to enjoy the meal.

George anticipated Alex's need and spoke a few words to the proprietor, two or three minutes later two large glass pots and two large chilled bottles of one of the local beers, "Tiger", being placed before them. Alex quickly revived as the beer went down. Life in Singapore was looking decidedly attractive! As might be expected, the ordering of the food was left to George. The placing of a pair of chopsticks at the side of Alex's plate gave him cause for concern, but he was relieved to note that there was also a spoon to hand. Within minutes a large bowl of some kind of soup was placed at the centre of the table and they were each given a small bowl of boiled white rice.

At George's invitation Alex ladled some of the soup from the large bowl into his own bowl and then, with George's smiled encouragement, proceeded to eat, finding the soup delicious. It was composed of a thin white gruel, rather like thin porridge, containing thin meaty rings of about an inch in diameter. Finishing his bowl, Alex's accepted George's invitation to serve himself another, eating this with relish also. Finally, Alex asked George what the delicious food was. George replied 'Pig's intestine porridge', which he explained was thin slices of cooked pig's intestine in a thin 'porridge' made by boiling white rice until the grains crumble and fall. Alex's initially aghast expression caused George to laugh, with Alex soon joining in, the laughter ending with George ordering another couple of bottles of beer.

The meal went on to include: steamed prawns; peppered crab; squid; and lemon chicken; along with chilli *kang kong* [22], chilli-flavoured "hollow vegetable", a kind of highly-spiced spinach; and *bai tai*, a small green and white vegetable, called in Cantonese *pak choi*; all served to the centre of the table, with each of them helping themselves. Additionally, they were both served with a bowl of *bai fan*, literally "white cooked rice", meaning "boiled rice".

Now emboldened by the beer, Alex followed George's example of eating the rice by lifting the bowl up to his mouth and scooping the rice up into it with his chopsticks. Within minutes he had a grasp of the technique and was eating about as much as he was spilling. A third bottle of beer for Alex, but with George declining, gave him all the confidence that he needed to use the chopsticks to pick up and safely deliver to his mouth even the more slippery of the items of food, such as tiny button mushrooms.

At the end of the meal Alex thanked George profusely for the warmth of his welcome and his generous hospitality. He looked across the table at George and thought what a pleasant chap he is. George looked at him in return, but his summing-up of Alex was more reserved. Certainly Alex was pleasant and friendly, but he had seen other foreigners who had come to Singapore to work who were just as pleasant at the outset, but once they had come under the influence of Major Horace Smedley (retd.) and had joined the ranks of the other expatriates in their exclusive little social circles, they had changed.

George smarted at the memory of what he had been told by his brother *Wing Chau*, who had worked for a short time for the British Army. The door of the sergeants' mess at the base carried a sign saying "No dogs or Chinese admitted." *Wing Chau* had told him that whilst the officers were alright, a few of the lower ranks were dreadful, enjoying a feeling of superiority that being in the army in Singapore gave them that compensated them for their feeling of inferiority from their lower station in the class-ridden society back in Britain.

Some of the wives of the lower ranks were worse than their husbands. They thought nothing of going to the NAAFI still wearing their dressing gowns with their hair in curlers and more often than not with cigarettes in their mouths. They would order the Chinese assistants around with false pretentious accents, and affect a preference for high-quality foodstuffs that they had never tasted, seen, or even heard of before. Back in their army apartments, they would give orders to their Amah, the cleaner, in a loud aggressive voice, and had no compunction in discussing on the telephone with their sister army wives the laziness of the Amah, even within her presence, not appreciating or even recognising the heat and humidity under which these ladies were expected to work.

The wives would meet in the circle of wives appropriate to the rank of their husbands, discussing the stupidity of the Chinese tradesmen who came to attend to any faults that developed within their apartments: 'So I told the stupid little Chinaman who came to repair a leaking tap "Now look here, I want you to get on with the job straight away, no skiving off and coming back tomorrow, or there will be a complaint to your boss", but the threat seemed to fall on deaf ears.' The sister-wives would nod emphatically and utter "Quite right" in agreement, and then proceed to tell their own latest example of the incompetence of the local populace. It was never considered that the workman might have spoken only a little English and could not fully understand what he was being told, or that he had had to leave the apartment to go and get a replacement part.

In their ignorance they believed that English spoken in a loud voice is comprehensible to even the most dim-witted foreigner, including, in their eyes, the Chinese. They themselves had no knowledge of any other language and didn't realise that they were the ignorant ones. George's eyes glinted in anger at these thoughts. The time would come, soon enough, when the British Administration would leave Singapore and Malaya, and then these expatriate '*gui lo*', "foreign devils", would find a drastically changed situation! However, for now he would reserve his judgement and do his best to help Alex.

After the meal George took Alex along to his apartment, which was in a block on a road just off Scotts Road, a very fashionable part of Singapore city. Alex expressed his delight at the luxury of the apartment, but George didn't tell him that the amount that the company paid for the rent of the apartment was greater than the combined wages of the four young Chinese lady clerks who worked in the company offices.

Alex had been advised by George that the removal of foot-ware was expected when entering a Singaporean home, and as he walked from room to room he was pleased with the ceramic floors that were cool to his feet. Alex particularly liked the completely tiled bathroom: the slope of the floor in the shower area to a central drainage point enabled a shower to be taken in the open room, instead of having to stand in the bath with a shower curtain drawn in place to prevent the floor from becoming wet, or stand within a telephone-box-size shower cubicle.

He noted with surprise that all of the plumbing and waste disposal piping was on the inside of the building, rather than being on the outside, as it was back in Britain. However, he didn't like to see the toilet waste pipe from the apartment above coming down through the ceiling into his own bathroom before being fed into the drain pipe running down through the floors below: in the event of a leakage from any of the joints, or a blockage in the system, this inevitably would have to be corrected from within the apartment. Still, a different country, a different system.

He experimented with the big overhead fans that were fitted in all of the rooms except for the bathroom, and found their breeze cool and refreshing. A thermometer hanging from the wall in the lounge read eighty degrees Fahrenheit, but it was not the temperature that was the source of discomfort, but the ninety-five percent humidity. Still, as George had said, he would soon get used to it, the main point being not to try to fight the humidity, but just to accept it.

That evening Alex walked down Scotts Road to Orchard Road, the main shopping area, and ordered a simple, but traditional, Chinese meal. "chicken rice", in a small coffee house, which really would have been better described as an eating house, as coffee was just a minor item on offer. Reassured by the way that he had coped earlier that day, he ventured again to use chopsticks.

After this, despite the heat, he walked west along Orchard Road until he came to a side street of Chinese shops, turning to walk along the five-foot way - introduced by Sir Stamford Raffles – in front of them, the awning covering the way providing protection from the sun and the rain. Although he was the only Westerner in sight, the shopkeepers and their customers were smiling and welcoming and he felt perfectly at ease.

He walked along, looking at the goods on sale, and delighting in the fragrance of the dried spices and the exotic fruit. Above the small shops were huge red boards, on which were painted large Chinese characters in gold, many of these characters being in relief. Alex looked at the characters in wonder, having no idea of their meaning, but being impressed by the strength and boldness of the strokes. He resolved to learn about the Chinese language as soon as he had settled into his new job and learnt his way around the city.

Feeling rather warm, he stopped at a tiny coffee house, where he sat at an outside table drinking a chilled "Anchor" beer. A Chinese couple passed by holding the hand of a young girl of about three or four years of age. When the young girl saw Alex, her eyes widened in amazement and she turned to her mother, whispering *"hong mao!"*, "Red head!", which was unintelligible to Alex, but which he learnt later was an often-used Chinese name for Westerners. The mother quickly told her to hush, and then smiled in friendliness at Alex, who smiled back. The friendly atmosphere of the street was like nothing he could ever have imagined back in Britain, and he was thrilled by how exotic it all was: it was marvellous!

Back in his apartment, Alex checked the thermometer, finding that it still registering eighty degrees Fahrenheit. He tapped it to make sure that the liquid level was not stuck. However, after living in the north-east of England, with its onshore winds blowing for six hundred miles over the cold North Sea from Scandinavia, he was beginning to enjoy the heat.

The next morning George met Alex early. As they drove out to the company premises, which were at Bukit Timah, these being Malay words meaning "Tin Hill", to the west of the city, they passed a group of workers repairing the road. Alex was surprised to see amongst them a middle-aged woman clad in a dark tunic and wearing a bright red headpiece of silk or cotton in the shape of a shallow rectangular box. He commented to George, who replied 'You are seeing a part of Singapore's history that will soon be gone. At one time there were many of these *"samsui"* women labourers, dressed in their distinctive clothing, but now they are few and far between.'

This brought a nostalgic smile to Alex's face, as he recalled Mike's memories of the trio of shawl-clad old ladies in his father's pub. Nothing lasts for ever. Soon, all those whom we ourselves love and know, and all that we find reassuring and familiar, will be confined to history, with perhaps a few old photographs serving only to amuse future generations with our simplicity and quaintness: they will not see us as having had youth and energy, loves and hates, ambitions and achievements, failures and disappointments. Yes, nothing lasts for ever.

After a short journey, they arrived at the company premises, which comprised a large fenced-off compound containing two large hanger-like buildings, and a small two-story office block. Parking spaces were marked on the ground in front of the office block, the space closest to the entrance door of the block being reserved for the Manager by being marked in large red letters with the inevitable "Major Horace Smedley (retd.)".

The major had been looking through the window of his upstairs office, waiting for George and Alex to arrive, but as soon as he saw them he returned to his desk and busied himself with some papers. His Chinese secretary, whom the major addressed by her personal name, *Yi Ling*, but whom the rest of the staff, being younger, addressed respectfully as Madam *Zhang*, announced their arrival, the major pretending to have been deeply absorbed in his work. He exclaimed 'What? Who? Oh yes, show them in.', but Madam *Zhang* wasn't deceived, knowing the pompous old man of old.

George brought Alex into the office and introduced him to the major, giving the latter his full title. Alex smiled at the major and shook hands with him, then accepting the proffered seat, whilst George was dismissed with a condescending 'Thank you George, that will be all.', accompanied by an obsequious and insincere smile.

The major was a decidedly unattractive middle-aged man: big, fat, red-faced and balding. He wore a three-piece suit and a tie, but due to the air-conditioner mounted in an outside wall, the temperature in the office was quite pleasant, at about only 70 degrees Fahrenheit.

For his introduction to the company and to its branch manager, Alex had put on his suit and tie, but he had already decided that in future he would follow the pattern of George and two other young men he had seen in passing through the lower floor of the office block, and simply wear a thin open-necked shirt. However, the major had noted Alex's formal attire, with satisfaction. It was necessary to keep up standards, particularly in front of these Chinese! He told Alex that he would have an upstairs office, next to his own, leaning over and whispering confidentially 'Must maintain our station, old man.'

Major Horace Smedley (retd.) had achieved his rank whilst serving overseas with the British Army during World War II. He had been employed in an administrative role, to which he was suited, not being a physically active man and having an obsession with minor detail. Other men who might well have risen beyond him, but who couldn't stand the monotony and boredom of administration, had applied for transfer to active service, leaving him with less competition for promotion, so that he was eventually able to reach the rank of major.

He would have loved to have earned a medal for bravery, or even a mention in despatches, but this wasn't in his nature. He had preferred the secure environment of his office away from the front, rather than to lead other men into battle. At the end of the war he had contemplated staying on as a regular officer, until he learnt that his war-time rank wouldn't carry through to peace-time, and that he would have to suffer a demotion to captain. Unable to contemplate such a loss of dignity, he left the army and took a job as a personnel manager with a manufacturing company in the English midlands.

Unfortunately, his dealings with the newly-demobbed workforce gave him daily mental anguish. They had no respect for his standing as a retired major, and indeed they ridiculed him for it. Their demands for easier working conditions and numerous concessions were outrageous. Given the slightest excuse they would down tools and make off for the nearest pub! If only he had had them under his command during the war, he told his wife, he would have shown them who was boss! He hated these upstarts, the new glorious British working man, returned from the war to make Britain a socialist paradise, with cradle-to-grave pandering of the work-shy!

What was more, he had heard tales, albeit unsubstantiated, about the "lack of patriotism" of some of the British industrial workforce during the War: they would take longer than necessary to machine urgently-needed components because they knew that if they produced them at a greater rate now, the company management would want to retain the greater production rate when peace was restored!

Not for nothing was the low-speed position of the gear-change lever on the machine tools known amongst the workforce as the "time-and-motion" position, which they used when the time needed to machine a work-piece was being measured by a representative of the company management; and the high-speed position known as the "piecework" position, which they used when they were being paid according to their output! Oh yes indeed, Major Horace Smedley (retd.) knew all about the lazy, skiving, British working man!

On one occasion the major was patrolling the shop, looking for signs of laziness amongst the workforce, when he decided to inspect the stores. He was delighted to find two men behind one of the run of shelves in the far corner, one man sitting with the second man standing cutting his hair. He was incensed and asked the 'barber' why he was cutting the man's hair "in the company's time". The man responded indignantly with 'Well it grows in the company's time doesn't it?' The major was livid and reported both of the men to the personnel manager, but the latter just laughed at the barber's response, only giving the two men a very mild warning.

The major's downfall came when, fed up with lateness amongst the workforce, he instructed the factory gate-man to lock the gates immediately after clocking-on time. Standing inside the gates, he told the growing crowd of late arrivers that they could come back again at the start of the afternoon shift, and that they would lose a half-day's pay. The mood of the locked-out workforce had then become aggressive, and he had had to retreat into the factory out of the way of projectiles of various sorts. Thoroughly incensed, he rang the police and instructed them to come and deal with the situation.

By this time the factory manager had arrived on the scene. Realising that the only way to defuse the situation was to allow the workers access, the manager instructed the gate-man to unlock the gate. The major was enraged at this "usurping of his authority", and immediately tendered his resignation, which the factory manager, in turn, immediately accepted.

The major had had enough of post-war Britain, with its bolshie, opinionated, workers and had sought somewhere to work where the old pre-war values still prevailed. The post in Singapore, offering him the opportunity to become one of the expatriate community, and to socialise with the officers of the British forces and the British administration, was just what he was looking for. One of the privileges afforded him by this appointment was in respect of the education of his only daughter, Caroline, back in England. She would be enrolled as a boarder at one of the more prestigious girls' schools, all fees and travel expenses involved being paid for by the company.

The major then took Alex down to the lower offices to meet the two assistant managers. He indicated the four female clerical staff with a sweep of his hand, not deigning to introduce them personally by name. The two assistant managers shared an office with George, with the four clerical staff sharing an adjacent office. The downstairs offices had fans rather than the air-conditioner that the major enjoyed, so the temperature was greater, at over 85 degrees Fahrenheit. Nevertheless, the staff seemed to be comfortable.

Alex stood with sweat soaking the front of his shirt, but he hoped that after a week or two, when he had had chance to acclimatise to the conditions, he wouldn't find them too bad. The major then left one of the assistant managers to take Alex out into the yard and introduce him to the yard foreman, *Siew Kong*, so that he could "learn the ropes", whereupon he then returned to his second-floor office to read the "Straits Times" whilst waiting for his secretary to bring his morning pot of tea in to him. It seemed to Alex that his life in Singapore could be very pleasant, Major Horace Smedley (retd.) apart.

Chapter Fourteen

As the days passed, Alex quickly settled into his new job, which wasn't really much different from his previous job in Newcastle. He learnt to rely on George and the two assistant managers, who had the admirable Chinese virtue of attending obsessively to every aspect of a transaction, until the dealings of a contract were completed. However, for most of their time they worked on contracts of their own, but usually having a word with Alex before accepting anything of an unusual nature, such as when one of them was asked to arrange the shipment to Britain of a client's collection of live tropical insects, some of them poisonous.

Alex also found that the Chinese lady clerks were equally admirable in this respect, dealing with all correspondence and maintaining all records without delay and with absolute thoroughness. They were a delightful group of ladies. During their mid-day break, after they had eaten lunch, usually some kind of noodles brought in from a nearby eating place, they would clear one of the desk tops and then play *mahjiang,* "Mah jong". The pieces that they used, known as tiles, were of traditional style, having faces made of bone dove-tailed into small bamboo tablets.

Despite watching them play for four consecutive days, he couldn't make out the rules, and as the tiles, running to one-hundred-and-forty or so, were not only inscribed with English numerals and letters, but also inscribed with confusing Chinese characters, this didn't make the matter any easier. Still, given time, he supposed that he might eventually learn how to play this ancient game.

After work that evening, he went along to the "Times" bookshop, where he was fortunate to come across an authoritative booklet "The game of Mah Jong" by Max Robertson.[14:1] Sitting down to read the book that evening, he learnt that a Mah Jong set comprises 144 tiles, which are divided into Honour tiles and Suit tiles. The honour tiles are made up of four red, green and white dragons, and four east, south, west and north winds; whilst the Suit tiles are made up of three distinct sets: bamboos, circles and characters, the tiles in each of the three sets thus totalling 136 tiles, the remaining eight tiles making up the set of 144 tiles being known as Flowers and Seasons.

Completing the set are four or six dice and a set of chips. There are four players and the game starts with each player throwing two dice to determine who shall have choice of seats, known as Winds. After this

---

14:1 "The game of Mah Jong" (24th impression) by Max Robertson, published by Whitcombe and Tooms, no ISBN number.

the tiles are shuffled face down: on account of the noise that the contacting tiles make, this step is called "the twittering of the sparrows."

After this the players build a square of four walls, each of two rows of 18 tiles placed one on top of the other, the walls then being pushed towards the centre of the table so that their ends touch the ends of the walls of the adjacent players to form a closed square, the objective of this being "to keep the devils out!", the square being known as "The Great Wall of China."

Alex's found the game to be very complex, and his brain was in turmoil as he tried to grasp the essentials of it. He learnt that the objective of the game is to secure a complete Mah Jong hand made up of four sets and one pair of tiles known as "Pung", "Kong" and "Chow", or any of several other hands. He read that a Pung is any three of a kind, although there are different forms of Pung, an "Exposed Pung" and a "Concealed Pung"; likewise with a Kong, which is any four of a kind, there being an "Exposed Kong" and a "Concealed Kong".

One reassuring thing that he learnt, with relief, was that the above rules, which had been developed in the West for playing Mah Jong, were much more complex that the traditional Chinese rules, which were simpler and faster, as the Chinese play this game mainly to gamble, whilst Westerners play for relaxation. This was all that he needed to decide that he would follow tradition, particularly as Robertson had said that whilst being simpler, the Chinese game is "far more mysterious."

By the time that Alex had got to "Chow" he had had enough for one evening, and put the book aside and decided to have a drink. However, after a couple of weeks, Alex was able to stand and watch the clerks play and follow their moves, whilst after a further couple of weeks he even ventured an opinion on the respective skills of the players. A few more weeks passed before he joined in with a game himself when, whilst not winning, he put up a fair performance.

On one occasion he found the lady clerks playing a board game that he didn't recognise, but which looked like some kind of drafts. However, they told him that it is *wei-chi*, known in Japan as "Igo", but usually shortened to "Go", one of the oldest games in existence, that had originated in China some three thousand years ago. There is much folklore about *wei-chi*. It is said that in the *Tsin* dynasty a long war had been fought with the loss of many lives. To bring an end to the conflict, it was decided that victory would be accorded to the winning side of a game of *wei-chi*. What a sensible decision to make!

The *wei-chi* board was originally made of a thick piece of wood with four supporting legs, but whilst the present-day boards are still of about an inch thickness, the legs are dispensed with. There is a rectangular grid of nineteen lines by nineteen lines drawn on the board, the stones not being placed on the squares, but on the intersection points of the lines.

This is a game of territorial gain. The pattern of the game is for the players to place one of their stones alongside one of their previously-placed stones, with the objective of joining up their stones so as to surround as much 'ground' as possible and capture the stones of their opponent. The complexity of the game includes handicapping, where a known weaker player, or the loser of three consecutive games, is allowed to take the advantageous opening turn. However, there were many other forms of handicapping that Alex found to be too complex to comprehend. Eventually he went along to the "Times" bookshop again and bought a copy of the excellent book "Go and Go-muko", by Edward Lasker,[14:2] and also a copy of an older book "Go for beginners" by Kaoru Iwamoto.[14:3] With the aid of these books on *wei-chi* his knowledge of the game improved dramatically, but it was still some time before he managed to win his first game.

One lunchtime he found the clerks using the wei-chi board, but playing a different, simpler game called *wu zi qi*, where the objective is to place one of one's own stones at each end of a continuous run, either orthogonally or diagonally, of five of the opponent's stones. The player with white stones first places a stone at the centre of the board, then the opponent, with black stones, places one of his stones alongside the white stone, either orthogonally or diagonally, after which the player with the white stones places a further stone on the board, in contact, again either orthogonally or diagonally, with one of the stones already on the board.

After losing a couple of times, Alex got the hang of the game, and successfully trapped a run of his opponent's stones, upon which the lady clerks burst out into peals of delighted laughter. Just at this instant the major returned from his lunch and glared at the group in an angry disapproving manner. The clerks leapt to their feet and hurriedly put away the game, even though their lunch break was not yet over. Later in the afternoon the major called Alex into his office. 'Just a word of advice, old man.' he said, in a quiet confidential manner, 'It is not good practice to socialise with the staff. They will only take advantage.' Alex

---

14:2 "Go and Go-moku" by Edward Lasker, published by Dover, ISBN 0-486-3-0.

14:3 "Go for beginners" by Kaoru Iwamoto, published by Penguin, ISBN 0-14-06259-2.

was incensed, but held his tongue as he knew that, if not by general standards, then certainly by the major's own standards, he was in breach of good practice. Nevertheless, he considered the major to be an unreasonable old fool trying to live in a bye-gone age.

He told George about being reproached by the major, asking him how he could tolerate working for such a pompous man. George smiled wistfully before replying 'The job provides me with a cast-iron rice bowl.' George was using an old Chinese expression to say that by accepting the Major's arrogant attitude his job was secure, in the same way that back in Glasgow, as elsewhere in Britain, a job with the local council, whilst sometimes undemanding or routine, is regarded as being comfortable and secure: few people have ever heard of anyone at the Town Hall being sacked!

As he waited for Madam Zhang to bring in his afternoon tea, the major sat back in his chair and concocted an addition to his 'rules of good practice' for company staff:

> "In the interests of staff discipline, members of senior management should not become familiar with employees. This applies particularly with regard to female employees, lest any unfortunate impressions be given."

then, satisfied with his creation, he smiled and reached for another digestive biscuit.

The personal name of one the male assistants was *Ying Hong*, "Brave Red", so named by his parents because, despite their being second-generation Singaporeans, they still felt a strong attachment to China, and admired the way in which Chairman *Mao* had stripped wealth and land from the rich landowners, whose words had previously been law, and distributed them to the poor and largely-illiterate peasants. *Ying Hong* was in his mid-twenties and had been with the company for five years. Quite a number of people in Singapore, as *Ying Hong*'s parents, felt loyalty to China, and this had lead to the administration in Singapore being concerned that there would not be any organised demonstrations in support of China's political and social policies, lest these should spread to Singapore itself.

The personal name of the other assistant was *Chonghai*, which had no political associations, as his grandparents had been rich merchants who had seen the way in which society was changing in China under the communist party, and had sold up and left, first making their way to Hong Kong, and then on to Singapore. *Chonghai* was aged about twenty. He spoke in somewhat faltering English, making up for this most of the time by a big beaming smile. He had been with the company for only a year, but he had a sound knowledge of its working.

A large proportion of the company's work was with expatriates returning to Britain, Alex often attending to such jobs. The people that he met were quite pleasant, but he found that even those with the simplest of jobs had a condescending manner towards the native Singaporeans, even though many of these Singaporeans were of superior intellect and education, and had made their mark from humble beginnings by hard work and dedication, and also by the great sacrifices to this end made by their parents. Many of the expatriates were not very bright, but had prosperous or socially well-connected parents who had spent a lot of money giving their children a veneer of culture and intelligence, this eventually leading to their being given a job, arranged by friends of their parents, that was well beyond their native ability, resulting in their having an exaggerated idea of their own importance and value to society.

This raised Alex's hackles and inflamed his sense of social justice: the nepotistic upper-class bastards! To listen to them speak so 'beautifully', with accents that had been carefully and expensively inculcated by private tutors, made him seethe. However, it wasn't just the middle- and upper-class of class-ridden Britain who wanted a position of superiority over their fellow man. He recalled the reply of a man whom he had met whilst working on the boats in Gourock to his question as to why the man, a welder in the Yards, was emigrating to South Africa. The man had replied 'I am sick of being at the bottom of the shit-pile. Now it's my turn to kick some-one else's arse.' referring to the native black people of South Africa. What an attitude towards his fellow man! This man's views on racial superiority closely paralleled the views on class superiority as felt by many others further up the social ladder, except for his views being expressed more directly and openly. Despite the many changes since the end of the Second World War, Britain is still a very class-conscious country.

As he relaxed into the job, Alex started to wonder what the social life of Singapore might have to offer. Without need of discussing this with George, the matter resolved itself one day when George suggested to Alex that he, *Ying Hong* and *Chonghai* go over the causeway into Johore Bahru in Malaysia on the forthcoming Saturday, for a "little entertainment". None of them owning a car, they took a taxi to the causeway, walked over the mile or so to the other side, and then caught another taxi to a seafront restaurant, where they sat at a table looking over the Straits of Johore to Singapore.

George took the lead in ordering the food. Before long, Ikan Bilis, whole fish of about one inch length mixed with peanuts, arrived; followed by Beef Biryani, curried beef with pilau rice; Lamb Biryani, curried lamb also with pilau rice; steamed prawns; and then sotong, known in the West as squid. Finally, they ate a dish of sliced mixed fresh fruit, most of the varieties of which were unknown to Alex. The meal was accompanied by four jugs of draught beer. As they split the bill, Alex was astonished at how cheap the meal, including the beer, had been.

Leaving the restaurant, George, *Ying Hong* and *Chonghai* led Alex a little way along the road, and then up a side track to a large building bearing the name "Mechinta", which George explained means "The place of love". Paying their admission fee, they proceeded into a large room, at the centre of which was a slightly raised stage, no more than about ten feet square. Tiered seats rose gently on three sides. The four of them sat at the back and waited for the performance to begin. After a few minutes the sound of "The Teddy-bears picnic" came from amplifiers placed at each side of the stage. Alex thought to himself, but saying nothing to his companions, 'What pathetic kind of juvenile entertainment will this be?'

Soon, "Little Red Riding Hood" came on, wearing the traditional red cloak and carrying a basket with its contents covered by a check cloth. After she had pranced around the stage for a minute or so, a man dressed in a wolf costume came onto the stage and made menacing gestures towards her, whereupon little Red Riding Hood put down her basket and threw off her cloak, to reveal herself clad only in a minute red skirt. The effect on the wolf was dramatic! After a few minutes of chasing Little Red Riding Hood around the stage, he caught her and pulled off her skirt, to reveal her in total nudity. What followed astounded Alex, and ended with simulated, but only just, copulation between Little Red Riding Hood and the wolf.

The show continued in this way, the gyrations and contortions of the naked female performers leaving nothing to the imagination. Some of the female performers were western women, with big wide hips and huge hanging breasts, whom Alex found unattractive, whilst others were slim tiny oriental women, with unlined faces, whom Alex thought delightful. How they had ended up in such kind of work he didn't like to think. Alex noticed that most of the eastern men in the audience reacted more enthusiastically to the performances of the occidental women than they did to those of the oriental women: clearly an instance of the novelty of something new to them.

Ying Hong and *Chonghai* had slipped away down the aisle to sit on the floor immediately in front of the stage, determined not to miss a thing. The performance ended with three tiny, but exquisite, naked young oriental ladies standing in what seemed like small dog-baskets containing an inch or so of water, inviting the audience to hire sponges, for a ridiculously small charge, with which to sponge down their bodies. *Ying Hong* and *Chonghai*, being well placed, and probably in the know, leapt up and hired a sponge each, washing the breasts and other more private places of two of the young ladies with great enthusiasm, whilst the young ladies conversed together in a bored fashion.

When the show ended, the four men took a taxi to a hotel in the city, where they sat in the lounge and ordered beer. After a little while, *Ying Hong* and *Chonghai* got up quietly and disappeared through a door at the back of the room. When Alex asked George where they had gone to, George told him, but without conviction, that they had gone "for a massage", but the suppressed grin on his face made it quite clear that their "massage" had more to do with the stimulation of the evening's performance that with the need to ease aching muscles.

The Chinese used to have a tradition of multiple marriages, many people believing that the first and subsequent wives would approve of the addition of a further wife to the household, as this would ease the sexual demands that their husband put on them. However, this is not the usual situation, where the wives in a multi-wife household would bicker and quarrel, and scheme against the other wives to secure dominance.[14:4] When in 1961 the Singapore Legislative Assembly outlawed multiple marriages except for Muslims, many men responded by going over the causeway in the evening, to seek their additional satisfaction elsewhere.

However, it would not do to think that the Malays have an easy-going attitude to sex. Whilst they do not appear to mind women of other races performing in such as the "Mechinta", there were no Malay Muslim women there. Any Malay Muslim, man or woman, found "in close proximity" to a person of the opposite sex, in a bedroom or other such private place, i.e. committing "khalwat", would be charged to appear in court, unless the man made an immediate proposal of marriage to the woman involved. Not a matter to be taken lightly!

[14:4] This situation is the theme of the dramatic film by *Zhang Yimao*, set in 1920's China, "Hang the red lantern" where the introduction of a fourth wife increases the level of domestic conflict, the wives scheming, lying, back-biting and telling tales to the husband, in an attempt to secure his granting to them of the control of the household, and also of his sexual attention, this being made known by the hanging of a red lantern over the door of the chambers of the wife chosen. The dialogue of the film is in Mandarin and there are sub-titles in English.

Following their trip to JB, Alex, George, *Ying Hong* and *Chonghai* started to go out for lunch together on most days. Normally this would be something simple, such as the traditional Chinese meal: chicken rice. This is a popular dish that appeals to both children and adults alike. To cook the chicken, it is placed in boiling water and the pan then taken off the heat source. When the water has cooled the chicken is removed and the water re-heated, prior to the re-insertion of the chicken, this being repeated several times, until the chicken is soft and tender. The stock in which the chicken is cooked is used in the cooking of vegetables and rice, as it imparts a delicate flavour. After the addition of a small amount of green vegetables and spice, the stock is often supplied as a clear soup along with the chicken rice. A small dish of chilli and often a few slices of cucumber complete the meal.

Sometimes they went along to a Malay food counter, where they would eat Laksa, a highly-spiced soup containing coconut and bean sprouts, noodles and other items, but with several regional variants, or Nasi Lemak, probably the national Malay breakfast dish, comprising rice cooked in coconut milk, served with a fried egg on top, along with Ikan Bilis that had been fried with unsalted peanuts, and pieces of cucumber; or another popular Malay dish, Mee Goreng, made by boiling rice and grinding shallots, chilli peppers, garlic, salt and other spices, to make a coarse paste, then heating the paste in a pan, after which the boiled rice is added and the lot heated for about four minutes. An alternative to Mee Goreng is Nasi Goreng, where noodles are substituted for the rice, the words "nasi" and "mee" referring to rice and noodles respectively.

Often when they were hungry enough, they would go for a "steamboat", which employs a large annular metal bowl set over a gas ring, where the heat from the gas can run up hollow centre of the bowl as well as up its outsides, the bowl being filled with hot water. The four of them would select for themselves what they wanted to eat from a nearby counter: fish, pork, beef, quail's eggs, sotong "squid", prawns and so on, along with *bai cai* and lettuce leaves, these items all being put into the hot water.

Periodically, they would lift the lid from off the metal bowl and retrieve the cooked food using small ladles and strainers, other items of food then being added in replacement. This would go on for a long time, the water in the bowl being replenished as it boiled away. Towards the end of the meal, the water, or soup as it had become, was allowed to reduce in volume, and then to finish the meal, the soup, of which the flavour was absolutely delicious, was drunk by the four of them: an elegant sociable meal, with much friendly quibbling as to who had stolen another's food from the bowl.

Other times they would go to a Thai food counter, where they would eat a simple meal along with the Tai specialities, Tom Yam Soup and Chicken's Feet. Tom Yam Soup is a spicy soup that even hardened chilli lovers find difficulty in eating. Alex soon started to call this kind of hot food an "A-B", as it sometimes burned just as much in leaving the body as it did in entering it. Alex found that chicken's feet are almost tasteless, being mostly gristle and skin. George, with a straight face, told Alex that the traditional way to cook chicken's feet is to put the chicken down on a hot grill. Initially the chicken stands up and tries to escape the heat, but when there is no feeling left in its feet and it sits down, the feet are cooked. Alex was horrified by this, but suspected that this could be George's idea of a joke. George had an unusual, almost British, sense of humour, as generally the Chinese tend to speak literally, as opposed to the British, and particularly those from Yorkshire, who often speak pure nonsense just to gain a laugh.

One morning Alex arrived for work early, to see the cleaning lady moving a long tubular vacuum cleaner, on four wheels and with a long tube extending from one end, by pulling the end of the tube. Feeling light-hearted that morning, he asked her in an innocent voice 'That's a nice little creature, what's its name?' The cleaning lady looked at him as though he were an idiot, before answering 'Vacuum', but, thankfully, Alex had the sense not to try to explain that he was pretending that the vacuum cleaner was a dog, otherwise the cleaning lady would have thought him to be deranged. Thereafter he toned down his humour.

They often visited "little India", on Serangoon Road. When Sir Stamford Raffles landed in Singapore in 1819, he had with him 120 Indian assistants and soldiers. As time passed, many more Indians came to Singapore to find work, both manually and in the civil service. Raffles wanted to develop separate ethnic districts for purposes of colonial administration, and Little India evolved as the home of Indian commercial activities. In this colourful area are many Indian shops selling saris and many other ethnic items, and small restaurants serving delicious Indian curries. Running parallel to Serangoon Road on the west side is Boundary Street, where the "Banana Leaf" restaurant serves Indian and Chinese food from metal containers onto a banana leaf set before the customer. Everything is very simple, the waiters being dressed in shirts with open necks and rolled-up sleeves, but the food is fine. In the proper Indian tradition, no cutlery is provided, the customers being expected to eat with their fingers, but those not able to cope with this method would be supplied with a fork and a spoon, upon request.

Close by the Banana Leaf is a food court where "pig's penis soup" is on offer, albeit written on the menu in Chinese so as not to upset the more sensitive and unadventurous western customer. On the occasion when the four of them visited this food court and Alex was invited to try it, he asked simply and innocently 'Is the penis sliced or is it whole?', which had the others in fits of laughter.

When time allowed, they would make their way north along Boundary Street until they came to the temple containing "The Reclining Buddha". This is a very large - about 20 feet long - and very impressive figure that attracts many visitors. Alex had become interested in Buddhism since his arrival in Singapore, particularly in its no-aggression and no-retribution philosophy. He resolved to study Buddhism[14:5] when, as with Mandarin, he had the time available.

One Saturday afternoon after they had taken lunch locally, they went along to the Bukit Timah Nature Reserve on Bukit Timah Hill, this hill, of some several hundred feet in height, still remaining as primary jungle, as opposed to growth that had taken place after the original jungle had been cleared, as in other parts of the island. This is the biggest hill left in Singapore, the earth of other hills that had originally been present having been used to fill in the mangrove swamps that used to cover a large part of the island.

They walked up the spiralling road that led to the top of the hill, and then stood and admired the view. George had brought with him a leaflet describing the range of wildlife to be found within the reserve, some of it being dangerous. A section of the precautions to be taken when visiting the reserve described a snake, a cobra, that is particularly aggressive when it is nesting and feeling protective towards its young.

When approached, it will shoot poisonous venom with great accuracy into the eyes of the disturber. The leaflet went on to describe what is to be done in the event of a person being so unfortunate as to receive venom in the eyes. George read out the instructions for the benefit of the others: "The first thing to do is to wash out the eyes with water. If water is not available, then the affected person should lie on the ground and have a second person urinate into his eyes to flush away the venom." The four of them grimaced at this, but the good sense of the advice was noted. Not having any water with them, they then took good care to stay well clear of where any snakes might be lurking for

---

14:5 Amongst many other books, the reader is referred to: "The heart of Buddhism" by Guy Claxton, published by Thorsons, ISBN 1-85538-274-1; and "The essence of Buddhism" by Traleg Kyabgon, published by Shambola, ISBN 1-75062-468-2.

fear that the remedial treatment might have to be called upon.

The four of them would often get involved in light-hearted arguments, during which the statements made grew in incredulity. After one particularly outrageous and impossible statement by George as to how many whole hot chilli peppers he could eat in one sitting, Alec snorted and declared in mock disgust 'And pigs might fly!', which caused the others to raise their eyebrows and look at each other in bewilderment. However, after a few seconds they spoke a few words together in Chinese and then broke into smiles. George said to Alex in explanation 'And the sun rises in the West!' The Chinese clearly have an expression to deal, in a gentle and humorous way, to leg-pullers, just the same as in the West. Alex was delighted in this further indication of the similarity between their two races.

On one occasion they ate at a restaurant offering *gali yutou*, "Curried Fish Head". When the bowl arrived, Alex could see in the dark soup the head of a quite large fish broken up into smaller pieces, along with long cylindrical dark green vegetables, rather like very small courgettes, known as "ladies' fingers". George fished into the bowl with his chopsticks and produced a fish's eyeball, which he offered to Alex, whilst *Ying Hong* and *Chonghai* watched with interest. Without batting an eyelid, Alex received the eyeball from George's chopsticks, and swallowed it down without a change of expression. The three Chinese were impressed: Alex was indeed a most unusual Westerner!

Alex asked why Curried Fish Head was so much in demand, when back on the Clyde everyone simply tossed the fish heads back over the side. George smiled wryly, and then told him that it may be that the Singaporeans want to remind themselves of the days when they, or their parents, had to eat all that was available as they couldn't afford to throw food away. Alex could understand this, as the traditional haggis of Scotland, now in great demand, was at one time just a means of using up offal rather than letting it go to waste and the same could be said of the black, "blood", pudding of the north of England.

Back in Glasgow, when children didn't want to eat their bread crusts, he had heard many parents say, but not in criticism: 'Get it 'et! People are starving in China for want of a bread crust', and it was said by many, in admiration, that 'The only thing that the Chinese don't eat of the pig is its whistle', although it is doubtful if any of those making these statements had any personal knowledge of their accuracy. However, from his recent eating excursions with his friends - who usually insisted that he use chopsticks rather than to use a knife & fork, so that his rate of consumption would be impaired, leaving more for them - Alex could give his definite personal assurance of the accuracy of the latter statement![14:6]

On the following Saturday, they all went along to Smith Street in Chinatown, towards the south side of the city centre. Here there was a great concentration of traditional Chinese shops, which had Alex fascinated. As they reached the end of the street, George pointed out the stained-glass figures of butterflies that adorned the windows of the upper-floor rooms. When Alex couldn't deduce what they symbolised, George told him that, in the past, they were to advise that "ladies of pleasure" were available there.

At one shop George drew Alex's attention to a large wicker basket containing a great number of large dark grey egg-shaped objects, which he advised him were "Century eggs". Seeing Alex's expression of incredulity, he went on to explain:

"These are called "Century eggs". Some six-hundred years ago, a man discovered several duck eggs in a shallow pool of slaked-lime that he had used in the building of his house, two months before. Upon breaking-open the eggs, he found that they were quite palatable, and decided to make some more, but this time with the addition of salt to improve the taste. The coated eggs are stored in cloth-covered jars or tightly-woven baskets. After a couple of months, when the mixture has developed a hard crust, the eggs are ready to be eaten. The practice has continued to the present time, but with many developments: coating the eggs with a caustic mixture of mud and rice husks; next to use a mixture of wood-ash, quicklime and salt to increase its pH and sodium content; and in recent years there have been several developments to reduce the curing time of the process. As a result of the process, the yolk becomes a dark green–to–grey colour, with a creamy consistency and an odour of sulphur and ammonia; whilst the white becomes a dark brown colour and relatively tasteless. Despite sounding quite unattractive, Century eggs are considered a delicacy by the Chinese, and are eaten on their own, or mixed with rice porridge, congee, or chilled bean-curd, *dou fou.*"

Alex was visibly impressed by George's knowledge, but declined his invitation to try an egg: perhaps next time!

Walking back along the street, Alex noticed again a most peculiar smell, like that of rotting fruit.[14:7] George smiled, as he and the two

---

[14:6] This statement is not completely accurate, as most Chinese do not like heavy Western meals such as the traditional Sunday lunch or Christmas lunch, with its bland and 'over-cooked' vegetables and its 'stodgy' puddings, nor are they keen on 'soggy' chips. In particular they tend not to eat lamb and cheese, both of which they say smell of vomit.

[14:7] Because of the strong and persistent smell of Durian, which many people find

assistants had one last food-test in store for him. The group stopped at a shop that had rows of spiky dusky-yellow fruit, of about the size of a child's football, arrayed outside on a large bench. He gave them all a good inspection, then picked one up, lifted it close to his ear and shook it, sniffed at the remnant of its stalk, tapped it with the handle of the vendor's knife, and then asked the vendor to open it for him, this requiring the use of a pair of strong gloves, a stiff knife, and considerable force. The vendor cut along one the five visible latitudinal lines on the surface where two of the sections meet.

George then inserted one of his fingers into the gap between two of the sections and touched the fruit within, after which he withdrew it, a small amount of the fruit adhering to the tip of his finger. He raised his finger to his lips and tasted the fruit, then nodding his approval. When the fruit had been separated into its sections and placed before the group, George said to Alex 'This is the king of fruit, the durian.'

Alex touched the fruit also, finding it sloppy and repulsive. Notwithstanding, he put it into his mouth and was astonished to find that it tasted delicious, somewhat like vanilla ice-cream, but with a much more pronounced taste and a creamy texture.

Alex asked George what the purpose was of the tests that he had performed on the durian before buying it, to which he replied 'When durian is not yet ripe, the fruit is stiff and sticks to the casing, but when it is ripe it separates from the casing so that when I shake it I can feel the fruit moving about inside, and when I tap it I can hear a dull thud instead of a higher-pitched sound. When the fruit is ripe, the stub of the stalk also has a stronger smell. The final test is to open the fruit and feel that is has a soft texture.'

Alex was visibly impressed! After they had finished the durian, George said 'You have tried the king of fruit, durian, now you must try the queen of fruit, mangosteen!', which turned out to be a fruit the size of a small apple, with a thin purple skin. The flesh was of a firmer texture and had a light, sweet refreshing taste, compared with the heavy taste of the durian: indeed the ideal complement to durian!

After they had finished eating, they washed their hands under a tap provided for this purpose, George advising Alex that the smell of durian is persistent, such that taxi drivers will not permit durian to be taken into their cabs, nor would hotels allow them to be taken into their foyers or bedrooms.

---

repulsive, passengers are prohibited from taking the fruit onto the Singapore MRT railway system. However, despite its off-putting smell, readers are asked to take the author's word that Durian has the most delicious, almost addictive, taste.

Two or three times each week Alex would leave his apartment to eat his evening meal at a Hawker Stall, most of these stalls being located within the basement areas of housing blocks and large commercial buildings. There was usually an extensive choice from perhaps a dozen different stalls – Chinese, Muslim, Tai, Indian, Indonesian, Western – with the different foodstuffs being freshly cooked and laid out in containers on the counters or on large tables in front of the counters, for the customers to choose from. The tables set out in front of the stalls are for general use, not owned by any particular stall, so he would select dishes from perhaps two or three stalls.

Other counters sold a great range of local fresh fruit, the stallholder cutting up the fruit as the customer made his or her choice. There were other counters selling beer and soft drinks and also fruit drinks made with freshly liquefied fruit. The meals were delicious and cheap, but more importantly, being cooked fresh, were absolutely safe to eat.[14:8]

For the odd few meals that Alex cooked at home, he would go along to one of the local wet-markets, that sold all of the fresh fish, poultry and fruit that he could want to eat, and also other creatures that he could not venture to buy, such as snakes, turtles an creatures that he hadn't ever seen before.

There was usually a range of shops nearly where he could buy groceries, hardware, medical items, and anything else that he might need, and also a branch of one of the banks. He was intrigued when the assistant at the bank called him forward by inverting her hand with her fingers extended vertically downwards, lowering her arm slightly and then making several rapid forward movements of her fingers: the usual British way of calling someone forward by extending the hand straight-out, palm uppermost, then curling the middle finger, is considered very impolite in Singapore. Indeed, in Britain this is the way that a teacher will call a mis-behaving pupil to the front of the class.

After he had visited one wet market several times, a lovely little old lady was awaiting his arrival, accompanying him as he made his way around the stalls, carefully checking any items he selected and replacing any that she considered to be of inferior quality, then haggling a good price from the stallholder: he has his own personal shopper!

[14:8] A recent regrettable trend in Chinese Hawker Stalls in Singapore is to rename them as Food Courts and not to display their food in open view at the front of their counters, but instead to give the customer a large card containing colour photographs of their various dishes on offer. Unfortunately, when the food arrives it is not always as attractive in reality, as it is when shown on the card. This is a misguided intention to become more modern and attractive to the customer.

She was a delightful, helpful kindly soul and he regretted that they were unable to communicate by other than gestures and smiles, but, alas, she spoke only Hokkien and he spoke only English and Mandarin. He felt perfectly happy living the lifestyle of the locals, and soon was passing a few friendly greetings with them as he became known: they were a grand group of people.

Before going to work some mornings, he would walk along to the open ground between the housing blocks and watch the locals, many wearing their pyjamas, performing elaborate and graceful *taiqi* movements. A lot of them had brought their pet cage-birds with them, hanging the cages at the top of long poles, where the presence of other birds encouraged them to sing as their owners danced. It was a delightful scene. However, he suspected that Major Horace Smedley (retd.) wouldn't have approved of his being enthusiast about the local culture.

Indeed, the major was beginning to feel disappointed with Alex. He had suggested to Alex that he join his club, but his suggestion hadn't been taken up. Also, Alex seemed to be spending all of his spare time in the company of George and the two assistants, which was not what was expected from an expatriate member of staff. He didn't appreciate that Alex's interests were totally different from his own. The major and his wife spent their spare time in entertaining, or being entertained by, other expatriates or people whom they thought worthy of cultivation. Being members of the 'right' bridge club or golf club was also important to them, and they were also very keen to buy the latest fashion in clothes and to be seen in the 'best' places wearing them.

When Alex unavoidably became involved in the company of the Smedleys, he found conversation difficult and strained. He wasn't interested in their polite chit-chat or their criticism and complaints about some of the aspects of Singapore that were not to their liking. Whilst not intentionally avoiding them, he had other interests to pursue. There was so much to see and experience in this new country, such as the customs and the traditions of the different ethnic groups, which fascinated him.

Mrs Smedley had been putting pressure on the major to involve Alex more in their social life, considering him to be a very handsome chap. She was also flattered by his polite manner towards her, and sometimes let her mind entertain thoughts about Alex that Major Horace Smedley (retd.) would not have been pleased about, had he but known. She liked nothing more than to hang on to his arm and take him around at company events, introducing him as 'My husband's right-hand man.'

She loved to see the look of envy on the faces of the older woman when they met Alex, taking this as a personal achievement. However, on a more practical basis, she was anxious for Alex to become involved when their daughter, Caroline, arrived on a forthcoming visit from Britain. What an asset it would be if Caroline were able to hook such a fine looking man! They would make a lovely couple! She would then ensure that the major looked after Alex's interests and promotion within the company. Alex was a very personable young chap and well thought-of by the company's clients. 'Yes,' she thought, 'he would do very nicely for Caroline.'

Despite enjoying all of his new experiences since arriving in Singapore, Alex still had one problem: he was missing female companionship, and when he learnt of Caroline's impending arrival, he realised that this might be the solution to his problem, having seen a photograph of Caroline on the Major's desk: she looked to be a very attractive young woman! When Caroline arrived, the major took the opportunity of bringing her into the office for all to see, particularly Alex. He was gratified to see that Alex gazed at her with interest, and spoke amiably and enthusiastically when introduced to her. By jingo, something might well come of this!

A welcoming party for Caroline was organised for the following day, to be held at the major's club. Alex had received his invitation personally from the major, who presumed that he would be overjoyed and available to attend. 'Formal dress, you know,' he said, 'black tie, white shirt and a dark suit if that's all you have.' Indeed, apart from casual clothing, a dark suit was all that Alex did have: be had no desire to equip himself with formal evening wear such as Major Horace Smedley (retd.) would be wearing.

Come the evening, Alex arrived at the club to be welcomed by the major and his wife and then led over to Caroline, who was wearing a low-cut gown, which emphasised her slim figure and her above-average height. She had long dark hair, which she wore in one of the popular styles of the day. She was a tantalising sight, especially to Alex, who of late had been feeling quite desperate for female company.

As the music started, Caroline cocked her head and looked at him questioningly, an obvious invitation for him to ask her to dance. He explained that he had not learnt to do the dance in question, a waltz, upon which Caroline reached out for his arm, told him that she would teach him the steps, then led him onto the floor. Within a few minutes he had learnt the elements of the dance and had started to relax. He started to open conversation, inquiring as to her journey from England, to which she responded enthusiastically.

When the music stopped, they walked over to her parents, who were beaming at them. The major spoke to him man-to-man. 'Well my boy, it's nice to see that you and Caroline are getting on so well together. You made a lovely couple out there on the floor.' Alex was aware of the implication butt smiled and said nothing. For the next hour Alex and Caroline chatted together, until she felt that she should mingle with the other guests. Alex soon realised that whilst she was an attractive girl, she was very class conscious and affected: as the evening progressed, she was beginning to bore him. Further, she had a cultivated home-counties accent that grated on his nerves.

Alex was torn between his physical desire for her and his dislike of her personality. However, he was like most, if not all, men in such a situation, in responding primarily to her sexual attractions rather than using his normal astute judgement of character. When Caroline returned, he suggested that they slip out onto the terrace and enjoy the cool night air. No sooner were they outside than he led her into a secluded part of the garden and then, without hesitation, drew her to him and kissed her passionately, Caroline responding in return.

A call from the major at the door to the terrace interrupted their activities, so they moved out of the shadows. When the major saw the flush on Caroline's face as they re-entered the ballroom he was delighted. He smiled and whispered to his wife 'They seem to be getting on very well my dear.'

When the Smedleys got home that evening, the major celebrated what he thought to be a great success in the coming together of Caroline and Alex by settling down in his study with a double brandy and a Havana cigar. However, his wife made her way up to bed complaining of a headache due to the excitement of the evening. Caroline followed her up to her room and sat on the edge of the bed. 'Mummy,' she said, 'there is something I want to talk to you about.'

Her mother came over to the bed and sat there, looking at her with a serious and concerned expression. Caroline continued. 'Do you remember Rupert, the chap from my tennis club whom I told you and daddy about? Well, things were a lot more serious than I had led you both to believe, but I don't want to talk about that now. It's all in the past and I want to put it behind me. What I do want to say is that it is time that I thought about settling down and I think that Alex could be the right man for me. He was very forward this evening and I am sure that it won't take long to make him fall for me. I know that he is rather coarse and unpolished, but he is from Scotland, where customs are different. There is nothing that I couldn't correct. It wouldn't take me long to mould him to our satisfaction.'

Her mother nodded, so Caroline continued: 'You and daddy have known him much longer than I have. Do you think that despite his background and everything, he would be suitable for me? He is different from every other man that I have known. There is something about him that attracts me even though we have only known each other for such a short time.' Her mother sat quietly, a faraway look coming over her face. Many years ago, at a regimental ball when her fiancé, then already a major, was away on a management course, she had danced for much of the evening with a handsome young Scots captain, who had charmed her with his simple sincerity. Later, they had walked in the grounds, where under the moonlight he had gently kissed her, and told her that he thought her divine.

One thing led to another, and before long they were kissing passionately. Although the captain had urged her to see him again she had refused, bearing in mind that with her fiancé already being a major, he had good prospects for further advancement in the course of time. The captain went away dispirited and she didn't ever see him again, whilst she went on to marry the major, who didn't ever achieve a higher rank. The marriage had not been a great success, as after the birth of Caroline the major had not approached her sexually ever again.

Many was the night that she had lain in bed and rued her decision, and thought of the young captain. If she had had the courage to follow her heart, she might now be leading a life of love and contentment, rather than being no more than a sounding board for the conceited outpourings of her pompous husband. She lifted her head and looked at Caroline, saying with utter sincerity, born of experience 'Yes, see Alex again,' but then adding with motherly caution 'but do be careful.'

Caroline thought a great deal about Alex as she lay in her bed that evening. Certainly he was coarse and uncultivated, but she felt that with time she could polish away the rougher side of his nature, and also teach him to speak properly, instead of with that horrid Glasgow accent. The next afternoon she called in at the office on her way home from the tennis club. She told Alex that there was to be a party at the club on the following evening for one of the expatriates who was returning to Britain, and asked him to accompany her. Alex told her that regretfully, he had already arranged to go out with George, *Xiao Hong* and *Chonghai* on that evening, and that he made a point of never letting anyone down once an arrangement had been made.

She reacted angrily, telling him that she wouldn't have thought that an evening with his Chinese 'cronies' would be preferable to attending a party with her, especially when so many nice expatriates would be present, but he told her that that is not the point: when an arrangement is made, it should be honoured. Caroline didn't see the sense in this, as on many occasions she had cancelled a social arrangement when something more attractive had turned up, and this was also common practice for mummy and daddy and their social set. She stormed off out of the office. However, on the following day, when she had calmed down, she rang him, having got over what she thought to have been a snub, to say that she would collect him at his flat on the forthcoming Saturday evening to take him to join her parents at her father's club, where they were to have dinner with some old friends.

The conversation during dinner was the usual polite talk on the usual point-scoring topics: their children's education; their forthcoming holidays and related travel arrangements; what they were having done to their homes back in Britain; the success of their children with their examinations, their ponies, and their dancing classes; and the problems they were having with their nannies or with their Amahs, the ladies who attended to domestic duties about the house. Initially, a few polite questions were asked of Alex, but he was unresponsive and the questions soon dried up.

Towards the end of the evening the wife of a prominent banker asked him which school he had attended back in Britain, but by this time he was feeling sick with the whole tone of the evening, and replied belligerently, but truthfully, 'Govan Infants, Govan Juniors, and Govan Secondary.' The lady did not grasp his intended sarcasm and continued. 'I just can't place Govan my dear', to which Alex replied, with a defensive expression on his face, 'It's a slum area about three miles west of Glasgow city centre. You wouldn't like it.' There was an embarrassed silence, then Caroline rose from her seat and said 'It's really time that Alex and I were leaving. I've had a few very tiring days and feel in need of an early night.'

As soon as they were out of earshot of the company, she could not contain herself any longer and turned on Alex, asking him how he could have behaved so boorishly, but he wasn't surprised or bothered. He had been expecting her outburst, but made no apologies, nor did he have any regrets about his manners or his words: it had been a satisfying end to a painful evening.

He was convinced more than ever that he had no place in the social circle of the Smedleys. However, a couple of days later he began to think that perhaps he had behaved unreasonably at the dinner table and had caused Caroline unnecessary embarrassment, and also, more to the point, he had been having erotic thoughts about her: it had been several months now since his sexual relationship with Aggie had come to an end.

He rang Caroline and invited her to dinner, mentioning that he wanted to take her to his favourite Chinese food court, to which he had been introduced by George. By this time she had got over her upset and gladly accepted his invitation. She reasoned that it was too soon to give up on him, when with a bit more effort she might yet be able to teach him how to behave properly in polite society. When Alex picked up Caroline, he was dismayed to find that she was dressed as though for a garden party, with high-heeled shoes, a long flowing silky dress and a wide-brimmed hat, and was also carrying a fashionable and expensive handbag, even though he had told her that they would be eating at a food court, not a restaurant. However, she had obviously made an effort to look nice for him, so he didn't comment on the unsuitability of her attire.

The food court contained a collection of different ethnic food-stalls, fruit-stalls and drink-stalls, surrounding a number of tables and chairs. As they sat down at one of the tables, a jolly, buxom middle-aged Chinese lady approached them and said to Alex with a friendly smile 'You back again so soon Alex? What you want to drink?' Alex ordered a jug of Tiger beer for himself and a glass of fresh fruit juice for Caroline, who was sitting looking at him questioningly. She said to him in a reproachful voice 'Why did that woman call you Alex? Are you always so friendly with waitresses?', to which he replied coldly 'That 'waitress', Mrs. *Ong*, is the owner of three of these stalls. She is an old friend of George and is now a friend of mine.'

Caroline received this news with a sniff of disdain. As Mrs. *Ong* returned with the drinks, she looked at Caroline, and then said to Alex 'This your girl friend then Alex? Nice girl, but a bit too posh for you.', upon which she broke out into peels of laughter, with Alex joining in, whilst Caroline sat po-faced. Alex responded with 'No, Mrs. *Ong*, you are my best girl friend. Get rid of that old man of yours and I'll come and join you in running your food stalls.' Mrs. *Ong* broke into hearty laughter again and then made her way back to her food stalls, chuckling. Caroline was furious! How could he joke with a Chinese serving woman like this, without regard for her own presence and his own dignity, when only a few evenings ago he had sat stiff, uncomfortable and uncommunicative, in the charming company of her parents and their friends?

Alex suggested that they make their way to the food stalls to select the dishes that they wanted. Caroline's eyebrows raised in astonishment as she realised that there were no waiters, and that, apart from drinks, the food court was entirely self-service. However, her eyebrows raised even further when she saw the range of exotic oriental foodstuffs on offer, with not one 'civilised' dish available. She stood there bewildered, as Alex pointed to one unrecognisable dish after another to indicate his requirements to the man behind the counter. Realising that Caroline was unable to cope with this system, he said to her 'Leave the ordering to me, just go and sit down at our table and we can share whatever I bring over.'

Caroline watched Alex as he indicated what he wanted. Mrs *Ong* came over to join him and at one point seemed to be telling him that he couldn't have one particular dish, but after they had argued for a minute or so she grinned at him and handed over to him a bowl of a dark green vegetable rather like spinach. He returned with a large tray of dishes, and then immediately went back and brought a second, similar tray, then spreading the various dishes around the table top.

Caroline looked with dismay at the food, as Alex pointed out to her the individual dishes: chilli crab; steamed king prawns; lemon chicken; curried fish head; chilli *kang kong* ; deep-fried baby sotong; and much else, including a bowl each of *bai fan*, boiled white rice. Caroline asked Alex what he and Mrs. *Ong* had been arguing about. He told her that Mrs. *Ong* had first said that he couldn't have the bowl of chilli *kang kong*, a traditional Singapore dish, as he had already eaten some earlier in the week, and its hot spicy taste was too rich for a Westerner to cope with more than once a week. Alex had responded to Mrs. *Ong*'s remarks by saying 'Alright, give me a bowl of laksa instead', this Tai dish being extremely spicy. Mrs.*Ong* had then relented, telling Alex 'If you die, don't tell anyone you came here for your food!'

Alex picked up a pair of the two pairs of chopsticks that he had brought to the table, and instructed Caroline in their use, using as demonstration the scooping up of rice from his bowl, placed immediately beneath his chin. Having always been taught not to place a hand onto a plate or bowl from which one is eating, and to retain one's head well above the plate or bowl, she found this manner of eating abhorrent, and refused to attempt it herself, asking him to fetch a spoon from the food counter for her to use instead, then eating the rice demurely and tidily.

Caroline tried the lemon chicken and found it delicious, telling Alex so. Then she tried the crispy-fried baby sotong, again finding it to her taste. This pleased him, as he had been beginning to feel that the meal would be a disaster. The chilli *kang kong* was too spicy for her, but she ate a little. Next Alex persuaded her to try the curried fish head, first ladling some of the soup from the bowl into her own small bowl, then sifting out some "ladies' fingers" from the soup, which she also accepted.

He then separated a few pieces of flesh from the fish head for her and placed them onto her plate, receiving her smiled thanks: things were going well! However, at this point, he unwisely rooted around the bottom of the bowl until he found a fish eyeball, which he then attempted to feed to Caroline using his chopsticks. She was repulsed! He had gone too far for her inexperienced western tastes!

Alex called to Mrs. *Ong* to bring him a pair of what looked like large nutcrackers and used these to break the limbs of the crab to expose the flesh within, holding the nutcrackers in one hand and the limbs of the crab in the other. Within seconds his fingers were coloured bright orange from the chilli powder that had been used in making this dish, but he simply wiped most of it off with a paper towel, then passing the nutcrackers to Caroline for her to use.

Gingerly, she picked up a leg in one hand and then tried to crack the shell of a crab leg with the nutcrackers, but the leg slipped and fell onto her lap, leaving a bright orange trail down her dress as it slid to the floor. She was horrified at the state of the lovely dress that she had worn especially to impress Alex. Mrs. *Ong* brought over a damp cloth and tried to remove some of the marks, but this only resulted in the orange trail spreading over a wider area. With difficulty, Caroline regained her composure and tried to recover the situation, saying to Alex 'Well, these things happen.' Following the main course Alex went over to Mrs. *Ong*'s fruit stall and after the required sniffing, tapping, shaking and tasting, brought a durian back to their table. Caroline was appalled at the smell. The major had warned her of this fruit, and told her how it was banned on public transport, in hotels, and in his club. Eventually she agreed to taste a small amount, but complained about its sloppy texture and spat it out onto her plate: unfortunately, she had become too prejudiced against durian by daddy's remarks to ever be able to give it a fair trial.

Alex was disappointed by her lack of adventure and ate the durian himself in silence. When his glass was empty, he called Mrs. *Ong* over to ask for another large bottle of Carlsberg, but she told him with great concern 'Best drink no more beer Alex. Durian is too "heaty" to take with alcohol. If you drink spirit, say whisky or brandy, with durian, you die straight off.' Caroline immediately implored Alex not to drink a further drop, with Mrs. *Ong* gravely nodding her agreement. Alex was feeling a little irritated by this time, but held his tongue and simply agreed: 'No more beer.'

He smiled to himself. He must buy a durian later in the week and try it with a glass or two of single malt, to see if it would kill him, which he very much doubted! The Chinese are very conscious of their health, and will not even drink chilled water, on the grounds that it will chill their stomachs. However, the Chinese are mostly fit and slim, with good clear complexions and unwrinkled skin, such that it is often difficult to judge their age. There are few fat Chinese, unlike many people in the West, who over-indulge in both food and drink and develop unattractive fat sloppy bodies, to the detriment of their health.

Although he was grateful for Caroline's attempt to make the best of the day after the ruining of her dress, Alex felt that there was probably an unbridgeable gulf between her lifestyle and his own, whilst Caroline herself was now having doubts as to the future of her relationship with Alex. Two days later Caroline called round at Alex's apartment in the evening. At first they were both somewhat uneasy, aware that their last two meetings had been disastrous, but eventually she took the first step towards reconciliation by getting up from her chair and sitting next to him on the settee. Her close proximity got the better of him. Reaching out for her hand, he told her that he was sorry for his lack of consideration, whilst she in turn told him that she should have made a greater effort to appreciate his background and interests.

Soon they were kissing passionately. After a few minutes he raised his hand to the cotton blouse that she was wearing and stealthily began to undo the buttons running down the front. As her blouse fell free, he kissed first her neck and then lowered his mouth to kiss the top of her breasts, rising above her brassiere. Her hands slid up around him, caressing his neck. He unfastened her bra and slipped it from her shoulders along with her blouse. Her breasts were full and shapely, and as her kissed her nipples he felt them harden and become more prominent.

In unison, they slid to the floor. Alex caressed the inside of her legs, causing her to moan in anticipation of his intentions, but she didn't attempt to stop him. She struggled free from the rest of her clothing, and then helped him to do the same. They rolled on the floor, exploring each other's bodies, until Alex could no longer bear the pain of his need for her. She sensed his urgent desire. She also was ready for the culmination of their love-making.

Later, as she lay by his side, she realised that she loved him, coarse and unpolished as he was. He was what she had been waiting for, and at last she was happy. However, Alex, now satisfied, was feeling guilty, as he had no love for Caroline. He had no intention of sharing her way of life. To ease his conscience, he thought to himself that she had got what she deserved, and so also had Major Horace Smedley (retd.).

She had already corrected him, in a superior manner, on the guttural way in which he had pronounced "bus", pointing out that all the 'best' people pronounce it to rhyme with "bass", and on the way he had pronounced "master", with hard emphasis on the "a", which word she said should be pronounced as if spelt "marster". She tittered when he used "Aye" instead of "Yes". She was beginning to exasperate him and she also had the typical expatriate attitude of superiority. In short, she was arrogant and over-cultivated, and convinced that the only proper lifestyle was that of the 'best' class of people, meaning her parents and friends and other members of their social circle.

He called for a taxi to take her home. Alex had no regrets. He had simply used her body for his own pleasure, nothing more, with no consideration for her feelings, or of the deceit that he had employed. There is a saying in the north of England that sums up the way that he had behaved: "A standing cock has no conscience." How true! Men are bastards, one and all! Alex had been an evil man when he had fled Glasgow, but had become a quite nice person by the time that he left Aggie and her son. Now he had regressed: his class paranoia had returned, as in his behaviour towards the Smedleys and their friends; as also had his lack of decency and his shameless cruelty, as in his seduction of Caroline. Perhaps a leopard is indeed incapable of changing its spots. It seemed that hope of his permanent conversion into a good man was receding.

Caroline came round to his apartment again a few days later, when they again made love. Alex noticed that Caroline was now acting as though they had a permanent relationship. She had expected him to tell her that he loved her, but this hadn't happened, which she put down to his reticence. After they had made love on a third occasion, she had questioned him about their future together, hoping that this might have encouraged him to propose to her, which would have thrilled her parents, but Alex wasn't drawn, just chatting about irrelevancies. She felt that he lacked the courage to cross the social gap between them, and decided to invite him to a cheese-and-wine party at her parents' home to meet a group of family friends, where the convivial atmosphere might give him the courage he lacked to ask the major for her hand. She told her parents to be especially careful to put Alex at his ease, and hinted that with luck they might soon expect "good news": they were elated!

On the morning of the party, Caroline came round to Alex's apartment to check what he intended to wear that evening. As he opened his wardrobe door, she spied Matt's old belt hanging from the tie rack. Dragging it from the rack, she dropped it onto the floor chortling. 'What on earth is this ugly old belt doing in your wardrobe Alex? It's the kind of thing a scruffy old dock labourer would wear. Get rid of it and buy a nice new belt that is more appropriate to your standing as a member of the expatriate community!' Alex glowered at her: 'Put it back. It belonged to my father.' Caroline did so, but she was most displeased, and began to wonder, yet again, if she would ever be able to make him into the kind of man that she wanted.

When Alex arrived at the Smedleys', Caroline was appalled to see that, in addition to a crisp long-sleeved cotton shirt, a well pressed pair of lightweight trousers and a smart silk tie, Alex was wearing Matt's old belt. She realised that this was his response to her remarks earlier that day. Taking hold of his hand, she led him through to the lounge and introduced him to the guests who had already arrived.

Whilst the major served wines, the Amah laid the table, not only with a range of cheeses, but also with a typical English afternoon tea, consisting of salmon and cucumber sandwiches; tiny sausage rolls; and scones served with fresh cream and strawberries; followed by deliciously-light Victoria cake: the Smedleys didn't do anything by halves!

After an hour of small talk, the major's wife suggested that they should play card games. Following this she suggested that they should play a party game, obviously having one in mind. At this point the major excused himself and left the room, claiming that he had some urgent business to attend to in his study. The idea of the game was to sing a song or recite a rhyme about a chosen theme: an animal, a book, a place, and so on. Alex was beginning to become bored, and suspected why the major had taken his leave. He was probably sitting in his study, enjoying a glass of single malt, having experienced these party games before.

The next theme was colour, Caroline starting off by singing "The white cliffs of Dover", then next person singing "Red sails in the sunset", and the next "The yellow rose of Texas", and so on, until it became Alex's turn. By now Alex was totally fed up with this pretentious contest and was increasingly angry that the major had not returned, or invited him to come and join him in his study. He fumed! The old sod had left him here, joining in with a pathetic little sing-song, whilst he himself was sitting comfortably out of reach, glass in hand. The party listened attentively as Alex recited a rhyme of his own creation relating to the colour blue:

"He couldn't make love to his wife,
'cos it had got '**blue**' off in the war."

There was a sharp intake of breath, followed by a stunned silence, which was broken by the ringing of the telephone. Mrs. Smedley jumped to her feet. She couldn't leave the room quickly enough. Caroline also got to her feet and started to refill the wine glasses, anxious to take advantage of any diversion. Her mother returned and took over this duty, informing Caroline that the call was for her.

After Alex and the other guests had left, she explained to her mother that the call was from Mr. Geoffrey Frodsham, the senior partner in a firm of solicitors to which she had applied for the post of Mr. Frodsham's legal secretary before she had left Britain. The news was good, but the appointment was conditional upon her being able to start work the following week, as the present incumbent of the post had been informed that a pending surgical operation was to take place then. Her mother interrupted her: 'But you can't cut short your holiday, and what about Alex?' to which Caroline replied 'That is precisely what I intend to do. After Alex's performance today and his behaviour over the last week, I think that this would be the best course of action.'

After one very brief and stilted telephone call from Caroline to Alex to advise him that she had an urgent need to return to Britain, there had been no further communication between them. Alex was relieved at this, as it was clearly a simple way to end what was becoming a messy situation. The major became incensed with the thought that Alex had tinkered with his daughter's affections, and perhaps more, with no intention of doing the honourable thing and proposing marriage. He suspected, with hindsight, that Alex had not had serious interest in her from their first meeting. Damn him! The major turned over in his mind the ways in which he could get Alex out of the company.

The main problem was that Alex had come to him with an outstanding reference from the Board of Directors back in London and, furthermore, since arriving in Singapore he had made a great contribution to the company's business in what is a competitive market, coming across favourably with all of the potential customers that he dealt with, mainly on account of his re-assuring Scottish accent and his wholesome appearance. Still, the major thought, one day he will make a slip and then he will be out on his ear, mark my words!

The Smedleys saw Caroline off on her flight to Britain from the airport, wishing her well, but saddened that things had not turned out as they had hoped. They loved her dearly, and there was nothing more that they wanted than to see her happily married. Three months later Caroline wrote to her parents to tell them that she was engaged to be married to her boss Geoffrey. He was twenty-five years her senior, which had given her parents concern, but this was compensated for by his having a very successful career and being financially sound. He was a widower whose wife had died shortly after giving birth to twin boys, both of whom were presently studying at university. He lived in a lovely big house on the banks of the upper Thames.

Caroline explained that although they had known each other for only a short time, they both felt that they wanted to start a new life together as soon as possible. She was sure that they would be happy. The wedding was to take place without delay, with the honeymoon to be spent later in the year. She implored mummy and daddy to come over for the wedding. Geoffrey would be delighted to put them up! The major was pleased that Caroline was to make a good marriage, but it did nothing to reduce his hatred of Alex: 'That evil, philandering Scottish degenerate!'

Mrs. Smedley was dismayed at the immediacy of the wedding. She and Caroline had often talked in the past about the kind of wedding that the family would have when Caroline fell in love. They would choose the wedding dress and the venue for the reception together, and they had even discussed who might be the bridesmaids. It was intended to be a wedding to remember and one that would outshine that of all of their friends!

The Smedleys made immediate arrangements to travel to Britain. Caroline and Geoffrey met them at the airport, but although Caroline looked radiant and happy at the prospect of her impending wedding, her condition couldn't be disguised from her mother by the soft folds of the expensive dress that she was wearing. A question that had worried Mrs. Smedley was now answered, but there was one further question that she couldn't bring herself to ask and, indeed, might never learn the answer to: is Caroline's new husband the father of her unborn child, or could that person be Alex? What was worse, she couldn't ever let her suspicions become known to the major.

Chapter Fifteen

In the weeks that followed, Alex and the major communicated as minimally as possible, and in a polite but icy manner. The major noticed that Alex had still not heeded his request to wear a tie at work, but decided that this issue was too insignificant for any damage to be done to Alex by any complaint that he might make to Head Office in London, and any such complaint might rebound unfavourably, with himself perhaps being regarded as somewhat small-minded by the Board of Directors.

Alex's friendship with George, *Xiao Hong* and *Chonghai* carried on strongly, with their now spending time together visiting places of interest around the city and beyond. These places included the Van Cleef Aquarium, the Botanical Gardens and the Museum, and offshore islands such as Pulau Ubin, taking a ferry from the harbour at Changi Village. Upon arrival at Paulu Ubin, they hired bicycles and pedalled along the dirt tracks free from disturbance by cars and other motorised vehicles. Partway around the island, they stopped at a tiny eating place, where they ate a plate of miscellaneous local fruit and drank a large bottle of Carlsberg each.

The eating place was just a roof made of rattan with four corner poles to hold it up, a table and some benches, which were just bare planks supported on empty oil cans. A refinement was table-covering made of a piece of oilcloth. The island was delightfully primitive, nothing like Alex had ever seen before, but the way that a large part of Singapore island itself must have been not too many years ago.

The pace of life on the island was slow, but many of the people there had turned down the opportunity for a 'better' life on Singapore Island, preferring to remain where they, and their forebears, had always lived. The houses were little more than simple huts set in jungle surroundings. Those few who had been seduced by the offer of an apartment and a job in Singapore usually came home at the weekend every few weeks and for religious and public holidays, to be with their families and to keep their children in touch with their small-island heritage, the peace of the island providing a nice relaxing contrast to their bustling weekday city life.

The Botanical Gardens were fascinating, with their vast range of orchids and other tropical plants. In particular Alex liked the exotic water lily known popularly as the "Amazon Water Lily" or the "Victoria Lily", having the botanical name Victoria Cruziana. In terms of appearance, this lily has little in common with the common water lily, Nymphaea, in that it has leaves in the shape of flat disks of about five feet diameter with turned-up rims of some three inches height. Floating on the surface of the water, the lily offers a resting place for frogs, terrapins, water tortoises and other small creatures. This lily can be seen back in Britain in botanical gardens having a warm-water pool, where in a single season it can grow from seed to its fully-mature size.

He also learnt the botanical name, Ravenala Madagascarariensis, for the tree that is known commonly in Singapore as the "Travellers' Palm", which is not actually a palm but is related to the banana. This tree grows to a height of about twenty feet and has a slightly tapering circular trunk, with all of its branches radiating out from the top almost in one plane, rather in the manner of a fan. When a large number of these trees are set out in a line, just as on a grass border at the side of a large swimming pool, or along the sides of a highway, the planes of the leaves of the trees are seen to have an almost identical orientation, suggesting that they are like a compass in giving guidance to the traveller. Alex couldn't decide whether the orientation of the trees was natural, in response to the sun and other climatic features, or whether it had been determined by the gardeners who had planted the palms. However, the tree has a large reserve of water in the leaf bases that can provide sustenance for the thirsty traveller, and it is more than likely that it is this feature that gave the tree its popular name.

One tall water plant with leaves that were curved into waves around their edges, and with beautiful large bulbous white or sky-blue flowers, caught Alex's attention. George explained to him that it was the *lian hua*, the "Lotus", the emblem of purity in China. Alex remembered having seen these plants before, growing in clusters in ornamental pools in the gardens of large houses, and even in uncultivated and neglected ponds in the gardens of kampongs. They are a prize possession, not only for their beauty, but also for their spiritual significance. Despite growing from deep in the mud of a pool, the Lotus reaches high above all of the other plants, to produce an immaculate flower, the message for the human race being that no matter how humble one's origins, by leading a good life one can rise to a position of prominence and respect in the community, and provide a shining example to all others.

Alex was impressed by the Botanical Garden's collection of orchids, amongst which was the orchid "Vanda Miss Joachim", named in honour of its discoverer, Miss Agnes Joachim.[15:1] Whilst tending her garden in Tanjong Pagar in 1893, Miss Joachim came across a new orchid growing between the two orchids Vanda teres and Vanda

---

15:1 http://www.mediav.com.sg/ossea/html/history/html provides further information and a photograph of this orchid.

hookeriana. Excited by her discovery, she took the orchid to show to the director of the Botanical Garden, Mr. H.N. Ridley, who declared that it was a natural hybrid of the two orchids growing alongside it. This was the beginning of Singapore's orchid history, leading to the honour of Singapore hosting the Fourth World Orchid Conference in 1963 and the later acceptance of the Vanda Miss Joachim orchid as the national flower of Singapore.

The Singapore Museum, although small, has an extensive collection of drawings, painting and artefacts relating to the development of Singapore from the time of the arrival of Sir Stamford Raffles. Alex was staggered at an early view of Boat Quay, with many rows of single-storey and two-storey buildings extending from the small road edging the river, to way back up the hillside, contrasting it with the present-day Boat Quay, where only the first row of houses remains, many converted into pubs and eating places, with the hillside to the rear now filled with enormous high-rise commercial buildings.[15:2] What a change! Progress indeed, but at what expense! However, such dramatic changes are a constant feature, not only of Singapore city, but of the whole of Singapore island.

Opposite to the Museum is a small area of parkland, alongside which are stationed many trishaws, the pedalled version of the old rickshaw, their drivers congregating together in groups to socialise. Alex and the others decided not to take a trishaw, these usually being hired by tourists, and therefore the drivers asking somewhat excessive fares. However, over in JB and in many other places in Johore and beyond, the trishaw enjoys great popularity with the local people, traders and private individuals alike, for carrying goods and passengers cheaply and reliably.

Frequently they would see a Chinese Opera set up on a vacant plot of land, or in the centre of a shopping precinct. The performances would take place in the twilight of evening or even later, adding mystery to the scene. Whilst Alex found the pitch of the voices and the oriental key of the singing alien to his western ears, he enjoyed the magic of the spectacle. Around the time of the Chinese New Year they would come across troupes of Lion dancers, often performing in front of shops, for a small fee, to bring good business to the shop in the forthcoming year.

15:2 See, for example, "Singapore: an illustrated history, 1941-1984", edited by Daljit Singh and V.T. Atasu, published by the Information Division, Ministry of Culture, Singapore, ISBN 9971-75-029-5 soft-cover; ISBN 9971-75-030-5 hardcover; which covers the history of Singapore and the developments taking place during the period.

Alex got into conversation with the leader of one Lion troupe during a pause in the dancing, and found that in view of its considerable weight they take turns in bearing the head of the lion, the person so relieved moving back into the body of the lion, which is of a comparatively low weight. Alex gratefully accepted the offer to try on the head, but declined the invitation, jokingly extended, to lead the troupe in the next dance.

One day George suggested that on the following Sunday they should take a ferry from Finger Pier over to Batam Island, an Indonesian island to the south of Singapore, the ferry taking only about fifty minutes to complete the crossing. He advised that they should take along mosquito repellent and sun cream, and pointed out that when visiting offshore islands, the complete absence of atmospheric pollution means that even greater care must be taken to avoid the harmful effects of the sun.

There are few mosquitoes in Singapore City, but in areas such as the zoo, the botanical gardens, and public parks, and in other places where there are many bushes and trees, the mosquitoes can cause discomfort, so the use of repellent creams or sprays are advisable. As might be expected, in the largely jungle-covered west of Singapore, mosquitoes can be a diconcerting and stressful, but unlike the dense hordes of midges that Alex was familiar with back in Scotland, they are less plentiful. Fortunately, malaria has been eradicated from Singapore, but there are still occasional outbreaks of dengue fever, and very infrequently deaths from malaria amongst tourists arriving from mosquito-infested areas.

The sting from the mosquito is more irritating than painful, first causing a reddish coloured swelling, and then a slight discharge that soon dries up to a small crust that falls off within a day or two, but outside of Singapore, malaria, and the even worse dengue fever, can be fatal, so to avoid this disease, midge repellent and long-sleeved shirts and long trousers are absolutely essential.

George advised Alex that he should never walk through long grass, or through the undergrowth, lest he encounter a poisonous snake, or a scorpion, or that horrid creature, the centipede, which when approached does not crawl away, but advances relentlessly and attacks, to deliver a sting that requires the poor stung person to be hospitalised. However, he pointed out, it is not that these creatures need to be avoided just in Indonesia, as the situation is the same in Malaya, but adding with a smile 'although in Malaya there are also wild tigers and elephants, to say nothing of crocodiles!'

When they arrived at Finger Pier, the departure hall was overcrowded with intending passengers, all clamouring at the desks of the different shipping companies to book their trips. Alex was astonished at the complete lack of orderly queuing, such as is usual in Britain, and which had been instilled in the British by the queuing that was necessary during the war to obtain most scarce items. Amongst the crowd were many young Chinese ladies hanging onto the arms of elderly but prosperous-looking Westerners. In most cases the visit to the island was a business arrangement, and it was likely that the same young ladies would be seen on the arm of a different elderly Westerner the following weekend.

Noticing Alex's interest in these couples, George advise him, with a smile on his face 'I can show you one of the booking offices on Orchard Road where you can hire a 'companion' for yourself the next time you come here.', to which Alex replied with a vulgar comment from his Glasgow days that left George's face with an expression of mock horror!

Eventually, the crowds round the desks thinned a little, so Alex and the others made their way to the appropriate counter, paid for the return crossing and handed over their passports. A short time later, after their ferry had arrived and the passengers had disembarked, the intending passengers again crowded around the desk, hands stretched out to clutch their tickets and their passports. When Alex got to the front of the crowd and gave his name, the clerk behind the counter said 'I'm afraid that your passport doesn't seem to be here Sir. Can you please wait just a few minutes?'

George, who was aware of the accepted practice of demanding brides, particularly from Westerners, who were thought, generally, to be rich, pushed past Alex and said 'Get his passport and ticket now, he's with me.' The clerk reached down to a shelf below his desk and produced the requested items, shrugging his shoulders philosophically, as if to say 'You can't win them all.' George explained that this was almost standard practice, the handing over of a few dollars by a foreigner who was becoming uneasy about missing the ferry immediately resulting in the 'lost' items being found. Alex had learnt another valuable lesson for those travelling to many places in the Far East.

When the ferry was about twenty minutes away from reaching the terminal, the passengers began to assemble close to where the disembarkation ramp, in earlier days called the 'gang-plank' would be run out, struggling and jostling, and trying to slip past each other to get closer to the head of the crowd. Alex thought that this was absolutely pointless, as the total time for the whole of the passengers to disembark was only about five minutes. The unwillingness for those in the Far

East to queue in an orderly manner is responsible for many of the elderly, or those with babies or small children, being unable to travel on public transport, as they would not be able to cope in the general crush.

There is a philosophy in Singapore of kiasu, "me first", which when applied to a person's desire to advance in business or commerce is admirable, but when this philosophy extends to fighting past others, old folk and women and children alike, to get a place on a bus, or to get to the front of the other spectators at a parade, or to snatch items out of the hands of other customers when the big stores hold their sales, it is nothing more than a gross lack of consideration for others. Those, usually men, who proclaim proudly and loudly so that all around can hear, with a smile of immense conceit on their arrogant, stupid faces and not the slightest trace of embarrassment 'I am kiasu!' should be treated with the derision and the contempt that they deserve.

As soon as they were off the ferry, they caught a taxi to the Batam View Hotel, where they each paid a small charge at the reception desk to allow them the use of the hotel's facilities for the day. They swam in the large pool in the grounds, and when they grew tired with this they sat on seats set within the pool at a small bar, drinking "Tiger" in chilled glasses. After this they ate a magnificent sea-food meal at an ethic restaurant sitting on stilts over the sea.

The life style in Indonesia was relaxed, but founded firmly on Muslim principles. The taxi driver who took them back to the ferry terminal on their return home instructed them in the way that they should respect the true believers. They should not hand over anything to a Muslim using the left hand, as this hand is used in the cleansing of the body, nor should they touch the head of a Muslim child, even in a friendly gesture. The taxi-driver told them that his father was a "strong man", as he had fathered thirteen children, with perhaps more to come. Life was simple for the people on this remote community. Food was plentiful, accommodation requirements were simple, and as long as Allah continued to shower favours upon them, life was good.

When they arrived at the terminal on the return journey home and went to the counter to receive their boarding cards, the clerk tried the same trick as his counterpart had at Finger Pier, but this time Alex simply leaned over close to the clerk, and with his face only inches away, said 'Get it now!' and was pleased at the immediate return of his passport, just as it had been when George had demanded it on their journey over to Batam.

Sometimes they just went along to Arab Street to admire the basket-work and the rattan furniture on sale, before calling into a nearby coffee house. Alex marvelled how the different ethnic communities of

Singapore live in harmony, but was told by George that this had not always been the case. Singapore had been a melting pot of people from many different races, and many different religions, and the Government had had to pay a lot of attention to ensuring that the rights of all cultures were respected.

After one visit to Arab Street, George suggested that they go along to Sungei Road, just a short distance away, to see the open air Flea Market. There were stalls selling second-hand items of all manner – car parts, radios and TVs, photographic equipment, clothing, sports gear and general bric-a-brac He came across a stall selling old coins, and bought, for a small sum, some big old Chinese coins, heavily ornamented with Chinese characters, and with a large square central hole. Alex was thrilled with all that he saw, and told George that it reminded him of the Barras' back in Glasgow.

George said that it used to be called the Thieves' Market and told him how, from about the 1930s, if a prosperous house-holder should be robbed, he would go along to the market, where there was a good chance that he could buy back the stolen item from one of the stallholders or from someone just standing there with the item in question. Alex asked why the authorities allowed such practices to continue, to which George responded with 'Because it was in the interests of both parties: the house-holder could recover his stolen item, perhaps a family heirloom or something of sentimental value, for a modest charge; whilst this 'modest charge' would be more that the seller could expect to get for the item from one of the locals.'

George went on to say that the practice was common in many towns and cities in the Far East, and that over to the south side of the city was a little alley - less than three yards wide and twenty yards long - that used to be called Thieves Alley, where such reselling of stolen goods - in Scotland this is termed "resetting" - used to be carried out, but on the odd occasions since his childhood when he had visited the alley there was no sign of such activity: times change and law enforcement becomes more rigorously enforced!

Out of interest - not sexual desire! - they went to Bugis Street, where there were many transvestites. Without body hair and having only slight muscular development, it was easy for them to resemble beautiful girls. They could be seen strutting the sidewalks, or sitting at pavement cafés, exposing a length of smooth shapely calf, in the expectation of meeting new friends. They looked lovely!

One evening they went along to Raffles Hotel on Beach Road. To

Alex this was another world, one of grandeur and opulence.[15:3] They sat at the Long Bar and drank Singapore Slings,[15:4] whilst watching others on the dance floor. Two sides of this area were open to the gardens, which, apart from allowing in the evening breeze, the cool air being distributed by large overhead fans to all parts of the room, also enabled people to stroll in the gardens. The dancers performed the waltz, the quick-step, the fox-trot and, in particular, the tango, this dance being exactly appropriate for the relaxed and elegant atmosphere.

Alex had now been in Singapore for several months and he was aware that he was getting very little exercise. In the past he had got all the exercise that he needed from his physical work, but this was not now the case. He decided not to have a drink and a meal at lunchtime every day, but instead go for a swim. At weekends he walked early morning and late afternoon when the sun wasn't as strong. This was an effort at first, but after a few weeks he started to feel much fitter and enthusiastically started to increase the distance of his walk.

One evening he called into at a bar on his way home, where he got into conversation with a group of expatriates. They were talking about walking across Singapore Island from east to west one Sunday in the near future. Alex was interested, and asked if he could join them. They agreed and told him to join them again on the following week to check the arrangements. Alex agreed, but found that the organiser of the walk, a man from Swansea, "Taffy" Evans, was quite despondent. For one reason or another, the rest of the group had dropped out of the walk, leaving only himself, and possibly Alex, willing to make the attempt. Alex assured him of his firm interest, and the two of them got down to making their preparations.

First, they agreed that they would need a hat with a peak and preferably also a flap at the back, so that both their faces and the back

---

15:3 Some years ago the Government of Singapore required the owners of Raffles to overcome its aging appearance and make it more attractive to visitors, particularly to affluent Japanese visitors. The result is now that the Long Bar, with its large unglazed windows open to the night air, is no longer a beautiful feature of the hotel. Much of the original atmosphere of Raffles was lost in its expensive and luxurious upgrading, and the accommodation charges are now astronomical. Disappointing to those who remember Raffles as it used to be: a glimpse of times of past elegance ... but you can't please everybody!

15:4 The Singapore Sling was introduced by a barman at Raffles Hotel several years before the first World War, and constituted Gin, Cherry Haering, Benedictine, and frsh pineapple juice. Later this was simplified to just alcohol and pineapple juice, and to the use of an automatic dispenser. Again, you can't please everybody!

of their necks would be shielded from the sun: Taffy remembered that he had a couple of these somewhere and said that he would find them and bring them along. They agreed that they would need to wear a long-sleeved shirt and comfortable shoes, and take with them plenty of sun-cream. Taffy suggested that they should apply Vaseline to the inside of their thighs so that the constant movement of one leg against the other wouldn't rub their legs raw. One last item that they would each need would be a small light-weight rucksack, to carry some fruit and cans of soft drinks to replace the inevitable loss of fluid that their bodies would suffer under the tropical heat. Finally, they arranged to meet at the corner of Orchard Road and Scotts Road at seven o'clock on the forthcoming Sunday morning. The rest of the group had stood by sheepishly as Alex and Taffy had completed their plans and were pleased to change the subject as soon as possible, so that they could relieve their uncomfortable feeling of being drop-outs.

They met as the agreed time and then caught a taxi to the coast road close by Changi, known for the infamous Japanese prisoner-of-war camp there during the war, some of the camp buildings being preserved and open to visitors. They asked the driver to stop at a curve in the road at the most westerly point, just short of the village. He was clearly mystified as to why they should want to stop at this deserted spot, but didn't say anything. He had obviously heard of the idiosyncrasies of the western expatriates.

It was fresh and cool at that time of the morning, but they both knew that the testing time would be in the afternoon, when the sun would be overhead and its heat at its peak. They set off following the coast road in a generally south-westerly direction, with the South China Sea on their left, until they reached the East Coast Road, when the road turned to the west. They made good progress, enjoying the warmth of the early sun on their bodies, and the relative absence of vehicles and pedestrians on the roads. After about three hours, as they approached the outskirts of the city, they turned right onto Fort Road, then, heading north, after about half a mile reaching Geylang, an area having a reputation for 'hospitable' ladies, always willing to oblige![15:5] They grinned as they passed a house with its number,"69", presented in enormous size on a board mounted on the house wall: they had too much ahead of them to contemplate such distractions!

15:5 A slim paperback by David Brazil, "No Money, No Honey!", describes the activities of these ladies in this area, and the steps that they take so that they can be identified easily. However, this book may not be available outwith Singapore, where it is reputed to have sold 20,000 copies.

Soon they turned west again, along Mountbatten Road and on to Kallang Road. They then turned to the right to travel along Rochar Canal Road, with the canal on their right. This changing of direction added considerably to the length of the walk, but was unavoidable due to the there being little orthogonality of the roads, and with many of them lying in a north-east to south-west direction or a north-west to south-east direction. However, it was pleasant to travel through the city to areas that were new to them, or to realise that they had been to a particular area before, but had not appreciated its exact location. They agreed that the best way by far to learn the layout of Singapore was to make one's way about on foot, albeit that this is slow, and can be uncomfortable because of the heat.

By this time they had both drunk the last of their cans of lemonade, but hadn't yet felt the need to urinate. Alex became a little concerned about this, so every time they passed a drinks stall they bought more cans, but it was only after Alex had drunk eight cans that he felt, with relief, the urge to pass water. Otherwise, everything was going well. They weren't suffering from the heat, they weren't tired, their feet weren't giving them any trouble, and the insides of their thighs weren't chafing.

Soon they arrived at *Sim Lim* Square, a busy intersection surrounded by tall buildings, with heavy traffic streaming from all directions. Although neither of them knew it, '*sim lim*', pronounced '*senlin*' in Mandarin, is the Chinese name for forest, with the character for '*sen*' comprising three trees combined with that for '*lin*' comprising two trees. It would have been difficult for them to imagine that this area was once a forest as they stood waiting for the traffic streams to be brought to a halt before they could cross the road and continue on their way.

At the junction with Serangoon Road on their right, the road that they were following changed its name to Bukit Timah Road. They carried on along this road all the way to Bukit Timah, and then went beyond through to Bukit Batok, coming out of Bukit Batok close to Jurong Road. The city was now well behind them, and although Jurong Road didn't have any walkways at its sides, it was pleasant to walk along it, passing many little kampongs on the way, with chickens scratching in the road and in the surrounding undergrowth. They stopped at a little eating house and bought further bottles of lemonade. By the time that they reached the end of this road, and had crossed over Jalan Bahar, "Jalan" being the Malayan word for road, the sun was starting to beat down on them fiercely.

They made their way along Upper Jurong Road, soon reaching on their right the tall and impressive arched gateway, smooth-faced and coloured brilliant-white, that was the entrance to the Chinese University of Singapore. Beyond this point there was little sign of human life, the roads and tracks leading off being few and far between. This was the low point of their walk, and they walked in silence, sweating in the heat and with their leg muscles turning to jelly. Eventually they reached Tuas Road, where there was an industrial estate, although this being Sunday, it was deserted.

They turned right at Tuas Basin Link, then left onto the last road of the walk, Tuas Crescent. They carried on along this road, knowing that the end of the walk was in sight, finally stopping when the road made a change in direction from north-west to north-east, the open waters of the Straits of Malacca limiting any further progress west. Alex and Taffy sank to their knees, and then lay down on the grass verge to the road, delighted to have completed a walk of over forty miles, in tropical heat and high humidity, in a little over ten hours.

Whilst during the working week, there would have been the possibility of stopping a passing taxi, they realised that this was out of the question on a Sunday, so they then had to walk back a few more miles to Tuas Seafood Village, a tiny little place comprising a shop and three of four seafood restaurants, their clientele coming almost entirely by either private car or taxi from the areas of greater population closer to the city. When they reached the village, they went into the first restaurant and ordered a jug or draught Tiger, sitting down to drink it in the shade of an awning.

The asked the proprietor to tell the first taxi driver dropping off customers that they wanted him to take them into the city, then they finished off the jug of beer. Taffy burped, and then said proudly 'Well Alex, we showed them. We'll not let them forget this in a hurry, the big girls!' but the twinkle in his eye belied the aggression in his words. Alex concurred heartily with this sentiment, but smiled as he did so.

The two of them were pleased with having accomplished the walk together and, full of euphoria, decided that one day they would set off at midnight to first walk across the island from east to west, and then go up to the causeway and walk from north to south, a total distance of some seventy-five miles, all within the same twenty-four hours. With this they got up and went to meet the taxi that would take them back into the city.

When Alex got into work on the following morning, with stiff muscles but otherwise in a fit condition, he told the staff what he and Taffy and done on the previous day. They all looked at him uncomprehendingly. One of them asked 'Why on earth did you do it? Could you not just have got a taxi?' to which Alex couldn't find an adequate response. Thereafter, he didn't again ever mention the walk, except for when he and Taffy met the bunch of English defaulters in the bar later in the week, where they ridiculed them mercilessly.

Alex's friendship with George, *Xiao Hong* and *Chonghai* was teaching him a lot about the Chinese and Chinese culture. After they had eaten lunch one day, they settled down to chat for a further few minutes before returning to work. George, finding that the teapot was empty, took off the lid, upturned it and then replaced it, whereupon a fresh pot of tea was delivered by the waitress within a couple of minutes. Alex was impressed: this signal was far better than trying to catch the eye of the passing waitress.

As she offered to fill *Ying Hong's* tea cup he quietly rapped the knuckles of his right hand on the table top, whereupon his cup was filled for him. Alex looked at him questioningly. He explained that a long time ago a Chinese emperor had wanted to see for himself, anonymously, the state of the country. Clad in a long gown and a hood, he had travelled far and wide along with several of his ministers, always hiding his identity.

Not speaking in case his accent should give him away, he had resorted to rapping his knuckles on the table-top to express his consent. Alex immediately joined in with this custom, and when the waitress next came round to refill their cups he rapped the table-top with a smile on his face. He would make a Chinese yet! Deciding to teach Alex more about the customs of Chinese tea-drinking, on the following Saturday the three of them took him to a well-known tea shop in Chinatown. They were welcomed into the shop by a smiling and bowing beautiful young Chinese lady, dressed in a traditional costume, the *cheongsam*.

After they were sitting down, the young lady placed before each of them the various items involved: a thin rectangular piece of polished and carved wood to serve as a saucer; a small handle-less cup of about one-and-a-half inches in diameter and two-and-a-half inches in height; and a further slightly bigger similarly handle-less cup. At the centre of the table she placed a crockery item somewhat like a milk jug. All of these delicate china items were beautifully ornamented. She then placed a tea strainer at the centre of the table.

Ying Hong said a few words to the young lady in Chinese, telling her which kind of tea they wanted to drink. She returned a few moments later carrying a tray on which were set a small tea-pot and a kettle. She put down the tray and then filled the pot with water. However, rather than to pour out the tea into the tea-cups, she poured the contents of the tea-pot onto the tray, where it drained away into a false base, it being customary to pour away the first mashing. Immediately, she refilled the pot with water and after a few seconds poured tea from it through the strainer into the jug, after which she poured the strained tea from the jug into the tea-cups.

Alex joined the others in placing the bigger cup, inverted, over the cup containing the tea. The young lady then left the table. Following the example of the others, Alex raised the inverted cup, whereupon the tea, a light refreshing green tea, was then ready to drink, the upper inverted cup being to prevent too much heat loss from the exposed surface of the tea between sips.

Ying Hong showed Alex how to hold the minute cup, encircling the top of the cup with his thumb and first finger and placing his second finger below the cup to stop it from slipping. He advised that the contents of the cup were to be drunk in three sips, the first sip being addressed to happiness, the second to longevity, and the third to the future. The tea-pot was refilled seven times before the tea-drinking ceremony was completed. They left the tea-house, to the bows and smiles of the young Chinese lady, Alex considering it to have been a delightful experience.

One day Alex noticed the youngest of the clerks, *Fu Rong*, "Cotton-rose", using what he knew to be an abacus. He thought *Fu Rong* to be aged about twenty or twenty-two although, in common with most westerners, he found it difficult to assess the age of the Chinese, in view of their smooth skin and relative absence of facial lines. Being curious, he asked her how the abacus works. *Fu Rong* had had a soft spot for Alex for some time, and now that his relationship with Caroline was known to be over, she hoped that they might become better acquainted, so she was thrilled to be able to demonstrate her knowledge.

She placed down the abacus before him and explained its features: 'The abacus has a rectangular frame, with nine columns of counters, or beads, spaced equally horizontally, running on rods from the top long side to the bottom long side. Partway down the rods is a horizontal crosspiece that separates the beads or counters, two being above the bar, and five being below the bar, the beads above the bar being equal to five of the beads below the bar.' Alex understood and nodded his head, so *Fu Rong* continued: 'Counting from the right, the rods represent units, then tens, hundreds, thousands, ten-thousands, and so on. There is spare space on the rods. When the counters are in use they are 'put in' by being pushed up to the crosspiece, and when they are not in use they are 'taken off' by being drawn away from the cross-piece.' Again Alex nodded his head.

Fu Rong showed him the best use of the fingers in putting in and taking off beads that enables the skilled abacus user to achieve an amazing speed. 'The easiest way is to use the thumb to put in counters in the lower part, and to use the forefinger to take off counters in the lower part and put in and take off counters in the upper part.' Then *Fu Rong* gave him an example of the use of the abacus. 'Suppose, as a simple example, I were to add 9 and 7. First, I would put in 9, which is one upper bead and four lower beads. Then to add 7, I would take off three and put in one bead on the immediately adjacent "ten" column. The result is then one bead in the "ten" column, one bead in the upper part of the first "unit" column meaning 5, and one bed in the lower part of the first "unit" column, meaning 1, so the answer is 16.'

Alex grasped the essentials and tried a few examples, and soon had *Fu Rong* applauding as he tackled more difficult additions such as 76 + 82 = 158, using the same basic principles. However, these were only simple demonstrative examples, and could been have solved just as easily with a pencil and a piece of paper, whilst the abacus is able to cope with much more lengthy and complex calculations, but they served the point of demonstrating the principles.

Pleased with his success, *Fu Rong* introduced him to subtraction: 'Suppose I were to want to subtract 3 from 10. As there are no "ones" to subtract the 3 from, 10 is put in as two 5 beads in the "unit" column. 3 is then subtracted from one of the 5 beads, the 5 bead being removed and the remainder of 2 being put in as two "one" beads in the "unit" column. Thus there is now one five bead and two one beads in the "unit", column, giving the answer of 7.' Understanding the principles of this simple subtraction, Alex went on to more difficult examples, soon subtracting long strings of numbers from other long strings of numbers. However, when *Fu Rong* tried to introduce him to multiplication and division, he was completely lost. 'Never mind Mr. MacAlister,' she said, 'I will always be pleased to help you at any time.'

Alex had thoroughly enjoyed his training session on this ancient Chinese counting machine, and thanked *Fu Rong* profusely. This caused her to smile and blush. As he walked away he thought what a lovely woman *Fu Rong* is: she has all the attractive features of a young Chinese woman, she is slim and demure; and, more importantly, she is kind, friendly and helpful. However, he didn't see the expression on *Fu Rong*'s face as he walked up the stairs: she dearly wished Alex would show some personal interest in her.

Chapter sixteen

Alex learnt that George had a sister, *Qiangwei*, "Rose". He was quite surprised that George hadn't mentioned her, as they had become close friends, sharing confidences, and talking about their different cultures, upbringing, education and friends, and their hopes for the future. Alex couldn't understand what reason George might have had for his not having mentioned her. However, George was very protective of his sister, and he didn't want Alex, or any other Westerner, to become involved in her life. George loved his sister dearly, and hoped to see her married to a good Chinese man, rather than becoming involved with a man who one day would return home, or worse still, take his beloved sister back home with him, away from the life and culture that she knew. No, he thought, the less that Alex knows about *Qiangwei* the better.

Reading the "Straits Times" one day, Alex was excited to see that the Extra-Mural Department of the University of Singapore, located just down Bukit Timah Road from where the company offices are, was to provide evening classes in Mandarin for beginners. He rang up and enrolled, the first class being on the coming Thursday at 7.00pm. He duly arrived for the class, finding his way to a lecture room where some thirty or so other students were sitting waiting. After a few minutes the teacher, Mr. *Zhang Chor Eong*, arrived and checked the register.

Mr. *Zhang* then opened his case and produced copies of the text-book that they were to use, the students each buying a copy from him. He started the lecture by speaking for some time about Mandarin, explaining that it is a very tonal dialect, a change in tone for the same character giving the character a completely different meaning. He then introduced the students to the four tones of the Mandarin dialect: the 1st tone, a level high tone; the 2nd tone, a rising tone; the 3rd tone, a falling then rising tone; and the 4th tone, a falling tone. The written tone marks, in order, are: a horizontal line; a rising line; a saucer-shaped line; and a falling line. Whilst the tone is usually indicated by a tone mark written above the character, a number is sometimes used instead, placed after the English spelling of the character.[16:1]

[16:1] Hereafter in this novel, tone marks will generally only be inserted for the first time that a character is used, to make the subsequent reading of the character easier. With personal names and names such as Beijing, that are well-known in the West, the tone marks are generally omitted and standard English is used in place of *hanyu pinyin*, "sounds combined into syllables", i.e. "Beijing" instead of *bei3jing1,* with the initial letter in upper case: with Chinese characters there is no such thing as upper case.

He introduced them to *han4yu3 pin1yin1*, "Chinese language joined up sounds", in which a Chinese character is written in the closest-sounding word in English to the Chinese sound, irrespective of whether or not that word has a meaning in English, followed by a number indicating the tone, giving to the class as an example the well-known question:

ma1ma ma4 ma3 ma? "Is mother scolding the horse?"

In the above example: *mama* with tone 1 means "mother"; *ma* with tone 4 means "scold"; *ma* with tone 3 means "horse"; whilst the final *ma* does not have a tone, but has a quiet level sound, the purpose of which being just to indicate that the sentence is a question rather than a statement. When Alex looked at him with an expression of bewilderment on his face, Mr. *Zhang* explained that whilst in English a question is indicated by a raised tone at the end of a sentence, this cannot be done in Chinese, as the final character would then be given a different meaning.

The class then went on to spend an hour chanting the different tones, which was almost like singing. Initially, Alex found this embarrassing, as he had not had any musical education or practice in singing in his whole life, as such would have been considered effeminate by the boys back in his school at Govan, and led to the risk of being mocked and called a "fairy", or worse.

Mr. *Zhang* presented the class with the most-common polite response to the question "How are you?", which is *wo3hen3hao3*, "I am very well", drawing attention to the three consecutive third tones, where the falling-rising, falling-rising, falling-rising of the tones would make the response cumbersome. He told them that in this situation the middle third tone would be replaced by the first tone, so that the words flow more easily.

Next Mr. *Zhang* pointed out that in Mandarin the final "g" in words such as *yang* is stopped short in a nasal manner, rather than being emphasised as in English, where the word would be pronounced rather like "yan-g". Before many minutes Alex was able to pronounce such words properly, without effort or thought. He was amused when Mr. *Zhang* told the class of the graphic Chinese phrase for a medical operation: *da3 zhen1*, "strike with the knife!"

When the class came to an end, Alex rushed home and sat down with a can of Tiger, not sure, in view of the complexity of the language, that he could cope with further study, but as the day for the next class approached, he had come round in his views, and resolved to give it another go. The number of students at the second class had dropped to only about fifteen. Having heard the way that spoken Chinese is presented in Hollywood Westerns, "Me wantee", "Me go town tomorrow", etc., and heard that there is only the present tense in the Chinese language, and that verbs are not conjugated, the defectors had thought that at the end of their first class they would be able to call at a Chinese hawker stall on their way home and order a meal in Chinese: no such luck!

The class learnt that the personal pronoun, "I", in Mandarin is *wo3*, i.e. using the third tone, and that it is converted to "we" by the addition of *men*, to give *wo3men*. Mr. *Zhang* then surprised the class the class by introducing them to another form of "we", *zan2men*, which can be used in a conversation between two persons to include in the "we" any number of other persons, who may or may not be present.

For example, in speaking to a foreigner in English, a Chinese person could say "In China, all of us work hard for the benefit of society.", but in speaking in Mandarin the use of zan2men would replace "all of us". If two students were waiting to go on a visit, and were joined by a third student who asked them "Where are you going to?", the reply "We are going to visit the town hall," might be taken, unless further clarifying words were added, to mean just the two who were waiting, but in Mandarin the use of *zan2men* in place of *wo3men* makes it perfectly clear that the new arrival is going on the visit also, or indeed, so the whole of the class might be.

Mr. Zhang carried on to explain that the character for the singular "you" in Mandarin is *ni3*, i.e. with the third tone, and for the plural is appended with *men*, to give *ni3men*, in the same way as with *wo3men*. However, when addressing a teacher, an employer, a parent, an older person or any other person to whom one wants to show respect, *nin4*, i.e. with the fourth tone, is used instead of *ni3*. Alex was beginning to think that he had bitten off more than he could chew, but decided to persevere.

At the third class the numbers had fallen even further, down to six. However, Mr. *Zhang* was not dismayed: indeed he seemed to have expected the fall, based on his experience in teaching Chinese to foreigners. The remaining students were generally pleased at the reduced class size, as it enabled them to be given tuition on a more personal basis. Amongst the remaining six was an elderly Chinese lady who had abandoned her native Chinese language in her youth, in order to concentrate on English so as to promote her progress within the English-speaking business community, but who now, admirably, felt the need to rediscover her roots as a Chinese. She was a living example of the Chinese proverb: *huo2 dao4 lao3, xue2 dao4 lao3*, "Live until old, study until old.", or simply "study all your life."

She was not typical however, as many non-Chinese-speaking English-educated Singaporean Chinese tend to regard themselves as "Westernised Chinese", and, regrettably, although it is doubtful that they would ever admit it, feel a little superior to those who are Chinese educated. However, the Chinese-educated have their own response, in describing the English-educated as: 'Like a banana; yellow on the outside, white on the inside.'[16:2]

Apart from just teaching the students Chinese language at his evening class, Mr. *Zhang* also taught them something about Chinese culture, including the everyday culture that was all around them. One student asked the meaning of the often-seen symbol made up of a circle split vertically by a curving line having a shape like a reverse letter S, the left-hand sign being coloured black and the right-hand side being coloured white. Mr. *Zhang* started off by explaining that ancient Chinese philosophers believed that the world is filled with a life-force called *chi*, of which there are two forms: the healthy and lucky *chi* being called *sheng1 chi*, where *sheng1* means "birth"; and the stagnant, misfortune-bearing *chi* called *sha1 chi*, where *sha1* means "kill", the favourable *sheng1 chi* being promoted by a proper combination of *yang2* and *yin1*. He explained that *yang2* is the positive component of *chi*, and is bright, active, masculine and energetic, represented by such as hot, light, heaven, solid, sharp and male, whilst *yin1* is represented by their opposites, cold, heavy, earth, hollow, blunt and female.

All of life is either *yang* or *yin*, but one is not more important than the other. Indeed, *yang* and *yin* contain the seeds of their opposites, represented by the small circle of the opposite colour found in the two parts of the symbol. What is important is to maintain a perfect balance between *yang* and *yin* so as to promote the beneficial *sheng chi*, the practice of this balancing process being called *feng1 shui1*, "wind, water."[16:3]

16:2 In a twist to "banana", in her book "Wild Swans: three daughters of China", published by Anchor books, ISBN 0-385-42547-3, *Jung Chang* tells how during the Cultural Revolution the Red Guards referred to those suspected of being capitalist 'roadsters' as "radishes", i.e. appearing to be 'red', loyal revolutionaries, on the outside, whilst actually being 'white', capitalist sympathisers, on the inside.

16:3 See, for example, "*Feng1 Shui1* from scratch" by Jonathan Dee, published by D & S Books, ISBN 1-5903327-1. In contrast to the above large-format book is the tiny book "*Feng Shui*" by Richard Craze in the "Collins Gem" series, ISBN 0-00-472316-3. Following a brief account of the history of *feng shui*, this back-pocket-size book

Mr. *Zhang* went on to explain some of the actions that are good *feng shui*: a south-facing front door; children's rooms in the south-east part of the house to gain the benefit of the morning sun; no clutter to restrict he passage of *sheng chi* through the house; plants with soft and round leaves in the house; halls painted in light colours; a ventilated lobby between the toilet and the rest of the house; and a curved path from the gate to the door of the house; whilst unfavourable *sha chi* is promoted by a nearby cemetery, refuse dump or industrial estate; a lamp post or telegraph pole outside the house; a visible aerial or a poster at the window of a neighbour's house; a direct passage from the front door to the back door, as *sha chi* prefers to travel in straight lines; a doorway facing the stairs; a toilet opening directly into the lounge; and dripping taps.

Alex came to the conclusion that *feng shui* is the suggestion of changes that are known by the *feng shui* practitioner, the "geomancer", to be likely to be well received, such as attractive ornaments in the living room or wind-chimes on a terrace, or comfortable dining-room chairs, such as will encourage dinner guests to linger; or else they are the application of 'rules' for healthy living that had been developed over many years, such as: toilets being located against outside walls so that adequate ventilation can be provided or, if not, that powered ventilation systems are installed; that kitchens are well lit and airy, with care taken that cookers, hot pans and kettles do not create a hazard; and that open fires are fitted with fire guards to protect the young.

He believed that the geomancer is a man with a great understanding of people and having a great knowledge of features that can improve a home, a garden or an office block, and of good practice for healthy living, the presentation of *feng shui* in terms of animals, mountains, trees and other symbolic forms being to enable its importance to be appreciated by the simpler and less-educated people of the past. Alex saw an equivalence between the *feng shui* 'rules' and the Ten Commandments of Christianity, the latter being no more than the formalising of well-known 'rules of conduct' to enable people to live at peace with each other. He saw that to some extent that the balancing of *yang2* and *yin1* has a counterpart in the western saying "All things in moderation."

However, he felt that features such as the "Eight directional trigram" and the "*lo shu* Magic Square" were just baggage that had been built up around *feng shui* to add mystery and apparent depth to it, as is the case

---

presents a mass of associated information along with many illustrations and also an extensive list of materials for further reading.

with most western religions, where depth is given by such as: the conducting of ceremonies using Latin or a long-since discarded form of wording; by ornate formal dress of the leaders of the religion; by the playing of beautiful organ music and the singing of stirring hymns; and by the building of magnificent churches devoted to the God of the religion concerned. However, he decided that he should study this topic in greater depth before passing judgement.

At his next lecture Mr. *Zhang* introduced them to the Chinese Almanac, a large volume considered popularly to be able to enable the ordinary Chinese person to make their own predictions as to such things as the most auspicious day on which to move house, to start a new job, to make a financial or personal decision, to get married, the most suitable person to marry, and the most suitable time to conceive, taking into account the particular year and the month of the year, the birth dates of the individuals involved, and other relevant information.

Alex was wary of the Almanac, but thought that its writer or writers must have a thorough understanding of Chinese customs and traditions and at the same time a sound knowledge of human behaviour. Similarly, he felt that fortune tellers back in Britain, who are consulted by many people seeking reassurance when facing important decisions, or who are fearful as to what the future holds for them, must call, similarly, on their knowledge of human behaviour, whilst at the same time trying to detect what it is that the person consulting them wants to hear, so that a prediction can be made that sends him or her away happy.

He did not believe that the consideration of a small amount of personal data relating to the person concerned and then using it in a mechanistic way in conjunction with the almanac or, in the case of the fortune teller, by an examination of the tea leaves at the bottom of a cup, could yield any useful advice beyond that provided by the personal experience of the *feng shui* practitioner or the fortune teller. Alex believed that the future lies out of the sight of mere mortals, and cannot be predicted. The most that anyone can do is to make a guess as to the future, based on the events of the past, on the prevailing social and political situation, and on the personalities and circumstances of those involved. Wiser and more experienced people can make better predictions because their data-base of human behaviour is broader-based and more extensive, such a person being the *feng shui* practitioner.

Slowly, Alex made progress with his evening class at the university, and he also started to attend evening classes in Mandarin at the Chinese Chamber of Trade and Commerce in the city centre, although these classes were more difficult for him to follow, as they were not for English speakers, but for those Chinese with some knowledge of Mandarin who wanted to become more proficient.

Upon his completion of the beginner's class at the university, Alex was awarded a Certificate of Attendance, and immediately enrolled to repeat the class. With the confidence gained after the completion of the second beginner's class, he then ventured to join the intermediate class. This class was to be conducted by Mr. *Loo*, a distinguished and senior member of the Department of Chinese Studies of the National University of Singapore, and the Singapore representative to many international committees and councils concerned with the Chinese language. At the first lecture, the class awaited his arrival with trepidation.

Mr. *Loo* entered the room, a well-built man with shortly-cropped black hair and a strong authoritative presence, like that of a senior member of the Chinese government. The class sat upright! He strode to the front of the class and surveyed them all with a stern eye. The class members thought to themselves 'What on earth have we let ourselves in for?'

Mr. Loo then exclaimed in a loud strong voice 'I am *Loo*.' After a silence of some five seconds he continued: 'My brother is James Bond!' which person was the secret service agent in a book written by Ian Fleming. The class was dumfounded. After a further long pause for dramatic effect he said 'Turn my name upside down and what do you have?' Still the class was dumfounded. 'Double-0-Seven! I am licensed to kill!' He then roared with laughter at having deceived them so successfully.[16:4] The whole class laughed along with him, relieved that he should have turned out to be such a humorous man

In his classes, Mr. *Loo* advanced their knowledge of Chinese rapidly, using the teaching books that he had produced himself. When the number of students inevitably dwindled, he told the survivors 'Now that we are down to the die-hards, we can make great progress.' This was indeed true, but the progress of one or two particular students was more spectacular than that of the others, as due the Chinese concern for loss-of-face, they were "false learners", this being an expression used for those who had already had some experience of the Chinese language, but who wanted to appear to be fast learners. Alex thought

---

16:4 Mr. Loo's humour was similar to that of the author of the classic "How green is my valley", which is set in a small Welsh village called Llados. This name thrilled Welch language purists, until someone noticed that "Llados" when read in reverse is "Sod all!"

mei2 guan1xi, "never mind."

During one class he told the students that the teaching of the Chinese language to foreigners used to carry the death penalty, but added 'For you, I will take this risk.' The class joined in with his laughter. Then he explained that this edict had been declared at the beginning of the Chinese period of isolationism, close on six hundred years ago, but no-one had yet told him that it had been withdrawn. Mr. *Loo* told them of the Chinese names for the fingers of the hand. The thumb is *muzhi3*, where *mu* does not translate into an equivalent English word whilst *zhi3* means "finger"; the first finger is *zhi3zhi3*, "the finger to point with", the character zhi3 meaning both "finger" and "to point"; the second finger is *wei4zhi3*, "the finger to taste with"; the third finger is *wu2ming2zhi3*, "the finger with no name"; and the fourth finger is *xiao3zhi3*, as in English, "the little finger." Alex was amused that the name of the third finger is that it has no name! In Britain, when referring to the left hand, this finger would be called "the ring finger".

One week Mr. *Loo* told the class that as they were now gaining an appreciation of the Chinese language it was time that he introduced them to ancient Chinese poetry.[16:5] A lot of the poems were about the sadness of leaving home or family to find work in some distant place, usually never to return. Mr. *Loo* sang the poems to the class in a plaintive voice that touched them emotionally.

Alex was moved by such poems of homesickness, and remembered with regret his treatment of old Mr. *Chan*, who had left his homeland to come to Britain and live amongst a community containing such a large unappreciative and hostile element. He cheered up when he had the thought that when he went back to Govan at some time in the future to apologise to Mr. *Chan* for his treatment of him, he would not do so in English, but in Mandarin!

During one class Mr. *Loo* asked the students, in turn, their place of birth. When Alex replied "Scotland", Mr. *Loo*, who was widely travelled, responded with '*su1ge2lan2! Zhen1 hao3! Su1ge2lan2 you3 shan1 you3 shui3!*', "Scotland! Really good! Scotland has mountains and lakes!"[16:6], the phrase "*you3 shan1 you3 shui3*" being a popular Chinese way to describe a country having beautiful scenery.

One thing that Mr. *Loo* pointed out was that Chinese poems written more than a thousand years ago still rhyme when read at the present

---

16:5 For Chinese, pinyin and English texts of the poems of some of the greatest Chinese poets, log onto: <http://www.chinese-poems.com/index.html>.

16:6 Being pedantic, the only enclosed body of water in Scotland described as a "lake" is the "Lake of Menteith", the rest being called "lochs".

day, indicating the steadfastness of the Chinese language. Indeed, although Mandarin was being promoted in Singapore to the detriment of Cantonese, the latter is a more complex dialect, with one more tone than in Mandarin, and having had even less spoken 'drift' over the centuries than had Mandarin.

Alex recalled the well-meaning effort of one of his teachers in Govan to introduce some culture into his teaching, in one lesson reciting the works of Shakespeare. The class had listened in silence and with total lack of comprehension, the language having suffered such an enormous drift over less than four hundred years that no-one knew what he was talking about. Alex thought to himself 'Ignore those who say "English is a living language" just to excuse their own sloppy treatment of it, and their ignorance of its structure and disregard of its grammar! Why change a beautiful logically-based language to suit the transient wishes of the younger, as yet not thoroughly educated, members of the community?'

Poems had not featured at all in Alex's education - excepting the illicit poems repeated by the children in the playground - as indeed they do not feature to any great extent in the education of British children generally. However, in ancient times, the candidates for the Imperial Examinations in China, held only once every two or three years, and in which no more than a few percent of the candidates were successful, were called upon to write a poem, as it was believed that this revealed the thought processes of a person more clearly than by any other means.

The later stages of the intermediate class introduced Chinese characters.[16:7] Alex marvelled at the beauty of the strokes: strong, bold and slashing, not like some of the Japanese characters, which are curly or wriggly. Many of the characters expressed their meaning clearly, such as the character for "horse", *ma3*, where the mane of a galloping horse can be seen streaming out behind it, as it gallops along on its four pounding hooves: however, he was saddened to learn that the simplification of some characters some years ago had led to the representation of an actual horse now being less close to the actual appearance of a horse: this had happened also with the character for "dragon", *long2*.

A character that looks very like its meaning is that for "goat", *yang2*, where the horns are apparent to everyone. The teacher told him

---

[16:7] An interesting book on Chinese characters is "Language, Art and Symbols from the Land of the Dragon: the Cultural History of 100 Chinese characters" by Ni Yibin, published by Duncan Baird Publishers Ltd., 2009, ISBN 978-1-84483-829-5, hardback, 192 pages. This is a book for the enthusiast, being quite expensive, but beautifully produced and illustrated.

that one of his favourite characters was that for "smile", *xiao4*, which looks very like the face of a woman smiling with seductively part-closed eyes! However, whilst Alex could see his point, he felt that in this instance a little more imagination was called for.

One character that amused Alex was that for "peace", *an1*, which shows a flat roof with a chimney and small facia boards, with the character for "woman", *nu3*, set beneath it. Mr. *Loo* explained, tongue in cheek, that the only time that a man can get any peace is when his wife is back at home under the roof whilst he is away elsewhere!

Another character that caught Alex's attention was that for "pig", *zhu1*, which shows a creature with four legs and a curly tail. When the character for pig is shown sitting below the same roof as that used for peace, this becomes "home", *jia1*: home is thus where the whole family lives, including the family pig!

The character for "pig", zhu*1*, whilst showing four legs and a tail, simply uses a horizontal line for the head. Alex was interested to find that when this line is surmounted by an addition looking like a trunk raised in anger, it becomes "elephant", *xiang4*: such a marvellous economy in strokes!

Mr. *Loo* introduced the class to *ping1*, which resembles a standing person leaning forwards over a table and has the meaning "the crack of a rifle or pistol"; and to its vertically-symmetrical counterpart, *pang1*, meaning "bang" When these two characters are placed together, the strong impression is given of two adversaries facing each other across a table. When account is taken also of the sound of the characters and of their meaning, *ping1-pang1* is seen to be a magnificent Chinese name, "ping-pong", for "table-tennis".[26]

When the Chinese began to run out of single characters, or more precisely, to run out of sounds, they made compound characters by placing two characters side-by-side, or one under the other, often one character indicating the sound with the other indicating the meaning. One compound character that Alex considered to be an ancient joke created by the learned men of the day was that for "fresh", *xian1*, which shows the characters for goat and fish, which can be amongst the smelliest of creatures.

A character that Alex found of interest was *ka3*, meaning "block the road", this character being a composite character - not a compound character - of *shang4*, "above", and *xia4*, "below": if nothing can pass above and nothing can pass below, then a road is well and truly blocked! When *ka3* is used together with *che1*, "vehicle", i.e. *ka3che1*, this is the very appropriate Chinese name for "lorry", as the latter vehicle is a common impediment, worldwide, to the smooth flow of traffic. What a beautifully graphic language Chinese is!

Shang4 resembles the ground - a horizontal line - with a trunk and a single branch of a tree growing above it, whilst *xia4* resembles the ground with a large root and a single side root growing from it.

There are other characters in which a horizontal line is used to indicate the ground, such as *shi4*, where a longer horizontal line, the arms, and a vertical line, the torso, standing above the ground, represent "an important person: a scholar, a person trained in a particular way or a commendable person" standing tall above the ground; and *tu3*, in which a slightly shorter horizontal line, set close to the horizontal line for "ground", together indicate "earth".

Someone in the class asked what the origin was of the "double happiness" symbol that is often seen in the Chinese part of the city, as ornamentation on furniture and particularly as written as wall and table decorations at Chinese weddings. Mr. *Loo* recounted that many years ago, in the ancient Tang Dynasty in China, a young student set off from his home village to the capital to attend the national final examination, in which the top performers would be selected as ministers in the court.

Unfortunately, the student fell ill on his journey to the capital whilst passing through a mountain village, but a herbalist doctor and his beautiful daughter took him to their house and treated him well. He recovered quickly due to the good care of the father and daughter.

When the time came to leave he found it hard to say goodbye to the beautiful girl, just as she found it hard to say goodbye to him: they had fallen in love! Before he left, the girl wrote down the right-hand part of an antithetical couplet for the student to match whilst he was away:

"Green trees against the sky in the spring rain,
while the sky sets off the spring trees in the obscuration."

The young student said to the girl 'Well, I can match the couplet, although it will not be easy, but you will have to wait until I have finished the examination.' The young girl nodded her agreement. In the examination the student won first place, and his efforts were appreciated by the Emperor. He was interviewed and tested by the Emperor, who wrote down the left-hand part of a couplet and asked the student to provide a right-hand part to complete it. The Emperor wrote:

"Red flowers dot the land in the breeze's chase
while the land colours up red after the kiss."

The young man realised immediately that the part-couplet given to him by the girl was the perfect complement to the Emperor's part-couplet, so he gave the girl's part-couplet as the answer without hesitation. The Emperor was delighted to see that the matching half to his couplet was so suitable and harmonious, and he authorised the young man's appointment as a minister in his court, but allowed him to pay a visit to the young girl's village first before taking up the appointment. The young man and the young girl met happily at her father's home and he told her of the Emperor's couplet.

They soon got married. For the wedding the couple doubled the Chinese character for happiness and drew the new character on a piece of red paper and placed it on the wall to express the happiness for the two events, the young man's appointment and the couple's wedding.

From then on it became a social custom to display posters bearing the new character at weddings. Some people say that the symbol resembles two people, a man and a woman, holding hands in wedded bliss. After listening to this lovely story, one of the class, with a cynical smile on his face, leaned over to Alex and whispered 'Not like nowadays, where the "double happiness" at the wedding ceremony often refers not only to the wedding but also to the knowledge that the married couple will soon be listening to the patter of tiny feet!'

Alex was intrigued to learn that the Chinese find names for foreign countries that sound like the name of the country, but at the same time flatter it, for example: *ying1guo2*, "brave country", for England; *de2guo2*, "virtuous country", for Deutschland, Germany; *fa3guo2*, "legal country", for France. The most impressive of all is the Chinese name *sha1di4*, "sand country", for Saudi. How admirably flattering or descriptive, whilst at the same time sounding just like the name of the country when spoken in English!

The Mandarin name for *Hong Kong* is *xiang1gang3*, "fragrant harbour" reflecting the situation before Hong Kong was colonised, but the pollution flowing down the Pearl River from China into the harbour, along with *Hong Kong*'s own contribution, has long since rendered this a misnomer: however, in the course of time the harbour may once again be fragrant.

Alex learnt that the Mandarin name for Singapore is *xin1jia1po4*, where *xin1* means "new", *jia1* means "add" and *"po1"* means "slope" or "sloping". These characters, therefore, were probably chosen on the basis of mnemonics, i.e. joining up sounds to make syllables rather than being descriptive. However, Singapore is **new**, and constantly **add**ing to its housing pool and it certainly has an upwards **slope** to the graph of its financial reserves!

The Chinese are considerate and flattering when giving Chinese names to non-Chinese persons, and to foreign countries, although in some cases the opportunity is taken for a little gentle ridicule.[16:8]

Some of the expressions used in Chinese are not to be taken literally. When, during the cultural revolution, Chairman Mao had said 'Let a hundred flowers of thought bloom', he had meant 'Let **many** flowers of thought bloom.' In the same way, when a superior gives a problem to a junior to solve he might say 'Try a thousand ways', meaning for the subordinate to "Do **all** that you can." The superior might ask the junior to carry out a task as soon as possible, by saying 'Do it *ma3shang4*', i.e. "on horseback", despite this rapid form of transport and communication having been surpassed for many decades.

Perhaps the most well-known example of this kind of exaggeration to emphasise a point was in the blessing, as seen on the front of the large building in *tian an men* square where the top Chinese party leaders address the Chinese people, that was given to the emperor of China in the old days: *wan4 shui4, wan4 shui4, wan4 wan4 shui4!*: "May you live ten thousand years, ten thousand years, ten thousand ten thousand years!", which is an enormous length of time,[16:9] but meaning simply "May you live for **a very long time**.

The Mandarin words for 'aeroplane' are *fei1ji1*, "flying machine", where both of the characters have the first tone. However, some unpleasant men would deliberately pronounce the first character with the second tone, i.e. *fei2*, changing its meaning to "fat", leaving the second character with the first tone, where it can also mean "chicken", suggesting that air-hostesses are "fat chickens." Even more unpleasant men would leave the first character with the first tone so that it still meant "flying", but give the second character the fourth tone, changing

---

16:8 The people of Hong Kong, however, did not display their usual kindness when just before the colony was restored to China they gave the nickname *pang4zi*, meaning "fat one", to its somewhat corpulent then-Governor, Patten. The Chinese name given to the author by his Chinese teacher in Singapore is *tian2wei1si4*. As the Chinese language does not accommodate "tr", the teacher chose the character *tian2*, meaning field, which, albeit mundane, is reasonable close to the "Trav" part of the author's family name, Travis. However, he gave the flattering characters *wei1*, meaning impressive strength, might and power, and *si4*, meaning to think, to consider and to deliberate upon, for the remaining part of the name. In all, a good Chinese name, albeit somewhat inaccurate in the flattering part!

16:9 Unlike English, the Chinese language has a character for ten thousand, *wan4*. In English, large numbers are expressed in multiples of 1000, e.g. a million is expressed as a thousand thousand, but in Chinese large numbers are expressed in multiples of 10000, so that a million would be expressed as *bai3wan4*, where *bai3* is a hundred. Thus "*wan4wan4*" is 10000 multiplied by 10000, i.e. a hundred million!

its meaning to "prostitute", suggesting that air-hostesses are "flying prostitutes." Although only intended to make a bad-taste 'humorous' play on words, these expressions are not just vicious and unkind: the Singapore air-hostesses are beautiful, slim and elegant, and are of unquestionable morality.

Alex learnt a little Chinese *xiao3hua4*, a "joke", based on some characters with the same sound and the same tone having several different meanings. He would ask his Chinese friends *'ni3 xi3huan1 shen2me jiao4?'*, meaning literally 'You like what religion?' After all of them had given him their answer he would say *'wo3 xi3huan1 shui4jiao4'*, meaning "I like to sleep": *jiao4*, i.e., pronounced with the fourth tone meaning, amongst several other things, religion and sleep. In a way, this is like the situation in English, where "jack" can be a man's name, or a raising device, i.e., a wheel jack, or the small flag at the bows of a ship.

There were other silly little jokes in a similar vein: *'ni3 xi3huan1 shen2me hua1?'*, literally "You like what flowers", meaning "What flowers do you like", with the eventual remark from the person asking the question *'wo3 xi3huan1 bao4mi3hua1'*, meaning "I like popcorn", although he or she could have said that they like peanuts, as the China name for peanuts is *hua1 sheng*: the word *hua1* in the question and the two answers means "flower". In English, the counterpart to this silly joke could be "I like cauliflowers".

In another joke, a young man travelled to China to learn Mandarin. Whilst there he developed a taste for *shui3jiao3*, "water dumplings", these being little pastry bags about the size of a golf ball that are filled with meat or prawns or vegetables and then closed up and steamed - as opposed to being baked or fried or boiled - until they are cooked, hence the prefix *shui3*, "water".

One day he decided that he would go to the local food store and buy some of these dumplings, but would order them in Mandarin! He entered the shop and said to the young lady assistant *xiao3jie3, yi1 wan3 shui3jiao3 dou1shao1 qian2?*, in which *xiao3jie3*, "little elder sister", is the appropriate polite form of address, *yi1 wan3* means "one bowl", *shui3jiao3* means "water dumplings", and *dou1shao1 qian2* asks "how much money?" He believed that he had said to the assistant 'Miss, how much is a bowl of water dumplings?'

Pleased with his efforts, the young man stood smiling at the lady assistant, but was shocked when she swung her arm and slapped him violently across the face! He was alarmed and mystified! What had he said? What he didn't know was that *yi1 wan3* means not only "one bowl" but also "one night", and that *shui3jiao3* means not only "water dumplings" but also "sleep" (with you), so that he had effectively asked the young lady how much it would cost him to sleep with her for the night! Young men in China wishing for a bowl of water dumplings should be careful what they say, as also should young men wishing to spend a night with a young lady assistant, or they may be surprised at what they get!

A similar story, also from Shandong Province, that Alex learnt, but again not from Mr. *Loo*, related to the efforts of a language teacher from Beijing who was in a small village in the province to attempt to teach the people in the village standard Mandarin, as opposed to the local version that they spoke. He explained to them that the words *ri4* and *tian2* both mean "night" and that there is no difference in their meaning. However, one young village girl spoke up, but with great trepidation, knowing that in her village *ri4* was the local word for sexual intercourse. 'But teacher, they don't mean the same. *yi1 tian2 yi1 ri4*, "one night one xxxx", is fine, but *yi1 ri4 yi1 tian2*, "one xxxx lasting all night", is too much!'

This joke reminded Alex of the couplet that is often seen in Britain on postcards and on larger cards mounted the walls of cafés and pubs:

"Once a Knight, always a Knight,
but once a night is enough!"

In one of his classes Mr. *Loo* told the students about the legendary creature, the *qi1lin1*, or "Kirin." Basic to Chinese mythology is that there are four spiritual creatures, each guarding a cardinal direction of the compass, these four directions being represented since the second century B.C. by four celestial animals: the Dragon for the East, the Bird for the South, The Tiger for the West, and the Tortoise for the North, these animals having no connection with the twelve animals of the Chinese zodiac. Over the course of time, the tiger was replaced by the mythological Chinese creature the *qi1lin1*, which is pronounced in Japanese as Kirin. The creature is said to have the head of a lion, the tail of an ox, the hooves of a horse, a body covered with the scales of a fish, and a single horn, although other accounts say the forehead is that of a wolf, the body that of a musk deer and that it has a fleshy horn.

The Kirin is said to appear only before the birth or death of a great and wise person. Legend has it that in the 6th century, a Kirin appeared before a young woman, *Yen Tschen*-tsai, and dropped into her hand a piece of jade engraved with the message that she would bear a son who would be "a king without a throne": the young woman gave birth to Confucius. The Kirin was said to appear again just before the death of

Confucius. Believed to live in paradise, the Kirin personifies all that is good, pure and peaceful, and it can live for a thousand years. One legend says that at one time a Kirin was killed, whereupon disaster fell upon the land. Because of its single horn, "Kirin" was sometimes translated into English as "Unicorn".

For Mr. *Loo*'s last class, he brought along a small tape recorder and played some traditional Chinese music. On the first tape, two instrumentalists played an *er4hu2*, a two-stringed type of fiddle that has a mellow haunting sound, and a *gu3zheng1*, a long multi-string zither-like instrument that is plucked with the fingers, the two instruments complementing each other admirably.

The second tape was of a symphony orchestra playing the ballad "The butterfly lovers." Mr. *Loo* told them the sad story behind the ballad. A long time ago in China, a young girl had wanted to study, but in those days the privilege of studying was restricted just to young men, young ladies of the time being expected to embroider, play a musical instrument, practice calligraphy, and so on. The young girl had then cropped her hair and donned boys' clothing, and gone off to study, pretending indeed to be a boy. She became very attracted to one of her fellow pupils, and very soon realised that she had fallen in love with him.

For a while she was in a quandary as to what to do, but one day she invited him to visit her home to meet her 'sister'. When the young man arrived, his fellow pupil was dressed in girls' clothing, and the young man realised why he had felt so attracted to 'him'. The two of them declared their love for each other, and the young man asked the girl's parents for her hand, but the parents refused, saying that she was promised in marriage to a rich old man.

The two of them were forbidden to meet again. The young man was distraught, and in his sadness became ill and died. On the day of the wedding of the young girl to the old man, the carriage taking her to the wedding ceremony passed by the cemetery where the young man was buried. Seeing his gravestone through the open gates of the cemetery, the young girl was overcome with grief and jumped from the carriage and threw herself down onto the grave, where she joined him in death. There was a sound and a movement in the air, and then two butterflies rose up from the ground, and flew away together, the two young lovers now re-united in death. The music reflected the sadness of the story and Alex was moved emotionally by the tragedy of the situation.

Alex had enjoyed learning various old Chinese sayings from Mr. *Loo*, one appealing to him in particular:

"If two men own a horse, that horse will be thin
If two men own a boat, that boat will leak."

He had also heard a similar proverb relating to the carrying of water for a monastery:

"If there is only one monk in the monastery
he will carry water and drink his fill,
whilst if there are two monks they will share the water that one carries,
but if there are three monks no-one will carry water
and all will go thirsty."

Alex considered that this summed up human nature in joint enterprises exactly: 'I will take things easy today and let the others get on with it!' Alex was pleased to find by these sayings that the Chinese and the British think along similar lines, and this view was reinforced when he started to learn Chinese idioms. There were many idioms[16:10] that Alex found to have popular western counterparts, such as those, including their tone marks, as follow: *bu4 jing4 er2 zou3*, 'run without legs', meaning "spread like wildfire"; *bu4 ru4 hu3 xue2, yan3 de2 hu3 zi3*, 'the only way to catch a tiger cub is to go into the tiger's den', meaning "nothing ventured, nothing gained"; *chen4 re4 da3 tie3*, literally "strike whilst the iron is hot"; *da4 hai3 lao1 zhen1*, 'fish for a needle in the ocean', meaning "look for a needle in a haystack"; *da4 zhi4 ruo4 yu2*, 'a man of great wisdom often appears slow-witted', "still waters run deep"; *dao4 shen2me shan1 chang4 shen2me ge1*, 'sing different songs on differet mountains', "when in Rome do as the Romans do"; *du2 mu4 bu4 cheng2 lin2*, 'one tree does not make a forest', "one swallow does not make a summer"; *fu4 shui3 nan2 shou1*, spilt water cannot be gathered', "no use crying over spilt milk"; and a beautifully picturesque idiom, *gua1 tian2 li3 xia4*, 'don't tie your shoes in a melon-patch and adjust your hat under a plum tree', meaning "don't draw attention to yourself by acting suspiciously".

16:10 A good reference book is The Times "Handbook of Chinese Idioms" published by Federal Publications (Singapore), ISBN 9810130686; whilst another book is "1000 practical Chinese idioms (speaking Chinese series)" by Luo Pingfeng and Zhong Zhenfen (editors) published by New World Press, Beijing, 2002, 1st edn., paperback, 460 pp, ISBN 78000563252. The internet is a route to many Chinese idioms: e.g. www.chinabooks.com.au/ provides details of many books on Chinese language topics - including many books that are illustrated - on such as Chinese idioms, proverbs, sayings and slang.

The young clerical ladies were normally very friendly towards each other, but one morning when Alex entered their office he found that one of the ladies had become quite angry with another of the young ladies by her persistent and unnecessary querying of the contract that she was drawing up. She eventually burst out with '*gou3 na2 hao4zi, duo3 guan3 xian2shi4!*', 'a dog trying to catch mice', meaning "mind your own business and let the cat (i.e. me) get on with it!" Alex smiled as he remembered the blunt direct Geordie response in such situations: 'Keep your nebbie (nose) out if it!'

Another popular idiom that Alex came across was *jiu3rou4 peng2you*, 'wine-and-meat friends' meaning "fair-weather friends"; and a further common Chinese expression that Alex came across was *gua4 yang1 tou1 mai4 gou3 rou4*, 'hanging out (over a shop) a sheep's head to sell dog meat', the English counterpart being "he cries wine and sells vinegar".

Alex understood this idiom, but was sickened by it, remembering his lovely dog Clyde: he would starve before eating dog flesh! The Chinese have no such reluctance, as, despite their high intelligence, sensitivity and unsurpassed loyalty, dogs are of little importance in Chinese culture except gastronomically, where they are clearly considered inferior to sheep, probably the most stupid and insensitive of creatures in existence, goats excepted. However, Alex recalled that the French eat horse-meat, and yet the British horse-loving nation doesn't protest: different nations, different cultures, different customs, so perhaps "live and let live" is the only sensible attitude.

There were many aspects in the thinking of the Chinese that Alex found of interest. The present-day Chinese way of inquiring if another person has already eaten, or simply to inquire if things are going well for that person, is to ask *ni3 chi1le fan4 ma?*, literally "Have you eaten rice?", which relates to the times in the past when food was in short supply, rice being the staple food, often eaten alone or sometimes with just a small amount of fish, meat or vegetable. If the person "has eaten rice", then all is well, the daily staving-off of hunger being of greatest importance in a person's life.

Alex was interested to discover that the Chinese see the heart as the root of all emotions, just as in the West. Whenever a compound character has the character *xin*, "heart", as part of it, then the compound character almost invariably relates to an emotion such as love, anger, jealousy, passion, compassion, heartache. The reason is probably because emotions can cause the heart to beat faster, but the certainty is that all emotions reside in the mind.

Alex also enjoyed listening to the Chinese folk tales[16:11] that Mr. *Loo* told them, many of which can be found in the literature, but not all. However, there were two tales that he told them that Alex couldn't find in any of the books that he read. The first tale told of how the king of one county sent an emissary to the king of a neighbouring county, who was known to be cruel and arrogant. When the emissary arrived at the gates of the palace of the neighbouring king, the king's guards looked at him, and seeing his stunted growth and his general ugliness, and wishing to humiliate him, told him to enter the palace by means of a very small side door meant for a dog.

When he was taken into the presence of the king, the latter asked why such an unattractive man had been sent by his king as emissary, and that the man's kingdom must be a poor place if he were the best man that they could find. The emissary replied that in his country, his king always thought carefully as to the most suitable man to send as emissary, choosing the man whose appearance was appropriate to the status and reputation of the king to be visited. He advised that in the present case, after careful thought on the matter, his king had chosen him as emissary, being the least impressive and the ugliest man in his whole kingdom.

The second tale told of how a man, Zhang, had worked hard and had saved the considerable sum of 300 taels of silver. However, Zhang began to worry about keeping such a large sum of money within his house, and decided to bury it in his field, which he did. Initially, he felt that his money so buried was safe, but then he began to worry that his neighbours might suspect that he had buried his money in his field and decide to go into the field and dig there to look for it. Zhang decided to put potential thieves off the scent and wrote a sign saying "No 300 taels of silver buried here", placing the sign over where the silver was buried. Feeling relieved, he ceased worrying.

His neighbour Wang saw the sign and, after much thought, saw through Zhang's subterfuge and went out one dark night and dug up the silver. However, after a while he began to feel disturbed that his theft might be discovered, so he wrote a sign of his own and placed it above where the silver had been buried: "Neighbour Wang didn't steal the 300

16:11 "Chinese Folktales" by Howard Giskin, published by NTC Publishing Group, ISBN 0-8442-5927-6, provides 95 folktales, under the headings: Dragon Tales; Love; Magic; Ghosts, Monsters and Evil Spirits; History and Legend; Fairy Tales and Fables; and Human Nature. An ebook containing forty-three Chinese tales and fables from 722 70 221 B.C., along with illustrations and music, is available from <http://www.popularshareware.com/Chinese-fables-transfer149.html>.

taels of silver buried here." The associated idiomatic meaning, that a guilty person gives himself or herself away by conspicuously protesting innocence, was expressed succinctly by William Shakespeare in Hamlet as "The lady doth protest too much, methinks."

Alex started to come to terms with Chinese grammar. Initially he had had to think what to say, and then translate this into Chinese. This was slow, and he had despaired that he would never be able to engage in Chinese conversation. However, the day came when he was able to respond to a simple unexpected question in Chinese, asked by a friend, with an immediate answer in Chinese, albeit that he may not have used the best choice of characters, or the most logical grammar. He was elated at his breakthrough!

He eventually began to understand the most difficult character, for an English speaker, in the Chinese language, *le*, which means a change of state or an action completed. In the simple sentence *ta1 lai2*, "he/she comes", the addition of *le* to give *ta1 lai2le* means that the action of coming is completed, and changes the meaning to "he/she has come". It thus seemed to Alex that *le* gives the past tense, but he had been led to believe that there is no past tense in Chinese. Further, in the sentence *ta1 hen3quai4 lai2le*, where *hen3quai4* means very soon or very quickly, the meaning is that he/she will very soon be in the changed state of no longer coming, or in other words "he/she will soon arrive", which seemed to Alex to relate to the future. What a complex language!

Alex was very impressed by the range of expression of the Chinese language. In English, if one asked another person, say, if they will come swimming, the answer "I can't" would inevitably lead would to the further question "Why can't you?" However in Chinese, the question could lead to three different answers: *wo3 bu4neng2*, meaning "I am not physically capable of"; or *wo3 bu4ke3yi3*, meaning "I don't have permission to do so"; or *wo3 bu4hui2*, "I don't know how to do so." How marvellous!

The more that Alex learnt of the Chinese language the more that it impressed him, particularly in respect of precision, where the Chinese would not say "Do you like tea?", but "Do you like to **drink** tea?"

There is a commonly held view amongst those unfamiliar with the Chinese language that there are no such words in Chinese as "yes" and "no", and that this absence must cause much confusion, but this is not so. Whilst indeed there are not specifically "yes" and "no", there are forms of sentence construction used that avoid the confusion that often arises in the use of these words in the English language.

If, back in Britain, Alex had arranged to go somewhere with a friend, but when he arrived at his friend's house and the friend seemed not now to want to go, he might ask "Don't you want to go?", to which the answer "No" would be taken as indicating that the friend didn't want to go, whereas the precise meaning in the use of a second negative is that the friend indeed wanted to go: exactly the opposite! In Chinese the repeating of the verb "go" in the answer "go" or "not go", is unambiguous. What must the visitor to Britain think of the extensive but incorrect use of the double negative in such poor English as "I haven't done nothing." or "I haven't been nowhere."?

No matter the difficulties he experienced, Alex forged ahead with his Chinese studies. Having acquired a reasonable knowledge of the grammar, he still needed to learn a great number of the total of some thirty thousand different Chinese characters that exist. However, it is considered that a knowledge of only two thousand of the most common characters is all that is needed to be able to read a newspaper, so he didn't despair. As it is, most Chinese have to consult their dictionaries quite often, when they encountered characters outside of their own range of study.

At one class a student who hadn't attended for a few weeks arrived, to be greeted by Mr. *Loo* with *hen3jiu4 bu4jian4*!, literally "Long time no see!", which was an expression that Alex himself had often used back on the Clyde when greeting the arrival of a fishing party that hadn't been out with him for some time: he thought 'what a further marvellous parallel between Chinese and English!'

Whilst walking home from his Chinese class one evening, Alex called into a store to buy a few cans of beer, in time to hear the proprietor call his young son, who had just knocked over a pile of tins, *ben4dan4*!, which means "stupid egg!" He was amused at this odd use of "egg", but then recalled that back in Glasgow almost every woman, young or old, to whom one wanted to speak in a friendly manner, even though they might be strangers, would be called "Hen": "Excuse me Hen, is this the way to the railway station?"

This easy familiarity between working-class strangers in Scotland is reflected in the use of "Jimmy" between males on the street in Scotland: "Can you give me change for the 'phone Jimmy?"; but such familiarity would be frowned upon in Kelvinside or in other middle-class areas of the city, as would the word "mate" if used by a working-class man when addressing a middle- or upper-class man back in Britain. Indeed, down in the south of England, what the Scots call the "deep south", any attempt at conversation with strangers - on the streets, on the tube or anywhere else - is treated with suspicion.

Mr. *Loo* showed the class how to use a Chinese dictionary using Chinese characters. The single-part character *kou1*, "mouth", is of the form of a square, and it might be thought that this could be drawn easily as just one continuous line, with three changes of direction, ending up where the line started, but this is not so. A strict stroke-order dictates that the left-hand side line of the square is drawn first, from top to bottom. Then the top horizontal line is drawn from left to right, the stroke order then allowing the line to be continued downwards as the right-hand side vertical line. Finally, the character is completed by drawing the bottom horizontal line from left to right, making three strokes in all.

A check in the short "radicals index" at the front of the dictionary for characters composed of three strokes tells on which of the following few pages, the list of "radicals", this character is listed. For *kou*, there isn't a second part to the character to be considered, so the reader is quickly referred to the correct page of the dictionary on which to locate the character.

For characters made up of two parts, such as the roof and the pig for *jia1*, "home", the strokes of the major part, the "radical", in this case the roof, are counted first, and found to be three. Checking in the "radicals index", as for the earlier example of *kou3*, tells where this radical is listed in the following few pages. Then checking under this radial for the number of strokes for the second part of the character, the pig, seven, the appropriate page of the dictionary is given. Whilst it may sound complicated, the method is quick and simple, only requiring knowledge of the prescribed stroke order of Chinese characters, whereas the English dictionary requires knowledge of the spelling of the word. The Chinese—English dictionary is even easier to use with *pin1yin1*, the dictionaries being arranged according to *pinyin*, and then according to the tone mark. Following the class, Alex made his way as soon as possible to the Times book-shop, where he bought their own publication, the "Times Chinese—English Dictionary [#23].

Alex was intrigued by the stroke order of Chinese characters and quickly learnt the names of each of the strokes: *dian3*, a dot; *heng2*, a horizontal stroke from left to right; *shu4*, a vertical stroke from top to bottom; *gou2*, a hook appended to another stroke; *ti1*, a diagonal stroke rising from left to right; *pie3*, a diagonal stroke falling from right to left; *duan3 pie3,* a short diagonal stroke falling from right to left; and *na4*, a horizontal stroke falling from left to right.

Whilst out on the street he had heard a young boy shout what was obviously an insult to another young boy: *ma3pi4*! That evening he consulted his dictionary to find that the word *pi4* means "fart". Fascinated he looked under this word to find *pi4gu*, which means "bottom" or "behind". From his dictionary he found two meanings of gu3 (the same written character but with the third tone) that could be relevant, one being "thighs" and the other the measure word for a "puff or smell of air", the latter seeming to be the more appropriate. The Chinese way of expressing "bottom" or "behind" is clearly "the vicinity in which farts are emitted". How delightfully graphic and earthy, albeit totally unacceptable in some strata of British society!

Alex's admiration for the Chinese language increased enormously when he discovered that the words for defecate are *da4 bian4*, "big convenience", whilst the words for urinate are *xiao3 bian4*, "little convenience". This was similar to the simple way these bodily functions are described by children back in Glasgow: doing a "number one" or doing a "number two". Alex had felt kinship with the Chinese from his first days in Singapore, and the more he learnt about their language, the more he wanted to learn. There was no doubt in his mind that he would pursue his studies of the Chinese language as far as is within his power to do so.

He hoped that one day, presently far off, he will be able to read Chinese as well as he can read English, and speak Mandarin fluently, but he realised that, in adulthood, his ability to learn a new language is greatly reduced, compared with that of a child. However, he took comfort in the Chinese saying *huo2 dao4 lao3, xue2 dao4 lao3*, "Live until old, study until old!"

Mr. *Loo*, had told the class that the written language had originally been in the domain of only the rich landlords, who had created extremely complex characters to impress their friends, one example being a complex character composed of four dragons, sixty-four strokes in all, meaning "to chatter". When the Chinese government promoted a change from the original *fan2ti3zi4* characters to the much simpler *jian3ti3zi4* characters in the 1950s and 1960s, in many cases reducing the number of brush strokes required to draw the character to as few as a quarter, there was criticism outside of China that this had been done to destroy cultural links with the past but, regardless, it certainly made the written language much simpler. One regrettable result was the appearance of the character for horse, *ma*, no longer showing so graphically its flowing mane and its pounding hooves, and this was the case with many other characters

To help him to learn the most common characters, Alex cut a thousand small rectangles of stiff white card, on one side drawing the character and on the other side writing the meaning in English. Such "flash cards" worked in two ways: they not only helped him to learn the meaning of the Chinese character, but also to draw the Chinese character after reading the meaning in English. He made steady progress, and enrolled for the advanced course.

Whilst described as advanced, this course would not have been advanced for native Mandarin speakers, except that many such speakers are illiterate in written Chinese, literacy usually being defined as a knowledge of five-hundred written characters, which target Alex soon met. He was therefore technically literate in Chinese and was delighted at this! However, he bore in mind the enormous number of characters in the Chinese language, realising that he yet had an enormous way to go in his studies.

George watched Alex's progress with interest, as he hadn't ever found an expatriate who had persevered to such an extent, *ni3hao3?*, "How are you", and *zai4jian4*, "See you again", and *ni3 chi1le fan4 ma?*, "Have you eaten?", normally being the extent of their vocabulary. He no longer saw Alex as an expatriate, but as his very good friend. In turn, Alex no longer saw the Chinese as a different race. With having stopped going to the expatriate clubs, and keeping out of the way of the major as much as he could, the only non-Chinese that he met were the company's clients. It was only when he looked into a mirror whilst he was shaving that he was reminded of his western origins.

Alex's interest in Chinese matters was increasing and broadening. In his spare time Alex visited all the bookshops in Singapore that he could find, looking in particular for books, new or second-hand, on Chinese history. One classic work that he was delighted to come across was the book "A history of Chinese civilisation" by Jacques Gernet, an authoritative illustrated work detailing the development of China from the Neolithic age down to the present time.[16:12]

Had he but realised it, Alex had now found his own particular obsession: Chinese language and culture! Lucky man, as many people pass through life without discovering theirs. Once a person finds his or her obsession, whether it be science, medicine, engineering, literature, music, archaeology, mountaineering, teaching, gardening, DIY or anything else, their future is secure, and free from boredom, dissatisfaction, discontentment, envy, clock-watching and lack of purpose or objectives. Pity those "couch potatoes" who do not find their own obsession, and criticise others for having found theirs!

Alex began to pay attention to the different ancient religions of China, some of which are still practiced in Singapore. He started with

---

[16:12] Translated by J.R. Foster, published by Cambridge University Press: ISBN 0-521-24130-8 hardback; ISBN 0-521-31647-2 paperback. Other books that can be consulted by those interested in Chinese history and culture are presented in "Further books on China" located immediately after the Appendices.

the teachings of Confucius, 551-479 B.C., whose formal name was *Kong3 Qiu1*, although as he achieved recognition he was awarded the name *Kong3 fu1 zi1*, or just *Kong3 zi3*, "Master Kong". Confucianism is not strictly a religion: it offers a moral code for living a good life by. According to Gernet: "Confucius attaches great importance to exercises of ritual behaviour, which forms the basis of a process of self-improvement rendering possible the mastery of one's movements, actions and feelings"; and "Wisdom can only be acquired after an effort lasting every minute of one's life, by control of the smallest details of conduct, by observation of the rules of life in society, by respect for others and oneself and by the sense of reciprocity". Further, Gernet states that Confucius "... identifies personal culture with the public good"; and that Confucius, as the head of a little school that was aimed at "forming good men", was ".. practical and pragmatic, taking account of each particular circumstance as well as of the individual character of each of his disciples."

In particular, Alex found that filial piety comes over strongly in the sayings of Confucius:[16:13] "Nowadays, to provide for parents is considered filial piety. But dogs and horses are so provided. Without respect, what is the difference?"; and "In the home the young should behave with filial piety, and in the world with brotherly love. They appreciate you. Be concerned with your appreciating others"; and one, "Action takes precedence over words", that is expressed succinctly in the English language by "Words are cheap!" He also said "The young should love the people and be close to the benevolent. Having so do, their remaining strength should be used to learn literature"; also "In serving parents, make suggestions tactfully and if your suggestions are not pursued, still respect and do not disobey, bear burden and do not complain".

Amongst the sayings, Alex found many that are good practice in present-day. How wonderful that Confucius's message can carry on down through the centuries for two-and-a-half thousand years with such relevance and impact! Alex was pleased to read a saying that conveyed to him how successful and worthwhile the life that Confucius had led had been: "At fifteen, I aspired to learning. At thirty, I established my stand. At forty, I had no delusions. At fifty, I knew my destiny. At sixty, I knew truth in all I heard. At seventy, I could follow the wishes of my heart without doing wrong."[#24]

There are many sayings that are as valid today as there were at the

---

[16:13] A great many of the sayings of Confucius can be found on the internet, but ignore 'humorous' fake sayings written in Confucian style.

time of Confucius: "When not in the official position, do not be involved with its policies"; and "What you do not want done to you, do not do to others".[16:14] There is much wisdom in the words of Confucius as to how to determine the character of a man that will benefit any present-day Employer: "Look into his motives, note his course, take heed of whether he is at ease, and how can a man hide, how can a man hide!"

Alex was in complete sympathy with Confucianism, some of the beliefs of the ancient religions seemed outlandish to him. "Legalism" seemed to be a totally inhuman blinkered pursuance of extensive rules for personal behaviour and for the conduct of state affairs, with no possibility for the exercise of judgement or compassion: he felt that living under such a system would be repressive.

On the other hand, "Daoism", or "Taoist", 'The Way', following the teachings of *Lao Tzu*, seemed to be totally concerned with personal rather than collective action, and involved preserving and increasing one's vital force by such as dieting, strenuous   exercise, breathing air in a closed environment so that it becomes depleted in oxygen, and by engaging in sexual practices such as discontinuing activity just before the point of ejaculation, in this way the 'energy' thus generated not passing to any other person involved, but being absorbed into one's own body. Not a practice for Alex!

During one lunch break, Alex got into conversation with a driver, Mohammad, at the offices on the subject of the Muslim faith, Islam. Appreciating his interest in Islam, a few days later Mohammad gave him a copy of "The Holy Qur'an" with a substantial English foreword explaining the fundamentals of the faith. Mohammad made the simple request that the book be kept above all other books on Alex's bookshelf, to which Alex agreed. Alex spent several evenings reading this great work, and was awed by the attention to the detail paid in its presentation, and by the amount of information and in-depth discussion that it contains.

He read that The Qur'an was written for the reform of the Arabs of the time, but later was meant for the guidance of the whole of mankind, and that the central theme that runs throughout it is "…the exposition of

---

[16:14] This saying is reported somewhat differently in "Chinese Wisdom: philosophical insights from Confucius, Mencius, Laozi, Zhuangzi and other masters", by Edward L. Shaughnessy, published by Duncan Baird Publishers Ltd., (2010), illustrated, hardback, ISBN 978-1-84483-15-1. When *Zi Gong* asked Confucius if there is a single saying that we can put into action throughout our lives Confucius replied 'Perhaps putting oneself in the other's place. What you don't wish for yourself, don't do to others.' This is a beautifully-presented authoritative book.

the Reality and the Right Way based on it": it discusses the aspects of man's life ".. that lead either to his real success or failure". Alex felt that the teachings have a universal message, in the same way that the teachings of Confucius have universality. He was impressed by the introduction, which told how God had created Man, and given him spiritual insight and a Will so that he should ".. experience the sublime joy of being in harmony with the Infinite", but how "Man fell from Unity when his Will was warped and he chose the crooked path of Discord", such that there was discord between kith and kin, and ".. men spread themselves over the earth, and became many nations speaking diverse languages and observing different customs and laws", whereupon ".. the brotherhood of man was doubly forgotten, - first between individuals, and secondly, between nations".

It was fascinating reading, and Alex was enthralled. He realised a great truth: the aim of most of the great religions of the world is the same, which is to improve the moral quality of their followers, and to turn them into good people, living in peace with their neighbours, not only locally, but internationally. It is only suspicion, ignorance and intolerance that lead to the troubles of the world, along with the exploitation of the faith of the followers by some leaders to advance their own political aims. He resolved to obtain further reading matter, in English, so that he could gain greater insight into the Muslim faith.

Alex learnt from his fellow-employee Mohammad that the Qur'an presents the guidance of Allah for mankind, expressed through the teachings of Mohammad, and that "Allah is the one true god and Mohammad is his prophet." His fellow-employee also explained that Jesus Christ has been considered a prophet of Allah. After consideration, Alex thought that if this is so, then isn't the god of the Muslim faith the same as that of the Christian faith? ... yet "the crooked path" has led Muslims and Christians to being in conflict from the time of the Pilgrimages. Discord has had many effects: in religion, to the formation of the Sunnis and the Shiites, in Christianity to the Roman Catholic, Protestant, and many other small churches, and in America to an even greater number of small churches, many of which are short-lived and bring disaster and death upon their members; in the political field it has led to Tribalism, Dictatorship, Communism and Democracy, often in conflict with each other; in mankind it has led to mutual distrust of other groups and nations, to racialism and racial discrimination, and to racial cleansing and civil wars.

Alex considered that there is no way to eliminate mankind's inherent following of the crooked path of discord, and that the only answer is to allow people of other countries to live as they themselves wish, but to give an offer of help – without any strings attached - in times of disaster.

However, he believed that there has been a positive effect of the following of the crooked path of discord: such as the ability of mankind in earlier times to explore the natural world, in face of religious persecution on the grounds that pursuing such research as exploring the movements of the planets is questioning God's work. In America in the early 1900s, a school teacher was persecuted for teaching his students Darwinism, in opposition to the churches' teaching of Adam and Eve and the Garden of Eden. Without such following of the part of discord, mankind would not have made its present achievements in science, in medication and in surgery, and in producing enough food to meet the World's increasing population. However, Alex found this topic too complex for him to see clearly.

Alex also decided that when a suitable opportunity arose, he would raise his interest in learning about Buddhism with George, whom he knew was a Buddhist himself.[16:15] Whilst he had not yet learnt anything about the Indian religions, he took pleasure in going to "Little Indian" on Serangoon Road, and in visiting the major Indian temple, Shri Miriamam, in Chinatown, between Smith Street and Temple Street, and other Indian temples throughout the city. As Alex and his friends usually toured the city in shorts, when required he would not only take off his shoes before entering a temple, but would also tie a length of cloth, provided by one of the temple assistants, around his waist to cover his bare legs.

Recently, Alex had been feeling the need for female company, but not now mixing with the expatriate community in their various clubs, he didn't have much opportunity to make the acquaintance of any young women, the women at the Chinese classes being more involved with their own culture. Alex had the desperate desire to become fluent in Mandarin. In his early days of learning Mandarin, he had got into conversation with an interpreter whilst drinking in a bar, and had complained about the difficulty of learning the dialect, to which the man had replied, somewhat crudely but pointedly 'If you want to learn a language, get yourself a xxxxing dictionary.'

Alex understood what he said, and thought that it would be a good

---

[16:15] A simple description of Buddhism advanced by Jo Durden Smith in "The Essence of Buddhism", published by Arturus, ISBN 978-1-84193-382-2, expresses its gentle nature: "A doctrine of salvation even older than Christianity, yet completely unmarked by violence, religious wars, inquisitions, crusades or the burning of witches". What a marvelous commendation!

idea indeed to find himself a young Chinese lady who could help him in his studies. However, he would have to wait for the opportunity. There were few young unattached ladies at his Chinese class, and it would ensure the wrath of Major Smedley (retd.), if he were to seek the companionship of one of the young ladies in the office, attractive as they are: Heaven forbid!

Alex's studies of Chinese continued. One character that at first he thought was not good Chinese, but soon realised the value of, was the character *ba*, added to the end of a direct statement to soften it and make it more in the nature of a question. This addition is very similar to the addition of "then" or "like" that Alex had found to be used so extensively in the north-east of England, where to say "Come here" sounds like a blunt and aggressive order, but to say "Come here then" takes off the sharpness. In exactly the same way, to ask the question "Are you coming?" sounds demanding, but, as used in the north-east of England, "Are you coming like" is friendly and inviting.

The Chinese in Singapore, making a little joke at their own expense, refer to the English that they speak as "Singlish". Indeed, there were some peculiarities of speech that Alex noticed at first, but he soon got used to them and began to use them himself. A peculiarity that Alex had noticed was the addition of "a" or "lah" to the end of complete statements and questions in English: 'How much did you pay for your new shoes-lah?; with the reply 'Twenty dollars over-lah', the response to which indicating incredulity: 'Twenty dollars over-lah? Ai-a!' In this exchange, 'over' is used instead of "more than", and 'Ai-a!' expresses mock horror and disbelief.

Other manners of speech that the Chinese ladies used were to say *deng3deng3*, when in English Alex would have said such as "and so on" or "and similar items"; and they might interrupt with "de de de de" delivered in a staccato, machine-gun style, to stop a person from continuing explaining something to them once they had got the gist of the message. However, he considered the latter practice to be impolite: somewhat like someone saying, in an exasperated and impatient manner, "Yes, yes! I've got your point!" when the person with whom they were speaking should have been allowed to complete what he or she wanted to say. The Chinese Singaporean would say 'advance it out', meaning "retract it"; 'on the light', meaning "put on the light"; and 'I send my children to school each morning.', meaning "I take my children to school each morning."

He found these to be delightful little 'mistakes', and realised that he himself made many such mistakes. Sometimes, as a Glaswegian, he would ask a question and at the same time indicate the expected answer: 'Are you coming, aye?' Whilst not a mistake, the lady clerks were amused when, in spelling a word, Alex pronounced the letter "j" the same as "gy" in "gyroscope", in the standard Scottish manner. Alex had found peculiarities of speech wherever he had been. In the north east of England, if he should ask someone if a person inside a house was ready to go somewhere, he might be given the reply 'Oh, he has already went', rather than 'Oh, he has already gone', whilst others would use "you" for the third-person singular, and "yous" for the third-person plural, just as was quite common back in Glasgow. In the depot at Newcastle, should he ask over the loudspeaker for someone to come to his office, the person would arrive and ask 'Did you sent for us?' albeit that the person was alone, but this was little different to the royal "we", as in 'We are not amused.', as is accredited to Queen Victoria when expressing her personal opinion.

Once one of the lady clerks asked him if had seen an item that she had mislaid. When he inquired as to its appearance, using the common Scottish form of words 'What is the like of it?' this had all of them in a great state of amusement. On another occasion he had had cause to remonstrate with one of the yard workers for repeatedly being late to clock-in, saying to him 'You're no good on the clock, so you are', the final "so you are" being to emphasise his point, this expression being common in Glasgow, possibly due to the large influx of Irish immigrants into Glasgow over a great many decades, as the expression is also common in Ireland. He had been overheard by one of the lady clerks, and soon the four of them were copying this style of speech, looking round first to ensure that Alex was not within range of hearing. One girl would say to another, with a stern expression on her face, and wagging her forefinger reproachfully 'You were late back from lunch today, so you were. You haven't filed that quotation yet, so you haven't. I'm going to report you to Mr. MacAlister, so I am!', the four girls then breaking down into fits of giggles.

One day Alex came down into the office just in time to hear the end of such a statement, and the commencement of the inevitable laughter. The lady clerks froze in their seats. Alex strode over to them and with an angry look on his face said 'You have just been mocking me!', whilst continuing to look at them with extreme annoyance, but after a few seconds adding 'so you have', then breaking out into hearty laughter, with a big smile on his face. After they had recovered their composure, the lady clerks joined in with the laughter, partly with pleasure because Alex had deceived them with his acting, and also partly because he had reacted to their pantomime in such good part.

As one of the clerks said to the others later 'After all, he is the deputy office manager, la! ... so he is!', and all four of them knew that Major Horace Smedley (retd.) certainty wouldn't have responded to their mischief with such pleasantness, friendliness, and indeed originality. 'People are the same the world over,' Alex thought to himself, 'none of us is perfect, thank God, or the world would be a dull place to live in.'

Christmas came and went, Alex having been in Singapore for a year. As Alex's second Chinese New Year approached, George decided that he should invite him to the home of his family on the evening of the second of the two holidays, the first evening being reserved for family members. Alex was delighted to accept, and asked what he should bring along for the occasion. George replied 'A selection of fruit would be fine, and also two oranges for my parents would be highly acceptable', these being the traditional gift when visiting at Chinese New Year.[16:16] The two principal varieties of orange are known in Cantonese as *kam*, which is homonymous with the word for gold and also with the word for sweetness, and *kat*, which is homonymous in Cantonese with the word for luck, so either variety is highly acceptable.'

Alex had learnt that because of the similarity in sound between a number of Chinese words in Mandarin, some gifts are not desirable, an example being *zhong1*, "clock", as this word also means "death", and no Chinese person wants to be given death as a gift!. Similarly, *si4*, "number four", is an ill-favoured number, as this same word means "dead". On the other hand, Chinese greeting cards often display *yu2*, "fish", for as this word also means "joy" or "pleasure", such a card is received gladly.

On many occasions Alex had seen the character for happiness, *fu2*, written upside down on a card pinned to a house wall or door. This puzzled him until George explained that the character *fu4* (fourth tone), meaning "overturn", combined with the characters *dao3*, meaning "fall or topple" and *le*, meaning that the action is completed, has the meaning "it (the sheet) has overturned." However, a further character, also pronounced *dao4*, has the meaning "arrive", so *fu2 dao4le* has the meaning "happiness has arrived", the two different phrases, apart from the different tones for *fu*, being homophonic! Thus, as the character is upside down, it can be 'deduced' that happiness has already arrived!

Alex had learnt that the Chinese consider *ba1*, "number eight", auspicious, and that this had arisen because of the respect they have for

---

[16:16] Chinese customs and festivals in Singapore, published by Singapore Federation of Chinese Clan Associations, 137 Telok Ayer Street, Singapore 0106.

the legendary *ba1 xian1*, "The Eight Immortals", who spent their time in righting wrongs committed against the poor and the weak. This is manifested in such things as the steps of staircases being in runs of eight, wherever this is possible, and the eight day of a month being regarded as favourable for moving house or getting married, or for buying a lottery ticket: there are great long queues outside shops and stores selling lottery tickets on the eighth day of the month, and particularly so on the eighth of August.[#25]

When Alex arrived at George's family home he found it to be an attractive two-story house in a pleasant street lying off Holland Road, to the west of the city centre. In front of the house was a small neat garden. Immediately inside the garden gate alongside the path to the house was what Alex believed was called a "Buddha House", but which he later learned was properly called a "Spiritual House", which had the form of an open-fronted box of about 2-foot-long sides set on a column of about 3-feet height, both the box and the column being made of concrete and painted bright red. Both the outside and inside of the box were adorned, in relief, with Chinese characters and scenes painted in gold. Inside the box was a bowl filled with flowers. Alex was intrigued!

George had seen him arrive, and walked down the path to meet him. He explained to Alex the meaning of the Chinese characters, in particular explaining one prominent set of four characters, which he said were pronounced *chu1ru4 ping2an4*, meaning 'come and go in peace'. He went on to explain that the flowers had been placed in the bowl to ask for peace and good fortune to those entering the house. Alex asked the meaning of one very complex character, to which George explained that it wasn't by itself a proper Chinese character such as could be found in a Chinese dictionary, but a composite of four Chinese characters, *zhao1cai2 lin2bao3*, meaning: 'attract wealth, receive treasure!', a sentiment held dear by the Chinese.

George then took him into the house and introduced him to his parents. They were a pleasant refined couple, who spoke only a little English. However, they used Mandarin in welcoming Alex into their *han2shi4*, using an old-fashioned modest expression from China, meaning "frozen hut", although their fine house was totally undeserving of such a description, and the temperature in Singapore rarely falls below 80 degrees Fahrenheit! Since emigrating from *Shenyang* in the north of China to Singapore some forty years ago, they had had very little opportunity, and perhaps also little desire, to mix with English-speaking people, so their progress in the language had been very limited and, in a similar way, working within their own ethnic group also limited their progress in the language.

During their earlier years in China, along with their family and friends, they had produced hand-crafted pottery that was sold locally. An enterprising businessman from Singapore had approached them with a view to their supplying him with ethnic pottery items for him to sell in several of his Singapore stores, where there was an increasing demand for them from tourists. Mr. and Mrs. *Yang* were anxious to find some means of making money in order to be able to buy a house and raise a family. With the idea of exporting their products from *Shenyang* themselves, rather than through an outsider, it was suggested to the newly-weds that, with financial help from their family and their friends, they should go to Singapore to start their own import business.

It had been very hard going at first, but once they had made the right contacts, the business had gone from strength to strength. More staff were needed, so it was arranged that four more family members and friends should come over from China to join them. The *Yang*s were able to make a comfortable living whilst also sending money back home to China, and gained particular satisfaction from having more of their family and friends around them.

The house was furnished traditionally. On an altar table in the entrance hall were set three statues that are found in a great many Singapore homes: the god of good fortune, *fu2*, carrying a child or a scroll at the centre; with the god of prosperity, *lu4*, carrying a sceptre or dressed as a Mandarin; and the god of longevity, *shou4*, carrying a peach or an ingot; on opposite sides of him. The Chinese sensibly believe that it is no good having prosperity and longevity if you do not have good fortune, and so accord the god of good fortune the prominent position. Nearby was a large carving of Buddha, which indicated the beliefs of the family. Alex was captivated by these statues.

The parents led him into the dining room, where members of the family and guests, all Chinese, were seated. Some of the guests greeted Alex with *xin1nian4-kuai4le4*!, "Happy New Year!", whilst others said *gong1xi1-fa1cai2*!, "Work hard, make money!", reflecting the inborn Chinese desire to do well in life. Alex responded to their greetings with suitable expressions in Mandarin, which brought forth smiles of pleasure. George's parents received the gift from Alex with thanks. George's father, Mr. *Yang*, in faltering English, asked Alex what he would like to drink. At that point Mrs. *Yang* looked across the room and said 'Ah, here is my daughter, *Qiang2wei1*', as a young Chinese lady entered the room.

Qiangwei, "Rose", was quite tall for a Chinese woman, with a slim shapely figure that was emphasised by the cheongsam – in Mandarin, the *qi2pao2*, known in the West as a "Mandarin Gown" – that she was wearing. Her pale complexion, high cheekbones and quite large nose indicated her ancestry as being from the north of China. *Qiangwei* wasn't wearing any make-up or jewellery, apart from a small wristwatch and a thin silver chain around her throat. Her expression was calm and composed, but not unfriendly: not for her the false western practice of flashing a big beaming smile upon first contact with strangers. Her eyebrows were thin and well spaced at the nose, but only as nature intended. Her hair was cut short with a simple fringe, in the style of a traditional Chinese doll: however, she was no Chinese doll, but a fully-grown serious young Chinese lady.

When Alex was introduced to her, she did not extend her hand, but made a slight bow. Alex had learnt that the Chinese do not favour physical contact with strangers, and often clasp their hands together in front of them to deter such contact, just moving them slowly up and down in greeting. He couldn't find anything to say, just returning her bow.

As *Qiangwei* greeted the rest of the guests, several of the older amongst them gave her a *hong2bao1*, a "red envelope", probably containing two bank notes, but with their denomination varying according to the wealth and generosity of the giver. Although an adult, being as-yet unmarried meant that she was still considered eligible to receive a monetary gift in the form of a *hong bao*.

The person giving the *hong bao* held it between the thumb and first finger of both hands, elbows drawn close to the waist, and *Qiangwei* received it in like manner, smiling gently and voicing her thanks whilst at the same time making a small slow bow: she was elegant, graceful and enchanting! Following Chinese custom, she did not open the *hong bao* immediately, and would not open it until later in the evening. The affection in which she was held by the gathering, both men and women alike, was clear from the fond way that they all looked at her.

Alex was reminded by the manner of giving the *hong bao* of the instruction he had received from George in the giving and receiving of business cards when the company had had some printed for him shortly after his arrival in Singapore, his name and company details being printed on one side in English and on the other side in Chinese. He had been told to hold the card with the tips of his fingers towards the ends of one of the long sides, with the details on the card facing the recipient for him or her to read, the recipient receiving the card in like manner, and then proffering his or her own card.

The dining table had been set out for ten persons, which is the Chinese tradition, with a "lazy Betty", a rotating circular table, set at the centre. The dishes were placed at towards the periphery of the lazy

Betty, as far as the number of dishes would allow, so that the guests could serve themselves without too much stretching. By good fortune Alex was seated directly opposite to *Qiangwei*. He looked at her with undisguised admiration, whilst she kept her eyes demurely averted. That she was a little younger than Alex meant nothing to him.

The meal went on for a long time, with a succession of dishes, which Alex thought amounted in total to twelve but couldn't be sure, arriving from the kitchen at regular intervals. He noted that many of the dishes were vegetarian and that *Qiangwei* selected only from these dishes. During the meal, strong clear Chinese wine, *Mao Tai Jiu*, was served, but Alex saw that *Qiangwei* drank only water. After the table had been cleared the company continued to sit there whilst Chinese tea and brandy were served. *Qiangwei* spoke to Alex for the first time, slowly and in a deep but gentle voice: 'I understand that you have been making good progress with learning Mandarin Mr. MacAlister.'

In response, Alex told the gathering about his courses at the National University and at the Chinese Chamber of Trade and Commerce, describing the course content, including ancient Chinese poetry. *Qiangwei* smiled at him warmly, her almost hypnotic eyes causing his heart to pound, then she said in an encouraging voice 'Please recite for us one of the poems that you have learnt.' Alex was trapped! How could he refuse her request? He recited in Chinese a poem that is learnt by all Chinese at an early age, just as British children are taught traditional nursery rhymes. This was the poem *jing4 ye4 si1*, "A tranquil Night [26], by the most popular of Chinese poets, *Li3 Bai2* (702-762 AD), about a man who left his wife and children on the family farm in the north of China to seek work further south and awakened suddenly one night in a confused state:

> *Chuang2 qian2 ming1 yue4 guang1,*
> *yi shi di4 shang shuang1.*
> *Ju3 tou2 wang4 ming1 yue4,*
> *Di1 tou2 si3 gu xiang4.*

After he had read the first line, the whole company, *Qiangwei* included, had joined in with him in the rest of the poem. Alex then recited the poem again, in English, whilst the guests listened in silence:

> "Before my bed a pool of light
> is it hoar-frost upon the ground?
> Head raised I see the moon so bright
> head bent in homesickness I'm drowned."

The meaning of the words is that the man awakened suddenly one night, to see the open ground in front of his bed shining brightly, and in his confused state he thought that he was looking at the frost-covered fields of his own farm. However, he looked up he saw the bright moon and realised that the light was just moonlight and that he was a long way from home, and he was overcome by home-sickness.

The company applauded his recitation. Alex both pleased and amused them when he closed up the fingers of his left hand and clasped the fingers of his right hand around them, then moving them slowly up and down close to his chest as he bowed slightly and said *guo4jiang3, guo4jiang3*, "You praise me too much", this quaint old-fashioned Chinese expression not usually being known by Westerners.

Alex went on to tell the gathering that *Li Bai* would have enjoyed the social evening that they were all enjoying, as he was known to have enjoyed company and certainly a drink, calling himself the "God of Imbibing", and having written his poem "Drinking alone with the moon":

> "From a jug of wine among the flowers
> I drank alone. There was no-one there with me –
> Till, raising my cup, I asked the bright moon
> To bring me my shadow and make us three.
> Alas, the moon was unable to drink
> And my shadow tagged me vacantly,
> As long as I knew, we were boon companions.
> And then I was drunk, and we lost one another.
> Shall goodwill ever be secure?
> I watch the long road of the River of Stars."

The gathering enjoyed hearing this poem, and applauded, then asking him to recite another poem by *Li Bai*. This time Alex recited a sad poem from the Tang Dynasty, 618-907AD, "The Moon at the Fortified Pass", which tells of the thoughts of home of the Chinese troops as they prepared for enjoining battle with the Tartars:

> The bright moon lifts from the Mountain of Heaven
> In an infinite haze of cloud and sea,
> And the wind that has come a thousand miles,
> Beats at the Jade Pass battlements....
> China marches its men down Baideng Road
> While Tartar troops peer across the waters of the bay....

And since no one battle famous in history
Sent all of its fighters back again,
The soldiers turn round, looking towards the border
And think of home, with wistful eyes,
And of those who tonight in the upper chambers
Toss and sigh and cannot rest.

The gathering again showed its appreciation and asked yet again for another poem. This time Alex recited *hui2 xiang1 ou3 shu1*, "Coming Home", by *He4 Zhi1 Zhang1*, first in Chinese and then in English. This poem is about a man who departed from his village at an early age to seek his fortune elsewhere, but left his return so late that when he arrived back at his village the children who ran to meet him didn't recognise the now white-haired old man and asked him where he had come from, thinking him to be a stranger:

shao4 xiao3 li2 jia1 lao3 da4 hui2,
xiang1 yin1 wu2 gai3 bin4 mao2 cui1.
er2 tong2 xiang1 jian4 bu4 xiang1 shi4,
xiao4 wen4 ke4 cong2 he2 chu4 lai2

Alex then recited the poem in English:

"I left home young and not till old do I come back,
my accent is unchanged, but my hair is no longer black.
The children don't know me, whom I meet on the way
'Where d'you come from, reverend sir?' they smile and say."

Sadly, this was not the home-coming that the man had expected. At the request for a third poem, Alex finally recited a poem that he had been struggling to learn for the last few weeks. This poem was much longer, and he was uneasy in case he should forget the words. It was the famous poem "Visiting the recluse on Mount *Tai-t'ien* and not finding him at home", written by *Li Po* - an alternative name, among others, sometimes used by *Li Bai* - over twelve hundred years ago. After having recited the poem successfully in Chinese, Alex then recited it again, this time in English, using the translation by Stephen Owen in his book "The great age of Chinese poetry: The High Tang", reproduced in "Heritage of China" edited by Paul S. Ropp:[16:17]

16:17 "Heritage of China" edited by Paul S. Ropp, published by the University of California Press, ISBN 0-52006441-0.

"A dog barks amid the sound of waters,
Peach blossoms dark and heavy with dew.
Where the trees are thickest, I sometimes see a deer,
Noon in the ravine, but I hear no bell.
Bamboo of wilderness split through with blue haze,
A cascade in flight, hung from an emerald peak.
No one knows where you've gone -
But I linger, disappointed, among these few pines."

Greatly simplified, the poem says that whilst seeking the recluse in the wilderness, the barking of a dog told *Li Po* of the presence of a human being, the master of the dog, whilst seeing peach blossom washed down by the stream confirmed that the recluse was living somewhere upstream. When *Li Po* saw a deer amongst the bamboo, that the deer did not run away told him that it was familiar with human presence, another confirmation that he was moving in the right direction to find the recluse. Whilst he was passing through a ravine, *Li Po* saw that the sun was overhead, which told him that it was noon, and as he could not hear a monastery bell, such bells customarily being rung at noon, he knew that he had penetrated far into the wilderness. In the overgrown ravine the light was dim, the "blue haze", and through this haze he could make out tall straight stems of bamboo, but he could see nothing to indicate the presence of the recluse.

However as he climbed up the ravine beyond the bamboo he saw a "cascade in flight", a waterfall, "hung from an emerald peak", falling from a high cliff, the sound of this waterfall being the sound of water that he had heard along with the barking of the dog: this must surely be the place where the recluse lives! As he reached the recluse's house, a servant informed him that his master was not there, and that no one knew where he had gone. The poet then stood amongst a group of pine trees, these being the symbol of the recluse, not just of the man he was seeking, but of all recluses.

He was disappointed at not finding the recluse at home, but he had learnt so much in his search for him, finding the surroundings that made the recluse what he is, that meeting the recluse was no longer necessary.

There was silence: the beauty of the poem had moved all of them: Owen's interpretation of the poem is masterly! [27] One of the ladies dabbed her eyes. *Qiangwei* said to Alex, using his personal name for the first time, 'Alex, that was beautiful. You really do appreciate Chinese culture.' Alex, filled with pleasure, was about to respond, when George stood up and said 'No, *Qiangwei*, that is no longer his name!' The company was startled! George walked around the table to where Alex was sitting. Placing his hand on Alex's shoulder said 'Henceforth, Alex is to be known as *Ai4-li4*. He deserves this on account of his interest in our culture, and on account of how much profit he is making for the company.'

Everyone broke into laughter. Alex joined in with them, realising that not only did *Ai-Li* sound very close to Alex, but also that *ai4* means "love" and *li4* means "profit". *Qiangwei* leaned as far across over the table as she could towards Alex, and said to him with a smile 'I am pleased to meet you *Ai-li*.', to which he replied with sincerity 'And I you *Qiangwei*'.

Chapter Seventeen

On the next working day, Alex thanked George for having invited him to his home, and gave him a small note written in Chinese addressed to his parents, thanking them for their hospitality. Alex seemed reluctant to end the conversation, the reason for which George understood fully. He had seen the way that Alex has looked at *Qiangwei*, with obvious admiration. His earlier suspicion and wariness of Alex had disappeared with time, but he still wanted the best for his sister and his determination that she should not become involved with a Westerner remained steadfast.

There was another reason why he didn't want to encourage Alex's interest in his sister, which was that she was a devout Buddhist, and that although she occupied a senior position in a leading bank in the city, she had the intention, once she had fulfilled her responsibilities to her parents when they passed on, of becoming a Buddhist nun. Alex was not the first man to have shown interest in his sister, but once a man had learnt of her long-term intention, he had reluctantly had to look elsewhere for a wife. He waited for Alex to come to the point.

'George,' said Alex eventually, 'is your sister spoken for?', using this strange old-fashioned expression for want of finding better words. George looked at Alex, seeing the concern in his face, and decided that the kindest thing to do would be to tell him the truth, to save him further misery. He sighed, and then told Alex of *Qiangwei*'s long-term intention. Alex wasn't put off, as he had been reading about Buddhism over the last few months and, whilst not accepting all the tenets of the faith, such as reincarnation, had come to the conclusion that it was one of the few beliefs that promote peace, as opposed to how he had come to view many religions, Christianity included, that seem to do more to promote hatred rather than love of one's fellow man.

He had read that in many far-eastern countries even Buddhist nuns and priests can marry and raise children, and he hoped that *Qiangwei* could come to accept and love him, and then marry him: indeed, he would become a practising Buddhist himself if this would help to win her affection. George realised that Alex had missed the point.

'Alex,' he said, as kindly as he could, 'what I am trying to say is that my sister will never marry, in readiness for her eventual celibate life as a Buddhist nun.' Alex was despondent.

The news of Alex's new Chinese name spread through the office, and within a couple of days all of the staff were referring to him as *Ai-li*, including even Madam *Zhang*. The major was livid with anger. Damn it! Not content with having jilted his daughter, the callous

316

Scottish lout had gone native, being addressed by all the staff by a heathen Chinese name and even speaking to them on company matters in some weird Chinese lingo! He thought of reporting the matter to the Board of Directors in London, but eventually realised that with Alex's excellent sales record since arriving in Singapore, his interest and participation in Chinese culture might be regarded as having been contributory to his sales success, as indeed they were. The major bit his tongue, but seethed. Sooner or later he would find a plausible reason to have Alex removed from the Singapore offices.

As the months passed, Alex and George continued to go out at week-ends with *Ying Hong* and *Chonghai*. Not only were there weekends and national holidays available for outings, but also there were the many religious festivities that were celebrated in Singapore: Christian, Chinese, Malay and Indian. One week they invited any of the office staff who were interested to join them on a trip on a bum boat from Keppel Quay to the Little Sisters Islands, lying just three miles or so to the south of Singapore island. The party met on the quay where the bum boats, small open boats of about 25 feet length and carrying a dozen or so passengers, were tied up. Alex saw with delight that George had brought *Qiangwei* with him. She was casually dressed in shorts, tee shirt, and open-toed sandals.

The day was hot and sunny, as are most days in Singapore, and the ladies present either wore sun hats or held parasols over their heads to shield them from the direct rays of the sun. Alex had thought earlier that the covered walkways in some parts of the city had been built to offer protection from the rain, but since then he had come to realise that they were also there to offer protection from the sun. When leaving one of the big stores on Orchard Road, the women shoppers would scutter from store to store to avoid being in the sun for more than just a few seconds. The Singaporean women feel that there is nothing worse than looking as if they are peasants accustomed to working in the fields, for the same reason many of them - and also some men! - leaving the nails of their little fingers uncut, to reach a length of an inch or more, to show that they do not perform manual work.

Alex contrasted this view of a tanned skin being associated with manual labour, with the opposite attitude towards a tanned skin in Britain, where both male and female members of the middle-class and upper-class strive to acquire a tan, on the ski slopes or on some Caribbean Island, so as to look more attractive. At the same time this will assure others that they are not associated with manual work: in Britain manual workers more often than not are stuck inside factories and coal mines, out of daylight for most of the time, leading to their

317

consequent pallid faces. This does not apply to fishermen, sailors, farm workers and others, who have ruddy coarse complexions from working out in the open in all weathers, but in the case of these people their quaint and blunt manner of speech easily identifies them as belonging to the working class, so there is not the embarrassment of those in the middle-class or upper-class being mistaken for them, perish the thought!

Alex noticed that many men with a small mole on their face from which a hair is growing, have allowed the hair to grow to a length or three or four inches. As hair is usually regarded as dead once it grows from the body, there is no reason why this single hair, if it would not be safe to pluck it out, could not be clipped short. Alex pondered on this, and was told eventually that, with the Chinese being very superstitious, those with such a hair think that if they do not allow this 'special' hair to grown to its full length, but cut it off short, this could result in their own life being cut short. Better safe than sorry!

Qiangwei made her way along the boat and sat down next to Alex. This caused the office secretaries to giggle in a childish way, except for *Fu Rong*, who was bitterly dismayed at what she saw. There had long been speculation as to whom Alex would eventually become interested in, and it now looked as though it could be George's sister. Sitting next to her, Alex had eyes for no other. As they rounded the western end of Pulau Blakang Mati, the swell of the open sea caused the boat to roll, such that *Qiangwei* lost her balance and fell against Alex, at the same time the top of her tee shirt opening such that Alex caught a glimpse of the soft flesh of her breasts. His breathing became laboured and he swallowed hard. It was three months since their first meeting at her parents' house and there hadn't been a single day when she hadn't been in his thoughts. He was deeply in love with her.

Upon arriving at the more westerly of the Little Sisters islands, the party first confirmed the time at which the skipper of the bum boat would return, and then unloaded their belongings and carried them to the picnic benches that had been located above the high-water mark, within a nearby bay. The island was lovely. Their party was the only one to have arrived that day, so they had the island to themselves.

Some time before at the East Coast Parkway Alex had seen some of the locals casting out large circular nets whilst standing in shallow water close to the shore The operation seemed quite simple, in that they gathered up some of the net in one hand, whilst piling the rest over their shoulder, then flinging out the net such that, under the inertia of lead weights at its periphery, it opens up into a perfect circle before the weights carry the edge of the net down into the water, a cord attached to the centre of the net with a loop at its other end secured around the wrist of the thrower enabling it to be retrieved.

After having seen this, Alex had gone along to Beach Road, where there are many chandlers and ships' outfitters, along with suppliers of fishing tackle and other marine items. The reclaiming of land had resulted in Beach Road now being a long way away from the sea, but it is still the centre of the fishing-supplies industry. Being confident of being able to handle it, he had bought the biggest casting net that he could find. He had brought this net along with him on the trip and, after changing into swimming trunks, marched down to the water's edge under the gaze of the rest of the party.

His first few attempts to cast the net were pathetic, the net simply falling into the water in a tangle, just a few feet in front of him. However, he persevered, and after half an hour was able to cast it so that it opened up to some extent before landing on the surface of the water. Encouraged by this success, and by the cheers of the party, he continued to cast the net, until eventually he found upon recovering it that he had caught a tiny fish of about three inches in length. With this success, he walked in triumph back up the beach to show his catch to the rest of the party, before returning it to the sea. He then sat down and drank a couple of cans of beer, during which time the size of his originally-four-inches-length catch grew gradually to eight inches in length, at which point the rest of the party called a halt to his exaggerations.

The ladies in the group started to lay the table for the pot-luck lunch. George had already lit the barbeque and was cooking spare ribs, chicken wings and large tiger-prawns. Each person had brought along their favourite dish, so that there was a delicious assortment of food. There was beer, and lots of fruit drinks made from freshly-squeezed limes, lemons and oranges. *Qiangwei* had prepared some vegetarian dishes that proved to be very popular. They finished the meal with an assortment of fresh fruit.

When all had eaten their fill, they sat under the palm trees away from the strong afternoon sun. There was a cooling breeze on the island and everyone was very relaxed. Alex stirred himself to get more beer for himself and George, lay back again, sighed, and then made the classic comment: 'It's hell in the tropics!'

Later, Alex and *Qiangwei* sat away from the group talking together. George could see that they were very content in each other's company. He had done his best to alert Alex to his sister's devotion to Buddhism at the expense of all else, and he did didn't want to see him hurt. To disturb them, he suggested that it was time for the group to get together for a couple of ball games on the beach to work off the food. Later the group settled down around the picnic bench, which had been cleared and was now set with more drinks.

Someone asked Alex to recite to a poem for them, knowing of his interest in Chinese poetry. However, under the influence of the beer and the sunshine, Alex felt in a silly mood and didn't want to speak of the traditional themes of sadness and home-sickness, so he jumped up onto the bench, squatted on his heels, and croaked in a deep voice "*gua1, gua1, gua1!*", before starting to recite a Chinese children's poem, *xiao3 qing1 wa1*, "Little green frog". By the time that he had completed the first line of the poem:

wo3 shi4 yi1 zhi xiao3 qing1 hua1, shui3li di4 shang4 liang ge jia1,

("I am only a little green frog, (but) I have two homes, one in the water, one on the land.")

the group had taken up his mood and were singing along with him, in loud, cheerful voices and with beaming smiles on their faces. The poem tells of the frog's amphibious life, and how it has two homes, one in the water and the other on land, and how it is as much at home eating the insects amongst the crops in the village fields, as it is swimming amongst the reeds in the stream. The poem ends with the frog telling how it sits in the moonlight croaking "*gua1, gua1, gua1!*" It is indeed a happy and contented little frog!

The party roared its appreciation of the poem and clapped tumultuously, but *Qiangwei* just stared in astonishment and disbelief at Alex. Although holding a senior position within the shipping company, he had just jumped onto a table, assumed the stance of a frog, and then recited a silly little children's poem, in the presence of office juniors! No Chinese man would ever abandon his dignity and behave in this way! Was he either supremely confident, or else very stupid? Would any of the office juniors have respect for him when they arrived for work on the following Monday morning? Moreover, she had heard the young assistants and the lady clerks calling him by his Chinese personal name, *Ai-li*, instead of calling him Mr. MacAlister.

Truly, she did not understand the Western mind. Was he not concerned at loss-of-face, as any sensible Chinese man would be? At the same time, she appreciated his love for the Chinese and for Chinese culture. *Qiangwei* was aware of Alex's feelings for her, and felt sad that she would never be able to return his affection, her path through life already having being laid out in accordance with her Buddhist

320

convictions.

On the way back to Singapore Island on the bum boat, the party sang popular songs of the day. Seeing Alex sitting alone on the fore-deck, *Qiangwei* joined him there. For several minutes they sat together in silence, enjoying the view and the gentle cooling breeze. Alex slid his hand over and took *Qiangwei*'s hand in his. They held hands for two or three minutes, after which she took her hand away. Alex realised with sadness the message that she was giving him: we can be good friends, but nothing more.

George had been watching them from further back in the boat and had seen Alex's gentle approach to his sister, and her equally gentle rejection. Apart from his parents, these were the two people for whom he felt the most affection in the whole world, and it saddened him to see the hopelessness of their situation. After thinking for a few minutes, he resolved to talk to his sister, and see if there was a way that a relationship could be established between them that did not interfere with her Buddhist interests. Perhaps Alex's own growing interest in Buddhist would offer a possibility.

A couple of days later, George said to his sister '*Qiangwei*, I have been thinking that *Ai-li* is becoming very interested in Buddhism. It would be nice if this Saturday afternoon we could take him around one of the temples in the city. What do you think?' Although George did not practice vegetarianism, he was still a sincere Buddhist. *Qiangwei* was initially non-committal, but eventually agreed, and the arrangement made was that, if *Ai-li* should be in agreement with the visit, they would meet outside the company offices when work finished at noon, and then go for a quick lunch, followed by taking a taxi to *Kong Meng San Kark See* Monastery on Brighthill Road in Bishan, which is the largest and most majestic Buddhist temple in Singapore.

When George told him about the proposed visit, Alex was enthusiastic, not only because it would give him the chance to meet *Qiangwei* again, but also because there were many questions about Buddhism to which he wanted to learn the answer. Come the Saturday morning, Alex watched the clock in the company office relentlessly: nine o'clock, then ten o'clock. 'Why doesn't the damn clock get a move on? At eleven o'clock George came into his office and said to him apologetically '*Ai-li*, there is a problem. I have to go out to see a client. He is leaving on Monday to take up a new job back in Britain, and wants to make sure that everything is alright before he leaves his wife to handle the removal. Can you and *Qiangwei* go off without me?'

Alex's feelings soared! A whole afternoon with *Qiangwei*, just the two of them together! George had difficulty in keeping his face straight when Alex expressed disappointment that he would not be able to come along, and he assured George that he and *Qiangwei* would be alright on their own, and that he would take good care of her.

At noon, Alex closed the door of his upstairs' office and came down to the ground floor to await the arrival of *Qiangwei*. Normally he would have heard the lady clerks chattering away, along with "the twittering of the sparrows", but there was silence. He looked into their room and was surprised to see the four of them standing in the centre of the room silently performing the slow breathing exercises that precede the chest-expanding movements of *tai4ji2 qi2gong1*. They then started to perform the movements.

He hadn't seen anything so controlled and so graceful before in his life. *Fu Rong*, who was dressed in a loose-fitting Chinese tunic, invited him to try for himself, but he was too self-conscious to accept her invitation. Under his gaze, she danced the slow controlled movements with inspiration, her face serene, the movements of her body fluid and precise. The other lady clerks stopped dancing and watched *Fu Rong* with wide serious eyes. They knew that she was now dancing just for Alex alone. Alex also sensed this, and was greatly drawn by the beauty of her dancing.

She went through the remaining of the eighteen movements: the rainbow dance; separating the clouds; the reversing arms exercise; rowing the boat in the middle of the lake; carrying a ball in front of the shoulders; turning to admire the moon; turning the waist and pushing the palms; the riding horse stance and swaying arms; scooping from the sea and reaching for the sky; pushing back the waves to bring in the tide; the flying pigeon spreads its wings; the flying swallow; the turning wheels, bouncing the ball and stamping the floor; and finally calming the *chi*.

As she performed the final movement, *Fu Rong* turned towards Alex and gave him not her usual cheery smile, but a mysterious and subdued - but nevertheless inviting - smile, that made clear her interest in him. Her face was covered with a gentle film of perspiration and her cheeks were suffused pink, not only from the strain of the exercises, but also from her emotions. She tried to covey to Alex at that moment how she felt about him. *Fu Rong* had many times wished to offer her help to Alex in learning Mandarin, which she hoped could have developed a bond between them, but had been too shy to do so. The other lady clerks would tease her mercilessly about this, upon which she would try to assure them that she had no personal interest in Alex, averting her eyes and blushing a deep red, to give lie to her words.

Alex was enthralled by her beauty as she danced, but this dance, and her message to him, had come too late, as Alex now had his heart set on *Qiangwei*. The other clerks realised the situation and felt great sympathy for *Fu Rong*. Alex smiled his appreciation to them for letting him watch them dance, but then turned and left. *Fu Rong* watched him leave with a great sadness in her young heart, whilst the other lady clerks pretended to be busy to give her time to recover her composure.

Alex walked to the front of the company offices, but *Qiangwei* was not to be seen. However, after he had paced up and down for ten minutes, *Qiangwei* arrived, explaining that because of a sudden downpour, all of the taxis had been occupied and she had had to queue until one was available. Before the taxi could dart away, he ushered *Qiangwei* into it and instructed the driver to take them to a well-known vegetarian restaurant in the city centre. Although Alex hadn't had much experience of vegetarian food, he found the dishes made from flavoured *dou4fou*, "bean curd", very tasty and likewise those made from lentils, which when cooked along with the traditional "five seeds" and known as "dahl" in the Indian community, he also found to be delicious to eat.

He told *Qiangwei* so, who couldn't resist a smile of pleasure at hearing his words, although she wondered whether his praise of vegetarian food was indeed genuine, or whether he was just trying to please her. For once, he didn't order beer with his meal, but simply asked for a pot of green tea. Things were going well!

After the meal, they took a taxi to a Buddhist temple on the east side of the city. *Qiangwei* was wearing modest clothing as befitted a visit to a temple, whilst Alex was wearing long trousers rather than shorts. Before they went into the temple, they walked around the grounds, stopping to look into a large pool in which a great number of *gui1*, turtles, swam. Alex asked *Qiangwei* as to why large numbers of Singaporeans once a year take ferries out to *Kusu* Island, which lies close by St. John's Island, for a religious celebration, in response to which she explained about the Taoist *Tua Pekong* Temple, where both Muslims and Taoists make a pilgrimage to honour the god of luck. In an old myth, a turtle transformed itself into *Kusu* Island to save a Chinese sailor and a Malay sailor from drowning.

Alex kept quiet about how he, George, *Yu Tian* and *Chonghai* had visited a restaurant where the presence of a turtle shell hanging in the window informed potential customers that stewed turtle was on the menu. George had told him during the meal that when turtle was called for by a customer, the kitchen staff would leave the turtle sitting quietly on a work-table, and then as soon as it had extended its head and neck from its shell they would quickly slip a noose over its head prior to cutting it off. As before with George, Alex hadn't known how true this story was, but nevertheless, he had found the stew, containing large pieces of turtle flesh, some still attached to pieces of shell, absolutely delicious.

The temple was surrounded by lawns composed of what looked like a very coarse twitch-grass. Alex had seen such grass being planted around finished apartment blocks and along the verges of roads, single tufts of the grass being planted at about a foot apart, and had been astonished when passing-by a month or so later to see that the tufts had spread out to form a thick carpet. He presumed that this grass was more suited to the climate and strong sunshine than the finer grasses used back in Britain.

The temple was huge and had many steeply pitched roofs, but with the slope of the roofs decreasing sharply towards the eaves and in some cases, at the ridges formed where two roofs met, the slope of the ends of the ridges proceeded beyond the horizontal, rising up substantially to impart a dramatic elegant appearance. Such curved roofs are typical of those found on many Singapore buildings.

Qiangwei explained that this is because of the belief that evil spirits coming down from above can only travel in straight lines, and can thus not negotiate the curvature of the roof, leaving the occupants of the building free from harm. She went on to tell him that it is for this same reason that many buildings - both homes and commercial and public buildings - have a short wall build in front of their entrance door, so that evil spirits cannot make their required straight-line entry into the building, leaving the building and its occupants free from their undesirable presence.

Alex was fascinated by this account, so *Qiangwei* carried on to tell him more: 'The roof of a building traditionally marked the point of spiritual communication between heaven and earth. Roof tiles of temples were designed to ward off evil spirits and bring good luck.' She drew Alex's attention to the lower ends of each of the sloping ridges of the roofs of the temple, where there were small figures, each forming an integral part of a ridge tile, the latter being known as a "guardian roof tile". The outermost figures were of a robed man riding on the back of a chicken, whilst behind these figures were lion- or dog-like figures, the numbers of these figures being one, three or more, but always in odd numbers. *Qiangwei* told him that in the state of *Qi* in China, there was once a cruel man, *Min Wang*, "Prince *Min*", whose reign ended in 283 BC. Legend has it that, on the Prime Minister's orders, Prince *Man* was hung from the roof of his ancestral temple for three days. Soldiers peeled off his skin and drew out his tendons, and the local people were allowed to each cut a small piece of flesh from his body.

His successors then had an effigy of Prince *Man* placed on the roof to protect themselves from his evil spirit, this effigy being mounted on the back of a chicken to give it greater presence. The dog-like creatures set behind him on the ridge were to prevent him from escaping. The legend continued, and during the *Ming* Dynasty (1368-1644 AD) guardian roof tiles had started to be made in pottery kilns.

Alex tried to imagine what was in the minds of the people that led them to set the effigy of the prince on the roof of his ancestral temple, and came to the conclusion that after the strong feelings that they had felt at the time of deposing him, there may have been illness and death amongst the populace or their livestock, or the failure of their crops, or some natural disaster, that in their ignorance they began to fear were the evil actions of the spirit of the late Prince. To appease his spirit, they created his effigy, dressed in long robes and reading - the prerogative of only the rich and powerful - from a tablet held in its hands. As it would be appropriate for someone of the Prince's station to be mounted rather than on foot, they set the effigy on the back of a chicken. Alex was intrigued by *Qiangwei*'s story and thereafter took great pleasure in noting the presence of Prince *Min* and his guardians on the roofs of building as he went about Singapore.

Qiangwei then took Alex to the door of the temple, instructing him, unnecessarily, as he knew already, to remove his shoes before entering. Once inside she stood and made her devotions. Across the other side of the entrance hall stood a Buddhist priestess, who seeing Alex, who was someone new to her and a westerner, came over and introduced herself. She was clad in a long plum-coloured robe held in place with a golden sash, and wore simple thong sandals. Her head was shaven. She looked poised and serene, free of the troubles of the world. Alex could see that she was Chinese, and ventured to speak to her in Mandarin, learning that she was from Indonesia, which, as with many other countries in the Far East, has a large Chinese population.

Alex asked the nun why the images of Buddha to be seen in different parts of the world have a different appearance and build, those from China and Japan being in the form of robust middle-aged men, whilst others are in the form of slim young women or young men, in some countries the male images of Buddha even bearing a moustache. She explained that since the time that Buddhism had arisen in India, some two thousand five hundred years ago, it had spread to many different countries, in so doing being modified and adopting some of the features of the host country, but at all times remaining true to its basic tenets. They spoke together for almost half an hour, until the nun was called away to religious duties.

As Alex and *Qiangwei* made their way around the many buildings of the temple they came across a large building from within which came the sound of many people, perhaps in their hundreds, chanting in slow, deep voices the same words, "*om mani padme hum*", over and over again. He looked at *Qiangwei* questioningly, who explained that it is a universal Buddhist chant that embodies all the elements of the Buddhist faith. By repeating the chant several hundred times a day, a Buddhist could atone for any misdeeds or acts of unkindness that they had committed, and in this way hope that following their death they will not be reincarnated as a lower-order life form.

Her explanation left him with many questions and with the resolve to explore the meaning of this chant further by reading about it in his spare time. However, although he read several Buddhist tracts, his understanding was little better: even the words of the Dalai Lama [28] on "om mani padme hum" left him with more questions that it gave answers to. He came to the conclusion that whilst Buddhism seems to be very complex, it is probably no more difficult to understand than Christianity would be to someone introduced to it for the first time. He decided that he would discuss the topic with other Buddhists whenever a suitable opportunity arose.

After leaving the temple, Alex and *Qiangwei* took a taxi to Kranji Cemetery, where many hundreds of servicemen from World War Two are buried. The atmosphere within the beautifully-maintained grounds was sombre, and Alex took *Qiangwei*'s hand in his as they walked along the rows of graves. One of the graves was that of a seventeen year old Indian serviceman, but the word "man" seems unfitting for one so young. *Qiangwei* was visibly overcome and a tear rolled down her cheek.

After this sad visit they carried on to Changi Harbour. From there they took a ferry over to Pulau Ubin, where Alex had been on an earlier occasion with George and the two assistants. They did not hire a tandem, but just walked along the street, little more than a dirt track, passing though the centre of the village, smiling and chatting to the locals. They stopped for a drink at a tiny food stall, Alex asking for a beer from the fridge, whilst *Qiangwei* asked for a glass of water. After this they continued on their walk, maintaining a leisurely pace in keeping with the peace of the village.

Qiangwei saw a small child, a girl, sitting on the grass verge at the side of the track playing with a tiny kitten. She bent down and spoke to the little girl in a gentle, friendly voice, asking if the kitten belongs to the little girl, and what its name is. The little girl responded with a few words and a beaming smile, and then lifted up the kitten and handed it to *Qiangwei*. Alex thought that the scene was beautiful and that *Qiangwei* would make a wonderful mother. As they carried on walking again, he told her so. However, *Qiangwei* didn't smile or acknowledge his words, but her face became sad and her eyes looked tearful. Alex realised that he had, unintentionally, drawn *Qiangwei*'s attention to the price she would have to pay for her planned future life as a Buddhist nun, and regretted having spoken as he did. They walked on in silence.

After having taken the ferry back to Changi Ferry Terminal, they walked along to Changi Hotel, where Alex had checked the day before that vegetarian food was available. The restaurant was elegant, with a piano playing in the background. They enjoyed a meal, before walking though the public rooms of the hotel, admiring the orchids and in particular the bougainvillaea, that most beautiful and prolific flower that typifies Singapore even more than does its national flower, the orchid, the bougainvillaea being set out in large pots, or dripping from hanging baskets, in all of the hotels in Singapore. The time was now getting late, so they went to the front of the hotel, where a doorman called a taxi for them.

Alex thought that it had been a lovely day, and he had spent it with the woman he desired most in the whole world. As the taxi made its way back to the city, for a second time he took *Qiangwei*'s hand in his, waiting for yet another rejection. However, she remained still, looking straight ahead of her. Alex gave her hand a little squeeze, then with his heart in his mouth he said 'I love you my beautiful rose.'

Still *Qiangwei* did not take away her hand, but after a minute she said '*Ai-li*, I have told you of my intention to become a Buddhist Nun', to which Alex replied 'Let me join you as a Buddhist. We are both travelling through life. Can we not take the Buddhist road together? What does it matter that I started life's journey before you, or that you took the Buddhist road before me? None of us know at which point our journey will end. If on our journey we can give support to each other in times of adversity, and rejoice together in times of achievement, then isn't this better than that we should both travel alone?'

Qiangwei was silent for a moment, then she said '*Ai-li*, you know that I have great affection for you, but the course of my life was set out long before I met you. If we travelled together, this would distract me from the mission that I have long been committed to.' She looked at him with wide sad eyes. 'There is no future for us *Ai-li*', to which Alex replied 'Then let us just enjoy the present whilst it lasts'.

Chapter Eighteen

When Alex and George next had lunch together, Alex took the opportunity to talk about *Qiangwei*. He wanted to reassure George that his interest in his sister was sincere, and told him that he felt that she was becoming very fond of him in return. George was very careful not to give Alex too much hope, just muttering a reply as to how she had enjoyed their outings together, but mentioning that she was interested in accompanying them on their next outing. The following weekend the three of them decided to visit an old pottery out at Jurong, in the still largely-undeveloped west of Singapore Island.

First they had lunch in a food court in the basement of a shopping mall. They each chose their own main dish, but shared a large jug of freshly-crushed lime juice, then a plate of sliced papaya, mango and rock melon. It was very pleasant sitting and chatting together and their conversation was happy and relaxed. Alex would have been content to sit for longer, but George and *Qiangwei* were anxious to make their way to the pottery.

They caught a bus on Bukit Timak Road, which would pass by Bukit Timah Plaza, and then go on through Bukit Batok until it got to Jurong Old Road. On boarding the bus and making their way to some unoccupied seats at the rear, an elderly Chinese lady leaned across quickly to the unoccupied seats and gave each of them a hearty thwack. Alex was puzzled, so George explained that the lady had been driving away from the seats any evil spirits that may have been left by the previous occupants. The Chinese believe that such evil spirits lie in wait for the next persons to sit there. Alex turned to the lady, nodding and smiling his appreciation to her, receiving a beaming smile in return. Initially, he was surprised at her action, but quickly accepted it as just another of the many delightful old Chinese customs.

For about ten minutes they travelled along this twisting old road, at the sides of which were little kampongs, "smallholdings", and open-fronted huts containing a small shop at the front and living accommodation at the rear. It was as if they were back in time, travelling through the undeveloped place that much of Singapore must have been like fifty or more years ago.

They passed by old Bulim Cemetery, with its time-weathered graves, many of which were the Chinese "armchair" graves, with a low horseshoe-shaped wall running from one side of the grave, around the back, and then down the other side. The walls of many of these graves were heavily ornamented, faced with tiles and with a small headstone set into them, bearing inscriptions in an old style that Alex, and probably many present-day Chinese, could not read.

A short way beyond Bulim cemetery they reached Jalan Bahar, where they alighted. Turning north along this road, after a few minutes of walking they came to Lor Tawas, "Lor" being the Malay work for lane, on their left. The lane was very narrow, little more than car width, with heavy jungle-growth on both sides. Small kampongs were scattered along the lane, with tall closely-spaced bamboo forming a tight hedge at their fronts. Scrawny chickens ran about unconcerned, but if any of them should stray into the jungle, there is no shortage of pythons to swallow them. A few lanes branched off, but they ignored these and followed the recent tracks of a vehicle in the soft earth, and after twenty minutes reached their destination, a very old Chinese-owned pottery, lying only a few hundred yards away from the Chinese University, which sat above them, clear of the jungle.

In this pottery was one of the few remaining dragon kilns. The kiln was brick-built, about thirty to forty feet long and of semi-circular shape of a height of about six feet, and lay on a gently sloping bank. The kiln was loaded from the lower end with alternate stacks of 'green' pots and lengths of timber. After having been loaded, the timber at the mouth of the kiln was set on fire, and then the end of the kiln was almost completely sealed with bricks. The gentle inclination of the kiln provided a chimney effect in sucking in air to feed the flames from the lower end and to draw out the combustion products from the upper end. They had arrived, fortuitously, at the stage of firing the kiln, and watched the firing procedure with interest. The owners of the pottery were a pleasant couple, happy to answer their many questions, and pleased at their interest.

Alex asked if, working out in the jungle, they had any trouble with snakes, monitor lizards, or any other kind of wild creature, the husband telling him that whenever they moved a pile of pots that had been lying around on the ground for some time, they had to exercise caution in case they should reveal a nest of snakes. Pythons were a problem in the area. Indeed, he told them, the local chicken farmers were constantly complaining to the authorities about the pythons that came regularly to devour their livestock. Whilst they are not poisonous, pythons can not only coil themselves around the body of anyone who approaches too closely, to squeeze them to death, but can also inflict severe injuries to the person by stabbing their fangs into the person's face.

The pottery owner told them about the monitor lizards that live in the jungle, with a body the size of that of a fully-grown Alsatian, but with a four-foot long tail, which they would swish from side to side with the strength to break a man's leg, whilst flicking out their great long tongues. They would come every few days looking for his dogs, or their frequently-produced litters, a pup from one of the litters making a filling meal for them. He spoke of the dangers of scorpions, which would stand their ground when exposed and raise their tails menacingly over their heads, in a clear warning to back away. However, of particular menace were the centipedes, rather like the ragworm used as bait back on the Clyde, with a length of a foot or more and a diameter of up to three-quarters of an inch.

When encountered in the open, they do not retreat, nor just stand and hold their ground, but advance quickly and aggressively, lunging at the intruder with the intention of injecting poison with their bite. It was common for someone bitten by a centipede to be hospitalised for two or three days, suffering from the toxic poison that they inject with their fangs. Having strong rubbery bodies, they are difficult to kill, chopping them into two pieces with a spade or a machete being about the most successful method.

In particular he hated the mosquitoes and "no see'ems", biting gnats, that flourish in the jungle environment of the pottery. He called that mosquitoes "horrid little buzzing creatures" and explained that they can be so dense at times that they look like a cloud and can cause distress to both animals and human beings alike by their sheer numbers. Although they are not usually disease-carrying in Singapore, their bites can fester and many people suffer badly from an allergic reaction. Mosquitoes can be kept from coming indoors by means of closely-fitting screens of very fine mesh on open windows and doors. However, he went on to tell them that this is not the case with the biting "no see'ems", as they are so small as to be almost invisible to the naked eye and can pass through the finest of screens. They tend to leave two or three bites about two-thirds of an inch apart, which leads many people to believe that they break through the skin with the first "bite" and then move along beneath it.

Alex considered this possibility, but thought it unlikely: his view was that as the gnats are so small, the distance apart of the bites is too great for the gnats to have travelled under the skin, so the second bites are simply from gnats stopping for a "fill-up" in travelling along the surface of the skin. The owner told them that despite the disadvantages of living in a jungle environment, he enjoys kampong life, as do most Chinese and Malays, and some Indians. Redevelopment has required that many Kampong dwellers relocate to one of the government housing schemes, but many of the Indians prefer to re-establish their shops and business premises in "Little India" in and around Serangoon Road.

Alex remembered his own 'wild animals' in his apartment in the city. On one occasion he had come across a small snake at the foot of the stairs up to his apartment. Having no knowledge of snakes, he had gone off to a bar on Scotts Road for an hour to give it chance to wriggle off, creeping cautiously up the stairs upon his return. In the apartment were a few cute little bright-eyed lizard-like creatures that the locals call "chitchats", which run all over the walls and the ceilings with a jerky twisting motion from the effort of having to break the suction between the bottom of their feet and the surface over which they are crossing, with every step that they take. Alex welcomed them to share the apartment with him, and would watch them with interest as they deftly caught and ate any mosquitoes, flies or other insects that were drawn towards the room lights.

He also had another 'lodger' living with him, a ten-inch long lizard. Sitting on his south-facing balcony one evening, just as the sun was starting to weaken, he had been surprised to see some of the foliage of his large pot plants swaying and moving. After a few seconds he was able to make out the lizard standing on a cross branch, weighing him up. Although he moved to and from the balcony several times during that evening, the lizard didn't move, but continued to stare at him with clear cold eyes. The next morning he went onto the balcony just as the sun was rising, to find the lizard in the same place, and giving him the same cold stare. However, a few minutes later, when the sun had risen clearly and the heat of the day could start to be felt, it had clumped down from its perch, along the line of pot plants, over the balcony and down to the ground. Thereafter, it was a daily pleasure for Alex to watch his lizard depart in the morning and return in the evening.

They retraced their steps to Jalan Bahar, then caught a bus heading further north along the road, passing many little timber-built stores on the way. The bus pulled up at a stop at a tiny hamlet at a road junction. Amongst the shops in the hamlet was an open-fronted barber's shop, with the usual red-and-white-banded barber's pole stuck out at a slightly upwards inclination over the front of the shop, just as in Britain. Inside the shop was just one old chair, where a man was sitting having his hair cut. The only piece of furniture was an old table with a few assorted items on top, including the mirror that the barber used to enable his customers to approve the results of the cut. Outside the shop was a bench where several old men were sitting, some awaiting their turn, but others just enjoying the chance for a chat. A pleasant relaxed scene!

Soon the bus reached a new cemetery that had been built on virgin ground in this outlying area, where they decided to get off. George told Alex that it was a multi-denominational cemetery, occupying two sides of the road, the larger left-hand side being predominantly Chinese, whilst on the right-hand side were the burial places of the deceased of minority religions in Singapore, such as those of the Jewish faith. Alex was surprised to learn that that was a Jewish population in Singapore, George then telling him about the Jewish Synagogue on Armenian Street in the city centre. Upon reflection, Alex realised that the Jews were similar to the Chinese in many ways, in travelling to different parts of the world to seek a better life for themselves and their families, whilst retaining their own strong faith and customs.

As they walked towards the entrance to the Chinese part of the cemetery, a lorry with its outside covered completely with fresh flowers came along the road. A large framed photograph set over the cabin of the lorry showed the deceased, whom the lorry's occupants were there to honour. On some days, half a dozen such lorries can be seen travelling towards the cemetery.

There was a burial taking place close by where they entered the cemetery, a new Chinese grave having being opened. As they approached, relatives of the deceased came up to them and gave each of them a carton of chrysanthemum tea, being pleased that they were present, as the presence of foreigners would give greater dignity to the occasion. The deceased, lying within a large wooden sarcophagus such as one would associate with the pharaohs of ancient Egypt, was borne over the surrounding rough ground by six men, and then lowered without preamble into the grave, the ceremony for the departed already having been conducted elsewhere, usually on the previous evening.

Neither Alex, George or *Qiangwei* knew whether or not the sarcophagus would be taken away before the grave was filled in. He had heard, back in Scotland, that before a grave is filled in, the polished-brass fittings and the beautifully-finished sides and lid of the coffin are removed, leaving the body to be interred in a simple timber box: however, he didn't know if this is the practice in Singapore, but presumed that the practical and common-sense Chinese would not want to bury such an expensive and re-usable item as the sarcophagus with each funeral.

At the thought of coffins, Alex recalled the story of the Yorkshire undertaker who used to denigrate his competitor's coffins to prospective customers by telling them that they are little better than a plain plywood box, and that if they chose to be buried in one, then "Your arse will be through the bottom of it within six months!"

Alex had actually been to the ceremony that preceded the burial of a deceased person. The foreman of the yard at the company premises on Bukit Timah Road, *Siew Tung*, knowing of his interest in Chinese culture, had invited him to the funeral service of his father-in-law, the service to take place on the eve of the burial. Alex had accepted his invitation, but he didn't know what to expect. The ceremony was to be held in the street outside the home of the deceased, where permission had been obtained, for a small charge, to close the street to traffic.

An awning had been erected against the possibility of a heavy downpour during the course of the evening. Alex was introduced to the family members, who thanked him for having attended. At one end of the space covered by the awning were piled the many symbolic items, made of coloured, heavily-ornamented tissue paper, that were to accompanying the deceased into the next world, to make his life there more comfortable. There were models of houses, cars, television sets, and even of servants who would be at the deceased's call. To honour the deceased, a party of monks had been hired for the evening. They first built a small open fire on a metal base to protect the surface of the street, and then they conducted an impressive gymnastics-like performance, which at one point included jumping over the fire and at the same time expressing a jet of fluid from their mouths onto the fire to cause it to flair up.

Siew Tung told Alex that his father had been born in China, where, after he had reached maturity, he had married a local girl. Several years later he had emigrated, alone, to Singapore to seek a better life. In the course of time he had married two Singapore women, one of whom was *Siew Tong*'s mother. The two wives had brought up their families in the same household, but *Siew Tong* said that there had sometimes been disagreement between them. Alex was introduced to the two wives, and expressed his sorrow at their loss.

The ceremony was not a sad event, but a happy acknowledgement of the long life of the deceased. Alex was moved by the philosophical aspect of the Chinese with regard to death. Instead of grieving and the shedding of tears, they remember the full life of the deceased and give their thanks. In the obituary columns of the Straits Times, it is common practice for the relatives to add five or six years to the actual age of the deceased, as the Chinese respect longevity. Indeed, the Chinese do not count a person's age from their date of birth, but add a further nine months to allow for gestation, the 'age' of a person starting from the time of the copulation of the parents, which has a kind of logic about it, although nowadays they would not extend this practice to formal documents.

The close relatives of the deceased then gathered together in a nearby private place whilst they waited for a sign that the deceased had 'passed over to the other side'. After about half an hour they returned to the main funeral party and gave everybody the news that the spirit of the deceased had now departed, upon which a large kettle was produced, from which cups were filled. Alex was surprised to find that the cups had been filled with beer, the use of the kettle to dispense it being so that the gods would not know that the mourners were drinking alcohol, and would thus not be offended. Alex considered this to be a delightful little deception and hoped that the gods would turn a blind eye to it should they ever find out! He thanked *Siew Tung* and his family and left, feeling honoured at having been invited.

Alex learnt that the Chinese dread the death of a child, irrespective of whether it is their own, before the death of its parents, this upsetting the natural order. He had heard that in some cases the parents of a deceased son or daughter will inquire as to other parents who have suffered the death of a child of the opposite sex, so that they could pray that the two deceased persons will meet 'on the other side' and have a happy relationship together. In some cases they would arrange a ceremony for the 'marriage' of the two departed souls, at which they would burn paper images of presents and vast amounts of both money and cheques issued by the Bank of Hell, so that they will be short of nothing in the afterlife. He also had learnt that it is not the Chinese practice to give a young child a gift of white clothes, this colour being associated with death. He reflected that this was no different than in Britain, where purple is seen as the colour of death.

Alex, George and *Qiangwei* then walked amongst the Chinese graves, Alex being able to make out some of the inscriptions. He enjoyed reading the names of the deceased to determine whether they were male or female, but in some cases he couldn't make this out, as the name was not of either a masculine or a feminine nature.

George smiled as he told him that it had been the practice in some villages in China for the parents of a male child to give the child a female name, or a neutral name, such as "final child", that did not show that the child was male, and sometimes even dress the child in girls' clothing, lest the gods become jealous of their son and steal him from them by death.

With his interest in Chinese characters, Alex had bought a book recently on calligraphy and also one showing different forms of Chinese script[18:1], starting historically with Oracle Bone, then continuing with other scripts, including Small Seal script, Clerk script, *Kai Shu*, *Xing Shu*, and *Cao Shu*. The writing of scripts originated

---

[18:1] *han zi jiu ti shu* (Book of nine styles of Chinese script), published by *he bei mei shu chu pai she* (North Lake Fine-Art Publishing House), ISBN 7 5310 0180 2/J.

around five thousand years ago as a means of keeping records, but the details became lost over the course of such a great length of time. Oracle Bone script was introduced, the characters being carved on the shell of a turtle using a pointed tool. Knowledge of this script also became lost over time, until the fairly recent discovery of several bones carved using this script.

Later there was the Large Seal style. These characters were tall, and of a uniform line thickness. However, the original Large Seal style wasn't standardised, so the First *Qin* Emperor, *Qin Shihuang*, known for his burning of many thousands of books to control the intellectuals of the day, introduced the standardised Small Seal script, such as is employed at the present day for the 'chops', "seals", used to authenticate letters and documents in China, and in some countries with a large Chinese population. Although of great interest and complexity, and in many cases representing closely the subject of the character, these carved or chiselled characters do not, and indeed could not, display the boldness of later scripts drawn with a pointed brush.

Following this the Official style was introduced, where a brush was used so as to be able to create both thick and thin strokes. The most frequently-used style at the present day is the Regular style, where characters can fit into squares, children's script-writing exercise books being provided with a pattern of squares to help the children to maintain the correct proportions of the characters.

Alex had learnt from his book on calligraphy that proper posture is essential for good calligraphy, with the body held erect, the shoulders not allowed to droop, the back straight, and the feet set firmly on the ground. The paper is held in the left hand and the brush in the right hand, with the tip of the brush about a foot below the level of the eyes. The brush is held vertically, with the thumb pressing outwards on the brush, the first and second fingers being on the outside of the brush pressing inwards. The third and fourth fingers are on the inside of the brush and act to balance the force of the second finger. Complete control of the brush is thus achieved.

Experts in calligraphy prefer to use the 'suspended position' for the wrist and the elbow, both being clear of the table, but this can be relaxed and the elbow or wrist supported when drawing larger characters. The basic strokes of calligraphy as explained in Alex's book were the dot stroke, the horizontal stroke, the vertical stroke, the rising stroke, the left-falling stroke, the right-falling stroke, the hook stroke and the turning stroke.

With his growing interest in calligraphy, Alex bought "The four treasures of the study", which comprises a brush, an ink-stick, paper and an ink-stone, the latter being used to produce the ink required by grinding the ink-stick on it with water, although at the present time most people just use already-prepared ink poured from a bottle. In earlier times, thin slips of bamboo or pieces of silk would have been used instead of paper. With this set he practised drawing the strokes in the prescribed order, using greater pressure on the brush to produce thicker downwards strokes when required, giving the brush a downwards 'dip' when changing the direction of a stroke, and taking off the pressure when giving the end of a downwards stroke a final upwards flick to form a *goul*, or "hook". He marvelled at the designing of the strokes, in some long-ago age, to enable the final stroke, whenever possible, to be made as a dramatic and bold horizontal slash.

What Alex couldn't understand was that often in displayed works of calligraphy, the calligrapher had allowed the tip of the brush to split, so that what should have been a thick down-stroke had become split into two or more parts, with a thin unpainted strip between them. Likewise, instead of withdrawing the brush from the canvas at the end of one stroke, the calligrapher had often allowed the brush tip to trail over the canvas on its way to the next stroke. He felt that such features were the result of poor brush-work, and that all strokes should be full, with a clear lifting of the brush at the end of each. However, those Chinese that he spoke to on this matter all said that such features were desirable in the work and displayed the individuality of the calligrapher. Indeed, any touching-up of what Alex considered to be defects is strictly forbidden and will render a good artistic piece of calligraphy worthless.

There was clearly a lot that Alex had yet to learn about Chinese culture. A personal dislike that he had was to see Chinese characters written with a ball-point pen, as opposed to a split-nib pen, which latter enables the strokes to be varied in thickness, to give beauty and artistry to the characters. In this particular view, he felt sure that he was not alone.

After leaving the cemetery they caught a bus to the end of Jalan Bahar, which led down over a short beach to the Straits of Johore. It was at this spot that the Japanese had first landed in Singapore after sweeping down through Malaya during World War II. This event was the turning point in British colonialism in South-East Asia. Although in greater numbers than the Japanese, and being dug in, the allied forces had been driven back from the Straits, towards Singapore City. The city depended for its water supplies upon reservoirs in the surrounding area. Knowing this, the Japanese quickly took over the possession of the water supplies, the fall of Singapore then being inevitable, this catastrophe being ascribed to over-confidence on the part of the British.

336

At the bus terminus just short of the Straits was a small coffee house, with a small temple close by. Just beyond the temple was a concrete holding-pit of some eight-feet sides and five-feet height. Inside the pit were two crocodiles, each of about six-feet length, that had been caught in the nearby mangrove swamps. In due course their skins would be sold for making handbags, belts and shoes, and their flesh would find its way into cooking pots.

This was truly a wild area, in great contrast to the sophistication of Orchard Road in the city centre where, along with the long-established Robinson's, a great number of fashionable stores flourish in great splendour, the equal of any to be found in London's West End. It was hard to believe that, as the owner of the pottery had told them, out here at Jurong there are crocodiles, pythons and monitor lizards roaming at will, not twenty miles from the city centre. However, Alex had had little experience of Orchard Road, as the only time that he had been there he had been subjected to the unwanted attention of numerous, persistent, touts selling copy 'Rolex' and other copy watches on every street corner and he hadn't yet felt a desire to return there.

With the growth of the city centre and the urbanisation of the surrounding jungle, many wild creatures had ventured to move into the city. To cope with the extremely heavy downpours that are almost a daily occurrence in Singapore, large-diameter drains and deep culverts are set along the sides of most of the streets, providing a home for "drain cats", wild cats, these poor creatures providing sustenance for the pythons that have also taken to living in the drains and culverts. On occasions, drivers are startled to see the head of a python lifting up from a culvert as they stop at traffic lights in the city. Indeed, once pythons have found their way into the service ducts of multi-floor apartments, they give a terrible fright to the occupants of the upper apartments when they discover them crawling along their balconies and stairwells [29]. Recent letters in the "Straits Times" from disturbed parents have drawn attention to crocodiles swimming in the reservoirs that provide drinking water for the city's inhabitants, fearing that their children playing at the water's edge might be attacked. What a country of contrasts!

On the bus home, Alex sat next to *Qiangwei* and again took her hand, despite being in clear view of George. He didn't care who saw them together, although many in the city who saw a beautiful young Chinese girl with an older Westerner would "tut-tut" and pass uncomplimentary remarks about the girl. As one middle-aged Chinese woman made her way past them she uttered an offensive remark to her husband that Alex understood clearly, so he released *Qiangwei*'s hand, realising her sensitivity in this situation. This had been a last-minute blight on what had otherwise been a perfect day.

They made their way back to George and *Qiangwei*'s home, where George diplomatically disappeared into the house whilst Alex made his farewell to *Qiangwei*. He took her hand into his, and told her again that he loved her, and that nothing would stand in the way of their continued friendship, as long as she herself wanted the friendship to last. The poor girl was torn between her growing affection for Alex, and her deep-rooted intention to become a Buddhist nun. How could she continue her friendship with Alex when she was dedicated to a future life of celibate devotion to the Buddhist faith?

Qiangwei eventually agreed to meet Alex the following week, but made clear to him, once again, that their relationship could not extend beyond friendship, even if Alex should become a Buddhist himself. This dashed Alex's plan of doing just this to win *Qiangwei*'s hand. Still, he was not going to give up. He would pursue *Qiangwei* for as long as it took. One day she might weaken in her intentions of becoming a nun, and then they could marry and live together happily within the Buddhist faith. No, he was not going to give up yet, not by a long shot!

The following Saturday afternoon he met *Qiangwei* outside her house, and then they took a taxi to the *Haw Paw* Villa, which is an oriental mystery park filled with traditional settings from Chinese mythology, some horrific in their cruelty, such as people being impaled on stakes, or having their bodies sawn in two from the top of their head downwards. It was all rather gruesome, but at the same time captivating. The villa had been set up by the *Haw Paw* brothers on the success of their "Tiger Balm" embrocation, which is rather like an oriental exotically-scented "Vick", and is well known for its efficacy in relieving muscular aches and pains.

As they made their way around the villa, walking side-by-side, Alex didn't take *Qiangwei*'s hand, nor did she take his. There was an embarrassed atmosphere between them, Alex not wanting to experience rejection and *Qiangwei* not wanting to give any false signals that might suggest that she had relented on what she had made clear to him the previous week. Alex started to feel guilty about what he considered to be perfectly natural feelings of a man for a woman, and he displayed this by increasing irritability and frustration: he wanted to have his own way, and that was that! In this, he was regressing towards the type of man that he once used to be. Perhaps it was more serious than that, in that a man can never really change his true nature, but only hide or suppress it temporarily.

After they left the villa they made their way along to the World Trade Centre, where they caught the ferry over to Pulau Blakang Mati. Sitting together on the ferry, Alex cursed his luck in having fallen for such a devout person as *Qiangwei*. If it had have been any other woman he would surely by now have won her over and they could have looked forward to a happy life together. Nevertheless, even in his distress, he admired *Qiangwei* for the strength of her convictions. She was also so marvellously and resolutely Chinese, as opposed to the majority of Singaporeans, who consider themselves not just Chinese, but Westernised Chinese. She didn't affect a Western personal name, nor burden her conversation with "of course", "my dear", "you know" and "actually", in an attempt to sound sophisticated; nor did she adopt any of the other Western mannerisms that would diminish her strong and beautiful Chinese personality.

They left the ferry and made their way around the island, stopping first at a building that housed a reconstruction of the surrender of the Allied forces to the Japanese forces that had taken place at the Ford factory down Bukit Timak Road. As they looked at the reconstruction, a party of Japanese tourists entered and although Alex could not understand what they were saying, they were obviously delighted, and chattered away animatedly and took countless photographs of one-after-the-other standing in front of the exhibit.

However, when they reached the next reconstruction, depicting the subsequent surrender of the Japanese to the Allied Forces, they passed by without saying a word. Alex held his tongue: he would dearly have loved to make a comment regarding the Japanese surrender just to see what effect this would have had on them! They made their way back to *Qiangwei*'s home with a measure of unease between them. Alex's romancing of *Qiangwei* was not going as he would have wished.

During the week that followed, and influenced by his visit to the cemetery, Alex reflected on his religious beliefs. From an early age, despite the piety and religious guidance of the staff at the home, he had felt that life is just a transitory experience, if indeed it ls an actual experience, as at times it seemed to him to have no more reality than that of his dreams. Back in Scotland Alex had believed that after life there was nothing, as with the snuffing out of a candle. Many times he wondered if indeed mankind has any free will, or if we are all acting a life-long play, with our actions and destiny pre-defined. He recalled an old Scots saying that at one time he had read on the tap-room wall of an old inn: "Whit's fur ye'll no pass by ye", which he interpreted as meaning "One cannot avoid one's destiny." However, if we take an action to avoid a situation, does this not then make the new situation our destiny? Is there a unique destiny, or is our destiny constantly changing to reflect our actions? Alex couldn't find an answer to this question.

In the West, a colony of bees can only survive the winter if in the previous summer the worker bees spend the whole of their short lives of about six weeks storing honey in the hive. However, only the queen and very few of the worker bees live on in the hive until the next spring, when flowers and trees start to produce pollen again. The all-day-long foraging of the great number of worker bees during the previous summer was not for their own welfare, but to ensure the continuation of the species. In the same way, shouldn't people devote themselves to working for the future good of the species, rather than for their own personal satisfaction, even if they cannot explain the purpose or even the existence of life?

Alex felt that we must all do what our instincts tell us is the right and proper thing to do, rather than just drift and see what happens. He had always felt uneasy when others would proclaim such fatalist remarks as 'If you number's up, your number's up', or 'If the bullet's got your name on it, there is nothing that you can do,' or 'With my bad luck I never had a chance.' Better that we follow the instincts that we feel and get on with our lives, seeking advancement when we can, avoiding danger when it threatens, improving our 'bad luck' by hard work and diligence, and helping others in genuine need.

In respect of existence after death, in the past Alex had always felt that when the heart has stopped beating, and the brain is no longer supplied with blood, all of one's memories and thoughts, indeed all that make one a person, cease to exist. When the last living persons who had known the deceased die themselves, there is no record of the deceased, except on photographic images, or in the personal possessions that he or she has left behind, except that such images and personal possessions would mean little to someone who had not known the deceased in life. There are always public records, giving the date of birth, marital status and date of death, but these are just statistical data that will allow future historians to write learned papers, without knowing anything about the persons involved.

He had heard that in the Middle Ages, a group of theologians had attended the bed of a dying man, first setting up his death-bed on a balance, and then checking for any weight loss at the instant of his death, when presumably his soul would have left his body. In the absence of weight loss, rather than accepting that the human body does not contain a soul, they had deduced, very conveniently, that the soul is weightless! What weight loss did they expect? Thoughts and memories and the 'soul' must all lie within the brain, and undoubtedly the brain matter that had enabled these thoughts and memories and the soul to exist in life would still be present, with the same mass, immediately after death.

Alex had always been of the opinion that the 'soul' within the human body is a person's conscience and sense of fair play. Exactly what the purpose of conscience is he didn't know, except that it prevents most of mankind from committing acts of extreme cruelty. However, conscience and sense of fair play are not confined to the human race. His own little dog Clyde had had a strong sense of fair play and a great capacity for love, but in no religion that he knew of would Clyde have been credited with having had a soul.

Alex felt that religion had been developed to fill the need of mankind for an explanation of their presence on the earth, so that they could then get on with their lives untroubled, without having to ponder matters that are beyond the understanding of even the wisest of men. Moreover, he believed that the trappings and rituals of all religions had been developed to provide more 'evidence' of substance to the various religious beliefs and, in complying with them, to provide the human race with a means of displaying the strength of their convictions: he was of the view that the playing of an organ and the singing of hymns at Christian ceremonies were to make the ceremonies more interesting and more of a social event. He wondered if the avoidance of the eating of meat on Friday was to give those of the Catholic faith the satisfaction of having denied themselves in the demonstration of their faith, likewise in the refusal of both those of the Jewish faith and those of the Muslim faith to eat the flesh of the pig, or even to eat from plates that might have been used in the past for this purpose: however, he would have to discuss such matters with a member of the appropriate faith before he could come to a firm opinion.

He had never felt any antagonism towards those of strong religious beliefs, of whatever faith, and sometimes he had even envied them the support and guidance that their faith gave them. What Alex detested most about many of those of strong religious conviction that he had met in the past was their hypocrisy: dressing in black and speaking mealy-mouthed platitudes in a pious voice, to give the rest of society the impression that they are 'good' folk, whilst the reality was that playing at being good is their hobby, just as others enjoy fishing or bowling. Goodness is demonstrated by what one does, not by what one wears, or eats, or says. Alex wasn't proud of his lack of conventional 'organised' religious beliefs, nor was he troubled about it: it was just the way that he felt. If a person believes, then he or she believes; if a person does not believe, then he or she does not believe: there is no 'good' or 'bad' about it.

He had had one embarrassing incident in his childhood, when the children from the home had been led along to the parish church to take part in a religious ceremony. As they were filing out from the pews at the end of the ceremony, his arm had been seized by an angry church warden, who led him to the pew in front of that in which he had been sitting and pointing at a wet stain had demanded 'Why have you pissed on the seat cover, you disgraceful little creature?' Alex had been too young to explain that he hadn't sat on that particular pew. From that time onwards he had had been put off from organised religion.

However, since arriving in the Far East, and particularly since meeting *Qiangwei*, he had experienced a growing interest in Buddhism. Although Buddhism also had its trappings, such as a belief in reincarnation, he had been drawn increasingly towards it because of its central belief that one must be kind to one's fellow man, never seeking retribution for wrongs suffered. Within limitations, of late he had tended to follow vegetarianism to some extent, in not eating the flesh of warm-blooded creatures that cared for their young, although he still ate fish.

Whilst he had initially accounted for the Buddhist belief that a grandchild might be the reincarnation of a deceased member of the family by considering that this 'reincarnation' is just the biological transmission through the family of the physical and mental characteristics of the deceased person; at the same time he subscribed to the giving of a newly-born child the name of the deceased family member as, for whatever reason, this is an emotionally satisfying way of remembering the deceased. As the child grow older, it will be of great pleasure to see it develop characteristics that resemble those of a departed loved one, and allow the family to believe that the loved one, or the qualities of the loved one, are not lost to the world forever.

However, the longer that Alex considered this subject, the more he began to think that the reincarnation of a loved one, and the biological transmission of their characteristics through the genes of the family members, amount to the same thing. Before there was knowledge of genes, who would not put family resemblances down to reincarnation, and why should people not continue to do so at the present time? The thought of the deceased do not pass on during reincarnation, so why draw a distinction between reincarnation and gene transmission?

Although he could not see what 'higher power' could determine in what form a person would be reincarnated, and how the person could avoid being reincarnated as a lower life form by the chanting of a sufficient number of mantras, he felt that perhaps the value of the chanting of the mantras comes from the belief of the chanter that he or she is doing something positive to secure a good re-birth, rather than just hoping, particularly when the mantras are addressed to the good of a child or other family member rather than for the benefit of the chanter. It is also possible that from the birth of Buddhism, attempts were made to keep adherents 'on the right path' by the warning of unpleasant consequences should they ever stray, which led to the chanting of mantras, in the course of time the number of repetitions of the mantras becoming excessive: better safe than sorry!

Alex was of the opinion that with all old religions where 'the message' has been passed down over many generations, it is inevitable that exaggeration or distortion of the message will have occurred: this is just human nature. Taking the case of Christianity, in the bible the reported changing of the side of the boat from which the disciples were fishing, without success, to the opposite side of the boat, leading to an enormous amount of fish being caught, is not necessarily a miracle, but something that all anglers can accept when fishing for shoaling fish: present-day nature programmes show the tightly-packed nature of such shoals and the rapidity with which they can move on, leading to a huge-catch or no-catch situation, that Alex had experienced himself many times.

In the same way, the feeding of the five thousand - probably greatly exaggerated with the passage of time - with seven loaves could be explained by the supplementing of the seven loaves by the food that some of the multitude had brought with them. It is not reasonable, nor is it of value, to question the exactness of the biblical or verbal teachings of all religions, but it is worthwhile to try to understand the basic message that is being passed on: it is the basic message that is important, not the way in which it is dressed up.

Alex was beginning to explore his long-term views on life. He looked down at the missing tip of the little finger of his left hand. If he had truly believed that there was nothing more after death, then why had he cut off his finger tip so that it could lie in the ground ever-after with Clyde's body? Was he not just the same as every other person in the hope that there will be eventual reunion with departed loved ones? Alex didn't know the answer, but he was no longer quite as sure as he had been in the past that mankind, or even the rest of the animal kingdom, was just a brief and unimportant flicker in the long history of life on the planet.

However, whatever his thoughts, even though mankind might now hold the centre-stage, he considered it inevitable that one day it will have to yield to some, perhaps as yet unknown, species or even to the carriers of a fatal disease, that will bring it to its end, just as the period of the dinosaurs came to an end after they had roamed the earth for millions of years.

Alex sometimes wondered if he actually existed, or if life is just some form of dreaming, his thoughts turning to the quotation of *Chuang Zi* (369-286 BC):

I do not know whether I was then a man dreaming I was a butterfly, or whether I am now a butterfly dreaming I am now a man

How sure can anyone be of their own existence? Are not one's dreams, at the time, just as real as one's living experiences? Could it not just be that living itself is no more than a dream? There is no help on this matter afforded by well-known statements such as "I think therefore I am", as in our dreams we are able to make decisions - i.e. to think - relevant to the dreaming situation, such as to run away from danger; and "Pinch me, I think I am dreaming", often advanced for confirming to a person that they are indeed wide-awake in the real world, as in our dreams we can experience minor assaults on our body without being awakened from the dream. Alex decided that he should not bother his mind unduly with such imponderables, but find what others, older and wiser [31], have to say on such matters, in the meantime just getting on with his life to the best of his ability.

He decided that he would ask *Qiangwei* where he could attend some classes in instruction in the Buddhist faith. Although Buddhism is not a religion, nor did Buddha want to be thought of as a god, Buddhism promotes a life-style of peace and consideration for both mankind and the animal world, that appealed to him After his earlier years of living a life of cruelty and brutality, he was now becoming truly concerned to lead a better life-style, although his recent treatment of Caroline was something that he should have been ashamed of.

The following Sunday Alex, *Qiangwei* and George took a taxi from Singapore over the causeway to visit the sea-side town of Kukup. Leaving Johore Bahru, they drove a short distance along the side of the straits, and then turned right up to the Istana, the palace of the Sultan of Johore, a large magnificent white-coloured edifice set in its own grounds. A strong boundary wall of highly-ornamented cast-iron railings enclosed the whole of the grounds, but allowed the passer-by to look at the immaculately maintained gardens within. There was a wide gateway with the gates drawn back, opening to a long sweeping drive, with armed, smartly-dressed guards standing at each side of the gateway to check the business of all who wanted to enter. Alex and his friends marvelled at the opulence of the palace and its grounds.

Coming down from the palace, they passed a Muslim cemetery, where Alex noticed how closely the graves were set from each other. George told him that it was the custom of those of the Muslim faith in Malaya to bury their dead in an upright position, as opposed to the Christian tradition of burying their deceased in a horizontal position: different country, different customs.

As they carried on they passed by the Zoo, then rejoined the main road, and continued westwards, leaving JB behind. After about fifteen miles they came to a major junction, where they turned left on the road that led eventually to Ipoh. They travelled through numerous little towns, such as "Pekinanas", which suggested to Alex "picking bananas", which would not have been entirely inappropriate, as bananas could be seen growing all the way along the sides of the road, together with sugar cane and small areas given over to the growing of coffee beans.

After a little while they stopped at a roadside fruit stall, where, after due ceremony, they chose two durian, eating them at a small table set out nearby. Then they bought some rambutan, small fruit with a prickly shell, of about the same size as lychee, but of a somewhat less-sweet taste. Following this they headed on, until they came to a tee-junction at the village of Pontian, the road to the right heading further along the south-west coast, whilst the road to the left led to the sea-shore village on Kukup. George had heard of the rest-house in Pontian, so after making a couple of inquiries as to its location, they duly arrived there.

The rest-house sits at the edge of the sea, a short distance outside of the village, and had been built originally, along with a string of other rest-houses scattered throughout Malaya, to provide a recreational meeting place for the mainly-British rubber planters. As they entered the rest-house seeking afternoon tea, they admired the decaying elegance of the place. There were still hooks in the ceiling from which cooling fans would originally have hung, manned by native Malayan labour. Since the departure of the British, the rest house had expanded into other areas in which it could serve the public, but naturally, in keeping with Muslin beliefs, there was no sign of alcoholic beverages. Two thrones were set at one end of the large lounge, for use at the wedding ceremonies of the local Malayan population.

It was a delightful place, living on beyond its heyday, but still able to give travellers a nice calm place in which to break their journey. They ordered tea and sandwiches and relaxed in the peace and tranquillity of the environment. A Mullah of the nearby mosque called the faithful to prayer, the emotion of his calls adding to their enjoyment. It was truly a place of rest.

They had asked the taxi driver to wait for them whilst they were inside, so when it was time to go they located him in the kitchen at the rear, and then set off for Kukup. On the way they passed a group of children making their way to a nearby mosque or school, all immaculately turned out. The young girls looked pristine: it was a credit to their parents that they could send them off from their primitive kampongs looking so clean and fresh.

Alex had formed the opinion that there are three ages of Malay womenfolk. First there are the naïve slips of young girls, modest and shy, and delightful to see; then there are the young women, mysterious and beautiful in their native dress, a loose wrap-around gown, the "sarong", and a head-scarf, the "tudong", and with alluring eyes, although modesty and custom often restrict their response to the pointing of fingers, whilst avoiding eye-contact, should one ask directions of them at the roadside; then there were the now thick-set mothers, who could usually be seen on a visit to the local markets or shops, accompanied by their daughters or daughters-in-law and their grandchildren. The Malay mother seemed to Alex to be like the Jewish mother, who loves her family and wants them to be always by her side and always be near to her to take her advice. Great matriarchs!

Alex reflected on recent visits to the East Coast, where he, George, *Ying Hong* and *Chonghai* would buy chicken rice or Laksa, along with their usual bottles of Carlsberg, and then sit on the sand under the shade of a palm tree, looking at the boats out at sea. Alex would watch the Malayan families arriving. First they would lay out a large cover, such as a lorry cover, on the sand, and then the mother and her daughters and daughters-in-law would unpack the makings of a substantial meal, whilst the grandchildren played in the sea. Any nearby children without friends of their own would soon be drawn into the playing, and when the time came to eat, welcomed to come and share the food.

The Malays are a lovely-natured race, with a relaxed attitude to life. Indeed, on one occasion when Alex had taken a ride in the taxi of a Malayan driver in Singapore, the driver had said to him that this was his last trip of the day, as he had earned enough money to provide the food for his wife and family on the following day, then going on to say 'These Chinese taxi drivers don't know when to stop and go home. Even when they have all the money they need for the next day, they carry on to earn money for the next week and the next month!'

After about half an hour they reached Kukup, where the taxi driver dropped them off at the sea-food restaurant at the end of the road, close by the jetty. They sat down at a table overlooking the sea, and ordered chilli crab, steamed prawns, sotong, chilli *kang kong* and fish poached along with *suan1 mei2*, "sour plums", together with fresh lime juice. The atmosphere was delightful. About half-a-mile away across the sea were several small islands, all with floating fish farms in the water in front of them. Small boats made their way to and from the islands and also between the islands and Kukup, many carrying visitors to the islands, out for a trip over the water.

When Alex asked the Chinese waiter where the *ce4suo3*, the "toilet", is, he was directed to the back of the restaurant where he found a small cubicle with a small hole at its centre, looking straight down into the sea some ten feet below. He trusted that the local boatmen knew to steer well clear of this spot!

Kukup is split into two almost equal parts by the main, and only, road running up its centre and ending at the jetty. On each side of the road are hawker stalls selling a range of goods: fruit, fish, and counterfeit watches and clothing. Most of the Westerners visiting these stalls had no idea as to how to bargain, criticising the goods or berating the seller for asking an exorbitant price, in the hope of securing a discount. The proper procedure is to examine the goods and comment on their excellent quality, but then to express concern as to how much they could afford to pay. The trader would already have marked up his price, in anticipation of being beaten down. After a suitable period of indecision, the potential buyer should then look the seller in the eye and ask in a sincere voice 'Now what is your best price?'

Upon the conclusion of the transaction, both parties would be satisfied, the customer leaving with a smiling face and the seller expressing the hope that they will return again soon. This is so much nicer and more civilised than the not-infrequent tourist behaviour of throwing the goods on offer down onto the counter with a nasty expression on their face, decrying their quality or their price, or both. If there is one thing that the street traders enjoy it is a pleasant bargaining session, followed by a transaction that is satisfactory to both parties.

The three of them then turned to explore that part of the village lying to the right of the road when looking towards the jetty. Immediately they were walking on walkways composed of narrow planks, of a total width of about five feet, sitting on top of piles that at first were no more than about eight or ten feet in height, but as they progressed away from the land became up to about fifteen to twenty feet in height. The piles were made from tree-trunks of about five or six inches diameter.

When the tide is in, the ground under the walkways is covered with water and everything looks clean and tidy, but the when the tide recedes, the refuse that has been thrown down from the walkways is revealed. Mud skippers and snakes can then be seen wriggling about in the mud, amongst discarded domestic items and old bits of netting. Nevertheless, Alex and his friends found the village ethnic and beautiful.

Along each side of the walkways are little timber houses built, like the walkways, on the top of timber piles. The houses are of simple and light construction, with windows open to the sea breezes that keep them cool in the heat of the sun. Further along, the walkway that they were on branched. They took a turn to the left, and soon found themselves opposite to a Chinese school. As they approached the school, the teacher, seeing Alex, and always anxious to expose her students to the experience of meeting Westerners, welcomed them in.

Alex greeted the teacher in Mandarin and then walked across to the blackboard where several Chinese characters were displayed. He took on the role of the teacher, with her smiling approval, in questioning the students as to the English equivalent of the Chinese characters. Soon the class was dissolved in laughter, in which Alex, George and *Qiangwei* were involved. They bid their farewell and carried on with their tour of this part of the village.

Later, after retracing their steps, they rejoined the main street, and then turned off along the walkways on the left of the main road. Despite the walkways being very narrow, there were many children riding bicycles along them, but ringing their bells in warning as they approached any pedestrians. As they made their way further into the complex of side walkways, they passed little shops, eating houses and simple open-fronted bars. At one point the walkway that they were making their way long opened up into a square, at one end of which was a stage, doubtless for performances of Chinese opera. It was a lively happy community, relatively self-contained, provided that one did not have a taste for the luxuries of the big towns.

Eventually they arrived at the sea front where fishermen were attending to their nets, or laying out huge numbers of shrimps on large pieces of canvas to dry in the sun. There were also octopus, and fillets of a range of varieties of fish, drying in the sun. They walked along to the extreme end of the village, where modern houses had been built over the water, but instead of having timber piles to support them, the piles were made of concrete. These new houses, instead of being made of timber, were made of cast concrete, with their outsides clad in small tiles of brilliant colours. Whilst they might have looked too garish elsewhere, in their exotic setting with the bright blue sea behind them, they looked perfect.

The future of this beautiful and unspoilt little town looked to be secure, although whether the village would eventually turn into a holiday retreat for the more prosperous of Johor Bahru and other places with easy access, such as Singapore, which is just a short boat journey away, would be something that might need to be contended with.

It had been a great day, and Alex suggested that some time soon they could head up north for a visit to Mersing, but George told him that this was not advisable, in view of the few communist guerrillas who still remained in the area, despite the presence of manned checkpoints here and there along the main roads. Soldiers carrying sub-machine guns would be stationed about a hundred yards beyond the checkpoints to ensure that no-one would decide to take off up the road at high speed.

As they reached the *Yangs*' house that evening, George went inside, wishing them good night. It was a warm still evening, so Alex suggested to *Qiangwei* that they take a short walk along to a nearby stretch of parkland. As they reach the parkland and Alex saw that it was deserted, he reached for *Qiangwei*'s hand, desperate to touch her. She smiled at him, relieved than the apparent rift in their friendship had been overcome, and he felt encouraged by her smile. He was tormented every time that he looked at her.

He gently turned her round to face him, and then kissed her on the forehead. She flinched a little, and tried to pull her hand away. Misinterpreting her reaction as being due to surprise rather than anger, he then put his hands around her waist and drew her close, kissing her hard on the lips and at the same time holding her body tightly against his, so that she could feel his state of arousal: a dreadful mistake! For two or three minutes he continued to hold her against him, hoping that she might calm down and accept his advances, but to no avail.

As he released her, *Qiangwei* reacted wildly, slapping his face and pushing him away from her. She told him that he was an "insensitive western barbarian", and said that she didn't ever want to see him again. He tried to tell her that this wasn't so, but he couldn't put into words what he wanted to say. He had only acted as many other men would have done in trying to show her the depth of his feelings for her. He hadn't ever felt like this before. It wasn't just sex: this was different. He loved her and wanted to spend the rest of his life caring for her. The women that he had met in the past had not been so important to him.

Alex was distressed and confused and didn't know what to do. Still *Qiangwei* railed at him, and reminded him once again of her intention to become a Buddhist nun. He felt his anger rising. Who did she think she was, this obstinate, inflexible woman? Wasn't he good enough for her? He had had enough of her strange ways and his anger spilt over 'What's wrong, scared I'm going to rape you? What pleasure would there be in that? I would rather find myself a good prostitute. At least she wouldn't think that I am some kind of sexual monster, you frigid pious sexless coward!'

As soon as the words were spoken, Alex regretted them. They walked back to her house in silence, and then separated at the gate, Alex saying in a subdued voice 'Goodnight', but with *Qiangwei* not uttering a word: she too was confused. Up to only a few moments ago Alex had shown only kindness and consideration towards her. He had a strong appreciation of Chinese culture and a love of Chinese people, so why had he now acted in the boorish, unsympathetic and barbaric manner that is found with many expatriates?

She had make clear from the start that the relationship between them could only be one of friendship, but he had refused to understand her position and her future intentions, nor did he appear to want to do so, arrogantly expecting her to fall in with his own wishes. His remarks had made her feel cheap and shallow, and she felt loss-of-face that she should have been treated in this way.

He had committed a grave mistake. Of all the characteristics of the Chinese, the inability to forgive a transgressor for loss-of-face is the most outstanding. None of the "Sorry love, are we still friends?" of the people back home after the speaking of harsh or cruel words during a quarrel, but the sad, stony, irreversible ending of a relationship: there is no chance of the acceptance of an apology for cruel words or actions, albeit that they may have been spoken or committed in the heat of the moment. Whether or not *Qiangwei* may have eventually come around to his way of thinking, it was now too late: she was lost to him for ever, and the fault was his.

When she came into the house, George could see that she was upset and asked her what was wrong. She told him what had happened, and how she had been shocked by Alex's behaviour. George, having had some experience of expatriates, could see the situation from Alex's point of view, and knew that perhaps Alex felt that *Qiangwei* had unintentionally 'led him on' to some degree. However, *Qiangwei* was his sister and it was his family responsibility to stand by her. She needed support rather than for her distress to be made light of.

He told her that he understood her position, and that he was completely in support of her intention to become a nun one day, and that he appreciated the price that she would have to pay for this, no matter how much sadness this might cause her. She eventually regained her composure, and went to her room. Before she went to her bed, she knelt and chanted a forgiveness mantra. She prayed for guidance, and for forgiveness for possibly having given Alex the impression that their friendship could lead to more. That night she had little sleep, but when she awakened in the morning her mind was made up: it would be best if she didn't ever communicate with Alex again, despite any pleas for forgiveness that he might make to her.

Chapter Nineteen

Alex was shocked and dismayed by *Qiangwei*'s rejection of him. He was indeed a barbarian by her standards of behaviour, but he had only acted in the way of most westerners. None of the women that he had known before had rejected him for his forwardness, and more likely would have sent him on his way before too long, as being dull and boring, if he hadn't have made some kind of approach towards them very soon in their acquaintance. Arriving at the offices on Monday morning, Alex went over to George to speak to him about the matter, but before he had had chance to say more than a few words, George cut him short: 'Don't waste my time with your expatriate drivel Alex.' Alex smarted that George had now reverted to his western name, and also at his snub in referring to him as an expatriate, whereas of late he had been referring to him, in humour and friendship, as a "newborn Chinese."

George felt guilty in speaking to Alex in this way, but he had to be fully supportive of his sister, and it was better that there should be a clean break between him and his sister and Alex. He hardened himself for what he was about to say: 'My sister and I no longer want to keep your company. I suggest that you go along to one of the clubs of your fellow expatriates, where your cavalier manner will probably achieve greater success.' George went on to say that he was dismayed that, despite the friendship between them, he had behaved towards his sister in just the same way that all of the other expatriates that he had known had behaved towards the local Chinese girls: no consideration of Chinese tradition, and no regard for their respectability and morality. He advised Alex that there were young Chinese girls of dubious morality in the bars and clubs of the city centre who would, for a price, put up with this kind of behaviour, but these were the exception. Let Alex go and seek this sort of woman in the future.

The word got around the company offices of a problem in the friendship between Alex and George and his sister. Madam *Zhang*, who was approaching middle age, and had seen the relationships of many Singaporean women with western men end in sadness, said that it was "probably for the best", whilst the younger clerical staff, who were romantically inclined, and more than one of whom had cast a glance at Alex when he was pre-occupied and would not notice, felt that it was tragically sad. They were silent and embarrassed when he approached, and kept their eyes averted.

The major could see that Alex had something troubling him, and asked Madam *Zhang* if she knew what it was. At first she said that she had no idea, but the dismayed expression on her face betrayed her, and begrudgingly she told him what she had heard. He was delighted at the news, but kept his face straight as he exclaimed in a deeply concerned voice 'Oh dear me! How unfortunate! The poor man!', but inwardly he was thrilled. Wait until he tells his wife that evening!

For the next few days Alex telephoned *Qiangwei*, but each time the phone was answered by her mother, who advised him that she wasn't free to speak on the phone. On one evening he left work early and took a taxi to the end of *Qiangwei*'s road, waiting until he saw her enter the house before phoning, but to no avail. 'Miss *Qiangwei* is not at home.'

For a few weekends after that Alex went out with *Ying Hong* and *Chonghia*, but they found him morose and poor company, so when he asked then about the next weekend, they both, regrettably, had "other engagements". To some degree, they also both felt that he had somehow behaved dishonourably towards *Qiangwei*, and wanted to avoid becoming involved. He decided to go out on his own and headed along Orchard Road, calling in at bar after bar, until before long he was very drunk. Then he noticed in a side street a sign over a door advertising an upstairs club with "adult" entertainment. Although it was supposed to be a members-only club, a few notes slipped to the doorman gained him admission.

The club was dimly lit, except for the stage, where two spotlights illuminated the performers, a naked couple, dancing to music played over amplifiers. The man had a huge erection, which the woman stroked repeatedly as they danced. After a little while they slid to the floor of the stage and commenced copulation. Under normal circumstances Alex would have found this amusing and mildly embarrassing, but in his condition it aroused his sexual urges.

A woman standing nearby had seen his reaction to the dancing and moved over closer to him. She was a Chinese woman who appeared to Alex to be of about his own age, and she was quite attractive, but in a hard cold way. In reality she was about fifty years of age, but in his inebriated condition and in the dim light of the room, he didn't notice this.

She was wearing a low-cut dress that was bit over-the-top, but to Alex, it seemed fine. She had had her eyebrows plucked out and replaced by tattooed ones, and she had also had a fold created in her upper eyelids by minor plastic surgery to resemble that in the eyelids of western women: she was a classic case of mutton dressed up as lamb!

After the performance had finished she caught Alex's eye and smiled at him encouragingly. He responded by stepping up to her and saying 'I would like to ask you to dance, but, much as I would wish, I am incapable of that kind of horizontal dancing at the moment.'

She laughed at this, and then accepted his offer to buy her a drink. They sat down at a table at the back of the room and started to chat, Alex learning that her name was Lily, and that she normally worked as a club receptionist, but was presently unemployed. After a few more drinks Alex asked her if she wanted to come back to his place "for a night-cap", an invitation that she had been expecting. She agreed, but suggested that Alex buy a last drink: "one for the road". After the drinks had arrived, Alex asked to be excused to "attend to a call of nature", during which Lily took the opportunity to take a small tablet from her bag and slip it into his drink.

They took a taxi back to his apartment where, with Lily's support, Alex made his way into the lift and then up to his front door. Lily took the key from him, opened the door, then helped him inside. After this she helped him into the bedroom, where he started to take off her clothes, but then he collapsed onto the bed and fell into a drunken stupor, awakening the next morning to find her gone, along with the notes from his wallet. He estimated the amount of the money that was missing: quite a sizable sum.

Lily was clearly a professional, and he had paid dearly for the experience. However, not as dearly as had others in this situation: from time-to-time the "Straits Times" reported cases of young foreigners found dead in their accommodation from drug overdose, following a night-out of heavy drinking.

Life became quite flat for Alex after the loss of his friends. The only relief from his own company that Alex received was when *Siew Tung* asked him if he wanted to come out fishing with a group of his Cantonese friends. Alex gladly accepted the invitation, and went along to Shore Road to buy himself a stiff boat rod, a multiplier reel and the miscellaneous other items that he would need. As he selected his fishing equipment in the tackle shop, a nosy fellow customer came over to see what he was doing, eventually, in a condescending manner, asking him what experience he had of fishing in the South China Sea. Alex told him that he was new to the area, but that he had fished a lot back in Scotland, mentioning, for want of something better to say, that fishing in Singapore waters would be a lot warmer than fishing in Scotland.

The man then said 'I could cope with the cold weather of Scotland with no trouble', which led Alex to inquire how this was so. The man went on to say 'I put my hand inside the fridge and left it there for five minutes. I didn't find it the least bit cold.' Alex was staggered at such stupidity. He explained to the man that cold still air, such as within the fridge, is not the least bit unpleasant, and when it is accompanied by a flat calm sea, a bright blue sky and snow on the mountain tops, there is nothing more pleasant. He told him that the worst weather is when it is wet, cold and windy. He didn't mention the time that he had been persuaded, against his better judgement, by the pleading of the fishing captain to take his party, on a freezing-cold winter's day, out beyond the Cloch Lighthouse and down into the open Firth, in face of a strong, force 4, south-westerly wind, which after a couple of hours had turned into an un-forecasted gale.

First, little spiralling whirlwinds had started to move up the Firth, drawing water from off the tops of the waves as they moved. Then the waves began to get bigger, soon reaching nine or ten feet in height, and the increasing wind had started to blow the tops from off them, creating a fifteen-foot depth of freezing-cold white spume, "spindrift", that shot horizontally over the surface at a speed of about sixty miles per hour and restricted visibility to less than a dozen yards. The force of the wind on the boat had snapped the weak link, but before Alex had had chance to haul in the anchor, it had dragged and then snagged on the bottom.

Unaided, as the fishing party, Fishing Captain included, had retreated into the saloon, where they would remain until the boat was tied up safely at the quayside, Alex had had to first motor the boat forwards to gain slack in the anchor rope, then rush out onto the fore-deck and draw in the slack before the wind could drive the boat back. After having done this three times, with fingers that had lost all feeling with the cold, he had gained enough anchor rope for the rope to be almost vertical, which would provide him with the greatest mechanical advantage when giving the engine full throttle to try to drag the anchor out of the snag on the sea bed.

After thirty minutes of motoring ahead, to port, to starboard, and in reverse, by which time he was on the point of cutting the anchor rope, he had managed to pull the anchor clear, after which he had to 'weigh the anchor' - draw it up - from the sea bed, unaided, before they returned to Gourock. By the time that they had got back, blood had started to flow again in his white freezing-cold fingers, and he had suffered acute agony.

The bumptious know-all standing in front of him knew nothing about being cold! Alex bade him a polite, but cold, good-day and left the shop with his purchases. He had seen on numerous previous occasions that some people are unaware of the depth of their own stupidity, and are prepared to give opinions on subjects of which they are totally ignorant and inexperienced. There was no point in trying to tell them anything. He was reminded of an opinionated man in the Puffer back in Gourock who, although never having flown in an aeroplane himself, had stated emphatically that 'There is no such thing as jet lag.', arguing that 'All you have to do is have a few drinks when you get on the plane and then get your head down for a few hours sleep', as though lack of sleep was the only problem. He knew nothing about the effects of changing the sleeping patterns of a lifetime and forcing the body's internal time-clock to make a violent step-change. This was yet another example of not being able to appreciate something that one has not experienced oneself.

The fishing party, comprising Alex, *Siew Tung* and ten of *Siew Tung*'s Cantonese friends, met at Punggol Jetty, and went aboard their chartered boat, which was rather decrepit and manned by an old Malayan man. On the way to Punggol, *Siew Tung* had stopped at a wet market, returning with a fresh chicken, along with the other items necessary to make a chicken stew whilst onboard. They intended to proceed only about three miles out to sea on their overnight trip, as they were aware of the repeated instances of fishing parties being robbed by groups of men setting off from the Malayan coast armed with machetes and sometimes guns. The Singapore authorities advised that fishing parties should stay within Singapore waters, rather than to proceed further north into Malayan waters and out into the lower end of the South China Sea.

As they motored along, even though their speed was some five knots, more than six miles per hour, Alex slipped over the side a six-inch long lure. He eased off the clutch on his reel, but left the ratchet on, so that should a fish take his lure, the sudden drag wouldn't break the line, but simply strip line from the reel, and the clicking of the ratchet would alert him as to the situation. After about ten minutes the ratchet began to make a fierce noise as a fish took the lure and then sped away. The skipper stopped the boat, and Alex began to play the fish, first drawing it towards the boat, but when it resisted, allowing it to take line. After a few minutes, the fish began to tire and was able to be brought alongside, whereupon one of the fishing party used the gaff to bring it aboard. The fish was what the locals called a mackerel, but it was nothing like the mackerel that Alex had caught on the Clyde, being some three feet long and weighing about ten pounds. He was elated!

When they got to the mark, an underwater reef, they baited up with some *sotong*, "squid", that the boatman had provided and settled down to fish. Within minutes they had hooked and landed several small brightly coloured and exotic fish, the likes of which Alex had only seen before in the van Cleef aquarium in Singapore City. Alex was reluctant to retain such fish, but the rest of the group had no hesitation and put them into their bags without delay, anxious to get on with catching the next one. Such fish, if caught in sufficient numbers, will fill their cooking pots when they get home, regardless of their colour and small size.

Eventually it was time to make a meal, so they approached the skipper to ask him to cook their stew for them, but to their surprised he refused, on the grounds that he could not be sure that the chicken that they had bought whilst in Singapore had been killed in accordance with Halal requirements, which is part of his religious beliefs: the killing of all livestock must be done in the traditional manner under the supervision of a religious leader.

Siew Tung tried to assure the skipper that the chicken had indeed been killed with proper regard for Halal requirements, but the man was adamant: he did not know the wet market from which the chicken had been bought and so could not be sure that these requiremens had been observed in its slaughter. No, emphatically no: he would not cook the chicken! They then suggested that they buy his pans from him and cook the chicken themselves, but again he refused, not permitting his pans, plates or utensils to be used in the preparation or eating of possibly non-Halal flesh. Siew Tung pleaded with the skipper: 'What are we going to eat today and tomorrow?' The skipper pointed to the bucket of *sotong* sitting on the deck: *sotong*, unlike chicken, do not contain any red blood, and thus are not subject to stringent Muslim requirements. In the event, the *sotong* stew was delicious.

As they fished, the rest of the fishing party laughed and joked, the only words that Alex was able to guess the meaning of being when the fishing became slack at one particular mark: *mo yu*, "no fish". They passed around their cigarettes in a gesture of friendliness. They were a wholesome group of lads. It was a big event for them to get away on a fishing trip and they were out to make the most of it. They were telling jokes to each other and generally were having a great time. *Siew Tung* came up to Alex and said '*Ai-li*, you should give up this Mandarin and learn *guangdonghua*, "Cantonese". These men tell the dirtiest jokes I have ever heard!'

Alex indeed wished that he could have joined in with the general hilarity. The group of Cantonese speakers had obviously come together on the trip to be able to speak their own dialect to each other, as opposed to having to speak English during most of every working day, or to listen to others speaking Mandarin. They were grand men, stocky and strongly built from their ancestors having worked the land for their livelihood for many generations.

With the fading of daylight, the skipper moved the boat to deeper water, where he put down an anchor. The party fitted bigger hooks, baited them with larger pieces of *sotong*, and then sat down to wait, leaving their reels out of gear, but with the ratchet engaged. Sitting on the deck, leaning against the gun'les, Alex had dozed off, but suddenly he was startled into consciousness by the roaring of the ratchet as a large fish took his bait and ran. He engaged the gear, and then put some tension on the line, feeling the resistance of the fish to capture.

Then followed a period of allowing the fish to take line and then recovering it whenever he could. He slowly brought the fish to the surface, where *Siew Tung* used the gaff to bring it on board. It was a beautiful slender fish, some four feet long and weighing fourteen pounds, known as a *ling*, although it did not resemble the *ling* that Alex's fishing parties had caught from time to time on the Firth of Clyde, which has a body like that of a conger eel but a with a barbule underneath its chin, and a taste when, cooked, like that of cod. He re-baited the hook, paid out the line, and then went back to sleep again.

Some time during the night Alex heard the sound of activity, but it wasn't loud enough to bring him fully awake. When he awakened the next morning, however, he found a ten-foot long tiger shark, *shalyul*, meaning, literally and appropriately, "kill fish", lying on the deck that had been caught by one of the other fishermen, and brought aboard by sliding a noose over its tail and then three of the anglers hauling for all that they were worth. Alex was surprised that he had slept through all of this action, but the excitement and the strenuous fishing of the previous day, and also the effect of the sun, together with its reflection from the water, had been tiring.

During the night the skipper had fixed a hurricane lamp over the side of the boat and caught many more *sotong* that were attracted by the light, not only to make up their bait, but also to provide another stew for breakfast, which he was now passing around in bowls. The day continued much the same as the previous day. Alex wasn't too unhappy when the time came to go home, as he was feeling the effects of the sun. Although shielded from the direct rays of the sun by his straw hat, there were still the effects of the reflection from the water to contend with. That evening, after he had cut up his catch and packed it into his fridge, he looked at himself in the mirror, and was amused to see a bright red face staring back at him. It had been a great trip: good weather, good food, and good company, albeit that, regrettably, he had not been able to understand the dirty jokes.

Alex was pleased when *Siew Tong* invited him along on a second fishing trip, this time embarking at the tiny port of Kg Sedili Besar in

Malaysia, which after crossing the causeway into JB involved a journey of about two hours by car, passing on the way through the fairly large market town of Kota Tinggi, noted for the nearby waterfalls that attract many visitors, and then through the tiny hamlet of Mawai. The fishing was even better on this trip, and the party caught a lot of good-size fish, not spectacular fish such as the tiger shark that they had caught on their previous fishing trip, and which Alex had found not very tasty, having taken home a stake of this shark along with everyone else, but fish that were highly appreciated for the pot, or for steaming individually along with a few *suan1mei2*, "sour plums". As they caught the fish, they gutted and stored them in insulated boxes, packing them in crushed ice that they had asked the skipper to buy for them at the fish market in Kota Tinggi.

On their way back home, they called into a small eating house in Kota Tinggi, where *Siew Tong* asked the proprietor to cook some of the fish for them, whilst Alex drank several glasses of beer and the rest of the party drank fruit juice, to replenish the fluid that they had lost in perspiration out on the boat. As they drank, Alex read the menus set up around the walls, written in Chinese. He was startled to see the character *shu3*, "rat". With some unease, he queried it with *Siew Tong*, who laughed before telling him to read the character immediately before "rat". Alex did so, and recognised the character as *song1*, which Alex knew meant "pine", as in *song1 shu4*, "pine tree".

After saying a few words in Cantonese to the rest of the party, who grinned at Alex's discomfort, *Siew Tong* explained that *song1shu3*, "pine tree rat", was the Chinese name for squirrel! The "rat" that Alex feared might be on offer was *lao3shu3*, "old rat", explaining further that another rodent with a name involving the character *shu3* was *xiao3 shu3*, "little rat", meaning mouse! Alex was somewhat reassured by *Siew Tong*'s words, but felt that the similarity, not only in their name but also in the general appearance, even before being prepared and cooked, between a squirrel and a rat was too close for him ever to have the confidence to choose 'squirrel' from a menu, at least until he had had a great many more beers.

Without friends to go out with in the evenings, and as he had not taken up the membership of expatriate and other clubs that had been offered to him, he was at a loss as to what to do. He came across some *mi3jiu3,* Chinese rice wine, in a supermarket and bought a few bottles to take home with him. Sampling the first that evening, he found it to be somewhat dry, but also fierce. Whilst wine fermented from grapes is normally twelve or thirteen percent alcohol, except for champagne, which can be fermented to about seventeen percent alcohol, the label on the bottle of rice wine said that its strength was thirty-five percent alcohol, so Alex deduced that if this were true, the wine must have been fortified.

The next morning, when he awoke two hours after he should have been at work, with a terrible hangover after having drunk two bottles of the wine, he realised that this was indeed true. The major was in the reception area when he eventually arrived at work, where he had been waiting for him: he wasn't going to miss any opportunity to find fault with Alex. 'Good morning, MacAlister,' he said, 'or should I say good afternoon.' Because Alex was late in getting out of bed, he hadn't taken time to shave or to pay the usual amount of attention to his appearance. The major seized on this, asking 'Have you not shaven today Mr. MacAlister? As I have told you before, appearance is important in this line of business.'

Alex was in no fit state to respond, as he would normally have done, so he just made an apology. This drunken pattern was repeated several times during the following weeks, but the colonel didn't feel that he yet had enough evidence to seek Alex's removal from the Singapore offices. Nevertheless, it was a start. He had his secretary record each incident in her desk diary. 'One day soon!' he would say to himself, 'One day soon!'

Alex's appearance and behaviour in the office started to affect his relationship with the rest of the staff. The young typists would drop their eyes to their work whenever he passed by, whereas previously they would have given him a friendly smile or said a cheerful word. After he had gone out of earshot, one of them would say, with nods of agreement from the others, "*fei1 e2 tou2 huo3*", "a moth darting towards a fire", meaning that Alex was seeking his own destruction.

George continued to ignore him until one day Alex's anger got the better of him and he blurted out 'What's up George? I wasn't good enough for your sister, aren't I good enough to speak to you now?' George looked him in the eye and replied '*cao3 mu4 jie1 bing1*', "grass trees all soldiers",[19:1] meaning "don't get paranoid". 'Your problem is

---

[19:1] This expression comes from a battle in China in AD 383, when *Fu Jian*, the leader of what used to be called *Qin*, led an 800 thousand strong army to attack *Dong Jin*, where the defending army's leaders, *Sha Shu* and *Sha Shuan*, had a force only 80 thousand strong. The second day, after losing the first round of fighting, *Fu Jian* went up close to the city walls to spy on the *Dong Jin* camp and was terrified when he saw the enemy camp in good order and the soldiers in high spirits. *Fu Jian* was even more alarmed when he glanced at the nearby mountains, for he mistook the swaying of the trees and tall grasses in the wind as the banners of rescue forces for the besieged defenders. Trembling with fear he told his generals that the mountain was full of soldiers. When the nervous Fu Jian led his troops into battle, it suffered a crushing

of your own making, not somebody else's. Give up this heavy drinking before it is too late.'

Alex was scheduled to call at the home of an expatriate couple who were due to return to Britain, and required a quote for the repatriation of their possessions for the husband to present to his company. The meeting was timed for two o'clock. Alex left his office at twelve-thirty and went for lunch in a nearby coffee house. Feeling rough from having drunk too much the previous evening, he decided to take "a hair of the dog" and ordered a large bottle of Carlsberg. This went down well, and helped to ease his hangover and the sense of guilt that went with it, so he ordered another bottle. On his way to the house, he stopped and bought himself a half bottle of whisky, the bottle fitting into his jacket pocket without too pronounced a bulge. He stopped a passing taxi and gave the driver the address of the client, which was a twenty-minute ride away towards the north of the city.

Although aware that he shouldn't drink whilst on company business, and already being under the influence, but attempting to justify his action by dwelling on his 'bad luck' in his relationship with *Qiangwei*, he took a swig from the bottle. After another five minutes he was beginning to feel even more sorry for himself, and took another swig. After a third swig, with the bottle now almost empty, the taxi reached the home of the clients. As he got out of the taxi he slipped and the bottle fell from his hand and smashed on the ground, but he was too drunk to notice. He fumbled in his wallet for some notes to pay the driver with, and then made his way to the front door. Before he had reached the door, it was opened by a young woman who had obviously been awaiting his arrival. 'Do come in.' she said, 'I have been waiting for you.'

Alex, making a great effort to walk straight, entered the house, whereupon the young woman led him into the living room. She asked him to sit down whilst she called her husband from his study. Within a few seconds a smartly dressed young man appeared and, with a smile on his face, introduced himself to Alex. 'Nice to meet you.' he said. Alex tried to put his mind to the business in hand, and asked if he could look at the various items of furniture, and the personal items of the couple, that were to be sent back to Britain. Standing up he swayed, but managed to regain his balance. The young couple looked concerned, but Alex reassured them by saying 'A damaged cartilage. An old rugby injury.'

---

defeat. Fu Jian was wounded and fled in haste. The moral is don't be paranoid, don't jump to a mistaken conclusion: try to see a situation as it really is.

The couple led Alex to the various rooms and pointed out the items that were to be transported. As they moved from room to room, Alex swayed on his feet, the couple noticing this but not knowing what to do. Entering the dining room, he fell against the carver chair at the head of the dining table and slipped to the floor. They then realised that he was drunk, and sat him down. Alex knew that he was incapable of carrying out the task in hand, and declared that he was feeling unwell and asked the couple to telephone for a taxi to take him home.

No sooner had Alex gone than the couple rang the company offices and asked to speak to the company manager. The major listened to what they had to say with delight, but expressed remarks of anguish as to what they had had to suffer at the hands of one of the employees of his company and, regardless of their insistence that this wasn't necessary, told them that he would come round to their apartment immediately to discuss the matter further.

The major was met at the door by the young couple, who took him into the lounge, sat him down, and then immediately embarked upon an account of Alex's behaviour. The major expressed great shock and great concern as he listened, punctuating their flow of words with 'Oh, how terrible!' and 'Did he indeed!', finally saying, as they came to the end of their account 'Well my dears, you can take it from me that I will treat this matter as of the gravest severity and of the utmost urgency. It would help your case if you were not to mention our meeting today, but write to me at the company offices detailing the experiences you have suffered at the hands of one of our company employees, and I will forward this to the head office in London, with my fullest support, to see what can be done.'

The couple could read into the major's words that there might be something in this for them, perhaps a discount on the cost of the shipping of their goods back to Britain that could be paid directly to themselves rather than to the husband's employer, or perhaps a couple of bottles of champagne delivered to the door, so they readily agreed.

Two days later Madam *Zhang* opened the letter of complaint from the young couple and placed it on the major's desk, awaiting his arrival. As soon as the major reached his office, he called in his secretary and asked her to take note of the receipt of the letter, before placing it in the "urgent" tray. He sat at his desk with a smile on his face, not of pleasure, but of malevolence, whilst his secretary was filled with dread as to what was to befall *Ai-li*.

She thought that perhaps she might warn him, but she didn't dare risk this. As she passed by the downstairs offices, she looked at him sitting at his desk: a sad man; a man who had taken to her own culture and in so doing had won the affection and respect of all in the company offices; but also a man who had lost the love in his life, *Qiangwei*, and was unable to cope.

The next morning the major called Alex into his office and told him about the letter of complaint. Alex, embarrassed, acknowledged that what the letter contained was correct, and waited for the major to continue. After a few minutes silence the major said 'I have managed to reassure the young couple that your actions were out of the ordinary and due to personal stress, and they have accepted this explanation. However, your behaviour must change.' Then he told an enormous lie: 'I think that I have been able to get you off-the-hook this time, but I won't cover up for you again, is that understood?'

Alex nodded, expressed his thanks, and then went back to his own office. The major then called in his secretary and said 'I want to dictate a confidential letter to the Chairman of the Board in London.' The secretary sat down, whilst the colonel paced to-and-fro in his office, seeking the best way to get rid of Alex whilst at the same time appearing to be acting in his best interests. Eventually he started to dictate:

"My dear Mr. Gleeson,

I am writing to you on a matter of some urgency concerning my Deputy Manager, Mr. Alexander MacAlister, whom you will remember joined us here with an excellent reference from the manager of the Newcastle depot. Mr. MacAlister has done sterling word for the company, winning the respect of clients and staff alike. However, I regret to advise that of late, Mr. MacAlister has been under some personal stress, which has taken its toll on him in that he has been finding solace in the over-consumption of alcoholic beverages. I have done my best to support him through this very difficult time, and believed that he was 'out of the woods': however, following his recent visit to the home of a client, I received the enclosed letter, which explains how he arrived to conduct an assessment of the client's needs in an inebriated condition. I have naturally visited the client and expressed the company's regret for this unpleasant incident, then sending another of my staff to attend to the client's needs. Nevertheless, my fears are that in Mr. MacAlister's present frame of mind anything might happen. It would be a dreadful loss, both to myself and to the company, if we were to lose Mr. MacAlister's services, but I am fearful as to what may happen if he were to remain in the Singapore office. Is there the possibility that he may be offered a post in one of the company's other overseas branch offices? I will naturally not discuss this matter with Mr. MacAlister but will await your reply and advice,

Your humble servant,

Major Horace Smedley (retd.)"

Madam *Zhang*, with regret, typed the letter, and then carried it through to the major for his signature. He checked the contents and nodded with satisfaction, added his signature and then handed the letter back to her, asking her to ensure that it went off in that day's post. This had been a good day for him. He would teach that uncouth Scots lout a lesson for having trifled with his daughter's affections!

Although she should not have done so, Madam *Zhang* could not resist telling *Fu Rong* of the major's letter to head office, knowing, as did everyone else in the office, of *Fu Rong*'s feelings for Alex. She could not help adding her personal opinions of the major's action, and of the devious way in which he was getting rid of Alex: *'kou3shi4-xin1fei1'*, "he says one thing and means another", to which *Fu Rong* responded with *'kou3mi4-fu4jian4'*, "honey-mouthed and dagger-tongued", meaning hypocritical and malignant. Madam *Zhang* nodded her agreement with *Fu Fong*'s words and then went back to her office.

Within the hour, all of the staff knew of Alex's misfortune, including George, who. despite being distressed at Alex's predicament, didn't see what he could do. He fumed at the shoddy way that Major Horace Smedley (retd) had managed to 'settle the score' in respect of the rift between Alex and his daughter Caroline: muttering angrily to himself *shu3bei4*: "mean creature!" That evening he told *Qiangwei* about the letter and how he was worried about what would become of Alex. She listened in silence, her emotions in conflict. She had spent hours, days and weeks in torment. On one hand she knew that Alex was a good man, with whom many women would be proud to be associated, yet on the other hand she knew him to have no respect for her wish to one day enter a Buddhist monastery. She questioned whether she was right to persevere with her intentions to become a nun, when she could instead accept a good life with Alex, sharing a loving home together and, in the course of time, a family.

The lady clerks in the downstairs office were upset to hear the news, but they were not surprised, as they had noted the recent changes in his behaviour. Nevertheless, they loved and respected him and would be sorry to see him go. *Ying Hong* and *Chonghai* were also dismayed, as Alex had accepted them both as good friends, indeed almost as brothers.

After three weeks the reply came from head office. Alex was to be offered the post of assistant manager at the Hong Kong branch, the level of post that he now held in Singapore, but with his salary to be increased substantially because of additional responsibility, that of being in sole charge of the import/export transportation service that the Hong Kong branch operated between Hong Kong and China.

The major called into his office with a beaming, but patently false, smile on his face. 'Sit down Alex.' he said, 'I have some very good news for you.' He went on to describe the offer, adding that the post would give him the advantage of using his knowledge of the Chinese language for the benefit of the Hong Kong office, as the manager there, Mr. Philip Gregson, had no such knowledge, and it was known that the Chinese are always wary in their dealings with Westerners: that Alex could speak Mandarin would reassure them. Leading him to the door, he shook Alex's hand warmly and said 'Well done, old man, give me your decision in the morning.'

Alex accepted the offer, to the great relief of the major, the date of the taking up of his new appointment being set for three weeks hence. The major said to him, apparently generously, but really because he wanted to see the back of him as soon as possible, 'Clear up your outstanding business here old man, and then take three week's well-earned holiday.' Before he left the office it was arranged that after two weeks *Siew Tung* and two of his staff would call at Alex's apartment to pack his belonging for transportation to Hong Kong.

Alex then took a taxi to the Buddhist temple that he had visited with *Qiangwei* earlier, the *Kong Meng San Phor Kark* temple, and spoke for some time to the nun whom he had met on that occasion. After he had finished telling her of his recent problems, she agreed to accept him in the monastery "in retreat from the world" until the day that he was due to depart for Hong Kong. Alex was relieved that he could spend his remaining time in Singapore within the monastery, as he had no wish to mix with the outside world.

She explained to him that he would receive instruction in the Buddhist faith, that he would be advised as to how to meditate, that he would attend the regular prayer sessions within the monastery, and that during the remaining time he would be expected to engage in private meditation. Alex agreed to this with thanks.

Alex's instruction in Buddhism began with an account of Buddha's life. Buddha was born into royalty about two-thousand five-hundred years ago, his father being the ruler of a state in north India. Although his mother had died soon after his birth, his father had taken care to ensure that he grew up to be a healthy normal child. He was named Siddhartha Gautama. So that his son's mind should not be confused by the many religions prevailing at that time, the king decided that he should not study any of these religions and advised his ministers that he should be taught only those arts and skills that would fit him, in the course of time, to take his father's place as king.

The boy grew to adulthood, and married and had a son, at which time the king's advisers agreed that he should start to encounter real life, as lived by the people within his father's kingdom. Travelling around the country, he pondered over the various human conditions that he encountered. The currently-prevailing view was that the truth about life could be determined only by one becoming an ascetic, which requires one to renounce everything in life: possessions, family and position in society. Siddhartha Gautama pursued this path, but after some years realised that self torture and other aspects of asceticism were not helping him in his aim. He began to practice contemplation and meditation, which led to the elimination of confused thinking from his mind, and enabled him to achieve his aim of seeing the truth of life. With the passing of time he was given the title of Buddha, which means "awakened", and he was called the "Enlightened One", in view of his being able to see things as they really are.

Alex's instruction then continued with an explanation as to how Buddhism had spread throughout the world since that time. Buddha did not claim to be a god, or an intermediary between a god and human beings, simply being an ordinary man who had being able to purify his own mind through meditation, so that he was able to see things as they are. Furthermore, Buddha said that this ability can be developed by anyone, irrespective of their social standing and cultural standing, their religious background, and their sex, and of whether they had the blessing of being able to pursue religious thoughts.

For forty-five years Buddha taught his philosophy throughout India, explaining that ordinary mortals are not fully conscious of the true world, because our minds are clouded by ignorance, confusion, misunderstanding and lack of insight, and that only when our minds are free of these "obscurations", are we able to see the true nature of things, this condition being referred to as the attainment of Buddhahood.

The instruction went on to describe two Indian traditions, the first being called Brahman, which is related to the pure nature of one's self and the reality of the world, which Buddha rejected as being an extreme position, as it over-values 'reality'. The second extreme position that he rejected, called Ajivikas, denies the existence of consciousness and moral responsibility, believing that humanity disintegrates upon death, leaving behind nothing. Those with these views are called nihilists.

Alex realised that whilst he originally had been of nihilist disposition, with the death of Clyde he had come around to believing that there could be more to existence than just self-gratification, the seeking of pleasure through over-indulgence, and immorality, with no final account having to be paid. His love of Clyde has continued since Clyde's death and will stay with him until his own death. He didn't think of Clyde as no more now than just a few decaying remains in a distant country, but as a loving friendly dog, still sailing out over the Firth with him on the "Westering Home" in his thoughts during quiet moments, or in his dreams.

He recalled the remark to him by one of his gang in Govan, saying, with conviction, when speaking of his young brother who was somewhat retarded 'But when he goes on to the next world he will probably have a brilliant mind to make up for his present problem', this belief giving the family hope, and seeming to reflect the Buddhist views that Alex was being taught.

Buddha believed that these two extreme positions do not reflect the nature of reality, so he advocated the "middle view." Alex's instructor went on to explain that the middle view is expressed in the "Fourfold Noble Truths", the first of which is the truth of suffering. Buddha realised that there is both happiness and sorrow in the world, and that happiness is only transitory. We cannot expect to find continuous happiness and must learn what is important and able to give us real happiness and what is not, if we are to gain true happiness.

Alex reflected upon the people whom he had met in the past who were constantly searching for happiness and, when unable to find it, complain at the unfairness of life, and are not able to accept that life is not necessarily fair. He thought of spoilt young children who weep bitterly and complain of unfairness when their parents don't buy them sweeties; he thought of these same children when they are older and can't find a chair in a round of musical chairs, and have to be kissed and consoled for their 'bad luck' by their parents; he thought of them in their teens, when they became paranoid and complain 'It always happens to me.' if their bike should develop a flat tyre or if they should be asked to do a few small jobs around the home; he thought of them as employees who complain that they are being picked on at work when they don't receive a bonus or a promotion, or are asked to work late; and he thought of them as husbands and wives who make little effort to improve their lives and the lives of their families, complaining self-pityingly 'I never had a chance to make much of myself.' with the excuse 'You're all right if your face fits!' or 'It's not what you know, it's who you know!' or 'With my bad luck, everything goes wrong sooner or later!'

Alex's own thoughts concurred exactly with the message of these teachings: unless one overcomes dissatisfaction, disgruntlement and self-pity, one cannot achieve real happiness: a simple message, but one that many people cannot understand, or do not want to accept, instead pursuing their own selfish and destructive interests.

The Second Noble Truth considered in the instruction was the origin of suffering. Buddha believed that the origin is within ourselves, and is not related to any external factor, although accepting that external factors can intensify suffering. We have to subjugate all excessive forms of desire: craving, grasping, greed and the like, as when we can't get all that we want, this makes us resentful and dissatisfied and more discontented. However, it was pointed out that Buddha was not opposed to moderate desire: it was excesses of desire, whether sexual, or material, or of any other form, that Buddha advised against.

Alex regarded these sources of suffering at the present time as being related to a large extent to commercial advertising, where one is led to think that if one can acquire all the wondrous products on offer, then perfect happiness will be the result. The reality is different, however, as advertising is endless and insidious, and at no point can one have acquired a full 'set' of the products that are 'essential' for happiness and therefore be able to relax and enjoy happiness, as "new and better" products are being introduced constantly. What is worse, such products are often directed at children, creating in them the cravings that will be the seeds of their own suffering throughout their lives.

These cravings extend through all ages and all classes of society: from the young who respond to the refusal of their parents to buy them the latest toy, or a pony, by endless, tearful, repetition of "please" and the wheedling "or but all the other kids have got one", to the angry "it's not fair!"; from late-teenagers who "set their heart" on a particular new dress, or on a particular motor-bike, and respond with a sulking silence; from married adults who must "keep up with the Joneses" and buy a particular new car, or go to a particular holiday venue, that is well beyond their means, and respond by being unhappy with their present circumstances and with each other. What a sad discontented situation they bring upon themselves by being unable to control their cravings under the "must have" pressure of the society in which we live!

The Third Noble Truth is the goal: the cessation of suffering, where we must first come to terms with the human nature of man, and how we must learn how to identify the cause of dissatisfaction, resentment and other burdens, followed by their elimination, to achieve the state known as nirvana. When one has achieved nirvana, it is then possible to see situations more clearly and to take more appropriate actions.

The Fourth Noble Truth was the path: the way out of suffering. This is the way towards promoting three features in an individual: moral values, meditation and the development of a focussed mind and wisdom. The path is eight-fold, and forms the basis of Buddhism. Much as he tried to understand what he was being taught, Alex found that the concepts are difficult to grasp and require more time than was available to him. However, he had learnt the essentials, and would be able to learn more by private study.

One last piece of information imparted was that Buddha believed that study and meditation should be complimented by the developing of a physical skill. This pleased Alex, who had been missing the pleasures of the sea after his trips out with *Siew Tung* and his friends. When he had settled in at Hong Kong he would try to find some means of taking to the water again, although he knew now that he would not be able to hunt and kill fish to the extent that he had done in the past, and there would certainly be no more instances of his netting and killing shoals of sentient fish such as mullet.

The next instruction was in group meditation, where Alex was taught how to assume the correct posture, how to relax and how to free his mind of the stress of daily problems. He soon found that meditation is a rewarding experience, and he would emerge from the meditation sessions with an untroubled relaxed mind, enabling him to see in clear perspective any troubling thoughts that he had previously pushed to the back of his mind rather than to face them. Group meditation led to private meditation, which at first Alex found unrewarding, as he tried, without success, to force himself to meditate, but on the third day he relaxed and allowed his mind to become free of stress.

He started to see his earlier life more clearly. He remembered Joe Bannion, whom he had cheated, and he felt guilty. He remembered his friend Greg, whom he had deserted without a word of farewell when he had left Govan. He remembered Flo, and forgave her for having had his beloved wee dog Clyde put down: she was a wicked woman, but this had been brought about by her upbringing and her life-style, just as in his own case.

He remembered wee Clyde himself, a loving friend, and he shed tears at the memory. He remembered Ernie and John, who had given him a new start in life when he was in need of help, and to whom he had not given a word of explanation when he left Gourock suddenly.

He remembered Aggie and Luke, and Aggie's husband Jack, and wished them continued happiness together. He remembered Matt, his 'dad', and he again wept tears of sadness. He remembered his lies and his deceit of Caroline, and he asked her forgiveness, as also he did of the major, who had only been acting in the best interests of the daughter he loved.

Finally, he recognised that he had been the sole agent in the ending of his friendship with *Qiangwei* and George. There is no other person to blame, much as he had tried to convince himself that this was so. He had not treated *Qiangwei* with respect, and he had not accepted her intention of becoming a nun, instead trying to force her to fit in with his own wishes. He had disappointed George, who had given him, a stranger and a foreigner, his friendship and affection.

Most importantly, Alex realised that he had been trying to blame others for the misery that had befallen him. He realised that no matter what he said or did to try to escape responsibility for his predicament, there was a quiet voice inside him, a voice that couldn't be silenced, and would speak to him in his quiet moments, or when he was lying in his bed at night: his conscience. The Buddhist beliefs that his instructor had explained to him, carefully and thoroughly, told him that there will always be retribution for wrongful acts, if not brought about by an external agency, then through the ever-constant voice of one's own conscience. He now knew this to be true.

Alex had come to terms with himself. He left the monastery at the end of his stay a renewed man. He had enjoyed the simple vegetarian food of the monastery, and resolved never again to eat the flesh of a warm-blooded creature. He would never again drink to avoid facing up to his difficulties. He had learnt forgiveness and humility, two big steps along the path to his becoming a good man once again. He had learnt much.

That same afternoon he called into the company offices to make his farewells. All of the staff were present in the downstairs office. The most senior of the lady clerks presented him with an ornamental Chinese scroll that had been painted by a master, to the purchase of which they had all contributed. Alex accepted the scroll with obvious pleasure, and expressed his thanks to them.

He then thanked each of the lady clerks in turn, for their unstinting help and support, and for the kindness that they had shown to him. They listened to his words with sad eyes: all of them would miss *Ai-li*. Tears ran down *Fu Rong*'s cheeks. Her friend, standing next to her, reached for her hand and gave it a reassuring squeeze. Indeed, they would all miss *Ai-li*, herself included, although, being older, and in greater control of her emotions, she had always taken care to ensure that her feelings for him were not evident to any of the other lady clerks.

Alex spoke to *Siew Tung*, and told him that he hoped that he would never again need to say '*mo you*', "no fish", on his fishing trips, upon which *Siew Tung* smiled and shook his hand. After this he spoke to *Ying Hong* and *Chonghai*, thanking them for being his good friends.

Alex then spoke to Madam *Zhang*, and in Mandarin wished her and her husband and their family happiness and good health for the future. Madam *Zhang* smiled, interlocked the fingers of her hands together, made a slight bow, and then moved her clasped hands up and down in the traditional Chinese way of expressing appreciation, at the same time saying to him *xie4xie4*, "thank you."

Alex then walked over to the major, who looked at him apprehensively, fearing that he might make some sarcastic or offensive comment, but Alex just said with sincerity 'Please give my best wishes to Caroline on the birth of your grandson, and my good wishes to her and her family for the future. I want to thank you major for the help that you have given me in my time here in Singapore, and to seek forgiveness for the troubles that I have caused you.'

The major was taken aback. He shook Alex's hand warmly, and experienced a twinge of guilt that he had been instrumental in Alex's removal from the Singapore offices. Whatever the major's faults, conceit, pomposity, no sense of humour and a boring personality, he wasn't normally vindictive. It was only that he had been incensed by Alex's treatment of his only child that he had done as he did. He smiled at Alex and in sincerity wished him success in his new appointment. Finally Alex turned to George and said 'Goodbye my friend. Please say goodbye to *Qiangwei* for me.'

With that he left the office and got back into the taxi that had been waiting for him outside. After arriving at Paya Lebar airport, Alex ate a snack in the cafeteria, and then waited for check-in time. He reflected upon his time in Singapore, and wondered what he would find in Hong Kong. When the check-in counter opened, he walked over to it, put his suitcase on the conveyor belt and handed his passport and tickets to the young woman behind the counter. As she completed the check-in and gave him his boarding card, he heard a voice that he recognised call his name: '*Ai-li.*'

Alex turned to see George standing behind him. They looked at each other for a few seconds, then George did something unusual for a Chinese, in stepping forwards and hugging Alex. He then said 'Goodbye my friend. *yilu4 ping2an1*': "one road level peace", meaning 'have a safe journey', before turning and walking away.

George walked to the far corner of the departure hall, where

Qiangwei had been waiting for him, and from where she had watched his farewell to Alex. She turned to him with sad eyes and said in a quiet voice 'I love him *yu tian*, and now he is going.'   After a moment George replied 'I know. I love him too. He was my good friend and I will miss him,' but then he added in Mandarin an old Chinese saying '*ou3duan4-si1lian2*': "the lotus root snaps but its fibres stay joined", meaning that *Qiangwei* should not weaken, but hold fast to her intention to maintain a clean break.

Part 4: Hong Kong

Chapter Twenty

As the plane rose above Paya Lebar Airport, Alex reflected upon his time in Singapore. He had made good friends there and now he was leaving them far behind for an unknown future in Hong Kong. Although Hong Kong was without the presence of the Malay and Indian communities that he had come to love in Singapore, it was Chinese, and would probably be more ethnically Chinese than Singapore, sitting as it did at the foot of the Chinese mainland.[20:1]

He looked down over the countryside of Johore, almost completely planted with palm-oil trees, the fruit of which, looking just like twelve-inch diameter raspberries, yielded the palm oil that made an enormous contribution to the economy of Malaya. There were also the slim birch-like trees that yielded rubber, with the downwards-spiralling cuts in their bark that channelled the sap into cups that were emptied at regular intervals by the plantation workers. Here and there were sugar plantations, the canes that contain the sugar-rich sap rising to a height of six feet or more. The villagers would cut these canes and run them through a press, rather like the old-fashioned clothes mangles that Alex had seen in his youth, the sap expressed being in great demand by the local populace. Less extensively planted were the lucrative coffee bushes, but these bushes needed nets to protect the crop from the environment and from the local wildlife. Also, because of its value, there was the need to keep the crop under surveillance. The scene down below was one of great tranquillity, as was appropriate to Malaya and its gentle people.

Alex closed his eyes, and remembered the friends that he was leaving behind him in Singapore, perhaps never to see again. He thought first of George, a true friend, who couldn't let him leave without friendship between restored between them. He thought of *Qiangwei*, whose friendship he had destroyed by his Western boorishness: would he ever forget her beautiful face, her gentle manner, and her soft kind voice, even though he had caused it to be raised in anger against him? He thought of his two friends, *Ying Hong* and *Chonghai*, who were almost like younger brothers to him. He thought of his fishing friend, *Siew Tung*. He thought of the sensitive and shy

---

[20:1] For a history of Hong Kong, see "The Hong Kong Story" by Caroline Courtauld and May Holdsworth, published by Oxford University Press, ISBN 0-19-590353-6.

young clerk, *Fu Rong*, who had wished for a closer relationship with him, but to no avail. He would miss them all. He would dearly miss them all, but of them all, it would be *Qiangwei* who would come into his thoughts during quiet moments.

For the rest of the flight he dozed, awakening with the message from the captain that the plane would soon be making its descent to *Kai Tak* Airport. His ears popped as the plane lost altitude, and then came into the flight path. He had been told of the difficulty of landing in Hong Kong, yet he was still amazed as the plane dropped down to the level of the surrounding tenements as it made its final approach. He had heard that one could see from the plane windows what the residents were cooking in their woks. Although this wasn't exactly so, it was a good enough statement to convey the extremely close proximity of the surrounding buildings and the very low margin of error that was allowed to pilots in landing here. No sooner had the plane's landing wheels touched the tarmac than the engines were put into reverse thrust as the end of the runway loomed large, with the waters of the bay immediately behind it. Indeed, some planes had actually ended up in the bay, when they hadn't been able to come to rest in time.

Alex collected his luggage, passed through customs, and then made his way towards the exit, where a crowd had collected. He scanned the crowd, and was pleased to see a thick-set middle-aged Chinese man wearing a driver's cap holding a board bearing his name. He went over and introduced himself, but the driver simply took his hand luggage from him and indicated that he should follow him. Clearly, there would be little conversation between them on this journey.

Alex knew that Hong Kong airport is in Kowloon on the mainland, although most people seem to think of Hong Kong as just being Hong Kong Island, or Victoria Island, to give it its original and proper name. With land values being high on Hong Kong Island, the company offices were in *Kowloon*, although the company depot was out in the New Territories, in the rapidly-developing district of *Shatin*. With there being many new high-rise apartment blocks being built out in *Shatin*, this was where accommodation had been arranged for him.

The driver stopped at one such block, took Alex's hand luggage from the boot of the car, and then led him to the lift and thence to his apartment on the tenth floor. Handing him his door keys, he made his first attempt to convey information to Alex, pointing to eight o'clock on his watch, and at the same time saying 'Morning, morning.' Alex thanked him, realising that it wasn't that the man was unsociable, but just that he was unable to converse with any fluency in the English language. That Alex could have spoken to him in Mandarin might have been of no use, as most of the people in Hong Kong are unable to speak this dialect.

Alex entered the apartment, and was pleased to find that it was well furnished, with a television set, fridge, cooker, washing machine, and a range of pots, pans and kitchen utensils. Opening the fridge, he was delighted to find that, in addition to a range of foodstuffs, it also contained a couple of litre bottles of "Blue lady" beer. He settled down to relax with a beer to contemplate the events of the day.

The next morning, at eight o'clock sharp, the door-bell of his apartment rang. Alex opened the door to find the driver, as he had indicated on the previous evening, ready to take him into Kowloon to the company premises. They set off out of *Shatin* and joined the stream of traffic making its way south into *Kowloon*, some of the traffic eventually to go further, through the recently-completed Cross Harbour Tunnel, to Hong Kong Island. Even though the distance to work was considerable, the cheaper accommodation in the New Territories compared with living on Hong Kong Island made the extra cost and time of travelling worthwhile.

On the previous evening, by the time that Alex and the driver had left the airport, the light had been was fading, so Alex hadn't taken much notice of his surroundings. Now, in the broad light of day, he looked around him, seeing the peculiar, almost uniformly conical, surrounding mountains, totally unlike the craggy and varied mountains that he had been used to in Scotland. It seemed to him that if a person slipped at the top of one of these mountains, he or she wouldn't stop rolling until reaching the bottom.

Soon the driver arrived at a tunnel and paid a small charge for passing through the mountain ahead of them. As they emerged at the other end of the tunnel, it was as though they had passed into a bowl, at the centre of which sat Kowloon. On all sides, mountains ranged above them. Alex learnt later that many centuries ago, a ruler of China had visited the area and had looked at these same mountains, counting their number and then saying to the party of local dignitaries that was accompanying him 'I see that you have eight dragons to protect you', whereupon an obsequious member of the party had replied 'No sire. We have you also, we have nine dragons to protect us.' thus giving rise to the Cantonese name for the area, *Kowloon*, "nine dragons", which Alex would have known in Mandarin as *jiu3long2*.

They made their way towards *Kowloon*, but turned off before reaching there to *Cheng Sha Wan*, which is less intensively developed than *Kowloon*, and offers business accommodation at a much more attractive rate. The driver pulled up at a small office block just off the main road and drove through a gateway into a parking area at the rear.

As Alex got out, the driver beckoned for him to follow, in the traditional Chinese way, by extending his hand horizontally with the palm down and with the fingers straight and pointing downwards, then drawing back the fingers towards him in several rapid movements, just as Alex had found in Singapore.

The driver took him through the back door and then led him to one of the offices. On the door was the name of the branch manager: "Mr. Philip Gregson". 'Great!' thought Alex, 'No "colonel blimp" to have to put up with here.' The driver knocked on the door, which was opened by a portly, balding, middle-aged man with a handlebar moustache as worn by members of the RAF during the War. He was dressed casually in an open-necked white shirt and sports trousers. The man introduced himself: 'Hello there old man, I'm Ginger, you must be Alex, nice to see you. Come in and have a snifter.'

Alex went into the office, where Ginger sat him down, and then said 'What's your poison old fellow? Being a Scot, I suppose it's a drop of the old single malt?' Alex nodded his agreement, upon which Ginger poured him a large measure of Talisker, a single-malt distilled on the Isle of Islay, off the west coast of Scotland, where on odd occasions he and John had made deliveries to the distilleries there. Alex declined the offer of water for his whisky, which brought a smile of appreciation from Ginger. 'No point in diluting the staff of life old man!'

Whilst the manager was referred to by one and all as Ginger, this nickname had been given to him by his fellow airmen during the War, when he had had a full head of bright red hair. However, what hair he still had left now, just a rim running round the sides and back of his head above the ears, was grey and thin. Initially Ginger had been the co-pilot of a twin-engined Manchester Bomber, built by A.V. Roe of Oldham, Lancashire, but when the Manchester was found to be underpowered and was replaced by the four-engined Lancaster Bomber, he had transferred to this new aircraft as a pilot. The Lancaster, a magnificent aeroplane, became the workhorse of Bomber Command during the war, and even when the War was over it carried on doing sterling service in Coastal Command as the Shackleton, where the long time that it could stay airborne enabled it to patrol many miles of coastal waters non-stop.

Alex was pleased at how affable his new manager, Ginger, was. Indeed, Ginger was described by all who knew him as a charming, pleasant fellow, with no 'edge' whatsoever. What none of them realised that this affability and imperturbability was simply a veneer that he had developed during the War to save him from suffering the emotional consequences of the deaths of his fellow airmen. After the death of the first friend that he had made when joining his squadron, he had steered clear of any further friendship, greeting all and sundry in a jovial manner, but never letting anyone get close to him.

When someone failed to return from a mission, and a place-setting was removed from one of the tables in the officers' mess by a steward, he would simply mouth the expressions that the others used under such all-too-frequent circumstances. 'I hear that old Harry "bought it" today over the Rhine. Bad show.', the euphemism "bought it" serving the same purpose as "gone west" used to do in the Great War, to avoid having to make a direct reference to the death of a friend or fellow airman.

No-one expressed their horror of war, or shed a tear for their dead comrades, although sometimes one of the aircrew would disappear into the toilets as soon as they had landed after a mission and emerge some time later with an ashen face, after he had vomited up the contents of his stomach. Such behaviour was frowned upon: 'Try to keep a stiff upper lip old man, don't let the side down.' was all the advice or comfort that was ever offered to the poor frightened man.

Ginger soon grew his handlebar moustache, so that he looked like all the other officers in the mess. He joined in with their childish games, drank to excess, and generally behaved as though the War was a great big game that had been arranged just for their benefit. This veneer served him well, and enabled him to carry on to the end of the War without cracking up under the strain.

After a series of dreadful missions, where half of the squadron had been shot down, he was given an immediate week-end pass. He set off for London where he stayed with his fiancée when on leave, just being in time to catch the last train from the nearest station to the airfield. After he arrived at London, he tried to telephone her to tell her of his arrival, but the lines were down following a raid by the Luftwaffe the previous evening. He caught a bus to the end of her street, walked to the house, and then quietly let himself in with his key.

The house was in darkness, so he turned on the living room light. Hearing a sound coming from within the bedroom, he walked over, gave the door a knock and then entered. The light from the living room was sufficient to show his fiancée lying in bed with a man: the uniform thrown over the back of a chair was that of a naval officer. The startled couple lying there naked stared at him aghast, not knowing what to do. With the strength of his veneer, Ginger said casually 'Now don't let me stop you, old chums. I'll be round for my things in the morning.', and with that he left.

When he called round the following morning, his fiancée was waiting for him, wringing her hands and full of explanations and abject apologies, but he quickly silenced her: 'No need to explain old dear. These things happen in wartime.' He packed his bags and walked towards the door, but then stopped, put down his bags and turned, holding his outstretched hand in front of him. His fiancée looked at him uncomprehendingly, so he wiggled his hand, palm uppermost, to indicate the need for her to hand something over. She realised what he meant, and slipped off her engagement ring and placed it in his hand, whereupon he turned and left.

He caught a taxi at the end of the street and asked the driver to take him to the nearest pawnbroker's shop and then wait there for him. Placing the ring on the counter he asked the pawnbroker how much he would give him for it. The man picked up the ring, studied it under his magnifying glass for a few moments, and then stated an amount that caused Ginger to raise his eyebrows in disbelief. 'What!' he exclaimed, 'I paid three-times that for it not six months ago!' The man was adamant. 'Take it or leave it!' Ginger took it, then went back to the taxi, instructing the driver to take him to the nearest drink store where he used the money to buy eight bottles of single malt. That evening, Ginger took the bottles along to the Officers' Mess, where he placed them on the bar counter and told everyone present 'The drinks are on me chaps!' His fellow officers were delighted and asked him if he had come into money. 'No', he said, 'but I have just had a narrow escape and want to celebrate.'

After this, Ginger didn't get emotionally involved again, but concentrated on the job in hand, taking his relaxation in the Officers' Mess and in joining his fellow officers on local pub crawls. At the end of the war, during which Ginger had been awarded a DFC, he returned to civilian life. As far as he was concerned, he didn't want to set foot inside the cockpit of an aircraft ever again. He went back to his job with an insurance company, and for a year or two was quite happy back amongst those of his old colleagues from the office who had not perished in the War.

However, he found that there were some there who resented his time in the War as a pilot, based back in Britain, whilst they had served overseas, often under atrocious conditions, not only whilst fighting, but even more so if taken prisoner. Because of his veneer, which had now hardened into a protective shell, he couldn't tell them about the appalling conditions that the aircrew of the bombers had faced, if not nightly, then quite regularly. Instead, he would just sympathise and say 'I know old bean, you had it rough while we aircrew stayed at home and shagged your womenfolk for you.'

After a few years, some of the recently-appointed junior staff, still only in their late teens and early twenties, who had just been children during the War, started to mock his "flying officer Kite" manner. Sometimes he would hear them in the tea-room: 'Wizard prang old boy! So I got old Hans in my sights and gave him what ho! Jolly good show what!' What was he to do? He couldn't come out of his shell and reveal his true self. Further, what was his true self?

Because he had seen so many of his fellow officers fail to return from a mission, he had become unable to develop a friendship with another man, and because of his betrayal by his fiancée he was unable to develop a sincere and loving relationship with a woman. In short, he was a casualty of the war, not displaying an obvious wound, but nevertheless deeply scarred emotionally. Where would he be in ten years' time? A dinosaur from an earlier age that had not been able to change with the passage of time, a museum exhibit, a relic from the War who should be carted off to a rest home?

His salvation came when he saw an advert in the paper for the post of manager in Hong Kong. He sent in an application, which was considered favourably by the board of directors, noting his DFC, and in due course he was offered the post. Ginger found his job in Hong Kong quite to his satisfaction. He joined a couple of the expatriate clubs, where he was given a warm reception: War heroes with a DFC were always welcome! He was able to retain his shell intact.

From time-to-time some of the club members would return to Britain temporarily, or go off elsewhere for a time on business, and he had plenty of opportunity to do his part in keeping their wives occupied whilst they were away. He was ideal for the job, as he never demanded any emotional entanglement, just disappearing when the husband returned, to be his normal urbane self at their next meeting in the club. As time passed by he put on weight and lost most of his hair, so that his opportunities for dalliances became reduced, but they were still frequent enough to keep him happy. Ginger was quite settled and comfortable in his lifestyle.

After his second whisky, Alex had taken to Ginger considerably, contrasting him with the pompous Major Horace Smedley (retd.). Ginger went on to explain to Alex how his particular responsibility was to be for import/export trade with companies in China. He said 'I have no knowledge of the lingo myself, so you will be of great help in getting our arrangements with the Chinese lads up north to go through smoothly. We'll go up there next month to get things rolling, and whilst we are there we will see if we can give some of the local girls a good

379

time. What do you say old man?'

Whilst not having acquired any knowledge of the Chinese language, it seemed that Ginger had acquired a liking for Chinese ladies! Alex was disturbed, in that he didn't want any fleeting paid-for relationship with a Chinese woman, forced on him by Ginger. His mind was still filled with his thoughts of *Qiangwei*. He just wanted to live quietly until he could decide what to do with the rest of his life. He didn't tell Ginger this, but just smiled at his suggestion, which Ginger took as expressing agreement.

Ginger took Alex for lunch at a Western restaurant, telling him 'I don't go in for this Chinese grub. One fart and you're hungry again.' Alex didn't tell him of the gastronomic delights that he had been missing over his years in Hong Kong, but simply smiled. There were many people that he had known back in Britain who wouldn't eat "foreign muck", by which they meant anything that wasn't served with chips or hadn't been fried in lard by their mother.

For that afternoon Ginger put Alex in the hands of his assistant, Albert, a somewhat dour young man with a serious acne condition. Albert wasn't a bad kind of chap, but his skin problem had given him a reluctance to mix with others, and he constantly tried to hide the left side of his face from view, as this was covered with a mass of red swellings, each of which was surmounted by a yellow spot, although the right side was little better. Alex felt uncomfortable for him, and tried to make light conversation, but with little response.

However, when George introduced Alex to the rest of the staff, it was a different matter. Alex found the Hong Kongers, or "Honkies" as many impolite Singaporeans call them, much more relaxed, and feeling more free to express their own thoughts than the staff in the Singapore offices. Within two minutes the two ladies and three men who constituted the rest of the office staff had found out his age, his marital status, if he had any romantic relationships, and his preferences in food. They were a happy bunch working for an easy-going boss. Alex thought that he would get along with them without any trouble.

After the office had closed for the day, Alex walked towards the city centre, feeling the need for some exercise. After a while he reached Prince Edward, a built-up area of mostly two-storey buildings, with shops occupying the lower floors. However, there were signs at the entrances of many of the passageways leading to the stairs to the upper floors advising such as: "Lily, young model: any position to please you"; "Obliging nude photographic model"; "Mandy, Masseuse. Let me take you in hand"; "Carol, exotic dance teacher."

The road, Nathan Road, was dense with traffic and the pavements were bustling with people. The activity of the district was intense, more than he had ever experienced in Singapore, except for perhaps in Orchard Road, Chinatown or Little India. He went into an eating house and ordered a bowl of *Wonton* Soup [30], small balls of thin pastry containing mainly minced pork, boiled and served in a clear soup, along with *pak choi*, "green vegetables", that in Singapore he would have called *bai tai*.

He ordered a bottle of Carlsberg, that the owner told him was called "gazsibaa" by the locals, where the "zs" was soft, sounding similar to "je" in French. The meal was tasty and satisfying, and he left the eating house in a relaxed frame of mind. Hong Kong is very crowded, and some parts look a bit care-worn, but it had a nice feel about it and he thought that he would enjoy life here.

He carried on walking towards the city, passing by Chunking Mansions on his left, noted as the cheapest and seediest place to stay at in Hong Kong. Eventually he arrived at the harbour, close by the arrival and departure point of the Star Ferry over to Hong Kong Island. For a few moments he contemplated taking the ferry over to the island, but then realised that it was about time that he returned to his apartment, and inquired of an inspector at the bus terminus as to which bus he would need to take, learning that he would first need to take a bus along Salisbury Road to the vicinity of the Cross Harbour Tunnel, and then the bus to *Shatin*. As he travelled towards the tunnel, he passed the massive and exclusive Peninsula Hotel on his left. He recalled that the Chinese name for peninsula was *ban4dao3*, "half island", and marvelled again at the graphic nature of the Chinese language.

There was no air-conditioning on the bus that he caught, but with all the windows open, the temperature inside wasn't too unpleasant, and likewise the bus to Shatin wasn't air-conditioned, As he paid his fare on the *Shatin* bus by proffering a handful of small coins to the driver for him to select from, he noticed a small board mounted close by the driver with several vertical strokes on it, separated by a horizontal stroke. After a few minutes he got into conversation with the passenger sitting next to him, an elderly Chinese gentleman who spoke good English, and asked him the meaning of the strokes. The man told him that the notice was to advise passengers of the fare to *Shatin*, and that the system was used in shops and other places, explaining the system to him as follows:

'There is a long vertical stroke in the middle of the top part of the board, and a horizontal stroke part-way down, dividing the board into four. Suppose that the board is to indicate a price of twenty three *yuan2*, "dollars". On the upper left is the MSD, "the most significant digit", in this case two, represented in Chinese as two horizontal lines, one above the other, rather like the "equals" sign; whilst on the upper right is the LSD, "the least significant digit", in this case three, represented in Chinese as three horizontal lines. On the lower left is the "exponent", in this case ten, represented in Chinese as a square cross, whilst on the right is the unit of currency, represented by the Chinese character *yuan2*. Sometimes there are three horizontal lines, so that as well as using Chinese characters for the MSD, the LSD and the exponent, letters of the alphabet can be used.'

The Chinese gentleman went on to tell him how as a child at school he had been instructed in how to find the number of days in each month, using the knuckles of the back of the hand, along with the troughs between them, the knuckles representing months of thirty-one days, and the troughs representing months of thirty days, or twenty-eight or twenty-nine days in the case of February. He demonstrated the method, stating the number of days in the month as he moved from knuckle to knuckle:

'Starting from the first knuckle: January, 31 days; trough, February, 28 or 29 days; knuckle, March, 31 days; trough, April, 30 days; knuckle, May, 31 days; trough, June, 30 days; knuckle, July, 31 days; then staying at the same knuckle and starting to count back in the reverse direction: knuckle, August, 31 days; trough, September, 30 days; knuckle, October, 31 days; trough, November, 30 days; knuckle, December, 31 days.'

Alex was delighted with this new knowledge that he had acquired, and thanked the man profusely, who smiled back in appreciation. It had been a good day. As he lay in bed that evening, he thought of *Qiangwei* and George. It would be a long time, if ever, before he would cease to miss them, but his life had to go on, come what may, and already he was beginning to enjoy mixing with the people of Hong Kong.

Two days later, Ginger invited Alex to join him on that evening at his club, "to meet some of my chums and have a drink or two." The club was well appointed, with a smoke room, a bar and a billiard room for the use of members only, along with a large waiter-service lounge where members and their wives and guests could sit and drink. Ginger introduced him to a couple of his pals, both ex-serving officers, who spoke in the same style as Ginger, but with the expressions that they used indicating the branch of their previous service. 'Welcome aboard!' said one of them, 'gin and tonic is it?; whilst later in the evening the other one asked him if he had yet found a lonely young wife to warm his bed for him, but advising him 'No names, no pack drill!'

They were nice enough chaps, but not the kind to whom Alex was accustomed. When mixing with them he was aware of his strong Glasgow accent and felt that he should perhaps try to modulate it a little, so that he wouldn't stand out so much in company. What he wasn't aware of was that many people were intrigued by his accent, whilst others were impressed with his natural, unaffected manner of speech. He enjoyed the club, but he didn't think that he would be able to find there the company that he was hoping to meet.

In Singapore he had enjoyed mixing with those of his male colleagues who were of his own age group and had similar interests, but there were no such male colleagues in the Hong Kong office, being either too young, or with family responsibilities, or else being Cantonese-speaking and uncomfortable when called upon to speak socially in English or Mandarin; and it was the same with the ladies of the office. However, he thought that it would be just a matter of time until he got to know a few people with whom he could be friendly.

To pass his evenings, Alex took to visiting different places in Hong Kong, although he found his own company depressing. Some evenings he would walk down Nathan Road to the harbour, often taking the Star Ferry to Central over on "The Island". There he would walk amongst the crowds, take a ride on the trams, have a coffee and a plate of chicken rice, then make his way back to *Kowloon* and then on to *Shatin*. There was no point in going back to his apartment too soon, and he felt a little less lonely when surrounded by countless others on the busy streets.

Other times he would jump onto a tram in Central and pass an interesting half-hour as the tram clanked its way along the middle of the crowded streets, narrowly avoiding running down incautious pedestrians or crashing into careless motorists. The trams were ancient looking and noisy, just like those that he used to enjoy riding on in his youth back in Glasgow, the main difference being that the Island trams were entirely covered with brightly painted advertisements. However, they were much appreciated by visitors, probably because of the nostalgia that they invoked.

Although Alex knew about the traditional, *fan2ti3zi4*, characters employed in Hong Kong from his studies in Singapore, he found many of them quite different from the simplified, *jian3ti3zi4*, characters, taught to him in Singapore. In particular, he admired the traditional character *long2*, meaning "dragon", which gives a vivid impression of a rampant dragon, whilst the simplified character is just a few unimpressive strokes. He also came across a few characters that he hadn't seen before, one of which was a single character for "twenty", which number in Singapore is expressed as two characters, *er4*, "two" and *shi2*, "ten", placed together. Another complex form of numeral was that for "one", *yi1*, which is normally written as a single horizontal stroke: the simple addition of a further one or two strokes changes the character to "two" or "three", thus offering little difficulty to a forger.

As the weeks passed, Alex learned a great amount more about the geography of Hong Kong and also about its history. Whilst he had experienced heavy rain in Singapore, the extensive system of large roadside culverts and drainage canals over the island avoided rain being more than an occasional problem. However, he soon found that the rains in Hong Kong are even heavier and that the hilly nature of the ground and the many deep cuttings that had been made into the hillsides in the building of roads cause severe local flooding.

To reduce the incidence of landslides from heavy rains, the steep sides of cuttings were faced with concrete. At times, when the winds are severe, storm cones are hoisted and storm warnings are broadcast over the radio. On the few occasions when danger level is approached, people are told to leave shops and offices and make their way home immediately. At other times, when the conditions are hot and dry, fires will sometimes spread over the hills and mountains above Kowloon, and advice is given to walkers to keep well away. When the weather conditions are hot and humid, condensation can sometimes be seen on the internal walls of air-conditioned buildings in the vicinity of doors letting in moisture-laden air from outside. All of this was quite new to Alex and each day brought something else for him to learn.

Alex took to walking in the evening in different areas of both *Kowloon* and Victoria Island, to take his mind off his growing loneliness and away from thoughts of *Qiangwei* and he soon became quite familiar with the layout of both of these places. He learnt the locations of the footbridges crossing congested roads, preferring to use them rather than to struggle with the crowds at traffic lights. One evening, as he was walking along Hennessey Road in *Wanchai* on the Island, there was a sudden heavy downpour, so he mounted the first covered footbridge that he came to in order to get out of the rain.

As he reached the top of the steps and turned to proceed across the footbridge, he encountered a line of hawkers sitting behind small folding tables along one side of the bridge, selling trinkets, cigarettes, lighters, and miscellaneous other items. He noticed a young Chinese woman sitting in a wheel-chair behind a table on which were displayed watches, lighters, cigarettes, and cosmetics. The young woman, in her mid-twenties, had large bright eyes set in a thin delicate face. The paleness of her skin and the tautness of her cheeks enhanced her looks, but also indicated that she was not in good health. Her long black hair was tied loosely at the nape of her neck. She was beautiful, but in a haunting way. Despite being of only slight build, her breasts were well formed, and her upper torso appeared to be normally developed. However, what of her lower body that he could see looked wasted, which he presumed was the reason for her being in a wheel-chair.

As he paused to look at her, not realising that he was now staring, her attention lifted from the table, where she had been re-arranging her goods, and as her head lifted she caught his eyes, then returning his stare with defiance and suspicion: she had seen other men looking at her before, deep in thought, and it disturbed her that she didn't know what they might be thinking. Alex flinched under her gaze, and hurried away across the bridge, but he couldn't get her out of his mind.

The next evening, Wednesday, saw Alex crossing the bridge again, but this time he stopped to buy a packet of cigarettes, smiling at the young woman as she gave him his change and saying *xiexie1*, "Thank you". The woman didn't return his smile, but just gazed at him coldly: she was suspicious of his motives in being friendly towards her. Not knowing what else to do, reluctantly he walked on. Nevertheless, he was there again the next evening. He had been thinking about her all day, but when he arrived the young woman was not to be seen. He crossed and re-crossed the bridge a few times, but to no avail. He was disappointed and wondered if he would ever see her again.

The following day he had intended to go to the footbridge again, but was disappointed to find that Ginger had arranged for him to go out to meet a client. He watched the clock anxiously, but by the time that his business had been conducted and he had rushed across to the Island and made his way to the bridge, it was deserted of hawkers. He was dismayed. He came back again on the next evening, Friday, and was delighted to see her sitting there, as before. As he approached her, he thought that he detected a look of recognition in her eyes, but he wasn't sure. He bought another packet of cigarettes, and as he paid her for them he took his courage into both hands and said 'You weren't here on Wednesday evening.' She stopped what she was doing, and looked him in the face: 'Yes, and you weren't here yesterday evening.'

Alex couldn't believe that she had noticed his absence, and said 'No, I had to work late.' The young woman replied 'Poor you', which made Alex laugh, his laughter bringing the suggestion of a smile to the corner of her eyes. 'I'll see you tomorrow morning.' he said. The young woman didn't reply. She watched him go with a sad, but resigned expression on her face. In her condition she didn't think that any man would have other than a voyeuristic interest in her. There were too many healthy young women available in Hong Kong for a handsome young man like him to want to waste his time on her. Nevertheless, the next morning, Saturday morning, she was at her stand nice and early, watching out for him, but by the time that noon came, she had given up hope. She reproached herself: 'What else can you expect, he was just being sociable.'

At five o'clock Alex came hurrying along the bridge. Although there was no necessity for it, he said to her 'I had to go into work again today', which brought the same comment from her: 'You poor man', but this time accompanied by a warm smile. Alex smiled back at her and said in Mandarin *ni3 jiao4 shen2me ming2zi?* "What is your name?" Although the woman spoke very little Mandarin, she knew this common question, so she replied in Mandarin "*xiao3 ma2que4.*" Alex beamed at her and said 'Little Sparrow! It's a lovely name to match a lovely young woman!'

Whilst *Xiao Maque* didn't understand exactly what Alex had said, she appreciated the gist of his words and smiled at him, feeling a warm glow in her heart. For the first time in her life a man had paid no heed to her disability, but had been kind and affectionate, and paid her a compliment. He told her that his name was Alex, which she repeated as "ah leek", but he didn't mind. He was too thrilled with the progress of their relationship to be bothered about such a small matter as that. He wondered whether he should leave things the way they were for today, or whether he might dare to make a suggestion. He decided on the latter, and cleared his throat nervously before speaking. '*Xiao Maque*, would you like to come out for dinner with me this evening?'

She understood what Alex was saying, and was pleased at his invitation, but it wasn't as simple as that. She would first have to go back to the hostel where she lived to shower and change her clothes. She told him this in her faltering English, but not mentioning the incontinence that made such an action necessary. Alex was pleased and suggested that he go along to the hostel with her. He waited whilst *Xiao Maque* packed away her merchandise into a large bag and folded up her table and attached it to the side of her wheel-chair.

Alex took hold of the back of the wheel-chair and pushed *Xiao Maque* along, taking great care whilst so doing. As they made their way to her hostel, he chatted incessantly about nothing in particular, to cover his shyness. She listened to him with a smile on her face. What a silly sensitive man he was, and how wrong she had been in her initial assessment of him.

Indeed, Alex was again a considerate and kind man. He was no longer the cruel insensitive lout who had terrorised Govan with his gang, nor the criminal who had worked for Joe Bannion, nor the conscienceless man who had seduced Caroline and distressed her father, nor the arrogant man who had paid no regard to *Qiangwei*'s wishes and thereby had lost her friendship and that of her brother. He had learnt the power of meditation and of forgiveness, and he had acquired inner calm and a clear untroubled mind. Yes, Alex was now a good man, almost as good a man as they come.

Chapter Twenty-one

The hostel was in a side street running off Des Vouex Road East. Alex waited on the pavement whilst *Xiao Maque* went inside. It was a run-down building, with some of the windows cracked, and with a drain pipe from one of the upstairs toilets leaking onto the pavement. Once inside, *Xiao Maque* wheeled herself to the shower, and afterwards to her room. There she opened the chest of drawers alongside her bed and took out her best clothes. Just as she had finished dressing, her friend Alice came in, saw her, and said 'My, you look nice tonight!'

Xiao Maque told her about Alex waiting outside, and how they were going out for dinner together. Alice was an understanding soul, who had been married for many years. She was a middle-aged lady whose husband had cared for her after she had developed rheumatoid arthritis, but upon his death, not having any children or family to take care of her, she had had no choice but to enter the hostel.

She said to *Xiao Maque* 'Wait just a minute', then walking away slowly to her room on the walking-sticks that she couldn't manage without, before returning a couple of minutes later with a small bag in her hand. First she took out some blue eye shadow with which she gently coloured *Xiao Maque*'s upper eye-lids, then she applied a small amount of rouge to give a slight blush to her cheeks, and finally she added a little lipstick. Standing back to admire the results, Alice said 'That's better!' *Xiao Maque* wheeled her chair out to Alex with trepidation, but without need. As soon as he saw her, he said '*Xiao Maque*, you look lovely!'

She didn't understand his words, but the expression on his face told her all that she needed to know. A blush crept over her cheeks that added to the colouring that Alice had applied and made her look even more attractive. Alex set off along the road with *Xiao Maque* to a Cantonese restaurant that he had noticed a few days before.

It was quite an up-market restaurant, with waiters dressed in crisp white shirts and immaculate black waistcoats and trousers. The head waiter was standing inside, ready to open the door for customers. Alex pushed the wheel-chair up to the large step in front of the door and beckoned for the head waiter to open the door. He then lifted *Xiao Maque* from out of the wheel-chair with ease, carrying her into the restaurant. The waiter indicated a table in the corner, but Alex ignored him and carried her to a table by the window. After he had set her down he told the head waiter to have her chair brought into the restaurant and put somewhere where it would be safe. *Xiao Maque* was impressed by his actions. Not only was Alex kind and gentle, he was also protective, and had treated her with consideration. She smiled at him and Alex was pleased with her appreciation.

When the waiter came to take their order, Alex left the ordering to *Xiao Maque*, telling her to order what she most liked to eat, and that he would enjoy whatever she ordered. To start with she ordered *dimsum*, "little hearts", which Alex had known as *dian3xin1* in Singapore. After this she ordered a sea-food salad, chicken noodles and a couple of other dishes, including the virtually standard *bai1fan4*, "boiled white rice", and also *mi3fan4*, "fried rice", which contains a selection of small shredded items and is a dish in itself. Alex asked for a glass of beer, but *Xiao Maque* said that she didn't want anything to drink: this wasn't strictly true, but she had to restrict her fluid intake because of her disability. She was self conscious and too embarrassed to explain her situation to anyone, and would have found it particularly difficult to do so upon new acquaintance with a young man such as Alex.

It was a very successful evening. As Alex wheeled *Xiao Maque* back to her hostel, it was her turn to chat away: he was happy just to be with her and to know that she had enjoyed herself. Reaching the door of the hostel, he said 'Goodnight Little Sparrow', then adding something that one of the older carers in the orphanage use to say to the little ones: 'Sleep tight and don't let the bed-bugs bite!', which mystified her. Why did he think that there were bed-bugs in the hostel? True, there were occasional outbreaks of bed lice, but the matron and her staff soon eradicated them. This kind of mild humour was alien to the Chinese, who tend to speak literally.

Xiao Maque thought that he was a very nice, but also a very strange, man. They arranged to meet again on the following evening, again at six o'clock. When she went inside, Alice was waiting for her, anxious to learn how the evening had gone. She needn't have asked, as *Xiao Maque*'s radiant face told her that all had gone well. 'Will you be seeing him again?' she asked, to which *Xiao Maque* smiled shyly, averting her eyes and then nodding her head.

Alice was pleased for her, and glad that Alex wanted to see her again, but she was uneasy that she might become too attached to him and end up being hurt. Still, it was not for her to say. Let *Xiao Maque* enjoy her new friendship for as long as it might last. There had not been much happiness in her existence up to this time, and she deserved, as do all young women, a chance of a little romance in her life.

The next evening Alex arrived at the hostel, as arranged, to find *Xiao Maque* waiting in the hallway, dressed in the same clothes, and again having been nicely made up by Alice. She was embarrassed that she only had the one set of good clothes. However, Alex smiled at her and said 'I'm pleased that you are wearing that dress. It suits you, Little Sparrow.', which eased her feelings. She liked him to call her "Little Sparrow": it was nice and affectionate.

As they made their way along the road, he asked her where she would like to eat. She already had somewhere in mind and directed him into a side-road, and then through an archway into a small square filled with crowded tables. Along two sides of the square were the stalls of food vendors, selling typical Cantonese food, but at a fraction of the price that they had paid the previous evening. *Xiao Maque* smiled at him and said in her quaint, but pleasant, English that although the food at the restaurant that they had been to last night was good, the food here is also good but much cheaper.

Despite the great number of people who had come to eat in the square, a group of people at one table, smiling and friendly, squeezed along and made room for the two of them. She told him to sit down at the table and wait, then wheeled herself along to the row of food stalls, choosing and pointing, and even stopping at a beer stall to order a large bottle of Carlsberg for Alex, before returning to her place alongside him 'My treat.' she said. Alex was filled with affection and reached over for her hand, saying, with sincerity 'Thank you little sparrow.'

They had both enjoyed each other's company, and for the next few weeks spent all the time that they could, evenings and weekends, together, their feelings for each other growing all the time: Alex was beginning to get over *Qiangwei*'s rejection of him, whilst *Xiao Maque* was thrilled with her first relationship with a young man.

One Monday morning Ginger called him in to his office to say that he had fixed up a visit for the two of them to see a company that they had dealings with in *Shenzhen*, a small but rapidly-growing town just over the border in China. They would take the early train on Wednesday morning up to *Lo Wu*, then cross the border into China, to be met by one of the representatives of the company that they were to visit. Rooms had been booked for them on that night and the following night in a *Shenzhen* hotel and they would return to Hong Kong on the Friday morning.

Alex was disappointed at the thought of not seeing *Xiao Maque* on the Wednesday evening, but at the same time he was excited at the prospect of visiting China and he told Ginger so. As he had done once before, at their first meeting, Ginger then made mysterious remarks to the effect that they might "have a good time" whilst in *Shenzhen*: 'You never know your luck, old man!' Alex wasn't quite sure what Ginger meant, but he had a suspicion as to what it would involve. He didn't press the matter, but just decided that, whatever Ginger's own intentions, he wasn't interested himself, not when he had his own little Chinese girl-friend waiting for him back in Hong Kong.

When Alex told *Xiao Maque* of his forthcoming trip to *Shenzhen*, she expressed indifference, although Alex could see clearly that she was disturbed at the prospect. She tried to pretend that she had no concern, but at the end of that evening she said to him, but in her own broken English, words that had the meaning 'I know that you have affection for me Alex, but I can't give you what you and all other men need. If you are tempted by a woman in China, then don't blame yourself, but please come back safe and sound.'

Alex set off with Ginger after work two days later from *Kowloon* Station. As they made their way through the station, Alex was surprised to see written below the English for "Platform" the Chinese characters *yue4tai2*, which mean literally "moon platform", as he couldn't see what the association with "moon" was. However, on reflection he thought that it might originally have been the name given for an area of flat ground outside a house where the occupants could sit under the moonlight in the cool of the evening, and had been adopted as the name for the flat area alongside the railway track.

The journey to *Lo Wu*, where they alighted, took little more than a half-hour. After going through the immigration control on the Chinese side, they walked out into the busy street outside the station. A young man was waiting for them there with their names written on a board. As they approached, he bowed and then introduced himself as an employee of the company that they were to visit. The young man's command of English was admirable, so the three of them continued to speak in English, Alex not wanting to exclude Ginger from the conversation should he speak to the young man, *Lim Kok Lun*, in Mandarin. *Kok Lun* said that before proceeding to the hotel that had been booked for them, they should take a meal in a nearby restaurant.

A waitress seated them at a table by the window, *Kok Lun* then ordering a variety of dishes. The waitress started to remove two pairs of chopsticks, whereupon Alex said *wo3 zhen1 hui4 yong4 kuai4zi*, "I really know how to use chopsticks", which brought a smile of pleasure to *Kok Lun*'s face, and the return of his pair of chopsticks by the waitress.

After the meal, *Kok Lun* took them to the hotel in the centre of *Shenzhen*, telling them as he left them in the foyer that he would be back at eight o'clock in the morning. They went up to their rooms, which were adjacent on the third floor. Alex could see from the window of his room that there was extensive development going on in *Shenzhen*, which had been selected for such development because of its close proximity to Hong Kong, which was due to be returned to China in 1997.

After Alex had sorted out his clothes for the next morning's meeting, he settled down to watch the television. However, within five minutes he received a call on the room telephone. 'I am a young and beautiful Chinese lady. Would you like me to come up to your room and keep you company? I am sure that we can find lots of things to do.' Alex explained to her in Mandarin that he was tired and needed his sleep, which the young lady accepted with grace. However, within two minutes he heard through the wall the telephone ringing in Ginger's room, when presumably the same offer was to be made. Ginger's words were not quite clear, but his enthusiasm certainly was. After a few minutes he heard the door of Ginger's room being opened, and them a few words of conversation. Before long the sound of activity on the bed came through the wall. Ginger was having the 'good time' that he had spoken about!

The next morning *Kok Lun* met them in the foyer, and took them to the premises of his company, where they were received in dignity by the managing director and his deputy, neither of whom spoke much English. *Kok Lun* introduced Ginger and Alex, taking the opportunity to inform his superiors that Alex spoke Mandarin. Thereafter, most of the conversation was conducted in Mandarin, with Alex doing his best to render a reasonable translation of the conversation to Ginger in English, with the frequent help of *Kok Lun*. Rather than feeling excluded by this arrangement, Ginger was delighted to be relieved of the effort of trying to understand the conversation, just saying to Alex in his usual unflappable manner 'Carry on old man, when you get to the important bits, just let me know.'

A couple of hours later the arrangements for their co-operation had been established, upon which Ginger said a few flattering complimentary words for Alex to relay to their Chinese hosts. As he spoke the words to them in Mandarin, the Chinese director and his deputy were highly delighted and called for *Mao Tai Jiu* to be served, before they all went off for a celebratory Chinese banquet. On the way to the restaurant, *Kok Lun* whispered to Alex 'Your company is very fortunate to have you Alex, and we can look forward to a great era of co-operation.'

The banquet lived up to its name, in that amongst the ten or so courses that were served were some that Alex had not eaten before, the first of which was Beijing Duck, the skin of a roasted duck with the underlying layer of fat still attached, that each of the diners themselves placed on very thin steamed pancake-like disks made of rice-flour, along with thin slices of cucumber, then topped with a thick and sweet plum sauce, after which the disks were rolled up tightly. Also, they were served short lengths of pigs' tail, stewed in a rich flavoured sauce; and pink-coloured slices of steamed lotus root, the regularly-spaced large length-wise cavities within the slices giving them the appearance of the cutting disks that are employed within manually-operated food-mincers that can be found in many British homes. The meal was elegant, and showed the appreciation of their hosts for the visit of Alex and George.

When they got back to the hotel that evening, Ginger also expressed his thanks to Alex for his help in smoothing-through the transactions, saying 'You can take a great load of my shoulders Alex, in dealing with these oriental lads. I can never tell what the devious buggers are thinking.' Alex smiled at his words. The Chinese are not in the least bit devious, but simply cautious in dealing with others who might in their Western arrogance think that they can get the better of them. Not the slightest chance!

After dinner that evening, Ginger said to Alex 'Listen old chap, what do you say to getting a couple of those girls up to my room tonight and having a bit of a party? Could be fun, what?' Alex didn't know what to say and, before he could find the words to refuse, Ginger, as he did on the day of their first meeting, took his silence for agreement. When the inevitable telephone call came from the lobby, Ginger said 'Yes indeed my love, and bring a friend with you.'

Ten minutes later two beautiful young Chinese girls, looking no more than about eighteen years of age, but because of the inability of Westerners to judge the age of the Chinese, could have been well advanced into their thirties. Ginger welcomed them into the room, sat them down on the settee, and then offered them a drink, at the same time deciding which one of them he would have for himself. He said to Alex 'Take advantage of all that's going old chap, they're both great looking girls.'

After a few drinks, Ginger indicated to Alex to take his new 'friend' back to his own room. As they closed the door behind them Alex could hear whoops of delighted anticipation from Ginger. After they had entered his own room, Alex started to feel decidedly uncomfortable. It had been a long time since he had had sex and he was feeling immensely frustrated, but at the same time he felt guilty that he should desire a woman other than *Xiao Maque*.

The woman moved over to stand in front of the bed. Realising that Alex was reluctant to take the first move, she slipped her dress from off her shoulders, then letting it fall to her ankles. She was wearing just a small black brassiere and minute black knickers. She turned her back to Alex, indicating with her hand that she wanted him to unfasten her brassiere. After he had done so, he slipped his hands around her and cupped her breasts in them: the woman had known that he would do this, and so break the ice.

She turned back to face him. Feverishly, he pulled down her knickers and stood looking at her in her nakedness, his desire for her rising to fever pitch. She then lay back on the bed, raising her arms and laying them on the pillow behind her, in a submissive gesture that said that she would do all that he asked of her. She had not removed her under-arm hair, which, although completely natural, Alex found erotic.

Alex took off his clothes. She looked at him with wide guileless eyes. She had had only limited previous experience of Western men, and was fascinated by his pale skin, the thick hairs on his chest, his heavy muscular development, and the size of his engorged erect penis: he was very generously endowed, even by Western standards.

For a whole minute Alex gazed down at her. She was slim and shapely, and though her breasts were small, they were well formed. She watched him as his eyes slid down to her lower body, where they came to rest on the tuft of black hair that sprang from the lower part of her Mound of Venus. The woman, with a professional eye, noticed Alex's reaction to the sight of her genital region, and lifted up her legs and opened them wide, so that he could see all that it offered. The reluctance that he had felt earlier disappeared in an instant. He didn't turn off the light, as he wanted to be able to look down on her: like most men, he had always been turned on by sight as much as by contact.

As he lay enjoying the sensation of being within her, she used one of her tricks of the trade. His penis was suddenly gripped tightly by the contraction of her internal muscles, but much more tightly than Flo had ever gripped him back in Gourock. The woman was pleased at his startled reaction, and a slow smile spread across her face. Alex saw the smile and despite there not being an idiomatic counterpart in Chinese, he said to her in Mandarin the closest he could manage to the most common English-language description for a sexually provocative woman: 'Prick teaser!'

She took the meaning of his words and, pleased at his professional compliment, started to laugh gently. Alex joined in with her laughter, and was delighted that as she laughed her stomach muscles alternatively tightened and relaxed, which gave him a very pleasurable sensation. He closed his eyes and groaned with delight. Although the relationship between them was a business arrangement, the use of her

394

body in return for a cash payment, he experienced a warm feeling of affection for her, and wished that such a young, beautiful and humorous woman didn't have to earn her living in this way. When he started to approach his climax, the girl, professional that she was, emitted simulated sounds of pleasure and imminent satisfaction to urge him on, and he responded accordingly.

After Alex had paid the woman and she was about to leave, he reached out for her and kissed her tenderly on the forehead, telling her that he was glad to have met her and that she was too nice to be in this profession. The woman was touched by his compassion, and asked him if she would see him again. When he told her that this was unlikely, her face saddened and she turned towards the door, giving him one appealing backwards glance as she left the room.

Never before had any of her clients been kind or considerate towards her. She had just been a body to be used: no need for words from the client other than to give her instructions to perform whatever act he had next in mind. She had just been an object, not a woman. She had left her tiny rural village at the age of fourteen, when a man had come seeking workers for a factory in *Shenzhen*, describing the marvellous working conditions and the luxurious living conditions in the factory hostel. She had hoped that her parents would implore her not to leave, but they were poor and wanted one less mouth to feed.

The hostel turned out to be no more than a large timber shack, with hard beds and single blankets, and just one cold-water tap and one door-less squat toilet for the use of the twenty girls who lived there. The food was mainly rice with a tiny amount of fish or meat, together with a mug of tea. She had worked for twelve hours a day, with only a half-day off every month. The girls were all so tired that on their half-day off they went back to bed to rest.

After a year, she had gone into the town on her half-day off and had been approached by a young man who spoke to her kindly and took her for a meal: not just boiled rice, *mi3fan4*, but fish, *yu2rou4*, dumplings *bao1zi* and "white vegetable", *bai2cai4*. Later he had taken her back to his apartment, where he asked her to stay with him whilst he found her a better job. Later that night, he had come to her room, where in gratitude for his protection and kindness she had allowed him into her bed.

After a further two days, he told her that she must earn her keep, and brought a man into her room. When she refused to allow the man into her bed, he scolded her and told her that he would report her to the police as a vagrant and that she would be imprisoned for breaking her contract with the factory, although she knew nothing about a contract and had not signed any documents. In fear she had agreed to his demands, and for the next few nights a different man had been brought to her room. Then her erstwhile 'saviour', now her pimp, had sent her out onto the streets and into the hotels, claiming most of her earnings from her each evening. For ten years she had lived this life, always in the hope that one day she might be able to escape from it.

She could not face the shame of running back to her village and telling her parents what she had become. Instead, she had clung on to the hope that perhaps one day one of her clients would take pity on her and take her for his mistress. She ached for the love of another human being, something that she had not felt since leaving her home village so many years ago. If only this kind Westerner had asked her to go away with him! Even if he had wanted her to continue with her profession, she would gladly have agreed: he was a good man, who would take care of her and might one day even come to love her, if but just a little. She could have attended to all of his sexual desires, however erotic, and there would have been no need for her to simulate pleasure when they were coupled, for she would have felt it, not just physically, but also deep in her heart. If only...

Later, Alex felt ashamed that his desire had caused him to be disloyal to *Xiao Maque*, but at the same time he had been desperate to satisfy his pressing sexual needs: *Xiao Maque* could not meet these needs, much as she wished that she could do so. The next morning on their way back to Hong Kong, Ginger said to him 'That was a great trip Alex old man, but mum's the word back at the office, what?'

When Alex met *Xiao Maque* upon his return, she suspected from his manner that something was wrong. He wouldn't look her in the eye, nor talk about his trip. She eventually asked him 'Alex, why are you so quiet? Are you unhappy?' He knelt down in front of her chair and laid his head on her lap. With utter sincerity, he said 'Yes Little Sparrow, I am unhappy and I am sorry.' He told her what had happened at *Shenzhen*. *Xiao Maque* reminded him that she had told him that it would be alright if he should seek the attention of another woman, as long as he came back to her, and here he was, sitting at her feet. What could she complain about? She couldn't provide him with the physical love that he needed. She ran her hand over his hair and said gently 'It's all right Alex, not a problem. Don't worry. Don't be sorry. You have a man's needs that I cannot satisfy.'

Alex was touched by her understanding, and lifting his head, leaned forwards and gave her a gentle loving kiss on the lips, the first time that he had ever kissed her. She was moved, and a tear crept down one of her cheeks. Alex was quiet for a few seconds before saying the Chinese idiom *ma2que4 sui1 xiao3, gan3 dan3 ju4 quan2*, "The sparrow may be small, but it has all the vital organs", meaning small but perfect. He was telling *Xiao Maque* that she was all that he wanted. 'I love you Alex.' she said, to which he replied 'And I love you too Little Sparrow.'

When *Xiao Maque* returned to the hostel that evening, she confided in Alice and told her that she didn't know what to do about Alex's needs. Alice had had a long and happy married life and was well aware of the sexual pressures that men feel, and the demands that they can put on the woman they love. She looked at *Xiao Maque* for a few moments before replying 'Because of your problem, you cannot offer all that a man desires, but you heart is full of love, and there are ways to give Alex pleasure.' She gently explained her meaning. *Xiao Maque* understood and was very grateful to her old friend.

Xiao Maque thought over her friend's words, and the next time that Alex took her to his apartment, she asked him to sit next to her on the settee. He placed his arm around her shoulders and drew her close. She took the initiative, kissing him and telling him how much she loved him. She slid his hand under her loose top and guided it to her breasts, at the same time looking at him with trepidation, lest he should think her wanton. Alex responded eagerly, and with his other hand he gently lifted her loose top over her head and dropped it to the floor. She averted her gaze as he ran his hands around her back and unfastened her brassiere.

Alex was stimulated by the sight of her perfectly-formed breasts. He took his hand away, gently kissed her nipples, and then laid his head there. He was touched that *Xiao Maque* wanted to give him some of the sexual pleasure that she felt he was missing. His tears ran down his face and onto her breasts, soon joined by her own, as they sat together whilst the light faded outside.

After Alex had taken her back to the hostel, she told Alice what had happened and how it had brought them so much closer together. Alice was pleased for her, and decided to give her one more piece of advice. Choosing her words carefully, she said 'Soon Alex will not be content just to fondle your breasts. He may need more.' *Xiao Maque* looked concerned, knowing her limitations. Alice said 'He touched you, now you must touch him.' *Xiao Maque* didn't understand what she meant, so Alice told her as gently as she could, what she could do for Alex, adding 'Alex will help you.'

The next evening Alex took *Xiao Maque* to the flower market in the north of Kowloon, where there were many exotic species for sale. He bought her a pitcher orchid that she could put on the window-ledge by her bed. Nobody had ever bought her flowers before and she was overwhelmed by his kindness. She thought that he was wonderful! As they set off on the following evening to do some shopping, the weather turned wet and windy, so they abandoned the shopping trip and went back to his apartment, where they sat on the balcony with a cold drink and watched the falling rain.

As it grew dark they went inside where Alex immediately lifted her onto the settee beside him. They kissed passionately. *Xiao Maque* remembered Alice's advice, and slowly reached out and placed her hand onto Alex's lap. Alex realised her intentions and helped her to loosen his clothing. He then lifted her gently onto the bed and lay down alongside her. Whilst he stroked her breasts and kissed her, she lowered her hand and fondled him in return. He placed his hand over hers and showed her what he wanted her to do. His breathing became laboured, but soon he stiffened and then lay still. Alex released his hold on her and kissed her gently on the eyelids, then saying 'I love you my own little sparrow. You have made me feel so happy.'

Xiao Maque felt that there was now an even stronger bond between them, and that she was now truly his woman. The loving relationship between them continued as the weeks went by. However, one evening, after they had lain on Alex's bed kissing and cuddling, he slid his hand down to her groin. *Xiao Maque* reacted instantly, grasping his hand and then looking him full in the face with a sad imploring look, whilst slowly shaking her head from side to side. In embarrassment, Alex moved his hand away and they lay there in silence, neither of them knowing what to say.

The next time that *Xiao Maque* met her friend in the hostel, Alice could see from the expression on *Xiao Maque*'s face that something was wrong. Eventually, *Xiao Maque* told her of what had happened between her and Alex, and the sadness that she felt at not being able to allow him to do as he wished. Alice thought for a moment and then took *Xiao Maque*'s hand in hers. 'Alex was not doing anything wrong Little Sparrow, but was just doing as all other men do, in following his instincts in trying to find your private place so that he can demonstrate his love for you. I know that because of your problem you cannot welcome him into this place, but do you not think that there is another such warm, soft, moist place, away from the lower untouchable part of your body, that you can welcome him into?'

Xiao Maque stared at her uncomprehendingly, but then the realisation of what Alice was saying became clear to her, and her face became clouded. 'But isn't that ....' Words failed her so she started again. 'But isn't that unnatural?' Alice gave a long low chuckle. 'My dear, all that takes place between a man and a woman in love is natural': Alice and her husband had had a long and happy sex life.

On the next evening, after she and Alex had sat on the settee in his apartment for a while, *Xiao Maque* slid down onto the floor and then drew herself up between his legs. She slipped down his zip, sought his manhood and, as it emerged, sucked it into her mouth, feeling it stiffen as she did so.

Later, as Alex lay with her in his bed, he told *Xiao Maque* that she fulfilled all of his needs and that he would never want to look at anyone else. He was completely content with this kind, understanding and considerate woman. In the weeks that passed, whenever he thought of her, on the bus, in the office, walking across *Tsim Sha Tsui* to the Star Ferry, or wherever, a smile would cross his face and he would quietly give his thanks to fate for having led their paths to cross. *Xiao Maque* on her part expressed her thanks to Buddha for having brought Alex into her life, and lit candles and incense sticks at the small shrine within the hostel.

However, as time passed, Alex began to have disturbed thoughts that whilst *Xiao Maque* had done so much to ensure his own sexual satisfaction, she had not realised the same pleasure herself, and might be suffering frustration as a result. He eventually raised the matter with her. *Xiao Maque* didn't reply for a whole minute, whilst she tried to find the right words to use. Then she took his hand and said to him in her limited English, the gist of which Alex realised was: 'Alex, my love, with my condition I would not be able to experience the pleasure that other women feel from full sexual contact with their man. There is nothing that can be done about this. However, you have changed my life from one of sadness and loneliness, to one of love and warmth. Every day I spend with you I thank Buddha for having brought you to me. There is nothing that I ask of you other than that you continue to love me, as I will continue to love you, until the day I die, and then beyond. I am completely happy and contented.'

During the following weeks, they spend all of their spare time together, doing simple things and enjoying simple pleasures: eating at the hawker stalls, exploring new shopping areas, visiting weekend markets, or just sitting on the balcony of his apartment. This was all that they wanted. Life was good.

On one of their trips to a weekend market Alex was passing by a stall selling little trinkets and oddments, when he spotted a very tiny spoon: the dished end of the spoon was of such size as to hold nothing bigger than a grain of rice, whilst the handle end was so small that it would have to be held within the fingers rather than to lie in the palm of the hand. *Xiao Maque* explained to him that it was an "ear-spoon", designed for the removal of wax from the ears, and made as if to buy one, but Alex stopped her: 'I had enough of the nurse in the orphanage poking paper clips and hair grips down my ears to last me a lifetime!'

Alex's next trip was to *Guangzhou*, "Canton". Ginger had another commitment, and left this visit entirely in Alex's hands. He travelled by an early train to *Guangzhou* on the KCR, the "*Kowloon*-to-Canton" railway. This was a fast comfortable train, travelling through open countryside, giving Alex clear views of the flat countryside of southern China. The city of *Guangzhou* was huge, the streets filled with such a mass of people that many times he was forced to step off the pavements onto the road, such as on some occasions he had been forced to do on some of the busier streets back in Hong Kong. It was an exciting experience for him to be amongst so many Chinese people, all hurrying about their business.

That evening, as Alex checked into the hotel at the conclusion of a successful day's discussions, he told the girl at the reception desk 'I don't want to take any calls this evening after 11 pm, particularly if they are from young Chinese ladies ringing from the foyer.' The young woman understood his meaning and nodded, the next call that he got in his room being a wake-up call at 7am on the following morning. Alex felt good that he had been loyal to *Xiao Maque*.

Another trip that was required to be undertaken was a one-day visit to the Portuguese colony of Macau, which is just over on the other side of the Pearl River Delta from Hong Kong. Ginger decided that he and Alex should make the trip together, not so much from necessity, but because he wanted to spend more time in Alex's company. They caught an early boat across to Macao, the journey lasting little more than an hour and, with good fortune, their business was completed soon after lunch. In the afternoon they took a taxi to the Chinese border, crossed over, and then took another taxi to the birthplace of *Sun Yat Sen*, the founder of the *Guo2Min2Dang3*, the "People's Party". They soon found *Sun Yat Sen*'s family home, and paid a small admission charge to be able to enter and look around it. The house was well, but not extravagantly, furnished and must have been comfortable to live in.

They then went on in the taxi to a nearby village that was noted for its pig racing. The race track was a short track of perhaps only three or four hundred yards length, which folded back on itself and ended alongside the starting point. Behind the starting gate were a dozen or so pigs, each of them bedecked in racing colours in the form of a band around its middle. Within sight of the pigs, an official tipped a bucket of swill just beyond the finishing line, the presence of the swill causing the pigs to squeal in excitement and to chafe at the starting gate, eager to be off!

After the stakes, all of small denomination, had been laid, the official raised the starting gate and the pigs were off up the track at a mad gallop, rounding the bend and rushing back just as eagerly up the return leg. It was exciting to watch, and Alex and Ginger roared with laughter, which pleased the crowd of locals surrounding them, some of them giving Alex and Ginger big wide smiles and the "thumbs-up!" sign with both hands: lovely, friendly people.

They then returned to Macau, where there was still a little time for them to see some beautiful old Portuguese churches and public buildings. They looked around the old castle, admiring the view from its ramparts, and then it was time to make for the harbour, on the way to which Alex saw an old lady selling items of hand-made lace, buying a small white collar trim that he thought *Xiao Maque* would like.

As the evening boat pulled away from the jetty, Ginger produced a hip-flask of Glenfiddich, which they passed between them. As they relaxed, Ginger said 'Tell me old man, it's none of my business, but are you fixed up yet with a lady friend back in Hong Kong?' Ginger was a great believer in the therapeutic effect of a good roll-on-the-bed with a young woman, and was relieved to hear that Alex had no problems "in that department", although he didn't press him for details.

A satisfied workforce leads to a happy office, with greater productivity and lesser confrontation, so Ginger considered it to be his duty to the company to make inquiries of this nature. They settled to finish off the Glenfiddich, followed by two further rounds of large single-malts of another distillate of similar quality: Scottish of course!

When Alex called for *Xiao Maque* one Sunday he told her that he was going to take her to see the Buddha on *Lantau* Island. They went along to the ferry terminal, where they caught a ferry over to the island, a journey of about an hour. It was a bright sunny day and they thoroughly enjoyed the trip. Then they waited to board a coach to take them for then ten or so miles to the site of the Buddha. Alex lifted her onto the coach and set her down on an aisle seat before folding up her chair and placing it close by the driver.

The other passengers were considerate, one person, with a smile, moving from his seat on the other side of the aisle across from *Xiao Maque* so that Alex could sit close to her during the journey. Similarly, when they arrived at their destination, instead of standing up and crushing forwards to get off the coach as soon as possible, the rest of the passengers held back until Alex had taken the wheelchair off the coach, opened it up, and then carried *Xiao Maque* to it.

The bronze statue of Buddha, *tian tan*, known popularly as "The Big

Buddha", is located at *Po Lin* Monastery, and sits on top of a lotus flower, to rise to more than 111 feet: it is breathtakingly impressive. Alex reached down for *Xiao Maque*'s hand and for two minutes they gazed at the statue in silence. [#32] There is first a 200-step climb to the base of the statue. Alex picked up *Xiao Maque* and carried up the steps, but stopping at each of the several landings to take a rest. *Xiao Maque* was thrilled at his strength, and was delighted at the many expressions of support and encouragement from other visitors making their way to the top: she was immensely proud of him! After they had reached the top of the steps, Alex put *Xiao Maque* down on a bench whilst he went back down to retrieve her wheel chair.

The statue and the base on which the Buddha sits are hollow. They went inside to find a temple in the form of a high-domed room, around the walls of which were religious relics and artefacts of the Buddhist faith. Alex stood to one side whilst *Xiao Maque* made her Buddhist devotions, and then he himself stood forward and did the same. She was both surprised and pleased to see Alex do so, for so far he had not made known to her the strength of his Buddhist convictions. Alex wheeled *Xiao Maque* around the narrow walkway encircling the base of the statue, the two of them enjoying the view over the surrounding countryside. It really is a beautiful place to visit.

Alex paid for two tickets to enable them to take a lunch that was available to visitors at the monastery's vegetarian restaurant. Although he still was not strictly vegetarian, with the passage of time he was slowly abandoning his carnivorous eating habits, apart from eating seafood and sometimes chicken. He had no compunction about eating prawns, sotong, crabs, and other creatures lower in the biological order, but he would never again eat the flesh of the cow or the sheep or of any other warm-blooded creature that suckled and nurtured its young.

They then returned to the coach stop, where the crowd gestured for them to go to the front of the queue. Alex smiled his thanks and said *xie xie*, "Thank you", to everyone they passed, in return receiving smiles and friendly little bows of the head from the kind Buddhist devotees. It had been a fine day out and one that he would long remember.

The next Sunday they took a taxi from the hostel to the highest point of Victoria Island, "The Peak." On their way up to the top they passed many residential areas known as "Levels", these levels becoming increasingly more desirable the higher they are. As they finally approached the peak, they passed the large, spacious, beautiful houses and gardens of the rich and privileged, a far cry from some of the overcrowded tenement blocks down below them at Central, and across in Kowloon and beyond. As luck had it, the Peak was clear of the mist that often clouds it. They sat on a bench and admired the panoramic view, not only of the island itself, but also of *Kowloon* and some of the offshore islands. They heard the Noon-day Gun.[33]

After this they took another taxi to Aberdeen, where they saw the many moored sampans on which families spent their whole lives. They took a small ferry out to the "Jumbo Floating Restaurant" moored just a few hundred yards offshore. This large boat is given over almost entirely to dining areas, where families and groups of friends can sit together at large tables. It was a noisy friendly place, where everyone seemed to be enjoying the atmosphere, the company and the food. *Xiao Maque* smiled around her at the mixture of locals and tourists.

On previous occasions she had felt a little uncomfortable at being seen out with Alex, as many of the local girls regarded a Westerner, young or old, as a good catch, who would give them a good time, and as a consequence were derided by the older 'respectable' folk. However, she no longer cared who knew her feelings for Alex. She reached across the table and took his hand in hers, to the smiles and the waving of raised hands, with drinks held in them, of the people at the nearby tables. Alex and *Xiao Maque* smiled back happily at them. It had been another lovely day. She had not known that life could be so good.

The weeks passed, Alex and *Xiao Maque* finding increasing pleasure and contentment in each other's company. They spent every evening and all of each weekend together, except for when Ginger required Alex to visit customers who were not available during the week, or for him to complete some urgent paperwork. One Saturday, Alex took *Xiao Maque* along to see the "Noon-day Gun"[33] fired from a compound on the north south of Hong Kong Island, facing across the harbour to *Kowloon*. As noon approached a group of spectators began to assemble, most of whom were Western tourists. An immaculately-attired British naval officer, accompanied by a Chinese seaman, then arrived and unlocked the gate of the compound.

After having made initial preparations for the firing of the field gun, the officer came over to the crowd and invited a middle-aged lady to join him in the firing ceremony. The lady was thrilled, but felt embarrassed and initially demurred. Then, encouraged by her husband, she walked with the officer to the breech of the gun. He told her to take hold of a lanyard connected to the firing mechanism, whilst he consulted his watch to determine the exact moment of noon. Spot on time he gave the lady a sharp command, upon which she gave the lanyard a firm tug.

The noise of the gun was much louder than Alex had expected. Obviously, the gun would not have been loaded with a live round, but with a pad of some kind, such as would offer some, albeit small, resistance to the ejection of the charge and thereby promote its greater consumption. Accompanied by a load explosion, the pad flew out from the muzzle a dozen or so yards into the harbour, to give the spectators a visual, as well as an audible, thrill. The crowd gasped and, as a body, took a step backwards.

Alex experienced a strange new sensation that made his spine tingle. Up to this time he had felt loyalty only to Scotland and had never acknowledged the enforced union of Scotland with England that had been secured only by the death of many Scots, but after this ceremony, carried out in a distant land on behalf of such a small country as Britain, he felt proud not only to be a Scot, but also to be British. *Xiao Maque* had flinched at the unexpectedly loud noise, which had left her ears ringing, but now she grinned with excitement. She reached out and gave Alex's hand a squeeze. She too had been impressed and awed by this simple traditional ceremony.

As they made their way along the road to Central, Alex tried to come to terms with his realisation that he now felt not just Scots, but also British. Perhaps his present feelings were because he was so far away from Scotland. What would Mr. Gilbraith have said of this? However, Mr. Gilbraith had not met Aggie, Luke, Matt, Taffy Evans, George, Ginger or any of the many other good sound British and foreign people that Alex had met and befriended since leaving Scotland. If he had have done so, he would surely have modified his xenophobic attitude.

Alex had come to realise the truth of the old saying: "Travel broadens the mind". There was no way, however, that such a bigoted person as Mr. Gilbraith could ever have had his mind broadened to reduce his hatred of the English: he would not travel beyond Scotland under any circumstances and see the

English as they really are, rather than as the commonly-caricatured arrogant, pompous buffoons as many Scots choose to see them, nor would he enter into the company of an English person without putting up the shutters of his mind and not heeding or even listening to anything that the person might have to say. It is possible that he could have found kindred spirits amongst some of the few Welsh and Irish extremists in a common resentment of the English; but his general acceptance of any non-Scot was unlikely.

The reality was that he would live the rest of his life poisoning the minds of his young pupils, and spreading his evil street-corner messages in the company of fellow misfits, and then die as an unreasoning, inflexible, intolerant and bitter old man, whose death would be no loss to Scotland.

The next weekend Alex took *Xiao Maque* on the bus to Taipo Market up towards the top of the New Territories. On their way out of Kowloon, high up on a mountainside, Alex saw the Lion Rock, a great craggy rock that resembles the head of a lion, and pointed it out to *Xiao Maque*, who was excited to see it, having heard of it from others in the hostel. Further along on the journey they looked to the right of the road, where in a prominent position on the mountainside is a column of rock in the shape of a woman with a child on her back. The folk-lore is that the woman is looking out for her husband, a sailor away on the sea, and has waited patiently for many centuries for his safe return, but to no avail. This time Alex's explanation brought a cloud of dismay to *Xiao Maque*'s face.

He was immediately sorry that he had caused this sensitive little person unhappiness, and quickly made up the untruth that the local people believe that before many years have passed the husband will return and then the figure and the husband will sink slowly from sight into the surrounding rock, the family then being reunited forever. She brightened at this, but Alex realised that he must be careful as to what he told her in the future. He took her hand, saying 'Just as you and I will stay together forever.' At these words, she beamed with delight and leaned against his shoulder, happy and contented again.

Not only was *Xiao Maque* very superstitious, just as are many

Chinese, she also had a great knowledge of Chinese mythology. When passing a Chinese craft shop one day she pointed out to Alex a painting of the *Ba1 Xian1*, the "Eight Immortals" [#34] of Chinese mythology, a band of seven men and one woman who roamed ancient China, righting wrong and protecting the weak and the down-trodden. However, 'mythology' is not quite the correct description, as some of the immortals are based on men of wisdom and influence who lived many years ago, as far back as the seventh century, albeit that with the passage of time they have been credited with the possession of incredible skills and with the execution of miraculous feats. Yetts many years ago made a scholarly study of the ancient literature relating to the Ba Xian [21:1]; this topic also having been researched by Margaret Medley.[21:2] *Xiao Maque* said that the mythology relating to the feats of the immortals is a way of passing over Daoist teachings to the illiterate and simple peasant folk of China, but it was clear that she herself gave great credence to their reported feats.

To this day, simple illustrated booklets, rather in the same form as children's comics in the West, relating to the adventures of the *Ba Xian*, are popular reading material in the East. In a way, the Eight Immortals are similar to "Robin Hood", whose reputed activities within Sherwood Forest and his legendary battles with the Sheriff of Nottingham, on behalf of the poor and the unjustly-treated, provide great entertainment value for the peoples of the West, but have a lesser moral message, apart from that of showing that those treating the poor unjustly will be brought to task. It is said that the Eight Immortals, whilst of Daoist origin, were also used in the past to promote the teachings of Confucius.

[21:1] "The Eight Immortals" by W. Percival Yetts, published in Journal of the Royal Society of Great Britain and Ireland, 1916, Chapter XXI, p.773; also available at <http://www.sacred-texts.com/journals/jras/1916-21.htm>.

[21:2] Margaret Medley, in her book "A handbook of Chinese Art", published by Harper and Row, ISBN 0-0643-0044-7, describes in simple terms the known history and the characteristics of the eight individual immortals, whose names are: *Li Tieguo*; *Zhongli Quan*; *Lan Cai*; *HeZhang GuoLao*; *He XianGu* (the woman of the group, who is believed to have lived in the 7th century); *Lu DongBin*; *Han XiangZi*; and *Cao GuoJiu*.

In the craft shop were several other statues of various gods held in high regard by many Chinese. *Xiao Maque* was very keen to advise Alex of the importance of the "Kitchen God", whose purpose is to watch over the household, in particular the kitchen, In the craft shop were several other statues of various gods held in high regard by many Chinese. *Xiao Maque* was very keen to advise Alex of the importance of the "Kitchen God", whose purpose is to watch over the household, in particular the kitchen, and report to the "Jade Emperor", the King of the Universe, on the 24th day of the last lunar month, on the behaviour of the inhabitants of the house, mainly that of the wife - in wasting money and food! - during the past year. To improve their chances of the report being favourable, some households will brush the lips of the kitchen god with honey or a sugar solution so that only 'sweet' things will be said about them. Other families leave out sticky buns for the kitchen god to eat, so that his teeth will be clogged by the buns and he will not be able to say anything untoward about them, or to leave out a glass of sweet wine, in the hope of securing the same effect. *Xiao Maque* was a fervent adherer to these old beliefs, so Alex was careful not to say or do anything that might ring of scepticism or sarcasm.

Taipo Market, just a short distance from the Chinese border, is a bustling market town, with crowded streets, a thriving wet market, and many busy shops and eating places, but too far out from Kowloon to encourage many tourists. Indeed, Alex was the only *ang mo*, "red head", Westerner, to be seen, which gave *Xiao Maque* a feeling of being special. She had him push her up and down the rows of stalls in the market, calling for him to stop at frequent intervals so that she could check the freshness of the vegetables and the ripeness of the fruit. When she made a purchase she haggled with the stall-owner until they were both satisfied that a satisfactory deal had been made.

Alex began to feel like a chauffeur or a taxi driver, in that he played no part in the purchasing, but simply followed her instructions. However, he was pleased to see *Xiao Maque* so confident and enthusiastic that he didn't say a word, but just smiled and carried on. After their shopping, they stopped at a small food stall, where *Xiao Maque* made a great fuss of selecting from the dishes on offer. Although Alex was by now quite familiar with Chinese food, even that particular to Hong Kong, he was prepared to stand back and let *Xiao Maque* do the ordering, as it clearly gave her much pleasure to 'mother' him in this way and to show off her knowledge: this was one situation when she was in charge.

Following their meal, they made their way to the railway museum built alongside the track of the KCR, the Kowloon-to-Canton Railway. This is a great coll9ection of engines, rolling stock and miscellaneous items from the early days of the railway. Alex couldn't understand why it was located so far out of Kowloon, but *Xiao Maque* said 'You want the museum at *Kowloon*, perhaps the Chinese want the museum at *Guangzhou*, so maybe the museum is best mid-way between the two at *Taipo*.'

Their visits out at weekend continued. One day they caught a bus to *Shatin* and then a second bus for a forty minute ride to *Fan Ling*, where *Xiao Maque* had told him was the "Ghurkha Market". This was held once a week on a field alongside a large base where Ghurkha troops were housed. A large hut within the base, presumably where the troops took their own meals, was put at the disposal of visitors to the market, where they could buy a range of good, local meals at a modest price. This outdoor market seemed to cater primarily for expatriates, and sold children's clothes, leather goods, soft furnishings, Indian-made ornaments in copper and brass, flowers and plants, and locally-grown vegetables. *Xiao Maque* was delighted with it.

One Sunday they again caught a bus to *Shatin*, and then, after this, a second bus to *Xi Kong*, a fishing village over to the east of the New Territories. The bus passed through many tiny villages and by many fields filled with a variety of crops. Some visitors associate Hong Kong only with the crowded streets of Victoria Island or Kowloon, but there are vast areas of open countryside and steep mountains in the New Territories without signs of human habitation. When they reached *Xi Kong* they made their way along the road alongside the sea wall, on the seaward side of which were tied up many boats: trawlers, netters and long-liners; whist on the landward side was an almost continuous run of business premises given over to the sale of fish, with a great display of exotic fish set out on counters in front of them, most of the fish swimming vigorously in big tanks into which air was bubbling.

Many of these shops must have been for purchases within the trade, and not just for immediate sales to passers-by, in view of the great quantities of fish on display. Apart from fish, there were octopus, lobsters, prawns and many varieties of shell fish. The whole scene was one of bustling activity. Alex became nostalgic, remembering his days on the Firth of Clyde, although most of the varieties of fish on display were unknown to him and certainly hadn't ever been brought aboard the Westering Home.

They left the front road and made their way along some of the quieter back streets. Here were businesses supporting the fishing industry: engine repairers, ships' chandlers, outboard-motor sales, communication and navigation equipment, nets and fishing tackle. The town of *Xi Kong* was flourishing, lively and self-contained. Alex was impressed.

Before they left, they ate a meal at one of the big seafood restaurants set amongst the premises of the fish traders and overlooking the sea. Although a Buddhist, *Xiao Maque* would eat fish from time-to-time. They gave their order to the waiter, who invited them to go outside and choose which of the fish within the different tanks that they wanted to eat. *Xiao Maque* became quite bothered, selecting one fish and then another, changing her mind because she thought that the fish that she had chosen had looked at her imploringly, or because it had looked sad. Eventually, Alex wheeled her over to their table and left her there, whilst he made the selection on his own. It wasn't that she objected to eating fish, but like many other fish eaters, she preferred her fish to be in the form of gutted and cleaned pieces, rather than having to face them as living creatures.

Alex remembered one occasion on the Firth of Clyde when he had caught about a hundred mackerel to give to the regulars in the Puffer and had taken them onto the shore to head, gut and tail. A couple had come along to see what he was doing, the wife emitting squeals of horror as he removed the heads, entrails and tails of the fish in rapid succession. However, after he had washed the blood from the fish in the sea, and then packed them neatly into plastic bags, the wife 'recognised' the mackerel as being the same as the fish that she bought in the local fish shop, and asked him 'Can I buy a bag from you?', upon which he had given her a bag, with his compliments.

It had been a great day out. Having a half-hour to spare before the bus was due to depart for *Shatin*, they walked through the streets at the far end of the town, eventually coming to a large square, along one side of which was a run of shops. They stopped at a tea shop with tables set out in front of it. Alex went in to order a pot of tea, and was surprised to find that the proprietors were a couple from England, and even more surprised to see that in addition to Chinese *baolzi*, "dumplings", which are made from flat disks of pastry topped with cooked meat or vegetables, drawn up into almost spherical shape with the edge crimped together to seal them, then steamed; and other Chinese foods of the region such as *dim sum*; they had on display traditional Cornish pasties and pies.

The tea shop also had a range of cakes, including vanilla slices, which had always been his favourite. He bought four vanilla slices that the assistant put into a box for him: these would be a treat for Ginger and himself to enjoy with their coffee on Monday morning. Alex surmised that these Western specialities were to satisfy the demands of Hong Kong expatriates on trips out to this area.

On the bus back to *Shatin*, *Xiao Maque* leant her head against his shoulder and hummed quietly to herself, clearly feeling very contented. Alex felt his love for her swelling up. He hated having to drop her off at the hostel each evening, and would much rather have had her spend the night with him in his bed, but she always refused. He knew that this was related to her problem, which he had now learnt a little about, and he didn't press the matter for fear of embarrassing her. He loved her so much that the prospect of having to assist her held no distaste for him, and he hoped that in the course of time she would come to realise this. However, *Xiao Maque* had already thought on the matter. She knew that Alex would willingly help her with her problems, but she also knew that romance didn't flourish and blossom under such conditions. No, better that she continue to stay at the hostel, at least for the time being.

As the bus left *Shatin* to take them back to *Kowloon*, *Xiao Maque* peered through the windows of the bus attentively, as though looking out for something. Alex noticed and questioned her. She explained that somewhere high on a mountain top above the tiny village of *Shatin Pai Tau* was "The Temple of The Thousand Buddhas". Many of her Buddhist friends had made a visit to the temple, and had told her about it, but she knew that she herself would never be able to make such a visit, as it required the climbing of many hundred of steps to reach the temple. She had been hoping that she might at least just catch sight of it. Alex felt sad for her, but didn't see what he could do to help. Although *Xiao Maque* weighed very little and he could easily have carried her up to the temple either on his back or in his arms, he was reluctant to suggest this because of the embarrassment that this might cause her: it was one thing to carry her up a few dozen steps to see the Big Buddha, and another to carry her up to the top of a mountain. Still, he would put his mind to the matter and see what he could come up with.

Alex continued to enjoy his work. Ginger was an easy man to work for and placed complete trust in him. This suited both of them, as Alex by now had a complete grasp of the company's business and Ginger was relieved to be able to hand over some of the responsibility. They would meet for half an hour or so each morning, but apart from that they got on with their jobs without needing to consult each other. Ginger had learnt of *Xiao Maque* from one of the clerical officers, who had seen Alex wheeling her along the promenade at *Tsimshatsui*, their animated conversation and smiling faces making clear the depth of their affection for each other. Ginger was pleased that Alex had found someone to spend his free time with.

One Saturday afternoon, after Alex and *Xiao Maque* had been to Happy Valley racecourse, and had been lucky in placing their bets, they celebrated their minor winnings by calling in for a drink at a nearby bar. Alex wheeled *Xiao Maque* to a table in a quiet corner and went to the bar to order their drinks. A group of men in seamen's clothing were standing at the bar, and he could not help but overhear their conversation, which was a general grumble about life at sea. One of the men, a big chap with a beer belly, was criticising his skipper for having reprimanded him for having been found drinking whisky whilst on duty. As Alex returned to the table where *Xiao Maque* was sitting he heard the man say 'So I told the old man, a couple of glasses doesn't do me any harm, but the old bugger sent me off-shift and told me he would dock my pay.'

The man began to work himself up into a rage, whilst his companions tried to calm him down. They ordered him a double whisky followed by a beer chaser, which seemed at first to have some effect in taking his mind off his problem, but then he said in a loud belligerent voice that he whole room could hear 'Sod the old fool! No man tells me what to do!' Alex was well used to drunks from his Govan days, but he was uncomfortable with *Xiao Maque* sitting next to him. The man saw Alex looking at him, and called across 'What's up with you, you nosy sod?' Alex held back his anger, whilst at the same time the seaman's companions remonstrated with him.

The barman warned him that if he said another word he would have to leave the premises. The seaman turned to his companions, and said a few words quietly to them and then roared with laughter. He seemed pleased with himself and repeated his words, but this time loud enough for Alex to hear. 'Aye, it's on the level, take my word for it!' The seaman's companions tried to shut him up, but without success. 'Aye, it's on the level. Take the word of one who knows!'

Alex stiffened in his seat, knowing full well the insult of the man's words. He got up and walked across to the man, and then standing square in front of him said 'I didn't quite catch what you said. Please repeat it for me.' The seaman just laughed and started to turn towards his friends, but Alex caught his arm and repeated his question. The seaman stopped his movement, and then grinned at Alex. 'Why don't you get yourself a proper woman instead of that Chinese cripple?'

The room fell silent. The seaman, standing six inches over Alex and weighing some five stone more than him, leered evilly, whilst his companions tried to get him to come to his senses.

Alex didn't move. After a few seconds the seaman said 'Well what are you going to do about it?' Despite the years that had passed since his time in Govan, Alex reacted instinctively. He smashed a blow into the man's face, then as the man reeled back against the bar he delivered a second blow to the man's solar plexus. The man started to double up and, as his head dropped down, Alex brought his knee up under the man's chin. The seaman once again reeled back against the bar, but Alex hadn't yet finished.

He took careful aim and then delivered a kick to the man's groin. The seaman's companions grabbed Alex's arms and told him that the man had had enough, but adding that he had deserved what he had got. As the seaman slumped to the floor, the barman said to Alex 'If he makes any trouble for you mate, just let me know. I saw how he started things and I'll speak up for you.' Alex turned and walked back to *Xiao Maque*. He had feared that she would be ashamed of him for his having fought with the seaman, but instead, although pale and a little shaken, she was pleased with him and immensely proud. Never before had she had anyone to look after her. When they reached the door of the bar on their way out, she stopped the wheelchair, turned it around, and then said in a loud clear voice, for all to hear 'You all see what happen. Better nobody mess about with my man!'

She smiled up at Alex as he wheeled her along, absolutely thrilled with him. Alex was pleased that *Xiao Maque* had taken the encounter in such good part, as he would have expected her to find his behaviour unacceptable in view of her Buddhist beliefs. However, he was troubled by his own immediate reaction to the seaman's insults. Had he not left violence behind him when he left Govan, in favour of responding to any transgressions against him with acceptance and forgiveness?

The more he thought about it the more confused he became. During the Sino-Japanese War, and during World War II, many thousands of Chinese and Japanese Buddhists had fought and killed each other despite their common belief in the sanctity of life. He wondered how these soldiers had been able to come to terms with their daily acts of what, before taking part in war, they would have described as acts of inhumanity. Are there some situations when a man has to react primarily to his instincts and emotions rather than to do what he has been taught is good and proper? Alex knew that he would never be able to stand by and see the gentle woman that he loved insulted or ill-treated, irrespective of the outcome. He knew that despite any efforts he might make, he would never be able to attain the Buddhist's desired state of Nirvana, where a person sees the world clearly and is no longer troubled by emotional conflict. Where *Xiao Maque* was concerned he would go to any length to ensure her happiness and safety.

Later that evening Alex took *Xiao Maque* back to his apartment at *Shatin*. As they sat together on the settee she asked him 'Alex, were you not afraid of that big sailor man today?' She then used a Chinese idiom: 'He *zhang1 ya2 wu3 zhao3* ', "bare fangs and brandish claws", meaning that he had made threatening gestures. Alex took *Xiao Maque* 's hand and told her gently that he had been very angry by the man's remarks and behaviour and hadn't had time to become afraid. After a few moments, looking apprehensive, she asked 'I know the word "cripple", but what did he mean when he said "on the level" and laughed?'

Alex though for a short while before replying. 'Little love, you know that, down below, all woman have a *yin3dao4*, "concealed path", and that the lips at the entrance to this path run just a short way from the front of the woman towards the back?' *Xiao Maque* nodded slowly, but kept her eyes firmly on his face, intrigued, but uneasy, as to what he was going to say next. 'Well some bad men say that with Chinese woman the lips run "on the level", meaning from one side to the other, instead of from the front to the back.'

Xiao Maque stared at him incredulously. 'That man is stupid! No such thing!' Alex took her hand and said 'I know that, and so does that seaman, but he was trying to be insulting towards Chinese ladies. That's why I struck him. I wouldn't let any man insult you, because I love you so much.' She gave him a beaming smile. 'And I love you too Alex. You are my man sitting on horse in shiny tin suit!' Alex knew what she meant. Later, he rang the matron at the hostel and told her that *Xiao*

Maque would be staying over in his apartment with him. The matron had been expecting this situation to arise for some time and expressed her concern: 'You know about *Xiao Maque*'s problem. I hope that you understand and respect what this means.'

Alex reassured her that he did and wouldn't do anything that would cause *Xiao Maque* embarrassment or distress. That night he and *Xiao Maque* lay together in bed in each other's arms. Soon she fell asleep, whilst Alex lay awake and listened to her gentle breathing. He felt happy and contented and realised that he and *Xiao Maque* belonged together. He came to a decision: he would ask her to marry him and come and live with him in his apartment, but first he would check with the doctor who visited the hostel that this would not present any problems. He could take her back to the hostel for any continuing medical attention that she might require, and he would hire a maid to clean the apartment and do any little jobs around the place that needed attention. In the meantime, he wouldn't put too much pressure on her. For the time being she could stay at the hostel during the week, from which it was fairly easy for her to wheel herself along to her pitch each morning, but she would stay over with him on Saturday night.

A week later, as Alex walked along to the bus depot at *Shatin* in the morning, he saw a group of Chinese who appeared to be making their way towards the foot of the mountain on which "The Temple of Ten Thousand Buddhas" sits. Some of them were pushing wheelchairs in which sat presumably infirm family members, whilst others were carrying what seemed to be small sedan chairs, these comprising a cut-down wooden seat mounted on two horizontal poles. He hurried to catch up with them. The group eventually reached a flight of steps at the foot of the mountain, where they transferred the infirm folk to the sedan chairs and then chained their wheelchairs to some nearby railings. They were obviously intending to carry their infirm charges up to the top of the mountain so that they could make their religious observances within the temple.

He walked across to one man who seemed to be the leader of the group. The man was not able to speak Mandarin, but fortunately had a good grasp of English. Alex told him that a friend of his, *Xiao Maque*, had a strong desire to visit the temple, but was unable to do so because of her physical condition. The man listened carefully, and then said 'Bring your friend here on Saturday afternoon at two o'clock.'

When Saturday arrived Alex met *Xiao Maque* at the hostel at noon for lunch. He didn't mention his meeting with the group, but simply told her that he wanted to take her out to *Shatin* to explore a lovely tiny old village, *Shatin Pai Tau*, that he had come across not far from the bus station. She agreed readily. By the time that they got to *Shatin* it was just after one o'clock. She was thrilled with the village which, whilst little more than a string of houses lying along a small stream surrounded by grass and undergrowth, was indeed beautiful. In some of the small gardens in front of the houses ornamental ponds had been built, in which swam huge coy carp.

Towards the end of the village there was a track leading to a small cleared area where there was a tiny provision shop with tables outside for the locals to sit at and drink the popular local beer, "blue lady". A little further on the track divided, a small track going to the left, whilst a larger track to the right led to the bottom of the steps up to the Temple of the One Thousand Buddhas. Those who had laid the steps must have decided, wisely, against a direct frontal assault on the mountain, in view of the severity of the incline, so the steps rose up around the side of the mountain, at no point becoming so severe as to deter visitors from making the climb up to the temple.

At the point where the track divided was a small hawker stall. Mounted in a table were two big cauldrons, one containing hot water for boiling *bai tai* and the other for boiling *wonton*. From time to time, the locals would come along and make an order, then picking up a pair of chopsticks from a container and plunging them into the boiling water of the cauldrons to sterilise them, whilst the proprietor dropped more *bai tai* and *wonton* into their respective cauldrons. Everything was cooked fresh and served hot.

They sat at one of the tables to eat their *wonton* soup and *bai tai*, Alex ordering a large bottle of "Blue Lady" beer, whilst *Xiao*

Maque ordered a bottle of *qi4shui3*, "gassy water" the name for soft drinks. Not seeing many expatriates in *Shatin*, and certainly extremely few in their tiny village, the locals showed a keen interest in Alex, smiling and expressing friendly remarks to him in somewhat limited English, being delighted when he responded to them in Mandarin. Others of the locals just gave Alex the international "thumbs up!" sign of friendship.

Just as they finished their drinks, the group arrived and the leader made his way over to Alex, who introduced him to *Xiao Maque* and told her of the kind invitation of the group for them to join them in their ascent of the mountain. She was delighted but apprehensive, and wheeled herself across to the others sitting in wheelchairs, being pleased to find that one of them was a young woman of about her own age, whom she learned was named Euphemia.

The group then pushed the wheelchairs over to the foot of the steps, helped their occupants into the sedan chairs, and then locked up the wheelchairs, *Xiao Maque*'s included, to the railings, as Alex had seen them do on the previous occasion. As the group moved forwards onto the steps, there was a lot of wobbling of the sedan chairs and much mock-fearful shrieking from the occupants, accompanied by laughter from the rest of the party. *Xiao Maque*'s face was radiant with excitement.

As they got further up the steps, at every bend she called out to her new young acquaintance 'Euphy, look at that lovely bird! Euphy, can you see the lizard in that tree?', not wanting her to miss anything. Euphemia too was finding the climb exhilarating and responded in like manner to *Xiao Maque* from her place in the 'caravan train' immediately behind her.

Before long they had left behind a couple of other eating places, a shop selling Buddhist artefacts, and the last of the houses and gardens set alongside the steps, which latter were twisting and turning to accommodate the contours of the mountain. The party was soon climbing past cultivated fields, the houses left far behind. By this time the bearers were beginning to get tired, so they pulled to the side of the steps and stopped for a break and to let others pass by.

They continued in this way for the rest of the climb, taking two further stops for a rest. Eventually the dining hall at the edge of the large terrace where the temple sits came into view, which inspired the bearers to a final burst of energy. As they reached the terrace the bearers dropped the sedan chairs unceremoniously, then slumped down onto some adjacent benches, one speaking for the rest: 'Made it!'

After a few minutes the party revived, and made their way into the dining hall. All around over the terrace were enormous carved and painted animal-like figures, but not really resembling actual animals, being more like the mythological beasts that Alex had seen back in Singapore at the *Haw Par* Villa.

After having had a drink, the group carried the sedan chairs over towards the temple itself, where through its open doors the ten-thousand small images of Buddha could be seen in row-after-row around the walls. At the entrance to the temple, a warrior-like figure, perhaps of fifteen feet height, was standing, protected from the environment within a great glass case. Other similar figures were standing around the walls. Alex lifted *Xiao Maque* from out of her chair and then gently took her into the temple and placed her onto a cushion on the floor in front of a figure of Buddha, from where she made her observances. After this he carried her around various other buildings, all devoted to Buddhism.

Finally, the group re-assembled for the long walk down the steps. They sang companionable songs as they made their way down. *Xiao Maque* had never had such an exciting day-out before. When they reached the foot of the steps she called the group over and thanked them for their kindness, in particular thanking Euphemia for her friendliness towards her. They made arrangements to meet again on the next Buddhist festival, when they would ascent the mountain and visit the temple once again.

As they lay in bed together that night, *Xiao Maque* thanked Alex for his part in giving her such a memorable day. She started to talk about what she knew of her earlier life, which amounted to little more than having been dumped on the doorstep of the hostel at about six months of age, with only the clothes that she was wearing. Her mother must have been desperate as to how she would be able to cope with a crippled and diseased baby. For the first few weeks the baby had sat in her cot in the hostel, silent and uncommunicative, her eyes wide and fearful. One of the staff said that she looked like a frightened little baby sparrow, and the name had stuck: "Little Sparrow."

In return, Alex told her of what he knew of his own early life, which also amounted to very little. He told her that he had been born as a result of a brief liaison between his mother and an American soldier whilst her husband had been overseas on active service. His mother had died soon after he was born, whilst her husband had been killed in action. As for the American soldier, he knew nothing.

Xiao Maque hugged him to her. They had both started off in the same way, knowing a mother's love for only a very short time. Thereafter they had no-one of their own to love or care for them. She would ask no more of her life than to be able to spend the rest of it with this fine, kind man. She needed nothing more. She snuggled against his chest and then fell asleep.

Chapter Twenty-two

One morning Ginger called Alex into his office and told him that he wanted him to go on an extended trip to China to strengthen contacts that the company had made with some Chinese companies in the import/export trade. Alex was pleased, although it meant that he would not see *Xiao Maque* for quite a few days. However, when he told her of the trip that evening, she simply said 'Work come first Alex, play come second.': *Xiao Maque* had the sensible Chinese attitude to work, unlike many Western women, who when faced with this situation would use it as grounds to sulk and complain, and also as a golden opportunity to extract promises of holidays, presents and other concessions from their husbands.

The trip was to cover: *Bei3jing1*, "northern capital city" (as distinct from *Nan2jing1*, "southern capital city", the former capital city of China); *Haerbin*, pronounced in English as Harbin; and then *Shenyang*; *Qinhuangdao* and *Dalian,* all in the north-east; followed by *Wuhan* and *Chongqing*, two large industrial cities lying on the *Yangtze* river towards the middle of the country.

The journeys involved would be made by train, although many of the journeys would be long and tedious: Alex realised that it would be necessary for him to book a 'soft' bunk rather than the cheaper 'hard' bunk in the trains whenever this was possible.

Ginger handed over to him a folder of papers and asked him to contact the companies concerned and then draw up an itinerary. Making all the arrangements took up a large part of Alex's time over the next two weeks, after which he visited the Chinese embassy to secure the necessary entry visa.

As the date of his departure grew closer, Alex could see that *Xiao Maque* was becoming increasingly unhappy, despite her attempts to conceal her feelings. 'Never mind' he thought, 'when I get back I will ask her to marry me and come and live with me here in the apartment.'

He sat off from *Kowloon* Station for *Beijing* on a Monday morning. The train would not arrive until Tuesday mid-morning, but he found the soft bunk that he had booked for his overnight accommodation warm and comfortable. However, he took great care to put his more valuable belongings safely below his bedding, well away from the occupants of the adjacent bunks: better to be safe than sorry!

The journey dragged on during the day, but was relieved periodically by the arrival of a food-and-drinks trolley under the charge of two young Chinese girls. Alex was impressed by their immaculate tunics and crisp white aprons and head scarves, and by the way that they bowed to the passengers as they made their entrance to the carriages, and again upon leaving.

Upon his arrival at *Beijing* he was met by what he found to be typical: a slim young man, smartly dressed, wearing a big smile, and speaking quite good English. Whatever the isolationist attitude of the Chinese in the past, this generation was outgoing, friendly and eager to make contact. The young man, *Chen Xinghong*, led him to a waiting car, which took them to the offices of *Chen*'s company, where they were met at the entrance by the Manager, Mr. *Qin Zhiliang*. The three of them went up to Mr. *Qin*'s office where he asked his secretary to bring them tea.

Initially, the atmosphere was all smiles but little conversation, as it seemed that Mr.*Qin* did not speak any English, but after a few minutes Alex said to Mr. *Qin* in Mandarin that he was grateful to him for having received him at his company, and that he hoped that their discussions would be of mutual benefit.

Mr. *Qin* was visibly delighted at this and, realising that Alex was a friend of the Chinese, ventured to say a few words in English in return. The meeting was now off and running! After two hours an understanding had been reached as to how the two companies would work together in the future, the formalities to be completed by correspondence between Mr. *Qin* and Ginger.

Mr. *Qin* then asked Mr. *Chen* to take Alex to the hotel that had been booked for him for the night, and told him that *Chen* would collect him later that evening for the three of them to take dinner together. The meeting had been a great success and Alex felt relieved. In the taxi on the way to the hotel he thanked Mr. *Chen* for the part that he had played in helping everything to go so well, but Mr. *Chen* simply said that he had just been doing his job and that it had been a pleasure. Once again Alex marvelled at the politeness and modesty of the Chinese.

Alex had been pleased to hear the *Beijing* people using the retroflex r, in Mandarin *erhua4yin1*, at the end of many words, as he had been told that they did this by his teachers back in Singapore. He couldn't see the reason for using the appendage, but Chen explained that the Beijing people like to use it as it seems 'more friendly' and gives them their own easily-recognised collective identity amongst those of the people of the many other regions of China.

Whilst initially this didn't appear logical to him, he reflected upon the many appendages to sentences that are used extensively in English, to make the speaker sound friendly or to ease the bluntness of direct sentences and questions, "Are you coming then?", and also serve to make clear the place of origin of the speaker,[22:1] "Why aye!" in the North-east of England and "Och aye!" in Scotland being obvious examples.

However, in some cases there is a difference in the meaning of a character when the "r" is added, for example: *tang1* with the first tone means soup or broth; whilst *tangr1*, again with the first tone, refers to the stock that is obtained when meat is cooked that is usually added to the *bai1fan4*, boiled rice, accompanying a meal to give it more flavour; and *bai2mian4* means "flour", whilst *bai2mian4r* means "heroin". A further example of the difference in the addition of the "r" is that in standard Mandarin *yi1dian1dian1* would be used for "a little", but in the Beijing dialect only *yi1 dianr* is required.

Before long he was able to pronounce *yi1dian* as '*yi di-ar*' and *yi1hui* as '*yi hwer*' without the least problem. In reality, he was quite pleased with this accomplishment, as to speak with a *Beijing* accent was considered desirable by the Chinese in Hong Kong and Singapore. He didn't consider it to be the same as if he had started to speak with a home-counties accent in Glasgow, as Chinese wasn't his native tongue and he could not therefore be regarded as selling-out on his heritage.

The restaurant was elegant and traditionally Chinese. A large carving of Buddha in marble stood in the entrance hall, whilst there were ornate statues of *Gwan Yin* and other reincarnations of Buddha set in alcoves in the dining room. There were decorations and scrolls mounted on the walls; and the "double-happiness" character [26] was carved into the back-rests of the chairs. All of the receptionists and the waitresses were dressed in cheongsams, the long vertical slits at the sides of which revealed their beautiful slender legs.

At one time the Manchu were referred to as qi2ren2, "banner people", and the tightly-fitting long dresses or gowns with long slits at the sides that their women wore were called qi2pao2, "banner dresses or gowns", the style becoming very popular in Shanghai in the 1920s. The Shanghainese term for this style of clothing was *zansae*, "long shirt/dress", and when Shanghainese tailors moved down to Canton, Guangzhou, the Cantonese pronounced the name as cheongsam, which then passed into the English Language as a loan-word.

[22:1] Many north-of-England men of working-class origin, including the author, who speak in a formal manner in their professional life, use "aye" instead of "yes", and when amongst friends or family, or fellow northerners, throw in the odd colloquialism or two, either consciously or sub-consciously, to show their feeling of familiarity, and to retain a link with their northern working-class roots. This may be scorned as inverse snobbery, but if so, then so be it … and long may the *Beijing* people retain their distinctive retroflex r!

The head waiter escorted them to their table, where Mr. _Qin_ called for Alex to sit at his side. The napkins of each of the guests had been folded ornately, but Alex's had been folded differently from those of the others, in that the folding had caused the napkin to rise to a much greater height. He realised that this signified that he was being honoured as an important guest.

As the first course of the meal was served, Alex picked up his chopsticks, lying on the table in front of him within a decorated paper sleeve. Whilst removing the sleeve, his attention was taken by the elaborate Chinese character printed on it, although he wasn't sure that the figure could indeed be classed as a proper Chinese character, as it was a composite of a great many, perhaps eight or nine, Chinese characters that he could recognise individually. Mr. _Qin_ noticed Alex's interest and asked him if he knew what the figure represented.

When Alex told him that he didn't, he explained that it was called _biang_, [26] and that _biang-biang mian4_ is the name of a type of thick broad noodle popular in _Sichuan_. However, Mr. _Qin_ told him that it is not a Chinese character, as it cannot be found in any Chinese dictionary, on the grounds that it is not possible for it to be located using the standard procedure of counting strokes. 'Actually,' Mr. _Qin_ said, 'it is a nonsense figure, requiring fifty-seven strokes to be drawn, and is not to be taken seriously.'

Mr. _Qin_ produced a pen and a notebook, and then proceeded to make quick strokes in a firm confident hand, identifying the individual characters set within the figure, then saying 'There is no logical connection between any of these characters, so how can the figure have any sensible meaning? It is just an advertising gimmick, rather in the way that in the West words are deliberately mis-spelt, so that "cream" becomes 'creem' and "telephone" becomes 'telefone' Also, it creates the impression that Chinese characters are ridiculously complex and illogical', to which Alex replied, mischievously, 'whilst in reality they are only **very** complex!' Mr. Qin laughed, and no more was said of _biang_.

Alex then joined in by recalling the character _zhe1_, that he had been made aware of by Mr. _Loo_, composed of the character for dragon, _long2_, written four times, the writing of which requires sixty-four strokes. Mr. _Qin_ smiled, then responding with 'That is so, but that composite, for it is not a character, fell into disuse some five-hundred years ago. There are other such composites, again not proper characters, some of Japanese origin, that can be mentioned, such as _taito_, said to represent a dragon in flight, composed of the character for cloud, _yun2_, written three times, set above the character for dragon, also written three times.'

Mr. *Qin* was warming to his theme. 'Amongst those true Chinese characters, meaning that they can sometimes be found in a dictionary, albeit a Japanese dictionary, the one requiring the greatest number of strokes, eighty-four, has the character for cloud three times, set above the character for dragon, also presented three times. One of the most complex characters found in some Chinese dictionaries requiring the greatest number of strokes, in this case thirty-six, is *nang4*, meaning poor enunciation due to a snuffle.'

Alex bowed his head in the direction of Mr. *Qin* in acknowledgement of his vastly superior knowledge, and then they both broke into smiles, with Mr. *Qin* calling for another bottle of wine to be opened. They had become friends in this intellectual sparring match!

Two young ladies dressed in long period costumes sat on a low platform at the end of the room, one playing an *er4-hu*, a two-stringed instrument played with a bow, as with a violin, whilst the second plucked a *gu3-zheng1*, a multi-stringed instrument rather like a zither, but larger, mounted on a stand set in front of her. The two young ladies then played a melody that Alex recognised, "The sorrow of the lady *Wang Chiu Juen*" and told his dinner companions this.

Mr. *Qin* was highly pleased, and said that it was one of his favourite melodies also. *Xinghong* took Alex to one side and said that Mr. *Qin* was very impressed with him, as in the past he had not trusted Westerners, quoting Mr. *Qin*'s view that they *cang2 tou2 lu4 wei3*, "show the head but hide the tail", meaning that they tell part of the truth but not all of it.

Early next morning, *Xinghong*, as Alex now called Mr. *Chen*, at the latter's request, arrived to take Alex, as arranged, to *tian1an1men2*, "Gate of Heavenly Peace". As they stood in the vastness of the square, Alex recalled television broadcasts that he had seen showing Chairman *Mao Tse-tung* addressing thousands upon thousands of adoring Chinese paying their respects to him in this square.

This great leader had brought the Chinese a long way from a country of cruelty and repression by landlords and warlords, to become the People's Republic of China and, despite making poor judgements towards the end of his reign, he was still revered by a great many of the populace.

After leaving the square, Alex and *Xinghong* walked the short distance to the former "Imperial Palace", or as it is often called, "The Forbidden City".[22:2] This huge complex, an enormous walled city in the

---

[22:2] For those intending to visit the "Imperial City", a DVD "Secrets of the Forbidden

heart of overcrowded *Beijing*, dating from the fourteenth century, covering an area of seven-hundred thousand square metres and containing almost ten thousand edifies of all kinds, had taken between two-hundred thousand and three-hundred thousand workmen fifteen years to complete: a thousand eunuchs had been at the service of the emperor and his family. If ever there was had been a need to overthrow a ruling system, this was it!

He thought it to the great credit of the Chinese leadership that at the overthrow of the dynasties, the last emperor, *Pu Yi*, had been allowed to take up a post as a gardener without having been called upon to pay a price for the excesses of his forebears. Next they went to see *Tian Tan*, the "Temple of Heaven", to which the emperor used to come to pay homage to Heaven, this homage being extended later to paying homage to Heaven and Earth, and then to include the Sun and the Moon.

About halfway along the wide stone-flagged terrace running from north to south over the whole length of the temple grounds, they came to the Circular Mound Altar, which is basically a large mound in the shape of an inverted saucer, over the flat top of which is a pattern of radially-orientated flag-stones, a large stone disk being set at their centre. Alex could see a group of visitors awaiting their turn to stand on the disk.

Xinghong explained to him the legend that a person who stands on this disk and closes his or her eyes in meditation can experience the sensation of actually being at the centre of the universe. Alex took his turn and stood on the disk, then closing his eyes, but the presence of so many other people awaiting their turn prevented him from achieving the required state of meditation, so he resolved to return again at some future time, possibly early in the morning, when there would be fewer people about.

Carrying along to the far end of the terrace, they came to the temple itself, its immaculate appearance belying the fact that it was built as long ago as 1420 AD. A crowd of people were standing at the open door of the temple, held back by a barrier. The inside of the temple was covered in Chinese characters in gold set on a red background and was richly furnished in ornate tapestries. The temple contained great thrones and religious statues. It was awe inspiring, and much as he appreciated the reason why the public was denied admittance to the temple, Alex dearly wished that he could have been able to see these beautiful treasures at close quarters.

City", made by Lion Television for the BBC and The History Channel, is available from www.demanddvd.co.uk, reference DEMDVD078.

Encircling the temple and the paved area immediately surrounding it is the "Echo Wall", brick-built with a tiled capping, of some eleven feet in height. Several people were standing close to the wall speaking messages to their friends standing close to the wall on the diametrically opposite side of the temple, the sound being reputed to be carried with great clarity from one person to the other. Alex had heard that the "Whispering Gallery" in Saint Paul's Cathedral in London is also able to provide this effect.

Xinghong asked Alex if he wanted to visit *Yi He Yuan*, "Garden of Good Health and harmony", also being called "The Summer Palace". Alex knew that this had been looted in 1860 by a combined force of British and French soldiers, who had burnt down many very-old buildings and carried away many precious objects.

Even so many years after the destruction, he didn't like the thought of being associated, as a Westerner, with such an act of vandalism. *Xinghong* smiled and assured him that he would not be called upon personally to face recriminations on that score. Alex, relieved, then agreed to the visit. In particular he was anxious to see the marble boat built there, as he had seen a replica of this boat built in the Chinese garden at Jurong in Singapore.[22:3]

Arriving at the Summer Palace, Alex was astounded by the size of the man-made *Kunming* Lake, the far shores of which seemed to be about half a mile away, if not more. Along the shores of the lake were clusters of *lian2hua1*, "Lotus", resplendent in bloom. They walked along the "Long Corridor" lying along the north shore of the lake, beneath the *Wanshoushan*, "Longevity Hill", its slopes covered with some of the 3000 halls within the grounds of the Summer Palace, the major of which are furnished in the style of the late *Ching* Dynasty. Eventually they reached the Marble Boat, which had been built by the Dowager Empress *Cixi* using funds diverted from the naval coffers. This beautiful structure sat firmly on the bottom of the lake, but looked so elegant that it was easy to imagine that it could sail away at any time.

To rest and cool off, Alex and *Xinghong* sat down on two vacant seats in the shade, with *Xinghong* on Alex's left, whilst on Alex's right a young Chinese woman was sitting. After a few minutes the young woman leaned across Alex and started to ask *Xinghong* questions about

---

[22:3] In the Chinese Garden at Jurong, Singapore, there is a large boat at the edge of the lake, also resting on the bottom, as is the Dowager Empress's boat, but similarly looking as though it is afloat. Although built in concrete rather than in marble and being somewhat smaller, it is nevertheless an impressive representation of the Dowager Empress's boat - and doubtless cost a very small fraction of that of its forerunner!

him in Mandarin: "Where does he come from?", "What is he doing here?", "How old is he?", and so on, until she eventually asked "Is he very rich?", at which point Alex could no longer remain silent. For devilment, he asked the young woman in Mandarin *'bu4 wen4 ta1. ni3 wei4she2nme bu4 wen4 wo3?'*, "Don't ask him. Why don't you ask **me**?", and then went on answer the question that she had addressed to *Xinghong*, using a quaint old Chinese expression: *'wo3 bu4shi4 yi1ge4 fu4weng4'*, "I am not a rich old man!"

The young woman was startled and her eyes opened wide! However, when Alex grinned she realised that he was just teasing her and broke into a beaming smile. The three of them then chatted away happily for about half-an-hour. Time didn't allow Alex and *Xinghong* to walk to the 17-Arch Bridge, but it looked magnificent from across the lake: *Xinghong* said 'Something to be seen close up on your next visit to our company!'

The next morning *Xinghong* arrived early in the morning by taxi to take Alex to see *chang2cheng2*, the "Great Wall". [22:4] There was a lot of traffic on the roads, and it took them the best part of two hours to complete the journey to *Badaling*, which is the closest part of the wall to *Beijing*. The taxi-driver chatted away, at high speed and using the *er* appendage to many of his words, so that Alex could only follow the drift of his conversation with difficulty.

He gathered that the man wanted to take him out that evening to a place he knew where he could "get a beautiful twenty-two year old young lady". The taxi driver then added 'But it will cost him more than for a Chinese man.' At this point Alex entered the conversation with *'mei2guan1xi. sugelan nan2ren2de "yu4jing1" bi3 zhong1guo2 nan2ren2de da4!'*, 'That's alright, Scotsmen's penises are bigger than those of Chinese men!'

Not recalling the correct word for penis, Alex had used the old and well-known Chinese euphemism [#35] *yu4jing1*, "jade stalk", which delighted the taxi driver and *Xinghong*, who both burst into laughter. Alex reflected that there was, however, some truth in his statement, as back in Singapore the condoms sold for Westerners were two centimetres, about four-fifths of an inch, longer than those sold for the local Chinese men. However, he also recalled the stories that had

---

[22:4] An excellent source of information on the history of the Great Wall is the DVD "The Great Wall of China", produced by Lion Television for Discovery Channel in association with Channel Four, available from www.demanddvd.co.uk, reference DEMDVD077.

circulated amongst the lads back in Govan, that the penises of men from the African races are **two inches** longer than those of Westerners! He consoled himself with the thought that the size of the penis is not as important as the confidence, skill and experience of the man standing behind it.

When they arrived at the wall, Alex made his way to the queue for Western visitors whilst *Xinghong* walked to the queue for Chinese visitors. The Western man in front of Ales turned to him and complained about having to pay more than the Chinese, to which Alex replied 'Seeing as millions of their forebears laboured for most of their lives to build the Wall, it seems quite reasonable to me for them to be given a reduced admission charge', whereupon the man glowered and turned away.

They walked up to the Wall, standing a few hundred feet above them. The Wall looked pristine, and gave no indication of having been built some two-thousand two-hundred years ago. Alex recalled what he had learnt of the scavenging of stone from Hadrian's wall by local farmers, who considered that the wall no longer had any purpose, whilst they could use its stone for building the bounding walls of their fields, and he was pleased that the Chinese had instigated a policy of reclaiming any stone that had come from Great Wall, wherever it was found, built into a house or used in any other way.

The Wall was a monumental construction, the large blocks of the wall fitting together with great precision. Alex was thrilled to be walking on a living part of Chinese history. It was a momentous occasion: however, there are many other places providing access to the Wall that merit a visit [36]. Twice a family group asked him to pose with them for a photograph, with which request Alex was pleased to comply. Alex asked how the Chinese had been able to accomplish such an enormous undertaking, to which *Xinghong* replied: *ma3yi3 ken3 gu2 tou2*: "ants knawing at a tree", meaning plodding away at a big job, bit by bit.

Late that afternoon Alex caught the train to Harbin, arriving late the following morning. He found Harbin to be a fine, big, well-laid-out city with wide multi-lane roads, and with large parks set out along a beautiful and impressive fast-flowing river. The buildings were strong and solid, due to the Russian influence in that region in the past. This city is home to the Harbin Institute of Technology, famous throughout China and in the West for the high-quality research that is conducted there to maintain and extend China's progress in science and technology.

That day followed the same pattern, with a very successful meeting and then dinner, but the meal was different in that the main course was "Mongolian Hotpot". This was very like the "Steamboat" that Alex had used to enjoy in Singapore, and he found it delicious. During the meal they drank Chinese tea, which was poured from what looked like a watering can with a very long spout. The waiter would raise the can high into the air before starting to pour, the hot tea emerging from the spout as a three-foot long column before falling without spillage into cups sitting not more than a few inches away from the drinkers' hands: a very impressive performance!

The restaurant was quite busy, and at times the waiters would call *re4shui3!*, "Hot water!", to alert the diners in the immediate vicinity not to move their chairs as they made their way past, laden with dishes. The use of "hot water" in this way reminded Alex of the use of "hot water" in Britain to advise someone that he or she was in trouble: "You're in hot water, take my word for it!"

Whilst the weather at Harbin was quite mild, Alex noted the three-bank radiator in his room and the triple-glazing of the window, which told their own story as to the depths to which the temperature can fall in winter in this region, lying right up at the top of China. He also had heard of the Winter Ice Festival held each year in Harbin, where majestic buildings and finely-detailed statues are carved from large blocks of ice, these blocks having been assembled from more-easily-manageable smaller blocks, and then illuminated to spectacular effect. Because of the low winter temperature, the display can survive for several months.

As he returned to his hotel that evening, he found a wedding party standing outside taking photographs. The bride, a beautiful slim young woman, was wearing a red wedding dress. As soon as he was noticed, Alex was led to where the bride and groom were standing, and set alongside the bride to have his photograph taken with them.

The crowd of family, wedding guests and interested passers-by, watched with interest, a Westerner being an unusual sight for them. For devilment, although he didn't know how well it would be received, he took hold of the bride's hand and assumed the pose of the groom, which cause the crowd to laugh and clap its hands in appreciation. Encouraged by the reaction of the crowd, Alex then leant forwards, looked past the bride to the groom, and inquired of the bride in a loud voice: *ta1 shi4 shui2?*, "Who is that?" Again the crowd was appreciative of his humour. No doubt, within the family, there would be much retelling of this event for years to come.

The father of the bride, who spoke reasonable English, invited Alex to take a drink with the members of his family, seating him near to the maternal grandmother.   Alex asked the old lady how many grandchildren she had, to which she replied *bal*, "eight". The father whispered in an aside to Alex that the old lady, as with many older Chinese people, only counted the number of male children or male grandchildren that she has, even in the presence of her female children and female grandchildren. Alex complimented the old lady on her large number of grandchildren, receiving the reply 'I was born in the year of the dragon, which made me strong and able to bear strong children.' The father went on to say that being born in the year of the dragon is considered so auspicious that many Chinese couples plan the pregnancy of the wife so that their child, hopefully a son, is born at this time, when he would grow up to be strong and be sure of a successful future.

Noting Alex's interest in Chinese culture, he told him that when his own wife had difficulty in conceiving, she prayed at the altar of *Gwan Yin*, who is the patron saint of childless wives and the Goddess of Mercy. When Alex asked him what he knew about *Gwan Yin*'s life, he thought carefully for a few moments, before he gave his response.

'*Gwan Yin* was a wealthy princess who sought enlightenment. She has been identified as the bodhisattva, or Buddhist prophet, Avalokiteshvara. During a long journey to seek the truth from a great teacher, she encountered many poor people of the countryside, to whom, item by item, she gave her riches, fine garments and possessions. When she finally reached the teacher and asked him the purpose of life, he told *Gwan Yin* that her selflessness in giving all of her possessions to the poor whom she had encountered on her search for him had shown that she already knows the purpose of life, which is to help those less fortunate than ourselves.'

Alex thought that this was a lovely story and smiled and voiced his appreciation to the father for having told it to him.   He recalled one of his outings with George and the two young assistants at Chinese New Year, when they had visited the temple to *Gwan Yin* on Waterloo Street, *si4ma3lu4*, "Four Horse Street", in Singapore City, and had watched the hundreds of devotees making their devotions within the temple, with many more who could not gain admittance making their devotions outside on the street. Most of them carried single stems of as-yet-unopened lotus flowers, of a pure sky-blue colour. It had been an impressive and moving experience. George had told him that because of her gentle forgiving nature, upon her becoming known in the West, *Gwan Yin* had been accepted as a representation of the Virgin Mary. She is given the description "The one who hears all the sorrows of the world", and is regarded as not only the patron saint of childless wives, but also the patron saint of sailors and fishermen.

The next place on Alex's itinerary was *Shenyang*, a beautiful large clean impressive city. After another successful meeting and enjoyable dinner, the next day his two hosts took him out several miles out of the city to see the famous *Benxi* Water Caves, which had been formed by an underground river. They walked down a tunnel to a landing stage, and there joined a group boarding a small motor boat, which took them for two or three miles along the river past huge illuminated stalagmites, stalactites and rock faces, each bearing a description as to what it resembled: a dragon, a petrified forest, a lava flow, and so on, the resemblances being remarkable. It was an impressive and novel experience and one that Alex would long remember.

There were many boats on the river. As the boats passed each other their passengers smiled and waved at each other. This reminded Alex of the many similar boat trips that he had seen on the Firth of Clyde. The Chinese were no different than the Scots, in enjoying a good day out in friendly company. Again he realised that if only the ordinary peoples of the world could meet each other free of the prejudices that had been implanted in their minds by the constant brain-washing of the politicians and the media, there would be no problems of world conflict.

Later that afternoon, whilst being taken around a large store by his hosts, Alex came to a stall where a man was cutting sheepskins to make long underpants, and selling them at a very fair price. The stall-holder quickly took Alex's measurements and then told him to return in one hour, when the underpants would be finished. *Shenyang*, like Harbin, must also be a very cold place to be in during the winter months!

The next stop on Alex's trip was *Wuhan*, noted, along with his subsequent destination *Chonqing*, as being one of the three 'furnaces' of China, the temperature during the Summer months staying at around thirty-five degrees Centigrade, with a humidity high in the nineties. Luckily, Alex's arrival did not coincide with a hot spell, and he listened with relief as the local told him, with a strange kind of pride: 'If you had have been here last week, you would have roasted!' *Wuhan* is at the confluence of the *Yangtze* River and the *Han* River, which causes the city to be divided into three towns.

It is known in China as "the homeland of white clouds and yellow cranes". The city is enormous in size, being twenty or more miles across and with nine million inhabitants. Alex found it hard to believe that the population of this one city is about three times that of the whole of Scotland!

The city was vibrant with activity and industry, reflecting the native instinct of the Chinese to work hard and make money. Everywhere there were people employed in businesses of a range of size, from the manufacturers of motorcycles in their thousands, down through their suppliers of components, and on down to the hundreds of small local eating places that fed the enormous workforce. It was a very impressive city! One company was reputed to produce about a million motorcycles each year which, despite being an enormous number, would only provide a motorcycle for one Chinese person in every thirteen hundred!

However, such a level of industrial activity brought with it inevitable pollution A haze hung over *Wuhan* such as Alex had not seen since his early years in Glasgow, but he realised that with the way that *Wuhan* was forging ahead in developing its industries, as were many other cities in China [37], the atmosphere must suffer, as had had to be accepted in the past by the developing West, but he had no doubt that, in the course of time, *Wuhan* would tackle this problem, just as the West had eventually tackled the same problem.

Alex recalled how many well-intentioned people in the West bemoan the environmental damage caused by industrial development in other countries, but ignore that this is virtually inevitable. The industrialisation of Britain had led to the creation of dense and harmful fogs in London and other major cities, and to the loss of salmon and other fish from most of its rivers, both of which problems took two-hundred years to be rectified.

Alex felt that the only acceptable way to avoid further environmental damage in the world is for the rich, developed countries is to give massive support to the undeveloped countries to help them to develop along less ecologically-damaging routes, so that their development will not lead to similar catastrophic results to those that arose in the West. If developed countries do not give such support, the developing countries will exercise their right to do what they themselves think best, pollution or no pollution.

After their business had been completed, Alex's hosts in *Wuhan* took him to visit the the site of the burnt-down "Yellow Crane Tower" [38], which had been one of the three most famous towers in south China, a beautiful five-floor, highly ornamented structure built in timber, with a history of more than 1700 years, overlooking the *Yangtze* River. Although the tower was gone, from what he had been told Alex was filled with admiration for the long-dead designers of this magnificent structure, and for those who had built it, and after it had been burnt down, for those who had then reconstructed it several times, although under what conditions and under what duress they had worked he didn't know. He realised that re-construction work would undoubtedly be carried out at some time in the future, in due course giving pleasure to countless thousands of visitors to this part of China.

Alex had read the famous poem by *Li Bai*, "Seeing off *Meng Haoran* (on his departure) for *Quangling* at Yellow Crane Tower", and could hardly believe his good fortune to be standing at the actual place. He recalled the poem, and then said a couple of lines of it softly to himself, imaging *Li Bai* to be standing at his side as he spoke:

"The lonely sail is a distant shadow, on the edge of a blue emptiness
All I see is the *Yangtze* River flow to the far horizon."

Next his hosts took him to the Hubei Provincial Museum showing the cultural relics that had been discovered when excavating an elaborately sealed tomb in the northwest of Suizhou City, Hubei Province. Inside the tomb were some marvellous items After having lain hidden for many years - from the early period of the Warring States some 2,400 years ago - the relics had been carefully restored and then put on view in the purpose-built museum. The tomb is now known as the *Zeng Hou Yi* Tomb , where the word *Zeng* refers to the kingdom, *Hou* is the title "marquis", and *Yi* is the name of the marquis, whose skeleton was found in the master's coffin within the tomb.

Amongst the main exhibits, the most impressive is the "*Yanghouyi* Chime Bells", regarded as one of the World's wonders, an enormous set of chimes mounted by stout cords within a timber frame of some seven feet in height and ten feet in length. These had been discovered buried within a cave. One of his hosts presented him with a scale model of one of the chimes, cast in metal, as is the original, which emits a clear sharp tone when struck by a small hammer. He was delighted with this beautiful gift.

The next stop on his itinerary was *Chongqing*, which was not very far away from *Wuhan* and also on the *Yangtze* River. Alex noted that the people of *Wuhan* and *Chongching* were on average not as tall as the people that he had met in the far north of China, where many of the locals had towered over him. Similarly, all of those he had met on this northern trip were generally taller and not as heavily built as those back in the south of China. This was similar to the situation in Scotland, where those from the Western Isles are generally two or three inches taller than those from the Glasgow region, Alex included.

By this time Alex had learnt a lot about the thought processes of the Chinese, and knew to allow them time to form their opinions instead of immediately rushing them into detailed considerations. He drank tea at the meeting with the senior staff of the *Chongqing* company, and then joined in with a discussion of the various merits of the different kinds of Chinese tea, telling them of his preference for Lychee Black and *Ti Quan Yin*, the former for a general tea to be drunk during the afternoon, and the latter for a light green tea to be drunk when accompanying a meal.

He told them that since arriving in the Far East he had given up the Western practice of taking *niu1nai3*, "milk", and *tang2*, "sugar", in order to be able to enjoy the pure clean taste of the tea. The others present nodded and smiled their agreement. They could do business with this civilised Westerner!

Later the group relaxed and celebrated their mutually beneficial discussions over a few glasses of *Mao Tai Jiu*, a very strong clear spirit that is served, very sensibly, in minute glasses. Knowing that Alex by now had visited several cities in China, one person asked him what he considered to be the best city in China. Alex didn't know quite what to say, not knowing the city of origin of all of those present, but found a suitably diplomatic response, turning the tables on his hosts by asking them which city they themselves considered to be the best.

After a little thought, the chairman of the company responded with his modified version of a popular Chinese opinion on this matter: 'There are several 'best' places in China: the best place to be born in is *Suzhou*, as it is a beautiful city and the people are also beautiful; the best place to marry in is *Hangzhou*, as this is a city of beautiful silk and beautiful ladies; the best place to eat in is *Guangzhou*; and the best place to die in is *Liuzhou*, as this city has the best wood for coffins'.

That evening at dinner they introduced Alex to what they called the *Chongqing* version of Mongolian Hotpot, where the liquid in the cooking bowl is a mixture of oil and water, as opposed to just water with the Singapore version. Because of the presence of the oil, it is not the practice to drink the contents of the cooking-bowl at the conclusion of the course, as is the case in Singapore. Further, as the liquid in the cooking-bowl is quite hot, as each item is removed from the bowl it is dipped into a small dish of a cold mixture of oil and water before being eaten. Alex found the food cooked in this way quite tasty, but it was too greasy for him: without telling his hosts, he decided that he preferred the less-rich Singapore Steamboat!

The day after the meeting, his host in *Chongqing* drove him by company car about fifty miles north to *Beishan*, *Dazu* county, to see the *Dazu* Rock Carvings. The oldest of these large carvings, set in a grotto within the mountain, had been made some three-thousand years ago, with other carvings being made over the following thousand years [#39].

One of the *Dazu* rock carvings in particular, standing in a niche 1.27 metres high, attracted Alex's admiration: "Avalokitesvara with a rosary", from A.D. 1131-1162. He read the description of her: "She stands gracefully and serenely, with her hands clasped in front of her and with her eyes looking downwards demurely, a gentle smile on her face. There are silk ribbons over her arms, and her skirt is blowing in the breeze. She looks so beautiful that she is known locally as the Charming Goddess of Mercy."

The carvings were divided into the southern and the northern section, the period of the individual carvings being indicated by their style: those of the late Tang Dynasty were dignified and plump; those of the Five Dynasties were small and exquisite; whilst those of the Song Dynasty displayed individuality and graceful postures. Many of the carvings were of Avalokitesvara, *Gwan Yin*, of whom the father of the bride in Harbin had spoken.

Amongst the other niches displaying carvings of Avalokitesvara was a niche 3.56 metres high, dating from A.D. 1116-1122, where Avalokitesvara is seated, solemnly, with six incarnations on each side of her, all wearing heavily-decorated crowns and gowns.

He was surprised to see a niche displaying "The Integration of Three Religions", in which there were Buddhist, Taoist and Confucian statues. He read with pleasure that this shows the social thinking of integration of the three religions underlined by the belief that "Confucius, Lao Zi and the Buddha are all great saints", and that "Confucianism, Taoism and Buddhism all look for the creation of a well-ordered world by punishing evil-doers and encouraging people to do good".

What a magnificent message from the past for the religions and political systems of the present day, where Catholics and Protestants, Jews and Muslims, Fascists and Communists and other opposing factions, fight and kill each other instead of devoting what they can of their short lives to living in peace and building a better world for themselves and for future generations to enjoy living in.

Alex spent several hours wandering from cave to cave, marvelling at the size, age and magnificence of the carvings, and trying to imagine the daily lives of the craftsmen who had spent many years creating such astounding works of devotion. Alex wondered whether these craftsmen would have expected their work to have survived for so long, and how many mistakes they might have made whilst undertaking the carving.

He recalled his visit to Tynemouth Castle with Matt, Aggie and Luke, when he had seen small blocks of 'virgin' stone inset into the gravestones to enable replacement characters to be carved where an error or an accident had occurred during the carving of the original lettering. However, this is life, and mistakes must be rectified as best they can, lest we all descend into an unhealthy obsession with perfection. To quote an expression that is used widely in the Western world: "The man who never made a mistake, never made anything!"

On their way back to *Chongqing* they passed through a small hamlet where a farm building was under construction, one of the workmen being in the process of laying a tiled roof. Alex asked the driver to stop the car for a few minutes, and then went over to speak to the workman. The man was very obliging and showed Alex the simple principles involved. First, long poles are run from the ridge to the eaves, parallel to each other, of such lateral spacing that the simple tiles, having a gentle concavity, lie with their edges on them without falling through. Then, proceeding towards the ridge, each successive row of tiles is set to overlap the previous row, to form a drainage channel for rain. To prevent rain from dropping into the gap between the columns of tiles, identical tiles are inverted and laid in the same manner, to cover the inter-tile space. No nails or other fastening devices are employed.

When Alex queried the absence of nails, the man told him that provided the poles were not set at too-steep an angle, little maintenance is involved, and if an odd few tiles should slide down from time-to-time, it is a simple matter to insert further tiles where required. The simplicity of the method impressed Alex, but he realised that whilst the method is fine for pigsties or log-sheds, it would not be suitable for dwelling places.

As they arrived back in *Chongqing*, Alex asked one last thing of his host, which was to take him to a jewellers' shop. After entering the shop, he told the assistant behind the counter that he wanted to buy an engagement ring for his young lady. Placing a tray of rings before him, she inquired as to the size required. Alex was stumped, but then asked the young woman to let him hold her hand so that he could feel whether her fingers were of the same size as those of *Xiao Maque*.

This caused all the other lady assistants in the shop to raise their hands to their faces to hide their smiles: it is not the practice in China to let strange young men hold your hand! However, when he found the hand of this particular lady to be too big, he called the other assistants over so that he could hold their hands in turn.

Finally, it was the turn of the junior assistant, a young girl of about eighteen who, whilst giggling with embarrassment, extended her hand. Alex smiled as he held her hand and found it to be exactly like that of *Xiao Maque*. He bought a gold ring surmounted by three small, but unflawed, diamonds. After his host had negotiated a good price, Alex bought the ring, and then they drove back to the hotel for Alex's last dinner of his visit to China.

Alex had enjoyed his trip immensely. He reflected on what he has seen in his few days in China and on the kindness and friendliness that he had encountered. He wished that more Westerners would visit China, to see its wondrous ancient treasures, to experience its different cultures, to enjoy its wide range of food and to meet its fine people.

On the following day; Alex couldn't settle on the train back to Hong Kong. The hours passed unbelievably slowly. He had hoped that there would be a train to get him back in the early evening, so that he could go straight over to the hostel to see *Xiao Maque*, but as luck had it, the only train that he could get didn't arrive until 10.40pm. He tried to pass the time sorting through the notes that he had taken of the different discussions that he had had, but soon gave it up, as he couldn't concentrate for more than a few minutes without his thoughts turning to *Xiao Maque*.

Eventually the train arrived in Kowloon, more than twenty minutes late, which put paid to the thoughts that had been growing in his mind about making his way to the hostel immediately, instead of waiting for the morning. The first thing in morning he caught an early bus into Kowloon and then went straight over to the island on the Star Ferry, then taking a taxi to the hostel. As he went into the hostel, the matron, who had been looking out for him, caught sight of him through the open door of her office and beckoned him in, then asking him to take a seat. Alex was alarmed, sensing that he was about to be told something ominous about *Xiao Maque*'s condition.

'I am pleased I caught you Alex', she said, 'I want to talk to you about *Xiao Maque*. She hasn't been well for the last few days and needs to take things easy. Take her out by all means, but please don't let her get over-tired or over-excited.' Alex was alarmed at the matron's words. As he waited for *Xiao Maque* to be brought down from the her room, he decided that it would be best if he didn't show her the ring at this time, but wait until she was in better health. After a couple of minutes her friend Alice brought *Xiao Maque* down and then, after a few pleasant words with Alex, left the two of them together. He could see from her pallor and the strained look on her face that *Xiao Maque* wasn't well, but he didn't draw attention to this, greeting her warmly and giving her a kiss.

Xiao Maque asked him how his trip had been, but it was obvious that she hadn't the energy to absorb a full account, so he just gave her brief details. Luckily, he had already bought some presents for her before his last-minute purchase of the ring. She was pleased with the main present, a carved jade broach in the form of a dragon, and had him pin it onto her cardigan. He had known that most Chinese set great store by the folk-lore associated with such objects. Whilst away up in

China he had seen for sale some hand-sewn bags made from soft leather and he had bought one just big enough for the few items that she liked to have with her. The bag had a handle long enough be attached to the handle of her wheel chair. Finally, he gave her a colourful quilted rug that she could put on her bed, or put over her legs when in her wheel chair.

Even though she was very weak, she was overjoyed. She had had very few gifts in her life, and to receive so many lovely things at one time was overwhelming. The conversation between them was strained. He was desperate to ask her what was wrong with her, but he knew that this would upset her, so he just kept his words to trivialities, whilst she felt that she should talk about her present ill-health, but hadn't the energy to do so. Alex would have liked to stay with her longer, but her hands were shaking and there was perspiration on her brow. He told her that he should be getting to work, and that he would see her that evening.

Ginger was delighted to hear from Alex how the trip had gone, saying to him 'If this new business goes through, and I can't see why it shouldn't, we will need to take on one or two new staff members.' He brought Alex up to date on the happenings during his absence, and discussed a couple of minor problems. He looked questioningly at Alex, who had been unusually silent and pre-occupied. 'Is there something wrong old man? You don't seem your usual self.'

Alex told him about *Xiao Maque*'s ill-health. Ginger was concerned and told him to go over to the hostel straight away. As he arrived at the hostel, Alex saw that the doctor was on the point of leaving after having made his weekly visit and asked if he could have a word with him. The doctor took him into the matron's office, shut the door and then invited him to sit down. The serious expression on his face forewarned Alex that he was in for some unpleasant news.

The doctor came straight to the point, repeating what the matron had said earlier that day, but adding 'You will know that *Xiao Maque* has never been in good health. Of late her condition has deteriorated and she is now suffering from diseased kidneys. We are doing what we can, but her long-term prospects are poor. I'm sorry to have had to tell you this.' The doctor's words struck Alex like a blow to the chest: 'What do you mean? Is she going to die?' After a few moment's silence the doctor replied 'Not immediately, but probably within the next year', but then, seeing Alex's stunned expression, tried to soften the blow by adding *'bu4 dao4 huang2 he xin1 bu4 si3'*, "Don't stop until one reaches Huang River", meaning carry as usual, hoping for the best, until all hope is gone.

Alex spent as much time as he could with *Xiao Maque* over the ensuing days, trying to be light-hearted whilst feeling that his world was closing in on him. *Xiao Maque* guessed that he had spoken with the doctor, and had learnt of her prospects. She had always known that she wouldn't make old bones, and had been resigned to this, there being little happiness in her daily life, but then she had met Alex and her life had been transformed. She desperately wanted to live and spend as long as she could with him. After two weeks she recovered a little, but the attack had left her weaker.

Chapter Twenty-three

The weeks passed, with Alex and *Xiao Maque* avoiding talking on the subject that was uppermost in the minds of both of them. They settled into a life of going on little outings, eating when they were hungry, resting when they were tired, and spending time together in Alex's apartment. They wanted to make the best of every minute that they could spend together. However, *Xiao Maque* no longer spent Saturday nights with him in his apartment, as they both knew that this would be more than she could cope with, so they found trivial reasons why such overnight stays were not convenient: his having to meet a potential customer with Ginger in his club that evening; her having a meeting with the matron early the next morning; and so on. Finally, one day *Xiao Maque* said to Alex, quietly 'I am going to die soon Alex', to which he replied 'I know my love, I know.'

They both felt relieved of a burden in no longer having to avoid mention of *Xiao Maque*'s condition. Now that the big secret was in the open, they could be their normal selves. They learnt to smile again, and to tease each other. When Alex ran his hand across *Xiao Maque*'s breasts inadvertently whilst adjusting her position in the wheelchair, she reproached him with mock annoyance: 'You hansap man!', which he got her to admit is a slang phrase for "dirty old man"! She went on to say that she wasn't sure of him when she first met him. He asked 'You used to think that I was a dirty old man? What do you think now?', to which she replied 'No longer just **think**,. now **know** you a dirty old man!'

They laughed together at this exchange, as though they didn't have a care in the world. Life had become happy again. They spent their time wandering along the streets of Hong Kong like the couple of lovers that they were, with *Xiao Maque* pointing out items of interest: the grill-enclosed balconies of the poorer accommodation blocks that enabled their occupants to spread out further without the risk of burglary; the even poorer accommodation for manual labourers without families or many material possessions, the "cages", where a man could lock his few possessions until he returned to sleep there at night, which comprised several strong grilled metal cages set three or four to a room, or in a line along the walls of a corridor; the "Barracks", the huge complex of buildings out near *Kai Tak* Airport where the spaces between the apartment blocks had been filled in with more floors to create a dark almost continuous 'village', not quite outside of the law, but where few law-abiding citizens would dare to venture.

They again took the funicular railway up to the Peak, and stood in admiration at the spectacular view across to Kowloon and beyond. In short, they were deliriously happy, living only for the moment, not daring or even bothering to think of the inevitable event that grew closer and closer to them, day by day. One evening, after they had eaten at a hawker stall, Alex took the ring out of his pocket and slid it onto *Xiao Maque*'s wedding finger. 'Now you are promised to me, for everyone to see.' *Xiao Maque* was thrilled with her engagement ring and took every opportunity to show it off.

When they stopped at a shop, she would place her left hand on the counter for all to see. Other times, when she spoke to strangers in a dining hall or in a shopping mall, she would introduce Alex as "my fiancée", having practised the pronunciation until she could say the word perfectly. This was the happiest time of her life.

Alex came to the hostel one evening after work to find the matron waiting for him in the hallway. '*Xiao Maque* isn't well. She was taken ill during the night and is confined to her bed.' The matron's face told Alex that the situation was grave. He followed her into her office where she invited him to sit down, and then he asked her what she meant by "isn't well". He asked hopefully 'Has she got a cold or something?'

The matron shook her head and then replied 'I don't know how much *Xiao Maque* has told you about her illness. The problem is that because of her paralysis her organs are under severe stress, particularly her kidneys. They are prone to infection, which is occurring more and more frequently. She needs increasing doses of medication, which has its side effects. At the moment she has a high temperature and is feeling very tired.'

One afternoon a few days later, Alex received a telephone call from the matron, explaining that the doctor had called to see *Xiao Maque* and was concerned about a build-up of fluid. He had had her admitted to hospital, as there was very little that he could do to help her himself at the hostel. The matron gave Alex the address of the hospital and the number of the ward and said that he could visit at any time.

When he arrived at the ward he found *Xiao Maque* sitting up in bed with a tube attached to her to drain fluid, but apart from that she looked fine. He was relieved, as he hadn't known what to expect. She was to stay in hospital for two days, but would need to return for twenty-four hours each week. However, *Xiao Maque* continued to deteriorate. When Alex collected her from the hospital after her regular weekly visit, she was becoming progressively weaker. After only about a further two months she was usually too tired to respond with enthusiasm to his remarks, just smiling when he fussed her. The matron confined her to bed.

One day *Xiao Maque* asked Alex 'How long have you known about my present condition?' He replied 'A little while, but that isn't important. What matters is that we are together now and we are happy. We must just take each day as it comes and make it count.' The inevitable day arrived. When Alex came into the hostel one evening the matron took him straight to *Xiao Maque*'s room, where she lay weak and pale in her bed. She hadn't the strength to raise herself to greet Alex, but smiled at him and said 'Hello my love. I'm afraid that my time has come.'

Alex sat down at the edge of her bed and reached for her hand. The matron withdrew, to leave them together for their last moments. Alex raised himself and put his arms around *Xiao Maque*. They cried and hugged each other, until the matron gently said to Alex 'It's time that you were going. She must rest now.' As Alex reached the doorway, he turned to *Xiao Maque* and said 'Goodnight my love.' *Xiao Maque* replied, but in a low voice so the Alex couldn't hear, not the words that he had just said to her, but more final, sad words: 'Goodbye my love.'

As she lay on her pillow her tears flowed, not tears of self pity, but tears of concern for Alex. What would he do when she was gone? He was such a gentle helpless man, how could he cope without her? He would mourn and grieve and be unable to move ahead with his life. She wished that she had made preparations for someone to enter his life after she had gone, and help him to pull himself together to face the future. After a while, her eyes closed, and she rested in peace.

When Alex arrived at the hostel the next morning, the sight of the matron waiting for him at the door told him all that he needed to know. She stepped forward and took his hand in hers. 'Alex, *Xiao Maque* passed away during the night. I'm so sorry.' She led Alex to a side room where *Xiao Maque*'s body was lying on a table, covered in a white shroud. She drew back the top of the shroud so that Alex could look upon *Xiao Maque*'s face.

Alex thought how tiny she looked. She had not been robust in life, but in death she did indeed seem to fit her name, "Little Sparrow". He reached forwards and touched her hair, and then he found her hand and held it in silence, his emotions in turmoil. He remembered the many happy times that they had had together, and the depth of their love for each other.

The matron touched Alex's arm, and told him that it was time that he should go. She said that she would arrange the funeral ceremony, and for the cremation of *Xiao Maque*'s body and everything else that needed to be done. As Alex walked out of the hostel, the matron said quietly, just as the night-watchman had said years before, but not using the same colloquial words: 'Poor man. Poor, poor man.'

Alex walked to the ferry terminal as if drugged, not heeding passers by, nor caring for the traffic on the roads. In truth, he would have been grateful if some speeding motorist had ended his life so that he could leave the world along with *Xiao Maque*. Somehow, he found his way to his apartment, where he drank himself into drunken tearful oblivion. The next day he went into work and told Ginger of *Xiao Maque*'s death.

Ginger, who had seen much death in his life under wartime conditions, but had learnt to cope with it, was sympathetic and concerned, and told Alex to stay away from work for a few days. However, during those few days, Alex simply roamed the places that he had visited with *Xiao Maque*, looking for her face in every crowd. He couldn't accept that she was gone for ever.

He walked up the ramp to the bridge where he had first seen *Xiao Maque*, and as he turned onto the bridge he saw a young woman sitting behind a table at what had been *Xiao Maque*'s pitch, and involuntarily called her name. The young woman looked up, and gave him the same kind of look that *Xiao Maque* had given him on that fateful day of their first meeting. However, the young woman then saw the anguish in Alex's eyes and averted her gaze. Alex stumbled away distraught, his mind confused.

The matron called him to advise him of the details of *Xiao Maque*'s funeral, asking him to call in at the hostel. She met him at the door and led him to her office. The funeral ceremony was to be a Buddhist ceremony two days hence, followed by the cremation of *Xiao Maque*'s body. Alex asked her for him to be given *Xiao Maque*'s ashes. Then she gave him the engagement ring that he had given to *Xiao Maque*.

The matron was not a young woman. She had lived long enough to know that there are many in this world who would rob a corpse, secure in the knowledge that the distraught family of the deceased would have too much on their minds to query a missing personal item. She asked him what she should do with *Xiao Maque*'s possessions, Alex advising her to leave this to Alice, who would know best the needs of the rest of the residents of the hostel.

Amongst the mourners at the funeral ceremony were the matron, *Xiao Maque*'s long-standing friend Alice, her recently-made friend Euphemia, and Ginger, who had come not just to represent the company, but also to support Alex in his time of need. The ceremony was simple, consistent with the Buddhist belief that death is not the end, but simply the start of a new life with the reincarnation of the deceased within the subsequent twenty-eight years. Alex took his turn to stand before the coffin, and with two lighted tapers in his hand he bowed his head three times to honour the deceased and wish the person a good life in the next world.

The next day Alex told Ginger that he had decided to return to Britain. He explained that, with *Xiao Maque* gone, Hong Kong held nothing but sadness for him. Ginger understood. After the deaths of so many of his fellow fliers during the war, the shell that he had developed had protected him from further personal grief, but he felt Alex's own sadness and knew that Alex was having difficulty in coping with *Xiao Maque*'s death.

Ginger was sorry that he would lose him, as he had made a substantial contribution to the profitability of the company, and he would miss him as a friend. He suggested to Alex that he contact the head office in Britain and try to find a suitable position for him, but Alex asked him not to. 'My mind's in a mess Ginger. I'm in no fit condition to think clearly. If I get myself sorted out, then I hope that you will be able to help me.'

Ginger agreed, and told him that he would arrange a flight for him back to Britain for the coming week. He then rose and shook Alex's hand. He hadn't made any friends since leaving the forces, yet he had taken to Alex right from their first meeting, even starting to think of him as a younger brother. He poured two large single malts and handed one to Alex. 'I wish you all the best in the future, old lad.' He watched through his office window as Alex left the building, and then he poured himself another glass of whisky and sat down at his desk. 'Poor bugger!' he said with feeling. 'Poor bugger!'

Alex collected *Xiao Maque*'s ashes from the matron at the hostel three days later. After leaving the hostel he stopped at a bar for two double whiskies, and then walked along Central for the last time. He would never return to Hong Kong with *Xiao Maque* gone. He boarded the Star Ferry to *Tsimshatsui* for the last time. The sun was starting to sink. He walked to the stern of the ferry as it moved away from the jetty and out into the harbour. After a few minutes he opened the box containing *Xiao Maque*'s ashes, then letting them fall into the wake of the boat, where they disappeared amongst the wash of the propeller. He dropped the simple wooden box over the side.

Finally, he took *Xiao Maque*'s ring from his pocket. No other woman would ever wear this ring. He raised the ring to his lips, kissed it gently, and then let it fall into the water of the harbour. As it hit the water, it flashed once in the light from the tall commercial buildings of the island, then it sank down into the depths.

Part 5: Return to Scotland

Chapter Twenty-four

As the plane taxied down the runway at Kai Tak Airport prior to take-off, Alex took his last look at Hong Kong. He wouldn't ever return, as the memories of *Xiao Maque* would still be strong for the rest of his life: her gentle smile, her sad eyes, her soft kind voice, never raised in anger, never spiteful, never vindictive, never cruel, never railing at her fate, despite her years of suffering.

The plane approached the end of the runway, with the waters of the Bay only a few yards away, then it slowed, turned and stopped. After a few seconds, when clearance for take-off had been granted, the engines roared at full power, the plane accelerated down the runway and then, at what seemed to be the last possible moment, it took to the air and cleared the roof-tops of the surrounding tenements blocks.

Alex closed his eyes and began to think what he would do upon his return to Britain. He didn't want to go back to Newcastle: Matt was gone and Aggie and Luke were no longer part of his life. Logic told him not to return to Glasgow, even though the best part of ten years had passed since he had left there, as Joe Bannion was noted for never giving up on a grievance. However, he didn't know much about any other part of Britain, and in his present frame of mind he had no wish to have to adjust to new people and to new places. He would have to make up his mind when he arrived at Heathrow.

The air-hostesses on the Cathy Pacific flight that he was on were mostly Chinese, and Alex took comfort from seeing them. He realised that he was in for a culture shock upon his arrival back in Britain, with the gentle oriental people that he had come to love in the Far East being few and far between. As one young air-hostess came down the isle serving coffee he saw a resemblance between her and *Xiao Maque* and unintentionally looked intently at her, but with his head filled with thoughts of *Xiao Maque*.

The girl misinterpreted his look as one of sexual interest and gave him a beaming smile as she poured his coffee, asking him if he had been on holiday in Hong Kong. He mumbled a flustered reply, which convinced the girl that he did indeed fancy her and for the rest of the flight she rewarded him with further beaming smiles whenever she passed.

By the time that the plane arrived at Heathrow Alex had decided that he would fly on up to Glasgow, taking the chance of Joe Bannion finding out about his return. If he felt threatened, he could move on, but as to where he had really no idea. However, he didn't think that he would go back to Govan, which would be too much of a risk, but would stay at a modest boarding house somewhere in Paisley, with luck out of Joe's way. He had saved a fair sum of money during his time in the Far East and had no worries about supporting himself in the immediate future, although he wanted to find a job as soon as he could.

As he left the aircraft, wearing the thin suit that he usually wore for business in Hong Kong, the cold air struck him, although by normal standards it was quite a mild day: something else he would have to readjust to. He booked a flight on the frequent service to Glasgow, checked in his luggage and then settled down to wait to be called for boarding. As he was sitting, he looked at the passers-by.

There were just two colourfully-dressed Orientals to be seen, the other people in the terminal being westerners. They stood patiently in orderly queues: this was something that Alex had not seen in his time in the Far East and was yet another reminder of the drastic change in his life that he was about to go through. His mind slipped back to Hong Kong and to *Xiao Maque* and it was only with difficulty that he roused himself as his flight was called.

The flight time to Glasgow was not much over an hour, during which time the cabin staff served drinks and a snack. As the air-hostess asked him what he wanted to drink, Alex was taken aback by her guttural Glasgow accent, even though it was little different to his own. Many of the passengers were business people returning to Glasgow from a trip down to London, and Alex was able to identify their different accents: the deep growling accent of the east-ender, the upper-class plum-in-the-mouth Kelvinside accent with its drawn-out vowels, the 'refined' accent of those educated in expensive public schools staffed by teachers brought up from England. He would have to try to forget the Chinese accents that over the years he had learnt to identify: the booming, rumbling Cantonese accent, the harsh, crackling Hokkien accent, the sharp, penetrating Mandarin accent.

After collecting his luggage, Alex took a taxi the short distance to Paisley, accepting the taxi driver's advice as to a clean but cheap place in which to stay. After being shown the room and agreeing the terms with the landlady, Alex took a walk around the town. Little had changed since the last time that he had been in the town: the same streets, with the same bars, the drizzle, a drunk staggering along the pavement: he was back!

He felt an intense loneliness, but who was there that he could meet? Certainly none of his own gang, who would soon put the word around about his return. He contemplated going into Glasgow and then taking the train out to Gourock to see his old seamen mates, but felt that this would be better delayed until he had decided what he was going to do with his future, in case Ernie, should he still be in charge, offered him a job. Finally he decided that he would go to Govan to visit old Mr. *Chan*, to make his peace with him and thereby ease his conscience for his past unpleasantness.

He took a taxi from the stand at the corner of the main road and asked the driver to drive him to Govan, once there telling the driver to drop him off in a quiet side street: no point in drawing attention to himself. As he approached old Mr. *Chan*'s fish and chip shop, he saw that its name had been modernised to "*Chan*'s supper bar", but all else seemed the same. The shop was empty of customers, but a young Chinese woman was busy behind the counter.

Alex looked at her with interest, as she was the first Chinese person that he had seen since his arrival in Glasgow. With a shock he realised that she was *Chan*'s young daughter who had been in the shop on his last visit, but she had now grown into a beautiful slim young woman. She had a kind sensitive face, albeit that she looked rather tired and over-worked.

Old *Chan*, his daughter *Mei Hua* and *Chan*'s son had originally run the shop together, all three living on the premises, but then the son had got fed up with the shop and with living under the eyes of his father, and had gone off to work in a restaurant in Glasgow. He had paid a couple of visits to them shortly after leaving, the second time to borrow money from old *Chan* to "get set up in a business" but then had not called again or given them his address. This had been four years ago and they had heard nothing more of him since. *Chan* had then become even more concerned with doing his best for his daughter.

Following the attendance of *Chan* and his daughter at a gathering of the Chinese community in Glasgow, *Chan* was pleased when a fellow Chinese businessman, *Loh Yung Tsui*, who ran a big restaurant in Larkhall, had told him that his only son, *Yu Wing*, had expressed an interest in *Mei Hua*. *Chan* had done his best to point out to *Mei Hua* what a good prospect *Yu Wing* was, with a family business to inherit.

Eventually *Mei Hua* had agreed to meet the young man, and a romance had bloomed, the two young people soon meeting on every free occasion. Mr. *Chan* and *Yu Wing*'s father and mother were delighted with the situation, and told each other what a lovely couple the young people made, and entertained thoughts of a wedding in the not-too-distant future, and then the prospect of grandchildren.

Yu Wing was allowed to use his father's big saloon car to take them out in the evenings, and one evening he drove *Mei Hua* out to see Loch Lomond, parking in a deserted lay-by. As darkness fell he persuaded *Mei Hua* to move to the back seat of the car. After kissing her passionately for several minutes, and telling her how much he loved her, his hand ran up to the buttons of her blouse. *Mei Hua* was alarmed: this was her first relationship and she was concerned about what he was expecting of her. However, *Yu Wing*'s soft words allayed her fears. With great reluctance she allowed him to undo the buttons and ease her blouse from her shoulders. He kissed her neck as he continued to remove her clothes...

When their lovemaking was finished, *Mei Hua* experienced a deep feeling of shame. Should her father learn of what she had let *Yu Wing* do to her, he would never forgive her.

This pattern followed for the next three weeks on the evenings that they went out in the car together. However, his calls to her then stopped. She didn't know what to make of this and after a week rang him up, to be given the explanation that he had been busy, but would soon get in touch. A month went by and *Mei Hua* still hadn't heard from him, during which time she became increasingly more despondent. Mr. *Chan* could see that something had gone wrong with the relationship between her and *Yu Wing*, but she wouldn't discuss it. He decided to go and see *Yu Wing*'s father, to see if he could throw any light on the matter.

As soon as Mr. *Loh* had taken him through into the family sitting room at the back, Mr. *Chan* could see from Loh's embarrassed behaviour that there was something unpleasant to come. He drew attention to the close friendship that the young couple had built up, and reminded *Loh* of how the two fathers and Mrs. *Loh* had all hoped that this relationship would lead in due course to marriage.

Mr. *Loh* agreed, but then went on to say '*Chan*, you and I both know how important chastity is in a bride. When a man takes a bride she must be unblemished.' *Chan* nodded his agreement. Mr. *Loh* continued: 'My son has informed me that your daughter is no longer innocent.' *Chan* was enraged! 'You know that my daughter has not kept company with any man other than your son!' Mr. *Loh* drew himself up straight and replied in a slow deliberate voice 'Yes, that is so.'

Chan realised the implication of Loh's remark. He replied 'What are you saying? Your son admits to having violated my hitherto innocent daughter and will not now pay the price?' Mr. *Loh* did not answer the question directly, but drew the conversation to a close: 'If a woman gives her favours to a man without his paying the price, then who is to know how many other men have enjoyed those same favours, also without paying the price? For the sake of his family and his ancestors, my son will marry only an unblemished woman. Good evening to you Mr. *Chan.*'

Mei Hua looked up from her work and said to Alex 'Yes?', expecting him to state his order, but as soon as she spoke she recognised him from his last visit, despite the years that had passed and her expression hardened to one of concern. Alex replied 'I want a few words with Mr. *Chan* please.'

Mei Hua's face expressed dismay. After his return from his meeting with Mr. *Loh* her father had withdrawn into himself, rarely speaking and not eating properly. He avoided all contact with the local Chinese community after he had learnt that *Yu Wing* was now keeping company with another young woman. *Chan*'s health had deteriorated from the time of the meeting, culminating in his death from a stroke just over a year ago.

Mei Hua told Alex that her father was dead, and was surprised to see that he was dismayed. Cautiously she asked 'What was it that you wanted to see him about?' Alex recovered his composure and replied 'I wanted to apologise to him for my behaviour some years ago. It is something I deeply regret and I came here to make my amends.' Her expression softened and she said 'Why don't you make your apology to me, as his next of kin?'

Alex felt better upon hearing *Mei Hua*'s suggestion, and went on to say, in a somewhat embarrassed manner, 'I also wanted to apologise to him in Mandarin'. *Mei Hua* wondered what had caused such a change in the man who stood before her, and said kindly 'Please make your apology to **me** in Mandarin.' Although her native language was Cantonese, *Mei Hua* had picked up a little Mandarin from some of her Chinese school-friends in Glasgow and was able to follow the gist of his words, at the same time realising the sincerity with which they were spoken.

After Alex had finished speaking, she drew herself to her full height and, looking at him with a serious expression on her face, said in a firm clear voice 'On behalf of my late father, I accept your apology.' After this she relaxed and smiled at Alex, who returned her smile, both of them feeling relief, Alex from having unburdened himself from the guilt that he had borne for many years for his cruel remarks to Mr. *Chan*, and *Mei Hua* from the concern that she had felt when she had recognised Alex.

They chatted in English for five minutes, but with *Mei Hua* throwing in the odd word or two of Mandarin whenever she could, at the end of which time they were both smiling at each other like old friends. *Mei Hua* didn't tell Alex that it would have been of no use for him to have tried to speak to her father in Mandarin, as he had spoken only Cantonese, together with a limited amount of English: and certainly not Mandarin. Somewhat belatedly, they introduced themselves, *Mei Hua* telling Alex her name in Mandarin, being pleased when Alex knew that her name meant "beautiful flower".

At this point two young men came into the shop, so Alex moved over to the far end of the counter and started to watch the television set mounted on the wall. The young men had clearly been drinking. They ordered two fish suppers, but when the order was placed before them, one of them said 'How about a discount for cash?', which had them both in fits of laughter. Alex stepped forward so that he was only two feet away from them. He looked in the eyes of the one who had spoken and said in a cold menacing voice 'Pay for your fish suppers and clear off.' One of the men looked as though he was going to challenge Alex, but the other saw the hard glint in Alex's eyes and said to his mate 'Come on then, pay up and let's be on our way.'

As *Mei Hua* thanked him for his help, Alex asked her if this kind of thing was a regular occurrence, learning that it usually only happened on Friday and Saturday evening after the pubs had closed. 'Okay then' he said as he left the shop, 'I'll see you on Friday evening.'

Over the next few days Alex bought himself some warm clothing, and a few cosmetic items. Coming from Hong Kong to a harsher climate, his skin had started to roughen, so he bought some moisturising skin-cream, which seemed to do the job. He had not suffered too much from jet lag, and in a few days was fully recovered from the effect of Hong Kong time being eight hours ahead of GMT. Although memories of *Xiao Maque* occupied most of his waking moments, he thought about *Mei Hua* from time-to-time and was pleased that he had been able to come to her assistance.

One evening he decided to pass an hour walking along the Govan streets, to see what changes had been made over the years that he had been away. He saw that many of the older tenement blocks had been replaced by smart two-storey apartments, with small but neat gardens set in front of them. The people he passed on the streets were generally well dressed and looked fit and healthy. Although still not an affluent area by any means, Govan had improved drastically, which pleased him immensely: the residents deserved a better lot than they had had when he had spent his childhood and youth there.

He reached the supper bar on the Friday evening just before the pubs closed, whilst business was still slack. There were half a dozen customers in the shop making their order from the list on the wall: fish suppers, haggis suppers, black pudding suppers, sausage suppers, white mealy-pudding suppers, meat pies, and so on. Once they had received and paid for their order, they made off for home before there was any boisterousness on the streets.

Alex sat in the corner ostensibly watching the television. As the pub crowd arrived, Alex noted two of them who looked liked the kind of men that Joe Bannion would employ for his protection work: rough, arrogant, all mouth and confidence, as he himself had been at one time. Although he did not know it, they in return took note of Alex. After they had left the shop with their orders, one of them made his way to the telephone box on the corner and spent a couple of minutes on the phone.

When the last of the pub crowd had cleared, *Mei Hua* closed the shop and asked Alex to join her and her assistant, Florrie, in the back room for something to eat. Florrie asked if she could be excused and take her fish supper back home with her, as she had to see that the kids were alright, but in truth she wanted to get back to give a fish supper to her man, who by now would have come back from the pub and would be becoming increasingly more belligerent by the minute at any delay in her return. *Mei Hua* turned a blind eye to the two large fish portions, rather than one, and the huge mound of chips, that Florrie wrapped up for herself before leaving.

As *Mei Hua* and Alex sat together, Alex told her about his time in the Far East, but leaving out any reference to both *Qiangwei* and *Xiao Maque*, whilst in return, *Mei Hua* told him about her own life, but not mentioning *Yu Wing*. They chatted on, until eventually Alex saw the time and asked to be excused, telling her that he would be back the next evening at the same time. However, the next evening an unexpected event occurred.

As he walked towards the supper bar, a black saloon car with a driver and two passengers drew into the kerb behind him, the two men he had noted the previous evening then emerging and coming up behind him. 'There's someone wants to see you Alex' said one of them. Alex thought of taking flight, but the bulge in their jackets warned him that they were concealing weapons of some sort, perhaps shortened pickaxe handles, so he got into the car quietly.

Alex cursed himself for having been such a fool as to ever visit Joe's territory. His fears were confirmed when the car pulled up outside Joe's office, as it had done all those years ago when Joe had had him brought in and had given him a good hiding. He would be lucky if he got away with a good hiding this time: more likely he would be thrown into the river from a jetty with his hands tied behind his back and a length of chain wrapped around his ankles. The two men led him up the stairs and into an office that he remembered well. Sitting behind the desk was a man whose face was familiar, but it wasn't Joe Bannion. 'Well, well, Alex' said the man, 'I knew that you would turn up again some day.'

With a start Alex recognised his old right-hand man, Greg, who chuckled at Alex's evident discomposure. 'You thought it would be Joe, didn't you, you old bugger, well if it had have been you would have been in for a bad time.' Greg extended his hand and shook Alex's hand warmly. He invited Alex to sit down, poured him a scotch, and then told him the story of Joe's downfall.

Joe had apparently become careless in his later years, and when a couple of brothers, the Fintry brothers, had moved into his area he hadn't taken his usual action of an immediate reprisal, but had let matters drift. By the time that he had decided to take action the brothers were well established and had built up a strong gang of hard men.

The word had somehow got out that Joe and his gang were to visit the Fintry brother's base for a sorting out, but the night before this was to take place Joe had been phoned by the landlord of one of the pubs under his protection and asked to come round straight away to discuss a problem. Instead of taking one or two of his men with him, Joe had been careless enough to have gone off on his own, never to be seen again.

After a week without a sight of Joe, Greg had stepped into Joe's shoes and taken command of the gang. However, during this time several of the gang had lost confidence and had drifted over to join the Fintry brothers, which left Greg's gang seriously under-manned. Realising that he would be at risk in running up against the brothers, he had gone round to see them, when together they had come to a mutual agreement as to which area each of the two gangs was to work. In addition, Greg proposed an alliance between the two gangs, such that if there were any future attempts to move into either of their areas, they would act together to suppress them. He pointed out to Alex that it wasn't a case of cowardice, but simply that the gang had run down to the extent that it was no match for the Fintry brothers' gang, and that it was better to have a smaller territory that he and his gang could work in peace rather than to go the way of Joe.

Having brought Alex up-to-date, Greg got down to the point of the meeting. His men had seen that Alex was giving protection to the supper bar and he wanted to know why he was doing this, telling Alex that if he wanted to work the area, he would have to do it as a member of his own gang, rather than as a freelance. Alex was relieved that he was not going to have to face Joe, but was also sorry at the fate that had befallen him.

He explained to Greg that his interest in the supper bar was purely personal and that before long he would be leaving the area. Greg grinned at this: 'She's a nice looking girl Alex.' After another scotch they shook hands again and Alex left, Greg calling after him that there would always be a job going if ever he wanted one. Alex rushed over to the supper bar and took up his place on the seat in front of the television.

When the shop closed that evening he sat with *Mei Hua* and told her about his earlier meeting with Greg. She looked alarmed and told him that she didn't want him to get into any trouble on her account, but he assured her that all was now well. Before he left, he asked her what she would be doing on the following day, Sunday. *Mei Hua* told him that her day was free and they agreed to meet mid-morning and spend the day together.

Lying in bed later, *Mei Hua* was troubled as she turned over her thoughts in her mind. She found Alex attractive, and wondered whether she had done the right thing in arranging to meet him, as surely no man would be interested in a serious relationship with her should he ever get to know of her lapse in morality.

The following morning Alex called for *Mei Hua*, being pleased to see her wearing a Cheongsam. She looked beautiful and he told her so, which brought a blush to her cheeks. She was pleased and flattered by Alex's words. He helped her on with her top-coat, and then they left the premises and set off for the city. Whilst he had not been there before, Alex suggested that first they visit Kelvingrove Museum and Art Gallery, in Glasgow's West End, with which *Mei Hua* happily agreed. Although the museum was impressive from the outside, as they entered it through the main entrance, they both stopped and stared in amazement at the magnificence of its interior.

Climbing one of the sweeping staircases from the ground floor, *Mei Hua* took Alex's hand, not so much in affection, as in wanting to share with him her feeling of wonderment and awe at all that she could see around her. Alex's spine tingled as he felt the warmth of her hand in his, but then he felt guilty that he could enjoy such a feeling so soon after the death of *Xiao Maque*. He would never cease to love *Xiao Maque*, but she was gone, whilst *Mei Hua* was a warm living person, and he was so very lonely.

They continued to hold hands as they explored the many galleries. After a couple of hours they were both in need of sustenance so Alex suggested that they make their way to the cafeteria, where they each had a bowl of soup, a bread roll and a cup of coffee.

Alex looked at *Mei Hua* as she chatted away confidently, pleased to be out of the shop for the first time since her father's death, and happy to be in the company of an attentive man. The cafeteria was warm so she took off her top-coat, her appearance then drawing many admiring glances from the other customers. Alex was delighted in the way she looked and realised that he was the envy of all of the men in the room. He reached over and took her hand, then saying to her quietly 'I'm glad that we are friends.'

In the afternoon they visited the Museum of Transport, where they wandered in wonder amongst the magnificent collection of old cars, bicycles, motorcycles, lorries, buses, tramcars, railway locomotives, and other memorabilia of years gone by. The section devoted to models of ships, both military and commercial, was equally impressive: in particular, those of Clyde-built ships sunk in action during the Great War and World War II, such as the Hood, gave Alex much food for thought. Less technically inclined, *Mei Hua* was fascinated by the handcart that was used in the old days to cart drunks away from off the streets.[24:1]

After seeing the lovely collection of old Argyll cars on display, the first of which was built in 1900, the output increasing when the company opened new premises in Alexandria in 1906, Alex was saddened to read that the relatively small Argyll company, turning out such high-quality cars, at the leading edge of the technology of the time, had been forced to close by the overwhelming output of cheaper cars by the massive highly-automated car factories of the English Midlands.

They then left the museum and took a journey on the underground loop that ran below the city, marvelling at the tiny Victoria carriages. It had been a grand day out, culminating in a meal at a Chinese restaurant, where Alex showed off to *Mei Hua* by conversing with the waiter in Mandarin. *Mei Hua*, in turn tried to impress Alex with her own knowledge of Mandarin by asking the waiter for another bowl of boiled rice, but instead of using the third tone for the character for bowl, "*wan*", she mistakenly used the fourth tone, which changed the meaning to ten thousand. One of the waiters said to her, whilst trying to keep his face straight, 'But Madam! You'll never eat so much rice!

[24:1] On his last visit to the museum, the author was disappointed to find that this cart is no longer on display and wonders if its withdrawal was misguidedly associated with Glasgow having been designated as a "City of Culture" some years ago.

Alex was thrilled with her attempt and told her so. He knew that at any moment she could have changed into Cantonese, which was the native language of most of the staff in the restaurant, and then he wouldn't have been able to contribute more than just a few words, and certainly not a single sentence, to the conversation.

Later, whilst waiting in the bus depot for the bus to take them back to Govan, a bus passed bearing the destination "Maryhill". Alex decided to try an old silly story on *Mei Hua*, saying to her 'Do you see the name of the place where that bus is going to? One time an Irishman got on the bus and sat behind a young girl. When the conductor came for the fare, the girl said "Maryhill, single", and as he reached the Irishman the man said Joseph ... ' At this point *Mei Hua* interrupted him with "Joseph O'Connor, married!", clearly having heard the story before, as would everyone else living in the Glasgow area. They both had a good laugh, but he decided not to tell *Mei Hua* any other silly 'tease the foreigner' Scottish stories, of the "How the haggis is captured" nature, as although she was born abroad, she was as good a Scot as any other young Glasgow woman and would resent any implication to the contrary.

Alex had had a lovely day out with *Mei Hua*, the only blight having been when he had learnt of the demise of the Argyll car company. However, as he reflected upon this, he brought to mind the new, modern car plant-built at Linwood, a dozen or so miles to the west of Glasgow. In this plant the automation was world-leading, particularly the under-floor scrap-disposal system, which enabled the manufacturing and assembly bays to be clean, bright and uncluttered, and the workers to enjoy a pleasant working environment. He then reflected on the recent launching on the Clyde of the QE2, which, after the correction of an initial problem in the transmission, had gone on to become the pride of Great Britain and to win the admiration of the world.

He considered the extensive microchip-manufacturing facilities in "Spango Valley", just to the south of Greenock, so-named, popularly, by the proud Scots as constituting the British counterpart to the Silicon Valley of the United States. Next he thought of the exploitation of the North Sea oil deposits, lying offshore of Aberdeen, the revenue from which was bolstering up the British economy. Then he considered the old Abbottsinch Aerodrome out at Whiteinch, which had been redeveloped to become the Glasgow International Airport, fed by the new M8 motorway running from out of the city, whilst down the Ayrshire coast, Prestwick Airport was the point of departure from Britain for many intercontinental flights.

Following this he thought of the achievements in other fields, as exemplified by the discovery of beta blockers by James W. Black in the late 1950s, which have improved the health and increased the longevity of millions of people worldwide. 'Yes,' he thought, 'things are looking good for Scotland.'

His sadness over the Argyll car was replaced by a warm glow of national pride. Whatever the problems Scotland might face in the future, they would be solved by Scottish brains, skills, ingenuity and muscle. His pride in being a Scot, in living in the most beautiful country in the world, amongst good sound people, was pure and simple, not tarnished by the bitterness that he would have felt in the past against the English 'repressors'. Alex had come a long, long way from his early days!

As they reached the supper bar at the end of the day, *Mei Hua* invited Alex to come in for a coffee, but he knew that she had a busy day ahead of her and declined. However, on a sudden impulse, he leaned forwards and kissed her tenderly on the lips. He had had a lovely day in her company and he wanted her to know this.

Their Sunday outings continued for a couple of months, with their visiting different places within the city that *Mei Hua* had never imagined existed, such as the "Rotundas", that were the entrances to the Glasgow Harbour Tunnel built in 1890-96, but closed to pedestrian traffic in 1980, these big round buildings, one on each side of the river, with domed roofs, originally housing the hydraulic lifts that took horses and carts down to the tunnel at one side of the river and then took then up to the surface at the other side, thereby avoiding the difficulty that the horses experienced in drawing their carts up and over the city bridges in wet or icy weather.

They visited the Botanical Garden at the junction of the Great Western Road and Byers Road, admiring the conservatories built in Victorian times that employed cast-iron frames to house the glass panels that flooded the buildings with light. On another occasion they visited the oldest house in Glasgow, the "Provand's Lordship", located on the west side of the top end of Castle Street, which has survived from the 15th century.

Close by the Provand's Lordship are the Glasgow Infirmary, the Glasgow Cathedral and the Glasgow Necropolis, the "city of the dead". The adjacency of the latter three places, the place to be born in, the place to be christened and married in, and the place to be buried in, causes Glasgow folk to remark "They get you coming and they get you going!"

Alex took *Mei Hua* across the bridge from the cathedral to the

Necropolis, known as the "Bridge of Sighs". In the Necropolis is the tomb of the illustrious John Knox, and also the tomb of William Baker, the Glasgow carpenter who in 1841 wrote the Children's nursery rhyme "Wee Willie Winkie". *Mei Hua* said that she had not heard of this rhyme, so Alex started to recite it for her, in broadest Scots:

> Wee Willie Winkie rins through the toon,
> Up stairs and downstairs in his nicht-goun ...
> Tirlin at the window, cryin through the lock:
> "Are the weans in their bed, for its now ten o'clock?"

Alex stopped after the first verse on account of *Mei Hua*'s bewildered expression, and repeated it for her in words and accent that she could understand, after which he carried on to the lesser-well-known second verse:

> "Hey, Willie Winkie, are ye comin ben (home)?
> The cat's singin grey thrums (purring) to the sleepin hen,
> The dog's speldert (stretched out) on the flure and doesna give a cheep.
> But here's a waukrife laddie, that wunna fa asleep!"

Whilst *Mei Hua* had enjoyed her visit to the Necropolis, as a typical somewhat superstitious Chinese she didn't feel at ease as they made their way around the impressive tombs and mausoleums of the rich Glasgow Victorian dead, and was pleased when Alex suggested that they make their way back home. She realised that she was falling in love with Alex, but what of her affair with *Yu Wing*? She eventually decided that the best thing to do would be to tell him of the affair so that he could decide for himself whether he wanted to continue with their relationship or bring it to an end.

The following Sunday Alex took *Mei Hua* to the Glasgow Zoo. As they walked around together, he took the opportunity to slip his hand around her waist. *Mei Hua* stared straight ahead, not giving any indication of her feelings, but with her brain in a turmoil. By now she knew that she loved him, and resolved to tell him about *Yu Wing* at the earliest opportunity. That night as they parted, it was *Mei Hua* who initiated the goodnight kiss, putting her arms around Alex's neck and drawing his mouth down upon hers. They kissed passionately, again and again, until *Mei Hua* pulled away and wished Alex goodnight.

She had troubled thoughts as she lay in bed that night, as she had had for many nights before: she desperately wanted Alex in bed with her. Alex for his part lay in his bed thinking of *Mei Hua*: he too wanted the two of them to lie in bed together and resolved to bring this about at the first opportunity.

The following Sunday they went into the city and took the train from Central Station to Gourock. As they walked from the station to the quayside, Alex looked for the boats that he knew, eventually spotting the Westering Home tied up alongside the quay, but there was no sign of Big John. They walked up to Ernie's cabin and entered, to find him sitting behind his cluttered desk, with nothing changed.

Ernie recognised Alex immediately, but greeted him coldly: 'I would have thought that you would have called in to see me before running off' he said, 'I would have liked to have said goodbye to that little dog of yours, even if not to you.' Alex told him of the situation of his leaving, and how Flo had had Clyde put down without his knowledge, leaving him so shocked and in such hatred of her that he had to get away as soon as he could. Ernie was incensed: 'Flo said that you had run off with a younger woman and taken your dog with you. The cow! Wait until I tell John and the other lads in the pub this evening. The bitch will get a few home truths I'm telling you!'

After Alex had asked Ernie how Big John and the other skippers were getting along, he and *Mei Hua* turned to leave. Ernie's parting words were 'If ever you need a job Alex, come and see me.' Ernie was a true friend, as Greg had turned out to be. Feeling that it was time for him to tell *Mei Hua* some of the details of his past life, Alex stopped a passing taxi and asked the driver to take them to Ashton Point. There he led *Mei Hua* up the mountain-side, with her not knowing why, but sensing that it was something important to Alex.

There were new houses on the lower slopes of the mountain but, as Alex had thought years ago, they did not extent very far up the mountain-side, and soon they were walking on open ground. *Mei Hua* marvelled at the view of the Firth opening up to her, but did not comment, as Alex was clearly deep in his thoughts.

Eventually they reached the place where Alex had buried Clyde. He sat beside *Mei Hua* on one of the rock outcrops and told her the details about Clyde that he had not spoken of in Ernie's office. Tears ran down his face as he spoke and when he told her how he had cut off and buried the tip of his finger with Clyde she wanted to hug and comfort him, but it was better to let him carry on. He then went on to tell her about *Xiao Maque* and of her tragic death. By this time *Mei Hua* was crying herself.

At the completion of Alex's account she moved close to him and laid her head on his chest. They cried together for several minutes, then

Mei Hua told Alex of her affair with *Yu Wing*, feeling so ashamed that she couldn't lift her head to look him in the face. When she had finished, Alex gently lifted her head and wiped the tears from her eyes. 'It doesn't matter love' he said, 'it doesn't matter at all. I love you and I want you for my own.' *Mei Hua* could hardly believe that Alex had spoken the words that she had longed to hear for many weeks. They cried together for a few more moments, but this time in happiness, and then they walked down the hill and made their way back to Gourock.

When they reached the railway station they found that the next train wasn't due to leave for Glasgow for another forty minutes, so they went into the tearoom at the corner of the street. On an impulse Alex asked *Mei Hua* if she would mind if he left her for a few minutes to look into the Puffer on the odd chance that one of his old skipper-mates might be there. He was out of luck: there was no-one in the place except for the barman and a middle-aged woman sitting on a stool at the bar.

The woman was grossly overweight, with her backside spilling over the edge of the stool, and her run of double chins disappearing down the top of her roll-top sweater. She had a statuesque mound of what she herself would have called blond hair, but in reality was straw-coloured and brittle from years of excessive bleaching with peroxide. As she leaned forwards in a confidential manner to say something to the barman, her huge shapeless breasts spread out onto the bar top.

She was clearly drunk and seemed to be trying to tell the barman some story or other, but her words were slurred and he was clearly not interested in what she had to say, just standing there looking bored. Alex caught some of her words: '…so I told the prick behind the desk that this is a free country and if I want to sodding well … ' She sensed that someone was standing behind her in the doorway and stopped speaking. Then, with difficulty, she heaved her upper body from off the bar top and turned her head, a look of aggression on her face, intending to give a 'piece of her mind' to the 'nosy sod' who had had the audacity to eavesdrop on her private conversation.

In her drunken state and with her eyes screwed up close in the late-afternoon sunlight streaming in behind him through the still-open doorway, she couldn't recognise Alex, but Alex recognised her: Flo, old vulgar drunken Flo, except that she had run to seed and now made a pitiful sight. Her puffy face was crazed with burst veins that she had attempted to hide with a thick coating of make-up, and dewlaps sagged from her jaws. Her lips were drawn into the shape of an inverted saucer to reflect her aggressive feelings. Alex was shocked. What an ugly specimen of womanhood!

Alex turned and walked out, whilst Flo, still resenting the

interruption, muttered angrily to herself 'Some bloody prick with nae cash looking to bum a bloody free drink!', before turning back to the barman to continue with her story. Alex was stunned by this encounter, which had brought back memories from an earlier life that were best forgotten, and he hurried back to *Mei Hua*, lovely kind sensitive *Mei Hua*, who represented the future.

Alex and *Mei Hua* held hands contentedly as the train took them back to Glasgow, whilst Alex thought over the events of the day. He had done something that he should have done long ago: he had cried for those he had loved and lost and he had shared his grief with another person rather than bottle it up inside himself. That night Alex stayed with *Mei Hua* at the supper bar, and in the morning he went back to his lodging house to collect his belongs.

Chapter Twenty-five

During the days that followed, Alex did as much as he could to help around the supper bar. Initially he only helped with simpler jobs that didn't call for much judgement or skill, such as seeing that the potatoes were peeled properly and their eyes removed where necessary, preparing the batter, and warming the mushy peas on the gas stove.

However, before long he was able to be trusted to fry the battered fish and heat the puddings, learning just when to remove the fish-pieces from the hot fat so that they would be cooked thoroughly without being over-cooked or, in the case of the pre-cooked puddings, heated throughout.

Mei Hua noted his progress with pleasure. Soon he was allowed to cook the chips, under her watchful eye. *Mei Hua* tried to get Alex to accept payment for his help, but he refused. However, after Alex had been helping for two weeks, the assistant, Florrie, gave in her notice. Whilst this would have been a problem to *Mei Hua* in the past, they just decided that they could do without replacing Florrie and run the supper bar on their own, with Alex as the new full-time paid assistant.

Life was good. They didn't get bored or irritable with each other from working together all week, although on one occasion when Alex dropped a tray of fish onto the floor of the back room he heard *Mei Hua* say under breath 'Shit!' Later that day Alex went around the back room of the shop saying 'Shit! Where is my clean apron? Shit! Where is the wrapping paper? Shit! Where is my clean shirt?', until *Mei Hua* laughingly apologised for her rude outburst. Alex wasn't shocked by *Mei Hua*'s use of this word, as both in Singapore and Hong Kong he had heard many people speaking a long run of Chinese, to be concluded by the expletive, in English, "Shit!" He supposed that the explosive start of this single-syllable word together with its sharp termination, as with the word "xxxx", made it a natural swear word, and one that has been adopted internationally: "Dear me!" and "Golly!" pale in comparison.

They still went out together on Sundays, but not every Sunday, as sometimes one or the other was tired from the week's work and just wanted to sit and relax. Putting in so many hours in the supper bar, they didn't have chance to make new friends, although they sometimes invited the young couple from the Newsagent's shop next door to come round for a chat on a Sunday evening, the men drinking a few cans of beer whilst the women drank coffee, the couple inviting them back to their place on a later Sunday.

On one of their Sunday trips out they went to Glasgow Green and spent a pleasant hour visiting the People's Palace, where they saw the exhibits relating to the rich industrial barons of the cotton and tea trade of a century before. Then they walked across the Green to the edge of the River Clyde, at this point no longer tidal, but more like a lake, due to the dam that had been built across it. Alex disliked the banks of tidal rivers, as when the tide is out they are usually muddy, smelly and unattractive.

Walking back towards the road they saw a crowd of people listening to a man addressing them from where he stood on top of a large box. Alex recognised the man as his old teacher, Mr. Gilbraith, and asked *Mei Hua* to stop and listen with him. As Mr. Gilbraith spoke vehemently against the English, as he had done so many years before, Alex thought what a sad old fool he was, with only his anger to sustain him. An ignorant, sad, old man. They moved on, without Alex giving a backward glance.

Mei Hua hadn't ever questioned their relationship, although Alex suspected that this was in her mind. Even though he had now declared his feelings for her, at times his mind was still filled with thoughts of *Xiao Maque*, but *Xiao Maque* was dead. With his growing love for *Mei Hua*, commonsense told him that he should marry her and bring up a family, although not in Govan, where he had spent his earlier, criminal life. He didn't want his kids to be told by the other kids that their dad had been a villain in his youth.

He raised the question one day with *Mei Hua* as to whether they could pool their resources and move to a new business outside of the city. To his pleasure *Mei Hua* agreed. They arranged for the trade papers to be delivered to them and scanned them eagerly as soon as they arrived. After a couple of weeks of reading the many advertisements, one day *Mei Hua* called out Alex's name in excitement, drawing his attention to a fish-and-chip shop up for sale in Dunoon, a beautiful coastal town just across the Firth from Gourock.

Alex read the advertisement with growing excitement, and then rang the selling agent in Dunoon to arrange a viewing, asking to be able to view on the coming Sunday. A little while later the agent rang him back to say that Sunday afternoon was alright with the owners, a Mr. and Mrs. Kennedy.

Almost hopping with excitement, they set off for Dunoon on the Sunday, first taking the bus to Glasgow city centre, then the electric train to Gourock, after that catching the ferry to the Dunoon ferry terminal. As they approached Dunoon, Alex pointed out to *Mei Hua* the statue of Highland Mary, the wife of the poet Robert Burns, standing in a small area of parkland high above the ferry terminal, looking out over the Firth.

The statue had been erected on the one-hundredth anniversary of the death of the poet, and gave an impression of elegance and history to the town. Alex thought that Dunoon, with its sweeping sea views from the West Bay to the East Bay, and with its good-quality shops and its houses standing bold against the background of the hills and mountains of the Cowal Peninsula, to face whatever weather might chance to blow up from the Irish sea and, beyond, from the Atlantic ocean, would be a grand place to start their married life in.

Alighting from the ferry, they asked their way to the address that they had been given, to find themselves outside a very dingy old-fashioned chip shop. The proprietor, Mr. Kennedy, had been looking out for them and opened the door. The inside of the shop was no better than the outside. The wall-paper was peeling and in some places held up by sticky tape and drawing pins; the paint-work had been discoloured over the years by the fumes from the hot fat to a dark ochre; the range was ancient and ugly; and dead flies were massed on the sticky fly-paper hanging from the naked light bulb: it was awful.

Mr. Kennedy could see that they were both dismayed by what they saw, and apologised, explaining that it had been a good shop in its day, but that both he and Mrs. Kennedy had grown too old to keep on top of the business and wanted to retire. He invited them to make an offer and went into the back room to give them chance to speak together in privacy.

Mei Hua wrinkled her nose and said that it would take a lot of work to restore the place to some kind of decency. Alex thought for a few moments, before saying 'Why restore it? Why not strip out the whole place, range and all? We could find enough money between us to fit it out in style, and we could open it as a combined chip shop and Chinese carry-out!'

Mei Hua knew that this was the present trend, as they had seen some of the attractive Chinese carry-outs in different parts of Glasgow city. She responded with enthusiasm, asking Alex what he thought they should offer for the premises. After thinking for a while, Alex replied 'We will be buying basically an empty shell, as all of the fixtures and fitting need to be thrown out. Depending on what we see of the rest of the premises, we can offer approximately a half of the asking price.'

They went through to the back room where Mr. Kennedy was sitting with his wife. After looking round the back room and the two upstairs rooms, Alex spoke candidly with Mr. Kennedy, telling him of their intentions for the place should they buy it, and of the necessity of stripping out all of the old fixtures and fittings. Mr. Kennedy had been half expecting Alex's words, and after thinking for a few moments simply said 'Okay then, how much will you give me for it?

When Alex told him his offer he sucked in his cheeks, tut-tutted and generally showed his displeasure at such a low figure. Whilst *Mei Hua* would have like Alex to increase his offer, he simply said 'Well that's our offer Mr. Kennedy. If you decide in due course that you are interested, your agent has our telephone number.'

On the way back to the Ferry terminal *Mei Hua* was silent and despondent. She could see in her mind's eye how the place would look when converted. Not only that, she had been thinking that the move to Dunoon might encourage Alex to ask her to marry him: she too thought that Dunoon would be a beautiful clean place in which to stay.

As the ferry moved off, Alex said to her 'Don't give up so easily Hen. We may hear from the agent.' Sure enough, two days later the agent rang to say that Mr. and Mrs. Kennedy had accepted their verbal offer and asked that they now instruct their solicitor to make a formal binding offer of acceptance to him in writing.

Now that their move to Dunoon was assured, Alex thought more about what life would be like there. He rang up Ernie at his office in Gourock and was pleased to find him in. After a few moments of chatting, Ernie told him that there was someone in his office who wanted to speak to him: 'Hello there, you old bugger. How are you keeping?'

Alex immediately recognised John's voice. They chatted companionably and then John said 'I was sorry to hear about what happened to Clyde. He was a fine wee dog.' There was a few seconds silence between them whilst they both brought back memories of Clyde, before the conversation got going again. Alex told John about his impending move to Dunoon and said that, if it would be alright with Ernie, he would come over to Gourock on the ferry one day and go out with him on the Westering Home, for old times' sake.

John replied 'Bugger the ferry! Whenever it suits you just ring up Ernie here and I'll come over on the Westering Home and pick you up at Dunoon Pier, and you can be her skipper again for the day!' Alex reflected on what a grand mate John had been to him in the past, and how he had now immediately welcomed him back into his life. It was the same with Greg and Ernie, who had both offered him a job without hesitation. He was lucky to have friends like this.

Now that their offer on the fish-and-chip shop had been accepted, Alex and *Mei Hua* had a problem, in that the law in Scotland is that once an offer is accepted it is binding, with no possibility of backing-out, as there is down in England. They had to complete the sale of their

Govan supper bar to find the funds to pay for their new place in Dunoon. However, as luck had it, within two weeks of putting their supper bar on the market a buyer came forward and they were able to arrange a date for the completion of the transfer of ownership of the two properties.

Alex decided that it would be better if they could arrive in Dunoon as a married couple and proposed to *Mei Hua*, who accepted his proposal without hesitation, having longed for this day to come. They decided upon a registry-office ceremony, and asked their neighbours at the newsagents' if they would be their witnesses. They also decided to close the supper bar a week before their departure to Dunoon in order to take a honeymoon, but as to where to take the honeymoon they were undecided. After much thought they followed the pattern of many Scots, in choosing Blackpool, down on the north-west coast of England.

Alex made a booking at the Travel Agent's for the"Chequers Hotel" at the north end of Blackpool, away from the young crowds who favoured the night-life and the excitement of Blackpool town centre. The description of the hotel advised that it was "modern and well appointed, standing boldly on the promenade, high above the beach, with steps running down to the beach through a terraced garden": it sounded grand!

For the wedding ceremony, *Mei Hua* wore a white wedding dress. At first, she had told Alex that it wouldn't be appropriate for her to wear white in view of her affair with *Yu Wing*, bur Alex wouldn't hear of it: he wanted his beautiful bride to look breathtaking on this important day. After a show of reluctance, *Mei Hua* eventually agreed, silently pleased that she had been persuaded to do so. In return, she wanted Alex to wear formal morning attire with a top hat, but, as a proud Scot, he wouldn't settle for this, and decided that he would not just wear a kilt, but hire full formal highland dress in the MacAlister tartan.[25:1]

After the morning ceremony, Alex, *Mei Hua* and their two witnesses had lunch at the Chinese restaurant where they had first dined together.

Having drunk the best part of a bottle of wine, Alex felt emotional

---

[25:1] The MacAlister family, a branch of Clan Donald, made their home in Kintyre, a peninsula over on the west coast of Scotland. The MacAlister tartan has a bright red background, with the "sett", i.e. the pattern of the tartan, varying somewhat in its dimensions, these having been modified over the years by the weavers of the tartan. See "The complete book of tartan" by Iain Zaczek and Charles Phillips, published by Hermes House, reference number 13579108642. A descriptive, highly-illustrated reference work is "Clans & Tartans of Scotland & Ireland" by Christopher Mcnab, published by Lomond Books Ltd., ISBN 978 1 84204 249 6.

and turned to *Mei Hua*, saying to her, oblivious of the presence of their guests 'When we have got our new restaurant off the ground, do you know that our next project will be?' *Mei Hua* was mystified. 'We will have a baby: if it should be a boy will name him after your father, to honour your ancestors and if it is a girl we will give her your mother's name.' *Mei Hua* was thrilled to hear his words, but with concern she pointed out to him that the choice of the name of a child is a serious matter, and has to take into account the birth signs of the parents, the year and month of birth of the child, and so on.

Alex quelled her outpouring by placing his fingers across her lips, saying 'Alright my love, when our child is born we will follow all the proper procedures, we will consult all the ancient books, we will take the advice of the *feng1shui3 xian1sheng*, the "geomancer", and we will do all that is necessary to give our child the right name.' By this time *Mei Hua* had become excited at the prospect and wanted to respond to Alex's kindness and understanding. 'But we will also give our children a western name!' Alex's eyes turned misty. After a few seconds he replied in a quiet voice 'Yes. If we have a son we will call him Matthew and if we have a daughter we will call her Beattrice.' *Mei Hua* looked at Alex with love and understanding. 'Yes, I would like that.'

The following morning, they dressed again as they had for the wedding, and took a taxi to Paisley, where they posed for formal photographs at a photographic studio. *Mei Hua* had protested at this suggestion from Alex, saying that the snaps taken by their witnesses with their small camera would be fine, but Alex had been insistent: 'These photographs are not for us, but for our children to see, and for our children to show to our grandchildren, in the years ahead.'

Alex and *Mei Hua* took the train from Glasgow Central Station to Blackpool, just as Madge had done almost forty years earlier. The station was almost the same as it had been in Madge's time, except that, although Alex and *Mei Hua* had no reason to know it, the announcement board mounted high up on one of the walls in the station hall, which had comprised a long bank of light bulbs that were illuminated in waves from right-to-left to carry various messages to the passengers, had been replaced by a modern electronic system.

The steam trains of Madge's time had been withdrawn many years ago in favour of diesel-electric trains, and their LMS logo by that of British Railways following the Government's nationalisation of the previous four major railway companies. However, Alex and *Mei Hua* would not have found this information of interest, with their minds filled with thoughts of their new life together.

The train arrived not at Blackpool Central, but at Blackpool North Pier Station, the closure of Central in 1964 leading to a new wave of redevelopment of the Golden Mile. However, such redevelopment was not new to the Golden Mile, as redevelopment has taken place there continuously from the beginning of the 20th century, despite long-standing opposition to such change. In 1899 the Blackpool Gazette had opposed redevelopment, stating of the Golden Mile: "If the front land is covered with howling cheap-jacks, swindling catch-penny trickeries etc. while the shops behind are let for giantesses, fat women, penny-in-the-slot indecencies etc. then what a disreputable pandemonium will Central Beach eventually become."

Despite such a sombre prediction, Blackpool and the Golden Mile still attract enormous numbers of holidaymakers and will continue to do so. The fresh breezes blowing in from the Irish Sea still invigorate those walking along the promenade; the donkeys on the sands still enchant the children; the Tower is still a thrill to those riding to its top. Blackpool will always be a magical place to all who visit, if they can accept its popular appeal and not criticise some of its less cultured attractions.

The Chequers Hotel was impressive, strong and solid to stand against the winds that blow in from the Irish Sea. After breakfast they walked across the road and then across the tramway to the promenade sitting on the cliff edge high above the beach. They took the path down to the beach, and then walked along the clean golden sands. Alex found a piece of driftwood and used it to draw a heart in the sand, which he then pierced with an arrow before adding their initials.

On their second day he called in at a general store to buy a small bucket and spade, and insisted that *Mei Hua* build a sandcastle on the beach and then use the bucket to mould turrets to fortify it with. *Mei Hua* was pleased with her efforts, and made a great fuss when the advancing tide threatened to engulf her castle, frantically digging a moat around it, but then having to accept its inevitable overwhelming, followed by its disappearance back into the sands whence it came.

Whilst many of the features of the town from Madge's time still remained, others had gone: the Tower Zoo had been closed; but the shop selling rock in the street behind the tower was still there, although the front of the shop was now glassed in and the table upon which the sticks of rock had previously been rolled was absent; the delightful Fairy Grotto had been replaced by a monstrous space-age kids' attraction, although the adjacent Madame Taussaud's Waxworks and The Huntsman public house still remained.

On their last day they decided to visit the Pleasure Beach, taking the tram from outside the hotel. Hand-in-hand they walked around the different attractions, but *Mei Hua* was feeling queasy and didn't want to go on any of them. Eventually they came to the Grand National. As they stood looking down through glass windows onto the tracks, two carriages came roaring down, neck-to-neck. Both Alex and *Mei Hua* flinched at the sight, as had many others before them, but at the last moment the carriages disappeared from view into a tunnel beneath them.

That night *Mei Hua* felt uncomfortable and restless. She awoke early in the morning needing to be sick. As she returned to bed, she looked down at Alex sleeping quietly and smiled to herself. He might just get to meet young Matt or young Beattie sooner than he had imagined! She said a silent prayer of thanks for having such a good man as Alex in her life. She knew with certainty that he loved her, but she also knew that he did not love her as deeply as he had loved *Xiao Maque*. However, this did not trouble her, for she knew that a man's first real love was special to him. For him, *Xiao Maque* would never grow old, her eyes would never dim, her beauty would never fade. Perhaps in the course of time he would come to love her almost as much as he had loved *Xiao Maque*. Time would tell, and she and Alex had plenty of time together ahead of them, years and years.

Alex indeed was now a good man. Since leaving Glasgow he had loved and lost a loyal friend, Clyde, and had grieved at the loss; he had gained and lost a man he loved as the father he never had, Matt, and had again grieved at the loss; and he had found and lost a family in Aggie and Luke, but had been happy for them in their reunion with Aggie's husband, Luke's father. He had suffered the death of a woman, *Xiao Maque*, whom he had loved more than life itself, and whom he would remember until his dying breath. Along the way he had learnt friendship, kindness, sympathy, humility, compassion, guilt and all the other human qualities that he had been lacking. All of these things had changed him from the evil man who had fled Glasgow many years before, into the good man that he was now. Yes, Alex was now a good man, a very good man: as good a man as one could hope to find.

Epilogue

The year is 1975; the place is the Pleasure Beach at Blackpool.

**

The day following Alex and *Mei Hua*'s visit, a family group walked up the gentle slope from the promenade and into the Pleasure beach. The group comprised a couple of about retirement age, an early-middle-age couple, and two girls, one of about seven and the other of about nine. They looked to be a typical American family of grandparents, parents and children, on a visit to the UK to see where Granddad had spent time during World War II.

The children looked healthy and were outgoing, with unlimited energy, determined to see everything that there was to see, whilst the parents were quieter, dressed in the baggy shorts that the Americans seem to favour, and recording all their experiences on a ciné camera for them to show to their families, friends and colleagues, and for them theirselves to look back on in the years to come. The grandmother was a little overweight, but had a pleasant, tolerant face that seemed made for smiling. They looked to be a successful middle-class family that got on well together and had a happy life.

The grandfather was tall and athletic looking, albeit a little bulky around the waist. His hair was beginning to turn grey at the temples. His skin was olive, not only from the sun of California where they lived, but also from his ancestry. He had dark gentle brown eyes and when he smiled he showed a mouth full of strong white teeth. He was a fine-looking man.

The group wandered around the various attractions, the children eager to try all of them. The grandfather seemed to be pre-occupied. He looked around him at the surroundings, as though not finding what he expected to see. They continued to walk around the Beach, until the grandfather stopped them at one point and spoke to an attendant at one of the attractions: 'Excuse me sir, but didn't there used to be a big hall around here somewhere, called the Fun Place or something like that?' The attendant was new to the Beach and called over a colleague to answer the question. The man told him that the Fun House had burned down some time ago. 'It was right over from where we are standing now sir. It had been a great attraction in its time, but, really, it belonged to a different age, so it was decided to replace it with something more modern.'

The grandfather flinched at the man's words. His eyes became glazed and vacant as he looked across to where the Fun House had stood, and he became lost in his memories. His wife brought him out of his reverie by saying that it was about time that they all got back to their hotel, ready for going to the show on the North Pier.

The group started to walk back towards the promenade, reaching the place where the carriages from the "Grand National" pass below the ground at the end of the 'race'. They stopped to look down at the track through one of the viewing windows. At that moment a pair of carriages came racing down their tracks towards them, their occupants crying out in excitement and fear. At the last moment the carriages dropped down into the tunnel beneath the family, and all of them laughed in relief, except for the grandfather, who closed his eyes and leaned his head against the glass in one of the windows.

After a moment or two he roused himself and walked over to an attendant standing by the entrance to the ride. 'Excuse me sir,' he said, 'but there is a question that has bothered me for many years now.' The man perked up with interest. 'What's that then?' he asked. The grandfather thought for a moment and then said 'When the carriages set off for the race, they are lying side-by-side, and when they return to the finishing post they are also side-by-side, but now they have changed sides. How can this be so?'

The man liked to be asked this question and had a well-rehearsed answer: 'This roller-coaster, built in timber in 1935, is a Mobius coaster. Although you, as many others, thought that there are two tracks, there is just one single track that makes its way round the course **twice**. As you rightly say, the two carriages set off and return level with each other, but they are actually half-way around the track from each other. Some distance after setting off, the two loops of the track separate from each other, one loop passes over the other, and then before the end of the race the two loops come together again.

By now the man had got into his stride: 'It's like if you want to hold a newspaper rolled-up tight you would use an elastic band, but if the band is too long you would give it a twist and wrap it around a second time. Two loops round the newspaper, but still only one elastic band!'

He beamed at the eloquence of his explanation, as the grandfather said 'Thank you indeed for answering my question so thoroughly.' He then withdrew a note from his wallet and gave it to the man with the request 'Please have a drink on me tonight after you have finished work.'

The grandfather rejoined his family and they all carried on walking again. Soon, close to the exit from the Beach, they reached the

"Casino", so named, but not offering any gambling facilities: the grandfather paused and looked into the big glass windows, almost as though hoping to catch sight of some long-lost friend. They then walked out of the Beach, first across the road and then across the tramway to the promenade,

They walked slowly north along the promenade, passing the South Pier. As they reached the Central Pier, the grandfather stopped, but then walked slowly up to the guard-rail at the edge of the promenade, and looked down at the sands. He was oblivious of his family, who stood back, realising that Granddad was reliving old memories.

His eyes turned to the patch of sand beneath the pier. He gripped the guard-rail firmly and then closed his eyes to bring back his memories more clearly. In his mind's eye he saw again a beautiful young woman with whom he had so quickly fallen in love. He opened his eyes and then looked along the promenade and remembered the despair in which they had clung together before leaving each other; he heard again the question of the young boy: 'Got any gum, chum?'

His wife looked at him with concern, but also understanding, in her eyes. She had long thought that he had had a relationship during his time in Britain, but had never questioned him about it. Despite their youth, they had married only two weeks before his departure for Europe. Her parents had protested initially, but had eventually relented and given their blessing, remembering their own situation when her father had had to go to fight in Europe during World War One..

The grandfather had been worried when he had had to leave, not so much for his own safety, but more for what would become of her, and the grief she would feel, if he failed to return. His lovemaking had been passionate, but also desperate, as thought he was trying to blot out from his mind any thoughts of what lay ahead. After they had made love, she would lie quietly, pretending to be asleep, whilst he would lie with his eyes wide open, staring at the ceiling.

It was understandable that upon arriving in England he would have felt frightened and lonely, and disposed to seek the comfort of a young woman. He was only a man, when all is said and done. However, she had not regretted a moment of their married life. His return to her at the end of the conflict had been the answer to her daily prayers.

After a couple of minutes she walked over to him and placed her hand on his arm: 'Come on my love,' she said gently, 'time to leave your memories behind.' He turned to her and smiled, and then took her hands in his. 'Yes', he said, 'it was a long time ago, a long, long time ago.

THE END

471

Appendix: further information

#1 In times-past in Scotland, porridge was the staple food, being a simple way to cook grain, in that it required only to be boiled in a pot, whereas to bake grain into bread required the use of an oven. A wife would cook porridge and then pour it into a "porridge drawer" - a drawer in a sideboard or kitchen table, sometimes lined with metal - where it would be allowed to set, before being cut it into squares or "pieces", to be taken by her children to school, or by her family members to their place of work, where it would be sprinkled with salt - sugar not being generally available until the mid eighteenth century - before being eaten: it could even be fried for an evening meal.

The use of "piece" has carried forward to the present day, where a child playing down in the court will call for his or her mother to throw down a "jam piece", i.e. a jam sandwich, or a man will pick up his "piece" before departing for work, irrespective of whatever that "piece" may comprise: sandwiches, a pie, fruit, biscuits, etc., but certainly not often nowadays a piece of cold stiff porridge.

#2 Many visitors to Morecambe Bay do not realise that the bay is some twenty miles across, and that at low water it dries out over virtually all of its surface. The outgoing tide exposes a great number of rivulets and gullies that run haphazardly, and then on its return comes in up these rivulets and gullies, sometimes from behind the unwary walking on the sands. By the time that they realise this, they can find themselves trapped on a sandbank, and if there should be even a slight mist they will not know which way to wade their way to safety. With the passage of time, these rivulets and gullies become too deep for them to wade across, whilst the sandbank continues to disappear beneath them, below the water.

It is an unwise person who remains out on the sands of Morecambe Bay once the tide has turned, and all persons should carry a compass and a torch, so that he or she will know which way to make their way to safety should darkness start to fall or a mist start to form.

Just a few years ago there was the horrific situation in Morecambe Bay where a party of 19 Chinese cockle-pickers was taken by their Chinese gang-master and left in the gathering dusk, without compasses and torches, to work the hours of darkness in order to keep their activities out of sight of the authorities and others who would be concerned for their safety. Their only light was that provided by the headlights of a vehicle.

Somehow the tide had been mis-judged and the Chinese party found itself trapped by a rising tide with no idea as to which direction to take to be able to wade back to the safety of the shore. Regrettably, all of the members of the party drowned. The dreadful situation arose where one of the party, with the tide now up to his chest, used his mobile phone to call home to his wife in China, to tell her of his plight, and make his farewell.

That such human tragedy can occur in the present day, for want of the provision of a few cheap compasses and torches, and, indeed, that inexperienced people can be set to work under such dangerous conditions, by indifferent gang-masters, is appalling: absolutely and inexcusably appalling.

In addition to the danger of becoming lost on the sands and then drowned, there are areas of quicksand that can draw people to their death. The locals say that "in the old days", upon the death of a member of the community, the funeral party would carry the coffin out onto the sands at low water and then set it down in a suitable area of quicksand.

They would then conduct a funeral service nearby whilst the coffin slowly disappeared from view beneath the sand. Presumably the coffin would be weighted with stones to counteract the effect of the buoyancy of the wood used in its construction. This kind of burial, partway between a land-based burial and a burial at sea, would have well met the needs of the local community at that time.

[#3] These 'drinking' birds, sometimes called "nodding ducks", used to be very popular for window- and table-display, but the author has not seen one for a great many years. He remembers that they were simple in construction, comprising a closed thin glass tube of about 8 inches length filled with a fluid that changes state from liquid to gas at around room temperature. The bottom end of the tube is bulbous, whilst at the top end an approx. three-quarters-of-an-inch length of tube branches off at $90°$ to resemble a bird's beak. A floppy wide-brimmed hat completes the 'bird'.

The tube is pivoted from a small stand constituting its legs, at such point that in the inoperative condition, i.e. when the liquid in the tube is in the gaseous form, the beak end is heavier that the bulbous end, so that the tube rotates and the beak descends.

If a glass of cold water is placed for the bird to 'drink' from, the chilling of the beak by the water causes the gas within it to condense, the liquid then running down the tube to the bulbous end, where its weight eventually results in the bird rotating and ceasing to drink. After ten or twenty seconds, when the liquid inside it has again become gas, the bird drinks again, and so on.

473

Whilst this might be seen as a perpetual motion device, it relies for its continued operation on the condensation of the gas effected by the glass of cold water. A fascinating little novelty: however, its disappearance may be a result of its having been withdrawn from sale on account of the easy breakage of the glass tube, with the consequent release of the enclosed gas, to the detriment of the atmosphere, as with the release of gas from aerosol canisters and the unintended release of gas from faulty 'fridges.

[#4] In his book "Culloden", James Pringle describes in great detail the Battle of Culloden, and the months of repression and cruelty that the Highlanders were subjected to following it: published by Penguin Books, number 2576; republished recently by Pimlico, ISBN 0-7126-6820-9. A book that includes in greater depth the events leading up to the Battle of Culloden is "Culloden and the '45'" by Jeremy Black, published by Grange Books, ISBN 1-84013-006-7. For an authoritative and all-embracing account of the development of Scotland from the Ice Age up to the 21st century, see "Scotland: history of a nation", edited by David Ross, published by Lomond Books, ISBN 0-947782-58-3.

[#5] See "No mean city" by A. McArthur and H. Kingsley Long, originally published in 1935, published by Corgi in 1957, ISBN 0 552 07583 3. This novel, presenting a horrifying story of gang violence and a young man's rise to leadership as the "Razor King" in the Gorbals area of Glasgow, also includes factual reports from the newspapers of gang violence in the late 1920s to the mid-1930s.

Three books by Robert Jeffrey, published by Black & White Publishing, reporting the recent crime scene in Glasgow, are: "Glasgow's Hard Men", ISBN 1-902927-33-8; "Glasgow Gangland: True Crime from the Streets", ISBN 1-902927-59-1; and "Blood on the Streets: A–Z of Glasgow Crime", ISBN 1-84502-017-0.

[#6] Probably the most well-known Puffer ever, the "Vital Spark" has been tied up for some years in Inverary Harbour, Loch Fyne. The author was originally told by locals that she was awaiting a refit, before being put into service taking parties on extended, comfortable, live-aboard trips in the Firth and beyond to the Western Isles, He hoped that the refit would not alter her business-like, any-cargo-shipped appearance: coal, timber, household goods, livestock, whatever the need may be.

However, he was told recently that an X-ray of the hull has revealed areas of excessive thinning. He hopes that this problem will soon be overcome and the "Vital Spark" will again be seen around the waters of the west of Scotland. This beautiful old boat, introduced by Neil Munro in his book "Para Handy Tales", published by Pan Books, ISBN 0-330-02277-6, featured in the Para Handy series shown in a series on television delivering and collecting cargo around the Firth of Clyde and the West Coast of Scotland under the command of her Master Mariner, the incredible 'Para Handy'. Great reading, although now a little dated, and great television, for those of a nostalgic disposition, as is the author!

[7] The Nautical Mile is defined as a unit of length corresponding approximately to one minute of arc of latitude along any meridian, but is approximately one minute of arc of longitude only at the equator, as the length of lines of longitude decreases with distance away from the equator By international agreement it is exactly 1,852 metres (approx. 6,076 feet).

[8] The test firing of torpedoes on Loch Long was discontinued some years ago and anglers are no longer disturbed in their fishing but, alas, the vast shoals of fish that used to visit the loch are also a thing of the past. The test range had provided a valuable contribution to Britain's efforts during World War II. In 1944 approximately 12,500 firings were made, seven launches being involved in the recovery of the torpedoes, with the recovery station towards the top of the loch employing many of the local women, and even having its own Home Guard unit.

[9] The Gourockian", a grand old lady of 60ft length, built in 1938 in Denny's Yard in Dumbarton, started life as a passenger vessel "Ashton", but in 1965 was renamed "Gourockian", and for many years took angling parties out into the Firth of Clyde from her namesake port, Gourock. She is now pursuing a quiet and sedate life in commercial trade as "Wyre Lady", based in Rotherham, but is remembered as a fine sea-going vessel.

The "Granny Kempock", built in 1944, to a length of 61.5ft and a beam of 18ft, as MFV (Motor Fishing Vessel) 137 for wartime tendering service and stores carriage, was one the larger, if not the largest, of the boats taking out anglers from Gourock, and was well regarded by the author and the hundreds of other anglers who fished the Clyde on her. She ended her service with Ritchie's, a Gourock boat-hire company, on 31/03/79, when she departed down the Firth of Clyde, being lost not long afterwards off Stornoway.

Until recently, the author had no knowledge as to the present whereabouts of the "Westering Home", his favourite Clyde-based fishing boat, aboard which he spent many happy days, and learnt much about fishing. He feared that she could have sunk or been sent to the Breakers' Yard, and was excited when a search of the web revealed that, close on forty years since he last saw her, she was listed as still sailing the Clyde, taking out divers to Clyde wrecks from out of Inverkip Marina.

The author left a message on the telephone of "Elaine" of Clyde Diving, who rang him back to say that, sadly, the Westering Home is not now afloat, but lying ashore awaiting being broken up. The surprising news that she had was that the skipper of the Westering Home in the old days, Alex Balfour, who was the inspiration for the character "John" in this novel, is still alive, at an advanced age, in a Greenock Nursing Home.

The author paid a visit to the marina to see the Westering Home before it was too late. She was just as he remembered her, except for a tragic degree of decay, and for navigational equipment that had been installed on the roof of the wheelhouse at some time. Her name could still be read on a plate mounted on the side of the wheelhouse; faded but legible.

The author would have liked to have taken the plate away with him, but decided against such a step: even a derelict boat has an owner who would not want to see his property tampered with. He spent a nostalgic half-hour reliving his memories of golden days out at sea aboard her, in the company of a party of friendly fellow anglers, and with Alex Balfour at the wheel, at a time when the Firth was filled with fish just waiting to be caught.

--.

[#10] There is a plaque mounted alongside the Kempock Stone which quotes the words of the Rev. D. Macrea, 'Notes about Gourock', 1988.

"The Kempock Stone is a bronze-age standing stone, dating from about 2000 B.C. This is the famous 'Lang Stane' of Gourock, more familiarly spoken of as 'Granny Kempock' … It is supposed that the Kempock Stone marks the site in Druid times of an altar to Baal … However that may be, the Kempock Stane was for many centuries an object of superstitious awe and reverence … Marriages in the District were not regarded as lucky unless the wedded pair passed round the 'lang stane', and obtained in this way Granny Kempock's blessing … It was chiefly in connection with the winds and sea that the Kempock Stane was regarded with superstitious dread … sailors and fishermen were wont to take a basketful of sand from the shore and walk seven times round Granny Kempock, chanting a weird song to ensure for themselves a safe and prosperous voyage."

[11] The strong sense of humour, albeit highly unusual, of Yorkshire folk is something that the author is long familiar with. Years ago, whilst travelling on a stopping train from Leeds to Manchester, a young man got on the train along the journey and sat across the isle from him, opposite to an attractive young woman. The young man was outgoing and friendly and within a couple of minutes was engaged in amiable conversation with the young woman.

As the train pulled into "Huddersfield" the young man saw the name of the station on a board on the platform and said aloud: "We're at 'Uddersfield now.", then smiling pleasantly at the young woman he asked her "Do **you** like your 'Uddersfield?" The author was astounded, but the young woman just laughed uproariously and then continued with their conversation, completely unperturbed! Who but a Yorkshireman would venture to make such a remark! However, Yorkshire people are grand and good company, and Yorkshire anglers are a pleasure to be out fishing with.

[12] Gavin Maxwell's book is an account of his commercial hunting of the basking shark in the Western Isles of Scotland. During World War II, because of the large amount of time that he spent afloat, he was given a machine gun to mount on his boat so that, in the event of his spotting an enemy submarine, he could attempt to seriously reduce its effectiveness by damaging its periscope. One day he came across his first basking shark and was urged by his companion to give it a burst from the machine gun, which he did, but the basking shark just carried on swimming, apparently unperturbed: what a great change in our attitude to wildlife preservation from that time to the present!

The main objective in the hunting of the basking shark is to obtain its oil-rich liver, but Maxwell made the disastrous decision to recover the flesh also, which meant a frequent return to harbour to attend to its processing in brine, whereas his main competitor just removed the liver and dumped the carcasses in deep water well offshore. An earlier edition of this book contained many black-and-white photographs, one of which showed a Lewis man who later became a postman at Strathclyde University, and with whom the author had many chats about fishing: the removal of the photographs from later editions may be because of the stark nature of the photographs showing the cutting-up of the carcasses.

On one occasion whilst fishing Loch Fynne in a small dinghy with a fellow angler, a basking shark passed close by. Anxious to take a close photograph of it, the author asked his companion to take over the outboard motor and follow the shark, then, as they drew close, he asked him to stop the motor. However, his companion was unfamiliar with the motor and instead of stopping it, he gave it full throttle. By the time that he realised his mistake, the dinghy had motored over the top of the shark, and the two of them then held onto the gunnels lest they alarm the shark, whilst watching its great tail fin swing under them from one side of the dinghy to the other, until it eventually moved away from under them.

The only reported deaths arising from encounters with basking sharks were when they were startled by the sudden appearance of a boat, leaped from out of the water, and then unintentionally destroyed the boat by landing on top of it.

[#13] A press statement by SEPA (the Scottish Environment Protection Agency) entitled "Sewage and waste on Scottish beaches", dated 21st Feb. 2001, draws attention to the concern of MCS (the Marine Conservation Society) over the amount of sewage debris on Scotland's beaches, which is more than twice the average reported for the whole of the UK. A large amount of sewage debris is reported for Kames Bay, Cumbrae, a holiday beach, which debris has been confirmed by SEPA as consisting of very large numbers of cotton buds, and it is stated that "SEPA can't rule out the possibility that they derive from the historic deposit of sewage in the sludge dumping grounds off Garrochhead": that the purpose-built sewage-disposal vessel "Garrochhead" was so named is doubtless because this vessel was to spent the whole of its working life dumping sewage at this location.

Sludge dumping ceased in 1998, but it is clear that the sea cannot accept, degrade and render safe all of the waste material that is dumped into it. The banning of sludge dumping was an admirable step, and important for the tourist industry, as it is not likely that a family on holiday in the area would to sit and play on a beach bearing evidence of the local dumping of sewage, or that they would want to paddle or swim in the sea in such an area.

[#14] Whilst it is delightful to drive through the Pass on a bright summer's day, the author once drove through the Pass whilst returning home from an end-of-year fishing trip up North, tired, late in the evening and with heavy clouds gathering overhead. Upon reaching a section where the valley widens to the better part of a mile, with the mountains on both sides forming fearsome natural barriers, brooding black clouds had descended to cover the valley from the mountains on one side to those on the other, closing it in as though from the outside world. The feeling of entrapment and vulnerability within the barren, tree-less and life-less valley was immense.

With nowhere to shelter and no signs of other human activity, it was easy to imagine some danger approaching, unseen, through the thickening gloom: the author couldn't get out of the valley quickly enough! Never before or since has he felt this primeval insecurity, such is the stark, awesome, yet majestic inhospitality of the Pass under adverse weather conditions. Try it for yourself!

---

[15] This sad, beautiful song, written by Lady John Douglas Scott, relates to the sadness at never again to see his "true love" that one of two of Prince Charlie's soldiers, who were captured and left in Carlisle after the 1745 uprising, expressed to his fellow captive, who was to be released, whilst he himself was to be executed. After his death, travelling in spirit by the 'low road', he would reach Scotland before his comrade, who would be making his way back slowly on foot, on the 'high road.'

There are several different versions of the song, in one version the differences starting at the third line "Oh, we twa ha'e pass'd sae mony blithesome days," and continuing in such vein as to suggest that the condemned soldier would never again meet his comrade rather than his "true love". However, the author prefers the romantic, commonly-accepted version, the latter possibly having been written to correct misinterpretation arising with an earlier version.

A further, less-attractive, but nevertheless plausible, interpretation, makes the suggestion that the meaning of "high road" and "low road" is related to the heads of executed Scottish soldiers being displayed, as a warning to others, along the 'high road', i.e. the major road (consistent with a major road at the present time being described as a "**high**way") between Carlisle to Glasgow, with the lover of the executed soldier bemoaning the she will never see him again, as she is not permitted to return to Glasgow by other than the 'low road', i.e. by a less-important road or track.

---

[16] The instructions of an old friend from Lewis on the making of Ceanncropic are as follows: 'Take the liver of a cod of about five pounds or more and pulverise it, preferably by pressing it through a sieve with the back of a spoon. If the liver is in a good rich condition there is no need to add oil, otherwise add a couple of table-spoons of olive oil. Mix oatmeal with it until it becomes sticky, but don't add too much oatmeal or the mixture will be too stiff, more like very stiff

porridge. Add pepper and salt and half of a chopped-up onion. Clean out the stomach of the cod, and then put the mixture into it. Seal up the openings to the stomach with pieces of string and then boil the stomach for about half-an-hour. Delicious!'

In books of old Scottish recipes can be found "Crappit Heids", which differs from ceanncropic in that the oatmeal and fish-liver mixture, together with onions and perhaps fish intestines, well seasoned, is put into the head of a large cod or haddock and then boiled. This method would have been employed on account of wanting to make use of the edible parts of the fish's head: the tongue, the cheeks, the part around the pectoral fins, and other pockets of flesh. The stock resulting from the boiling of the Crappit Heids would have made a good basis for a fish stew: Crappit Heids, as with haggis, reflects the frugal nature of earlier generations of Scots and their admirable determination not to waste anything edible. It is very likely that the words "crappit"; and "cropic" from "Ceanncropic"; have the same source. Recently the author heard a cook from the east coast of Scotland describe the making of "Crappit Heids" without including the liver, but has not tried this for himself.

---

[17] The author found reference to an unofficial guide for Doncaster Museum and Art Gallery, www.aeroflight.co.uk/c-e/doncastermusart.html, which advised that on display there is a Mignet HM.14 Flying Flea, built in the 1930s and flown locally; and also a locally-built Bensen B.7 autogyro: he hopes that he will be able to make an early visit to the museum. Mignet is the designer who played the leading role is producing many of the types of flying flea before the French Government banned their manufacture in 1936 on account of numerous fatalities. Photographs and information on Mignet and his flying fleas are available from the Hendon & Cosford RAF Museum at www.rafmuseum/org.uk/mignet-flying-flea.htm. Within the Aircraft Museum in Malta there is a Mignet flying machine that was built by local enthusiasts.

---

[18] A plaque mounted alongside the ship advises that the history of the Turbinia had begun with the invention and patenting by Charles Parsons in 1884 of the steam turbine, a high-speed engine in which steam is applied to the blades of a rotor to effect motion. This success of this invention led Parsons in 1893 to proceed with plans to build a boat to demonstrate the advantages of the turbine in marine propulsion. Initially he conducted model tests of the hull of such a vessel using a two-foot long model said to have been towed by a fishing rod and line,

and then by a six-foot model driven by a twisted rubber cord, on a local pond.

This simple beginning led to the eventual construction of the Turbinia at the Parsons' Heaton Works in 1894. To reduce the weight of the ship, it was constructed in very thin steel sheet, its displacement being only 44.5 tons, and its dimensions being 103 feet 9 inches length and 9 feet beam. The power from the three separate turbines used was so great that it had to be fed via three separate shafts, each with three propellers mounted on it, making nine propellers in all. The ship had a very low freeboard and, if the sea should be other than dead calm, a trip on the boat for the ten-man crew and any passengers usually meant a soaking for all concerned. To reduce such soaking, the wheelhouse was eventually enclosed within a torpedo-boat type 'conning tower'. With her sharp bows and slender build, the ship was nicknamed "The North Sea Greyhound".

After early problems, the Turbinia eventually achieved a recorded speed of about 34.5 knots, which is nearly 40 miles per hour. This success led Parsons to think as to how to impress the admiralty with the power of the marine turbine. The Turbinia was motored down to Queen Victoria's Diamond Jubilee Review of the Fleet at Spithead in 1897, where it astounded all present by an unauthorised dash through the fleet at a speed of 34.5 knots. After this, the Admiralty was convinced of the supremacy of the marine turbine and Turbinia was allowed to pass into history, having made her own magnificent contribution to marine propulsion.

---

[19] Each barrel had a liner that had to be shrunk-fit into place, securing by heating the barrel to several hundred degrees and at the same time chilling the liner, prior to assembly. The bore of the barrel was a few thousands of an inch smaller than the outside diameter of the liner, this "interference" when the assembly reached a common temperature producing a tremendous compressive stress between the two components, the compressive stress on the barrel liner effecting a substantial offset to the tensile stress imposed on the liner when the gun was fired. After the shrink-fitting operation, the bore of the liner would have had to be machined to size, and then rifling – spiral grooves - machined into the liner so as to cause the projectile to spin when discharged, so that it will not wander appreciably from the desired trajectory.

---

[20] A year or so after moving into this district the author developed a bad chest, which required that for four years he join many other local

children in being taken by bus each day to an "Open-Air School" located in an area of fresh air outside of the city. Fortunately, the treatment worked, restoring him to health. Thank goodness for the promoters of the banning of the burning of fossil fuels, which ban will have avoided damage to the health of many thousands of other people, men, women and children alike.

---

[21] Close by the author's village of Arrochar is Balleyhenan Burial Ground. A plaque mounted on the boundary of the burial ground in 2004 on the 100th anniversary of the completion of the building of the West Highland Line, for which the labour force was mainly Irish navvies, advises that "Beyond this wall are buried some of the 17 men who died in the Parish of Arrochar while building the West Highland Line." Another source says that 37 navvies were killed in the Parish during this time, so unless the total of 37 is incorrect, it can be presumed that these 17 men who were buried **outside** of the graveyard were Irishmen who weren't, or weren't known to be, Protestant. Racial and religious bigotry have a lot to answer for!

---

[22] Chilli Kangkong is very like spinach, and grows wild in swampy tropical areas. During the occupation of Singapore in World War II it formed a major part of the diet of the local people. Its flavour is enhanced considerably by the addition of a small amount of sambal blachang, sometimes spelt balachan, which is made from shrimps, sardines and other small fish that have been allowed to ferment in the sun. The resulting very pungent and odorous mass is then mashed and minced with fresh chillies and possibly lime leaves, and in some cases then dried, being available in paste, powder and cake form.

In his book "King Rat", published by Coronet Books, ISBN 0-340-20445-1, describing life in Changi Prison Camp during the Japanese occupation of Singapore, James Clavell provides an account of how blachang was made by the local populace at that time. Essentially, this involved: digging a hole in the sand on the shore; lining the hole with palm leaves; using a net to gather the small creatures, shrimps and whatever else, that were living in the shallow water at the water's edge; putting these creatures into the hole and covering them with further palm leaves; replacing the sand; and then waiting for three months or so; by which time the buried sea creatures had become a stinking, putrid mass!   "Shrimp paste", as found in Chinese supermarkets, is similar to blachan, and is used along with lemon grass in such as *tom yam* soup, a hot spicy Tai soup.

[#23] The "Times Chinese–English Dictionary", reprinted frequently, ISBN 981 01 3906 3 paperback; ISBN 9971 4 6098 X case-bound; has printed characters that are of quite large size, and for almost every character the most common phrases using the character are presented and their meanings are explained.

The "Oxford Chinese Desk Dictionary: Chinese–English/English–Chinese", ISBN 978-0-19-800596-4, is supplied along with a "Talking Chinese Dictionary and Instant Translator" on a CD-ROM, enabling words and translations to be found by entering Chinese characters, *pinyin*, English, or a mixture of all three. A valuable addition is that Mandarin pronunciation is provided for the 4000 most-frequently used single Chinese characters.

For several years the author has found that the particular features of the word-processing software "NJStar", available from www.njstar.com.au, makes it very easy to type, edit, format and print Chinese documents. Different versions of NJStar are available, offering features from the following: simplified and traditional Chinese characters; instant English-Chinese/Chinese-English dictionary/translation; Chinese hand-writing recognition input; Chinese text-to-speech function; more than 20 Chinese input methods; up to 10 Chinese true type fonts; Chinese character vertical printing; typing of simplified Chinese, traditional Chinese and English on the same line; and a range of Chinese learning tools.

Also available from the same company is a program "Chinese Master" which is of help to those learning Chinese, giving instructions in pronunciation, providing the sounds of the characters as read by a native Chinese speaker: there are many other features of interest, not least of which are 300 poems from the Tang Dynasty, presented in both Chinese and English.

[#24] The illustrated book "The house of Confucius" by *Kong Demao* and *Ke Lan*, published by Corgi Books in 1989, ISBN 0-552-99345-X, tells the story of the Confucius family, down to *Kong Demao* herself, a seventy-seventh generation descendant of Confucius, describing how the family continued to live in *Qufu*, in *Shandong* Province, north-east China, from the time of Confucius until the late 1930s.

The adoption of Confucianism two hundred years after the death of Confucius lead to the leader of the family, the *Yansheng* Duke, acquiring great wealth, a mansion, large areas of land, a private army, and an importance equalling that of the Emperor himself, this power and influence remaining with each successive Duke, despite the rise and fall of many ruling dynasties over the same time-period.

That the opening ceremony of the 2008 Olympics in Beijing was held on the eighth of August is doubtless due to this being regards as an auspicious date. All races have their own idiosyncrasies, whether in the west or in the east, which are part of the interesting differences and similarities between us. Long may these idiosyncrasies exist.

#26

Above left The nonsensical composite *biang*. The figure is presented at a large scale - as it would be on bakery and food-shop signs - so that some of the various *fan2ti3zi4*, traditional, characters from which it is composed can be identified: at the top, the strokes that resemble a flat roof, with a fascia board on each side and a central chimney, as seen in such characters as *jia1*, "house"; immediately below this is *yin4*, meaning "sound"; below this is *ma3*, "horse"; on both sides of *yin4* is the 3-stroke character *yao1*, meaning "one", that is only used orally; below *yao1*, on both sides of ma3, is *chang2*, meaning "long"; next below is *xin1*, "heart"; whilst running down the left-hand side and along the bottom of the composite figure is the radical that looks like the bows of a boat and, indeed, some Chinese call the "boat", which is used in characters that refer to movement, such as *guo4*,"to cross or pass". From their similar size it could be thought that *xin1* and the "boat" together make up a compound character such as the above-mentioned *guo4*, but no such character can be found in a dictionary. Below the 'fascia board' of the roof are two short oppositely-running diagonal strokes that do not seem to have a meaning.

Above right This symbol, called "double happiness" or *shuang1xi3*, comprises the lateral merging of two *xi3*, 'joy', characters. The symbol is always displayed at Chinese weddings, painted in red on large white sheets or posters, hanging on the walls.

靜夜思
床前明月光
疑是地上霜
舉頭望明月
低頭思故鄉

静夜思
床前明月光
疑是地上霜
举头望明月
低头思故乡

龍馬乒乓國個

龙马乒乓国个

籲豔豐雲

吁艳䒤云

Top five rows The title and the four lines of *Li Bai*'s poem, *jing4 ye4 si1*, "A tranquil night": on left in *fan2ti3zi4*; on right in *jian3ti3zi4*. In most cases the *fan2ti3zi4*, traditional, and *jian3ti3zi4*, simplified, characters are identical or only slightly different, but in some cases they are so different as to appear to be unrelated.

Penultimate row Interesting characters: *long4*, "dragon"; *ma3*, "horse"; *ping1-pang1*, which constitutes an onomatopoetic phrase for "ping-pong", "table-tennis"; *guo2*, "country"; and *ge4*, a common

485

measure word: on left in *fan2ti3zi4*; on right in *jian3ti3zi4*. The simplification of *long4* and *ma3* is such that the characters bear a much lesser resemblance to the objects that they represent, which is regrettable. However, in the case of *guo2*, its presentation as *yu4*, "jade", a gemstone held in high regard by the Chinese, surrounded by a protective wall, makes it an admirable representation of "country". The delightful almost-horizontally-symmetrical characters "ping" and "pang" thankfully remained unchanged during the simplification process.

It is easy to imagine the creation of a character representing a noun or a verb, but difficult to imagine how one would arrive at the representation of a measure word, in this case *ge4*. However, *ge4* is a general measure word that is used extensively in Chinese, so its simplification to just three strokes from the original ten is well justified.

Bottom row These *fant2ti3zi4* characters, on left, are some of the very complicated characters to be found in Chinese dictionaries, being presented here at a large scale so that the details of the strokes can be compared with those of the corresponding *jian3ti3zi4* characters, on right. The justification for simplifying such complex characters was mainly in enabling Chinese to be used commercially in the modern business world. The characters from left to right are: *yu4*, "appeal"; *yan4*, "gorgeous, colourful, gaudy"; *xin4*, "quarrel"; and *yun2*, "cloud". Although the simplified character for "cloud" can be seen within the traditional character, there does not appear to be an association between the simplified form and the tradition form of the first three characters, except that the lower-right-hand side of the composite character *yan4* is the character for colour, s*e4*.

#27   Alex chose to read Owen's interpretation, as in what is a difficult task, a literal translation, or too little an appreciation of Chinese culture, would not convey the beauty of the words. As illustration, a literal translation of this poem would lead to:

> Sad lean two three pines
> Dog bark water sound in
> Peach blossom bring thick rain
> Tree deep occasionally see deer
> Stream noon not hear bell
> Wild bamboo divide green mist
> Fly stream hang green peak
> Lack person know place go

#28 H.H.Tenzin Gyatso, the 14th Dalai Lama, has provided a definition of *om mani padme hum*:

"It is very good to recite the mantra *om mani padme hum*, but while you are doing it, you should be thinking on its meaning, for the meaning of the six syllables is great and vast. The first, *om*, symbolizes the practitioner's impure body, speech, and mind; it also symbolizes the pure exalted body, speech, and mind of a Buddha."

"The path is indicated by the next four syllables. *mani* meaning jewel, symbolizes the factors of method: the altruistic intention to become enlightened, compassion, and love."

"The two syllables, *padme*, meaning lotus, symbolize wisdom."

"Purity must be achieved by an indivisible unity of method and wisdom, symbolized by the final syllable *hum*, which indicates indivisibility."

"Thus the six syllables, *om mani padme hum*, mean that in dependence on the practice of a path which is an indivisible union of method and wisdom, you can transform your impure body, speech, and mind into the pure exalted body, speech, and mind of a Buddha."

It is often said that *om mani padme hum* is the "jewel in the lotus", or more dramatically, "Behold! The jewel in the lotus!", in that it contains within itself the essence of the Buddhist faith; although it is also said that *om mani padme hum* can not be translated into a single phrase or sentence.

#29 Whilst living on the campus of Nanyang Technological University, surrounded by jungle, the author and his wife frequently encountered wild creatures within and around their apartment, such as a snake crawling up the stairs to their second-floor apartment; a monitor lizard coming out of the nearby jungle that was as big as an Alsatian dog, with a 2 ft long slashing tongue; a 20ft long python that had crawled onto the road to bask in the morning sun, but had been run over by a bus bringing in staff to work; swarms of termites, that can devour a shelf of books overnight; and great big cockroaches that fly in through the open windows; but fortunately, being on the second floor, we were spared the centipedes, scorpions and huge stinging spiders that seemed to plague some of our ground-floor neighbours.

One morning the "Straits Times" reported that a groundsman at a local golf course had temporarily ceased work to relieve himself in one of the toilets, a ladies' toilet as it happened. Whilst sitting there comfortably, a python came from around the S-bend and seized his testicles in its jaws. He managed to struggle free to seek medical attention. The following day, a trap was laid for the python by leaving a dead chicken, tied to a strong rope, alongside the toilet. In due course the python started to emerge, saw the chicken and seized it, whereupon several groundsmen rushed forward and pulled the python - which wouldn't let go of its find - completely out of the toilet and waste pipe, then overpowering it. It was reported that the python was released into the jungle at some distance away from the golf course.

----

[30] A recipe for Wonton Soup is as follows. Ingredients: 300g of lean minced pork, 1 stalk of spring onions; salt and pepper to taste; 4 tsp. soy sauce; 1 tsp. sugar; 1 packet of wonton skins (available from a Chinese supermarket, but if not the author believes that suet pastry rolled until it is very thin will suffice); 3 cloves garlic; 9 cloves shallots; about 300-400g *tang oh* (Chinese celery, available from a Chinese supermarket, but if not then British celery will probably suffice, although, as Chinese celery is thinner and greener, it would be advisable to use also the green leafy ends to the sticks that are normally discarded. The original recipe stated 1kg, but this seems excessive). Steps for cooking wonton soup: slice six cloves shallots and fry in oil; when golden brown remove shallots, drain oil and place aside; slice spring onions, add to minced pork and mix well; add soy sauce, sugar, salt and pepper to the minced pork and mix well; put 1 table-spoon of minced pork mixture onto each sheet of wonton skin; wet the edges of the skin with water, fold into a ball, and press the edges together to seal the ball; put water, garlic and shallots into a pan and bring to the boil; add the wonton - initially the wonton just lie in the surface of the water, but after about six minutes they expand and bob-about, partly out of the water; remove from the wonton from the water; add the celery to the water; when cooked, remove the celery; place into a soup bowl a small amount of celery and the wonton, soup and shallots.

----

[31] It is not always the case that the "older and wiser" amongst us can provide the answers that we seek. Two common questions that trouble mankind are: "Where did the universe come from; and what is reality?" The usual answer given by the experts to the first question is the "Big bang" theory, that the universe sprang into existence about 13.7 billion years ago by a "singularity": which latter is infinitely small, infinitely hot, infinitely dense. No-one knows where it came from, but before it came there was nothing! A possible answer to the second question was advanced on a recent television programme on "Reality", in which it was suggested in all seriousness that the world may be no more than a hologram created at the edge of space! These scientific

explanations are no more credible or reassuring than those in the bibles of the various faiths in the world.

The author prefers the following delightful explanation as to where the Universe and human life came from, as recounted by Michael Sullivan in Chapter One, "Before the Dawn of History", in his extensively-researched book "A short history of Chinese Art", published by Faber and Faber, 1967 (no ISBN number):

"In far off times, the Universe, according to a popular Chinese legend, was an enormous egg. One day the egg split open; its upper half became the sky, its lower half the earth, and from it emerged P'an Ku, primordial man. Every day he grew ten feet taller, the sky ten feet higher, and the earth ten feet thicker. After eighteen thousand year P'an Ku died. His head split and became the sun and moon, while his blood filled the rivers and seas. His hair became the forests and meadows, his perspiration the rain, his breath the wind, his voice the thunder - and his fleas our ancestors.

A people's legends of its origins generally give a clue as to what they think most important. This one is no exception, for it expresses a typically Chinese viewpoint - namely that man is not the culminating achievement of the creation, but a relatively insignificant part in the scheme of things; hardly more than an afterthought, in fact."

The above folk-view of the unimportance in the universe of the relatively-late arriver, man, accords well with that implied in the following Chinese proverb:

"Modern people see not the ancient moon,
but the modern moon once shone upon ancient people."

[#32] In addition to there being many large statues of Buddha, there are also a great many large statues of *Gwan Yin*. During the mid 2100s, the author visited the *Kek Lok Si* temple, "Tmple of supreme bliss", in the village of Air Itam close by Georgetown, Penang, Malaysia, to see the magnificent 36.5 metres tall bronze statue of *Gwan Yin*. At the time of the visit, enormous columns were being erected to support a canopy above the statue.

[#33] Whilst the firing of the Hong Kong Noon-Day Gun is an event not to be missed, the gun itself is a fairly modern breech-loading gun, whereas the Noon-Day Gun fired at the former Saluting Battery at the

Upper Botanical Garden in Valetta, Malta, is a muzzle-loading 1807 Bloomefield twenty-four pounder, fired by the ignition of a length of fuse. The firing is under the control of a five-man squad of volunteers of Fondazzjoni Wirt Artna, <info@wirtartna.org>; <www.wirtartna.org>, wearing appropriate Victorian military uniforms.

This organisation is also responsible for Fort Rinella, a magnificent Victorian Fort housing the largest cannon every made, the Armstrong 100-ton Gun, a muzzle-loader capable of firing a 1-ton shell eight miles, sufficient to protect the nearby Valetta Harbour. The author was present at one of the few firings of this great gun since it was withdrawn from service more than 100 years ago. However, the charge used was only 8kg, which is minute compared to the rated service charge of the gun of 100 pounds (45.4kg), and as a projectile was not in place, leaving the charge not pressurised sufficiently to ensure complete combustion, a part of this charge was ejected unburnt, and the noise of the explosion was modest. Nevertheless, it was an experience not to be missed! The author was also privileged in being allowed to join the firing team and fire, with full ceremony, an ancient eight-inch muzzle-loading howitzer at the fort.

It is reported that a Noon-Day Gun is fired at Signal Hill in Cape Town, this practice being started to enable ships to check their chronometers. It is also reported that a Noon-Day Gun is fired on Janiculum Hill, Rome.

---

[34] During his time in Singapore, a Buddhist friend of the author gave him a copy of "The Eight Immortals", illustrated by Chan Kok Sing and translated by Koh Kok Kiang, published by Asiapac Books, 1996, ISBN 9813029-96-6. This slim, stiff-bound book is largely visual, but with sufficient text to convey the clear and simple message that wrongdoers will be brought to justice and made to see the error of their ways, and that the sick, poor and oppressed will be relieved of their suffering by the interception of the Immortals. The stories are of a traditional nature, and contain an element of both Buddhism and *feng shui*, The Chinese belief in the good fortune associated with the number 8 is said to have been based on the good actions of the "8" Immortals. An adult form of this type of booklet is distributed free-of-charge by the Buddhist faith to show the consequences of not having lived according to Buddhist principles, where the non-observer is shown reincarnated with mental or physical difficulties, or born into a life of misery or personal tragedy, or even reincarnated as a lower form of life.

---

[35] The use of "jade" in sexual euphemisms is not confined just to

male genitalia. The extensively-researched book "Shanghai", John Murray (Publishers) Ltd., (Feb. 1999), deals primarily with information on Shanghai from the 1920s obtained from author Harriet Sergeant's interviewing of many of the older residents of the city, together with accounts of her own visits dating from the time of the Cultural Revolution: however, it also contains a mass of information on the general history of China and the Chinese that will delight the Sinophile. The book is available through Amazon in hardback and paperback from several suppliers, in both used and new condition.

In her book, Harriet Sergeant recounts a scene on the Bund in Shanghai where coolies were loading and unloading cargo under the direction of a foreman. To keep his men hard at work, the foreman would shout out whatever might inspire them. As a fat Western lady passed by, he led his men in a chant: "Look at that fat, white foreign woman coming past now"; with the men, in a sing-song voice, responding with "Oh, look at her, look at her", the foreman continuing with "Imagine getting lost up her Jade Gate", with the response from the men "What a fate! What a fate for a poor man!"

It is a universal very-satisfying practice for the underdogs in a situation such as the above to be able to quietly and effectively ridicule anyone 'lording it', or in this case 'ladying it', over them, without fear of detection or reprisal: critical or offensive words that are not understood by the persons against whom they are directed are much safer to employ than both anger and dumb insolence.

However, what the underdogs intend is not always what transpires. The coloured slaves of the southern plantations of America in around 1850 developed a parody of the movements of the dancers up at the 'white Master's house', in creating the "Chalk Line Dance", with dance movements including high-strutting promenading whilst bending the body backwards and dropping the hands at the wrists. Some masters, as could be expected, resented the slaves' intentions of ridiculing them, but others enjoyed and appreciated the dance, leading to the masters of neighbouring plantations organising competitions to see who owned the most impressive dancers, with the prize of a cake being awarded. The name of the dance soon changed to the "Cake Walk Dance", leading to the popular present-day exclamation at another person's incredulous, impressive or astounding actions: "Well, that takes the cake!"

The dance grew in popularity such that by around 1890 it had become immensely popular with the fashionable upper-class and middle-class white people of the big northern cities: not what the slaves had intended! It has been suggested that, in a similar way, the traditional white handkerchief held by Morris men - who originally were of basic peasant stock - and some of the movements in their dancing, are a parody of the affectations of those dancing up at the squire's or the lord's residence, in holding up a handkerchief whilst so doing, and of their elaborate dances, such as the minuet.

[#36] Whilst making a lecture tour of several universities in the northeast of China some years ago, the author visited Qinhuangdao City in Hebei province. This is a fine tourist city, with many hotels, restaurants, and places of cultural interest. Popular attractions are the beach, with its many miles of clean sand; and its wide sweeping promenade - where a great many friendly Chinese families throng - with its gardens, large public areas, eating places, shops, and stalls selling souvenir and other items.

The Great Wall is quite close to Qinhuangdao. About nine miles to the northeast of the city, forming part of the Wall, is the small town of Shanhaiguan, expressed with tone marks in Mandarin as *shan1 hai3 guan1*, literally "mountains", "ocean", "pass", meaning "The pass between the mountains and the ocean", the mountains being the Yanshan Mountains and the ocean the Bohai Sea". This part of the Wall was built in compacted earth faced with stone in early years of the Ming Dynasty (1368-1644) and the Pass, built 1368-1381, was regarded as of strategic importance, being the most easterly checkpoint. The Wall in and around the town is still well preserved. The town can be reached easily by public bus from Qinhuangdao, and there is much for the tourist to see in the town area, i.e. mountains, temples and the Great Wall Museum.

The Great Wall is often regarded as being like an enormous dragon, lying across China for approximately five-and-half thousand miles, with its western end now disappearing beneath desert sands and its eastern end reaching 23 meters into the Bohai sea as if to drink: the latter location is known as *lao3 long2 tou2*, "Old dragon's head". The author was pleased to be able to spend some time there. Laolongtou is about three miles south of Shanhaiguan. The name of the site is linked to a legendary dragon-head carved in stone and built into the Wall there, but lost with the crumbling of the Wall. However, in the 1980s the authorities replicated the original dragon-head.

Close by the end of the Wall is the two-storey Changtai Tower, with the Temple to the Sea Goddess set within it, built in 1579. The author read that this area has now been provided with replica soldiers in Qing Dynasty uniform, to give the visitor an impression as to how it would have looked during its period of military occupancy. He recommends a visit to Qinhuangdao, such visit to include trips to Shanhaiguan and

Laolongtou.

[37] China's economy has continued to grow, year by year. It was reported on the UK television news that in 2005 China's economy grew by 9%, overshadowing the growth in the economies of the countries of the West over the same period of just 2 or 3%. It was reported in the Daily Telegraph Business News on 17 April 2006 that China's president, *Hu Jintao*, disclosed that in the first quarter of 2006, China's gross rate of domestic product increased to 10.2%, leap-frogging France and the UK to become the World's fourth-largest economy. By 2011, China's economy had become the second largest economy in the World after that of the United States. This is a magnificent achievement by China, and vindicates Napoleon Bonaparte's prophesy: "Let China sleep, for when she awakes the world will tremble." The World now knows that the sleeping dragon has awakened, lifted its head, and roared!

A recent book by James Kynge, published by Weidenfeld & Nicholson, "China Shakes The World: the Rise of a Hungry Nation", ISBN 0-297-85229-9, describes his observations, after living more than twenty years of living in China, of the economic growth of the country, to become a major industrial power. The book is written in a readable, relaxed and descriptive style, like that of a novel, without the aid of graphs, pictures and tables of data, and recounts many of Kynge's discussions with working-class Chinese.

[38] The latest re-construction of the Yellow Crane Tower began in 1980 and was completed in 1984. The author was able to visit this magnificent structure, which is built in the elegant style of its predecessors, whilst on a visit to *Chongqing*. A beautifully illustrated book, "Yellow Crane Tower", ISBN 7-5430-1705-9/J, published by *wu han* publishing house, 1997, introduces the tower, describes its ancient origins and the fairy tales and legends associated with it, details the military actions that took place in its vicinity, tells how the tower fared over successive dynasties, and finally describes famous scenic spots in the area, then concluding with an extensive explanation of the culture and customs of the region. An admirable book.

[39] It is astounding that the carvings at this site have survived for so long. Where the carvings are in a deep niche, they have not suffered a great degree of weathering and their painted surfaces are fairly intact, but in other cases, time has led to some of the carved detail having been lost. In recent times, in order to protect such carvings from further

damage, light roofs had been built above some of the niches.

One impressive sight is the 8.2 metre high niche containing the "Three Saints of Huayan School of Buddhism", which houses a total of 119 statues, with Vairocana in the middle, Samantabhadra Bodhisattva on the left and Manjusri Bodhisattva on the right, the three statues reaching as high as 7 metres - about twenty-three feet. Held in the hand of Manjusri is a stone pagoda weighing close on five-hundred kilogrammes - almost half a ton - which has remained securely in its place for more than eight-hundred years, supported just by the carved cassock draping down from the elbows to the feet of the figure.

An impressive niche is that dating from A.D. 1174-1252 displaying Sakyamuni entering Nirvana. The reclining Buddha forming the centrepiece is 31 metres long. One niche, the "Niche of the Nether World", dating from A.D. 1174-1252, containing 133 statues, shows scenes of horrific barbarity, including the "Hell of Knee-Chopping", the "Hell of Freezing Ice" and the "Hell of Cauldron of Boiling Oil", some of the eighteen hells of the nether world.

The "Hell of Knee-Chopping" was considered to be particularly appropriate for those who could not control themselves after drinking, lest under the influence they do something immoral. Although this scene is from a bygone age, it was quite surprising to the author, who had always believed that the essence of Buddhism is that people should be good because they want to be good, not because they are afraid of being caught doing something bad, as is the case with most present-day religions and political systems. However, it may be that in the 'old days' even Buddhists needed a sharp visual reminder of the possible consequences of straying from the good path.

There are also carvings of other Buddhist figures: Manjusri, Bodhisattva of Wisdom; Samantabhadra, Boddhisattva of Universal Benevolence; Maitreya, future Buddhist Sutra; and many others. Inquiry of a Buddhist monk who was passing-by revealed that "Boddhisattva" means "God" or "Goddess", although Alex had also been told that the word refers to one who has achieved enlightenment but who remains on the earth to guide others along the same path: perhaps both meanings are applicable.

A beautifully illustrated booklet, "*Dazu* Rock Carvings of China" has been compiled by the Art Museum of *Dazu* Rock Carvings, edited by *Tong Dengjin* and published by the *Chongqing Ziyi* Advertising Company Ltd. Those wishing the visit the *Beishan* Grotto can contact Tourists Consulting, Tel: (023) 43722268; 43789147. Some photographs of these carvings are presented in the book "China revealed: a portrait of the rising dragon", by Basil Pao, published by

Wedenfeld & Nicolson, ISBN 978-1-407-20811-4

Further books on China

An authoritatively written novel on China, "Jade", by Pat Barr, published by Corgi Books, ISBN 0 552 12281 5, opens in the turbulent 1850s and carries through until the early 1900s, telling of the life of missionaries of the period and the influence of "Western Barbarians" on traditional Chinese culture. This long book contains a great amount of well-researched factual material that captivated the author, as it will others interested in Chinese matters.

An unusual insight into Chinese military thinking is afforded by "The Art of War" by *Sun Tzo*, translated by Samuel B Griffith, published in hard-bound by Watkins Publishing Company, 2009, ISBN 9-781844-831791, hardback, 272p. This illustrated, beautifully-presented, book shows the influence of *Sun Tzo*'s views as to how war should be conducted, starting from his own time, in about 500 B.C., through the ages up to the time of *Mao Tse-tung*. Despite its somewhat sombre title, the message of the book is essentially that " ... the skilled strategist should be able to subdue the enemy's army without engaging it, to take his cities without laying siege to them, and to overcome his State without bloodying swords." The book is based on the translator's doctoral submission and is understandably written in an academic style, but at the same time the topic has been researched exhaustively and authoritatively.

An extensively-researched book is "1421" by Gavin Menzies, published by Bantam Books, ISBN 0-553-81522-9. The title of the latter book is the date that a Chinese fleet is believed to have set sail with the remit to proceed all the way to the end of the earth. This book is well illustrated and contains much well-reasoned discussion extending to the political atmosphere developing in China at that time: fascinating reading!

The Overseas Chinese Affairs Office of the State Council China Overseas Exchanges Association commissioned three Chinese academic institutions to write a series of books, "Chinese Common Knowledge Series", written in both Chinese and English, to acquaint overseas Chinese teenagers with basic knowledge through class education and self-teaching. These books are well illustrated and written in a straightforward manner, such that they are of interest to all ages and, in particular, to non-Chinese readers of all ages. "Common Knowledge on Chinese Culture", ISBN 962-8746-49-9, covers: Ethnic groups; Folk customs; Traditional virtues; Ancient science and technology; Spoken and written languages; Literature; Artistic work and sport; Ancient architecture; Arts and crafts; and Cultural relics. The two further books in the series are: "Common Knowledge about Chinese History"; and "Common Knowledge about Chinese Geography,"

Other books on Chinese history are: "The search for Modern China" by Jonathan D. Spence, published by Hutchinson, ISBN 0-09-174472-5 and "Return to Dragon Mountain" by Jonathan Spence, published by Quercus, ISBN 978-1-84724-343-0; and for those interested in Chinese pottery, there is "The Chinese potter" by Margaret Medley, published by Phaidon, ISBN 0-7148-2593-X.